CW00673091

HENRY CROWNE
PAYING THE PRICE BOOKS 1 TO 3

In the HENRY CROWNE PAYING THE PRICE series
SPY SHADOWS
IMPOSTOR IN CHIEF
(Coming out in Winter 2021)

In the NANCY WU CRIME THRILLER series
BLOOD DRAGON

Don't miss FREE access to the backstories that underpin these books as well as FREE chapters.

Go to www.freddieppeters.com

HENRY CROWNE

PAYING THE PRICE BOOKS 1 TO 3

FREDDIE P. PETERS

Henry Crowne: Paying The Price Books 1 to 3
First published 2019 by Freddie P. Peters
www.freddieppeters.com

Text copyright © Freddie P. Peters 2019
This edition published 2021

The right of Freddie P. Peters to be identified as the author of this work has been asserted by her in accordance with the Copyright, Designs and Patents Act 1988.

All rights reserved. No part of this publication may be reproduced, stored in or introduced into a retrieval system, or transmitted, in any form or by any means (electronic, mechanical, photocopying, recording or otherwise), without the prior written permission of the publisher. Any person who does any unauthorised act in relation to this publication may be liable to criminal prosecution and civil claims for damages.

ISBN: 978-1-9993373-8-4

A CIP catalogue record for this book is available from the British Library.

Cover design by Ryan O'Hara.
Typesetting by Aimee Dewar.

This is entirely a work of fiction. Names, characters, businesses, places, events and incidents are either the products of the author's imagination or used in a fictitious manner. Any resemblance to actual persons, living or dead, or actual events or localities is purely coincidental.

This book is sold subject to the condition that it shall not, by way of trade or otherwise, be lent, resold, hired out, or otherwise circulated without the publisher's prior consent in any form of binding or cover other than that in which it is published and without a similar condition including this condition being imposed on the subsequent purchaser.

BOOK ONE:
COLLAP$E

Henry, mon ami,

This letter took me a while. I realised I had not put pen to paper for such a long time. I do not mean emails or texts. I mean actual writing, the act of my hand on paper, the slight hesitation that precedes putting down what cannot be erased. Mais enfin la voici.

A sketch of it came on the day I left you behind. The heavy doors closing on you brought a chill to my heart. So it felt right, maybe even necessary. And I have come to realise that a good letter must divulge something intimate about its writer, so I will start with my own news. I have decided to reconnect with my previous life, the one I thought I had left forever behind. Don't be alarmed and think I am recanting after talking so much about giving up the rat race. I have found an unexpected use for my old talent, my new-found bohemian style joined up with the impeccable training of this legal mind – well, you have seen the result!

Of course, you may already have gathered that I received a little nudge. It came in the shape of our mutual friend Mr P. I want, no … I need to plunge into the City once more, but this time on my own terms. A final test, maybe? Time will tell. To be completely honest, the gentleman in question attracts my interest terribly. There you are. How about this for a confession – ha!

I think I should finish swiftly, and now that my letter lies in front of me I hope it will be the first of many. Please reply, for I know that coming to terms with the act of terror you lived through and the deceit you endured will bring you resolve. But for today I simply say – I understand. The rest is up to you.

A très vite
Nancy

1

Chapter One

A stretch, a barely disguised yawn … Henry Crowne was nonchalantly sitting in front of his four plasma screens on GL's trading floor. He propped himself up in a sudden move, once more focusing on the vast room spread in front of him. He loved the position of his desk, not his office, no … his desk. From here he could see rows of machines and men, plugged into world markets, ready to take action as the markets moved, action that was wiping out, in seconds, billions of dollars.

Today however the atmosphere on the floor was subdued. Henry started rocking slowly on his leather chair again. He was not a trader but a structurer. He knew himself to be good, in fact remarkably good, yet the takeover had unnerved him. His reputation and that of his team were spectacular. He had flair, nevertheless competition at HXBK was fierce. He knew his rival only too well, hard working, hand of steel. Anthony Albert was a force to be reckoned with. The two men had been unspoken enemies ever since they first met. Everything served to make them opposites, not only their attitude towards people and work but also their very cores.

The phone ringing brought him back to reality with a jolt. He looked at it with suspicion. Should he answer? His black phone was hanging at the side of his desk. He preferred it the old-fashioned way and was one of the few people on the floor not yet wearing a headset. One of his team picked up for him; a phone never rang more than twice at GL.

"Ted for you, line two."

"OK, thanks. Hey Ted, what's up?" asked Henry, pleased to hear one of his best mates at GL.

"I need to speak to you outside the floor. Can you get to your office right now?"

The voice on the other end of the phone sounded shaken, hardly recognisable, very much unlike Ted whose sense of humour had defused many an argument they'd had.

Henry stood up, towering over his desk.

"Sure, I will call you back on your mobile," said Henry already moving towards his office. The distance he had to walk was minimal. Time was money. Henry closed the door and dialled Ted's number.

"Ted, what on earth is happening? Has the committee come to any decision about the team, I thought–"

"Listen," said Ted cutting him short, "nothing to do with your team Henry, Anthony Albert is dead."

The enormity of the news and its implications hit Henry in slow motion. It unfolded gradually, a mixture of relief, shock and disbelief. The phone stayed silent.

"Henry, are you there?"

"Impossible, I just can't believe … what happened? I spoke to him only yesterday."

"Look. I don't want to talk about this over the phone. I am at Canary Wharf. I want you here as soon as possible. Can you make it now?"

"Sure, sure. On my way."

He stood at his desk for a few minutes, fighting the strong emotions raging inside him. The sombre news was confusing him, so much had been at stake and so much done because of Albert and now … now, the old enemy was dead, a twist of fate, brutal and unbelievable even by City standards.

"Guess who is going to head the combined team now?" muttered Henry as an enormous weight was lifted from his shoulders.

Henry was still standing at his desk, his CV spread across it so that he could give it the final touch before submitting it to the integration committee. It wasn't as though the committee members were unaware of who he was and what he had achieved, but it was the rule.

His last year at Dublin University; a first in mathematics; his interview at BZW, the then investment banking arm of Barclays. Mathematicians earn nothing but it's the bankers that make the money, he remembered saying to Liam, his old university pal as he celebrated his departure for London. And the first innovative structured transaction he completed there. He touched the CV lightly and a smile rose on his face.

"Yes, the combined team."

His own words shocked him. This relief, this near elation, was based on someone's death. The rapidity at which his mind had assessed the situation, decided it was a 'good thing', without regard for Albert, unsettled him. But Henry knew how to rein in his feelings.

Come on, come on, he was a manipulative little shit – still. Henry had always prided himself on being a considerate man.

His PA tapped at the glass partition, she needed to have a word.

"Are you OK? You look as if you've seen a ghost." Her strong Scottish accent grounded him into reality.

"Morag, that is not funny."

"Why? You really look pale. You're not losing your sense of humour. I couldn't bear it." Her intelligent smile beamed at him.

"Sorry, sorry – a lot on my mind. I need to go to Canary Wharf straight away. Cab, please."

"Done," said Morag.

He grabbed his jacket and mobile and strode towards the rear of the building where his black cab was waiting. The cabbie would wait fifteen minutes before calling the office to enquire about his passenger. Henry walked out of the building and took a sharp right. The small newsagents he had earmarked in case of emergency a few months ago sold burner phones. Henry picked one up and paid cash. He walked back towards the building checking his watch. It had taken him less than ten minutes.

Henry had hardly sat in the back of the cab before he was setting up the burner phone to dial a number.

"Liam, it's me. Are you still in the UK? … OK, back in Dublin then."

Henry listened to what was being said on the other side of the phone and frowned.

"This mobile is not traceable … I know, but a situation is developing and I might have to speak to the cops."

"I don't think it has anything to do with our business."

"Listen. LISTEN. It probably has no bearing on the transfers. I will contact you again only if I need to. OK. Bye."

Henry inhaled deeply and put the mobile back in his trouser pocket. He would get rid of it as soon as he could.

Henry started scrolling down his emails on his BlackBerry. The call with Liam had been securely stored in the impenetrable part of his mind. He was not expecting to see any details of the Albert incident yet but the habit of using his time to do business whilst on a cab ride gave him a sense of security. He noticed a mail from his art dealer and was tempted to call but he chose not to. A conversation about his latest acquisition would unfocus him. Henry however smiled at the challenge surrounding the purchase of the piece. Anthony Albert and he had found themselves invited to the same preview of a young up-and-coming talent.

"Sorry mate but I think we're there, right?"

The distant voice of the cab driver reminded Henry that he was on his way to meet Ted. Henry bent over to see the building on his left-hand side through the black cab window. He could now see the slick glass and steel offices of HXBK.

"Yep, we're there."

Whilst the cabbie was looking for a place to park, Henry took a meticulously rolled Hermés tie from his top pocket and quickly knotted it around his neck. A few years back GL had adopted a dress down code on its trading floor but Henry felt uncomfortable without his Savile Row suit. The only concession he made to what he regarded as a ridiculous policy from Silicon Valley was to wear his shirt with rolled-up sleeves and without a tie. However, tie and matching cufflinks were always kept in his pocket, ready to be used on the first occasion. Henry stepped out of the cab, his shoulders squaring up to the imposing building.

HXBK's atrium was rumoured to be the largest in Canary Wharf and spread over two floors. The ground floor resembled an art gallery with its Andy Warhol that covered the far side of the entire wall – four immense panels of pop art.

Henry walked up to the reception desk where a well-spoken Japanese woman took his name. He climbed the escalator two steps at a time, passing on his left another valuable piece of art, this time an installation by Damien Hirst. The reception area lost its serenity when he reached the first floor. Two large metal gates had been installed in the wake of 9/11. He was met by a couple of security guards who approached him with the required stern expression.

"Please put your keys and mobile in there, sir."

The man was pointing at a small tray on the side.

"I know, I know … been here before," Henry grumbled.

The news of Albert's death had started to sink in. It remained incredible, an insane joke only the City could produce.

Ted was sitting down, stirring a cup of coffee when Henry opened the door to the meeting room. The pool of liquid in Ted's saucer indicated his nerves. He looked tired, his curly blond hair was a mess, shadows lodged deep beneath his baby blue eyes. Lack of sleep and extreme pressure were the lot of those appointed to serve the integration committee. Ted did not complain.

"Coffee … Henry?"

"Thanks, I'll pour. You tell me the story so far."

"I'll tell you what I know. Got a call this morning at around 8am, I was with Jason Gateway and Mathias Wunderlink. We were reviewing the consolidated presentation to be handed over to the integration committee. Anyway."

Ted took a mouthful of coffee, pulling a face at its bitterness.

"Apparently the plane carrying Albert crashed early this morning. He was flying on one of the bank's private jets. A rumour was circulating that you also were on board. They don't know what happened but I have been told that they may not be treating this as an accident."

Ted had spoken the last words quickly, swallowing yet another mouthful of his over-stirred coffee. Henry frowned and pulled his chair over, sitting uncomfortably close to Ted.

"No. This is ridiculous. Which bloody newspaper has been stirring it up this time? BANKER MURDERED IN HOSTILE TAKEOVER BID. I can see it from here." Henry gestured in the air as if to underline a title.

"This is not a takeover. This is a merger."

The company approved mantra had clearly sunk in with Ted.

"Anyway. Nobody knows yet, Henry … this has not been released to the press. The police are involved … hell I don't know. I am so bloody tired. This is going to be such a fucking nightmare."

"We are all tired Ted, but who would realistically want to murder the old fart? You, me? Half the City …"

"Don't say that," Ted protested. "This is not funny."

"OK … OK," said Henry, dropping his sarcasm.

"I still can't believe he is dead, let alone that there's foul play. I have a shedload of catching up to do here. Maybe I am just too bloody whacked to take it all in."

"I have been told the police will want to interview anyone who has been in recent contact with him," said Ted without looking at Henry.

Henry observed Ted closely for a few seconds. Was his friend holding back information? No, he wouldn't dare.

"Understood. Let me know when," replied Henry standing up. He left the room without waiting for Ted's response.

Henry walked out of HXBK's building and took a sharp left towards Canary Wharf's main concourse. He turned left again onto a large plaza and crossed towards the water's edge. He spotted a small bench on the waterfront, secluded enough. Henry sat down and placed his work mobile to his ear. He looked around. There was no one in sight. He stood up abruptly, still pretending to be involved in an animated call, took the burner mobile out of his pocket and let it slide into the water. Still no one around. Good.

Henry retraced his steps and terminated his fake call. He hailed a black cab. He so wished he had called Charlie for the return journey. This thought propelled him back to a trip he had taken three months earlier with his driver.

Charlie had rung the doorbell at 5.25am on the dot. Henry's private car had been booked for 5.30am. Charlie made it a point to arrive five minutes early, avoiding for his best client the where-is-my-wretched-car morning stress. Henry was ready and acknowledged his driver as soon as he rang the doorbell, a little punctuality game the two men enjoyed playing. Charlie had been Henry's chauffeur for the past five years and was always made available to him by his Limo service. Henry managed to smile at the memory.

"Morning Charlie, quick trip to Biggin Hill today. Boy, it's cold."

"Good morning Mr Crowne, indeed dreadful weather for late spring," Charlie had replied in his reassuringly manicured voice. Henry appreciated Charlie's eccentricity. He spoke an impeccable English unexpectedly combined with the bulk and allure of a CIA agent.

As he left his building Henry had looked up towards his dwelling. He had moved in a few months ago. The sumptuous old building still impressed him. He had noticed a light on in the duplex apartment opposite his. His neighbour, the enigmatic Nancy Wu, was already up. Their brief encounter had aroused his curiosity. But Charlie was standing at the door, patiently holding it open. It was time to leave.

Henry sat in the S-Class Mercedes and reached for the large cup of Assam tea waiting for him in the cup holder in the middle of the rear seats. One of Charlie's many personalised touches. He was about to switch over from Jazz FM to Radio 4 to catch the early morning news when Henry stopped him.

"A little jazz will do us good. I am not sure I want to hear more news about the global collapse of the financial markets right now."

"As you know Mr Crowne, jazz is always my music of choice."

"I have not asked for a while, Charlie ... how is the jazz club doing?"

"There may be a financial crisis but we are doing fiendishly well. Our latest Arun Ghosh Sextet show has been a roaring success."

"I'm not surprised. You guys know your stuff. I did listen to the Miles Davis CD you recommended. I might be getting the hang of it, I think," said Henry.

"A genius, all about timing of course."

"Timing is everything Charlie – everything."

"I am glad we share the same view, Mr Crowne."

"Talking about timing. How is your other business going?"

Charlie features tensed. From the very moment Charlie had become his driver Henry had guessed that he had done time. A childhood in Belfast had made Henry more familiar than he would ever admit with the Nick – or rather the Paddy. He had managed to gain Charlie's trust and convince him that his past did not worry him, somehow impressed by Charlie's determination to rebuild his life. Charlie would be on parole for a little while longer though.

"My parole officer is not a bad person, but I am looking forward to not having to meet him again."

"But all going fine, right?"

"It is. Thanks for asking. The jazz club and my driver's job make all the difference."

Henry nodded and Charlie turned the radio up. They fell into a comfortable silence.

Henry's mind drifted towards his trip to New York, trying to anticipate the reason why Douglas McCarthy, CEO of GL, had asked him to join him on his way to the US. DMac, as he had been nicknamed by the market, had spent over forty years in the financial sector. His reputation was as a ruthless man, whose success at the helm of investment banking had been impressive. He was a man of extremes, capable of arguing the most desperate of cases and winning support in the tightest of spots. Henry had been working as one of his few direct reports for nearly three years. He had an affinity with McCarthy that few enjoyed. Henry had developed the habit of speaking his mind and in return was consulted on matters relating to the overall running of the firm.

He had won this privilege during the negotiation of a protracted but essential transaction with Morgan Stanley which had put GL on the front pages of the *FT* and the *Wall Street Journal* for weeks. Henry had been clever enough to let some of the more senior management bask in its glory, while taking a voluntary backseat.

Upon arrival Charlie had resumed his role of chauffeur, opening the Mercedes' door and confirming he would be there for the return journey. "Much appreciated," Henry had said, discreetly placing a £20 note in Charlie's hand. He was now eager to join DMac. The invitation had been unusually formal. He needed to know why.

Chapter Two

Nancy switched on the news as she was drinking her first cup of tea of the day, a strong Sichuan with a little milk. Breakfast TV bored her but she enjoyed the early morning programmes on the Bloomberg channel. She always found snippets of information that would not be repeated during the day, news that was usually very telling to the discerning mind. The Asian commentator was exploring the implications of the announced merger between GL and HXBK and questioning whether this merger between two of the giants of investment banking was not a merger but rather a reverse takeover. Nancy poured herself a second cup of tea and frowned, too much milk. Her mind wandered back to the programme, paying a little more attention. She had spotted her neighbour, Henry Crowne, leaving the block of flats early that morning as she was opening her curtains. She had surmised he was working on the trading floor of a large investment bank, hence the early hours, and recollected he was indeed working for GL. The commentator speculated for a while as to the reasons for the merger and Nancy got a little irritated.

"A bank the calibre of GL would only agree to merge for one reason, lack of capital, of course," she said aloud.

Nancy opened up her agenda and looked at the day's schedule. She had a meeting late morning with a young artist who was hoping for a grant to support her next show. The Bloomberg programme was going nowhere in its exploration of the GL-HXBK story. Nancy switched off the TV and turned her attention to the world of art. She had a few hours to review her notes and make herself ready to meet her young friend. She grabbed a large portfolio of prints that had been left with her and delicately lifted the sheet of light tissue paper protecting each of them. Nancy gave a wide smile, so much talent for someone so young. She forgot all about the news and slowly slid into a world of intensity that engulfed her.

* * *

The bombshell hit all Bloomberg terminals at 11.47 GMT. A short but speculative piece announcing the death of Anthony Albert AKA … AA the recovery man:

In the bitter battle for the reverse takeover of GL and HXBK, a dramatic development has rocked both stocks in this morning's London session. Anthony Albert, a major figure at HXBK, has been killed in a tragic plane crash. Police are treating the incident as suspicious after several eye witnesses reported what seemed to be an explosion shortly after the plane took off. HXBK and GL have been contacted but so far have not been available for comment.

Henry had been told to prepare his team for the news. They had just walked out of their meeting room when the news hit their screens. James Radlett, Henry's number two, said aloud what everyone else was thinking privately.

"Hey guys, look at Bloomberg. Mr Recovery Man is famous at last. I am sure the little prick would never have thought it would come to him that way."

"Not appropriate James," snapped Henry.

James shrugged whilst most of the team privately enjoyed the rebuff.

Henry was exposed, knowing he must be the last person to have had contact with Albert. Something was wrong, very badly wrong. With a long career on the trading floor Henry had developed the ability to sense danger, to feel and recognise the dark undercurrents of a disastrous situation. Now that the news had settled in, a sense of disquiet had started to rise within him. Then again what could he possibly be scared about? His planning had, so far, been immaculate.

James went back to work whilst Matt, another senior member of the team, cautiously hedged his bets.

"Bad for the stock though," said Matt, tapping furiously on his Bloomberg terminal to check GL's latest share price.

"Gee … Well spotted, genius," replied Harriett. She removed her glasses with a swift gesture, wiping the lenses with the sleeve of her cashmere cardigan methodically. The heavy frame had left two deep indentations below her light brown eyes. She rubbed the soreness away slowly and pushed the glasses back into position.

She had not said a word during the team meeting, Henry had noticed the out of character silence. Harriett had been patient, positioning herself within the firm for the past three years and now stood to be made an MD at the next promotion round as did Matt. Of course, the merger could still ruin their plans and so could any unfortunate associations with a losing leader. Henry was under no illusion that they had joined his team for no other reason than because he could guarantee high visibility. But the death of Anthony Albert could only mean 'issues'. Henry sat at his desk outside his office. He surveyed his team one more time, as an uncomfortable thought started to settle in. He knew them all well, but then again, he knew his people only within the confines of banking. He had seen them weather some tough situations and difficult people, take knocks and come back up, strengthened by the experience. He had seen them compete against one another and other banks to win the deal and the limelight, but this was different. He had chosen them for their complementary skills and personalities and taken risks in welcoming and training these ambitious characters. Whilst he could normally provide an environment where their various aspirations could be fulfilled, the combination of the takeover and this latest drama would put strain on his ability to keep the team together. He needed some space to think. A cup of tea grabbed from his favourite patisserie would do the trick.

L'Epi d'Or was buzzing with customers. Henry frowned at the idea of queueing. He spotted Marianne serving a young woman. She had multiple orders that would most certainly feed an entire desk of traders. He was about to wave when Marianne grabbed a large paper cup and waved it at Henry with a smile. He smiled in return and gave the thumbs up. Someone in the queue turned around and looked displeased. Henry recognised Cindy, McCarthy's PA. He shrugged and mouthed 'sorry' with a grin. Cindy collected a large paper bag and walked past him.

"H, you're incorrigible."

Henry turned back to see her disappear. He had not seen McCarthy since their flight to New York three months ago. The memory of that last meeting made his stomach churn with anger.

He is there once more.

Henry steps into the Gulfstream G400 full of the confidence an indispensable adviser has. The rich smell of leather rises to his nose. This is the smell of unabashed luxury and power. No matter how many times he has flown in the private jet that smell always excites him.

McCarthy is in his seat, documents scattered around him, a cup of coffee in his hand.

Henry has managed before to hitch a ride with McCarthy for a great many of his own clients' meetings. His deals have profile and McCarthy enjoys that association too. Henry's last $3.5 billion convertible bond issue has been yet another exceptional success.

But times have changed and when McCarthy lifts his head, he presents a tired face, deep lines etched onto his forehead.

"Hello Henry, how are you?"

"Hello Doug, haven't seen you for ages," Henry says.

"I know, should've been in touch sooner but I have been considering various options … we'll talk later … Christie at the back will fix you a drink."

To McCarthy all stewardesses are called Christie. Henry has never had the nerve to ask him why. He assumes that remembering the name of an air hostess is fairly low on McCarthy's priority list.

The plane has been in the air for about thirty minutes when McCarthy signals Henry to approach. Henry has opted for a seat at the back of the plane, judging by his boss's demeanour that he does not want anyone around. Time to himself is precious for McCarthy, whose involvement with the Bank's affairs is a constant, gruelling 24/7 schedule. McCarthy has been reviewing his diary for what would be a typical visit to the New York office. The aircraft phone rings and Cindy, McCarthy's PA, is on the phone confirming last minute changes.

"Breakfast at 6.30am with Apple is fine if you tell me that Gary will join us," says McCarthy whilst inviting Henry to sit down.

"Good. Calls and meetings after that fine but I am not giving up on consolidation time … I need to review the CDO file … don't care if Steve needs a quick answer. Tell him I am reviewing the figures and that I understand our position on the AAA tranches."

McCarthy scribbles some notes on the side of his timetable and glances at Henry.

"Yes, I'll take a late call from the Asian office as long as it does not compromise my dinner with Paulson … At what time does his flight from Washington arrive? Table booked at the usual place? No agenda in writing please, just say collateralised debt obligations."

McCarthy hangs up and takes a mouthful of coffee.

"This market is too fucked up for words. One day I am gonna lose the plot," mutters McCarthy.

Henry does not envy McCarthy's CEO position. Rather, he relishes the role of éminence grise, that of favourite counsellor in keeping with the feudal ways of the City. He feels certain that no essential decisions will be taken without his consultation.

"Henry, we need to talk without being disturbed. I'll get straight to the point. I have been speaking to Roy, our Global Head of Debt. You know we are very stretched at the moment in terms of core capital. We have missed one very large trade and are *about to miss another one … you know the story … capital cannot be freed easily at the moment … the situation will not in my view improve … unless you tell me otherwise?"*

Capital, capital, capital, *Henry knows* – lifeblood of any company from multinational to small cap. *He nods, there is very little he can add since one of the transactions being turned down is one of his own.*

"Well, Doug you know that my team and I have been working on this $5 billion structured convertible for months. We can only innovate and convince the market if we take a fair chunk of the deal ourselves. The Hedge Funds want to feel that we believe in our mathematical modelling and our pricing before they commit—"

McCarthy interrupts by waving his hand in the air with a snappy gesture.

"I know all that Henry. I am trying to find imaginative ways of stretching our capital and there are none. We can't come to market, we would be slaughtered, the share is pricing at US$13.47 down ten per cent. We have used a number of structures to reduce our capital exposure but off balance sheet products can only help so far. The Securities and Exchange Commission and the FSA are going to start asking difficult questions soon … so … what's next?"

His voice is impatient. He is rehearsing his arguments, a dry run for a future intervention in front of the Board. Henry shifts on his seat, conscious of the uncomfortable distance established by McCarthy.

"I know you know Doug and I am also aware that we have sold all the assets we could," Henry says with some equal impatience. *The subprime investments wrapped into CDOs GL has kept on its books are pulling them down and Henry has warned them about it.*

"Are you only now trying to tell me that something major is about to happen, such as a sale?" His voice remains calm but his face has lost some of its colour. *If GL is being taken over or merged then Doug has not confided in him.*

Henry's remark brings a spark of amusement to McCarthy's eyes.

"Well, yes … I am talking about hanging a 'for sale' sign in the shop window. You admit yourself that your team will not be able to perform unless we broaden our capital base. Even you, Henry, can't bloody well deliver a structured solution despite your experience so what else can I do? We have to take the initiative … Force a takeover of the reverse kind."

McCarthy's eyes now glow with a mixture of cruelty and excitement at the prospect of what lies ahead. After so many years he is still thirsty for blood.

Henry's heart starts racing and his mouth has gone dry. He has not felt this taken aback for years. The matter of fact statement, the absence of communication, can only mean that he is not in the running, that he and his team are not a core part of the protracted negotiation process. Henry can feel anger gripping him, an incandescence burning in his chest.

Betrayed.

Control is essential. He cannot, will not, allow himself to show the turmoil inside. Henry reaches for his coffee, takes a long sip and sits back. The colour has returned to his face, he is calm.

"Mr Crowne ... Hello?" Marianne's voice propelled Henry back into L'Epi d'Or. His hand had been moving in slow motion towards his pocket, fetching a few coins to pay for his tea. Time speeded up again. Henry gave Marianne his best smile and left with the cup of tea warming his fingers. He turned into Gresham Street not yet ready to rejoin his team. He started walking towards Poultry, drinking his tea slowly. But no matter how good the weather and the tea, Henry could not shake the memory of his NY trip.

McCarthy's voice rings clear in his ear, the arrogance ... the coldness.

"I presume you have a counterpart in mind with deep enough pockets or shall we discuss options?" Henry asks.

"A valid question coming from you Henry!" McCarthy still needs his cooperation in the process. "However, I think our options are limited. I told you, I won't be taken over. I want a reverse, I want to be in the driving seat when I am at the negotiation table ... in the interests of us all of course. There is therefore only one bank that can fulfil that role in my view."

Henry does not volunteer a name. He is still hoping that the forbidden word won't be spoken.

"HXBK is the only one." McCarthy's eyes have not left Henry. The anger is rising again in Henry's chest, much harder this time to control.

"Are you telling me that you are seriously contemplating a merger with this sleeping dinosaur?"

"More like a sleeping beauty, needs to be awakened – and OK some may not see me as a charming prince but what have I been paying my bloody PR consultants for?"

The deal is done, you motherfucker, *Henry knows*, just like that.

"So, what would you like me to do now, Doug."

To be part of the integration committee is vital.

"I am going to ask you one of the most difficult things to do Henry, but I know you well, you will be able to handle it," McCarthy pauses, takes a sip of coffee before putting the cup slowly back in the saucer.

"I want you to do nothing."

Henry goes to stand up. His seatbelt stops him dead. He unbuckles it with rage. He is now towering over the older man who remains impassive. McCarthy looks up into the younger man's face without the faintest hint of emotion. His faded blue eyes don't blink.

15

Had Henry been in a room, a car – dammit even a boat, he would have walked, swum … but at 10,000 feet his options are limited. He sits down again.

McCarthy has organised the meeting wisely. Mind manipulation, also referred to as 'coaching' in most leadership courses, is a strong skill of his and for the seven hours the flight lasts Doug 'coaches' Henry into his way of thinking.

* * *

At home, Nancy was still going through the portfolio of prints, meticulously taking notes on each of them and only looked up when her doorbell rang. She grabbed her BlackBerry to check the time. The bell rang again. It had to be a lunchtime delivery but she was not expecting anything. She gave a sigh and moved to the intercom.

"Yes, can I help?"

"A delivery for Mr Crowne," replied a polished voice.

Nancy was intrigued. It was not the usual coarse greeting of a courier eager to get to his next job.

"Is he expecting you?"

"I had arranged to deliver late morning, so that he could take the time to look at the painting during his lunch break."

"I am coming down," replied Nancy.

Could Henry also be a collector? She arrived at the main entrance door to see a well-dressed young man in a hat. He was carefully balancing a large painting covered in bubble wrap.

"I am happy to take delivery for my neighbour. But you must let me see the piece. A little nosy but well …" said Nancy with an engaging smile.

"Certainly. It is rather contemporary," the young man replied hesitantly. "I am Phillippe Garry by the way."

"The wilder, the better."

Nancy and Phillippe engaged in a lively conversation about galleries and artists, while he unwrapped the piece destined for Henry. He said nothing more, but positioned the painting on one of Nancy's sofas.

Nancy sat down for a few moments, stood up and walked away without losing sight of the piece. She came back, sat down again.

"*The Raft of the Medusa*. A powerful reworking of Géricault. Who is the artist?" she asked, admiring the daring interpretation.

"Tom de Freston. A very promising painter we represent."

"Why the *Raft*? It was a controversial painting in 1819 when exposed in Paris. The story of this shipwreck caused much embarrassment to the newly restored French monarchy. I am right, *n'est ce pas*?"

Phillippe nodded in admiration. He had found an unexpected art expert and French speaker in Nancy.

"Tom enjoys the depiction of epic narratives and draws much from art history."

"Does he believe history will repeat itself?" asked Nancy, turning towards Phillippe.

"What do you mean?"

"Well, so much despair. People plunged into such barbarism. I can't help feeling an association with today's economic crisis, terrorism. Perhaps we are on the brink too. *La fin est peut-être proche!*"

Nancy paused. The idea struck her as a chilling revelation. She shrugged but Phillippe agreed.

"*Absolument*. To be honest it had not crossed my mind but Tom has an uncanny way of seeing the world, of trying to introduce order into chaos."

Nancy was about to launch into a discussion about artists' ability to sense the future but realised she had to prepare for her first meeting. Phillippe left his details and promised he would arrange a lunch with Tom.

As she was getting herself ready Nancy could not help but wonder why Henry had chosen this piece. Was he also stricken by its premonitory power or was it simply an attempt at capitalising on an early talent before Tom's pieces reached unimaginable levels? The question intrigued her. This could surely be debated over a drink. Nancy would extend an invitation to Henry and quench her curiosity.

* * *

Henry was returning from his walk. He had forced his well-trained mind to stop dwelling on McCarthy. Henry had a plan and so far, so good … The weather had suddenly turned cold but the sharp wind was doing him good. His mobile rang.

"Henry Crowne," he said in his smooth baritone.

"Good afternoon Mr Crowne, Inspector Jonathan Pole, Scotland Yard. I understand that you have been informed I may want to speak with you. Would it be convenient for us to talk at some point?"

Henry would have dropped his tea had he not been balancing it on the railing of the pedestrian crossing opposite his office building.

"Well … yes … what exactly are you expecting from me? Anyway, I am outside the office – can I come back to you?"

"We do not need to talk now. Shall I come at 5.30 tomorrow afternoon? I will text you my number in case you need it."

The voice was harmonious yet unequivocally firm. There would be no arguing. Henry knew he would be made available by his firm to the Yard, he had no choice and the voice at the other end of his mobile knew it full well. Inspector Pole would tolerate no setback.

"Fine I'll book a room."

"Excellent, see you then."

The wind that had invigorated Henry was now assaulting him, making him shiver. He rapidly crossed the street and disappeared into the building.

Back at his desk Henry was assailed with urgent calls and emails. The market had moved dangerously again and some of the products his team had helped launch recently were now under stress. The Albert story disappeared in a flash as Henry engaged with the issues at stake.

It was late when he finally reached his home that night. He had jumped into a black cab whilst still scrolling through his emails on his BlackBerry and swiftly replying. At the last traffic light before the cab reached his home, he had stopped. Henry enjoyed this small ritual, a way of preparing himself to let go of the day's pressure.

He entered the imposing yet welcoming hallway. Before he reached the lifts he passed a modern steel and wood table. The janitor was on holiday and his replacement was a disaster. Henry swore in a low voice as he noticed his mail mixed up with that of his neighbour, Nancy Wu.

"If this moron can't put it through my letter box, at least he should allocate it properly."

He separated his mail from Nancy's in an angry gesture and dropped a bunch of letters on the floor. He swore again, this time louder. The little he had seen of Nancy intrigued him. The Chelsea Flower Show Committee had sent her a large envelope. The Henry Moore Foundation had sent her what looked like an official invitation, both letters indicating that she must be a trustee. Another letter from the Inns of Court attracted Henry's attention. He placed his own mail underneath his arm and moved towards the lifts, still perusing his neighbour's mail. Some more mail from abroad, China and France. Henry smiled at his own preconceptions. He walked out of the lift and rang her doorbell. No one replied. How irritating. He could have done with a little company. He could keep the mail and try later perhaps. Nancy had given him her phone number as the mixed-up mail incident was not the first of its kind. Henry realised it was the only time he'd had a conversation of any length with her and been invited into her home. But the mood soon faded. He slid the mail through Nancy's door.

He might not be such good company after all. Besides, Nancy might not live up to his expectations. Henry was about to step into his flat when a white envelope on the floor of the hallway stopped him. His name was elegantly penned across it and underlined.

Henry impatiently tore it open.

Dear Henry,

Your painting, The Raft of the Medusa, *arrived this morning. I was hoping I could deliver it to you but a prior evening commitment prevents me from doing so. I thought you would want to see it as soon as you came in tonight and therefore asked the janitor to be allowed into your flat. I hope you won't mind.*

I could not resist taking a look. I am impressed by the quality of the execution and the strength of the content. Would you care to join me for a drink later on this week? I would so much enjoy discussing this provocative piece with you.

Yours, Nancy

All ideas of grabbing the janitor by the throat for having allowed a stranger in vanished. Instead, Henry felt flattered. He dropped his mail on the low table at the centre of his lounge.

The painting was still wrapped and had been carefully positioned against one of the bigger sofas. Henry had forgotten how large the piece was, not as large as the original Géricault but still imposingly sizeable. He did not bother to change but ran to his kitchen to find a pair of scissors. He placed the painting on the sofa against which it had been leaning and started meticulously unwrapping it. The joy of knowing and yet not fully remembering gripped him until the bubble wrap paper lay discarded on the floor like the abandoned dress of a lover.

Henry took a few steps back. Opposite sat *The Raft of the Medusa.* The shock was intense, the nakedness and the vulnerability, the despair and the savage need to survive. A few days ago death had been a controversial theme that called only for words. Today it had become reality. Why had he chosen such an uncompromising painting?

Henry stood up, incapable of taking in anymore, rapidly covering the piece.

"I am not in the mood," he said aloud, as if it was a sufficient reason.

Henry took off his jacket, threw it on the sofa and unknotted his tie in an irritated gesture. He looked around the room and the elegant antiquities reassured him. They were some exquisite dancing Shivas, a benevolent Buddha and his prize piece, a miniature terracotta warrior from the Emperor Qin Shi Huang's Terracotta Army. All were expensive and suitably safe. Henry had never reflected on the decorative nature of his collection. The pieces had been purchased at a price. He had taken monetary risk, or perhaps that of fraud but what other risk had there been? And was it art?

He climbed a flight of stairs to his bedroom and there again the large Matisse painting on the wall felt kind, a gentle presence, comforting in its origin and execution.

Should art be more than simply pleasing to the eye? Why collect? And why *The Raft of the Medusa*?

Henry shook his head again.

"I am not in the mood," he repeated. He would call Phillippe tomorrow. Maybe this piece was not the hit he thought it would be. Yet he had fought for its purchase against no other than Anthony Albert himself.

Most surprising, they had both been invited to the exclusive preview of Tom's work. Henry's newfound love of contemporary art had led him to follow Phillippe's gallery and its many young up-and-coming artists. When Albert walked in, Henry knew he was there to close a deal. Anything as long as it was a good investment.

Henry had challenged his rival with flair by welcoming him openly.

"Anthony, how nice to see you here."

"Likewise," Albert had replied unfazed.

Henry had turned away towards Phillippe declaring in the low voice of a conspiring man. "I would buy the whole lot but it would feel very Saatchi-like."

"Why, bonus on the decline?" Albert had butted in, unashamed of his uncouth eavesdropping.

"Noooo, but as you know at your own cost, I do not buy in the manner a rug merchant does. I pick and choose!"

Henry had raised his champagne glass in humour and moved on. Albert had then walked straight to Phillippe and asked for a quote on the entire display. But Albert was no Saatchi and Phillippe knew to exercise caution. Henry had become a good client and both men managed to catch up whilst the artist presented his work and was interviewed by the *FT* art correspondent.

"The gentleman you spoke to wants the whole lot," Phillippe had said. "This is unusual for a first-time buyer."

"My fault, Phil. I mentioned Saatchi… but I think *The Raft of the Medusa* is the one I truly want so just tell him I desperately want *Minotaur*. He will buy that one and a few more I am sure."

"Understood. By the way… *The Raft* is an excellent choice!"

And today *The Raft of the Medusa* was sitting in Henry's lounge.

Chapter Three

The room Henry had booked was small but comfortable. He assumed Pole would be coming on his own. He was standing by the large bay window overlooking the City's roofs. The top floor of the newly converted building was solely dedicated to meetings. The place had been given a professional but pleasant feel. Teams of staff were dedicated to the welfare of the bankers and their clients. Henry would press a button on a remote control lying on the small desk adjacent to the meeting table and refreshments would appear swiftly, a well-rehearsed choreography Henry took for granted and hardly noticed.

Biscuits and cakes came to mind … He remembered some of his first meetings where the joke invariably turned on the 'quality' of the snacks provided. It sounded rather frivolous now but the memory made him smile at his own reflection in the window. He was trying to spot the roof of the Bank of England when the phone rang. A male voice announced his guests, asking Henry whether he should send them through. Henry noticed that the plural had been used.

"I'll be with you right away," replied Henry.

Fucking hell. How many coppers does it take to interview one bloody banker?

Inspector Pole was a tall man, with greying hair. Henry noticed that he was also sporting a well-trimmed goatee. His colleague was an equally tall Asian woman.

"How do you do," said Pole whilst extending his hand to Henry. "I am Jonathan Pole and this is my colleague Nurani Shah."

"How do you do?" said Henry.

Henry shook hands with both of them. He had kept his right hand in his trouser pocket ensuring the tissue within it absorbed the moisture of his sweaty palm.

"Shall we move to room sixteen?"

"Certainly. Thank you for taking the time, I am sure you are very busy."

"Well business is not exactly as usual. A merger imposes restrictions on what a bank can do as you know." Henry's voice stayed remote, matter of fact. He had no need to befriend Pole.

"Of course, I suppose the acquiring company wants a period of status quo to ascertain past performances and risk levels in particular in the current subprime context," replied Pole.

"This is not a takeover, this is a merger." The firm's mantra Henry did not believe in would however do for Pole. He pushed open the door of room sixteen.

"Tea, coffee, water?"

Everybody went for tea. Henry placed the order and sat opposite his two unwelcome guests.

The conversation started with a bland exchange of information until refreshments had arrived. This took less than three minutes after the call had been made.

But the biscuits looked sad.

"Well Inspector Pole, I presume you have not come here to enquire about the rate of inflation so let's get on with it, shall we?"

"Certainly, I know that Ted Barnes has given you a quick summary of what happened to the flight Anthony Albert was on. We have also contacted GL's internal legal team to ensure that we can gain access to relevant information. This is important since I am afraid we will be treating the incident as suspicious."

"Do you have any proof of this?" said Henry in a tone he thought too eager.

"Very sorry but I can't discuss this with you Mr Crowne." Pole's voice remained even. "However, in this context we have to try to map with exactitude the movements of Mr Albert. So, tell me, when did you last make contact with him? Is there any information you think is relevant?"

"Sure," said Henry, settling down into his chair comfortably. "Today is Wednesday. We spoke on Monday. Anthony was asking for details of all structured products we were working on. I was preparing this report but wanted a bit more time."

Henry shifted slightly, he was suitably vague, knowing that the subsequent conversation had been made from an anonymised phone in one of the meeting rooms.

"Could you be a bit more precise, was the conversation tense, amicable?"

"Well this is a difficult merger, it is not easy but in the current context it was professional and sufficiently courteous."

Anthony Albert and Henry had had a courteous enough conversation on the Monday, however the subsequent call had degenerated into an almighty row. Henry knew the game too well. Under the pretence of 'future cooperation' and teamwork, Albert was trying to find out what the competing team was working on. His aim was also to adapt his own pipeline of product development and tailor it accordingly. The idea was of course to look at least as good if not better than Henry. They had exchanged information but both camps had surrendered ideas that were already known to the market. The cutting-edge technology that made Henry's team so spectacular remained hidden.

"I understand that you and Mr Albert were not particularly friendly," said Pole.

His eyes rested on Henry and he let him feel their weight. Pole was in the game of information gathering, an opponent worthy of Henry's attention.

"Well, this is a tough environment, banking is hugely competitive, at best people may respect each other …"

"Would it therefore be fair to say that there was respect between you and Mr Albert?"

"I think that is right," Henry gave a soft roll to his r. Pole did not seem to blink at Henry's first lie.

"Could we now show you a number of documents that have come to our attention this morning? We recovered them from Mr Albert's computer."

* * *

To: Roger Kodorov Global Head of Equities Trading
Date: 08 September 2008
From: Anthony Albert European Head of Structured Products
Subject: Henry Crowne

Roger,
A quick mail as agreed to update you on the latest conversation with Crowne. I simply cannot understand the man. He suggested we fly together to Switzerland tomorrow and now he has changed his mind. He will not take

the plane with me! He was the one who suggested we take the company's jet so that it gives us some privacy for a discussion about the teams which I thought was the first reasonable idea I have heard from him so far.

However, Crowne is now too busy, this is frankly a lame excuse. Anyway, I will see you later in Geneva. At least and at last … Crowne has prepared some documents I can work on. I will pick them up myself so that I can work on them on the plane before we meet.

Best,

Anthony

Anthony Albert, ACA, FTII
European Head of Structured Products

* * *

Henry read the note once, and again. He finally pushed the page back to Pole with two fingers. He folded his hand on the table, lifted his head and took a moment to speak.

"I do not understand this email at all, he had mentioned a trip to Switzerland but never firmed up on it."

Henry's mind was now working quickly and in anger. *Why would this crazy fucker want to send such an email?* Henry had expressed surprise but had he been convincing to the well-trained eyes of Pole?

"You have no explanation why Mr Albert wrote this mail?"

"None whatsoever."

"What about the papers Mr Albert mentioned in his mail, would he have really come to pick them up or send for them? Why not email?"

Henry had delivered some papers but all had been done by mail and the latest batch had not been ready on time hence the row with Anthony Albert. Henry knew he was late and pressure had been mounting. The game had to be played with precision, too much resistance and he would lose the hand.

"Well, the papers were ready but he never picked them up," Henry's voice dipped a little – his second lie.

"You mean there was a bundle to be picked up prepared by you, specifically for Mr Albert, with all the required information?"

"No, not printed, but that could have been printed had he asked for them. He never did."

"Well, we have another email dated two days previously asking for the documents to be delivered, what do you make of this?"

"Can I see it?" asked Henry slowly sinking into the half-truth that made survival in his job possible. His answers would not be incorrect but would always be open to interpretation.

Control at all cost.

"The documents refer more, I believe, to general figures about P&L."

"OK, but I presume P&L can be gathered from your accounts department."

"Yes, but we also have projections."

"Now Mr Crowne, what do you make of this mail?" said Pole moving around pieces of papers so that they landed precisely in front of Henry.

This time the mail was addressed to Albert's PA. It was asking her to confirm the booking of one of HXBK's private jets and inform security of Henry's identity and details. Albert was also giving specific instructions about Henry's pick up at his home address.

"I have absolutely no bloody idea, Inspector. I can't give you any answer to this apart from the fact that Albert and I never discussed this trip in detail ... and I mean never." An alternative reality was unfolding around Henry. He was part of it ... yet a powerless spectator.

Remember, Control at all cost.

"But I thought you said Mr Albert had mentioned a trip?"

"I mean we never firmed up on it. It was not even a discussion more ... a vague suggestion. Absolutely nothing more."

Pole sat back in his chair, looking at Henry, sizing him up. Henry knew exactly what Pole was thinking ... Yes, this man was intellectually arrogant, an excellent negotiator. Probably hideously ambitious, but could he kill for it?

Pole took his time, giving Henry space to measure the impact of his thinking and what would come next.

"Understood, but we will need to talk to you again. You realise that the gap between your account of the facts and what we have as evidence is let's say ... unreconciled ... I am afraid Mr Crowne I am about to become a regular feature in your timetable."

Having shown his two unwanted guests out Henry grabbed his mobile and speed dialled number one.

"Pam, I need to speak to you urgently!"

"Darling, you always need to speak to me urgently," purred Pam in a husky voice.

Pamela Anderson had worked with Henry on most of the complex deals he had put together since joining GL. Her name had been a constant source of sarcasm, mixed, of course, with the inevitable dirty joke. Pam had cleverly used this unfortunate homonym to her advantage, playing for or against it according to circumstances. After all, it was a name to remember and she certainly made sure that her contacts did exactly that. Pam was tough. Some argued that the City had taken its toll as it did on so many women. Truth be told, Pam simply paid lip service to the female condition but enjoyed the company of men more. She was one of the few equity partners at Chase and Case, the largest law firm in the City. Equity partnership meant sharing in the revenues of the firm, an enviable position with a foreseeable substantial income. This of course came with large responsibilities too, a state of affairs which many City critics preferred to ignore. But Pam had more than it took to preserve her position.

"Pam, do you have a good criminal lawyer in your contact list? There is a crazy situation developing at work and I may need to check a few things … in private …"

"Where are you?" interrupted Pam, switching immediately to her professional voice. "Has someone screwed up on one of our deals?"

"No, no, not a deal Pam … something more personal … I'll explain."

"I am completely stuffed at the moment but I could squeeze in twenty minutes for coffee at 4 o'clock."

"I'll be there."

Henry looked at his mobile in disbelief, anger … a constant companion as faithful as a dog, as hungry as a wolf.

Fuck … No, I did NOT screw up. How could she be so bloody quick off the mark? She has collected enough fees from me, been so goddamn ass covering in each transaction. She was bleating away to me when one of the partners opposed her elevation … and without me where the hell would she be?

Henry could not stay mad for very long at Pam. He would not question that feeling of slight helplessness whenever they started a new deal together, getting used to her proximity again after a few hours. But the keen anticipation would always be there after a few months of separation.

* * *

Inspector Pole settled at his desk, stretched his long legs and waited for Nurani to free up the only other chair in his office. She dumped the files at her feet and sat at the edge of her seat.

"So, Nu, what do you make of our particularly exciting case?"

"You mean Crowne? Interesting. What I expected from the City …

with something extra ..."

"And what would that extra exactly entail? Apart from the fact that he is single, probably a millionaire, rather presentable," teased Pole.

"You mean frankly, sexy ..."

"Great start ... a frank assessment of The Banker of the Year 2006, 2007, 2008 ... You look surprised Nu, but we have here quite a pedigree animal," said Pole.

"Not very politically correct, Jon, we are not at a dog show," Nurani grinned.

"And addressing the sex appeal of Mr Crowne is not exactly PC either... Is he sexy?" Pole mused.

"I thought we were staying strictly professional, avoiding any crude sizing up of Mr Crowne."

Nurani was still smiling wryly at her boss.

"Quite so my dear ... quite so. Anyway, the question with Mr Crowne despite his numerous attributes is—"

"Has he got the gumption to commit murder? Could he literally pull the trigger? I am sure he has done so at least in his mind many times in the past, you don't get to be where he is without having slaughtered a few opponents on the way."

Nurani whilst speaking was firing an imaginary gun at the level of someone else's head.

"Well, this is the preconceived idea anyway, you assume that he has had to do some pretty bad things to get where he's got to, but has he? And as you know we are not in the business of assumptions but facts so ..."

The phone rang and Nurani picked up

"Some preliminaries from forensic, I'll go. Shall I also call the team in?"

"No, just bring the results back to me. We'll have a look, you and I, before drumming up the troops."

Pole watched Ms Shah (her preferred title) as she disappeared down the lift to the basement. Nurani had been his first choice when the case had come through. What she lacked in experience, she made up for in sheer determination ... no one in the City could faze Ms Shah.

"And ... she can find a needle in a haystack," Pole muttered as he made room on his untidy desk. His office was permanently cluttered, files, papers, various documents strewn across the room or mounting in piles of various heights. The department's common joke was that any piece of missing evidence would be found in this ridiculous mess.

Pole didn't care. "My favourite detective is Columbo," was the equally common reply given to anyone attempting to introduce their order into his chaos.

He moved a couple of piles with precision, uncovered a blue file, reached for document three, pulled it out with a small flick of the wrist. He had exactly what he wanted. Pole sat down again while surveying his office with a contented grunt.

Pole enjoyed the job because it was 'totally him'. An odd answer for the many who had not reflected on why they were doing what they were but a highly enlightened one for those who had. Pole's propensity to philosophise was regarded with irritation at the Yard. Yet his ability to zero in on a suspect's motivation and get results were respected in equal measure.

As he started reading, Pole proceeded with impeccable logic, creating an elaborate web of possibilities.

There are a number of hypotheses, he thought whilst scribbling some notes. *First accident or homicide-murder. Let's see what Nurani brings but my gut … Murder.* Pole wrote the word in the far-right end side column on his paper. *Then … People known to Albert, either close family friends or within his wider social circle, work … the takeover, past deals, promotion-bonus … any other link to a network of influence. Money, power …a good recipe for a bad outcome.*

Simplicity was paramount as many answers to crime resided in the immediate environment of the victim but the Albert case was already proving different. He had, just this morning, gone through a preliminary interview with Anthony Albert's widow. Pole opened his notebook.

Shockingly calm she was … a high profile hit job … Possible.

Pole looked at the far side of the corridor. Nurani should be back any minute now.

Yes … it's got to be murder, the signs are there, a new plane and one of the most reliable on record, an explosion near the tail of the aircraft where the luggage is stored … Pole had, however, another niggling feeling, difficult to identify, a vague and contradictory sense that although he wanted to keep matters simple, the way evidence was presenting itself was almost too neat. A thought he would keep in the back of his mind for the time being.

"Yep, 'tis a murder case," said Ms Shah.

She had pushed the door open without knocking and was still reading the report.

"Traces of Semtex were found on some of the remains of the private jet, a fairly common but very effective type of explosive."

"Have you asked for the origin of the sample to be traced?"

"Yes Sir, Forensics are on it. It may take a little while unless it is already on the data bank. The guys from the IAFA have also left a message by the way, hope they will not want to interfere too much"

"You bet ... There is a clear security breach at the airport. It's bad enough at a large airport but how can it happen on a private jet. No guaranteed security for the high flyers ... as welcome a problem as a pork chop in a synagogue."

"Wow, goodbye political correctness ... seriously, Jon."

"First thing ... we need to eliminate the pilot from our potential suspect list," Pole said satisfied with his little bad joke.

"Do you think the pilot could be involved? That would be very odd."

"Everybody is a suspect as you know ... don't assume anything in the first instance. And yes, I understand what you mean. But it is possible ... mental illness, less unusual than you think ... frighteningly so."

"OK, that is definitely frightening. I will speak to the company and do a full background check on him."

"Although I have to admit, with a banker on board, my gut is telling me we won't find anything on the pilot."

"So, what do we do next?"

"Now, we follow the trail Ms Shah ... We follow the trail."

"Motive, means, opportunity," she said.

"Correct. Do we think this guy Crowne is on the list?"

"He hates his rival who may be about to take over his team."

"OK, motive!" Pole said.

"He was supposed to be on the aircraft with him."

"Opportunity, I sort of buy that."

"He might have given him docs to carry, or ... something else."

"Yep ... means to achieve his purpose."

Pole was looking through the report without paying real attention to it.

"That is a bit obvious, not a very clever way of covering one's tracks, for a guy who I think is pretty bright."

"Yes but, this is only circumstantial for the time being, he may have involved a pro. I don't see him doing a DIY job on this one, I agree."

"He may lose in the battle for power, but this is common in the City. You live by the sword. You die by the sword ... then get reborn and move on to yet another guaranteed bonus."

"Is that right?" said Nurani, incredulous.

"Yep, absolutely. But granted, Crowne may no longer be thinking straight."

"Exactly. Have you seen his face? He looks as if he has not slept for a hundred years and he lied at our first meeting, several times. You said so yourself."

"*Bon.* Mr Crowne, you're number one on our suspects' list."

Nurani opened up her notebook and slowly penned Henry's name. She was about to suggest another name when Andy Todd knocked at the door. The youngest recruit in the squad, he had started two weeks ago and was eager to show commitment.

"Hey, Nu, got the tapes you wanted. Do you want to view them now?"

"Tapes?" said Pole raising one eyebrow in his inimitable fashion.

Nurani blushed a little.

"Yes, I asked to see the video cameras at the entrance of Crowne's place. Just in case Albert or someone else came to pay a visit. Just to make sure …"

"I see, no flies on you Missus."

Pole was grinning at the speed at which Nurani was following her own logical path.

Pole looked in amusement as his little team vanished in the distance. He stood up and closed the door. A sign he wanted no disruption and started meticulously reading through the file.

* * *

Henry was pacing up and down the small cosy lounge of Chase and Case. Pam had said twenty minutes at 4pm. It was already ten past four and Henry was growing irritable. He stopped his restless walk to pick up a newspaper when someone grabbed his arm. Pam placed a peck on his cheek in a mechanical fashion and pushed him through the exit doors.

"Let's go."

She was looking tanned and relaxed in her grey designer suit, having just come back from two weeks in Barbados where she owned a large flat in one of the secluded parts of the island.

"Right, Henry, what is this garbage about a criminal lawyer? You look like shit by the way, you need to rest my friend."

"Thanks. I feel so much better after that reassuring comment."

Henry was staring at his tea, adding yet another sugar and stirring it cautiously. Contacting Pam may not have been such a good idea after all, however here she was. He told Pam pretty much everything including about Pole's visit. Pam frowned for the entire time he was talking, her dark brown eyes fixed on Henry. She said nothing until he had finished.

"The first thing you must do is ensure you have the GL legal team involved, you don't want to say anything unless you know they are. GL's gators are pretty fierce."

"Who?" asked Henry.

"I mean the litigation team, nicknamed gators after the creatures that hunt in swamps."

"Right ... right," Henry nodded, not amused.

"Henry, what are you concerned about anyway? You seem to imply you are targeted."

"These emails are strange. I've never seen them, I am pretty sure. I am tired not senile."

"Albert was trying to make you sound like an uncooperative little shit. What's new? It's classic merger tactics."

"Unlikely, he would have been found out pretty quickly."

"Look, I'll have a think, don't panic. It is nothing for the time being, OK?" She glanced at her watch. "Got to go. Hang on in there, big boy."

Henry was one of Pam's best clients. She owed him her elevation to the enviable position of equity partner and would call him a friend. These events were, however, strange and dangerous for a young partner. Pam tapped him on the shoulder and left. Henry watched her energetic silhouette move away and noticed that her hair had become blonder in the sun. She had spent exactly twenty minutes with him.

* * *

Back at Scotland Yard, Inspector Pole was still reading the file when he got an excited call from Andy Todd.

"Boss, I got something. I can come up and ..."

"I'll come your way. I need to stretch my legs," said Pole amused at the enthusiasm. *"Ah, to be young and keen again!"*

Pole entered the room in which Andy had been sitting without noise.

"So, how many wine gums packets has it taken you?"

"Er, only three. I mean, I know it's not really mature and all that but it helps the concentration."

"Just kidding, show me what you've got."

They both leaned forward, as Andy rewound the tape and played it back. A man resembling Anthony Albert was pressing a doorbell, hunched over as if speaking into the intercom system, then keying some numbers into the entry door pad. Andy froze the image.

"And now Boss, may I introduce you to Mr Albert," Andy grinned.

"Well done, young man. Keep at it. And have another packet of wine gums on me," said Pole leaving Andy to his task.

Andy punched the air, several hours of viewing not spent in vain. He carried on with the tape to see Anthony Albert walk into the building and come out of it ten minutes and thirty-seven seconds later with not one but two briefcases. Life was hotting up for Henry Crowne.

Chapter Four

Henry decided to walk home. Work was piling up at the office but he could not shake off the events of the past few hours. It was only 5pm and anyone back at base would have called it a half day. He took his BlackBerry out of his jacket pocket in a mechanical gesture and started scrolling down the messages, only paying attention to those that seemed important. The sun was out and despite the bitter cold it felt good to be walking at a quick pace. Henry recognised St John Street. He had somehow given up on the BlackBerry and for the first time in years found himself looking at the buildings in the street. Some of them had been freshly renovated, some replaced by new premises. A strange mix, yet not disharmonious, he was taking the time to notice.

Unlike many City professionals, Henry had chosen to live away from Chelsea, Belgravia or Holland Park. He found these upmarket places stuck up and predictably bourgeois. He had decided to remain in Islington, the area he had moved to when he had secured his first job in investment banking. He had been hunting for the perfect flat for years and had finally found it at great expense. A cash purchase, no mortgage. The estate agent had taken two seconds to persuade the vendor to accept Henry's offer.

A large warehouse with an unusual glass entrance appeared on his right-hand side. The place had been converted a few years ago into a meditation centre for aspiring City MDs. Henry had always resisted the training programmes that might come too close to deciphering who he truly was. He knew he had ambition and that was enough. Henry did not distrust psychology as a science but had little respect for those selling their so-called coaching skills to the banks.

He slowed down as he passed the entrance and shook his head at the thought. He had been in competition with Anthony Albert to win the same client and had engaged in the battle mercilessly. The CEO they were wooing had discovered the power of meditation recently and was enthusiastically visiting this City outpost of St Augustine. Henry could now see himself, kneeling on an uncomfortable cushion trying to stay still without too much wriggling. Albert was sitting a little further in front and closer to their prospective client. Keeping one eye open, Henry was surveying the situation. Albert's heavier body was constantly tensing up. He would not last an hour. To Henry's satisfaction Albert had had to bow and retreat, the cramps in Henry's own legs indicating that he would not last much longer either. At least he could withdraw without his target noticing.

"*Nil points for both of us*," thought Henry as he now saw the line of trees that sheltered his own building.

Tiredness gave way to a warm feeling of reprieve from the events of the day. He was fingering the keys in his pocket. Soon he would be home, a place to reflect and stand at a distance from today's drama.

His solitary life pleased him. The work hard, play hard reputation of City traders was too cliché or perhaps out of date. The eighties were long gone. The days when traders snorted coke at their desks before markets opened had vanished. Banks had decided that the bonuses of their higher paid employees should preferably not disappear up their noses. The expression of power had shifted; expensive tastes of a different nature had replaced the exuberance and carelessness of that era. There were still the second homes in the south of France, the cars, the exclusive restaurants and fine wines but there was now contemporary art, a new battle ground on which to unleash vanity and buying power. Henry's own private collection had moved from antiquities to modern art. He had no interest in spending a fortune on school fees when he could direct his hard-earned cash to the purchase of a masterpiece.

Henry knew that his monastic existence raised eyebrows in the City and so what? Wild speculations about his character fuelled malicious gossip. Was he gay? Was he impotent? Did he have an even darker secret to hide? Henry brushed these aside. Ambition had been his sole mistress and she had never betrayed him.

His mind switched back to the painting sitting in his flat, wanting to close further speculation on his emotional landscape. *The Raft of the Medusa* had not been touched since he had first looked at it. Henry decided to call on Nancy – he felt the piece would be better viewed in someone else's presence. Nancy had mentioned drinks. Why not accept her invitation sooner rather than later? The thought comforted him and the prospect of a conversation with someone in the know presented an irresistible intellectual challenge.

* * *

At Scotland Yard Nurani and Andy had been busy and were now sitting in Pole's office. He was listening intently to what the pair had to say about Albert's visit to Henry's flat.

"So, you are completely positive, Albert came in with one briefcase and left with two."

"Absolutely boss," said Andy. "No mistake! He spoke to someone. You can see him bending towards the entry phone and saying something after he's rung the bell."

Andy kept glancing at Nurani to take his cue.

"Someone else could have been in the flat?"

"Crowne is single, no girlfriend, broke up with someone a few years or so ago, it seems, and the cleaning lady comes on Fridays. His family, well, father is deceased, mother still alive, lives in Asia," said Nurani.

"Did you get a shot of Crowne coming into the building himself?"

"No, but he could have taken the car or simply walked in through the garage door. The CCTV camera was vandalised a few days before, not repaired yet. So we would not have seen him. He takes his car regularly, he's got an MD parking space at the office," replied Andy.

"Anyway Jon, why don't we go and ask him ourselves?" said Nurani. She enjoyed using Pole's abbreviated name when most of his other reporting lines addressed him as Jonathan or Inspector Pole.

"You just want to take a look at how the City bankers live, don't you?"

"Now what would give you THAT impression," she said, not flinching.

"OK, let's go and visit our favourite banker. And Andy, check the log of the GL garage. If Crowne took his car there will be a record of him parking there."

Ms Shah was driving her brand new car, a yellow Beetle with a small flower vase stuck to the dashboard. Today a flamboyant red rose sat proudly in its miniature holder.

"Nu, you don't like this guy but don't let it cloud your judgement."

Pole was right, she did not immediately reply. Pole was one of the few senior officers who had taken time not only to work with Nurani but also to train her; a man for whom welcoming an Asian woman into the force was more than fulfilling the 'diversity' quota. His opinion counted.

"I know Jon. I won't make the wrong remarks. I just think it's such a shame that someone as bright as that should be letting himself down by spoiling his talents in a City job. The only guy I have sympathy with at the moment is the poor bugger who was flying the plane."

Pole remained silent. These two men had died a tragic death, which was now murder. Nothing else mattered. He was not here to judge, that task would be left to the jury. He was here to do his job so that justice could be served. After so many years in the force Pole had reflected many times on the clear difference between revenge and justice, between justice and the law. Profile cases blurred these lines and yet he knew that, to be good at his job, this clear-cut definition had to be understood.

"At his best, man is the noblest of animals, separated from law and justice he is the worst," said Pole.

"Wow, did you come up with that? Profound," replied Nurani with a grin. She had been warned about her boss's philosophical inclination.

"I wish! No, it's a quote from Aristotle."

"Was he not a Greek philosopher?"

"Correct, around 400BC."

"So you are telling me we are here to make a difference?"

"Well I am. And to know that revenge in whatever form is neither law nor justice."

"Right. I will need to ponder that a little if I may," said Nurani, unwilling to be drawn into what she considered a superfluous debate.

Pole observed his young colleague sideways and judged that Nurani was not ready yet for an in-depth conversation. But whether she liked it or not he would one day have that discussion. It was the way he taught.

"Here we are."

Pole opened the door and took time to look at the imposing building. It had been the headquarters of Thames Water in North London at the turn of the last century, displaying sumptuous architecture of heavy stone and classical art deco design. They entered through the gate and walked a few yards, past a series of well-kept grass and flower beds, before reaching the main entrance. The bells pertaining to the flats bore no names. Albert must have known where to go. Pole pressed bell number seven. There was no reply. He moved away from the building and glanced up. There was light in the duplex flat occupied by Henry. Pole persisted and was prepared to ring Henry's mobile when a voice answered.

"Mr Crowne, Inspectors Pole and Shah, may we come in? We called your office, but you had left already."

The main door opened without a sound. They moved along a large hallway of stone, wood and steel. It felt solid and yet light at the same time, a peaceful harmony that was home. Pole and his DS reached the private landing of Henry's flat, and the large door on the far-right hand side opened. Henry leaned against the door frame, one hand in the pocket of his jeans waiting for them to make their way towards him. He looked quite different now that he had changed clothes, more carefree. He had swapped his expensive Savile Row suit for a pair of cheap jeans and an old Dublin university T-shirt. Pole took this opportunity to observe him before the mask of control had time to settle back upon his face.

"Could it not have waited 'til tomorrow morning?" said Henry.

"'fraid not," said Pole, cheerfully.

Henry led the way into the flat. The entrance gave a feel for the eclectic taste of its owner. Sober yet elegant; a small collection of Asian antiquities was displayed round the hallway and as centrepiece a fourteenth-century Buddha from Cambodia rested in a carefully lit niche.

In the main lounge an immense tapestry was hanging on the far wall, it looked old and its distinctive blue revealed its origin to Pole.

"Aubusson," he murmured.

Henry tried to ignore him but felt both impressed and gratified. Pole was not just some ignorant copper to have identified the piece so quickly. Pole glanced at the rest of the room, a few other statuettes had been carefully positioned on dedicated shelves, a large cream sofa with a couple of armchairs added to the peaceful comfort. Henry's lounger in brown leather, matching the frame of the sofa, was surrounded by newspapers and files. A quirky teapot sat on a side table still exhaling the scent of its fragrant tea.

Henry let his tall body slump into the chair, he vaguely gestured to his guests to take a seat.

"We are intrigued by a visit we suppose was for you, Mr Crowne. You did not mention it at our last interview."

A faint smile brushed Henry's lips at the word 'interview', which had in the banking world a much more exciting meaning. Pole took out of his pocket a CD, Henry thought he recognised the initials AA on the cover.

"Do you think we could play this for you?"

"Be my guest."

Henry leaned backwards and grabbed a small compact remote, a large screen appeared over the fireplace. He took the CD from Pole and shoved it into a dark sliver below the screen. Some scrambled images shot across the screen, then froze to present a picture of Anthony Albert speaking into the ground floor intercom of the building. Henry had not had time to sit down and any desire to do so was stopped by the scene. He spotted the date and time at the bottom of the screen 08-10-08//21.57.03. His mind raced back to the time only a couple of days ago, trying to remember whether he was still at the office, at a client's. He needed … an alibi, a word he thought would never enter his vocabulary.

Pole let a couple of minutes pass, he was in no rush to break the silence. Henry felt Pole's focus was total, he was reading his reactions, absorbing every detail, studying the lines on Henry's face, the tension in his body, all information useful to harvest.

"Well it seems to me that Mr Albert was trying to invite himself to a decent bottle of wine," said Henry finally.

Humour always saved his day. But this time the attempt at levity failed. In the silence that followed, Henry heard himself speak,

"Why do I have the feeling Inspector Pole that you do not believe me?"

"Play the DVD further, you will see my dilemma."

And so it was that for the next few minutes Henry witnessed, incredulous, Anthony Albert buzzing his doorbell, entering the building and finally walking out with not one but two briefcases. The images finally vanished, leaving a grey screen. Pole waited, again in no hurry to suggest a possible scenario. Nurani had made herself invisible by studying the surroundings with great care. Henry followed Nurani's glance. She had noticed the large parcel still in bubble wrap lying against the wall at the far end of the room. It looked incongruous in Henry's well-orchestrated décor and *The Raft of the Medusa*'s power shook Henry's confidence.

"What is the crazy asshole doing? He was not supposed to collect them himself, anyway."

"What was the a-hole not supposed to do?"

Pole sounded amused by this sudden lapse in political correctness.

"The papers I told you about yesterday. He was not supposed to collect them himself."

"Well, Mr Crowne, it looks as if he found them after all."

"Correction Inspector. What he found was a briefcase. God knows what was in there," Henry struggled to regain control of the situation. After all, he was right. Who could prove what was in the case?

"Point taken. But you must admit this is rather strange."

"Strange as it might be, I certainly did not see him that evening."

Pole sat back in his seat. The amazement on Henry's face was genuine enough, he felt he had passed that test.

"So where were you that evening?"

"I was here. Later that is. What was the time again?"

Pole grabbed the DVD case.

"Time 22.57."

Henry had seen Liam that evening. He had no intention of saying any more for the time being. Liam was not the type of character he wanted to discuss with Pole. He needed to leave him out of the discussion at all cost.

"Yes, I was back at home."

"From where?"

"The office actually." This was not a complete lie since Henry had dashed back into the office to grab some documents he needed for an early morning meeting. One of the trainees had stayed late to prepare the pack for Henry.

"You are not going anywhere in the next few days I presume. We may need to talk some more," said Pole. "We need to understand what Mr Albert was doing at 22.57 … at the bottom of your building."

"Absolutely Inspector."

* * *

Henry was walking back toward the lift. He had insisted on accompanying Pole to the door of his building and watched the two speak as they entered their car. He had not performed well and suspicions would be mounting. In a strange way, Albert was suddenly in control of his life. But Henry shrugged, Albert was dead. He was about to press the lift's call button when a voice stopped him.

"Henry, what a happy coincidence," said Nancy as she walked towards the lift herself.

"Nancy, how nice to see you," replied Henry, forcing a smile.

"Would you care for a drink? That is if it is not too late of course."

Henry took time to assess his neighbour. He liked her energy and elegance.

"Excellent idea, I could do with a drink and a good chat," he said.

Nancy smiled amiably.

"Let me bring the wine if I can be that forward as to come to yours. I would love to take a second look at your new acquisition."

"Something tells me that you are not going to take no for an answer," said Henry, seeing the humour in the situation. His flat, his sanctuary would be invaded again although he had to admit he was looking forward to this latest intrusion.

By the time Nancy entered his lounge, Henry had positioned the painting on the sofa again. He had not removed the bubble wrap. She thought it strange but said nothing. Henry poured two glasses.

"Are you a collector yourself?" asked Henry.

"Yes, but I also support a small gallery."

"I thought you were a lawyer? The head of Chase and Case mentioned your name a while ago," said Henry intrigued.

"I was, a barrister to be exact. It feels like a lifetime ago and no longer that interesting," replied Nancy.

Henry was torn for a moment between the desire to know more and that of speaking about his own collection. Surely a successful lawyer would not give up such a lucrative career.

"We can talk about my old profession some other time if you are interested," said Nancy, relaxed. "How about discussing something that matters much more: YOUR collection."

"Absolutely," replied Henry.

Had he been that transparent?

"I must say … This is a daring piece to acquire."

Nancy drank a little wine and carried on.

"Do you have a particular affection for the original?" she said as she stood up to move towards the painting.

"In truth, I have never seen the original. I mean, I have seen it in books but not in the flesh, so to speak, and … I don't see why it makes any difference," said Henry failing to hide his annoyance. This was not an art history course.

"I agree, a painting can have an immediate effect on the viewer but in this instance, it presents a background story with considerable significance."

"Which is what exactly?"

"Well, Géricault's *The Raft of the Medusa* depicted a tragedy that shocked the world and reinforced in France the distrust in the old monarchy."

"I still don't see the point."

"The *Medusa*'s wreck was largely attributed to the incompetence of its captain, Viconte de Chaumarey. He was perceived to be acting under the authority of the restored French monarchy."

"Why would the monarchy be involved in such an appointment?"

"*Absolument* and a very astute question indeed," acknowledged Nancy. "It is almost certain that King Louis XVIII had nothing to do with it. But remember the whole affair happened at a point in time in French history where democracy, as defined by the revolutionaries of 1789, has failed and yet monarchy is still unable to make a full come back."

"The event was pretty horrific. How many survived?" asked Henry, sensing the potential of the original story.

"Only fifteen out of the one hundred and forty-seven crew survived. And those who did had to suffer starvation and cannibalism, murder, despair."

"Do you see an analogy with the way French people saw the monarchy?" said Henry.

"I see two analogies. Yes, I see the incompetence of the French captain confirming the view that France had of its monarch but," said Nancy, pausing as if to find the right words.

"And the second?" said Henry, eager to put forward the idea that had just dawned on him. "Are you going to tell me you see a parallel with what is happening in the markets?"

"Artists have an uncanny sense for what comes next. *Il me semble*," said Nancy.

"Nancy. This is only a painting."

"Then why do you want to buy it?"

"It is well executed, and the theme powerful."

"It is not enough, Henry … it has meaning for you, not an intellectual one, a deeper one. *Oui, quelque chose de profond.*"

Henry poured some more wine in the two empty glasses, searching for a response and trying unsuccessfully to summon his French.

"There are a number of other pieces that represent the *Raft*. To me this is significant. The collapse of the old, the coming out of the new," finished Nancy.

"I don't see it myself but then again I have not spent ages intellectualising this purchase, *et puis, je parle mal francais.*"

Henry had hoped for a diversion from today's events but instead found himself dragged into a philosophical debate he did not want to have. Nancy sensed the mood. There would be nothing to gain in arguing with a very tired Henry.

"You might be right, I might see too much in this piece," replied Nancy. "But I hope you will indulge me if I speak French, a necessary contribution to my mixed cultural background and reminiscence of intellectual pride." She smiled at Henry and the intelligence he read in her eyes struck him. She had defused his anger with unexpected calm.

Nancy changed the subject and spoke about the coming Frieze Art Fair, the latest big names who would be displaying their work. Henry finally relaxed. He could not resist a few good insider tips.

Chapter Five

The global structured equity 7am conference call had just finished. All participants from either Asia-Pac, Europe or the US had left the call but Henry was kept behind by one of his nosier colleagues. He was keen to gather information about the 'Albert case' as he put it. Henry had no intention of volunteering anything meaningful but had not moved quickly enough from the room to avoid him. Despite claiming he had an urgent appointment, he was unable to shake the limpet who accompanied him for part of the way to his phantom destination.

Morag saved the day when she spotted Henry's attempt to extricate himself from the little man.

"Henry," she shouted across the floor. "Your call. Starting. Five minutes ago."

She walked over to them, ignoring altogether the other man. She looked annoyed at this lack of punctuality. The limpet let go, not wanting to be accused of wasting Henry Crowne's valuable time.

"Well done. That guy is such a moronic prick! Why do we bother keeping people like that?"

"His father sits on the Bank's board. He is such a leech too, always trying it on. Anyway, you had a few calls. I've left messages on your desk."

"Anything from Pam?" asked Henry

"Nothing, but internal legal called."

Henry nodded and swiftly entered his office. Since the plane crash, he had spent more time there than he usually did. This was very unlike him and would not remain unnoticed on the floor for very long. As a rule, Henry liked to be among his people. He always sat at the same bank of desks as they did and was content for his office to be used for calls or meetings. The Floor could be noisy when activity flared up, to the point where no decent amount of thinking could be done. Most people who had spent time working there could cope with it. Some even claimed they could never work in any other environment such was the energy emanating from it.

Henry sat down and flicked through his messages. Pam had not called. Did it mean anything? He would give her a couple of hours and call again. This lack of contact was more upsetting than he liked to admit.

James Radlett knocked on the glass partitioning, Henry waved him in. It would be good to talk business, something familiar he knew he was good at.

"Hi, do you have a minute?"

"For you James, always," smiled Henry.

Out of his twenty-three strong team, Henry had chosen James as his number two. James had had a very unusual career path which made him ideal for the job. James had started in the army. He had joined the Intelligence Corps and had been deployed alongside the 2nd Rifles, but an injury during his time in Kosovo had cut short his time on the field. He had decided to change his career altogether and found himself on a 'programme for mature students' at GL. His training in the military had multiple advantages for his reporting line which Henry had immediately recognised. He respected the chain of command and showed Henry absolute loyalty. James could withstand pressure better than most, having had to face the prospect of death for a meagre army salary, but never spoke about his time in combat. In return, James demanded absolute transparency from Henry, which Henry gave him unreservedly.

"So how is the deal with Google doing? Last time we spoke the strike on investors' put options was still under discussion."

"Still waiting for back-test results, the Quants team is reviewing the model. I think we are close; probably a one-year and a three-year put with a 110 and 130 strike."

Henry arched his eyebrow. "Quite a risk for the issuer."

James nodded feebly in agreement, showing he was not particularly interested in pursuing the discussion on their $5billion star deal.

"Henry …"

Henry stopped juggling with his pen, startled to hear James call him by his full name rather than the usual 'H'.

"What is happening with this AA story? People are starting to gossip. Some really screwed up rumours are doing the rounds and the team is getting worried."

"Such as …?"

Henry straightened himself up in his chair.

"Well, speculation as to who would gain the most from his murder. I am sure that the guys at HXBK have put your name in the hat. Such a bloody good opportunity can't be missed."

"And what do you think James?"

His voice remained calm but his entire attention was focused. He was not prepared to take any of this fucked up crap from anyone, certainly not his own team.

"You tell me, Henry."

James had remained equally calm in his response.

"Do I understand your question correctly? Are you actually asking me whether I —" (the words stuck in Henry's throat) "have bumped off Albert?" His hands stretched over his desk as he was speaking, his body leaning forward. One move and he could reach James.

"A valid question," said James leaning forward as well. "It is direct but I have seen some bloody awful things in service."

"James, firstly we are not '*in service*', secondly what do you think I am about to say? Even if I had done it, which by the way is completely ridiculous, I certainly would not tell you the truth."

Henry's voice had gone up one notch, the burn of anger setting fire to his throat. But James' time with the Intelligence Corps had taught him all about information gathering. Was he already onto something?

"I had to ask, you know I like to get to the point," replied James as he sat back in his chair. "By the way, I disagree with you on one point. We are at war."

"James, let's take a reality check here shall we? I have worked with you for what – six years? You know me well, do you really think I could dispatch a guy just like this? OK, OK, we are talking about AA, Mr Recovery Man, I know, but still. This is a completely different ball game. I know we use some pretty shit even murderous language on the floor but it stops there! Bloody hell, you know that as well as I do."

"Fine, fine, but be aware that rumours are starting to circulate. Everybody knows that with the IRA's arms decommissioning it is not that hard to dispatch someone, as you say."

A chill went down Henry's spine. Although he had not given it much thought since he had acquired dual nationality, Henry still held his Irish passport, his nationality of origin. And of course there was Liam. Henry was about to reply but thought better of it. James stood up slowly as if to give his last remark time to sink in.

"We will not have any further discussions about this, James. I mean, this is not only bloody ridiculous but also frankly unacceptable."

Henry had got up as well, James left without another word. Henry followed and shut the door. He knew he had not handled the situation as well as he could have but it was now too late to call James back in. He would let things settle a bit and go out for a good bottle of wine; anything could be settled over that. The idea reassured him somewhat. He looked at the various clocks in his office marking the time in different time zones, chose the NY one and subtracted five hours, a silly game he loved playing. It was time to chase the elusive Pam again.

* * *

Young Andy had now been officially appointed to the case. He had spent the last few hours with a permanent Cheshire cat grin on his face, to the annoyance of his colleagues. His first assignment was a full background check on Henry, which he had initiated with enthusiasm.

Pole was having breakfast at his desk when Nurani entered his office.

"I have the transcript of our interview with Albert's merry widow. Shall I leave it with you?"

"Please, we need more time with her. I also want to know what is in Anthony Albert's will, including insurance policies and the like," said Pole.

The first task when opening the case had been to inform the family. Pole had gone to visit Anthony Albert's wife as soon as he could to offer support as well as collect the necessary information. When he arrived Adeila Albert had already been informed of what was considered a 'great tragedy' by the head of Human Resources at HXBK.

Anthony Albert had recently moved to one of the most expensive parts of Belgravia. One of Albert's main objectives in life must have been to become part of the establishment Pole had surmised. The purchase of a large property there was a decisive step in the right direction.

Pole had asked Dolores Patten, the team's psychologist, to join him. He had delivered the same dreaded message so many times and yet he still hated doing so.

On arrival Pole pressed briefly, almost shyly, at the doorbell. The door was opened a minute later by a small woman, dressed in black. Mrs Albert had already decided to rise to the occasion by choosing the appropriate dress code. The sobriety of black was, however, undermined by the ostentatious jewellery. Two diamonds, too opulent to be fake, hung from her earlobes.

The necklace of solid gold reached her waistline; the various rings she wore on her left hand dwarfed her modest wedding band.

Pole offered his condolences as he entered the house, introducing his team in the most tactful fashion. Mrs Albert mumbled an inaudible thank you, interrupting him to ask whether they wanted some refreshments.

"We would not want to cause you any unnecessary work," said Pole.

"Absolutely not. I just dashed to Harrods to buy some food when I heard you would be coming."

"Well, that is very kind."

She disappeared into the kitchen. Pole and his team looked at each other in disbelief. The wait was interminable. The team used that time to observe their surroundings in silence, noticing the collection of antiques that left the place feeling cold and heavy. Adeila Albert returned with a large silver tray, on which sat a delicate bone china tea service. Pole stood up and helped her, placing it on the low table in front of them. It was more a high society tea party than a distraught family gathering. He patiently took his cup and waited to speak, again, at what he thought would be the appropriate moment.

"I am sorry to be intruding at this difficult time but we will need to know more about your husband."

"How could he do this to us? Anthony has always been so unreliable. How am I supposed to cope with all there is to do in this house?" Adeila Albert spat angrily. She was furiously twisting her wedding band round her finger.

Dolores Patten, the police liaison officer, softly intervened.

"I am sure your husband was unaware of the danger he was in."

"And how would you know?" Adeila replied.

"We know this is a difficult moment," said Pole again trying to exercise patience and tact.

"You have no idea! I have two children to look after because Anthony refused to send his beloved daughter to boarding school. That is a fatal mistake. The child needs discipline."

"Mrs Albert, we do need, if at all possible, to ask a few questions about your husband."

"Ask away, ask away," said Adeila Albert with a small disparaging wave of the hand.

"Are you aware of anyone who may have a serious grievance against your husband ?"

For the first time Adeila Albert seemed to pay attention to what Pole was saying.

"Why do you ask?"

"Well, certain preliminary tests have led us to believe that this plane crash may not have been accidental."

Pole paused to let the devastating piece of news sink in.

"I know it is yet very early days but we need to inform you of this," he continued.

Adeila Albert stayed silent for the first time. Pole carried on.

"We need to establish whether there was anything troubling him? Did he confide in you? Are there any indications you can give us at this stage? Of course, you can think about it and call us later if you would like."

"There is the takeover of course, Anthony was very busy, and, well, concerned about it." Adeila Albert's voice sounded less confident. "He had mentioned some other person who wanted him out. Anthony is not the most courageous of men you understand, Inspector, but he sounded more scared than usual."

"Did he mention any names?"

"Some Irish person. I don't really remember. Henry – Brown – no, Crowne?"

"Anything else?"

"I have given you a name. Is that not enough? Anyway, Anthony was working in the City."

"So, there was no one else, in your view, either in the City or outside?"

"No."

Adeila Albert brushed her hand through her hair in a seductive fashion.

"More tea?"

Without waiting for an answer, she poured tea into the half-drunk cups.

"We should probably leave Mrs Albert, Inspector," said Dolores Patten softly. Pole nodded.

"If you need any assistance please call me, this is my card," added Dolores.

"I can cope perfectly well on my own," said Adeila, ignoring the card.

"And this is mine," said Pole, leaving his card on the table in a determined gesture.

Adeila rose and walked her guests to the door. The interview was over.

* * *

Henry had left the door of his office closed.

Time to call the elusive Pam.?

He could not stay annoyed with her for long. She was, after all, a 'very busy girl' as she liked to put it. The scent of Chanel N°5 floated out of nowhere in his room. Henry's pulse jumped a beat. He had not seen Pam for a few weeks. Time spent apart always gave her a more intimate presence. Something he had learned to tame but felt hard to control today.

Pam's PA answered. She recognised Henry instantly and apologised profusely. She would nudge Pam again. She knew it was urgent. Henry grumbled a vague thank you and frowned. What the hell was Pam playing at? He needed her now. He grabbed a large deal tombstone lying on his desk and read the text inscribed on it. Their first deal together. He looked at his watch. He would call her mobile in thirty minutes.

* * *

Pole was rearranging his tallest pile of documents, fishing for a file he knew was near the bottom whilst Nurani updated him on progress.

"Meeting this afternoon with the IAFA at 2pm," said Pole.

"Background check on Albert in good shape. Started on his wife and family, will have more late afternoon. I have prepared a request for the court to grant us permission to hold and question Crowne plus remand in custody if necessary."

Pole ruffled his goatee but said nothing.

"I have updated the list of people who saw Albert a few days before the crash. We have a few more to see but he seemed to have very much kept himself to himself, at least in the past few months."

"I've also made a list of people close to Crowne, team, colleagues, friends and foes. Will call on them as well."

"Good, what else?" said Pole finishing a cup of coffee that was precariously resting on the side of a notepad.

"Nearly finished the background checks on the pilot. Nothing coming up. As you rightly predicted, Jon."

Pole shook his head, flattery would never get anybody, including Nurani, very far with him.

"When are we going to have the pleasure of interviewing Mrs Albert again? Can't wait," carried on Nurani, carefully wiping a crumb off Pole's desk.

"I have left a message on her answer phone. No reply yet. We may have to invite ourselves for tea again," replied Pole. "Block out some time in both our diaries. I want to have a good stretch to go through all the info with you after this afternoon's meeting."

"Will do Jon."

Nurani paused.

"Anything on your mind, Inspector Shah," asked Pole leaning towards her with an over-serious face.

"Not yet Inspector Pole," she retorted, leaning forward towards her boss, mimicking his gesture. She could not hold it for very long and started laughing.

"I'll tell you later. Suspense is key."

Chapter Six

Henry finally got an answer from Pam. She had placed a heavy caveat on her choice but had at last given him a name. The barrister was a certain Harold Wooster QC, a specialist in Corporate Criminal Law. Even Henry had heard of him. He had been material in successfully defending a couple of investment bankers in a notorious insider dealing case. Market manipulation of share price had occurred on a large scale, resulting in a quoted company on the LSE declaring itself bankrupt. The trail led the regulator straight back to the door of the well-known institution and yet Wooster had demonstrated that the evidence gathered was not beyond reasonable doubt. The traders had walked free. Holding Wooster's address had pacified Henry somehow, and yet the conversation he had had with James lingered.

What evidence could have pushed James to suspect he could be involved? Yes, it was true that the City was a cruel and unforgiving place and thinking of 'murder' could indeed take place in many forms. It happened every day, battles for positions, battles for transactions. James was right, in a sense they were constantly at war. He remembered one of his colleges saying arrogantly, "My mind is my sword, my will my armour", as if to introduce some semblance of chivalry into his selfish attitude to work. What a lot of bullshit. Maybe fifteen, twenty years ago ethics still meant something to people in the City but the increased domination of the trading floors where the stakes were unimaginably high had put an end to this.

He had done what he had to do. First to survive, then to grow and finally to reach the position he so desired. He admitted he was ambitious, in fact fiercely so, but he never saw anything wrong with it. His childhood in Northern Ireland had not been easy, then again it had not been disastrous either.

Or had it?

It had fostered in him the desire to live intensely, to take risks, to challenge himself, find his limits. He never wanted to feel fear again.

But the old question came back to him.

Could he *actually* kill?

Could he bear the sight of the body torn and lost? He was ruthless, he knew. He had removed people from his team who did not perform to the highest standards he imposed on himself. He, Henry Crowne, had done so in what he considered to be a tactful and humane way. But the choice between the black bin bag and the quiet chat on the side was the only attempt to appear considerate. The careful words selected to make the point that, "*you did not make the grade*", or "*sorry you batted for the wrong team*" were always the same, picked more in an attempt to avoid a lawsuit rather than to show compassion. He pondered, but then again there was Belfast. Henry forced the image of his native city out of his mind. He once more focused on the ways of the City, the subtle back-stabbing, the gossip and opinions directed at colleagues or competitors to gently discredit them. An activity repeated every day, so common that it became hardly noticeable after a while.

Henry was still deep in thought when Morag tapped at the glass partition.

"I am off for the day. Do you need anything else tonight H?"

"No, that will be it. Thanks." Henry smiled.

Morag had been superb, not a word about the events of the past couple of days, business as usual. Amazing.

He had not noticed the time or the fact that the desks were already deserted. At 7pm it was rather unusual, then again the past few months, certainly the past few days, had been anything but. He was himself glad to be able to escape early. He made his move.

* * *

The meeting with the IAFA had been predictably tedious. The question of the breach of security was clearly on everyone's mind as no new details had emerged from the interrogation of personnel at the airport or from the pilot's background checks. Pole had decided not to mention the second briefcase until it was clear it was a material piece of information. He wanted to gather more but also force the IAFA investigators to dig deep on their side, a strategy that could backfire. He was prepared as ever to take the risk. Pole was unhappy at the cosy way evidence was lining up and he was willing to stretch his luck.

Nurani had not attended the meeting. She was to fully concentrate on the background checks. Information was starting to arrive thick and fast. It was time for Pole to carry on completing the picture of the murder he had started to formulate.

There was a great deal of activity at Pole's office when he arrived. Nurani was on the phone, frantically taking notes. Andy was organising documents on the meeting table. The team had been busy in his absence and Pole felt invigorated at the thought of plunging into the nitty gritty of the case again.

"Hi gang," said Pole cheerfully.

"Hi Boss," said Andy.

"What have you got for me?"

"Followed your advice and got my own thinking organised on the white board and then file. Hope you don't think I am, sort of, lacking initiative," blurted Andy.

"To give orders it is essential first to know how to receive them. That's always my first piece of advice to you young people," smiled Pole.

"You like training people," said Andy.

"Is that a question?"

"No, no, I can see that and I sort of really like it."

"Well, I am sure you have been told that I am a bit of an oddball. And don't worry, I don't mind a bit," carried on Pole. "Just tell me if I start acting like your dad though."

"Boss, I can tell you there is zero chance you'll be like my dad." And with that Andy closed the discussion.

Pole nodded, he would elucidate Andy's last remark over a more convivial pint of beer.

Nurani waved as she finished her conversation and put the phone down. She looked triumphant.

"The travel agent confirms they sent the tickets."

"OK." Pole dumped his mac on his chair. "Rewind will you. Which travel agent and which ticket and where?"

"Sorry. Plane tickets to go to Zurich on HXBK's private jet were delivered to Crowne's flat the day before the trip. The travel agent says someone signed for them. I have asked for the documents to be scanned and sent to us."

"Very good. Bring them along as soon as you get them. Andy, what have you got for me?"

"Quite a lot actually, Boss."

Pole was about to ask Andy to stop calling him Boss every time he opened his mouth but thought again.

"Right. Shoot."

"Background check on Albert and his family nearly completed, lots in there. Statement from the integration committee – they have been willing to release this before they do so to anyone else but it's very general. We'll need a lot more detail. Finally background on Crowne, I have not got all the basic but there are a few bits that may be interesting already."

"Sounds excellent. Let's begin with Albert."

Andy adjusted his thick glasses on his nose and started flicking through the tags he had arranged in Albert's file.

"For a start, his original name is not Albert but Albertini. His father was an Italian immigrant. He owned a small pizzeria near the train station in Southend. He and Albert's mother never got married and it was a real struggle for him, I mean the father, to stay in the UK before the EU. We have a wad of applications for work permits and so on. He died when Albert was very young, five or so. The mother never married, she had a small allowance from her family but was always on the breadline from what I can tell."

"Is she still alive?"

"No, died a few years ago."

"So, Albert had no money as a kid, no real family around him and what does he do next?"

"Well, he gets into accountancy. Safe job and all that. He is a bright guy because he gets his diploma with distinction. He gets married to someone else on the course and as soon as they are married he changes his name, making it more English, I suppose."

"So, from Mr and Mrs Albertini, we now have Mr and Mrs Albert."

"Right, then." Andy was flicking through the file. "He spends five years at Arthur Andersen, works as an adviser to City Group for some of their structured products and makes the big move into banking. Spends another five years there and gets headhunted into HXBK for the small guaranteed bonus of US$200,000. That was thirteen years ago, not bad."

"Actually, not that great Andy. Even thirteen years ago some of the big boys earned a damn sight more! So Albert did not negotiate his welcome pack into HXBK that well, probably because he moved from Arthur Andersen after the Enron scandal. Please check … What else?"

"His wife stopped working eleven years ago. They had their first kid, a daughter called Anastasia, now age eight, and a son Alexander, age four. They only moved to Belgravia two years ago, before that they lived south of the river," said Andy flicking through his notes more vigorously. "Aaannnd … a few more bits. He and his wife may have had some marital problems – they went to see a marriage counsellor about five years ago."

"Before the second kid was born?"

"Yep."

"Had a second kid to try to shore up the marriage. Anything else in that vein could open up possibilities, in particular if he is the one playing away … oh, and for that matter is she playing away?"

Pole remembered how Adeila Albert's attitude had changed during their first encounter when he had mentioned potential enemies. He was about to call Nurani to check on their next meeting with Albert's widow when Ms Shah appeared in his office.

"Got the scanned documents. Don't recognise who signed for the tickets. Might be the janitor but we need to check. I will give him a call to see if he remembers slotting them into Crowne's mailbox."

"Regrettably, it looks as if the delightful Mrs Albert will have to wait for a while," said Pole.

"So we think Crowne got the tickets. That would confirm Albert was expecting him but does not confirm Crowne had agreed to be on the flight."

"Maybe but why would Albert send the tickets then?"

"To force Crowne to be on that very flight, in particular if he, Albert, wanted to have a meeting which the other guy, Crowne, was trying to avoid."

"Surely Crowne would have made an excuse even at the last minute – unless … unless Crowne did not want people to know he had agreed to be on that flight."

"That's a point."

Pole pondered this for a while.

"What happened to the second briefcase? Albert would have wanted to open it before the flight to check the contents. He would have wanted to look at the presentation or whatever Crowne was supposed to deliver to satisfy his curiosity, and anxiety. Why take a second case full of documents if you can't open it?"

"So, we need to establish whether he opened the bloody thing," said Nurani.

Andy, who had not said a word, raised a timid hand.

"Yes," said Nurani turning towards him, unhappy at the interruption.

"If I remember correctly, from what I saw on the CCTV camera, I should be able to tell you what type of lock it is, I mean, was."

"Can you?"

"If it is a simple key lock, then it is easy enough to open even without the right key. If it is a combination lock well, then, it is much more difficult."

"Excellent, go and find out. I need to know whether there was an issue with opening the case. Did Albert try to contact Crowne to get it open? We did not spot anything on email, Nurani, so check for text messages, voice messages. I want to know whether Albert was carrying a case he had not and could not open."

Both disappeared leaving Pole to immerse himself in the fast-growing case. This would be a welcome late night.

* * *

It was 6am when they came for him. Henry had just switched off the alarm when there was a ring of the main entrance bell. Henry knew immediately who it was. The sound of his doorbell had the effect of a cold shower, he was wide awake, his mind totally alert. Inspector Pole and Ms Shah stood in front of him as soon as he opened the door. They had a search warrant for his apartment. There was no point in protesting, so he moved sideways with a welcoming gesture as if to invite them in.

Irony …

The only way to remain in control. Henry got dressed quickly and grabbed the piece of paper on which he had jotted down Harold Wooster's telephone number.

Nurani had spent a good part of the night searching through various emails, text messages and phone records to find any piece of evidence that would link Henry, Anthony Albert and the second briefcase. She had been rewarded for her efforts with the discovery of a text asking for the PIN number of a briefcase, textbook evidence. Andy had also confirmed, through his work on the CCTV videotape, that the briefcase lock was a combination one. It could not be opened unless the PIN number had been entered into the lock. The text read, *Number invalid, please resend code.* There had been no reply from Henry.

The accumulation of evidence necessitated a formal chat with Mr Crowne. Henry was also a flight hazard and Pole was not taking the risk.

Henry sat down without a word, finding space at the back of the police car. Pole took his seat next to him. Both men remained silent until they reached Scotland Yard. The smell of early morning disinfectant assailed

Henry's nostrils as soon as he entered the building and was suddenly back to being a boy in Northern Ireland.

He is no more than seven. It is the first time, but not the last, he ends up in the nick – no … the paddy! Some street fight with another gang of kids descends into chaos, bricks thrown, windows smashed. The police are called and catch up with them pretty quickly. In those days any scuffle attracts an instant police response. Belfast is not a playground for young boys. After a couple of hours, his mother comes to collect him. A quiet English woman, she came to Ireland as a teacher, married his Irish father and decided to stay. But she has never managed to find her place among the Irish, and found herself shunned by the English as well. Why does he have to hang around with the Irish mob? She tries and fails to scold little Henry. He remembers her crying. On that occasion he feels ashamed but anger prevails … always.

Pole's voice had shaken Henry back. He had directed him towards the interrogation room. Henry had barely noticed he had been processed in the *customary fashion*. Pole had offered a drink.

"A good cup of tea would not go amiss," said Henry with his usual hint of irony.

His renewed confidence at holding Wooster QC's address, had pushed him to start without his lawyer. There would be plenty of time to call at a later stage. Calling him too early might indicate guilt and he had no intention of giving Pole ammunition.

Inspector Pole started the interview with Dolores observing. A trained psychologist was helpful now that serious questioning was underway.

Both men went over old ground, the sequence of events, the CCTV tape, the takeover, Henry's relationship with Albert. The answers came back identical. The interview had been going on for an hour and a half when a text message flashed up on Pole's mobile phone. He excused himself and left Henry alone in the room. Dolores waved as Pole appeared in the observation room.

"Are you taking five so that you can see how he will react on his own?"

"Yes and no. I've received a cryptic text from Nurani, more evidence rolling in and it was time to take the pulse with you. So, what do you think?"

"On the surface, self-assured, focused, excellent memory. He is going to use the same words for the same questions no matter what. He has formidable self-control. If you go deeper and I mean much deeper, there is a lot of anger."

"Interesting, you mean old anger coming from way back?"

"Yes, past events, not surface aggression."

"OK, keep up the good work. I will be back."

"Count on me. Don't often study a specimen coming from one of the largest trading floors in the City."

Pole was about to make his way to his office when Nurani appeared. She could not resist the temptation of observing Henry in the cage and had come to deliver her piece of information to Pole.

"I was on my way."

"I know, but this is massive Jon. Henry has some connection with the O'Connor brothers, Liam and Bobby."

Pole's focus became absolute.

"Any recent contact?"

Nurani nodded slowly as if to emphasise her response.

"Two days before the crash."

Chapter Seven

Pole resisted the temptation to go back into the interrogation room and savage Henry.

Was he getting soft?

If Henry had the serious IRA contacts he seemed to have, anything, absolutely anything was possible including taking a plane down. After the IRA decommissioning, the O'Connors had remained on a small list of hardcore operatives; a recent fusion of three IRA splinter groups meant reinforced vigilance in Belfast and London.

Anger was not part of his temperament but Pole was angry. Angry at himself for having given Henry the benefit of the doubt, but more importantly because he might have made a fundamental mistake, one which an officer of his rank and experience should never make. He kept asking himself why as he walked towards his office, but could find no answer.

It was unlike Pole to ask anyone in his team to get him a coffee but nevertheless he asked Nurani to fetch him one. He always looked upon his colleagues who abused their juniors with disdain. But Pole was annoyed, he wanted space. Nurani left him, deciding on a particularly good coffee shop. Inspector Pole needed a treat and space to brew.

She came back ten minutes later and placed a cup of coffee in front of Pole.

"Here we are Jon, strong latte, one sugar."

His fist was still clenched in front of his mouth. He was not looking at the file.

"Thanks, Nu, much appreciated. Give me the lowdown on the Irish connection."

"In the background check, we noticed that Crowne had gone to school with the O'Connor brothers. This rang a bell and so we tried to see whether we could trace any contact they may have had after they left school. Crowne and Liam O'Connor shared the same house with a number of other students when they went to college in Dublin."

"They could not have gone to uni together. I thought Henry's mother was English. And after his father died she looked after him on her own," interrupted Pole.

"Correct. Crowne went to Trinity, which would have been very usual in those days. The O'Connors went to UCD but they shared the same house."

"Did Crowne leave straight after uni to come to London?"

"Correct again. It seems that after uni, Crowne saw them far less but whenever he went back to Ireland, he called Liam and they might meet, with or without Bobby."

"How do we know all this? Was he under surveillance?"

"No, not him, but the O'Connors were."

"Obviously," said Pole. "Henry must have known that his friends would be tracked. He can't have been that naive."

"Perhaps. Or maybe he didn't think the Counterterrorist Squad would find anything. I don't know but he met with Liam again about six months ago. Now, the amazing thing is that it was after the closing of a large transaction in Dublin and guess what? Anthony Albert was there as well."

"Crowne and Albert hated each other's guts … a meeting on Crowne's turf. We need to know more."

"Albert's team had little to do with the transaction but I get the feeling that he invited himself to the party anyway. It was a very big ticket – $3.5 billion."

Pole could not help smiling as Nurani used the term *ticket* like a pro from the banking world.

"Don't think I am going mad, I did get the number right. I guess Albert wanted to be part of the glitz. May have cost him his life, of course."

"Are you not jumping to conclusions a little fast here?" said Pole.

"Well, hear me out, this is NOT the end of it," she said emphatically. "Liam hardly comes to the UK for the reasons we know. He did, however, visit last week, arrived on Sunday and left Tuesday night for Dublin. On the Monday he had a drink with Henry." She was about to carry on when Pole lifted his hand.

"So, he has lied to us again. How did we find out about the meeting between these two?" he said.

"Liam is not involved these days, apparently, in anything too dodgy but since the IRA decommissioning some of the old members have remained active," Nurani replied.

"Liam? Now a faction IRA member?" said Pole dubious.

"Well, I'm not sure, but Bobby may be one of them, the Counterterrorist Squad was a bit vague. They keep an eye on Liam as he could be a go-between."

"So, they were following Liam?"

"Yep, although again they were a bit circumspect about this but I gather they have continued tailing Liam ever since the IRA gave up on their terrorist activities."

Pole stood up abruptly.

"Time to reconvene with Mr Crowne. Want to join the fun?"

Henry had been sitting by himself. He knew that behind the tinted glass someone was observing him. He was still relaxed. Waiting games were common in the banking world, in particular around the negotiation table when final terms were being discussed during closing sessions. He had been taken aback by the delivery of the so-called tickets. Then again, the replacement janitor was not the sharpest knife in the drawer. Something he thought would need to be discussed at the next landlord's meeting. If he can't do the job well, plenty of competent people can. Just give the moron the sack.

Henry decided to control his anger by reflecting upon his successful career. He did not want to allow his mind to wander, to feel the pressure of the moment. He chose to go back to the closing of one of his most impressive deals. *People have a vague idea of what goes on in the City*, he thought. Large bonuses and expenses paid were all that was ever spoken about in the papers. The unacceptable level of risk, sometimes irresponsibly taken, was also a favourite subject. Of course, the high level of technical knowledge, the heavy regulatory environment, the sophistication of the entire machinery that enabled an investment bank to exist was completely ignored by the media whose appetite was solely for scandal and scoops. Henry was proud to be part of what he regarded as an elite of 'thinkers' who could apply their mind to finding innovative financing structures and do it properly. He had to admit that the greed and stupidity of some idiots might one day bring the entire system to its knees. Cracks were already appearing in the Credit Derivative Market but he was an Equity man and thus keen to distance himself from the bullshitters who sold CDOs.

The trading floors were places of innovation where astronomical amounts of money transited every day, but they also created an environment where egos flourished untamed. Making money had become the sole purpose of the floor and the sense of service that had once been at the centre of banking had disappeared. And yet it had not always been so. Henry remembered, at the beginning of his career, the words 'ethics' and 'client service' had meant something and had mattered. His first interview had been with a grand old bank, now long gone, absorbed and dismembered by a number of takeovers and restructurings. There were two men interviewing him, a young chap marginally older than himself, who had been hired to expand the trading capability of the bank, and an older gentleman whose attitude as investment banker and relationship manager was diametrically opposed to his younger counterpart. Henry had hesitated to fulfil his ambition and enter the banking world. He had sensed the voracity and harshness of the youth, the face of tomorrow's banking. The older man had been running the interview with professionalism and consideration. He was focused on assessing Henry's capabilities but nevertheless strove to be fair. Henry remembered how thick his Irish accent was then, a matter that had long been remedied. He had felt clumsy in comparison to the well-polished and sophisticated interlocutor. The young man had been, on the other hand direct, explaining what he wanted and immediately pressing Henry for weaknesses, challenging his power. Little did he know, for Henry had had more than his fair share of challenges in Belfast, a mistake that would soon cost this cocky little chappie his job. In the fight for supremacy, Henry was a winner.

Yes, today he recognised it – he was the man in *The Raft of the Medusa* climbing on dead and live bodies in order to survive.

The slam of a file on the table brought Henry back to the here and now. He lifted his eyes slowly to meet Pole's. Pole was standing in front of him, his hands resting on the back of a chair, his body tilted forward, controlled anger showing on his face.

"Henry, how about an honest conversation about Liam O'Connor?"

A quote Henry had seen on Bloomberg sprang to his mind 'Always tell the truth and you won't have to remember what you've said'. But truth was about to become Henry's worse enemy.

* * *

The plane had been delayed by two hours. DMac had experienced delays before but this particular episode was testing his endurance. The head of Legal at GL called him on his emergency number at 1am in NY.

McCarthy had hardly gone to sleep when the news of Henry's arrest arrived on his BlackBerry, guaranteeing a sleepless night. Whether Henry was guilty or not was not a consideration for McCarthy. Henry had by virtue of his involvement in Albert's murder case become a liability that needed to be dealt with swiftly. He called his PA Cindy and asked her to ensure his private jet would be ready as soon as possible. Cindy called back fifteen minutes later, departure time would be 6am EAST. His next call was to Roger Pearce, Head of Corporate Communications. GL had to be ready to make a formal announcement. It was imperative at this critical stage in the takeover that they wouldn't lose the upper hand. Any argument would be used by HXBK to establish dominion over its rival and he, Douglas Sullivan McCarthy, CEO of GL would not tolerate it. McCarthy's next call was to Ted whom he had to extract from yet another meeting of one of the integration subcommittees.

"Hi Douglas, what can I do for you? All on track, as discussed. I am doing my best to—"

"Yes, yes, Ted, you are working on the integration of the two businesses – Albert's and Crowne's – are you not?"

Ted gave a very slow, "That's right."

"Good! I will be back from NY in seven hours. I want to see you then, come to pick me up at the airport, contact Cindy, nothing moves on this before we have spoken."

McCarthy had hardly finished his conversation with Ted when his BlackBerry flashed, announcing new mail. Roger Pearce had been at work, a short statement from GL was ready for McCarthy's consideration. The old man smiled. He could certainly get his people to produce. He started reading, satisfied with the speed and quality of response of his management team.

* * *

Pole was sitting opposite Henry. Nurani to his right had also taken a seat.

"I am waiting Henry."

Pole was tightening his grip over the man opposite him and he would not let go until he had the truth.

"We went to school together in Belfast," said Henry, his eyes shifting quickly away from Pole.

"Henry, you should stop playing this smug game of yours right now. You may be excellent at negotiations, you may be the king of the big deal,

64

but that game is over, understood? I want to know everything and make no mistakes, I will."

Pole paused to face Henry full on.

"So, now, I want everything on you and Liam O'Connor and if I can't have it the easy way, I will have it the hard way. Are we clear?"

Henry nodded, his expression unperturbed. He knew that it was time to call his lawyer. Henry duly made his request. He would stay put until his lawyer arrived. He was disappointed at Pole's calm reaction when he announced that Harold Wooster QC would represent him. It had not been the bombshell he had expected. Pole was becoming a serious adversary. Henry felt the fever of the hunt. He had thought through everything, all the better if the opponent was of a serious calibre.

* * *

McCarthy's plane had landed at Biggin Hill. His delay had cost him a meeting with the Global Head of Legal, and his counterpart at HXBK wanted an immediate face to face as soon as he arrived. This meeting, if unprepared, could undermine his current position, strategising was essential. The outcome of the integration committee, including past deliberations, were critical too and should be reworked to indicate a choice of candidate that left no place for argument. McCarthy was creating as much distance as necessary between the bank and Henry.

Ted was waiting for him at the small airport gate. From a distance McCarthy could see the small silhouette of Ted, a young man of Henry's age but with a tenth of his intellect, a fortunate state of affairs in the current circumstances. He would have no problem in getting from Ted what he wanted.

"Integration committee still on standby?" McCarthy had no time for small talk.

"Hi. Yes, yes as you said."

McCarthy entered the limo and closed the partition inside the car, isolating the driver.

"Any record, deliberations or any other documents relating to the choices to be made for the new head of the combined structured product business?"

"I will need to check, I am not sure."

Ted was trying hard to recall the events of tens of meetings.

"This is a yes or no answer," exploded McCarthy. "Are you on that committee or not? Unless you have been missing meetings?"

"No, yes, I mean I have not missed any meetings," said Ted retreating in his seat.

"So, do I need to repeat my question?"

McCarthy's eyes were on Ted, drilling into the young man's.

"I am sure that there is nothing in writing."

Ted was unsure but had decided to give his boss the answer he wanted to hear.

"Check again and report to me, no phone calls or emails directly. I want a definite answer in the next hour."

McCarthy's limousine pulled up in front of GL's headquarters. Ted disappeared in an instant, eager to fulfil his task. The car carried on into the MDs' car park and parked in the CEO's allocated space. The driver got out, opened the door. McCarthy did not move. He was still weighing up the odds that Ted would deliver. At the time that the committee was formed Ted had been the right choice, bright enough but more importantly scared of losing his job, and of McCarthy – an ideal element to manipulate. Ted knew his limits, he knew he had exceeded the level at which he could comfortably operate a long time ago. His only chance of survival was to squarely stay in McCarthy's camp.

The parking space was directly opposite a private lift. McCarthy exited his car and started the ascent to the penultimate floor of the building, exclusively reserved for top management.

Cindy was waiting for him as he walked through the doors, the driver always rang her as her boss entered the elevator. Everyone would be waiting for the 'Big Man' as he walked in. She took his coat and went straight to business.

"David James-Cooper has called again himself, he wants to see you ASAP."

"I know, I need you to give me time, find some credible excuse."

"I will. The head of communications wants confirmation that the text concerning Mr Crowne can now be released."

McCarthy noticed that Cindy had switched from H to the formal Mr Crowne, self-preservation in the corporate world was already at work.

"Confirmed."

"Some reports on the various integration committees have arrived."

McCarthy stopped as he reached the door to his office, his steely gaze on Cindy.

"Anything on structured products?"

"No."

"Thank you, Cindy."

McCarthy opened the door and sat at his desk, he had hardly slept in the past thirty hours. He dialled Ted's number, Ted answered before the end of the first ring.

"I am ready to come up."

McCarthy put the phone down and waited. He knew with certainty that Ted would do what he had to.

A few minutes passed before Ted appeared. He sat silently, his small frame looking lost in the large armchair facing the CEO's desk. McCarthy interlaced his fingers, and rested his hands on his desk, observing Ted as he spoke.

"You are positive this is the only thing in writing that we have, nothing on email?"

"Yes," nodded Ted.

"Good – good." McCarthy leaned back in his chair.

"Are you able to antedate a document?"

Ted gave a small gasp of panic as the impact of what was asked of him registered.

"Yes, it can be done but—" faltered Ted.

"This is not the time to show lack of guts, I reward guts as you know. Ted, shall I ask someone else to help?"

"Well, I suppose the conclusions of the report were not final and we still were discussing I mean, although, of course Henry was the clear favourite and—"

"Ted!" interrupted McCarthy. "Do you think I give a shit about who thought what? I want the right conclusions to have been reached at the right time. Can you deal with it, yes or no?"

"The committee will remember …"

"Are you running this committee Ted?"

Ted nodded.

"Good. Then IT will remember what is good for IT and what you tell IT to remember, right? What do you think the proposed appointment of a murderer will do to our share price?"

"Henry has not yet been—" Ted had no time to finish his sentence. McCarthy was already reaching for the phone.

"I'll speak to Archie, he can take over."

"I could alter the document in that way," said Ted hastily throwing one hand towards McCarthy as if to stop him short.

There was no reply from McCarthy, his hand was still in mid-air.

"I will alter the document in that way."

Ted had spoken slowly.

"Let me know when it's done."

Ted was looking down and McCarthy knew his hesitation. Ted was thinking about Henry who had been a good friend, thinking about the task ahead, thinking that any other course of action would mean the end of his career.

A slap on the desk brought Ted back in an instant and McCarthy met Ted's scared look with the cold gaze of his faded grey eyes.

Ted stood up and left the room without a word.

* * *

As Ted was walking out of McCarthy's office, Henry was contemplating his next move. He was allowed to call his lawyer and had been left on his own to do so. He took out of his jeans' pocket a scrap of paper on which was written Harold Wooster's number. Henry reached for the phone and dialled slowly, making sure he composed the number correctly.

A male voice answered promptly.

"Harold Wooster's chambers, may I help you?"

To his surprise, Henry felt embarrassed.

"Hello," said the voice with impatience.

"Yes, may I speak to Wooster QC please? My name is Henry Crowne. He is expecting my call."

There was a short silence.

"I very much doubt that is the case, sir."

"Well, Wooster QC may be very busy but I have a personal introduction from Pamela Anderson of Chase and Case," replied Henry, irritated.

"Are you certain?" insisted the voice.

"Absolutely," Henry was about to lash out when a terrible thought entered his mind. He broke into a sweat. The words that came next hardly surprised him.

"I am indeed surprised that Ms Anderson" (the voice trailed slightly on the name) "would have managed to reach him. Wooster QC is currently on a sabbatical. He will not be back until next year."

"Who are you?" were the only words that managed to escape Henry's blank mind.

"Harry Lewis-Cooper, his clerk."

Numbness overcame Henry as he dropped the phone down on the table, a small tremor coursed through his body – unbearable panic, then an explosion, a wave of raw anger carried him across the room. He slapped his hand so hard against the wall that his entire body shook. How stupid had he been, the great Henry Crowne, the number one negotiator, fucked – fucked like a beginner.

A distant voice was calling, "Hello? Hello?"

He walked back to the table and slammed down the receiver with hatred.

Ms Anderson had been too busy to make the call or was it that she had not wanted to make the call? Henry's rage had to abate before he could think straight. There was little time left. Pole would soon walk through the door, asking for confirmation of who the lawyer was. Henry felt pain cutting through him, he would look moronic, ridiculous, a joke.

Henry closed his eyes. He forced himself to breathe, to regain some stillness in which he could think outside the predictable pattern; friends and estimated colleagues would have vanished by now.

Henry opened his eyes. Picking up the phone once more, he started dialling.

Chapter Eight

Henry was waiting for Nancy to answer the phone. It had rung five times and he suddenly wondered why he had dialled his neighbour's number. He was about to hang up when Nancy answered in her warm yet firm voice, happily surprised to hear from him.

Henry wondered, she was rumoured to have been a first-class QC, but their last encounter had put a dampener on this image.

"Nancy, I am not around. I was wondering whether you could check on the flat for me?" said Henry.

"Of course. Tell me what you need me to do. By the way, I am horribly nosy. It's my old profession, you see. I hope you won't mind me asking where your travels have taken you."

"Ah." Henry marked a pause.

If he had had a coin he would have probably tossed it: heads a lie, tails the truth.

"Scotland Yard, small dingy interrogation room."

It would have been tails.

"How uncomfortable," replied Nancy unfazed. "Tell me what needs doing but first let me grab pen and paper."

Henry did not have time to reply before the phone went quiet. He remembered that Nancy had purchased an old fashioned 1930s telephone which she was using in her lounge.

Henry hesitated. He did not know her that well and yet he had made the impulsive decision to rely on her to find a defence lawyer in what was rapidly becoming a turning point in his life.

"Actually Nancy, I may need a bit more than just help with the flat."

"Are you referring to my previous expertise as Queen's Counsel," she said, in amusement.

A door had opened, Henry rushed headlong through it. He summarised as best he could the events of the day.

"I am on my way. You do not say or do anything until I have arrived," ordered Nancy.

"I certainly won't," replied Henry, hoping his voice did not betray his gratefulness.

"These bad boys never change."

As the phone went dead Henry wondered whether he had heard the last remark correctly. He managed a smile, she would be an unusual ally.

* * *

James was speaking to one of the option traders when Ted entered the trading floor. Ted rushed into his office and closed the door. He looked pale even from afar. James hovered, speaking to some of the people he knew well. Everyone had a story to tell, the market was diabolical. Ted left his office again and walked quickly towards the gents. James suspected that Ted's rush had little to do with a bad curry but rather a discussion with McCarthy. After all, James had been part of the Intelligence Corps during his stint in the army. He had learned to read the signs. Ted's PA had just disappeared with a wad of documents, James noticed. She would be busy for a while. There was an opportunity.

James dialled his PA's mobile. "Morag, I am sending you a text." Morag knew the drill, a text when James was only a few paces away meant something important was afoot.

Create a diversion for Ted, I need five minutes after he gets out of the gents. Text me when he is on his way.

Morag stood up and James knew she had understood.

James casually entered Ted's office and closed the blinds of its bay window. He moved swiftly to Ted's desk. He was in luck – the PC had not yet gone into sleep mode. Ted's working documents were open for scrutiny.

James shook his head. *What a cretin.* He sat down and inspected the files. Ted was working on the P&L reports of Henry's team but also and more surprisingly Albert's.

"Motherfucker. What the hell are you up to?" murmured James.

James had worked on the P&L figures with Henry. He knew them by heart. He would spot any changes. Yet, the task of amending these papers was not straightforward. Part of the text in the report had to be modified but more importantly so had the figures. Such a change would be more problematic. The final numbers referring to the P&L of the Crowne and Albert teams came from data prepared by the finance departments of their respective banks. James flicked through the screens and consulted his watch, only three minutes to go. Audited figures of the past years were difficult, if not impossible, to amend.

"Bastard. You're going to change the current year and projected figures aren't you? Much easier than the audited," exclaimed James.

Only two minutes to go. James pressed the print button and paper started to spew out of the printer in Ted's office. He was about to get up when he spotted a yellow Post-it. *Andy Todd from Scotland Yard asking for you, it's about who you know.* Henry? Was Ted truly about to commit the unthinkable?

Only one minute to go. His mobile flashed – a message from Morag. He grabbed the documents on the printer, stuffed them into his shirt, opened the blinds again and got out. Everybody was too busy salvaging their job to have noticed him.

James walked back with no rush to his desk.

"Well done," he said to Morag. She simply smiled. Ted had entered his office and closed the door. James waited a few more minutes before disappearing into Henry's office. He needed to take a look at Ted's reworked numbers. The police were looking at gathering evidence, anything that could provide a motive. James pondered on what this all meant. *Ted is working under orders, McCarthy's? ... Got to be.*

But how could he get away with such falsification? Once the documents had been sent to the police there was no turning back. James concentrated on what was lying on the desk in front of him.

The first document showed deliberations about the merit of both candidates, the profile of the teams together with previous, current and projected income figures. The second document showed tables of figures and had been used to feed into the first one. These documents were sensitive, disclosing insider information. They were kept in a separate drive, which only a small number of people had access to, including Ted and the other four senior members of the integration committee.

"*So, Ted has been granted the IT privilege to go into Henry's drive as well as Anthony Albert's,*" muttered James, incredulous. "*This is bloody unbelievable.*"

Ted would have to open the original documents and make the required changes without arousing suspicion.

"*But the system logs any amendments made with names, dates and time of changes. The log would therefore show that Ted, had made some modifications. It would not show where.*"

Mmmm. Maybe the little arsehole has not thought about that." This cheered up James until he noticed a note left at the end of the document.

Documents printed and sent to Scotland Yard re Henry Crowne enquiry.

"*Shit, shit,*" said James through greeted teeth. "*Ted has left a note on the docs so that people think he has only sent them but not amended them.*" A very valid move if questions were asked as to why he opened these reports. All Ted had to do was to make the modifications of text and figures after he had called Scotland Yard and all would look above board.

Henry's face, laughing at one of Ted's jokes, flashed in front of James. He flicked through the documents again. A sudden urge to go in and savage the little git grabbed James, but no.

You want to play with the big boys, fine. Let's see how far you go. James took out the USB key that never left his trouser pocket. Opened the relevant original files and saved them onto it. He would disclose these when the time had come. Revenge was a dish best served cold.

* * *

Cindy knocked at the door of McCarthy's office and entered without waiting for a reply. She had a way of banging on the door which meant matters were urgent. David Cooper-James, CEO of HXBK, had called again. Cindy had gained time by inventing a call from Whitehall but it wouldn't be long until he called back.

McCarthy smiled, revealing that he had been a handsome man, before the City had claimed its price.

"Well done, the pompous arsehole must have been impressed. I am ready to talk to him, wait another half hour and call him back and don't make it easy to find a slot."

McCarthy was preparing his strategy and indeed would make a call to his contact at Whitehall. He left his office and started towards the lift. The place was silent with activity. The floor was reserved for the members of the executive Board as well as their PAs. Most of them were in meetings frantically preparing for the imminent takeover. DMac took the elevator to floor four, which was dedicated to Mergers & Acquisitions. He needed to find a meeting room the phone lines of which would not be recorded as was the case on the trading floor. He also did not want to leave a trace

– dialling from his office or his mobile was out of the question. He turned the corner, ignoring the glances from a couple of employees who recognised him. One of the rooms was empty. He dashed in, pulled the blinds shut and flicked the sign to *occupied* on the door. McCarthy looked at his watch, it was 11am. Exactly the right time to call his contact for an update. He swiftly dialled the number he knew by heart.

"Douglas," exclaimed a voice. "How timely of you to call, I believe we must catch up."

"I could not agree more," replied McCarthy.

"Well, how about this evening at the club? There will be a couple of people joining us, Timothy from the Treasury and Edwina from the Bank of England. Shall we say 6.30?"

"Very well, I will see you there."

"Good, good. Oh, by the way, since I have you on the phone, do you need anything done on the slight issue you are facing at the moment? Such an unfortunate affair."

"Crowne – it is under control, at least so far, but we need to discuss some of the ramifications."

"Certainly, I'll make sure we have time."

McCarthy walked back to his office by the back door, climbing four flights of stairs without taking a break and finding that his stamina was still very much with him. He was now ready for a particularly demanding task, a meeting with his rival, the CEO of HXBK.

* * *

Henry had sent a short text to James twenty-four hours ago, asking him to *look after the shop*. Since then nothing.

Unusual, worryingly so.

James noticed Ted coming back from the executive floor where McCarthy sat. He must have been reporting to McCarthy that the task of amending the P&L had been completed. James still found it hard to believe but the evidence was there, securely locked in his desk.

The words of Gordon Gekko in *Wall Street* still rang true after all these years: "*If you need a friend, get a dog*". A pitbull would have been better than a friend like Ted.

James was right. It was war. It was war every day, without the much-needed camaraderie expected between brothers-in-arms. James' experience of the army was that of harshness and bullying. He felt these were just as present in the banking world if only more subtly evident. The City was feudal. People formed clans, allegiances, in order to protect their positions; a small cluster of people looking after each other's interests, come what may. It was not unusual for these clans to move together. The leader of a team would be headhunted and would inevitably, either immediately or over time, bring across his own people. This generated seismic shock waves for the unfortunate employees whose boss might have been replaced. Some survived, most didn't. Everyone in the square mile would have a view on the amount of money that might have been paid to move the new team. Numbers would be running high, reaching in some cases into tens of millions of dollars. Would the team work in their new environment? The gossip would carry on for months. Despite wanting to establish its reputation as a place of strong intellect, the City was a place of tawdry gossip where reputations and abilities were constantly trashed by competitors who sought to undermine their adversaries at every possible opportunity.

James tried Henry's BlackBerry one more time. He was sitting in Henry's office, playing with his pen, swinging it across the back of his hand, round his thumb and catching it again before it fell. A trick he had learned from his boss, he smiled at the thought. James lifted his head. Someone was watching him. Matt had been observing him and stood up abruptly to mask his distraction. Lack of information was quickly destabilising the group. The usual banter had stopped and people had become unexpectedly quiet, even guarded. Morag herself, Henry's PA, who took no prisoners when it came to nonsense was subdued. Henry needed to be back soon, or at least to communicate. Henry had to know that the team would not hold together for much longer, and as importantly he needed to know about the P&L but Henry's BlackBerry rang engaged, the mailbox was full.

Chapter Nine

Nancy had not bothered to change when she arrived at Scotland Yard. She was still wearing her old faded jeans and gardening T-shirt as she walked into the interrogation room. Henry had not been expecting her in person. He had wanted a professional reference. Both men looked at each other in disbelief. Pole could hardly contain his amusement, whereas Henry looked momentarily horrified.

"I believe you intend to interrogate my client again," said Nancy without greeting Henry.

"That is the idea," replied Pole.

"May I remind you, Inspector, that you started questioning my client twenty-four hours ago and collected him from his flat ten hours ago, without proper representation."

"Your client, Ms Wu, was very willing."

"Understood," said Nancy lifting her hand to stop Pole continuing. "But unless you can show more than circumstantial evidence, my client and I will be leaving you to your conjecture."

"Are you still practising, Ms Wu?" said Pole squaring up for an argument.

"Sir, I have done enough criminal law in my time to know what I can and can't do. To answer your question, yes, I still belong to chambers." This was not exactly an answer but it would do for the time being. "I need some time with my client, now, if you will."

Pole had not expected anything less from a decent barrister. He and Nurani withdrew, leaving Henry and Nancy alone in the room.

"Don't worry," she said, laying her hand on Henry's shoulder in an appeasing fashion. "I will find someone for you. What matters, now, is that you say nothing and you get out of here."

Henry shook his head, uttering a relieved, "Thank you."

* * *

"So, Andy, ready for your big conf call?" said Pole.

"Yes Boss, ready to go."

"OK, put us on the loudspeaker. I won't say anything but will be there in case you need me."

Andy grinned and released the mute button.

"GL, Ted Barnes' office."

"This is Andy Todd from Scotland Yard, he is expecting my call." If there was to be no courtesy, Andy was going along with it. Pole was impressed.

"Mr Barnes, Andy Todd. Many thanks for sending me the information I requested. I have a few questions if I may." Pole gave Andy the thumbs up.

"Certainly, Andy, shoot," replied Ted.

Pole narrowed his eyes. His face said it all, this conceited little git was too clever for his own good. Young Andy gave him a nod. Ted's elation did not last long. Young Andy started to ask searching questions, on the process of integration, the documents required, the people involved, demonstrating that he had been well trained in the art of extracting information. Pole pressed the mute button whilst Ted was trying to answer as best he could.

"Make him feel like the interrogation room is around the corner."

Andy depressed mute.

"Mr Barnes, I am still a little confused on processes. Surely you can't arrive at these conclusions without consulting the heads of team and yet it seems neither Mr Crowne nor Mr Albert have been heard. Maybe you should come to our offices and we could discuss this more extensively."

Pole mouthed *Brilliant* without a sound. Andy was on a roll.

"No, no. No need," blurted Ted. "Why don't I send you some more docs and you can decide whether this is what you are looking for?"

"Good idea, it will save us both time, for now."

Pole had detected Ted's uneasiness. He was fearful.

"You realise I will have to run all this past my 'gators," said Ted trying to assert himself by mentioning GL's legal team of litigators.

"Of course, I have cleared this call with them already, but be my guest."

Young Andy scored another point as Ted had not asked whether Andy had cleared it, before speaking to him. Pole signalled to Andy to hang up. He did with minimal courtesy.

"Well done, Andy. This guy is not telling us all he knows."

"And he is scared out of his wits. I'll chase him in a few hours. Can't let him think I don't mean business."

"You mean business all right, keep up the pressure," said Pole, with a kind shake of Andy's shoulder.

* * *

James had been observing Ted's moves in and out of his office. Ted had come back and yet again promptly closed the door of his office behind him. James thought about the defrauded P&L. But now was not the time to give Ted a bloody nose, further intel gathering was needed. By now Henry's future must have been discussed extensively and the revised number would not help. James walked decisively across the floor and knocked at the glass partitioning of Ted's office. Ted jumped and looked up.

"Hey Ted, what's up?" said James as he opened Ted's office door.

"Busy, good. You know …"

"I was wondering whether you'd heard from Henry. Can't get hold of him."

"What do you mean?" demanded Ted abruptly, fidgeting with his Montblanc pen.

"Nothing more than that Ted. I can't get hold of him."

James had sat himself in front of Ted's desk in one of the leather chairs, attitude relaxed and mind alert.

"Well, I haven't either, sorry but I've got tons to do, you know." Ted gestured vaguely.

"Sure, sure. Well, if you hear anything let me know. How is the integration committee going anyway?" asked James boldly.

"What do you mean? I can't talk about it as you well know," said Ted with disdain.

"Of course, you can't give the specifics but surely an indication. Our P&L results have been bloody good despite the crisis," said James.

"What? What do you mean? How do you know?" replied Ted, on the verge of losing his cool. James had scored better than he thought.

"No worries," replied James as he slowly stood up.

James took his time to leave his office. He stopped to chat with one of the traders, a burly chap with a large paunch – a little too much beer with the lads. James kept looking in the direction of Ted's office.

Ted was speaking to his PA, no doubt instructing her to let no one in before closing his door again. James had seen fear in men's eyes so many times; Ted was terrified.

Henry was in deep trouble and the firm was about to cut him loose. James pondered over the expression 'cutting loose', a mountaineering term, the last man on the rope may have to be cut loose if his weight became a danger to the team of climbers above. An extreme act of last resort in the close-knit community of climbers, alas a technique frequently used in banking and Henry was its latest victim.

* * *

Nancy and Henry were alone. She was sitting opposite him, her dark brown eyes resting on him with a sense of calm and something Henry had not felt for a long time.

Kindness.

"So, Nancy what is the game plan?"

"As I said, you need to get out of here first, then we decide on strategy. We'll discuss it in the privacy of my pad."

Henry liked her voice. It was smooth and yet authoritative. Henry wanted to ask her the question that was burning on his lips when Pole entered the room. Pole's face was closed to scrutiny, his voice neutral.

"I am prepared to release you on one condition. You must surrender your passports."

What? Henry's reaction was one of anger at the thought of giving up his freedom. What if a client needed him? He was about to protest but Nancy read his mood.

"My client accepts your conditions, Inspector."

"I do not," burst Henry.

Nancy stopped his sentence short with a sharp move of her hand and a glare that cut him to the quick.

"Yes, you do," she replied.

Pole left the room to prepare the documents. Henry turned towards Nancy, his chair screeching on the floor, his body leaning half way across the table..

"What the fuck is the matter with you?"

Henry blushed for the first time in a long time as he realised he had insulted his neighbour, a woman he hardly knew, and more importantly someone he needed to rely on. Nancy paused before replying with a mixture of humour and implacable determination.

"This is no longer the trading floor, my dear fellow. You do not make the rules. I do. And I know this will be mighty hard, but you do not swear at me either."

"But my passports? What if I have to see a client urgently," replied Henry without conviction.

"I doubt you will be let near a client in the next couple of days. Don't you think?"

"Why the hell not?"

"Because YOU are involved in a murder investigation, Henry. GL will have taken notice of this somehow. Don't you think? And so will your clients."

Henry stood up but Nancy had not moved.

"You won't be allowed outside the country. Get used to the idea."

Henry gave a conceding grunt.

"Good, this is your get-out-of-jail card. We play it and we move on."

Henry felt reassured by the 'we'. His experience in the City had taught him to detect lack of substance. Nancy had plenty of firepower and he liked that.

Nancy looked at her Chanel watch and stood up. Henry raised a quizzical eyebrow.

"The papers are ready," she said.

Henry looked towards the door, doubtful. The door opened. The papers were indeed ready.

* * *

An hour before, Dolores Patten had taken a phone call that could change everything.

Jon, need an urgent chat with you, a significant development in the Crowne–Albert affair, read the text to Pole.

Dolores was working at profiling Henry from what she had so far seen but Pole knew it would take time before she could deliver her findings. It had to be something else, something major. Dolores was not the sort to get him out of an interrogation with a prime suspect for nothing.

Chapter Ten

Pole had left Nancy and Henry. He had swiftly turned towards Dolores' office after receiving her text. Pole saw her in the distance waving at him. Her face, which usually reflected calm and composure, was concerned.

"I know you are keen to go back but I truly need to speak to you," she turned towards her office and sensing Pole's hesitation looked back at him.

"It's urgent."

He followed her. She gathered notes scattered on her desk, Pole perched himself on a side desk that leaned against the wall, his preferred spot when speaking to Dolores.

"I just had a long conversation with Anastasia Albert, very disturbing."

Pole frowned.

"You mean Albert's daughter?"

"Yes, I do. I have taken a copious amount of notes, we can discuss this later but in a nutshell she believes her mother is responsible for her father's death."

"Are you serious?"

"Absolutely, it was a very distressing call. She managed to speak despite the tears. A courageous little girl."

A heavy silence settled. Pole took a deep breath and let his head lean against the wall behind him, closing his eyes.

"Is this credible or is she overreacting to his death?"

"I can say two things for sure. She knows this is a murder case. She is absolutely convinced her mother is involved, bear in mind she is only eight years of age." Dolores stopped again. "She has also had, in my opinion, a traumatic childhood that leads her to think this."

Dolores looked at Pole. He tugged at his goatee.

"I am listening," said Pole and jumped from his perched position, to sit in a chair in front of Dolores.

The situation was grave enough that he owed it his full attention.

Dolores explained the details of the conversation. Mrs Albert had, according to her daughter, a lover who sometimes visited when her father was away but whom she also visited often, leaving Anastasia and her brother alone, terrified. The details given by Anastasia were far too vivid to come from her imagination. When Dolores asked tactfully how she was getting on with her mother the little girl erupted. She had had to grow up too fast, pushed by the demands of overzealous parents, who wanted her to be what they had never been and more importantly could never be. Dolores stopped for a short while, allowing Pole to take the information in. She had worked with him long enough to know that cases involving children always disturbed him.

He stood up and moved a few files on her desk, then sat down again.

"So, you think that there is enough content in this little girl's call to investigate?"

Pole knew the answer but braced himself for the reply.

"Yes, Jon, I do. This is not only the trauma of a major loss speaking here."

"Don't go anywhere please. I know you are on half day but I need to dispatch Crowne first. This latest development forces my hand. I'll be quick."

Pole found Nurani and Andy processing fresh data and keen to share their findings. Pole interrupted his two assistants courteously but unequivocally.

"Yes, I will need to review them with you but before we do this could you please prepare the documents for Crowne's release."

Nurani and Andy exchanged a glance of disbelief. Henry was getting away.

Whilst his team was following the release procedure, Pole went back to Dolores' office. She was reading her notes again, making some additions here and there, ensuring that nothing of her conversation was lost. Pole had not bothered to knock at the door and Dolores did not mind. She lifted her face and shook her head.

"There is a lot in this conversation. We are looking at some serious psychological abuse I fear."

"How old is Anastasia again?" asked Pole.

"She is eight." Dolores clasped her hands underneath her desk and leaned forward. "The procedure for interviewing minors is very rigorous,

I will have to talk to social services. Her mother is no longer fit to be the adult present at her interview I fear."

"How can this happen in an environment that is so privileged?" said Pole. "I know it shouldn't surprise me but after all these years it still does."

Dolores smiled at him.

"That's why you still do your job so well after all these years, Jon. You still care about the human soul."

Pole coughed, not knowing how to react to this compliment.

"Anyway, to answer your question. I can think of many reasons unfortunately. A powerful combination of mankind's worst features, greed, vanity, devouring ambition, you know these as well as I do. You keep up with colleagues," Dolores said, "the neighbours, you move up and up and you become so obsessed by it to the point where you fail to ask yourself the real questions, dead to the values that should really matter."

Dolores lifted her face towards Pole. Her dark eyes resting on him, her head tilted so that her mass of heavy dark locks fell to one side. Pole had never asked her why she had chosen the job.

"I also presume that no one in their environment would have noticed anything."

"Unfortunately, it is hard to be honest with yourself. The pressure of what others will think, the need to comply and be accepted. This means not allowing for signs of dissent to appear as much as possible."

"When are we going to get the OK to pay Mrs Albert a visit?" said Pole deliberately moving back to the case.

"I need to follow procedure, call social services. You know the drill. I will do this now. We won't get an answer until tomorrow morning but I don't think the little one is in immediate danger."

"Your call, Dee."

Dolores nodded and started ringing her contacts.

* * *

Henry shivered in the open air when he stepped outside Scotland Yard. Nancy had wrapped a bright orange pashmina around her shoulders, it barely sheltered her from the cold October wind. Her walk was alert – a woman at ease with herself. Henry slowed down and let her move a few paces ahead. He could not quite believe his present situation; the prominent City banker, walking out of the Yard, accompanied by a retired QC who just secured his release, albeit without a passport.

"I'd laugh at the situation, if it weren't mine," said Henry.

"Humour is a powerful tool, don't lose it just yet."

She grabbed his arm and pushed him into the cab she had just hailed.

"Yes, Mum."

Henry grinned at the familiarity he had just displayed to someone he still considered a perfect stranger. Nancy smiled in return and gave their address to the cabbie.

They rode home in silence. Henry was enjoying his freedom. He had thought he would feel exhausted after his lengthy interrogation but he only felt joy. He was free. What mattered, he discovered, was the moment. The cab took a wrong turn, it was going to take longer to get home. Henry would have normally jumped at the cab driver and got him to change his route; not today. He swallowed what would have been a heated argument. It was of very little importance, after all.

Henry took in the scenery. He *saw* the embankment for the first time in years, admired the square clock of the Savoy Tower, spotted King's College disappearing on his right as they went through Aldwych. It felt good simply to be alive and able to take it all in, not needing to block out all that was happening around him, always projecting towards the next meeting, the next deal to close, the next battle to win.

* * *

Nancy pulled a yellow pad out of her orange rucksack and started writing. An old habit from her lawyer's days she had never lost. She took notes on everything and arranged them in folders fastidiously organised in her office. Her note-taking method was renowned in the profession. She captured the words of course but also the minor details she observed, those that made all the difference. Communication of vital importance was always the non-verbal she had observed.

Henry dropped his guard as soon as he entered the cab. His body was relaxed, slightly slumped in the corner of the back seat and his attention focused on the magnificent spectacle that constituted the building outline along the Thames. Nancy gave Henry a side glance. Without knowing yet why, she felt sympathy for him. She trusted her instinct as to Henry's character but also knew something personal was afoot. *The Raft of the Medusa* had told her so.

Vivid images of Paris materialised. The original painting hanging at The Louvre, then The Sorbonne Law School final year results. The students smoking *Gauloises sans filtre*, terrible taste but so trendy among her left-wing friends. She was part of that community that rebelled. She had escaped communist China with her parents at the time of the Cultural Revolution and felt welcome amongst *la gauche française*. The young woman standing in front of the panels with all her friends had undergone such transformation. Nancy wondered whether it could have been different.

The cabbie used his horn and swore at a cyclist. Nancy's past evaporated as quickly as it had surfaced. She went back to her pad. Henry had not moved, still savouring his release. Nancy read what she had jotted down and added one final comment.

Check Jonathan Pole, know the name.

As they were approaching home, Henry noticed that Nancy was looking at him with an amused smile.

"Freedom is good, *n'est-ce pas?*" she whispered.

Henry nodded. Nancy exuded an unusual mix of confidence and empathy. Henry could never trust easily but today he seemed more at ease with her than any of the numerous friends he had in the City. Nancy had stopped writing and relaxed in silence. Time for an in-depth conversation would come later. She let Henry enjoy a few moments of peace. The hard work was still in front of them.

* * *

McCarthy walked out of the building and jumped into a cab. He enjoyed these few moments of complete anonymity away from the well-orchestrated timetable that Cindy laid out in front of him every day; the penance of a CEO he often said. He enjoyed meeting with the UK political elite. Unlike their American counterparts, the British still had a sense of decorum and cultivated the cosiness of exclusive gentlemen's clubs. By some quirky twist of the law, the Club that McCarthy visited was still reserved for gentlemen only, something that he approved of wholeheartedly.

His taxi turned into St James's and stopped at the corner of Jermyn Street. He would walk the last few yards on foot, as was customary. McCarthy left the cab driver with a reasonable tip. He did not want to be remembered either for tipping too much or too little. He disappeared down a small passageway. The door of the club was open and the small plump doorman, who was waiting at the entrance, recognised him. With a short nod of the head and the customary *Good evening sir*, he ushered him into the club's lobby. McCarthy was led through a series of rooms where gentlemen sat in small comfortable meetings. He finally reached a corner of one of the smoking rooms and was left to settle. McCarthy was a tad early. He pursed his lips, a fault in protocol. He knew his contact well enough though to avoid playing games about timing.

At 6.30 on the dot McCarthy's contact entered the room and came to sit opposite him in one of the deep leather armchairs.

"My dear Douglas, I hope I have not kept you waiting long."

McCarthy stood up rapidly and, with a grin, extended a short energetic hand.

"I've just arrived."

"Good, good," the other man said. He turned towards the waiter and then McCarthy.

"The usual I presume?"

"Yes please." McCarthy felt a slight pinch of pride that his contact remembered his taste in beverage.

"Two Glenfiddichs, as they come, Martin, thank you." The man settled comfortably into his chair and joined his hands in front of him, fingertips touching.

"So, Douglas, where is this market going?" asked the slender gentleman without any further niceties. "We entered the subprime crisis nearly a year ago now. There are some signs of optimism which I don't believe will last. How bad is the housing market in the US? You are the expert." He gestured with deferral at McCarthy.

McCarthy pushed his stocky body into the chair and considered his answer. There was no point in trying to sell William bullshit. He had been in government for far too long not to recognise the smell of it.

"Yes, it is going to get a lot worse. We are only at the beginning I am afraid," McCarthy paused.

"And? I feel there is an 'and'."

"And GL has already incurred a heavy loss," said McCarthy clearing his voice.

"So you invested in that market too? Billions?"

McCarthy nodded.

"Tell me more about Collaterised Debt Obligations," William asked.

"They are instruments that use mortgages as investments."

"Like subprime?"

"Correct, but they have tranches of risk." McCarthy replied.

"And you believe that the rating agencies have verified each investment that goes in there. There must be thousands?"

"I am – not sure," said McCarthy promptly taking another mouthful of whisky.

"I see. But GL is the master of the CDO business, right? Any risks of contamination to the UK?"

"Quite possibly, in fact almost certainly. US CDOs sold to UK investors and of course you, in the UK, have your own subprime market!" replied McCarthy almost defiant.

"Mmmm, thought so. Timing is obviously appalling for the Labour Party. Gordon will not survive this crisis but then again a change in the governing party after twelve years is overdue."

"Are you not worried?" asked McCarthy dubious at this even-keeled response.

"No, I am the glue that keeps all governments together," said the man with a distant smile and a spark of humour in his eyes.

"I see." McCarthy paused for a moment before deciding to be unequivocally frank.

"To continue on the subject of subprime," said McCarthy. "We are going to see a spectacular collapse at the lower end of the market very soon, certainly before the end of the year. I don't think the banks know exactly how bad their inventories of subprime products look yet."

McCarthy paused, took another mouthful of whisky.

"Hell, I don't understand some of it myself, CDO squared, CDO cubed," he uncomfortably volunteered.

"Neither do we," the man replied after an equally lengthy pause. "As you know, a number of economists during the Blair era warned us of the impending crisis. The mortgage rates were too low, the level of borrowings too high, etc. John was quite vocal about it but then who in government would volunteer to stop the fun? Gordon got into a world of his own. Intellectual arrogance and stubbornness are unfortunately the main character traits of successful politicians. We received a number of reports from the Bank of England that were sounding caution. Of course, no one had the appetite to do anything about it."

"What about the FSA?" ventured McCarthy.

"Come, come, Douglas, buffoons as you well know yourself. Most of them have a salary one tenth the size of the salary of those they seek to regulate. A farce really."

McCarthy smiled.

"I am aware."

His contact reciprocated the smile.

"The difficult thing here is that all of us are to blame, including the public, but who will be frank or crazy enough to tell the story? It is much easier to concentrate on the obscene amount of money made by the banks."

McCarthy was about to protest when his contact raised a hand.

"I know you don't want to hear this but how many people earn $10m bonuses? Not even the president of the United States, and yes you are going to tell me you work terribly hard, but then again so does he. The banks have been irresponsible but then so have we and so have the regulators. We all know that bankers are bad boys! What the government is not doing is acknowledging the snowball effect of it all."

"The public was equally quite happy to consume without checking whether they were doing so above their means. And the regulators content with mortgages exceeding by a ridiculous amount the value of property."

"True enough but here again Douglas, when you earn £20,000 a year, have to feed a family and want to provide a roof over their heads, I can sympathise," said the other man with some feeling. "How many billions will it take?"

"By the time we have finished probably over one trillion."

McCarthy's Whitehall contact stared at him for a few seconds. McCarthy had created the effect he wanted to create. His contact was assessing the information. Was McCarthy bluffing? Was he implying that GL was too big to fail? Was he expecting some help with the takeover that would involve giving McCarthy support? McCarthy was not yet sure that any of these questions merited a yes but they might soon do.

"Some people are going to brandish the spectre of the Great Depression in front of us. My latest conversation with the Fed convinced me of it."

"I wouldn't be that dramatic," replied McCarthy. "But yes, the papers are going to have a field day."

"Murdoch is going to make even more money, how depressing. One trillion you say?"

"Yes, as far as I can tell from our own exposure, it may be more."

"Your bank is very long in this type of debt?"

"Enough to sink us, unless I can close the merger on time."

"Will you?"

"Definitely," said McCarthy putting his empty glass down. "As long as this story between Albert and Crowne does not derail the process, matters should proceed quickly."

"I expect you have the upper hand at the moment?"

"I have, but – and there is a *but* – " said McCarthy.

"You said there were some ramifications you wanted to discuss."

"As you can imagine very few of HXBK's top management will survive."

McCarthy's contact seemed unsurprised.

"I think it is cruelly ironic. But the combined structured product team would have gone eventually to Anthony Albert."

"That is truly surprising. Do I want or rather need to know the reason?"

"Albert was involved in a lot of subprime structuring. He sourced the majority of these loans and GL is on the other side. He knows or rather knew where some of the skeletons were buried. One of them is Northern Rock and you need to keep an eye on other UK banks too."

"I see," said the other man putting his near empty glass to his lips.

"I will do all I can to control matters at my end however …" finished McCarthy.

"I need to do my bit – understood. Did Anthony Albert know too much?"

"It is no longer our problem, is it?" replied McCarthy.

"Northern Rock is only the beginning, good to know."

McCarthy said nothing, he had given enough. He felt it was his turn to be on the receiving end.

"Your views on the US elections? Obama? McCain?"

"Obama."

McCarthy did not comment. If he had his finger on the pulse of the financial market, his contact had his on the political arena.

"Timothy and Edwina will arrive in a minute," said McCarthy's contact. "Are you ready for a spot of dinner?"

"Most certainly, William," replied McCarthy.

The time for confidences was over.

Chapter Eleven

Nancy had insisted that Henry come to hers before retiring to his apartment. She needed to understand more about the background, more about Henry whom she knew too little before choosing the right QC. She had dashed into the kitchen to prepare a cup of tea, something the British presented as a remedy to all ills. She smiled. She was not all that British after all, but perhaps keen to feel she was, a good cup of tea was indeed needed.

Henry had nodded his approval and sunk his tall body into one of Nancy's comfortable armchairs. For the first time since he had met her, Henry was looking around. She owned the opposite penthouse to his and had already been there for a while when he moved in. Although Henry had visited her a couple of times, he had never bothered to pay much attention to her home, his mind always racing in another direction.

One of the walls exhibited a painted mural representing a stylised bamboo forest, a *camaieu* of greens (Henry remembered this French word with pride) that gave the room a clear sense of space. The mural had texture and an inviting depth, enough to make him want to wander through the exotic landscape. Henry's eyes moved slowly across the room, noticing the sofa's fabric in intense green, embroidered in various shades of the same colour; large and luscious tropical flowers were enticing birds of paradise to suck their nectar. The other walls were white, it should have been a severely minimalist room and yet it exuded a sense of peaceful welcome, a rich tranquillity. Nancy had arranged on opposite walls two massive paintings, two single canvases in shades of a single colour – white.

Henry smiled. Could it be, he wondered, Pollock? Rothko?

The small clunk of a tea tray interrupted his wandering gaze. Nancy sat down on the same sofa and began pouring the tea.

"I know you need a rest and that you have already spoken at length about the story but I need to form my own opinion. You understand?" she said whilst handing over a cup.

Henry bent to grab his tea, took a sip. He drank his tea very hot just as his mother did.

"I understand," his voice had regained its composure.

"Good, now before you give me the details of what has or has not happened, I need to know more about your connection with the O'Connor brothers."

Such a bold question showed Henry unequivocally why Nancy had been a brilliant barrister. She had within minutes identified where the weakest point of his defence lay. Then again, Henry felt that he should not make it so easy for her. After all, he was out and his instinct told him that Pole had another lead. Henry had so far played his hand rather smartly. And why had Nancy agreed to help him so readily? Nothing was ever given for free in his world.

"Is this relevant?" He sipped again at his tea.

Nancy stopped him taking another sip with a kind but un-compromising gesture.

"Henry, you are out and you feel the pressure is off and maybe you are right, but if you are not, trust me, you need to work at your defence, and right away."

She paused as if she could sense his anger rising.

"I know," she carried on. "You are tired, you are used to being in control, and you may not be willing to speak to someone who is not bound by the conventional client-lawyer confidentiality."

"People do not make decisions for me," said Henry.

"It goes without saying. However, you need to decide right now whether you trust me and, if so, please, give me some credit for my knowledge of mounting a defence."

Henry leaned back into the sofa and studied Nancy. She let him.

"I don't trust people easily."

"That comes with the territory. You can't be working in the City and be a friendly, trusting sort of guy, agreed, but you are way beyond your everyday negotiation, Henry. I am sorry to have to break this to you so abruptly, but life will never be the same again. Not now, not ever."

"You have no idea where I come from and how much I am able to sustain."

"I know it takes a lot to have risen to pre-eminence as you have but let me repeat this, you MUST focus on the here and now."

"We are not going to have a philosophical debate."

"Henry, you have chosen to speak to me because you may not trust people but you trust your instinct. I know what I am talking about and you know I know."

Henry was silent, he suspected but he had hoped. When he had left Scotland Yard a few hours ago he had tasted freedom and it was sweet. He had felt safe again, as if it had all been a big mistake, a deal gone wrong that he had just managed to fix.

"Henry?"

He did not like to be pushed. No, he would not be pushed. Everything he knew about influencing, negotiating, manipulating, flooded back to him. He was a master at it, and practice at the game had made him perfect.

"I will fix this too, Nancy, mark my words."

"And when was the last time you spoke to your team?"

Nancy had done it again, gone straight to the point. Henry realised he had not spoken to his team for twenty-four hours. He had been completely engulfed by the events of the past day and by now GL would know about his interrogation. His team would not have seen him or heard from him for a ridiculously long amount of time by City standards. Nancy was right, his life was rapidly unravelling in front of his eyes. He put his cup down. He needed to make contact with his people urgently.

In an instant the comfort of Nancy's home became suffocating. Henry needed to escape this flat and its art. He wanted to rewind the tape of his life and forget about the stranger in front of him. Nancy's voice came as an irritation to him.

"You can call them if you like and in fact you should but I can assure you that, by now, you will have received a number of messages from Human Resources asking you to call them. I would be surprised if GL allows you to go back at all, Henry. At best they may allow you in for a clean transition but in the middle of a takeover–"

"A merger," interrupted Henry forcefully.

"You know I am right but please call, do whatever you need to do and when you are ready we can talk again but I say this to you: the more you delay the worse it will get."

She poured some more tea into his cup, an invitation to stay. Henry was torn. A part of him knew that she was right and yet the thought of losing his team, *his* team, was unbearable. He had reached his goal, he had earned respect, he could impose his ideas, his enemies feared him.

He stood at the centre of his world, his will unchallenged, his mind in absolute focus. He had forgotten at long last what fear felt like.

Henry stood up and looked at Nancy. Despite the Asian skin, the difference in personality, she reminded him of his mother. It was the look in her eyes, the same expression of concern. Henry had not noticed he was still holding his tea. He bent forward to put the cup back in its saucer, reached for his BlackBerry in his jeans pocket. Looking finally at the screen, he saw that he had fifty-eight missed messages.

* * *

Pole had spent over two hours with Dolores going through the details of her telephone conversation with Albert's daughter. Although sceptical to start with, he now felt as sure as Dolores that this was a serious lead. Pole was still struggling with the prospect of having to conduct an interrogation on an eight-year-old girl. He was grateful that he had had to deal with very few cases involving children, thanking a God he did not believe in.

"When will we have the OK to," he paused, looking for the right words, "bring her in?"

"Tomorrow morning, at the latest," replied Dolores.

"Doesn't leave me a lot of time to prepare," muttered Pole half to himself.

"I know but we need to act quickly."

"I am not contesting that."

Dolores nodded. She knew he would be as tactful as he needed to be. "I am here, remember."

Pole shook his head and left her office. He took a left turn and moved rapidly towards the open-plan area where his team was working.

"Nurani, any further info?"

"Yep, more in the direction you wanted us to look into."

"What precisely?" said Pole, irritated.

She hesitated, taken aback by Pole's uncharacteristic grumpiness.

"There is a man on the scene. I don't even think they have been that discreet to be honest, or not until more recently that is. The neighbours talk about him, as do AA's work colleagues, they all talk of a marriage on the rocks," said Nurani, placing a fist on her hip in a disapproving manner. "Some of these guys talk about a marriage on the rocks as if it were a drink."

"Compassion comes in short supply in the banking world."

"All that feels more like an acknowledged lover than a secret affair until a few months ago. Matters seem to have cooled down quite a lot or, at least, become less visible."

"And the gentleman is …?" said Pole with a small elaborate movement of the hand, indicating he was expecting more.

"Brett Allner-Smith, works with Sotheby's. He is an antiques' dealer specialising in classical stuff." Nurani was a little vague, ill at ease in the arcane world of rare antiquities.

"He is not married, although divorced twice and has private wealth coming from his family, his mother more precisely. Got a picture, rather stuck up if you see what I mean."

"Any convictions? Divorce case ruled against him?"

"No convictions apart from the odd speeding ticket. Actually, he likes speeding apparently. He lost his licence a few years ago, and yes divorce ruled against him, naughty boy it seems, was conducting a number of affairs and eventually shacked up with another bird."

"The very technical terms the court was using too, I expect", said Pole amused.

Nurani pulled a face.

"Not quite. I am giving you the condensed version."

"In short you are telling me that Mrs Albert is having an affair with a philandering, speed-loving, rich-but-now-poor-because-of-his-two-divorces bloke who flogs antiques?"

"Eh, yep," replied Nurani, putting a pen to her mouth to suppress a grin.

"Interesting, interesting," said Pole. "How poor has he become?"

"Well, he now owns only one house in Belgravia," hesitated Nurani.

"All is relative, Nu, I have one house in Clapham and that is more than enough for me but …"

"If you have been used to being rich." Nurani was picking up on Pole's idea.

"It might be a tad hard to let go of the habit."

"Yep, very true." Nurani opened the file again. She usually could give Pole a complete and detailed account of events without any help, having committed it all to memory.

"He had a house in Exeter, mansion, sold to his half-brother, then he lost the house in Grasse, south of France, pretty exclusive."

"True, where perfumes are made. Lovely part of the world and unbelievably expensive too."

"... and a flat in New York – apparently he does a lot of business in the States, and," Nurani carried on leafing through the file, "... a fleet of sports cars, one Aston Martin DB9, one Bentley – no two Bentleys, Bentayga and Mulsanne, aaaand a little Porsche."

"This is getting more interesting by the minute," said Pole, moving from his chair to join Nurani and look at the file over her shoulder. "Do carry on."

"A collection of drawings by Leonardo da Vinci, a painting by Vermeer called *Woman seated at a Virginal*."

Nurani kept reading from her notes.

"This is unbelievable." Pole stopped Nurani mid flow. "In fact, jaw-dropping."

Nurani stayed silent. The prices of the various items had been submitted as undisclosed and she was starting to understand why.

"I can see why someone losing all this might get tempted to do something really stupid to get back a fraction of what he owned." Pole could hardly believe it. "These pieces belong to a museum."

"Well, Jon, you have your wish. Yes, they do now. This guy Brett managed to lose everything."

Pole burst into roaring laughter.

"This is incredible," he repeated. "OK, we need to have a look at the will as soon as possible, including any recent changes made to it. We also need to know whether Mrs Albert was aware of its most recent content."

"The solicitor dealing with this will never let us see it before the formal opening date in front of the beneficiaries," said Nurani confidently.

"That is what you think, my dear," replied Pole, absorbed again in the pages in front of him, "and strictly speaking you are right of course. However, I don't need the text, I need a direction. I need the number of Albert's solicitors. Let's try to get a meeting today."

"Done. I'll call the solicitor straight away," replied Nurani. "And Jon?"

"Yes Ms Shah, I feel a burning question coming my way."

"How come you know so much about art?"

"Ah, yes, why would a copper like me know about these things? Well, believe it or not I was brought up in an artists' family, destined myself to become one of them."

"What happened? It must have been a hell of a shock when you told them."

"A story for another time," replied Pole ruffling his goatee.

The phone rang. Pole looked at the screen, it was Dolores' extension. She had an answer for him he might not like.

Henry was pacing up and down his lounge, impatiently listening to his voicemails. He had left Nancy's flat in a hurry, with a few mumbled words of thanks, preoccupied by the time he had already lost. The first message was from James Radlett. The familiar voice had pacified him. James was being his usual controlled, factual self but it was clear from his messages that matters were not looking good back at base.

He was longing to get back. If he could be there, he knew he would be able to control his team again. He would take the questions they had head on. They might give him a rough ride but he would handle it. Henry decided he would call James first. He needed to reconnect but also wanted to avoid hearing what he could not cope with, a message from HR. James mobile rang once.

"H, bloody hell. I have been trying to—"

"I know, Jamie, I know. Can't explain right now, just wanted to check how things are going with our star transaction?"

"Quite a few technical points to go through."

"Shoot," said Henry feeling the tiredness slip away from him. He was at his best problem solving. They discussed a number of complex points relating to pricing and structuring of an equity linked transaction. James would not want to discuss these with anyone else.

"We need to be cautious," emphasised Henry. "I want to avoid the usual feeding frenzy. You know the sort of crap that goes on with the closure of large transactions."

"And the other teams sticking their noses into our business. Pretending they are part of the deal to get credit. Yes, I know."

"Usual shit. And the traders have lost too much money not to try anything that will give them additional P&L," replied Henry.

"Agreed. H, we also need to speak about the team."

"What about it? Are they missing me?" asked Henry.

"Yep, in particular as they have not had anyone to sign their expenses."

"OK, let me guess now. Matt and Harriett have had a big ding-dong, actually no, by now they have had a number of ding-dongs."

"Yep."

"And Matt has been trying to behave as if he is the head of the team, correct?"

"Correct."

"But you showed him who was boss," continued Henry. *Nothing unpredictable there* he thought.

"Just the way you've showed me," replied James sounding amused. James regained composure for his next question "Have you spoken to Ted recently?"

"No, why would I want to do that?" replied Henry, the association between Ted's name and his team seeding unwanted thoughts.

But a persistent noise interrupted Henry. It was the voicemail reminding him that he had forty-five unanswered messages. Henry cut the conversation short. James was doing a good job holding the team together. Henry was ready for whatever GL would throw at him next.

Quite a few messages rolled through, all uneventful. In the absence of any major calls, Henry started to relax. He sensed the return of his confidence, stronger than before, further invigorated by his conversation with James. He looked at his watch and started calculating how much time it would take to shower, get dressed and take a cab to the office. Then the message from HR came through. The voice sounded impatient, it was someone he did not recognise, his old Human Resources' contact had resigned a few months back, dreading the aftermath of the credit crisis and the takeover.

"Mr Crowne, I am sure you are extremely busy."

What a bloody stupid thing to say.

"But could you please call me back."

And who the fuck is ME?

"It is, as you can imagine, incredibly urgent."

"I am not ignoring your call, you stupid bitch. I return calls within the hour, unless of course I am in the frigging nick."

Henry looked at his phone, he was furious at this lack of professionalism. And then he recognised the number of the off-boarding team. His anger erupted. He wanted someone to lash out at, someone he could defeat the old way, the only way he knew. His fists were clenched. He had not wanted to hit someone like this for many years and had forgotten what it felt like. He started screaming at his phone, obscenities, threats of retribution. The more vulgar and disgraceful, the more appropriate. He screamed until he felt his face distorting uncontrollably, a sharp pain surging in his chest. When he was done, he slowly sagged into his armchair, utterly empty. Anger would not get him out of this mess. His eyes fell on a wrapped parcel he had almost forgotten.

The Raft of the Medusa sat against the wall. Despite the wrapping, the potency of its images flooded Henry's mind. The image of death and defeat made him queasy. He was exhausted, spent, an eerie calm came over him and for the first time since he was a kid, he felt like crying. He hid his face in his hands. The BlackBerry had dropped to the floor, still scrolling through the messages. Leaving it where it had fallen, he walked through his lounge, across the corridor and rang Nancy's doorbell.

Chapter Twelve

The two police cars carrying Pole and his team had parked in the middle of the street in front of Anthony Albert's Belgravia house. Dolores and another woman from social services shared one car, Pole and Ms Shah the other. Pole said little during the journey. He was concentrating on his delivery. His face turned to the car window, looking out at the rolling streets he did not see. His mind rehearsed once more what he would say to Adeila Albert, to control her, how he would speak to Anastasia, to reassure her. He would never be pushed in a direction he did not want to go, something his superior called lack of vision or at best stubbornness. Pole found that knowledge to be his strength. The understanding of his own limits, the one he wanted to surpass, the one he would never cross, gave him freedom.

Pole emerged from the car first. His team was waiting for his signal. He stood for a few seconds looking at the imposing yet elegant house. He moved swiftly to the front door and rang the bell. As he stood waiting, Pole thought he could hear music coming from inside the house in an attempt to cover the noise of two people screaming at each other. He rang the doorbell with insistence, ready to get one of his men to break the door down if necessary but the music stopped and a few seconds later the door opened. A dishevelled Mrs Albert stood in the doorway, wearing an expression of fury. Pole saw a slender silhouette flying up the stairwell behind.

"Mrs Albert, may we enter?" said Pole already pushing his way through.

"This is not a good time," replied Adeila Albert dryly.

"Whether it is or not, is irrelevant," said Pole. "We need to talk to you and your daughter."

"What is this nonsense about my daughter?" she replied, mad anger flashing in her eyes. "She is a very difficult child. Her father used to indulge her without restraint. Anthony never had any discipline."

Adeila was about to continue when she spotted Dolores and the woman from social services. Her face turned livid. She had been overheard and was desperate to give her side of the story first.

"This may be so Mrs Albert but we would like to speak to your daughter directly."

"I am her guardian and will decide whether or not you can speak to her," said Adeila Albert in a shrill voice.

"I am perfectly prepared to file for a search warrant and I have a protection order Mrs Albert. You no longer decide whether we speak to your daughter. I do."

Pole's calm determination sent shock waves around the room. Adeila Albert stepped toward Pole, ready to do battle, when a small child appeared in the doorway of the lounge in which all had gathered.

"I am here," said a young girl in a shaky but decisive voice.

Dolores moved forward gently and swiftly placed herself between mother and child.

"I am Dolores, we spoke on the phone."

The young girl nodded.

"Would you like to come with me?"

Dolores crouched in front of Anastasia, who was twisting a small hankie in her hands. She had been crying. The little girl nodded and Dolores softly took her by the hand. Mrs Albert leaped forward with a demented scream, but Nurani barred the way. Adeila started speaking in another language, which no one could understand, although there was no need to. The distorted expression on her face and the vehemence of her voice could only mean abuse. Pole moved next to Nurani, both of them remaining calm until the front door of the house had been closed. Pole let the crisis rise and fall, waiting for a panting Adeila to stop.

"Could you please now follow us to Scotland Yard, we have quite a lot to discuss, Mrs Albert."

Pole's voice carried the undercurrent of some unbreakable will. She would follow them and would be questioned. Adeila Albert clenched her jaws and moved with disdain. She would follow *after* she had changed into more appropriate attire.

* * *

The coffee machine was making its familiar grinding and buzzing noise whilst Pole leaned against it, his eyes not seeing the coffee that was being prepared. Adeila Albert had been led into one of the interrogation rooms and offered a tea that she had turned down. She had called her lawyer and refused to say a word until he arrived.

"Your coffee is ready, Jon," said Dolores, squeezing his arm gently.

"Ah, yes, thanks. I was miles away."

"She is a brave little girl, and more resilient than you think," continued Dolores, trying to alleviate Pole's concerns.

"What has she decided?"

"She wants to stay with a foster family, for a while."

"Why do people take it out on their kids? I know it is always complicated and I should not judge but by God – why?"

"Ambition and vanity engulf people without them noticing."

"I know Dolores but it still makes me mad," said Pole. "Then again I don't have any kids."

"Well, you don't need to have any to see the absurdity of all this." Dolores had also asked the machine for an espresso, no sugar.

"Your coffee is ready, Dolores," said Pole with a smile.

She smiled back took her cup and lifted it to Pole in a sign of acknowledgement.

"And what is my excuse?"

Pole finished his drink and crushed the cup with one hand. He had nearly reached interrogation room twelve where Mrs Albert was impatiently waiting when Andy caught up with him.

"Boss, just very quickly, I have reviewed the documents sent by this guy Ted Barnes from the integration committee at GL."

Pole's mind switched swiftly back to the other matter.

"The committee that is in charge of merging a number of businesses after the takeover is finalised, in particular Crowne and Albert's businesses. Go on," said Pole.

"Yes, well the numbers are interesting, plus the comments. I am pretty sure Albert would have got the top job."

Pole lifted a quizzical eyebrow and ruffled his goatee.

"Mmm, *not* really what I was expecting," he paused.

"How old are the numbers Andy?"

"Last year's unaudited and this year's projection."

"OK, get me some figures for, say, the last five years, audited, plus a list of deals closed for the past five years and the one that should close this year."

"I am on it, Boss," said Andy turning around to dash out.

Pole shook his head in amusement, paused and inhaled.

He walked into interrogation room twelve. Nurani was already there checking the equipment that would be used to record the conversation, keeping an eye on Mrs Albert and her lawyer.

Adeila Albert had complained that she needed time to change before leaving for the Yard. Pole had had no intention of indulging her ridiculous request. Considering her circumstances, Mrs Albert was pretty focused on the non-essentials. As luck would have it, she had managed to spill a cup of undrunk coffee on her dress – clever move. There was no alternative but to let her change.

With an air of triumph, Adeila had retired, accompanied by Nurani, to her bedroom and effected at speed the much-wanted switch of clothing.

She had emerged wearing an elegant black and white trouser suit from Escada and managed to name drop the designer when calling her lawyer. She had decided on a pair of classic Chanel shoes to match her handbag. This time neither Pole nor Nurani could avoid recognising the unmistakably intertwined Cs. Her jewellery was equally impressive. Finally, and despite the lack of sun, Mrs Albert drew from her bag a white pair of D&G sunglasses.

Pole observed with interest and some surprise the effect on Nurani, the mixture of disdain and what he suspected was envy. Adeila Albert had walked into the police station as though she were entering a recording studio. The show was on.

Pole started with simple questions but soon decided to cut to the chase.

"How close are you to Brett Allner-Smith, Mrs Albert?" asked Pole.

"We are *good* friends," replied Adeila .

"How did you meet Mr Allner-Smith?"

Pole had picked up on her emphasis but decided to avoid the obvious question for a while. Adeila launched into a description of auctions at Sotheby's and Christie's. How she had spotted an incredible piece of antiquity. How her husband had thought it was unaffordable, of course poor Anthony could not tell the difference between a two-thousand-five-hundred-year-old Grecian vase and a flowerpot from IKEA. She, however, was a natural. Her lawyer looked unhappy but simply expressed his growing unrest by indicating that these details were superfluous. Brett had been marvellous, Adeila continued, spotting her skills at detecting unusual pieces. He had recommended she attend a course he was running at one of the auction houses. She babbled along for a while and Pole let her go on. Her lawyer tried politely to redirect the conversation yet again. Adeila was too engrossed in her world to notice.

"Is Mr Allner-Smith your lover?" Pole demanded abruptly.

"Brett is," said Adeila before her lawyer could stop her. "Anthony was never of the right calibre."

"How long have you been having this affair?" Pole asked in a flat tone.

Adeila's face changed colour, her lips tightened. She abruptly turned towards her lawyer.

"Why did you not stop me?" she spat at him vehemently. "You incompetent nerd."

The older man's cheeks reddened with anger.

"Could I have a moment with my client please?"

"Certainly," replied Pole.

The interview would carry on now, no matter what. Adeila would not get much sympathy from her lawyer.

Good result.

* * *

Brett Allner-Smith had arrived at the Yard. He was coming voluntarily, no doubt very keen to give his side of the story and clear his name. Brett was waiting. He had accepted his cup of tea and looked pretty relaxed. His control was different from that of Henry, softer and yet surprisingly more effective. Pole had asked Nurani to start the process without him, giving her the lead. He would observe for a while through the one-way mirror.

His very English tailoring had made Nurani cringe, the Prince of Wales jacket, the silk cravat, the small moustache and the very blond hair made her feel uncomfortable. His perfectly manicured hands showed no sign of real work and his nonchalance irritated her, yet something about him was intriguing.

Brett had become nervous when she entered the room, but then again this was not a particularly relaxing experience. Brett Allner-Smith was somewhat shaken at the idea of where he was but managed to hide his nerves surprisingly well. Pole detected something else. Until Nurani entered the room, the man was bored. Adeila might have provided a distraction for a while but he had moved on. He needed something new. In dilettantish fashion, he was surveying the young inspector sitting opposite him.

The chase is so much more interesting with a female police officer, thought Pole. He entered the room.

"Mr Allner-Smith, Inspector Pole," said Pole, extending a hand. "I hope you have not been waiting too long." Pole smiled.

"Absolutely not," Brett replied, looking annoyed. "I can, of course, spare the time to assist in these terrible circumstances. What a tragedy."

Pole sat down. A few long hours of hide and seek with the truth had now begun.

Chapter Thirteen

Henry rang Nancy's doorbell twice, in short impatient bursts. He wanted to get on with it, wanted to get definitive advice from a *proper* lawyer. She would recommend someone tough, someone who could deal with HR, this entire mess. He wanted to go back to his team, his life. Nancy took what Henry thought was an interminable amount of time to reach the door. He had rested his tall body against the wall, arms folded across his chest, when she finally opened up. She gestured him in, she was on the phone to what seemed to be an old colleague.

She carried on her cryptic conversation whilst Henry stepped into her living room, not knowing what to do. She left him there, going back to her notes. He noticed that she was writing once again on a yellow legal briefing pad.

Reassuring – once a lawyer, always a lawyer.

The room wrapped itself around him. Henry felt it again, this deep sense of peace, unaltered by the charged activity. Nancy had now finished her conversation and looked at her watch.

"I thought it was going to take you longer to come over," she said with an amused smile. "A good sign indeed."

"You mean it took me less time than you thought to admit that you were right," retorted Henry.

"No," said Nancy. "I am not trying to enter into a battle of wills with you, Henry. I am simply glad you have realised that denial works against you. I have nothing to prove to you." Her tone of voice was conciliatory. "I have just finished a conversation with Gavin Pritchard QC, a good friend of mine and ex-colleague. He can take the case on. His record in criminal law is second to none. We have an appointment first thing in the morning."

Henry did not respond. She waited a few more moments until Henry finally relaxed, reassured by the news.

"You now need to think about a number of important things. Firstly, do you want to get a recommendation from someone else?"

Henry opened his mouth to speak but Nancy lifted her hand to stop him in his tracks.

"Secondly, do you want me to still be involved and, if so, how? Your barrister will be bound by client confidentiality. I am not, although I am very happy to enter into a form of agreement tying me to the same rule if you so wish. Finally, you must think about what you are accused of and decide what you want to say and how you want to plead. Telling the truth to your lawyer is advisable, then again you need to decide what this all means to you."

Henry sat down on the sofa, bending his body forward, elbows on knees.

"I need time," he said eventually.

"You have some time but not much, at least to decide on the first two questions," said Nancy.

"Could I stay here a bit to think?" said Henry, feeling awkward at invading her privacy. But he needed to stay away from his flat at all costs, the temptation to call his office still far too strong.

"Sure," said Nancy in a relaxed tone. "I need to tend to my flowers, so help yourself to whatever you need in the kitchen. I make a mean *tarte aux citrons* and there is some left in the fridge."

With this she disappeared into the second floor of her duplex apartment. The idea of a slice of cake made Henry's mouth water. He had not had any proper food for forty-eight hours and decided to investigate Nancy's fridge. The association cake and fridge reminded him of his mother. She too kept cakes in the fridge. *Keeps them nice and moist for you my love.* For years, as a child, he had enjoyed sneaking in there for a slice. He had discovered only much later she had been fighting a losing battle with the various rodents that haunted her kitchen. The fridge was at least a safer place to store food. Henry shivered in disgust, wondering why he was reminiscing about the past. He helped himself to a large, possibly too large for good manners, piece of *tarte*. He had never tasted such delicious food until he had come to London. There was still some tea in the pot so he poured himself a mug, visited the fridge again for milk and settled in Nancy's living room. It was so easy to be here. He sat back, looking at the unusual decor of the room, took a deep breath and fell asleep.

* * *

McCarthy had been updated by Ted twice already, each time after a discussion with Scotland Yard. Ted had been creative in a way McCarthy had not expected, his friendship with Henry soon forgotten. McCarthy consulted his watch. It was nearly time for another key internal meeting. Ted would be there doing what he was told. This total compliance would have been nauseating at other times but with the takeover strategy to finalise McCarthy needed it.

* * *

Ted also consulted his watch. It was five past two in the afternoon, and his meeting had started already. He had been compiling the next lot of documents to be sent to the Yard. McCarthy would probably want to be updated after the meeting. He had to be ready. Pushing the door of the meeting room open Ted uttered a barely audible, "Sorry, lots to do" and grabbed the nearest seat.

A pile of documents had been distributed, waiting to be opened. Anish Gupta, Global Head of Debt Capital Market at GL, was running the meeting. He had paused briefly to allow Ted to enter before carrying on.

"We are checking our combined numbers with the other team, but the low estimate exceeds $20billion at the moment. It will depend how finance wants to calculate the losses on our complex, illiquid and long dated instruments."

Another young man in the team, with a ponytail and a small beard, got very excited. "The accounting standards are going to bloody crucify us. Any mark to market in the current climate is a fucking disaster."

"I know Nick," said the short Indian man pursing his lips in disdain. "But this is what enabled us to take our profits when the going was good. It is going to take a lot more than $20 billion to get the accounting standards to be changed. So we have to be creative."

"You mean a complete meltdown of the whole effing market," Nick replied.

Heads turned from one man to another as if he had uttered the worst of obscenities. Unperturbed, Anish Gupta carried on.

"We now have on the books a number of mispriced instruments, why? Because the original assumptions on growth, interest rates and sustainability were wrong. The leverage on these is tenfold what it should be. We are not going to be able to sell these on, so the balance sheet is eroding at a speed

I have never seen before. In fact, at this rate we will be in default in the next two months."

The people around the table protested loudly at the same time, producing an inaudible jumble. Again, unperturbed, Anish carried on.

"The way I see this, we can accept HXBK's offer now and subsume the business into theirs or we can try to play hardball and miss the boat. We still have the upper hand, no need to deny what is happening. We are amongst ourselves today." Anish paused for effect. "If the deal does not go through now, we will all become the underdogs and the next lot of negotiations will *not* be fun. By the way we can argue until we are blue in the face that our financial models have been reviewed and agreed with the regulator, this will make zero difference if the markets tank once more."

This time the room remained uncomfortably silent. A few shuffled on their seats. Suddenly the door opened, the timing was impeccable as McCarthy made his entrance. Each of the men assembled in the room greeted the old man in their particular ways, vying for attention.

"Have you discussed?" said McCarthy without any other form of introduction.

"We have," Anish replied equally abruptly.

"Then you all know what you have to do, don't you?" carried on McCarthy, this time facing the room full on.

The question didn't call for a debate, and the room was plunged into an icy silence. Douglas McCarthy scrutinised faces. There was little his men could hide from him. The room stood still. McCarthy waited to see who would move first.

Ted shuffled on his chair.

"Ted, do you have a question?"

All heads turned towards the young man. Ted's dishevelled blond hair, and wary eyes made a few of his colleges snigger. He was not one of them. It took a few seconds for Ted to realise that McCarthy was addressing him, a few more seconds before he could start formulating a remotely sensible response.

"No! Good."

McCarthy had decided to spare Ted the humiliation of making a fool of himself. Ted needed to do a lot more for him in the Crowne affair. McCarthy spoke again.

"I am expecting you all to push for a close. This means that the final due diligence is to be done swiftly, the contracts ready for signature inside two weeks."

A murmur went around the room, McCarthy lifted his hand. He had not finished.

"If you have issues to clarify I do not want emails, I do not want calls, I want direct face to face contact. If you can't do this because you are travelling, I will make sure that Cindy sets up a secure line through our video call network. I am also expecting you to communicate in the same fashion with the members of your staff that you trust."

McCarthy paused and waited, this time no one moved until he did.

"When it comes to the Crowne incident, I will handle this personally together with the Head of Legal. Any queries I want referred to me in person, no mail, no voicemail."

He did not bother to ask whether there were further questions. He knew there would be none. McCarthy left the room having spent less than fifteen minutes with his direct reports.

An efficient meeting, he thought.

McCarthy avoided the lift but walked the three flights of stairs separating the meeting room floor and his office. He had hardly reached his desk when Cindy entered in her usual fashion, asking whether he had time for Ted. McCarthy had expected Ted would need to speak. The young man was fretting during the meeting.

"When is my next available slot?"

"Tomorrow, 9pm."

Cindy never hesitated to push his schedule beyond the call of duty. She had learned, in all the years she had worked for McCarthy, to identify the people he would want or need to speak to. Ted had become one of them. But McCarthy needed to see Ted sooner. Cindy suggested a rearrangement that disregarded rank and seniority. McCarthy managed a smile – this was why he respected Cindy.

* * *

The phone call with Henry was over and yet James had not moved. As their dialogue progressed, Henry had come back into his own. No one but him could have helped James navigate the complex matter they were debating and certainly not Ted. The intricacy came from a number of angles, one was the mathematical modelling of the embedded option. The technology was cutting edge and only a handful of people comprehended it fully. James understood well enough what his quantitative team, in charge of this new model, was talking about but then again, he wanted to make absolutely sure, never fazed by admitting he did not always know. Henry made a point of encouraging his people to speak freely about their doubts, something that the CDO team hardly ever did.

Henry had little respect for a team that created what he regarded as artificial products. *A lot of bullshit and hot air!* His take on sophistication and risk was simple. There is no such thing as a free lunch. If the rewards were high, so were the risks. Anyone pretending otherwise was guilty of shameful, intellectual dishonesty.

James was invigorated by their chat and almost optimistic, almost. But they had not spoken about Ted. On reflection, the discussion about Ted needed to be face to face. For the time being he would hold the fort as Henry had asked him to. Would GL ever allow Henry back on the trading floor? Certainly not until this mess had been sorted out and possibly not even after that.

"Yes, you are in deep shit my friend," uttered James.

He sat back at his desk and started checking his mailbox. One of the messages caught his eye. It was from Cindy Freeman, McCarthy's PA.

James,
Mr McCarthy would like to see you at 7.00am sharp tomorrow morning.
Regards
Cindy Freeman, Executive Assistant to Douglas McCarthy

He read the message again for clues and finally pressed the only button he could possibly press, accepting the invite.

James looked up and saw that both Harriett and Matt were missing.

He leaned towards Morag.

"Where are those two?" he whispered.

"No idea," she replied. "I have a feeling that Matt is in New York."

James took in the information, flinching at the thought.

"Doing what?"

"Again, no idea," whispered Morag.

"Harriett?"

"I suspect still at the lawyer's. She is trying to close her deal this week. She was working on it late last night, in fact early this morning. She sent me an email at 2am."

"Who is he using?"

"Pamela Anderson."

In other circumstances James and Morag would have made the expected joke but the mood was missing.

"Find out for me where Matt is please. This is urgent," said James in a low voice.

"Understood, I am on it."

Morag put on her headset and was immediately on the trail.

Chapter Fourteen

Pole spent over an hour with Brett Allner-Smith, talking about his two marriages, his work and finally his relationship with Adeila Albert. He was proceeding gradually, moving in deeper with each question, so he could get a different angle. In this meticulous job that he enjoyed doing, Pole felt like a surgeon moving closer to the epicentre of the disease.

Currently, however, both Pole and Ms Shah had retired to exchange views, leaving Allner-Smith on his own.

"This guy is starting to interest me more," said Pole.

"Why? He is so removed from real life," replied Nurani, dubious.

"Well, you look at him and you think 'antiquities' that few people can afford, at least at the level he operates. That makes him remote. OK, true enough but—"

Pole paused. He sat on Nurani's desk whilst she took the chair.

"It does not mean that he is not after money the good old fashioned way. And that he is not capable of scheming to get back what he has lost or even pushing someone to commit the worst."

Nurani considered Pole's proposition for a few moments before replying.

"I find him creepy in a seductive sort of way," she volunteered. "So, yes, he could manipulate, be the brain."

"It is a simple calculation. Right?" said Pole. "Anthony Albert dies, Adeila gets the money, he moves in or even better he marries her. She probably does not know the extent to which he has lost his own wealth. If all goes well he stays married for a while and spends her money the way he has been used to all his life. Worst comes to the worst, he gets a divorce and asks for a settlement. People have killed for less – he simply needs to put the right idea in Adeila's mind."

"I agree that Adeila is besotted enough with this guy to do anything for him and, well – if her own husband had an affair then maybe. But then again, it is pretty obvious."

"We are dealing with people who are arrogant. Do you think they think we are going to catch them? No, no, no – they are convinced they are going to fox a bunch of dumb coppers like us."

"Yes, Guv," carried on Nurani, crossing her eyes.

"And conveniently, this murder takes place in the middle of a protracted takeover."

"Does Adeila really measure the huge tension between her husband and Crowne?"

"All we have seen of the competition between these two men indicates that this has been going on for some years. She knows. She also is the sort of woman who will want to find out whether her lifestyle is going to be affected by the changes in her husband's financial situation. If he is likely to fail, a life insurance cheque may not go amiss."

They both stopped to assess this latest statement. Neither Pole nor Nurani had noticed Andy standing at the door, listening intently to what was being said.

"Actually, I might have found something … interesting," exclaimed Andy.

"Mmmm," said Pole, his mind still on Adeila and Brett.

"I think Brett Allner-Smith knows Henry Crowne and also Douglas McCarthy, the CEO of GL."

"What?" Pole said with a sideways look. "That IS news, go on."

"I have been checking Crowne's bank account for movements that might be of interest and I've found some large sums of money being paid to Sotheby's. He buys and sells a fair bit of Asian art, so I called Sotheby's."

Andy was about to enter into a lengthy account of his findings when Pole interrupted him.

"And?"

"Sorry, sorry," replied Andy, blushing slightly whilst adjusting his glasses. "Allner-Smith sold a statuette, a Guanyin, in ivory, sixth century AD, to Crowne in March 2004. The statuette came from his own collection but had to be authenticated by Sotheby's, at Crowne's request as far as I can tell."

"Very good. A nice bone of contention between those two," exclaimed Pole. "And what of the McCarthy connection?"

"Allner-Smith always invites McCarthy to all sorts of previews when Asian art comes to auction, but I haven't had time to dig deeper."

"Well done, young man – keep digging and you, Ms Shah, you go back and have a little chit-chat with Brett."

Nurani's face twisted, cringing at the thought.

"I will put Mrs Albert on ice and join you for a more in-depth conversation with the English gentry."

Pole dealt swiftly with a furious Adeila. Yes, she would have to wait, yes, she could have a coffee but no, it would not come from Caffè Nero. Pole rejoined Nurani for a new round with Allner-Smith. Brett was very animated, seeking Nurani's attention. Pole could see that Ms Shah had dropped her guard significantly, admiring with slight annoyance the skill of the other man. Inspector Pole walked straight to the table and slid a picture of an ancient ivory statuette in front of Brett.

"How about giving me an expert description of this particular object, Mr Allner-Smith, together with, if you please, an even more detailed description of its sale?"

Pole's eyes ran over Brett, ice cold. Nothing would escape his attention until the interrogation was over. Brett Allner-Smith took a small pair of half-moon glasses out of an old leather box and pushed them up the tip of his nose.

You can try to buy time, thought Pole, *I am still getting the truth out of you.*

Allner-Smith remained composed, yet Pole detected the man's mood swing, a mix of irritation and disquiet. Pole was satisfied with the reaction he had just triggered. He now needed to tap into its source. Brett finally responded, his voice was low and his lips quivered.

"I used to own this Guanyin," he paused. His fingers went lovingly down the picture as he spoke again. "A magnificent piece attributed to the Tang dynasty. It came from my great grandfather," he paused again his eyes resting still on the picture. "A well-travelled man."

"And you sold it?" interrupted Pole tearing the man away from his fond memories.

"Yes, I did," replied Brett, still composed. "I had to sell it to this – Irish peasant." The words escaped Brett but he did not seem to care. "New money you see," he said in a vague attempt to redeem his outburst. "They think they can buy style or appreciate the finer things in life but what do they really know about the exquisite pieces they acquire?" he finished with a sigh.

The room fell silent, leaving Pole to acknowledge the strange intensity of Brett's feeling for his world of art and aesthetics.

"Crowne, the buyer – after a massive bonus. God knows what unholy transaction he must have done to deserve that one."

Pole shrugged, "And so …"

"It is hard to relinquish such a phenomenal piece to such an amateur," carried on the antiques dealer adopting an expert approach to the argument, still hoping for sympathy.

"Why did you not mention this before?" asked Pole, not letting go of his grip.

"It was a while ago Inspector."

"You must be aware that this is a murder investigation," replied Pole.

"Well, you're the policeman. Details like these escape me."

"Well then, let me therefore remind you of the insignificant details. You received £250,000 from Henry Crowne on the 27th of March 2004 and delivered the object on the 22nd of June, the reason for the delay was?"

"Inspector, you cannot be serious," said Brett barely able to refrain from laughter.

"Do you really believe that that was the full settlement for such an exceptional piece? You must be out of your mind," exclaimed Allner-Smith, his outrage sounding genuine.

Allner-Smith had managed to unsettle Pole. Inspector Pole took it on the chin and sat back.

"OK, enlighten me Mr Smith." Pole consciously dropped the double-barrelled name.

"It cost Mr Crowne the ridiculously low sum of £580,000," exclaimed Brett, now fired up.

"How did he settle the rest of the sum?" asked Pole.

"Ask my accountant," replied Brett, crossing his arms over his chest.

"I will," carried on Pole.

"Now let's move onto another subject if I may. What is your relationship to Mr and Mrs Albert?"

Allner-Smith pushed his chair back in a move to go.

"I am not sure I want to carry on with this conversation, Inspector. I came in good faith and you are now throwing some pretty unpleasant suggestions my way."

"And we appreciate your cooperation greatly, Mr Allner-Smith, as well as your contribution in enlightening us as to the true value of these antiquities."

Pole sounded sarcastic but no matter. Brett Allner-Smith still wanted to get his side of the story across before, or at least at the same time, as Adeila did. Pole now simply wanted to listen, to hear the man speak about himself and the Alberts. But Allner-Smith had decided on another tack altogether.

"Well, Inspector, may I interest you in another relationship? One that was worthy of a Greek tragedy, Mr Crowne and Mr Albert," said Allner-Smith resuming his emphatic tone.

"What about it?" said Pole.

"Ah, well, you must be aware that Mr Crowne and Mr Albert were rivals in many ways?" Allner-Smith paused for effect. "Everyone knows of their rivalry in the City. Although I cannot speak of this as it would only be hearsay on my part but I can certainly vouch for it in the auction rooms."

"Please indulge us and do enlighten us further."

"I have witnessed, as you can imagine, many a battle at both Christie's and Sotheby's but Crowne and Albert had a memorable confrontation a couple of years ago."

Pole stayed silent. Allner-Smith was on a roll. "The desired piece was another oriental artefact, a small terracotta warrior that was almost certainly a miniature version of the larger and well-known terracotta warriors of Emperor Qin Shi Huang, first Emperor of China." Allner-Smith cleared his throat and continued. "We presume that the small version had been used as a miniature copy of what the larger pieces would look like. A sort of proof, to be shown to the Emperor for approval before the production began."

Pole nodded in acknowledgement but Allner-Smith did not notice.

"It is very rare that an auction is participated in by the bidders directly. Usually agents are involved to shield the identity of the purchasers. It is equally unusual to have the bidders in the same room. Exceptional pieces attract bids from all over the world."

"Albert and Crowne were there in person?"

"The bid started relatively low for such an exceptional artefact, at £150,000. Crowne has always had a fascination for Asian pieces and even I have to admit his collection is rather good."

"What about Albert?" asked Pole.

"Albert had not noticed it until the bidding started. I can't imagine where it would fit in his collection. Mrs Albert is not particularly fond of Asian pieces, unfortunately."

"This battle was more a 'mine is bigger than yours', I presume."

"That is a rather crude way of putting it, Inspector! But I suppose yes it was. In fact, that's a rather fitting description of the mentality of the two protagonists."

Allner-Smith had become very animated, the electric atmosphere of the auction still in his mind.

116

"Crowne immediately doubled the bid to £300,000, a clear indication that the bidder was not going to mess about. It does away with small opponents but Albert added another £150,000 right away, £450,000 – within three minutes the price had tripled."

"£150,000 per minute, the auction house must have been ecstatic," remarked Pole.

"An exceptional piece, Inspector. Still Crowne would not give in; he added £50,000. Half a million pounds, just like that. Adeila was furious. She had her eyes on another object and Anthony was ruining her prospects of getting it. I could see her arguing with him but he was not having any of it. He was on the phone to his private banker. How far could he go?"

"So, Albert increased the price?" guessed Pole.

"Indeed. Albert increases the bid by £30,000. We are talking £530,000. The entire room is on edge. We are all holding our breath, me included. But Crowne was magnificent. I have to admit it, on that occasion, I was impressed. Final bid £580,000. Adeila left the room. She had said only one word to Anthony and the hammer fell. The room did not move, unbelievable. The sale was sealed in less than five minutes."

"Albert must have been gutted," said Nurani.

Pole smiled at the expression. But Allner-Smith shook his head in complete agreement.

"That he was."

"Did he stop because of his wife?"

"I am not quite sure, Inspector. I did not think it wise or discreet to discuss it with Mrs Albert."

"Could you say a little more maybe? The relationship with Mrs Albert and her husband seemed tense."

Allner-Smith relaxed. He had set the scene the way he wanted. He described the first meeting with the Alberts and an evolving relationship that developed through various organised auctions and grand receptions. Pole knew that Allner-Smith had rehearsed his story. He was a good storyteller though. He used his talent to make the events credible and enjoyable, without too much flourish, peppered with plausible anecdotes, deliberately vague or forgetful when asked for details by Pole or Nurani. To an untrained ear it would have sounded honest and justifiably imprecise, suitably depicting Adeila Albert as a highly charged, difficult woman whose marriage was at an end, a deluded woman when it came to other men. In short, he thought her to be a modern Madame Bovary, as he put it to himself. Pole and Nurani listened, nodding encouragingly, letting their interlocutor unfold his story without interruption. Pole saw the art of the conman in Allner-Smith. He modulated his voice, his speech, his body language effortlessly. It was clear that he had managed to convince Nurani of his story. Her first reaction of distrust was now replaced by a neutral or perhaps favourable opinion. She was not enthusiastic but she was finding him plausible. Pole had to rein in his own judgement, consciously standing back.

"Adeila was desperate to buy a new painting, a portrait by a small Dutch master from the seventeenth century. Anthony was not at all convinced. A great shame as the painting was well executed. Of course, events overtook us." Allner-Smith had finished his story. Albert's death did not seem to either bother or concern him.

"Many thanks for this very thorough account," said Pole. "It will help us greatly in forming a picture of the situation."

Pole emphasised the word *situation* in a conciliatory voice giving Allner-Smith the reassurance he was looking for. He rose, pressing a button on his mobile and signalling that the interview was over. Nurani stood up and managed a small smile at Allner-Smith. He responded with a courteous bow, extended his hand towards her, making contact.

"Let me show you out, Mr Allner-Smith."

Pole's voice sounded almost friendly. Brett looked content, hiding his feeling of success.

Both men walked down the corridor, exchanging banalities about taxi availability outside Scotland Yard. Allner-Smith was keen to get back to work even at this late hour; an impending auction needed his full attention. They were turning the corner and descending a flight of stairs, when a small woman dressed in a black and white designer suit and a podgy man passed them, on their way up. Brett Allner-Smith and Adeila Albert came face to face. Adeila could not contain a short shriek, her eyes wide. She might have run towards her lover had her lawyer not prevented it with a solid grip of her arm. She pulled herself together, calling upon her sense of decorum. Allner-Smith was unfazed. He nodded and moved away to let the pair through, hardly stopping his conversation with Pole. The encounter was masquerade, and Brett let the moment pass.

Pole was reluctantly impressed.

Pole went back to his office to take stock of the events of the day. He was deep in thought when a familiar voice startled him.

"A penny for them?"

"My God, Nurani, I have not heard that expression for a while."

"I am old school you know."

"So am I," sighed Pole, "anyway, I think this guy is a cool customer. Our little charade between him and Adeila yielded very little emotion. I think Henry Crowne has just found a serious competitor on our list of suspects."

* * *

Nancy returned to her lounge to discover Henry fast asleep on her sofa. She wasn't surprised. She moved silently closer to observe him at his most vulnerable. His face had relaxed and sleep revealed deep emotions. Henry moved slightly as if Nancy's scrutiny disturbed him. She stood back a little and continued looking at his face. The unhappy arch of his mouth was telling the story of pain, loneliness, certainly feelings that were never expressed. The furrows that ran along his face and gave it its attractive sculpture had deepened, carved by a heavy chisel.

Nancy looked around at the spacious room in all its delicate femininity and contemporary aesthetic. She enjoyed the contrast. Memories of her darker past floated unexpectedly in front of her eyes.

She saw a much younger Nancy walking the streets of Paris and entering the premises of one of France's most controversial lawyers, Jacques Vergès. She had just finished her dual law degree between La Sorbonne and King's College and was looking for an internship. No one had dared approach him but she knew her own cultural background would be key, a Chinese father and an English mother. He had warned her. The Law, in particular the Bar, was not a place where kind souls thrived. Egos flourished there just as they did in the City. He relished it, but would she?

She inhaled deeply and was grateful that the desire for power had left her many years ago. And yet here she was, reconnecting with that past she had so desired to give up. The idea merited some thought.

Henry moved again. She cast a last look at her unexpected guest. He would be asleep for a little while longer. Nancy disappeared into her kitchen, closing the door behind her softly. Time to indulge in another of her favourite activities, cooking.

* * *

The cab had dropped him a few yards right in front of his apartment. Brett Allner-Smith entered his building rapidly, not wanting to be noticed, a habit he had developed after the sale of his Belgravia family home. His flat was spacious and comfortable but it was a flat! Brett got in, threw his mac onto a Louis XV armchair and walked straight into his office. He opened the door of a small cabinet and poured himself a large whisky. The tumbler was elegant, part of an antique service he had managed to salvage. It was late enough and the work he was about to undertake required concentration. A small tonic was much required.

Brett placed the glass on a low table and pulled aside the Hereke rug that lay in front of it. He pressed a small wooden square etched into the floorboards and a medium sized opening appeared. He pulled a couple of files from the vault, a small laptop and a USB key. Brett shut the safe, replacing the rug. He walked to the sofa, placing the items he had just picked up on the table next to his glass.

The phone rang, but he took no notice. The voice with a foreign accent recorded a message. His Chinese contact was getting impatient. Too bad he would have to wait. The auction for the newly discovered Ming pottery was in a week's time. He would call after he had finished.

The laptop was now connected. Brett opened the first file entitled Henry Crowne. He chose a couple of pictures and some neatly typed notes. The first picture showed Henry and a friend having a drink in a small inconspicuous pub in Dublin. The second showed Henry and Anthony Albert celebrating the closing of a large transaction, again in Dublin. The man in the first picture was there too. He spread the pictures on the table and took a large mouthful of whisky. He savoured the quality of his drink. He could still afford the best. He closed his eyes and let the delicious malt flavour linger on his tongue. Adeila's image flashed in front of his eyes. He pushed it away. Brett would deal with the woman and this afternoon's events later.

Brett leaned towards the table again and opened the second file. He scrawled through some documents that had come up on his screen. A list of all major sales closed with the Alberts appeared. Brett smiled at the thought of two of his best clients tearing each other apart in business. Competition sent commissions rocketing up, splendid – but Brett Allner-Smith wanted something more substantial. He longed to move his collections into a large house again. He longed for the standing he had lost. His plan had been executed with elegance and the call from Scotland Yard had not surprised him.

The phone rang again. The same foreign accent. Brett sighed. In the meantime, he would answer the phone.

Chapter Fifteen

The homely smell of cooking enticed Henry. He opened an eye and woke up with a jolt. Where was he? It took a couple of seconds to realise that he was in Nancy's flat. She could not refrain from bursting into laughter.

"You were out for the count. I did not want to wake you up."

She was still smiling an amused but kind smile. Her face was so different when she laughed, much younger and much more Asian. The high-set cheekbones that delicately shaped her face became accentuated and her almond eyes gently closed. She was a very attractive woman, maturity seemed to have softened her.

"Was I?" said Henry, his mind still wandering.

"Oh, yes. You were."

"What are you cooking? It smells very good."

"Sichuan chicken curry, my family's special recipe – or so they claim. Most people enjoy it."

"You should not have gone to so much trouble."

Henry felt embarrassed, assuming she was cooking for him and she indeed put him right.

"My dear fellow, it wasn't just because of you. I cook for myself. I simply added a bit more."

She was standing in front of him with a closed fist resting on her hip. She was still wearing her oven gloves. Henry burst into laughter and felt better for it. The scene was so unreal.

"Can I help?"

"Yep, you can set the table, crockery in this cupboard and cutlery this one." She was pointing in various directions as she returned to the kitchen. "And you can select the beer you prefer too. I have some in the fridge."

"Beer? I thought wine?"

"Well, you thought wrong I am afraid. Wine with curry is an aberration. A good beer. Nothing else will do!"

Henry nodded, a good beer would always please an Irishman. Moving towards the kitchen he found that he had not done simple things such as setting the table for quite some time. Most dinner parties he held in restaurants. The friends he kept were always keen to try the latest and the best. If he had dinner parties at home he organised these through a caterer. All he had to do was choose the menu, since staff would be in attendance to wait on them. Yet Henry remembered a time when he had enjoyed cooking. The joy of discovering new types of food in London was still vivid in his mind. He'd never thought food could be so enjoyable, a whole new world of excitement and possibilities opened up to him.

They sat at the small dining table in the kitchen and Henry tried not to wolf down what was in front of him. He had survived on very little since Scotland Yard. He did not quibble at the offer of a second helping. Nancy was also clearly enjoying her meal. As predicted, it was excellent and they both savoured it in the half silence that befits appreciated food.

"Tell me more about yourself, Henry," said Nancy after bringing a plate of fruit, cut and prepared, to the table.

Relaxing, Henry wondered whether Nancy had waited for the opportune moment to plant her question. He looked at her and smiled. He did not mind. In a couple of hours, he would meet with her contact and would include her in his legal team. He cast a glance at Nancy's iPhone and remembered his own BlackBerry had been abandoned on the floor of the lounge but resisted the urge to return and look at his emails. Nancy was right. He had to get himself out of this unforeseen mess before he could reclaim any of his territory.

"Where shall I start?" he said.

"The beginning is usually a good place," said Nancy pushing her chair back and turning it sideways to extend her legs. She was elegantly slim.

"OK," said Henry gathering his thoughts.

"Where did you grow up?" asked Nancy to get the conversation going. A shadow moved over his eyes.

"I grew up in Belfast."

Nancy could not hide her surprise.

"I know," he added very quickly. "I don't sound Irish at all any more. You won't believe how effective elocution lessons are when you really want to learn. The City eighteen years ago was not exactly welcoming."

"I've had plenty of racist jokes in my time."

"I was five on Bloody Sunday." Again, Henry hesitated but now he could hardly backtrack. Why stop? After all, it was only a piece of history.

Nancy folded her hands in a meditative fashion, her left hand cupping her right in a most peaceful gesture. She was giving him her utmost attention.

Henry had not cast his mind back to his childhood for a long time. He remembered it as a dark place full of fear, anger, and yet he could not say that he had been unloved. He spoke about his mother, a young woman who had come to Belfast to teach English, escaping her family in England. She had wanted to take risks, to establish her own independence, thinking she could always go back if matters did not work out for her. Life had decided otherwise when she met Henry's father, Irish Catholic and strongly militant.

"Forty years ago," added Henry with little emotion in his voice, "Ireland was a nation on the verge of destruction." He sounded remote, an observer of a city long cast away.

"An Irish boy marrying an English girl – that must have been …" Nancy stopped searching for the right word.

"Disastrous," ventured Henry, with a small sad smile.

"I was going to say dramatic but, I suppose, very difficult at least."

"Yep. I remember two things from my very early years. My father swinging me on his shoulders, grabbing Mum and dancing to some crazy tune, we were all laughing and then …"

Henry grabbed his fork and toyed with a piece of fruit. He no longer wanted to conjure the memories back.

"The shrieks of sirens after bombs had struck, the predictability of the bombs. So much violence ready to erupt for little reason, it becomes part of who you are, you don't even – well, notice it."

A long, drawn silence elapsed before Henry continued.

"My mother and I were on the street that day, why? I don't know, she never said. Anyhow, miraculously, we survived."

"Are you angry?" asked Nancy.

"Wouldn't you be?" replied Henry, without hesitation.

"Yes, I was angry too, for different reasons but yes, I understand that sort of anger well."

"Are you still angry?"

Henry could not imagine Nancy being anything but charming and relaxed. Yet behind her eyes was a light that sometimes lit up. He had seen it when they were both at Scotland Yard.

"Not anymore, I have made my peace with what was eating me alive," she said, serene, "and so should you. Late thirties is the right time to start letting go."

"Maybe. I will have to think about it," said Henry. Anger had filled him with energy for success. He was not prepared to yet let go of such a potent fuel.

"Was your father IRA?" Nancy asked.

The question surprised Henry by its directness, but then again, she knew nothing yet of his complex links with the O'Connor brothers.

"I am not sure. If he was he never said. Anyway, it is irrelevant now. He died many years ago. It was not the cause that killed him I think but the bottle."

"Sorry to hear that."

"I was young when it happened. It belongs to another life."

"What about you Henry, are you IRA?"

Henry opened his eyes wide and roared with laughter, shaking his head.

"Nancy, I know you are my brief but I am not sure what you expect me to say to that?" He was still grinning at the question.

"The truth, of course," said Nancy in complete focus. Henry's face fell a little.

"If you are referring to my friendship with the O'Connors, yes I knew them as kids and Liam and I went to uni at the same time. Bobby was older."

"Did you know they were involved?"

"It always was a hot topic of conversation with them, although Liam has been much more, let's say, conciliatory of late. Bobby has been a staunch follower of Gerry Adams from the time he discovered who Adams was. However, I am sure you have read the news. The IRA has been decommissioned."

"So, you are Catholic Irish, on your father's side," continued Nancy.

"Yep, my lass," replied Henry in an Irish accent. "Although a little complicated by the fact that my mother was Anglican and in charge of my education."

"Henry, your life is so different now. What keeps you close to these guys?" Nancy asked with genuine interest.

"I have asked myself that question many a time. Maybe old bonds don't die so easily. I don't really know, Nancy," carried on Henry after a while. "We did some silly things together when we were kids. You know, boys stuff. We looked after each other even more so after our fathers died.

To them I was not an English brat, the invader that deserved to die. I was their friend."

Memories of his past propelled Henry back to the Troubles. Some lads at school have started calling him names, one spits in his face and soon he is on the ground fighting. The whole class is ready to join in but Liam intervenes. Bobby, always ready to throw a punch even at eight, savages the most vicious of the boys whilst Liam issues his warning: *you mess with Henry, you mess with us.*

Henry inhaled and the memory faded away.

"Mmmm," Nancy said "I am not sure this explanation is going to wash with Inspector Pole."

"Possibly not but it will have to do. In any case I hardly see Liam these days and never Bobby."

Nancy looked at her watch, the conversation was over.

"A final cup of coffee?" she asked.

"Now, let me do that one. I do a mean cup of instant coffee," replied Henry with enthusiasm.

Nancy looked at him in horror. He had pronounced the forbidden word *instant*. Henry clapped his hands and with a wink continued, "Got you there … Just kidding, let me make a proper cup of well brewed Jamaican coffee."

Nancy face relaxed slightly, still not entirely convinced that Henry's standard of well brewed coffee was up to hers.

* * *

Ted looked at his watch and made his way to McCarthy's office. As usual he would be too early. Cindy saw him step outside the lift and sigh. When would he ever learn?

She indicated to him with a short wave of the hand that he had to wait a few minutes. She was on the phone to New York. Ted made his usual gesture of apology and stepped into the visitors' waiting room. He stood in front of a print, depicting the image of an androgynous man. The picture was a William Blake and featured as one of GL's most impressive pieces of art. He read the text yet again, as he always did, a form of symbolist poetry which still eluded him.

"Mr McCarthy will see you now," Cindy said formally.

Cindy always referred to McCarthy by his surname, preserving the distance a CEO should have with his people. Only a few direct reports enjoyed the privilege of having her refer to him as Douglas. Henry had been one of those people. He was a rising star who would have eventually been elevated to a position as high as that of McCarthy. Ted was a different kettle of fish. But today, as he was about to enter the CEO's office emboldened, Ted looked like a puffed-up sparrow, lots of feathers and very little weight. Cindy walked past him, did not knock at the door in her usual way and introduced Ted. McCarthy did not move. He carried on reading an email.

"I spoke to James," said McCarthy, now typing his reply.

Ted was standing in the middle of the room not knowing whether he should approach the great desk or simply take a seat at the meeting table.

"Oh good," he hesitated.

"Did you have another conversation with Scotland Yard?"

"Yes," mumbled Ted.

McCarthy was waiting.

"They want more information," said Ted.

His stomach did a somersault, in fear of the old man's reaction.

"Not surprising," replied McCarthy.

He stood up and moved towards the meeting table at which point Ted sat down.

"Have you prepared the next set of information needed?" asked McCarthy as he sat down himself.

"Well, I thought we could have a conversation about this, maybe."

McCarthy gave Ted a cruel look.

"Do I have to dictate the numbers to you or will you be able to cope on your own? Should I ask someone else to deal with this?"

"No, no. I can cope, I just need general direction," replied Ted.

Their eyes met and Ted was doomed. The young man had crossed the threshold whence one does not return. There would be no further heart-aching questions. He would now simply think about how to execute the task with ruthless efficiency. Thoughts of Henry, his colleague, his friend, had stopped haunting him. He had tasted real power and it was good.

McCarthy and Ted spent a few minutes on what McCarthy expected and then Ted was gone.

Walking out of his office after Ted had left, McCarthy turned to Cindy.

"No calls or meetings for the next hour. Reschedule. I need to think."

Cindy nodded. Nothing and no one would cross the threshold to his office for the next hour.

McCarthy went back to his desk, unlocked a drawer with a key permanently kept on his own key ring and pulled out an unlabelled file. McCarthy took a deep breath. The contents of this file were only known to him and the head of the CDO team. What it contained was capable, even after all these years, of taking his breath away. He had not checked the latest figures. McCarthy did not bother to consider the rows of numbers and the text that justified the findings contained in the document. He jumped straight to the aggregated figures, one indicating the current loss on the portion of CDOs GL had kept on its books. The second was an estimation of the potential loss going forward should the subprime markets not stabilise. The second figure was accompanied by a number of scenarios. The first figure was already very alarming. McCarthy paused. In his entire career he had never considered bankruptcy of a financial institution the size of GL, a bank of such stature simply could not disappear the way Bankers Trust did. He clenched his fist, his mind racing to find a way out of this predicament. It was then that the second number hit him, $31 billion. He pushed his chair back in horror. He was speechless. He came back to his desk and muttered to himself.

"Who the fuck chose the parameters for this set of projections?"

Still standing, he read the figures again and again, as reality slowly and inexorably began to sink in. Were the markets to move down again, there would be no salvation. McCarthy went back to the text and speed read the content. The complexity of the subprime products that had been designed by his team eluded him but the equation that could cost GL bankruptcy was simple. The level of risk that GL had retained with its CDO business had been grossly miscalculated. Even the AAA tranches, reputed to be the most solid part of the CDOs' tranches were collapsing. The rating agencies had cocked up, the regulator had cocked up, and his senior team in risk management had cocked up. No one had checked the content of what they were selling.

McCarthy sat down slowly, the battles of the past few days now taking their toll. He had to make the call.

Chapter Sixteen

The background checks on Brett Allner-Smith confirmed Pole's suspicions. The suave English gentleman hid well the ruthless dealer. Pole smiled into a stretch, his arms folded behind his head. In a strange way, Henry Crowne had met his match in the antiquities world. A number of deals had been questioned – the value given to certain 'priceless' objects, the authentication of a variety of pieces. There was never enough evidence to conclude that there had been foul play. Allner-Smith, although sailing close to the wind, knew how to protect his rear end. Pole had called in a specialist from another squad so that he could understand the level of sophistication such a fraud would demand.

Eugene Grandel had worked on some of Allner-Smith cases. He was, for his part, convinced that something was afoot.

"This guy is incapable of being completely straight."

"Not surprised. Anyhow tell me more about this chap."

"Smooth operator, extremely knowledgeable and connected. If I were a betting man I'd say secret services of some sort. The little git gets himself out of the tightest of spots." Eugene lifted his hands before Pole could ask for more. "Don't ask me to substantiate – can't. Just the view of an old copper but one thing I can definitely say – can't keep it in his pants. He has a soft spot for the ladies, young ladies."

"How young?"

"Young enough," added Eugene.

Eugene gave Pole a naughty grin and raised his eyebrows.

"How far would he go for money?" continued Pole.

"Very good question."

Eugene crossed his arms and rested his head on his chest. He looked at Pole.

"Murder? Yes, possibly but it would have to be sophisticated."

"Really?" said Pole unconvinced.

"No direct involvement, as I said, but he could be the mastermind. He could manipulate, in fact, come to think of it he would enjoy manipulating. There is a case," he continued, now following his own trail of thoughts, "Might be helpful. Let me come back to you on this."

Eugene walked away, promising Pole more information and soon.

Pole was alone in his office having refused his team's invite for a break. He needed time to reflect. Henry no longer remained the only suspect. And then some disturbing information had arrived on his desk exposing Anthony Albert's transaction pipeline. Albert was involved in the structuring of subprime products. Pole had just started scratching the surface of what Albert was up to at work. There were rumours of enormous deals being closed and astronomical sums of money being made. A billion dollars had been mentioned as the average size for a transaction.

The AVERAGE size – these guys had really lost the plot.

Now Pole had two key targets in mind. He wanted to hear what Liam O'Connor had to say about his friend Henry Crowne. The police in Northern Ireland had been informed and were on his trail. Liam was a smart operator, it might take some time. Pole also wanted to speak to Albert's solicitor. The will would be open and read – soon. Pole would arrange for a sneak preview. Still, Pole was not satisfied. Something else was afoot and he had not yet found out what. He was deep in thought, creating a picture of all that he knew when Nurani knocked at the door. Without waiting for a response she poked her head through the door.

"The guys in Ireland have traced Liam O'Connor," she announced, excited at the thought of meeting her first IRA sympathiser.

"Good work!" said Pole. "That is a bit of luck. Any details on how it happened?"

"He was trying to get out of Switzerland."

"And going to?" asked Pole whose interest had been piqued by the location.

"North Africa, Libya to be more precise."

"Where did they pick him up?"

"Zurich Airport," replied Nurani. "Big banking there. Any coincidence?"

"That would be a very big coincidence," said Pole stretching his arms wide. "How quickly are they going to extradite him?"

"Pretty quickly. I think he should be home tomorrow. The Swiss are keen on banking secrecy but not so much so on terrorism. This is happening as we speak."

"OK. Get two tickets to Belfast, we are paying our friend a visit," said Pole.

"Yes Boss," saluted Nurani.

Pole rolled his eyes. She grinned before disappearing. He settled down, immersing himself once more in the files piled on his desk.

* * *

Henry was back in his flat with a long list of to-dos. Nancy had focused his attention on the task. She hoped the exercise would be long and tedious enough to prevent Henry from contacting GL again.

Nancy for her part needed to follow one of her hunches. She had stored her own to-dos in the back of her mind as methodically as she used to when a barrister. *Old habits die hard*, she smiled inwardly, surprised at the speed at which the dormant QC had resurfaced in her. Her reputation had been built on the sagacity of her observation, her phenomenal determination. She never spoke about her other weapon – intuition. Not to be discussed in this male dominated profession, they might have called her a witch. But she had learned to listen to her inner voice. That voice had made itself louder during the day.

She grabbed her lime green coat, stuffed a pad into her matching handbag and rushed out. She looked at her watch. She had some time. The library on Russell Square would not be shutting yet. Before hailing a cab, she cast an eye towards Henry's window. The light was on. She derived some comfort from it. He was doing his homework, maybe? She pushed that idea aside to concentrate on the task at hand.

The library was slowly emptying. It was much more functional than she remembered, PCs everywhere. Still the smell of books lingered, sweet and subtle. One of the librarians had been particularly helpful. She sat in front of the oldest PC in the room, letters almost erased by so many eager fingers. She started scrolling through old newspapers. She remembered the tedium of perusing the press for information. This was so much easier and yet she had enjoyed the feel of the pages unfolding beneath her fingers.

Nancy had reached the year 1992. She had a date in mind, 10th April of the same year. The date the last IRA bomb had killed in the City of London was linked in her mind to a face and a name: Jonathan Pole.

The search engine threw a number of newspaper articles onto the page. Nancy skimmed them; *The Times*, the *FT*, *The Daily Telegraph* and finally the *Evening Standard*. Here it was, a large front-page article describing the bombing, accusing the Met and the Counterterrorist Squad of poor communication. The article was condemning the lack of efficacy of both forces in failing to anticipate the blast, despite a serious but last-minute tip-off. The same article showed a picture of a young police officer fielding the press as best he could. A much younger Inspector Pole was looking straight at Nancy with a serious look in his eyes. Nancy smiled at the young man. He looked rather dashing, she thought. But no flirting with the enemy or at least not yet.

The printer spewed out two copies of the various articles. She grabbed them and made her way to the coffee shop. The library would close in one hour and was already completely deserted. She ordered Darjeeling in a proper teacup and was pleased to discover that the old crockery had not been replaced. Nancy chose a deep chair and settled in to reread the news articles. The IRA bomb had cost three lives. The usual IRA message had been sent to the Met only thirty minutes before the blast. Slow communication between the Met and the Counterterrorist Squad had been blamed for the tragedy. Pole looked ill at ease in this bad picture of him. The article presented him as a spokesperson for the Met, the liaison officer with the CT Squad. Not an easy job in those days. She took a sip of tea, refreshed by its delicate aroma. She sat back and wondered whether this new piece of information mattered. Henry was Irish, brought up in Northern Ireland. Should this imply some connection? The explosion that killed Anthony Albert had necessitated access to explosives and an expert knowledge of bomb production.

The cup was warming Nancy's hands. She took another sip. What would Inspector Pole make of this? He had experience of the IRA and its techniques. Pole was bound to create a link between Henry's Irish past and the murder. She finished her tea and stood up.

"Jonathan Pole. It's time to have a little chat," she murmured.

* * *

Pole looked at the clock on the wall. He rolled his head around in a welcome stretch before moving his seat away from his desk. He could see the desks emptying slowly. Nurani and Andy had gone to check some key details with Forensics. The phone rang. Pole frowned. What now? But his professional self tapped him on the shoulder.

131

"Pole."

"Guv, Nancy Wu is downstairs. She would like a word."

Pole remained silent. How unexpected. The intriguing Ms Wu wanted a word, and why not.

"I'll come down Reg. Ask her to wait please."

"Okey dokey, Guv."

Nancy was standing in the lobby, absorbed in considering the space when Pole reached her.

"Ms Wu, what brings you to my neck of the woods?"

"*Good evening*, Inspector," said Nancy. "I was admiring your new lobby. It's a lot more impressive than it used to be ... but could do with a good piece of contemporary art."

Pole smiled at the remark.

"Apologies! *Good evening* Ms Wu."

"Don't worry, I have not come to discuss the merits of the new interior decoration. What exactly was your role in 1992 with the Met and the Counterterrorist Squad?"

Pole's face turned to stone.

"I could try to find out indirectly but why not answer the question yourself," carried on Nancy.

"May I ask why it is of any concern of yours?" replied Pole dryly.

"Henry is Irish, from Northern Ireland as you know by now. I just wanted to decide whether the Inspector leading the case had particular views on this key fact."

Nancy was squarely facing Pole. Her ebony hair clasped with an ivory pin, her almond eyes sparkling with intelligence and wit.

"If you are trying to establish whether I will be biased—"

"I am not implying anything, Inspector," Nancy interrupted "I am simply asking some honest questions. I do not shy away from these issues, in particular if I feel they may be material to the case."

Pole remained silent. Part of him just wanted to give Nancy a piece of his mind, while the other part wanted to yield to the openness she had shown.

"Well, I presume you will find out. I was with the Met but worked as liaison officer with the Squad. And before you ask, it was complicated and mistakes were made in 1992. It was a long time ago, so no, I do not hold a grudge."

"That I can believe Inspector," replied Nancy. "It takes a certain type to join the Squad."

"A compliment?" replied Pole.

"No, a statement of facts," said Nancy unperturbed. "I like to determine very quickly how I can work with people Inspector. I am not trying to be argumentative but I will get to the point and rather quickly at that, if I feel it is in my client's interest."

"Very good, Ms Wu, and I will certainly be more than happy to oblige," retorted Pole, invigorated by this honest discussion.

"We now understand each other, which is excellent," said Nancy. Pole had expected her to bid him farewell but she was not finished. "And to show you I think we can work together, I have come to give you an important piece of evidence."

"Why now? Should you not have come forward earlier on?"

"A valid question of course but I needed to know how to approach this. Are we to talk here or in your office?"

Pole pursed his lips.

"It depends how long this will be."

"Very short indeed. I received post for Henry a day before the flight. The janitor is on holiday and his replacement is quite absent-minded I am afraid. In that post were a couple of plane tickets which I suspect were for the fated trip to Switzerland. I asked the young man to redirect them to Henry and was a little short with him. Probably because I felt guilty I had not done so myself more swiftly."

"In short Henry did not get the tickets on time because you could not be bothered," said Pole.

"A harsh but good summary of the position," replied Nancy unfazed.

"Does Henry know?"

"That is between me and my client, Inspector. With due respect of course."

"Anything else I need to know?" said Pole bluntly.

"Absolutely nothing."

"Fine," Pole grunted. "I will get one of my team to record your statement."

"Thank you for your time Inspector, no doubt we shall speak soon. *A bientot.*"

"*Certainement. Et au plaisir,*" finished Pole in impeccable French.

Pole gave a short nod, turned back, disappeared into a lift and walked back to his office. He went straight to his computer and clicked on the Scotland Yard search website. He entered Nancy Wu's name. He scrolled through her bio quickly and returned to the beginning. Her mixed cultural background did not surprise him, but the history of her family both intrigued him and resonated with his own personal experience. The internship with Jacques Vergès however was utterly unexpected. He jotted a few words on a pad, a reference to the Klaus Barbie affair. Ms Wu must have been fiercely ambitious to agree to be one of the defence lawyers for a war criminal. Pole would not cast judgement on whether Nancy Wu was also devoid of all moral principle to have accepted this assignment, knowing the answer to this question was more complex than it seemed. Then again, she had left France and entered pupillage at Gray's Inn. Her career had been stellar, becoming a Silk at such a young age. She should have been called to the bench but in 2008 Vergès' name reappeared. Pole jotted down a few more words and sat back in his chair. Something important had happened in 2008. The Nancy Wu that had managed to get under his skin a few moments ago was a very different woman to the one he had just encountered on the page of the Yard search website.

Why?

Chapter Seventeen

As Nancy turned the corner of her street, she looked up. Light was still on in Henry's flat. She consulted her watch, it was past 9pm. Henry had followed her advice or perhaps not. There was to be no contact with GL until he had spoken to his lawyer, the notorious Pritchard QC. Pritchard had defended a number of high-flyers in the City. Finance was his domain. If Henry had focused in the way he should have, then his list of to-dos was finished. Nancy anticipated that it would be executed to perfection, with certain omissions of course. She couldn't imagine a man like Henry disclosing all at a first meeting. Then again Pritchard was a man of extreme sagacity. A small pang of anticipation entered her heart. She smiled. Could it be that she was missing the old profession? It only took a few seconds for her to answer with a categorical no, or at least no to the way she conducted her affairs a few years ago. Nevertheless, she had to admit that she was enjoying the intellectual challenge.

The door of her own apartment appeared in front of her. She paused before opening it. Should she check on Henry? Was he actually there or had he left? She decided against it. She would call when she had settled herself back into her flat. Another cup of Darjeeling would do the trick. The flashing light on her answer phone told her that she would not have to call. The small replay button was pressed and Henry's baritone voice filled the room, poised but expectant.

"I have completed my list. But I think I have to come back to you with a couple of questions. One or two points to clarify."

There was a small silence.

"Happy to cook, by the way, although my standards are unlikely to compare to yours – takeaway perhaps. Let me know."

Mr Crowne is starting to come around. She had left the door ajar on the off chance and Henry a few moments later leaned against the frame, knocking inside the door.

"Evening," he said informally.

"Good evening, my dear. How is it all going?"

"I am very clear on most of it," replied Henry as he sat down where he had sat before.

He took the tea that had been poured for him, bringing the cup to his nose. The gentle and fresh scent of first flush Darjeeling satisfied his senses. He took a sip.

"Do I really have to say a lot about Albert? I have to admit I disliked the guy but it feels futile and rather strange to speak ill of him now."

"Speak no ill of the dead for fear they may come and haunt you. That is a tad irrational for you, Henry," said Nancy gently mocking him.

"I don't like speaking of someone whom I can't challenge any longer."

"Fair enough. Why don't you give examples? Show us events that have happened between you and him that you think best describe your relationship and who Albert was. The prosecution will use these too and your defence team needs to be prepared with your version of facts."

Silence.

"I can imagine that you must have done business together, closed transactions."

After some more hesitation, Henry succumbed to the most human of temptations, the pleasure of talking about himself.

"I suppose I could talk about Dublin?"

"I think you should," said Nancy. "You know as well as I do it is an important moment."

"I am sure you are knowledgeable about my speciality," continued Henry.

"You mean the fact that you run the Structured Product Team at GL?"

A smile and glance of admiration lit up Henry's face.

"So you know that GL arranges some pretty large deals for its clients?"

"My old profession, Henry, I dealt with a lot of City people. I know your business."

"Well then you will appreciate … My team had closed a particularly large complex transaction, in fact the first of many. It was an accounting play that improved EPS, I mean Earning Per Share, for corporates. I must add that these transactions did not cause any negative effects in the markets."

"You mean this has nothing to do with subprime, of course."

"Absolutely nothing remotely to do with it. In fact, I think those guys

136

got exactly what they deserve but that's another story." Henry poured himself some more tea.

"The transaction had taken us nearly a year to construct and the amount raised was the largest ever raised for a quoted company, and still is, I believe."

Henry stopped, mentally perusing the record of the deals he knew had been done.

"Yes, I am sure. Anyway, we had used HXBK as partners in the transaction. GL had taken a portion of the deal on its trading book and needed someone else to come along that the company would trust. There was no front running, of course. But our Head of Marketing is pretty good. He knew what we had to offer to place the deal with them."

"Was Albert's team involved?"

"They had to review the technicalities of the deal, legal structure, pricing."

"How so?"

"Well, for a start this company had been their client for years. The CFO would derive some comfort if they joined. We were testing our ability to explain the deal and the impact of the parameters of pricing and kept a little black box that would give us an advance on the market."

"You mean, you protected your intellectual property because it did not impact on the buyer's?"

"Correct!" said Henry. Yes, Nancy would have been superb in his team.

"And I presume Albert was livid."

"Oh yes, you bet. We had managed to market to one of his major clients right underneath his nose. Of course, the little motherfucker, sorry—"

Nancy waved her hand. "Go on."

"But, we needed them buying into the deal alongside us. Very few clients enjoy being first to market, let alone with a bank they are not so familiar with."

"I suppose Albert did his best to scupper the deal?"

"To start with he did, but we were confident and GL's structure was very robust. He could do nothing but pretend he was working on a similar idea; pathetic really but so typical of him."

"And why Dublin?" said Nancy wanting to hear about what she suspected was a loaded subject.

"We closed the deal there because we needed an offshore Irish company to structure the transaction."

"So, Albert was at the closing?"

"Well, yes, and bearing in mind that HXBK came to the table and he knew the client. It was very hard to tell him to get lost."

"Who else was there, then?"

Nancy poured herself a fresh cup of tea. Henry measured the impact of the question, admiring Nancy's ability to lead effortlessly.

"The usual suspects. That is, a cast of thousands: structurers, traders, marketers, lawyers, accountants, the client and his own team of course."

"And Albert."

"And Albert," acknowledged Henry. "We all got pretty drunk."

"In a good Irish pub?"

"Wine bar, Michelin star restaurant and then a good Irish pub."

Henry's mind drifted back to that evening.

The face of his Chase and Case lawyer Pam hovers very close to him. They are both laughing. She is teasing him about drinking Guinness. She grabs his pint and drinks from it, pulling a face. He remembers her words after she has wetted her red lips with the dark liquid. *Henry, babe, how can you drink this stuff?* He can't quite recall his answer but he feels the opportunity, the intimacy.

"As a matter of interest, who was your lawyer on this deal?" asked Nancy, dissipating the last image.

"Why?" replied Henry. Had she read his mind?

"Well, once a lawyer always a lawyer as you must have guessed by now," said Nancy. "I am interested in finding out who the next generation of high profile solicitor is."

"We use a number of law firms at GL but usually for these deals Chase and Case."

"A good choice. And do you have a partner assigned to your deals? It is rare to chop and change. Important to trust your key lawyer, it's fine and dandy when it goes smoothly but when a deal goes sour …" continued Nancy.

"Well, yes. I agree. It's when a deal goes south that …"

The memory of the Wooster QC debacle came back to Henry like a slap in the face. He had thought there was something special between Pam and him. Physical attraction, he knew, but perhaps something more. Trust he had relied on and the hope she cared.

"And the lucky partner that looks after you at Chase and Case is?" said Nancy.

"Pamela Anderson."

"Anybody else to help you celebrate the pinnacle of your career?" asked Nancy. She would come to Pamela later on.

"What do you mean?"

"Well, you are Irish after all. And Dublin is a small place. I don't wish to offend you by saying this of course. Are you not bound to meet people you know when you get out there?"

"I know the owner of the pub quite well. I always bring a good crowd when I sign a deal and he gives me good service."

"Was it the pub you frequented when you went to uni?"

"Nancy, really, Dublin was a hell of a different place when I went to uni."

"Mmm, so no uni pals to help you celebrate your big day?"

The ring of Nancy's phone spared Henry. He would not have to speak about Liam and Bobby. Nancy stood up. It was Pritchard QC.

Henry no longer hears Nancy's voice. It is sound rather than words, replaced by the buzzing noise of a pub, glasses ringing, laughter bubbling up.

Henry does not notice his two friends at first. But Liam raises his glass in the distance with a large grin on his face. Henry goes to them cheerfully, inviting them to join his crowd for another round. The moment is too big not to ask his best pals to share in his glory. He feels invulnerable. Liam and Bobby stay with his party well into the night. Who have they been speaking to? He cannot remember.

Nancy was standing next to her 1930's phone when she turned to Henry.

"Pritchard will see us first thing in the morning."

The memories of Dublin lingered in Henry's mind. He stood up as if to shake off the image of his two friends. He bade Nancy goodnight and left.

Nancy waited a few minutes before crossing her flat to her office. She opened her computer and started a search for the pub Henry had mentioned in their conversation. She knew something material had happened there.

Chapter Eighteen

Henry walked into his flat and was about to go to bed. He had nearly forgotten his BlackBerry. He had left it where it had dropped and not looked at it since. But the little red light was flashing in a hypnotic fashion. Henry tried to ignore it and was about to toss it into his briefcase when his last conversation with James resurfaced. What had he meant by speaking to Ted? He looked at his watch. It was gone 10pm but James would take a call.

He dialled without hesitation. James mobile was engaged. Henry sent a quick text and the reply came back swiftly.

Still @ office, finalising docs, anything you need?

No txs, keep going, was Henry's equally cryptic reply.

He could be at the office in fifteen minutes if he took the car. Nancy had told him to stay away but so what? She was not his mother and he had already breeched her recommendations once by trying to call McCarthy. There had been no negative consequences, but then again McCarthy had not taken the call.

Henry turned towards the door but something was holding him back. He hated this state of indecisiveness. It wasn't him. His eyes fell on the wrapped-up painting. He had not looked at it or moved it since the night Nancy and he had had drinks. Henry walked decisively towards the piece and tore the bubble wrap in one violent move. The painting nearly crashed on the floor. Henry held it back and pushed it into position. Now he could see it better. He liked the ferocity of it and its uncompromised violence. Yes, he would once more bend the rules.

He grabbed his car keys, tossed them once in the air. He pocketed his BlackBerry and walked out of his flat.

The car park underneath the block of flats was brightly lit, Henry's Aston Martin parked close to the entrance in one of the larger bays. Henry stopped for a few seconds, someone must be in the car park as the light was on. He looked around but could not spot anyone. He was about to deactivate the car alarm when he felt a firm hand on his shoulder.

Nancy was standing in front of him.

"Going for a spin?"

"Absolutely. The car needs to take the air."

"And would that spin take you back to the office, by any chance?"

"Look Nancy, you're my lawyer not my guardian," he raised his voice.

"Frankly Henry, it feels as if I am turning into just that, otherwise stop being so childish."

"What the fuck has childish got to do with it? I need to have a chat with one of my guys. It's strictly business."

"It has zip to do with business, Henry. You just can't control yourself."

"Control myself! What planet are you on? I have a multibillion dollar deal in the pipeline—"

"Stop the crap," interrupted Nancy. "If this is important you can deal with it on the phone. I am sure that you have perfect backup. Your team are not a bunch of incompetent nerds, right?"

Henry did not have time to reply.

"You do what you have to do, I won't interfere again but I will not be working with some chap who is going to annihilate his chances of salvaging his case – clear?"

Nancy turned and walked away.

"And what is my case to you anyway Nancy, hey? An attempt to crawl back into the limelight?" shouted Henry.

"No, a vague attempt at redemption. And since we are getting down to it, I had received the plane tickets in my post by mistake and forgot to deliver them back on time to you. Yes, the police know. Yes, I feel bad about it. And no, I don't give a damn whether you're peed off." Nancy was speaking over her shoulder as she was waiting for the lift. She disappeared into it when it arrived.

"Shit," shouted Henry throwing his keys against the door of the lift.

* * *

McCarthy had checked his mobile earlier in the day and could see he had missed a call. Henry's name was showing on the small screen and McCarthy was only surprised it had taken so long. He must have been informed of GL's decision by HR. McCarthy had not made the time to speak to Henry directly and for a moment he felt regret. After all, Alexander the Great had been known to give the *coup de grâce* to his dying soldiers himself, but then again McCarthy was not Alexander the Great. More pressing matters were requiring his attention besides his philosophical beliefs or Henry's need for explanation. He walked out of his office in search of an empty meeting room. He needed urgently to call his Whitehall contact. McCarthy walked purposely. Anyone meeting him would imagine he was on his way to an urgent appointment. He would not be interrupted. To his annoyance all the meeting rooms were full. This sign of renewed activity did not cheer him as most meetings were internal, his firm was on the brink. His people were starting to get too agitated, the takeover combined with a gasping market that could not find its feet was destabilising GL's well-oiled platform. Disaster scenarios were being run daily. It was now only a matter of time. McCarthy dove into the staircase and went down one floor. Thankfully, a small meeting room was free. He swiftly entered the room and dialled his contact number.

"Douglas," said the voice, genuinely surprised. "So soon! How are you my dear fellow?"

"We urgently need to talk," McCarthy said. There was no time for niceties.

"I suggest lunch tomorrow. I may be a little late. Say 2pm, same place? I'll be there, alone."

"As you see fit, William," answered McCarthy.

"Can you give me a hint?"

"We are on the verge of a global financial meltdown," replied McCarthy without hesitation.

* * *

The rain had started falling in the early morning, a fine drizzle that made the cold even more penetrating. James Radlett shivered as he crossed the street towards GL's offices. It was 6.30am. The trading floor began its day with cash traders on European markets arriving as early as 6am to prepare their day, listening to the analysts' reviews of the economy, reading the financial papers and scrolling through Bloomberg and Reuters.

Information was key, not only published but also inferred; each trader trying to create a position of favourable arbitrage before the London market opened, a discipline that most traders would respect.

The derivative people would arrive at 7 or even perhaps 7.30am, their reliance on market data different from their cash colleagues unless the markets were turbulent.

James showed his card to the security guard – since 9/11 GL had introduced drastic security measures. He progressed towards the turnstile in the vast atrium, scanned his card again and moved to the third floor, rapidly climbing the escalator. The trading floor was already full. The subprime crisis was spreading fast, reaching areas of the market that under normal circumstances would have been spared.

One young woman had been working the Asian market and, looking away from her screens, dropped her head into her hands in a gesture of defeat. She could do nothing but lose time and time again.

James logged in, and quickly perused Bloomberg. He was not focusing on the debacle, but rather was hunting for any announcements relating to the takeover between GL and HXBK. Interesting news had the habit of appearing early morning and brusquely disappearing from the news panel as the day moved on. He searched under the GL ticker, then HXBK's then financial institutions. Nothing. He quickly looked at the clock at the bottom of his screen which indicated 6.47. He would make his way to McCarthy's office at 6.55. He had no intention of arriving ahead of time.

* * *

Ted had also arrived at the office early. He had parked his Porsche 911 in GL's private car park, a luxury only MDs enjoyed. The congestion charge did not worry him. His property had had the good fortune to fall on the right side of the line when Ken Livingstone had extended its perimeter. His house in the West End was indeed well positioned. Something he liked to brag about with less fortunate colleagues. Ted reached the elevator and looked at his watch; 6.55 exactly.

When the door opened again, Ted found himself face to face with James. A small yelp escaped from his mouth. James nodded stiffly and stepped into the lift, forcing Ted to rush out.

"*Little fucker, I'll get you one day,*" James said through gritted teeth.

The lift pinged again, reminding James of why he had entered it in the

143

first place. It took him to the executive floor where Douglas McCarthy was expecting him.

Unusually, McCarthy's door was open. Cindy was nowhere to be seen. James was about to wait for Cindy to return when McCarthy's authoritative voice summoned him in. He was seated at his desk and well advanced in his day's work. He asked James to take a seat at the spacious meeting table. James sat down and McCarthy joined him, neither man had greeted the other.

McCarthy's attention rested on James, a heavy weight that the young man felt immediately. His army training and military career, albeit short, had familiarised him with the implacable authority of his commanding officer, and yet the proximity of McCarthy made him uneasy. Whether he liked it or not his CEO was a force to be reckoned with.

"I am sure you know why you are here James," said McCarthy without any further formalities.

"Well, since I have not seen Henry for over thirty-six hours, I think I do," replied James.

There was no point in being coy. If McCarthy intended to have a straightforward conversation with James, James was intent on giving him just that.

"Our legal team informs me that matters look difficult for Henry," said McCarthy.

No reply from James.

"I consequently have a major decision to make regarding the future of the team," carried on McCarthy.

James remained silent. He had prepared himself for this outcome. McCarthy paused once more. James, still sitting straight in front of him, rested his gaze on his CEO. Without Henry or Anthony Albert around, McCarthy had a much broader choice. He held an additional chip that could be played to his advantage. Something that would not have crossed his mind thirty-six hours ago now became a distinct possibility. HXBK's people knew this too. They were on tenterhooks.

"HXBK is putting pressure on me to transition the team immediately. It would be a quick and viable answer but I am not sure it is the right one," carried on McCarthy.

McCarthy was waiting for a reaction. James, still sitting straight in front of him, had folded his hands calmly on the table. He looked at McCarthy straight in the eyes. He would not compromise.

"For the time being, I would like Ted to take control of the team. He

144

will be relying on you heavily, of course, to keep the technical side under control. But when it comes to management decisions Ted will take over from Henry."

James finally shifted. This was preposterous. Ted had neither the kudos nor the market credentials to take control of Henry's team.

"I am sure there is a rational reason why this is so but I am sorry, I just can't see it myself."

McCarthy remained relaxed. He would not employ the same technique as with Ted. In fact, Ted bored him, he was so easy to scare and manipulate, so repulsively weak. James was more of an interesting challenge.

"I agree that at first sight it does not seem a good move. I know Ted does not have, let us say, the same credible image as Henry does but …"

McCarthy paused for effect and poured a fresh cup of coffee for both of them. James was taken aback by his willingness to explain his decision.

"Ted is heading the integration committee on this segment of our business and you seem to work well with him. He has only good things to say about you."

"I am glad Ted feels comfortable with me," replied James, unmoved by the compliment. Ted had no option but to claim he got on well with James. He needed James' technical expertise to control Henry's team.

James felt awkward. If he had any ambition to succeed Henry, he had to seize the opportunity now.

"Excellent," McCarthy said, turning James' hesitation to his advantage. "Then the matter is settled. I will confirm by email the arrangement."

"Which I am sure is only temporary, until a final decision is made," added James, still seated and not prepared to move.

McCarthy may have decided the discussion was over but James had not.

McCarthy shot an ice cold look at James, but indulged him. After all, it would have been too easy. James glanced at the clocks on the wall. McCarthy had another ten minutes to spare. If he wanted to check how much guts James had, James was up for it. McCarthy was game, he moved back to his desk, checked a couple of emails as he was speaking to James.

"You are referring to the outcome of the merger. I agree," replied McCarthy still looking at his screens.

James was still in his seat.

"I am not sure I am actually referring to the ultimate conclusion of the merger, no," carried on James.

Now or never.

"The first question is, will Henry come back, the second, if he ever does, in what capacity, and finally does it make a difference anyway?"

McCarthy stopped browsing through his mailbox and leaned against the front of his desk, arms crossed, a faint smile on his lips. He was enjoying this battle between ambition and integrity.

"You mean, if Henry returns, does he have a chance of getting his job back? Assuming he is cleared of all charges, his reputation will have been damaged beyond repair. This is *not* something you recover from. Henry is finished. Consequently, yes. I need to make up my mind on long-term succession."

McCarthy stopped there, not prepared to make things easy for James. If he wanted it, he would have to ask, possibly even beg. James would have to descend into the pit, fighting in the mud like all of them.

Despite his rising anger, James felt that maybe, just maybe, McCarthy was right. What right did he have to judge so readily? He had chosen banking and not any type of banking. He had chosen to work on the trading floor of one of the largest banks in the world. These were the rules of engagement.

A sharp pain in his left leg surprised James, his face closed to scrutiny and he quickly pressed his hand upon it to stop the shaking. The wound he had suffered in battle had decided to make itself known again. He mechanically massaged it whilst trying to formulate his next question. A battle scene flashed before his eyes. He stood up.

"When you have, Douglas, please let me know," said James.

The moment had passed. James would never become one of McCarthy's men. He returned to his desk. Usually keen to know what the markets were doing, James would normally stop to chat with a trader. Not today. Morag had kept the meeting quiet, secretly hoping James could take over. Her fresh news about Matt's whereabouts would do nothing to cheer him up.

Arriving at his desk, James sat down without a word. He activated his screens not paying much attention to what was scrolling in front of his eyes. Morag shifted in her seat, still hesitant.

"Yes Morag," said James, without looking at her.

"Do you want the bad news or do you want the *very* bad news?"

"It's going to be one of those days," replied James with a grim smile. "Come on. Give it to me."

"I know where Matt is," she said, lowering her voice and leaning towards him.

"Mmmm," James moved towards her, his solid face now close to hers.

"New York," she whispered.

"And?"

"HXBK's offices."

"Definitely one of those days," sighed James. "OK, fill me in."

Morag passed on all the details she had managed to glean. James walked into Henry's office and shut the door. He looked at the last text from his boss.

Keep going …

Chapter Nineteen

Nancy had rung Henry's doorbell in three short bursts. She could hear, from behind the door, a fumble of activity and it finally opened. Henry had switched his jeans for the expected dark suit, white shirt and, *oh*, a red tie. Nancy took a step back.

"You're with GL, aren't you?"

"I like your newly found optimism Nancy. I thought you might have said, *you were.*"

"I am referring to the colour of the tie my dear. You look very Goldman Sachs. Red tie."

"Correct. I am going incognito. This is camouflage."

"Anyway, I approve."

Henry grinned but did not reply. As they went down in the lift, he observed Nancy. Her elegance was sober yet striking. Her suit was dark grey and the shirt an unusual pattern of soft greys and black. The final touch was a large ring featuring in its centre an equally large pink pearl. Her style made him feel confident. He was dealing with a professional woman who knew how to power dress.

"You mentioned your driver would be here to pick us up. Should you not have checked?"

"No need, Nancy. I have used Charlie for over five years. He is the most punctual person you can ever meet. He would have called if he had been delayed."

Henry opened the door of their building, making room for Nancy to go first. She spotted the black S-Class Mercedes waiting for them. A heavy man with dark glasses emerged from the driver's side. Nancy thought she was meeting Agent M from *Men in Black* and immediately approved of Henry's decision to stick with Charlie.

* * *

The meeting with Henry's brief was going well. At the outset Henry had required Nancy to be included in his team; documents were being drafted to that effect. Henry repeated what he had said to Pole. Nancy gave details about what she had witnessed. One of Pritchard QC's pupils was taking notes. For the first time in thirty-six hours, Henry was feeling in control. He had regained the upper hand. He had also managed to avoid looking at his BlackBerry for a couple of hours. Yet he fiddled with it with the intensity of a religious devotee fingering prayer beads.

"Shall we have a tea break?" Pritchard QC offered.

He signalled his pupil to organise it. Henry stood up and escaped, to be alone finally and scroll through his emails. A sense of new possibilities had given him hope. The call he had received from HR could wait. He could never take these people seriously anyway. But no new emails had come in for several hours. Henry checked again, no emails since 10am in the morning. It was already 3pm and there was only one explanation: his email service had been suspended. The searing burn of anger flared inside him.

"What is that stupid bitch thinking of? Fuck you."

He scrolled through his previous emails and furiously dialled the HR number. Henry exploded on the phone when she answered but she was having none of it. She kept asking him to calm down and listen to his voicemails. Henry decided to shut her up by requesting to speak to McCarthy immediately. He had viewed this request as his ultimate defence. The old man had not responded to Henry's missed calls but then again how could he in the midst of a takeover? Henry would have to swallow his pride and try again. He asked to be put through to Cindy. She would arrange a call with McCarthy to clear up this ridiculous mess.

"Mr Crowne," insisted the woman on the phone in a high-pitched voice. "The decision to discontinue your email service was signed off by Mr McCarthy himself."

Henry could not remember having been slapped so hard in the face, more used to throwing the punches than receiving them. He recovered swiftly, not prepared to admit defeat, yet.

"I want to hear this from him in person," said Henry.

"Well, call him directly if you'd like," retorted the voice on the other end, "but I will not disrupt him for what are clear instructions—"

Henry hung up without waiting for her to finish her sentence. He dialled McCarthy's personal mobile number once more, a privilege he had never abused before. He had just put the mobile to his ear when a strong hand grabbed his arm. Nancy had witnessed the whole conversation.

"This is not a good idea," she said calmly. "What are you going to achieve?"

DMac's private mobile had started to ring.

"WHAT?" she repeated, still squeezing his arm.

Henry was furious. He tried to yank his arm free from her grip. Nancy's hold must have been stronger than he thought. They exchanged angry looks. The mobile was still ringing. This time Henry pushed her hard and freed himself. The BlackBerry escaped his hand, flew into the air before crashing on the ground with a metallic crunch.

Henry's eyes opened wide as he yelled, "No," – a cry of agony. He dropped to the floor where his phone lay in pieces. "No," he moaned each time he picked one up. Nancy's face had reddened, her hand frozen in mid-air. Henry darted toward her, a demented look in his eye.

"I need to get a new phone right away, right NOW."

"We have not finished our meeting with your defence lawyer," replied Nancy with as much composure as she could summon.

"I don't give a shit," shouted Henry. "I need to get another phone RIGHT NOW."

He had grabbed her arm, screaming.

"I understood you, Henry, nevertheless—"

"What the fuck am I doing here? I must be completely out of my mind. I should be at the office and you," he said, pointing at her with a menacing finger, "you have not practised for years, you have no idea what goes on in the City anymore."

His body shook with uncontrolled laughter whilst shaking his head, looking at the bits of phone mangled in his large hand.

"It is just not happening. I am getting a new phone. Tell this lawyer of yours I will come back when I have done what I need to do, you stupid cow."

"And your QC will tell you that he is fully booked until next month," came a curt response from behind Henry.

"By the way, Ms Wu may not have practised for a while but she still is regarded by the profession as one of the best, so you may care to apologise. I will be in my office. You have five minutes to consider whether you want to continue our conversation."

Nancy closed her eyes slowly, still shocked at the violence of the outburst. Now that it had passed she realised she was more *surprised* than upset by what had triggered it. Letting go was never going to be easy for Henry.

She heard the bench in the corridor groan beneath the weight of his body. He sat there motionless, staring at some invisible images.

"I am really losing it," said Henry finally, rubbing his hands over his face a few times. He could not face Nancy or apologise.

"You may not believe it," Nancy replied. "I went through it myself. It is hard to give up the rat race."

"Don't say it, please," Henry murmured, eyes cast in the distance.

Shifting on his feet, he could feel renewed anger in the pit of his stomach. He had no time for a lesson he did not want to hear.

Nancy was choosing her words carefully.

"To let go of old anger."

"Is this a lesson in Eastern philosophy?" replied Henry with sarcasm.

"No," said Nancy calmly. "I think you will find the same idea being tackled by most of Western theology."

Henry looked surprised. Nancy had gone down a path that he had never trodden himself.

"Come on," said Nancy, extending her long delicate hand towards him. "Let's finish what we have started. You can buy another BlackBerry after that. OK?"

Henry stood up and walked into the room alongside Nancy. His expression was inscrutable.

* * *

Nurani had booked the early morning BA flight to Belfast. She had originally hesitated between BA and a low-cost alternative, but Pole was categorical. He was not flying a cheapie airline that almost certainly shirked proper maintenance. So, the great Inspector Pole was scared of flying. She cast an eye at her boss sitting next to her and saw the relief on his face when they eventually touched down. Pole grew positively euphoric when they reached passport control.

A short, ginger-haired man was waiting for them at the arrival gate. Pole recognised his colleague of old and they shook hands warmly, delighted to see each other again.

"It's been a while," said Inspector Murphy in his distinct Northern Irish accent.

"It has," replied Pole still smiling. "May I introduce you to my colleague Nurani Shah."

"Good to meet you," said Murphy. "Couldn't get a better boss."

Nurani smiled in turn and shook his hand, not knowing what to reply to a remark that may have sounded patronising but somehow did not feel that way.

"She doesn't need much of that these days," said Pole.

Nurani blushed at the compliment and they all moved towards an old battered car.

"Don't tell me they can't do better than that," said Pole looking at Pat's official car.

"Na, it's my car. Pay could be better though," replied Pat unconcerned.

"Yep, London's the same. Can't complain too much though. At least I am not trying to raise a family of four."

"Five actually Jon. My little one is already six years old."

"Congratulations Pat, Niamh must be busy."

"Thanks, she loves it though. And what about you Jon. Still single?"

"'Fraid so. I am a lone wolf after all," said Pole, increasingly conscious of Nurani's curious silence.

"And still south of the river?"

"Can't leave the house, too many memories there."

"Plus the artworks she left you. I remember them well."

Pole nodded slowly and Pat picked up on his unease.

"Liam has not been that cooperative, but he's got the message – we softened him up a bit for you," said Pat, tactfully reverting to the case.

Pole cast a somewhat alarmed eye at Nurani. Pat had always had a way of getting what he wanted and sometimes not in an entirely orthodox fashion. He was about to reassure her that all was legal and above board when she poked her head through from the back seat of the car.

"How do you do that," she said, enthusiastically.

Pole sat back amazed. *What, one foot in Northern Ireland and she was ready for some serious interrogation techniques. Ms straight-laced-and-by-the-book shows her true colours.*

"Well," said Pat, now sounding coy, "it takes a lot of – training."

Pole decided to stay out of it, almost miffed that his old chum had stolen the limelight.

Pole recognised the police station from a distance, the same sad building earmarked by years of terror and neglect. The sight of the Troubles' effects reminded Pole of days he still could not forget.

Without much formality, Pole and Nurani were led into a meeting room where Liam O'Connor was waiting. Nurani's face showed her disappointment. Liam did not look like much.

"Less impressive than you may think," whispered Pole, reading her expression.

"Hello Liam."

"What a pleasant surprise," replied Liam. "I've said all I need to say to these guys." Liam indicated to Murphy with his head.

"So I was told but I always like to hear a good story for myself," said Pole.

"If you have time to kill," replied Liam, shrugging his shoulders.

For the next hour Pole and the team took Liam O'Connor through some key facts; his connection to Henry, his job in the Dublin Docks providing IT support to some of the banks settled in the Irish financial centre. The same story was rolled out, which was identical to the transcript Pole had received before he took off for Belfast that morning. Inspector Pole was starting to wonder whether Liam had anything new to offer when a last question on his meeting in London with Henry focused Pole's attention. Liam had a plausible reason to be in the UK, since his company was organising the maintenance of a number of offices situated in the Dublin Docks. He was sent to London regularly to check on clients. Pole smiled at the thought that Liam O'Connor was running quality control checks for a number of English companies. This sounded all very much above board. Pole decided to ask an unrelated question regarding the takeover and its impact on Henry. After all, Liam was also supposed to be in finance.

"Do you think Henry will survive the takeover? His competitor is well positioned, I understand."

For some reason Pole used the present tense and noticed a surprised reaction from Liam O'Connor.

"Well, unless GL and HXBK play the Ouija board, I don't think that snooty bloke will trouble Henry anymore," responded Liam with a hint of sarcasm and smirk in his voice.

"Unless Henry is convicted," retorted Pole, trying to yank open the door.

Liam looked at Pole with ferocity, "You have nothing on Henry."

This was the answer Pole had been waiting for. The game was on. He mentally praised his colleague. Pat certainly had softened up Liam considerably. Nurani discreetly disappeared at the sound of her BlackBerry buzzing. She moved noiselessly, hardly disturbing her chair as she rose.

"Why do you think Anthony Albert was snooty, anyway? Did you discuss him with Henry? I thought you said you hardly spoke business."

"I can just imagine it," replied Liam.

"Why do you think there is nothing to be found on Henry?"

"I don't know. I'm just making assumptions," carried on Liam.

Nurani had returned as discreetly as she had left and placed a number of pages in front of Pole. Pole stood up, turned away and took the time to read through them. Liam could wait until he was ready to continue.

"Let's talk Switzerland."

"Why?"

"You know why," said Pole evenly, producing the document he had been expecting since his arrival. "I am sure you are aware that the secrecy surrounding banking law in Switzerland has been greatly reduced? If you're not, you should be. We are getting much more information from our Swiss colleagues these days. They have learnt the word *speed* when we mention the word *terrorism*."

Liam took it in, but still offered no reply.

"My colleague Ms Shah will tell you more about what we have learned. The world is becoming a very small place," continued Pole.

In front of Liam Nurani placed several snapshots showing him walking out of Zurich Airport, spanning three years. There were also photos of Liam taking the tram and finally entering a bank, a discreet institution specialising in private banking.

"So what? I have a bank account in Switzerland, big deal, a lot of my clients have too," said Liam unshaken.

"Sure," said Nurani. "But how many of them do so under an alias and please let us have a list. It might make for some interesting reading."

Nurani slammed a list of transactions from a bank statement in front of Liam.

"Do they also receive large sums of money from numbered accounts registered in the Caymans, the owner of which is another numbered account from Lichtenstein? If so I really, really, want to know."

Nurani was enjoying herself. She was not going to be intimidated by some guy with or without IRA connections. She was ready to take on the little git. Liam had no idea what it meant to be at Scotland Yard for an Asian woman.

"Well, if you are so clever, why do you bother questioning me at all?"

"I am not. I am telling you," she said vehemently.

Liam's light green eyes had changed colour, growing darker. His round placid face hardened up.

"Another very large sum of money arrived a few days ago, another new client from Saudi Arabia," Nurani pushed a copy of the Swiss bank account details in front of him.

"I have a lot of generous friends."

"Me too. But maybe not of the same calibre."

The change in law had not been part of the plan. Liam had hoped to be quick enough to move accounts around. He had been a little too slow in taking Henry's advice … shame. The great network of clandestine help had started to dissolve in Ireland after the IRA decommissioning, making large movements of cash much more difficult to engineer. But the old links with other terrorist networks had remained. Switzerland still played a part in the money laundering chain. Liam sat back and looked at everyone in the room. There was no doubt in his mind that they would eventually find out, but he would be damned if he made their task any easier.

"I want my lawyer," he said folding his arms over his chest. "This discussion is over."

"Sure," said Pat. "Do you have a name?"

Murphy, Pole and Ms Shah left the interrogation room to recap.

"Do you hope to link Crowne with those payments?" asked Murphy, knowing that Pole would share his thoughts.

"Of course, that would be a major step forward. Although I suspect it won't be all that easy. After all, Crowne is a banker. He uses tax havens to structure his transactions. I suspect he can create enough screens for us to find it difficult to track him down. Then again, even the most intelligent of people make the most obvious of mistakes sometimes."

Pole was now sitting comfortably in Pat's office.

"And you missus," he said, imitating Liam's Northern Irish accent. "I would like you to stay and continue our discussion with O'Connor."

"Great," replied Nurani, her dark almond shaped eyes shining with pride. "Looking forward to this."

"I know, I know," said Pole. "Just don't savage him too much, will you? You, on the other hand, Mr Murphy, you're not allowed to teach Ms Shah the many different ways of softening up witnesses or, in other words, beating the bejesus out of them."

Pole waved a reproaching finger at Pat. They all laughed. Other officers in the neighbouring offices lifted their heads at the raucous noise.

They were preparing to go back to the interrogation room when another officer knocked at the door and opened without waiting for an answer.

"We have located Liam's brother, Bobby. I think you guys should get down to central. It's not going according to plan."

The relaxed atmosphere faded in an instant.

"Let's go," said Murphy, his spirit dampened.

He knew what to expect and did not want to cast his mind back to the days of the Troubles.

"Talk to me," carried on Murphy as they all started running towards central control.

"Bobby must have heard about Liam being picked up. He was trying to leave the country following the usual arms smuggling route. Unfortunately for him it did not go as smoothly as he'd hoped. Some of the old guard are prepared to grass on the splinter groups. They don't belong anymore," replied the other officer.

"He has barricaded himself in an office at the Docks. There may be hostages. We are not sure yet. What we know for sure is that he has fired a few gunshots at the local guys."

"Shit," blurted Pat. "This idiot is going to get himself killed with some other poor sods who have nothing to do with the whole affair. He just can't give up."

Murphy and his guests burst into the control room, where other officers were giving directions on the ground.

"Have you spoken to him directly?" asked Pole.

"We have tried but nothing doing at the moment."

"Pat, are you going to engage with him?" said Pole.

"Do I have a choice?"

"I have not done this for a very long time, Pat. You're the man on the ground. I am no longer part of that team anyway and ..." Pole hesitated. "Nurani is with you. She will handle it. Just keep me in the loop."

"It will be done and I am sure it will be safe."

This was not what Pole had intended but then again it was part of the job and he trusted Pat implicitly in the affair. They shook hands with no further words exchanged and Pole headed towards the exit. He had a plane to catch.

Nurani wanted a word. Pole wondered whether his decision to leave her behind might be too much too soon and he was about to change his plan when she spoke.

"This could be a breakthrough Jon."

"How so?"

"Well, if Bobby can't or won't give himself up maybe this helps with Liam."

Pole gave a little nod. He knew where she was going. He felt both impressed and shocked. She certainly was the person for the job.

"You want to cut a deal with Liam?" he said, focusing his full attention on her. She had never experienced this before and recoiled under his glance.

"Well, I thought …" her voice trailed off.

"It has to be considered. Bobby's life against the name of the account holders," said Pole. "But," he stressed, "before you cut a deal, I want to know every detail of what it entails. Do we understand each other? I want consensus with Murphy. This is not going to descend into a political disaster or the evidence being tainted by foul play."

"Of course Jon, I would not want to do anything without you knowing," replied Nurani.

Pole relaxed in the knowledge that his stark remarks had hit home. He looked at her with kindness.

"These guys are very dangerous Nu. Don't be fooled by what you see. Even the C-T squad in London is scared about what they can achieve." He turned around, grabbed his bag and disappeared into his cab. Nurani would miss his guidance terribly.

Chapter Twenty

The plane was taxiing down the runway and Inspector Pole was strapped into his seat. He was not looking forward to the flight back on his own. His dislike of flying was usually alleviated by conversation but Nurani was still in Belfast and by all accounts shouldering the considerable task of bringing Liam home to roost. Pole closed his eyes and gripped the armrest when the pilot revved the engine for take-off. His stomach somersaulted as the plane left the ground. Pole opened his eyes again to see the little boy seated next to him observing him with curiosity.

"It's fun to fly," said Pole, embarrassed.

The boy nodded once and went back to his comic book perusing it with the seriousness of a business man reading the *FT*. Pole exhaled deeply and dived into his briefcase which he had placed underneath the seat in front. He was not going to stand up to get it out of the overhead locker. Carrying a briefcase was bad enough. He had never believed in the need to own one and always borrowed the one he had to use occasionally from a willing colleague. He took out a wad of papers he had printed before leaving Murphy's office – emails and reports. A mass of documents he might want to read once more.

Pole sank into the case with the feeling of familiarity and ownership. The first document was confirming the meeting with Anthony Albert's family lawyer the next day. Albert's solicitor had been away but was now back in the office. He would make the time for Pole, although he was asking for a few hours' grace to organise matters appropriately (in his own words). Pole was asking for the rules on confidentiality to be bent and had to give way a little himself.

The second email was from Eugene. He had sent him a long account of Brett Allner-Smith's recent dealings. Pole managed a smile.

Brett was a controversial figure who enjoyed sailing close to the wind, in Eugene's words. A number of antiquities which he had brokered had questionable origins. He did not seem to mind too much who the seller was as long as he had a buyer to match. Evidently, Brett Allner-Smith enjoyed a few connections with the underworld of trafficking although there had never been enough evidence to convict him. Pole nodded. This guy was surprisingly good.

The stewardess offered Pole a much-needed drink. A small bottle of red wine would help with a very sad looking sandwich. He was not strictly off duty but needed a bit of help with his air travel. Pole carried on reading the lengthy mail, details of specific art pieces, valuations, contacts. He was starting to lose interest when a piece of information attracted his attention. Allner-Smith owned an account in Switzerland with a small private bank well known to Pole, one of the last strongholds of the much-denigrated banking secrecy. There secrecy meant secrecy. Pole had never managed to get one iota of information out of them and nor had his Swiss colleagues. Pole sat back in his seat muttering to himself.

"Now this is interesting, another coincidence? Mmmm."

He immediately felt the heaviness of another set of eyes on him. The little boy sitting in the adjacent seat did not seem amused.

"Sorry," said Pole with a silly smile.

"Accepted," replied the little man and dived back into his comic book.

Pole was about to make some comment but thought otherwise. *Children these days*, and as the thought crossed his mind, he did feel like an old fart.

Pole returned to his own stack of papers. He started constructing a plausible scenario surrounding Albert's murder. Would Allner-Smith want to frame Henry? Could he frame Henry? It would not be too tedious to find out about Henry's Irish links. He knew about Anthony and Henry's rivalry. Allner-Smith had witnessed it first hand in the auction rooms of Christie's and Sotheby's. Motives were plentiful; greed would always be at the centre of this case, then revenge, power, vanity. All of these qualities Brett exhibited in spades. But then there was the briefcase, Pole stopped. He straightened himself up and cast an eye at the little lad next to him. He was still engrossed in his comic book now furiously chewing on a piece of gum.

Pole smiled, sitting back in his seat.

So where was he? The briefcase. Pole drew a blank. How could Allner-Smith have orchestrated the delivery of this explosive item? *That is a very bad joke*, thought Pole, still unrepentant for having cracked it. Maybe with the help of Albert's wife? That did not sound right either or maybe it was – a switch in briefcases? By all accounts Allner-Smith would have wanted to stay in the background to manipulate Adeila. Discussing the delivery of the briefcase directly with her would give her immense power over him. They would be accomplices, and Allner-Smith operated on his own. No, he would want to be the sole mastermind, or so Eugene said. Then again, he had never, as far as they both could see, gone that far.

Pole stopped, took a sip of wine from the plastic glass and pulled a face. He looked at the label which was claiming a full bodied red exploding with wild berries. In short, a passable plonk. As the plane started to give a couple of small jolts, Pole emptied his glass. He spent a few minutes still considering the motive, there was a lot of money involved.

Actually, how much money exactly?

Pole reached for his colleague's briefcase again and pulled out another document. A summary sent by Albert's accountant of the dead man's assets, *give or take a few £100,000* read the email.

Ridiculous, but then so many things sounded ridiculous at a few thousand feet in the air. Pole shifted. Not an idea to dwell on. Back to the case.

The mail was well constructed and showed in a very concise form what a City senior MD can make in a few years of hard earning.

1) *Belgravia House (latest estimate @ 30/08/2008)*	£10,500,000
2) *Art collection (including pieces over £1,000)*	
See appendix 1 for details	£5,650,000
3) *Jewellery*	
See appendix 2 for details	£1,100,000
4) *Flat in Nice (latest estimate @12/07/2007*	
Fixed @ 11/10/2008)	£1,750,000
5) *Investments in Funds and other*	£9,584,000
6) *HXBK unexpired options*	£7,500,000
7) *Cash on account*	£70,800
8) *Aston Martin DB9*	£115,000
Grand Total	£36,269,800

Pole read the numbers one more time and mused at what he would do with £36 or so million. Then again did he really want that much money in the first place? He could have followed in the footsteps of his grandmother or indeed his entire family for whom art did not mean meagre revenues. He remembered the artists visiting her house, the debates, the excitement and the falling out. Her sense for talent was unique. He could have lived in her shadow, or that of his father, a remarkable saxophonist who still played, at the age of seventy-eight, with the greatest jazz fusion musicians. But he had chosen to be different. Why? Pole looked at his watch and decided to park the question for later on knowing full well what the outcome would be.

So, it was evident that Anthony Albert had done well for himself since joining the banking world. Pole remembered the sum Albert had negotiated when he had first joined HXBK. The shy young man had learned to monetise his talents, fast. Such a quick rise in revenue, however, must have indicated only one thing, a ruthless desire to take risks, and a lot of them.

Large and risky transactions were about to come undone, or so the financial press claimed. Albert was not the sort of man who looked closely at the ethical consequences of the deals he put together. What simply mattered was the bottom line and the bonus he would derive from negotiating such large deals. The idea focused Pole's mind again. In the context of a takeover matters became much tenser. He jotted a note down on the side of the document he was reading. Albert dealt in the subprime market. Andy had collected a list of the latest deals by Albert, with counterparties' identities and revenue streams. He also had a detailed account of Albert's bonuses in the past four years. HXBK's HR had finally provided a list of bonus figures that were as impressive as his total wealth. The last bonus in particular was explosively large both in cash terms and HXBK options.

Interesting, thought Pole. *Looks like HR are dragging their feet. Why?*

Pole was interrupted when the plane gave yet another jolt. The seatbelt sign lit up. Inspector Pole grabbed the armrest. The pilot came on the intercom. They would be encountering some turbulence until they landed at Heathrow which was only twenty-five minutes away. Pole grumbled and prepared himself for a very uncomfortable final ride.

* * *

Back on terra firma, Henry, Nancy and his barrister were about to conclude their findings. The BlackBerry incident had put a dampener on what would have been otherwise a very successful meeting. Nancy's choice of barrister had proven to be very judicious yet Henry could not reconcile the incident. He had lost control but then again, why interfere with his business?

Gavin Pritchard QC's voice brought Henry back to the meeting room, a large space filled with books and faded furniture. The chairs looked as if they hadn't been changed since Pritchard had started his career, which Henry took to be a very long time ago. Yet it felt cosy, even familiar.

"I am feeling clear on all the facts and evidence surrounding your matter," declared the barrister with confidence.

"I will step in the next time Inspector Pole wants a meeting. It is essential. I recommend a solicitor I work with regularly to attend meetings." Pritchard QC leaned forward and tapped his pen on his notes.

"So far WE take the view that WE have a series of coincidences which are fortuitous. WE believe in the circumstantial nature of the events. The police of course will not accept this easily. Pole is a methodical man. Nevertheless, it is OUR intention to pursue the argument."

"Precisely," replied Henry.

He felt drained of energy and knowledge. Pritchard waited a few seconds. His thought process was nearly palpable to Henry. Beyond his tiredness Henry gathered Pritchard might have something else in mind.

"Excellent," carried on Pritchard.

He jotted down a few more notes. Henry had been tense for several hours. He felt a release from pain. *Fight or flight*, he thought, as he gathered himself to stand up. Maybe, just maybe, he could escape further scrutiny.

"One final point if I may?"

Henry's barrister adjusted his round glasses and pushed his body back in his chair. He had kept the meatiest morsel for the end.

"Your IRA faction connections?"

Pritchard had not bothered with the word alleged. To him all Irish men from Belfast had IRA connections.

"What about it?" replied Henry, non-committal.

Pritchard QC looked at his client and remained silent. He was simply waiting. Nothing Henry could say would convince him to drop the question. It hit Henry to see the anticipation of success, the challenge – and what a challenge, a banker blowing a plane out of the sky through IRA contacts. Magnificent. Even more so after the IRA had renounced violence. A splinter group would make matters more complex to defend. Possibly the challenge of a lifetime. Henry suspected he might have done it for free, but Pritchard would know as well as Henry did that money was not only worth the pleasure it gave, it was also a benchmark against which all professionals aspired to be measured. Was Pritchard giving him a reflection of his own image when he himself was going for the kill?

Henry stared at his lawyer, anger burning his gut. The moment passed. Henry kept looking intensely at the face in front of him to make it give in, but the smooth round oval did not budge. The slightly overarched eyebrows, the large forehead etched with waves of lines, all was calm and decisive. Henry inhaled deeply. Pritchard would not take the case unless he knew. Henry sat back in his chair.

"Where do I start?"

"The beginning is usually a good place," said Pritchard picking up his pen once more. He leaned forward with avidity.

"It was a long time ago."

* * *

The officer at passport control greeted Pole with the requisite stern face when Pole handed over his passport. Pole had received news from Nurani by BlackBerry. He was trying to reach her now that matters had moved decidedly forward in Ireland. He was concerned. Bobby was a dangerous man, hardened to the core with a hint of lunacy thrown in for good measure. Pole had tried many times to imagine what the IRA decommissioning would do to such an extreme mind. Bobby was a zealot, his dedication to the cause more a way of life than a political battle. Over the years Pole had suspected that the reasons why had become secondary to the means. Nothing else really mattered. It was all about the fight, regardless of the peace process.

Pole had recognised the impact Henry's upbringing in Northern Ireland had had on him. The violence would have been in the background, a constant present, an unseen filter potent enough to distort all that it touched. Pole remembered reading a book a few years back describing life in Belfast: the prejudices, the people trying to make a living out of so very little, but above all the bombs. The book's description of one bomb blast had made a lasting impression on him. It was not so much the torn bodies and the atrocious violence that made an impression on him. It was the incomprehension, even the absurdity so clearly exposed. The stubborn attitude of the perpetrators, the total disconnect between rhetoric and death. Pole did not believe in God or indeed that the Church had any valid role to play in guiding man on his ethical search but he believed in humanity.

The ringtone of his mobile brought him back to the now. Nurani was calling.

"What news?" asked Pole without further greetings.

"Bobby is refusing to talk at the moment," replied Nurani, eager to give her news. "We still don't know why he turned up there, probably to see Liam. However, things are getting more complicated. We are almost certain it is a hostage situation."

"What do you mean by 'almost certain' about the hostage situation?"

"Bobby got in as people were leaving. One person has not arrived home yet. We have to presume he is still in there unless we hear from him."

"Agreed, we are not taking chances," replied Pole now regretting he was in London. "Who is on the scene?"

"The situation is pretty advanced. Pat called his contacts in Dublin. Special forces are there as well as a hostage negotiator."

"Can you deal with it?" asked Pole abruptly, unconcerned about sparing Nurani's feelings.

"Yes, Jon, I can," she replied with absolute certainty.

"Very well, what are you suggesting?"

"Bobby has already fired a few rounds. The guys in Dublin are very twitchy. The Docks are a popular district for business. They are deciding whether to storm the premises or not. The only thing that stops them at the moment is the hostage story. An IRA incident is not what the authorities want at the moment, even if this comes from a splinter group."

"Pat has no jurisdiction over that part of the world though."

"Yeah, but he knows the boys in Dublin pretty well. And he knows the O'Connor brothers even better. The Dublin guys have already asked him for his opinion and they now know that we have Liam in custody – to storm or not to storm?"

Pole took it in. Nurani had accustomised herself to the situation pretty fast. She was hard and uncompromising, she would do well.

"Pat is prepared to cut a deal. Liam gets to reason with his brother to give himself up and gets him out of this alive but–" .

"Liam gives us Henry," Pole interrupted

Nurani coughed.

"OK, do it," replied Pole after another brief silence. "I am on my way to the office and will call you two from there. I want to discuss the terms of this agreement if there is going to be one."

Pole dashed into his waiting cab.

Chapter Twenty-One

Henry was walking home. He had left Nancy behind with little ceremony. He needed to be on his own and desperately wanted to replace his lost BlackBerry. It took some considerable time for Henry to find what he had in mind. He had not previously taken the trouble to investigate the multiple options that were available to him. His PA Morag always chose the most up-to-date version available, irrespective of whether it made sense or not. One simply had to have the latest at GL. Henry never had the time or indeed the inclination to be a 'geek', however the subject matter had become of intense interest to him and the young woman who first tried to serve him did not fare well. Henry could not admit it, thinking himself a progressive, but he had to be very convinced before he relied on a woman for anything technical.

Her boss had spotted the issue and moved in to help. It was too late and Henry had already worked himself into a contentious mood. He was furiously enquiring about functions and apps that he had barely noticed let alone used, and then, of course, the phone was too bulky, the keys too small, the iPhone he was offered did not have the right security protocol. The intervention of another sales assistant only made matters worse until Henry eventually looked at his watch.

He decided upon a particular model much to the disbelief and relief of the exhausted staff. Henry left the box behind, had the SIM card installed, grumbled a final question about mail access and pocketed his phone. He walked slowly down Chancery Lane revisiting his time with Pritchard QC. He would not be a man easy to lie to. Could Henry risk jeopardising the relationship with his defence lawyer? The thought of succeeding gave him a pang of excitement. He had done well but the day was young and he would not presume success.

Henry was about to cross Holborn when he spotted a small cafe on his left. He decided to do what he often did in the City when he needed to take a step back. He settled himself in the window of the cafe shop with a large Assam tea and a biscotti. For a while he observed the passers-by. He tried to guess which firm or employment the men and women who walked past were coming from. The young man with a white shirt, sober but noticeable red tie, and clean-shaven was unmistakably Goldman Sachs, the middle-aged woman with her severe black suit and large briefcase one of the barristers. Henry could not help but notice that none of these people had a smile on their faces. No matter how much he tried to brush it away it kept coming back. He looked at his watch, he should be going home despite a half-drunk cup and unopened biscotti. Yes, home – he saw his lounge, his favourite armchair, the collection of expensive antiquities and art. Henry listed his prized pieces, his beloved Guanyin he had stolen from the shady Allner-Smith and the miniature terracotta warrior he had won from Anthony Albert. What a coup that had been. The savagery of triumph stirred him up. Albert was a coward. He would never have matched him when the price became truly hot and he certainly would never have opposed his wife. But now there was *The Raft of the Medusa*. Everything he had chosen up to now had created a sense of wealth, an easy decor to live with. Had it been all for show? Nancy had made the point and he had to admit reluctantly that she might be right. Was it an attempt at probing what art truly meant for him or a message of doom? Henry shrugged. What a ridiculous idea!

But no, Henry pretended all was good, opened the biscuit wrapper and wolfed it down. He washed it down with the now lukewarm tea. It occurred to him that he had had no desire to see any of his friends. This thought put a derisory smile on his lips, the only man he would want to speak to at this moment in time was Liam. There never would be any confidants among his City pals. Friendships had been built on a show of power or self-interest. He had made particular choices and was not surprised by the result.

But then there was Pam. The debacle with Wooster QC's sabbatical had left him raw. Forgiveness was impossible, his throat tightened up. Henry shifted on his chair, struggling with his feelings. He praised his ability to stay detached and clear-headed but was it not a lot of nonsense? Henry had to laugh, he was anything but detached. He simply did not want to admit he cared. Pam was safe, she was his lawyer, she was forbidden territory for a man of Henry's ambition. He saw her face close to his in the pub in Dublin.

She had drunk Guinness from his glass and pulled a face. He had moved a strand of hair away from her eyes, hardly brushing the skin of her forehead.

His BlackBerry started to buzz, he hesitated for a second not yet prepared to let Pam's face fade away. He finally pressed the answer button. The voice at the other end startled him.

"This is Henry."

The familiar voice of James shoved GL back into his life, the sea of desks, the constant tension on the trading floor, the highs, the lows, a wild energy that he had found hard to leave behind. Sitting in the window of this small cafe, he suddenly felt the urge to belong again.

"Hey Jamie, what's up?"

"H, bloody hell, WHERE have you been? I thought I was never going to get hold of you."

"That bad, hey," chuckled Henry.

At least James had called him, there must be some hope.

"Have you spoken to DMac at all?"

"Nope, can't get hold of the old man and I had a little mishap with my phone, I'll call him later," continued Henry, trying to sound confident. "In fact, why don't I call him right away and call you back afterwards, I might—"

"H. Henry," said James. "Listen, I am so sorry mate, I am sorry to have to tell you that you're wasting your time. He won't take your call."

"And how would you know?" said Henry now squeezing his BlackBerry to breaking point.

"Because McCarthy called me in to discuss succession—" James had no time to finish his sentence.

"What! I am gone for less than three days and you shits have already decided to screw me over."

The entire cafe went silent.

"Of course not," replied James. "Do you think I decide for McCarthy? Wake up Henry. That guy has always been a selfish bastard and he certainly—"

"I don't give a flying fuck about what you think of McCarthy. I don't believe … I know he would have spoken to me."

"Henry where the bloody hell have you been for the past fifteen years? This is investment banking, my friend. This is the trading floor and YOU are in the deepest shit because you've got a murder hanging around your neck."

James was also shouting.

"And," finished James, "because DMac wants to be the CEO of the combined bank. Do you really think he is going to stick by you?"

"So bloody what! He WILL lead the combined bank," replied Henry emphatically. The sudden realisation of truth punched Henry in the guts.

"NOT if he sides with you he won't," replied James. "Ted has been named head of your team."

A heavy silence fell between the two men. James was about to ask whether Henry was still on the phone when the noise of a smashed piece of crockery deafened him.

"That motherfucker cannot, will NOT, head up my team. I'm coming in."

"H, let's meet outside. We can come up with a plan. We are the A-Team aren't we?" said James trying to coax Henry away from an impending disaster.

Too late, the phone had already gone silent. The whole cafe had been hanging onto Henry's words, no coffee had been stirred, tea drunk nor pastry eaten.

Henry smashed the phone on the small table. He closed his eyes, the beast within was loose. Henry had not yet reopened his eyes when he felt the pressure of a small hand on his arm. He turned around with a jerk.

"The cup is broken," said one of the young female waitress.

Henry did not bother to reply and slammed a twenty-pound note on the table.

"And your hand is bleeding," she added, handing over some tissues.

The hand holding the shattered cup was dripping, Henry looked down, used to the sight of his own blood. He had not felt a thing and started laughing. Blood was indeed on his hands.

Henry dislodged a piece of porcelain that had planted itself inside his palm and grabbed the tissues as he stood up to leave. The waitress offered more assistance that Henry ignored.

He walked out of the small cafe without a reply and was transported thirty years back, to a squalid street on one of Belfast's estates.

Three against him, no chance, a rain of insults and then one of the boys starts pissing in his direction. Henry's rage propels him. He strikes the first boy in the throat, the boy falls, his eyes bulging in pain and amazement, the other two stop laughing. Within seconds their astonishment has been turned to Henry's advantage, a quick punch in the head and the nose of the smaller boy explodes, a well-adjusted kick to the groin of the last boy brings him to his knees and then it happens, a frenzy.

Henry carries on kicking and punching. He cannot hear the screams. He cannot see the blood. Nothing else matters but this elated release, the joy of inflicting pain, a newly discovered power.

* * *

Nancy was walking at a pace, her hands deep in her coat pockets. The satchel on her right shoulder felt heavy. She had not felt the weight of her lawyer's bag for a long time. It was uncomfortable. She quickened her steps and realised that her high-heeled shoes were hampering her. She stopped at a traffic light. The light turned green. She waited. Some young man grumbled past her. She was in his way. He pushed forward and crossed the road towards Temple Inn. What was she doing? Henry's outburst was predictable. She had known it would come. Could she handle the case at this moment in her life? Could she even be bothered? For so many years she had removed herself from the circle of power. She had done it deliberately, with the utmost determination, a slow process that had finally borne fruit. She liked the Nancy she had become, but was her life sterile? Henry's encounter was a passage she knew, his story a vital moment between old and new. She also knew that the air tickets debacle had shaken her complacency. She could still make mistakes that endangered others.

Her time with Jacques Vergès resurfaced. Defending a war criminal: it had sounded so daring, so impossible. The Klaus Barbie affair in France had made the front page of the papers for months.

The light turned green again. She started walking, wincing in pain. *Damn shoes*, she thought. Her chambers were thankfully very close. She needed to reconnect with her old practice, in a fresh way. She entered the familiar rooms. In seven years nothing had changed. The wood panels, the smell of ancient leather and books. Her sore back relaxed as she spotted that her favourite armchair was free. She sank into it and paused for a few moments. The severe face of her tutor, the first barrister for whom she had worked, materialised in front of her. She had learned from him that appearances were indeed deceptive as he had taught her everything he knew. No fuss, no need for thank you, he simply liked to impart knowledge. And after the Klaus Barbie affair her admission to the Bar was not a trivial matter. She remembered the ambition and disliked now what she was then but it had been a necessary transition. She thought she had moved away from it all and yet here she was. A young barrister brushed pass and apologised, intrigued by this face he did not recognise. Nancy pulled her satchel onto her lap and retrieved her old address book. Leaving her belongings behind, she moved slowly towards an old telephone booth. The old-fashioned devices were still there. Chambers operated in the past, how refreshing.

The number rang a few times and Nancy wondered whether her contact's number might have changed. She had not called Whitehall for a few years. A polished voice finally answered. That voice had remained the same in the twenty-five years she had known him. He was then a young barrister intent on entering the civil service. She smiled at the thought.

"Nancy Wu," exclaimed the man, a little taken aback. "I cannot believe it is you."

"It is good to speak again, William. I should have called you earlier. It must be at least a couple of years."

"Possibly more."

"You might well be right and yet, here I am calling you to ask for a favour."

"Well, my dear Nancy. In the spirit of our old friendship, I take no offence and will make an exception for you. I do not speak much with lawyers these days."

"You may want to know a little more about the subject matter before accepting."

"Very true, how considerate."

Nancy had never abused his friendship and probably never would.

"It is about the Albert–Crowne affair."

The phone remained silent for a moment.

"You have come indeed to the right man," replied William slowly. "Let's meet at Tate Britain in thirty minutes. I make the habit of escaping there to gather my thoughts and grab a tea."

"I remember. The William Blake room."

"The William Blake room indeed."

Nancy put the receiver back into its upright holder. She gave it a tap of satisfaction. Her Whitehall contact had a view.

* * *

"Pat, I am sorry to labour this with you but …" Pole was going to get what he wanted out of his Irish colleague. He knew Nurani was also on the call and he wanted to reaffirm his instructions.

170

"Jon, the deal with Liam will be solid. It won't be done in writing, no lawyer present. Liam knows I can only request it from the guys in Dublin but if I don't, all hell will break loose for Bobby."

"Right," replied Pole, still measuring the impact of this next move.

"Liam has gone around the block a few times Jon, think about it. He has always been smart enough to protect his brother and, after all these years, he won't let go. He won't let him down," carried on Pat with absolute certainty.

"I think you're right. Christ, what a choice: his best friend against his insane brother." Pole was now convinced, blood ties would be the strongest.

"Will you do this on your own?" asked Pole.

"Yes. We have discussed it with Nurani," hesitated Pat.

"It is better that way, not an easy discussion," added Nurani quickly

"Fine, we are all on the same page. The floor is yours, Pat."

* * *

The 'chat' with Liam lasted five minutes at most. Pat entered the room alone as planned. Nurani observed through the tinted glass although the sound had been cut off. Liam stood up abruptly as Pat put the deal to him, no introduction, no soft landing. Liam walked to the wall and, facing it, leaned against it, smashing his fist into it. Twenty years of hatred and destruction came flooding back. He sat back at the table. He could not look at Pat at first and when his cold blue eyes locked with his, he uttered only two words.

"Take Henry."

Pat handed over a pad and a pen. Liam started writing.

* * *

Tate Britain was buzzing. The Turner Prize was on display, creating the predictable degree of attention. Nancy was a little early and decided to pay a visit to the new installation that had won the much-wanted recognition. She surveyed the display of Richard Wright's work. Her mind could not quite focus. The piece in front of her had to be intellectualised to be appreciated. She decided she was not in the mood and made her way to the William Blake room. Her contact was there already. She could see the delicate frame of his body standing in front of a favourite piece, an illustration from Blake's book *The Marriage of Heaven and Hell*. Nancy glanced at the room around her, it was a little too full for her liking. She moved slowly forward.

"Good afternoon, my dear."

The slender man had seen Nancy enter the room, but waited for her to approach, a gentle way of reconnecting with an old friend.

"Good afternoon William. I thought I might be late."

Nancy extended a graceful hand which the man took with warmth.

"No matter how often I come here, Blake always inspires me. Something profound about human despair, and hope, maybe."

Nancy turned towards the piece she knew well and smiled.

"He is still one of my favourites although you may balk at what interests me these days."

"Do not tell me you have gone contemporary," William said.

"I'm afraid I have."

"Well, we must debate this although perhaps later. I gather we have a more serious matter to discuss."

"Indeed, shall we find a corner?" Nancy asked.

"The members' room is usually quiet at this time."

They found a couple of comfortable armchairs and settled there, waiting for their orders to be delivered.

"I am advising Henry Crowne in the Anthony Albert murder case."

Nancy had decided that there was no point in fishing for information. William was far too astute to play games and he was also a friend.

"Are you fed up with retirement? Selfishly, of course, I would very much enjoy seeing you again at the Bar."

Nancy accepted the compliment but shook her head.

"The profession is no longer for me. Let me simply say that I am helping a friend."

Her contact raised an inquisitive eyebrow but said nothing more.

"I am convinced that there are many moving parts still in this affair. Call it intuition if you will. I know I can mention this to you," said Nancy, touching her friend's arm with warmth. "And you won't think I am a female lunatic reading the runes."

"I am all ears, Nancy but you will have to give a little more. Your intuition is right as always, however. I can't comment as openly as I once could. Seniority is a burden to bear."

The sentence had been spoken with no vanity, a pure statement of fact. He was indeed a very senior man at Whitehall.

"Let me therefore elucidate. I believe that the crux of this particular matter is rooted in the intense rivalry between Crowne and Albert."

Nancy paused to observe her contact and allow the waitress to serve their tea. The slight tension in his jaw and bat of his eyelid encouraged her to go on.

"It is an unusual form of rivalry, something visceral, rooted in the deepest of hatred."

"Although I do not know these people personally, let's be clear. I know enough of them through their work to be in utter agreement."

"In the battle for pre-eminence during the takeover, I wonder who would have been designated to head up the combined team. As I suspect there would have been a merger between Albert's team and that of Crowne."

Her contact took another sip of his tea and considered his answer.

"Albert," he said, a statement of fact, no speculation.

"And this is not a last-minute change?"

"It is a very good question. I was assured it is not."

"So even before Henry's fall, Albert's name was going to be put forward as head of the combined team."

"Are you in doubt?"

"On the face of respective aptitude very much so. Which begs the question. What did Albert know to warrant this good fortune?" said Nancy, still incredulous at the outcome. "Was Albert aware?"

"You mean, would he have been told informally?"

"Or seen the signs and for that matter what about Henry?"

"They might have suspected, but then again these very large deals make rational people behave in the most unpredictable of fashions."

"Was McCarthy being blackmailed?"

"I could not possibly comment," William replied with a faint smile.

Nancy paused. She drank a little of her tea. William had chosen well.

"Is GL's financial position seriously affected by the current subprime crisis? I mean, beyond the fact that all banks are affected? I remember reading they are big in the CDO business."

"I do not see the relevance."

"I am trying to establish whether there would be any particular reason to frame Henry or to sacrifice Henry?"

"I don't think Henry would have been *framed*, as you put it. Sacrificed, well – it's a takeover."

"Are you protecting someone, William?"

Nancy's contact shook his head in deep approval.

"This is your strongest quality, Nancy, and whether I reply one way or the other, you will make something of it."

"How very kind of you to say so. But you have not answered my question."

"Not someone, my dear, something."

Nancy looked at her contact with a frown, slightly taken aback. After a short moment her questioning look was replaced with astonishment.

"Do you mean …?"

"Yes, the UK financial system. I leave the rest of the world to the Americans."

"And I thought this affair was complex."

Nancy's contact shrugged his shoulders. He would not be fazed by the enormity of the task or indulge in the absurd idea that he could defeat the monster he was facing.

Their exchange was nearly over. Nancy decided to enjoy a few moments with her friend and moved the conversation onto other interests they shared. They soon parted and Nancy decided to hail a cab. She raised her hand and a black Mercedes S-Class slowly pulled alongside the pavement where she had stopped. The window came down with a mechanical purr.

"Good afternoon Ms Wu. Would you care for a lift? My current commission is taking me to the City. I could make a small detour?"

Nancy recognised Charlie's voice.

"Most kind of you Charlie. But I would not want to impose."

"It would be my absolute pleasure."

"In that case, to Islington."

Chapter Twenty-Two

The black cab screeched to a halt but Henry did not notice. Nor did he, as he stepped out into the road, remark upon the cabbie opening his window, shouting insults and gesturing in an unequivocal fashion. Henry was going back to the bank. No traffic lights, men in suits or uniforms would stand in his way.

His mouth was dry, the blood pumped in his ears, his security card had not left his wallet. It had probably been deactivated by now but he knew most of the security guards by name. He might find a way. No, he *would* find a way.

Henry was rehearsing what he would say, if the card didn't work. He saw himself going up the flights of escalators and launching into Ted's office. The concern for his team had vanished with the news they were no longer his. They could have put up a fight for him and they had not. Still a pang of pain hit him and he clenched his fist. It was Ted he now wanted to see. The little shit had taken his job away, he who called himself a friend. Yes, he would see Ted. Henry could already savour the pleasure of savaging him, this nobody, this coward – Henry would grind him to nothingness, a worm beneath the sole of his shoe, less.

The side of his office building was now visible, an eighteenth-century edifice only the facade of which had been preserved. Henry fetched his wallet and checked his hand. It was no longer bleeding. He took his security card out, the face in the photograph was smug and slightly heavier. He had had the good idea of wearing a suit to visit Pritchard QC and was carrying a small black satchel for paperwork. He looked at his watch, 16.42. He could have been coming back from a meeting. The timing was good, the early morning security team would be eagerly waiting for the next shift to come in. They started work at 6am.

Despite all his mental calculation since he had left the cafe, Henry felt nervous as he strode along the large bay windows of GL's front atrium. He was annoyed by this lack of control. He replaced the security pass in his wallet and stuck his wallet in his back pocket. He started composing himself, trying to look casual yet absorbed by the task at hand. GL's entrance hall was large and imposing but the walk to the escalators leading to the trading floors didn't take long.

As predicted, most of the security guards had retreated to the far end of the atrium leaving only one young man in charge of the turnstiles. Henry recognised him instantly. He had started his job only a couple of months ago. He was keen but impressionable. Henry pushed the revolving doors with confidence, his coat unbuttoned. He stuck his mobile phone to his ear and walked with what he judged a measured but assured pace towards the escalators, taking his wallet from his back pocket in an irritated fashion. The phone got stuck between ear and shoulder, as Henry tried to get his pass out of the wallet, pushing, shoving as if the card was stuck and with a sudden move the card sprang out, flying over the turnstiles to land on the other side. Henry looked annoyed, muttering his apologies, now curtailing the non-existent conversation on his mobile to give his full attention to the young guard.

"So sorry, John. Could you please?" said Henry gesturing at the gates.

The young fellow jerked upright and stuck his own pass over the electronic eye.

"Certainly Mr ..." he had forgotten Henry's name.

"Much appreciated," replied Henry with one of his best grins, picking up his security ID and starting his speedy climb to the third floor.

He was in.

He had to be fast, his next goal, Ted's office. He carried on climbing the stairs two at a time as he always did and within seconds found himself on the Equity Trading floor. He inhaled deeply, the atmosphere was intense. Out of habit Henry cast one eye over the screens that were hanging at regular intervals across the immense open-plan room. Five hundred traders were packed together and the herd smelt fear. All major indices had dropped by over ten per cent since the opening. Henry made a quick calculation – $900 billion had just been wiped off the market since the opening in Tokyo. Henry kept going. He had slowed his pace but was still crossing the floor in haste. Ted's office was at the far end. He saw from the corner of his eyes the incredulous look of Morag his PA. He quickly moved his finger to his lips. Silence. She closed her eyes in acknowledgement and with this, anger burning, Henry found himself in front of Ted's office. The door was shut. He spread his hands on the glass wall and took a few seconds before entering.

The expression of terror on Ted's face was exquisite. Ted was reaching for the phone in slow motion, his hands weighing a ton. Henry moved swiftly. He opened the door, crossed the office in one stride and tore the headset from Ted's hand. Without a word he turned back, closed the door he had left open and closed the blinds, ensuring privacy. Ted had picked up his mobile but fumbling with it, did not manage to place the call before Henry threw the first punch. He caught Ted in the stomach, the young man's eyes opened wide, his mouth agape in a silent scream. Henry grabbed the mobile and crushed it underfoot. His attention turned now to Ted, who was still leaning against his desk but had not yet recovered his breath. Henry pulled a petrified Ted to his chair. The little bastard had never thrown a punch in his life, he reflected, with a smile on his face. It was one thing to play hardball at the bank, another on the streets.

"You and I are going to see the old man," said Henry calmly.

He was sitting on Ted's desk, his hands ready to throw the next blow.

"You're mad," stammered Ted, his face growing redder.

He had grabbed the armrests of his chair, his eyes still wide open, bracing himself.

"You try to prevent me from reaching McCarthy and I will break your neck before anyone can rescue you, understood? Understood?" repeated Henry, slamming his hand on the desk.

Ted nodded and stood up, grimacing in pain. Henry gestured for Ted to move and open the door. Henry ignored the havoc of the trading floor. He stood uncomfortably close to Ted who was already in front of the lifts.

"I forgot my pass," said Ted lamely.

"*Voila*," replied Henry, with a sarcastic grin on his face as he produced the much-needed item between his index and middle finger. "Thank God one of us has got brains."

Henry pressed the ninth floor button and shoved the card in the security slot. Ted eyes grew dim, there would be no escape.

The elevator pinged open. Henry pushed Ted out.

"Not one sound or you are dead."

Ted simply nodded and started moving. At the far end of the large open space was Cindy. She was typing and Henry knew Cindy would not be diverted from her task. She was not expecting anyone but must have heard the lift. She would probably be preparing one of her spectacular rebuffs. Henry smiled at the thought.

As predicted she finished her typing before looking up. She would not be distracted by unacceptable behaviour. She had no time to utter one of her scolding remarks. Henry and Ted had crossed the hallway, Henry shoving Ted abruptly forward, Ted's panic etched across his face.

Cindy had barely stood up when Henry pushed her back into her chair with a rapid harsh movement. She nearly screamed.

"Don't," commanded Henry with a menacing finger.

He looked around. There was no way he could silence these two for long enough to do what he had decided to do. Cindy sensed the hesitation and made a small gesture towards the panic button. Henry stopped her with a sharp move of his hand. He had to act ruthlessly right now or give up. He pulled the telephone cord from the wall in a firm and precise move, a sharp pang and the wire sprang up. Henry caught it with the same hand, he had not left Ted for a second.

"Tie her up," he ordered Ted, rummaging in Cindy's desk.

"I can't," stuttered Ted.

Henry's fist tightened and Ted took the wire with a feeble hand. Cindy made a second attempt at screaming but a large piece of gaffer tape covered her mouth in an instant. It was way too late despite Ted executing Henry's order at the slowest of paces.

"Tighter," ordered Henry.

Ted pulled the wire and Cindy winced. Ted proceeded, he was not doing a bad job thought Henry. Little Ted had succumbed to fear. Like Cindy, little Ted never saw the fist coming down on him for the second time. Henry caught the side of his head, below the eardrum. Ted fell to his knees. The other blow sent him into the middle of the room, unconscious, the deep and luxurious carpets muffling the sound of his falling body. Henry used the rest of the gaffer tape to tie him up.

McCarthy was alone in his office, no interruption. Henry turned towards the old man's office. He was only a few feet away but suddenly he felt he had a gulf to cross. If he crossed that gulf, Henry knew the consequences would be devastating, not only for him but also GL and so he slowed down. Cindy had followed him with a sceptical eye. Would he dare? Henry's hesitation gave her hope. He saw the fever in her eyes and stopped. He marvelled at that hope, anchored in the belief that there could be at this very moment restraint or consideration. The slow motion gave him an immense sense of power that he savoured silently.

"The time has come," said Henry and with one single push fuelled by the fire burning in his gut he opened McCarthy's door wide.

McCarthy was facing the large bay window. He was standing in his favourite corner of the room, a place that overlooked the City. He enjoyed that position in which he felt he held dominion over the world below. McCarthy was making a call on his private mobile, with headphones on. He certainly did not want his call to the Global Head of Risk to be recorded in any way, shape or form. The door opening with force did not startle him, Cindy entered his office in such a fashion at least once a day, when she felt matters required his full attention. No other member of staff would have dared cross the threshold without his say so. It was only the much heavier footsteps moving behind him and a tall shape profiled in the window that caused him to interrupt his call abruptly, and turn. As he did so he found himself face to face with Henry.

Henry saw the unmasked shock in the CEO's eyes and enjoyed it. A mixture of fear and astonishment was swiftly replaced by anger. Henry sat on the corner of DMac's desk, his leg squarely masking the panic button. Henry and DMac had locked eyes when they faced each other and their gaze had not shifted. Henry leaned backwards, running his fingers along a small shelf on McCarthy's antiques desk. He pressed the secret button twice and a small drawer no bigger than a matchbox opened. Henry reached inside for a key. McCarthy shouted,

"Don't you dare you little shit."

He lunged forwards, instantly meeting Henry's fist. The punch to his face made him retreat but it had not managed to bring him down. He fought back, finding his footing and lunging again. His last move had given Henry enough time to turn the key of the top lefthand drawer, pulling a loaded gun out of it.

Henry sat down calmly in his boss's chair, a triumphant grin now on his lips.

"Good afternoon Douglas."

McCarthy did not reply, he needed the gun back. His eyes darted from Henry's face to his hand, assessing the determination of the other man to shoot.

"Don't try Douglas, I didn't come here to kill you." Henry's voice was a strange blend of excitement and anticipation.

McCarthy changed tack. Confrontation was not an option, neither was reasoning. He had to anticipate Henry's next move if he had any chance of surviving.

"How?" asked McCarthy, no longer hiding his amazement at Henry's knowledge of the secret drawer.

"You hired me because of the accuracy of my observations, Douglas and so I observed. The undisclosed documents, the hidden cache. I know all your dirty secrets Doug."

McCarthy was about to try another tack when Henry interrupted him.

"I know what you are trying to do Douglas and time is of the essence."

"That's the name of the game, I guess," shrugged McCarthy.

A touch of admiration for the old man ran through Henry, under threat and still unfazed.

"Open the top drawer nearest to you," asked Henry.

McCarthy did not flinch.

"No."

"Suit yourself," replied Henry.

The gun discharge deafened them, resounding against the windows, shattering the wood in a burst of violence Henry had not experienced for decades.

Fear and shock showed for the second time in McCarthy's eyes, both men facing each other, on their guard. McCarthy moved first, desperation and rage overtook him, the thought of his impotence in front of Henry unbearable. Henry avoided the charge and McCarthy came crashing down on the side of his desk, displacing it. He was about to turn back and resume his attack when Henry gave a single kick, hitting McCarthy in the face. The blow threw the old man flying across the room. He landed on his back with a harsh muffled thud.

The drawer was pulled open frantically and Henry grabbed the file that McCarthy had concealed there only a few hours ago.

"What are you going to do with it?" mumbled McCarthy, incapable of getting up.

"What you should have done, Douglas, had you had a shred of honesty," replied Henry.

McCarthy lifted himself on one elbow so that he could see Henry but rolled on his back again. Through a mouthful of blood, he started laughing, stopping and starting in pain.

"You are not going to give me a lesson in ethics, are you Henry? Not you."

Henry did not reply. He took his new BlackBerry out of his pocket to find a number and punched the digits on McCarthy's phone.

"The office of David Cooper-James, HXBK," replied a male voice.

"Is he there? This is extremely urgent. My name is Henry Crowne."

"Mr Cooper-James is in a meeting."

"I have vital information concerning the takeover of GL," interrupted Henry. "This information will change the value of the bid. What fax number can I use?"

McCarthy took a few seconds to realise what was about to happen. He summoned his last ounce of strength and lunged forward one last time. He met Henry's foot again, this time in the stomach. It left him crying in agony. Henry had pressed the mute button just in time. McCarthy's body curled up in the middle of the room, in a heap, motionless.

"David Cooper-James," announced a very nasal voice on the loudspeaker.

Henry depressed the mute button.

"You wish to give me core information," carried on the voice.

"I do indeed, sir. It concerns the exposure of GL to the subprime market – several billions worth of it."

"How can I be sure?"

Henry did not have time to justify himself, instead he read a string of figures to HXBK's CEO. The phone stayed ominously silent. Henry thought he heard some noise in the reception area. He needed to act now.

"Are you still on the line?" asked Henry.

"I am," said the other man in a strangled voice.

"The fax is on its way to you."

Henry dashed to the fax machine. It swallowed the document, a familiar strident noise started.

From the corner of his eye Henry detected movement.

* * *

Inspector Pole had finally received the transcript of Liam's interview. He had read the document in one breath, after each page assessing the impact of its content, increasingly aware that this case was about to escape him.

The document had landed on Pole's desk with a soft feathery sound, so little noise for such heavy content. Pole had to locate Henry fast, before the Counterterrorist Squad took over. Something about the interview worried Pole. He wasn't satisfied, a sense of unfinished business began to set in. Pole opened the door of his office and called Nurani who had just arrived back from Belfast. She turned, the phone pressed to her ear and indicated she had nearly finished. Pole then called Andy.

The young man pushed his heavy glasses up from the tip of his nose where they had slid and rushed into Pole's office.

"I need to find Crowne as soon as possible. Call his lawyer to check whether he is there. I have tried the mobile. No response."

Andy nodded and disappeared. Nurani made her own entry, knowing that the transcript had just arrived.

"Bloody good job, no?" she said with pride.

"It is pretty compelling. Not in Henry's favour as you can imagine."

Pole found himself annoyed at this admission. Nurani sensed this but not knowing how to respond, remained silent. Pole handed over the report and closed the door of his office. Nurani started reading. She remained standing throughout and moved, as she was finishing, towards the chair in front of Pole's desk. She cautiously pushed it with her foot and sat down slowly before handing the document back to him. She was looking at Pole with a broad smile on her face. For the first time since he had started working with Ms Shah, Pole resented her sense of victory. He liked, and cultivated, restraint in shows of success.

"So, Mr Crowne, the darling of the structured product world in the City, is contributing to an undisclosed Swiss account, which turns out to be run by his good friend Liam O'Connor, who in turn uses it as a slush fund for his IRA pals. Mmmmmm, naughty!"

"Used to," Pole corrected her. "The IRA is now officially decommissioned."

Nurani waved her hand in the air; that was but a small technicality. Of course, she was right. Henry Crowne had been contributing to an undisclosed fund for years and it was only a matter of days before the link with that fund and the IRA would emerge. These donations stretched as far back as his first big City bonus, Liam had said with a hint of admiration for his friend. Pole had no intention of sharing his new line of thoughts with his young colleague. What other terrorist organisations were linked with this fund and why had Liam been heading to North Africa when he was caught?

"I've asked Andy to locate Henry," said Pole changing the subject. "I want to get to him before the other guys do."

"They can't take the case over, can they?" said Nurani.

"You know the rules as well as I do – yes they can and they will without hesitation. Careful what you wish for my dear," said Pole, satisfied his DS was about to learn a valuable lesson.

"Don't tell me you are going to roll over just like that Jon!"

182

"No, it's not my style. We may still have a chance to salvage the situation if we can prove the case is not related to a terrorist act," continued Pole.

"But you need to speak to Henry to get him to confess to us first." Nurani sounded sceptical.

Pole did not have time to reply before Andy burst into the office.

"There has been a disturbance at GL's offices. The security guards think Henry has entered the building without authorisation. They don't know where he is."

"Let's go," shouted Pole, "Andy you're on."

Pole's car screeched down Waterloo Bridge, turning onto Aldwych and then Fleet Street. The flashing light was making it easier to move but Pole still cursed the traffic.

"Shit, we've hit rush hour."

"We should have taken the tube," replied Andy.

Nurani looked at Andy with an expression reserved for the demented and Pole flashed a black look at the young man in the mirror.

A voice came on the radio and they all focused on what was being said. The Counterterrorist Squad was on its way. Pole doubled his efforts to avoid the traffic, using the horn, winding the window down and waving madly at the cars that would not move. His car finally burst into King Edward Street and came nose to nose with another police vehicle. Pole rushed out without closing his door.

"Who is the ranking officer?"

"On his way," answered a tall middle-aged man as Pole presented his ID card, "The traffic's holding him back."

"I am Inspector Pole, I am going in to assess the situation."

"You should discuss with Commander Jeffries," replied the other man aggressively.

"Not if we are in a critical situation that involves my case and your commander is miles away. He should have taken the tube!" replied Pole with a grin.

The other officer grabbed his radio and made contact with Commander Jeffries. Pole, Andy and Nurani did not wait to hear the conclusion of the conversation. The three moved swiftly towards the entrance of GL's offices and barely noticed the shouts calling them in the distance.

Chapter Twenty-Three

The bay window exploded into Henry's back. He had dived onto the floor seconds before rolling onto his side to avoid the shower of glass. The dark silhouettes of the Counterterrorist Squad moved into the room but Henry was running. He ran towards the lift deaf to the shouts and noise behind him. He shoved Ted's ID card into the slot, turned the switch back on to reactivate the elevator, pressed the fourth floor button all in one. A hand poked in as the doors were shutting but it was too late and the lift started moving. Henry's tall body collapsed against the wall, sending reverberations into the side of the elevator. He was shaking uncontrollably.

Henry had not given any thought as to what he would do next. The fourth floor was Mergers & Acquisitions. He noticed he had blood on his jacket. He removed it, slung it casually over his shoulder and composed himself. When the doors opened, Henry had regained some control and opted to go in the direction he knew best. He veered swiftly to his left, meeting rooms on both side of the long corridor. Each room that was occupied had an engaged sign below the name of the room. He dashed into the first free room he found. He closed the door and sat on the floor. He did not want to think about the last hour. He simply wanted to enjoy a few more moments of freedom, a few more minutes of respite.

Loud voices startled him, they were coming down the corridor, he held his breath as they walked pass. He stood up. As he retraced his steps back to the lift, he noticed the door of one of the rooms was open, papers spread over the meeting table, laptops showing figures and diagrams, jackets on the back of the chairs. Henry looked into the room – no one there, how careless! Henry managed a smile and picked up one of the jackets that looked large enough to fit him, in exchange for his blood-stained one. He slung it over his shoulder again. Henry started walking in the opposite direction, the elevator might not be such a good idea. He remembered that there was a set of stairs between the fourth and third floors. This enabled the M&A people and their analysts to communicate without having to share lifts with other parts of the bank. He still had Ted's ID, it should be good enough. He accelerated his pace, grabbing a pile of documents that were being photocopied as he walked past. He looked over at the far side of the large open-plan office and stopped in his tracks. A figure he thought he recognised was walking towards him.

* * *

Pole had flashed his inspector's ID at the security guard, demanding to be led immediately to the control room. The security team was on high alert. One of the men at the entrance door accompanied Pole to a room behind the reception desk, a couple of people were scrutinising the CCTVs, all other staff dispatched throughout the entire building to search for Henry. Information was being exchanged but nothing concrete had yet emerged, the hunt for Henry was picking up pace.

"Have you seen him?" asked Pole with minimal introduction.

"We think he is on the fourth floor, but not sure yet. Some of your team have just stormed the CEO's office where Crowne previously was. The lift on the ninth floor dropped someone on the fourth a couple of minutes ago."

Pole clenched his fist. He did not have time to question why the rapid intervention team of the Counterterrorist Squad had been put in position without his being informed. That would come later.

"The fourth floor you said, which lift side?"

"The right-side Inspector," replied the older man in charge, without looking at Pole.

Pole turned around and started running towards the lifts. Nurani was at the entrance surveying the arrival of the Counterterrorism Squad commander. Pole called her on the mobile and she turned around.

"Nu, don't follow me but go back to the car and get into the MD's garage with Andy."

He did not wait for a reply as the elevator had arrived. A few people walked out unaware of the drama unfolding a few floors above.

The doors opened onto the fourth floor. Pole walked out and quickly tried to get his orientation. He decided to turn left away from the meeting rooms, he would get a much better view of the entire floor from the other side of the open-plan office, a 50/50 chance of getting it right.

Pole recognised Henry before Henry saw him. He stopped. Why should Henry trust him? Why wouldn't he try for a final escape? Pole decided to stay still, waiting for the other man to see him, signalling his willingness to talk, to give Henry the option of a less violent outcome. He waited, knowing that in a few seconds he would be noticed. The silhouette that Henry had seen in the distance was now staring at him, no movement, an immobility that was waiting for acknowledgement and Henry understood. It was Pole, giving him the time to take a decision, expecting him to make the first move. The two men faced each other for a moment. Henry slowly moved towards the internal staircase, his eyes riveted on Pole. Pole could catch him if he moved fast but he remained still. Henry stopped, Pole immobile, both men aware of the other's proximity. Henry started moving fast, he accelerated as he reached Pole's side.

"There is an internal staircase to the third floor," said Henry before Pole could say anything.

"Can we get to the garage from there?" replied Pole as he started walking swiftly with Henry.

"We can do better, we can get to the CEO's parking bay." Henry managed a smile as he took Ted's security pass from his pocket.

"Do I even want to know how you got that?"

They reached the staircase. Henry flashed Ted's ID again in front of the electronic eye. The door released silently and they ran down the narrow passage.

Pole called Nurani on his mobile. "Nu, find a way to wait for me at McCarthy's parking bay."

He terminated the conversation abruptly and shut down his mobile altogether, not wanting to get his mobile tapped into. He gestured to Henry to switch off his BlackBerry too.

"Left mine behind and borrowed McCarthy's – don't want to be traced either."

"For someone with no criminal record, you are doing pretty well."

"I am a man of many talents."

Henry was trying to sound amused but a cloud passed over his eyes as he spoke. Pole remembered Henry's IRA links. They reached the third floor and entered the executive lift in silence. Ted's card was put to use again and the elevator glided to its destination. When the door opened, Pole's car was waiting with Nurani in the driving seat. Henry and Pole got in the back, she accelerated, barely stopping as she flashed her ID card at the security guard who had let her in. The car radio picked up a message.

The CT Squad were not getting their way and they did not like it.

A couple of calls came through for Inspector Pole whilst Nurani was driving them back to the Yard. Inspector Murphy told him that Bobby had been caught without a struggle once Liam was involved. Pole would not elaborate with Henry in the car. Pat had managed to extract a statement from Bobby, the transcript of which was on its way to London. Pat sounded amazed at the content but gathered that his friend was in no position to talk. Then again Bobby had the reputation of being a crackhead. Pat surely knew that and it was unlike him to overdo the evidence. Pole went back to his passenger. Now that the chase was over, Henry's face had sagged into that of a much older man.

"What happened in McCarthy's office?" asked Pole, not expecting an answer.

"I settled a few scores," replied Henry.

"You did not—" said Pole.

"No, Inspector Pole I did not," cut in Henry.

He turned and Pole noticed his clear blue eyes.

"Although I had a moment of hesitation."

"Hesitation is good," said Pole nodding.

"I also sent some documents to HXBK. Compromising documents, of course. I will be surprised if this takeover is one of the reverse types, to quote my former boss," said Henry through gritted teeth. "In fact, I will be very surprised if this takeover happens the way McCarthy and his team had envisaged."

"What do you mean exactly?"

Like most people, Pole had been following the market meltdown closely but he had also assumed, as everyone did, that GL was above the mess that the less worthy banks had succumbed to.

"GL is up to its eyeballs in the subprime business." Henry said.

Pole raised an eyebrow, surprised.

"I know," continued Henry. "Who'd have thought? Such a respectable firm! McCarthy thought I did not know. What a stupid man, too wrapped up in his superiority. The only way we can survive the next big drop in the market and there will be one, mark my words, is to merge with HXBK. Of course, the guys at HXBK don't know that or rather did not know that until this afternoon that is."

"But surely, they have looked at your books," said Pole unconvinced.

"And so what?" said Henry. "Do you really think that the complex derivatives structure we have on the books can be understood and valued easily? Neither the FSA nor the accountants fully understand the ramifications of what has been bought. They rely on the rating agencies having done their work. The best credit is AAA, for example a country like the UK is AAA. GL created the famous Collateralised Credit Obligations, these are full of US subprime loans. These CDOS are tranched, like a cake. The best part of the cake, the one with icing and a cherry on top is AAA rated. But if you start eating at the cake from the inside both the icing and the cherry will collapse. This is what's going to happen – today, tomorrow, very soon. I just don't know how big the bubble is going to be."

"Are you telling me, Henry, that even you don't know what the hell is going on?" said Pole, incredulous.

"Yep, I don't know what it means for the financial markets, let alone the economy. It will all depend on how much leverage, I mean borrowing, has been created around these structures."

Pole absorbed the information but refrained from asking his next question, keeping it for later, when it would be properly recorded as he suspected the answer would be Anthony Albert. Instead he came back to the documents that had been sent out.

"So, what was it exactly that you sent HXBK?"

"The summary, with simulations, of our exposure to subprime, unadulterated. It does not make good reading – at the moment at least $30 billion."

"Should you … " Pole stopped, this was a stupid question.

Henry smiled.

"I came to an abrupt but very clear realisation that no matter what, I will never work in the City again."

"Is this justice?" said Pole.

"Revenge," Henry didn't hesitate. "We are all wired very simply in investment banking despite appearances. The most we can do is think about justice in a biblical sense, an eye for an eye."

Pole remained silent, he would no doubt read the results of Henry's fax in the press tomorrow. It was indeed an unforgiving world.

A new mail flashed on his BlackBerry, it was Dolores. She was chasing Albert's solicitor and was promised a call as soon as his will had been read.

* * *

Nancy was standing in one of Scotland Yard's waiting rooms looking through one of the windows. Her mind had drifted towards art. She had been neglecting her role of patron and mentor, aware of the several missed calls she had not yet replied to. *The Raft of the Medusa* emerged from the depths of her mind the way it must have emerged on the horizon of the ship that rescued it. Its power, reinforced by the events of the last few hours, struck her. The despair and violence it described could be read at two levels: society and individual, such was the power of the *Raft*. She knew something extreme had happened when the BBC reported the CT Squad intervention at GL Headquarters. She was on her way to the Yard already when her mobile rang. Henry and she exchanged very little. Nancy's patience was about to be tested to the full. For a fleeting moment she wondered why she had ever got involved. A last remnant of ego, a moment of intellectual vanity? Yes, there was the mistake she had made with the airline tickets, but she had owned up to it, she could have moved away with a suitably clear conscience. Whatever it was that had pushed her, she also had a sense of duty. She would see this case through just the way she had all those years ago in France.

She had been mesmerised by Jacques. He was a powerful intellect and a true showman in court. The law was a means, a tool he used to take on the most controversial of cases. She had dived into the world of criminal law head first, moved by her own background, a Chinese father, an English mother and a childhood between Mao's China and France; Jacques Vergès shared a similar background, a French father and Vietnamese mother together with an association with communism. Was it what she shared with Henry? The impact of a cross-cultural upbringing in a world hardly ready for it? The anguish of not knowing where to belong?

Nurani interrupted her thoughts by calling her name. Nancy composed herself before facing the young inspector. She gave an affable smile and followed without a word. When she entered the meeting room, she sat in front of Henry and listened. He did not omit any details this time, including the impact of Liam's confession. Nancy still listened when he finally spoke about the regular payments into the Swiss bank account.

"You knew it would support some IRA operations, even though Ireland is trying to move on." Nancy did not intend this as a question.

"I never asked," replied Henry.

"You knew it would support the IRA," repeated Nancy. She would not be put off by some non-answer. The Irish cause could be fought through other means but Henry gave a small shrug.

"Why? Henry why?"

"You and I are very different, Nancy," said Henry.

"That is rubbish and you know it," replied Nancy.

"You think there is always some goodness to salvage in someone but I don't. I was born with anger and violence around me and that has become part of me, forever."

"That is not a good enough reason, I understand anger more than you can imagine–"

"Do you know what my first childhood memory is?" interrupted Henry. Nancy would not have the last word.

"A wall full of hatred, murals and slogans that spoke of death and retribution. Did I ever want peace? No, I wanted revenge and then I compromised; money makes you complacent. I wanted to grind those stupid bastards underneath my foot and I became one of them. So, somewhere I still had to have some truth in me, not to forget 500 years of abuse and exploitation. OK I am a manipulative arrogant bastard of a banker but at least …"

Henry paused as if considering the veracity of his statement.

"I have remained true to my only friends."

A total and yet childish admission, a boy who had never grown up was speaking. Nancy extended a hand as if to reach Henry's.

"Did you have to go that far? You had escaped."

"You never escape Nancy. I can still hear it all: the bombs, the sirens, the gunshots, the insults and the cries of those who had lost someone they loved. It will never go away."

"It will never go away if you keep fuelling it. Did you kill Anthony Albert?"

The question startled them both.

"NO."

"Are we having a discussion about semantics?"

"NO."

"Bobby is giving evidence as we speak."

"Bobby is a crackhead; he will do anything."

"Anything for you?"

"What do you mean?"

Henry paused, as the unthinkable began unfolding in his mind. Unwanted thoughts, now unleashed, rushed around his head. The door opened and Pole appeared, alone.

"It won't be long before the Counterterrorist Squad arrives."

"On the strength of Liam's deposition?" asked Henry.

"No, on the strength of Bobby's."

Chapter Twenty-Four

The will itself was particularly short. An up-to-date statement of assets had been appended to the document. This attracted Pole's attention as it was only a couple of months old. The entirety of Anthony Albert's wealth was meticulously accounted for. The appendix was longer than the will itself but the decision unequivocal. All of Albert's assets were settled in trust for his children. The forceful Adeila received nothing.

Pole read the document again, motivated by professional habit rather than a need to check the content. Pole dialled Dolores' extension. There was no reply. He looked at the clock, the reading of the will had been over for less than an hour. Would Albert's widow contest it?

"She will have to. What a mess."

The phone rang, he picked up without checking the number. The voice was unfamiliar, but Albert's solicitor introduced himself.

"Have you received the document?" enquired the voice.

"Yes, certainly. I have read it too. May I ask what the reaction at the reading of the will was?"

"You mean Mrs Albert?"

"Were there other relevant parties attending?"

"Yes, the appointed trustees but to come back to your question, well …". The voice on the line was searching for a proper way to qualify the scene, "we thought she might be surprised, but there was not a moment of astonishment or even anger."

Pole took note. That was out of character.

"In fact, I am almost certain she knew the contents of the will. I find this amazing because Mr Albert was very particular about keeping the new will from his wife. In any case she was prepared. She immediately declared she would contest the will."

"When did Mr Albert decide on the changes?" asked Pole.

"Less than two months ago."

Pole exchanged a few more words with the solicitor then the conversation was over. He had picked up the phone again to call Dolores when the humour of the situation hit him. There had never been any real discussion between Adeila and Brett about Anthony Albert. All must have happened through innuendoes and half-spoken words. Brett thought he was wooing a woman who might become rich, she was hedging her own bets trying to attract a man whom she thought was wealthy. If Adeila knew about the will, which now seemed likely, she certainly did not want her husband's death. Allner-Smith did not know but it was now unthinkable he would have planned the murder on his own. All this amounted to a laughable game of deceit, smoke and mirrors. Adeila was, Pole had to admit, pretty good at it. He looked at his watch; time to reconvene with Henry.

* * *

"We don't have much time, Henry," pressed Pole. "This is Bobby's deposition, take a look."

Henry lifted an eyebrow and took the piece of paper with a lack of interest. He could imagine Bobby's disjointed mind coming up with some insane storyline. A convenient tale the police would pursue but easily torn to shreds by his lawyer.

Both Nancy and Henry started reading. They read all ten pages in absolute silence. Henry put the document down before Nancy did. She was surprised. Henry could still, under exceptional strain, retain a distinct capacity for absorbing and interpreting information.

"Bobby is insane," said Henry softly but it did not sound like a reproach to his friend rather a realisation that was long overdue or perhaps a reproach to himself.

"What do you mean," said Pole perceiving the unexpected change in the tone of Henry's voice.

"I need to think, Inspector," carried on Henry, "… alone please."

Pole was about to mention again that time was running short but thought better of it. Something was happening. He ruffled his goatee and signalled to Nancy that they should leave the room for a few minutes.

The scales of justice were now starting to move imperceptibly, a momentous decision was about to take place. She knew. She had witnessed it before. The turning point in a life that had suddenly veered off course.

Pole arrived with coffee, which they drank in silence. When they had finished, he gave a small sign that it was time.

"Give him a few more minutes, please," said Nancy.

"We are cutting it very fine."

Nancy nodded but did not reply.

"Since we have a few minutes Ms Wu, may I ask what happened to Jacques Vergès? You worked with him once upon a time."

If Nancy Wu was prepared to dig into his past, he surely was in a position to do the same with hers.

"Who?" asked Nancy in earnest.

"Jacques Vergès," said Pole.

Nancy's look of surprise gave way to a short laugh.

"Well Inspector. Serves me right for digging around people's past."

"You still have not answered my question."

"It is a long story Inspector and you said it yourself, we don't have that much time."

Pole was about to protest when she continued.

"Those were dark days in which I learned a lot about being a barrister, about myself too. I worked with Jacques once, when he defended a war criminal called Klaus Barbie. I was a very young lawyer then."

"An affair in Bordeaux, in the late eighties," said Pole.

Nancy looked at her watch.

"You're right, let's go."

"How about a contact with Vergès in late 2008?"

Nancy was already walking down the corridor.

When they had reached the room Pole opened the door, gallantly pulling back to let Nancy enter first. She acknowledged him with a small movement of the head.

"I had introduced Bobby to Anthony Albert," said Henry as both Nancy and Pole sat down.

"It was a completely fortuitous meeting," he carried on in a knotted voice. "We were celebrating a closing in Dublin, we found ourselves all in the same pub. Albert was there and I could not care less anyway. I had just closed the biggest god damn deal ever!"

Henry stopped, it now sounded so meaningless.

"Bobby caught onto us I vaguely remember, although by that stage we were all pretty drunk."

Henry's eyes stayed focused on his friend's written confession.

"Albert had invited himself to the party, we were closing the transaction with HXBK. Hardly anything to do with him but it was a high profile deal. This little shit had to pretend. We went for drinks after the closing dinner. Liam has a job now in Dublin, turns out he was at the same pub as we were with Bobby. Still we hardly spoke. He does not feel comfortable outside Belfast and does not like me in my work clothes."

Henry could not help a sad smile.

"You mean Bobby and you hardly spoke?"

"Mmmm, he just wanted to know who the guy who was left on the side was. I gave him his name. I probably told him he was a waste of space," continued Henry.

"Did Bobby speak to Albert?"

"I don't know Inspector. As I said, Bobby does not feel comfortable outside Belfast. I certainly can't remember him leaving, I don't even think I said goodbye."

Henry sat back for a minute. His hands had not left his friend's confession. He kept looking at it.

"I think I might have …"

Henry stopped and Nancy stood up.

"Henry, we need to discuss this," said Nancy. She must control the next few minutes.

"Bobby seems to dislike Albert a great deal, there is an entire page on why it was a good idea to do what he did."

Pole was ignoring Nancy. He knew Henry was wavering, almost ready to talk.

"Bobby has never had a clear view as to why he hates. It is a rant, a long-lasting condition, he simply hates, with passion and without reason. I am surprised he could be so precise," answered Henry.

"Henry, I need to speak to you in private," said Nancy, in a final attempt.

"He said he spoke to you a few times and got instructions through voice messages. He could have dreamt it but then again it takes a lot to circumvent the security of any bank, let alone of an airport. Henry?" Pole was pushing on.

"Inspector that is enough!" interrupted Nancy.

"Nancy, this is OK," said Henry.

"I need to know, Inspector. It could only have taken a few hints."

"What do you mean?"

Pole looked at his watch, they had five minutes at the most. If Pole was to extract Henry from the clutches of the Counterterrorist Squad, Henry had to admit to the unthinkable. Nancy knew Pole was right, she had no time left to coach Henry. She changed tack.

"Henry, speak to us if this is truly your choice, we don't have much time," urged Nancy.

Pole turned towards her, amazed.

"Is that the QC's advice?" said Henry.

"And your friend – you do NOT want the Squad to take over."

Henry nodded

"We had a plan, it was such a long time ago. At university," Henry hesitated. "It now sounds ridiculous, arrogant or simply crazy, but during the Troubles, in Belfast it was so – normal."

"You mean the bombings?" asked Pole, pushing Henry back to darker times.

"Politicians used to fly a lot from small airports. Getting a bomb through was not all that difficult."

Henry paused and a sense of clarity took hold. He knew what Bobby had done, and he now knew what it meant to him.

"I was a student at Trinity College. I took it as a challenge, a way to see whether I could outsmart them all. I don't even remember whether I believed they would actually do it – I didn't care."

Henry stood up unexpectedly.

He was deliberating, his thoughts nearly palpable. For so many years he had skirted around the issue. Was he in, was he out? Could he truly have done what Liam and Bobby had done? The time had come to find out. He wanted it, at this very moment and in this room, with a passion he thought had deserted him when he left Ireland.

"Is the Squad on its way?"

Pole nodded.

"You can still save yourself, Henry."

"No. Not any more. Bring them on." Henry's eyes blazed with hatred.

Pole faced Henry. Henry held Pole's gaze – the desire for a fight in the air. Henry wanted to feel the sweet taste of blood, just once more, the crush of bones beneath his fists. What respect could he have for a man who wanted to compromise, a man he realised was trying to save him?

Pole understood immediately, it took a few more seconds for Nancy to see it. He opened his mobile and dialled Nurani's number, a few words were exchanged. He would not reason with Henry any longer. Pole felt strangely disengaged.

Henry was at the gates of Hell and wanted a taste of it – so be it.

It took all but the best part of a minute for the Counterterrorist Squad commander to arrive with four more men. Henry was handcuffed roughly but did not wince.

Nancy and Pole left the room and shook hands without exchanging a word, there was nothing else to add. Pole walked back to his office. His view of the situation had been proportional. Yet a moment ago he had stopped caring. Now an infinitesimal feeling of regret, an imperceptible sense that the job was not altogether finished started troubling him. Pole hesitated and changed direction, time for a quick catch up with Dolores.

Chapter Twenty-Five

Henry was sitting in the police van that was taking him to Paddington Green station for interrogation. He was preparing himself, anger pumping through his veins, the rage of years long past rising once more. *Had he been so careless?* he wondered. Everything had worked so well: the financial arrangement, the multi-tier structure, the tax havens, the numbered accounts in Switzerland. Did he truly want this fight? A fight with Pole was not worth it but the Counterterrorist Squad was. Excitement replaced anger. How far could he go? He looked at the three officers sitting in the van with him. They knew violence and death all right. He carried on inspecting them. A strange form of combat had already begun. He had been pushed to the far end of the van, the three men were gathered near the door. Henry tried to remember Belfast, the Troubles, the sounds of the bombs and the blasé remarks of those who had escaped.

"It's near College Square."

"Na, it's Victoria Street, they have done the Europa again."

And so it would carry on for a while until the news confirmed the location.

Henry moved position to discover that the back of his shirt was wet with sweat.

Not that tough anymore, Henry. A small ironic smile curled his lips, a good thing he had learned from the English – the power of self-deprecation.

He moved again. The three guards looked at him and decided he wouldn't be trouble. The cuffs were pretty tight, very small but so effective a tool. The van was taking an eternity to cross the red light, this time Henry shuffled his feet. Were they stuck in a traffic jam, surely they could sound their siren and get through?

It all happened in an instant, a surge of energy never experienced before. An uncontrollable force threw Henry against the walls, the floor, the ceiling of the van, his ears incapable of taking in the noise. Space had been torn open and consciousness ripped from him.

Yells of agony and anguish brought him back. With all his might Henry willed himself awake, reaching new depths he had never suspected existed inside him. He drew deep to stay alive.

For an instant it all sounded quiet again as if nothing had happened. The cries started again, a siren in the distance, then a second one. Amid the suffocating smell of burning flesh, Henry wanted to open his eyes, he wanted …

A hand shook his shoulder and someone was shouting.

"I need to move you, mate, can you hear me?"

Henry mumbled, he could see a vague shadow over him, an awkward shape, a heavy weight was pinning him down as he was trying to move.

"Can't," he tried to articulate, his eyes still out of focus.

"You must, mate, the van is on fire, it's about to explode. Come on, you can do this," the voice was pressing.

Two hands grabbed his shoulders and started to drag his body. Henry moaned, and summoning all the energy he could, pushed something away from him. He opened his eyes, finally able to focus, to look at what was preventing him from moving. The severed body of one of the guards lay on its side, the explosion had ripped open the door, tearing apart his torso. Henry's mouth opened, his eyes bulged. He was looking into the eyes of the guard, empty and glazed. A scream that never came suffocated Henry. He crawled forward ignoring the helping hands that were trying to move him out. The van rocked heavily on its side. Two arms pinned him down to stop the van toppling over altogether. Someone else dragged him onto the road. One of the other guards, who had been fiercely searching for his keys, released Henry from his handcuffs.

"The driver is still trapped in the front," urged the man, "help me."

A small woman, a passer-by, ran towards the scene. Henry did not move, she followed the guard to drag the driver out. The smell of burning petrol was overwhelming.

For all his years in Belfast Henry had never been close to a bomb blast as it happened. He had heard them, seen the aftermath, read about them. He had imagined all the gory details. He had become blasé about them to the point where his only concern was to pinpoint with precision the site of the explosion from the sound it made. He had always been prepared – the mangled bodies, the smell of burning flesh, the yelling of the wounded. But reality had now dug its claws into his belly, twisting and turning like a hook. He fell to the ground, limp. People were running around him, strangers helping strangers. Henry thought he should be there too, his eyes turned towards the van, he bent forward and threw up. It was not easy to kill a man. Henry tore his jacket away from his body and wiped the blood and vomit from his face. He stood up, looking but seeing nothing. Henry started walking, his mind filled with images he needed to escape.

He walked past the screaming ambulances, the howling police vans. He walked, blinded by emotions. Faster and faster he went, chased by the furies of destruction. Henry was running, escaping what had always been a part of his life. He was running when a cold sensation hit his face. He could not understand it to start with, a thousand needles attacking his skin. The rain fell harder; he welcomed it, its vicious bite bringing him back to life, his chest burning. The torrent drenched him, blinded him, pushed him to run faster. Where was he? He did not care.

Henry turned into Marylebone. He was running. His clothes clung to his wet body. But suddenly the rain stopped, subsiding like an ocean wave, its violence gone and with it the promise of relief. Henry's pace slowed. His hand found the cold strength of an iron gate, he was spent. He clung to the metal frame with a ferocious grip, gasping for air. He was wrecked, just as those men must have been who clung to the Medusa's raft. There was no hope left.

A black Mercedes stopped beside him. The driver's door opened and a gloved hand grabbed Henry, pulling him into the car. Henry collapsed on the back seat.

"Mr Crowne, I think you need a lift," said a familiar voice, a voice that came from a past not so distant and yet that belonged to another life.

Charlie started the car again and drove off. He looked with kindness at the heap collapsed on the back seat of his car, the man he had so often driven to one airport or another. Henry knew he was safe, he did not know why. Finally, he sat up, articulating with great difficulty.

"Charlie, you should not ..."

"Nonsense," replied Charlie. "I would be a poor limousine driver if I could not offer a much-needed ride to my best client."

"You don't understand," protested Henry, each word requiring a crushing effort.

"What don't I understand – that you are a wanted man?" Charlie kept his eyes on the road ahead. "It takes one to know one. I was once in a very bad place too, as you well know."

"You don't owe me, Charlie," said Henry.

"It is all about respect, Mr Crowne, that which you give and that which you receive."

A comfortable silence fell in the car.

"There are some fresh clothes in the boot of the car and I won't take no for an answer," said Charlie still looking ahead. "Where are you going to go Mr Crowne?"

"Charlie, I think you can drop the Mr."

"As you wish … Henry."

"I don't know is the answer. I just don't know."

The comfort he had felt vanished. He thought about Nancy but the police would know. He had no money, no ID. He was stripped bare.

"I have finished my day. We could go for a drink."

Charlie spoke slowly in a manner that seemed hesitant. Not knowing whether it came from discomfort or anxiety, Henry was about to decline the offer. He met Charlie's eyes in the rear view mirror. There was genuine sympathy.

"You know that the cops are after me?"

Charlie smiled at Henry, a generous smile that said it all. He became serious.

"As I said earlier, Henry, very few bankers were prepared to give an ex-con much of a chance."

"You don't have to repay me. You have always done your job well. In fact, more than well."

"Have you done time?"

"Not exactly."

"But you know what that means …"

"I am probably about to find out sooner than I would have wanted to."

Henry closed his eyes and inhaled. Could he ever give up being an arrogant ass?

"If you need to get out of this country, you have very little time." Charlie's tone had changed. It had a palpable urgency.

"What do you mean?" Henry looked up suddenly, his heart jolted with a pang of hope.

"I know people."

"I need to think," said Henry, nodding slowly.

He froze as a police car screamed past them. Charlie kept his composure.

"Let's have that drink. I know a good place in Hackney. You will be fine there, for a while."

Henry remained silent, the siren still echoing in his ears. He recalled the earlier vision of *The Apocalypse* by John Martin. He clenched his fists so hard his fingernails cut into the palms of his hands. He thought about the mangled bodies, he saw Liam and Bobby's faces, he saw *The Raft of the Medusa* waiting for him in his apartment.

"Don't do this to yourself. It won't solve anything."

Charlie's voice saved him from the abyss. Henry sat back, surrendering to the moment. He looked at the streets around him. He had lost track of where he was.

* * *

The distant noise startled Nancy. It was unfamiliar and yet not unknown. She looked at the large clock hanging on the wall of her conservatory. It indicated half past six exactly, evening rush hour at its peak and she knew a bomb had gone off.

She threw away her gardening gloves in an angry gesture and ran across the length of the room. She climbed down the stairs, nearly tripped, grabbed the banister. She swore as she found her balance again and rushed to the nearest phone.

Nancy dialled Inspector's Pole number from memory.

"Pole," he answered.

"Inspector Pole, where are you?"

"Good afternoon Ms Wu," replied Pole in an amused tone. "I thought I was the one who—"

"No time, Inspector," interrupted Nancy. "I think a bomb has just gone off in Central London. I can't quite be sure but if I can hazard a guess. I'd say west of me, possibly Hyde Park, Marble Arch – that sort of way."

"Do not hang up, my other phone is ringing."

Pole voice lost some of its clarity but Nancy could still hear his side of the conversation.

"Where exactly? I see. I am on my way."

Nancy could hear him fumbling with both phones.

"The bomb exploded at Paddington." Pole hesitated. "It caught the van in which Henry was being transported. It's chaos over there."

"Is he dead?" asked Nancy.

"I don't know. I am going, right now," replied Pole.

"I'll meet you at Paddington," she would not be told otherwise.

"Fine, ask for me."

Nancy sat down. The news nearly overwhelmed her. She thought of Pole and drew some comfort knowing he would be there. She had to find Henry. Nancy stood up, grabbed her coat, checked again that she had put her mobile in her bag and left the safety of her flat without hesitation.

Chapter Twenty-Six

Tube and buses had stopped. Nancy managed to convince a cabbie to take her as close as he could to Paddington. She could hear the distant howling of ambulances. Her left hand started to shake uncontrollably and she grabbed it with her right to make it stop. An image was slowly forming in her mind, people running and screaming, the smell of tear gas, but the cabbie's voice dispelled it.

"It's as far as I can go, love."

Nancy gave the driver a £20 note and rushed out without asking for change. The acrid smell of smoke and melted plastic assaulted her. People were walking in all directions, some still fleeing the scene, others frantically moving towards it. She could make out a number of police vans in the middle of the road. She saw officers stopping people. She needed to find Pole. Nancy grabbed her mobile and, still walking, pressed the redial button. The number was busy. The engaged tone played with her nerves. She gritted her teeth and tried again. She was about to terminate the call when Pole's name appeared on the screen. She switched line.

"Where are you," asked Pole.

"At the corner of Paddington and Westbourne Grove."

"I am coming for you."

Nancy stood still in a sea of people – injured, helpers, relatives in search of their loved ones. A strong grip on her arm made her turn around. Pole was standing in front of her. His pale face stood out against the darkness of night. He had seen the bomb site. She did not know how to ask the question.

"Henry is alive," Pole managed.

Nancy simply shook her head. Words meant very little and she could not find the right ones. They faced each other speechless. Pole was still holding Nancy's arm, the way a drowning man may cling to his rescuer. He realised it and reluctantly let go. She managed a quick smile.

"Is it very bad?"

"Atrocious," replied Pole, his eyes now avoiding hers. "I need to go back – and you need to find Henry."

Pole did not move and Nancy knew he would not until she did. She shook her head and put her hand on Pole's square shoulder, pressing it gently. She was finding it hard to move away too but a yell of despair in the distance jolted her into action.

She took a step back, still facing Pole and finally turned around. She moved faster and faster, her chest pounding. She felt nauseous. She stopped abruptly but the moment passed.

She must indeed find Henry.

* * *

The Vortex Jazz Club was a busy place, an intimate setting for the jazz aficionados who came to listen. Henry followed Charlie into the club and noticed his driver giving a quick gang style handshake to the bouncer at the door. They found a free table at the back of the room. The redheaded woman on stage had just started her first song.

"She is Irish," said Charlie, "the best Jazz fusion in town at the moment. Beer?"

"Guinness."

Charlie simply nodded and disappeared.

Her song had the broken, intellectual rhythm of original jazz yet peppered with some melodious, melancholic undertones. Henry drifted into the music. Jazz had never been his favourite but somehow he felt carried by the tune or maybe the words. It was familiar. Henry realised she was singing in Gaelic, the wheel of time spinning in reverse.

He was seated at a similar table in Belfast. Bobby had brought a wad of papers to the pub and Liam had gone mad at him for it. It was a partisan pub, but still. It had been agreed that they should not discuss their latest plan in public. Bobby had disappeared into the crowd and not reappeared until the following evening. Henry could see the papers but the pages were blank. He did not want to look at them, to turn those pages and remember.

"Good stuff!"

Charlie's voice startled Henry. His Guinness was sitting in front of him. Charlie raised his own pint of lager and Henry raised his drink, clinking Charlie's glass softly. He took a sip. He liked the gentle sensation of the froth hitting his lips before the bitter taste engulfed his tongue. He took another sip. The wad of papers reappeared in front of his eyes.

Liam was talking to him about the airport. He had gathered good quality intelligence. The airport was small and therefore ideal. A lot of high ranking civil servants and even royalty flew from it. The perfect target.

The song ended and Henry noticed that his glass was nearly empty. He was about to offer to pay for a round but remembered he had no money. A sensation of helplessness he had never known choked him. A plump waitress dressed in black and wearing the requisite piercings brought some chips. Charlie signalled for another two drinks. He had said nothing, content to be listening to his favourite music. Henry finished his pint and regained some composure.

"We can talk if you'd like," said Charlie looking at the stage, "but it may not be what you want, that's fine by me. No pressure."

Henry nodded. He knew he had to make the effort soon, but maybe not just yet. He let himself drift into the redhead's next song.

* * *

Nancy walked all the way home. She felt she was losing valuable time but there was no other option. She wondered how she could find Henry – no BlackBerry, penniless. Who would he turn to? She did not know his friends although she suspected his City pals would never be his first port of call. Who?

Henry had been betrayed but was it not of his own doing? A harsh situation, thought Nancy, but one she knew only too well. The core of Henry's belief was unravelling. He was at a crossroads but would he recognise it? Nancy remembered the events that had tested her in much the same way. Pole had been right when he had asked about early 2008. Jacques Vergès had offered to defend Tariq Aziz, Saddam Hussein's close adviser, and after all these years contacted Nancy. She knew full well why. Vergès was getting old without losing his appetite for controversy. Nancy had just won a spectacular case against the extradition of a world-renowned hacker. Her name had been in the papers for days and coming out of the Old Bailey, she had addressed the journalists with the mixture of tact, humour and defiance that so characterised her. She knew Vergès' decision was a media stunt, she saw straight through it and yet the temptation was too great.

She had arranged to meet him in Paris. A good shopping trip along the Rive Gauche would not go amiss if she decided not to work with Jacques. She was about to board the Eurostar when an old friend spotted her. They had both studied at The Sorbonne and corresponded for a long time until Nancy's professional life took over, consuming all hours of day and night. They were sitting in the same carriage, a strange turn of fate which Nancy would reluctantly interpret as destiny. They sat together and talked the way old friends can sometimes do, with candour. Nancy heard her own voice describing what she did and it sounded alien, false. She was not lying of course when she was recounting her successes at the bar. But doubt was slowly creeping in. Her friend nodded and smiled. Nancy could see on her face a mixture of admiration and regret. When the train arrived at the Gare du Nord, Nancy's friend embraced her warmly with only a few parting words: *"I am glad you enjoy this all-consuming job so much, take a little time for what else matters will you?"* There was some sorrow in her voice, which did not betray envy but gentle disappointment. Nancy took the cab that was waiting for her but never saw Vergès. She instead walked the streets of Paris the way she had done so many years ago. She took time again to look at life unfolding around her. At the pinnacle of her career Nancy had started the process of self-transformation. She knew now why but it would take her time to see clearly the root of it all.

The rain surprised her with its intensity. She shivered. She yearned for the tranquillity of her home. She wanted to get rid of the acrid smell of smoke and death. Her mind would not settle until she had reached her destination. She accelerated her pace. She would be there very soon. Then the answer would present itself.

* * *

The music had banished his anxieties for a while. Jazz had been the perfect music and he thanked Charlie for it. The first part of the show had finished, a young saxophonist was now filling the room with a doleful solo.

"Have you ever been betrayed, badly?"

Henry's question came as a surprise, its frankness almost unbearable.

"Don't you mean to say, have I ever grassed on someone, in a way that is unforgivable ever for best friends?"

Charlie's rephrasing of the question felt brutal. His voice had lost its manicured tone but not its precision. Charlie looked at Henry as he replied. In the darkness of the club, Henry felt his eyes on him.

"I have paid my dues. I decided it was enough, my slate is clean. It's hard to acknowledge who you are."

"Was it worth it?"

"You already know the answer to that."

"I am not so sure anymore. It's easy to think about it when all is good but today ..." Henry's voice trailed off.

Charlie's phone buzzed. He looked at it with distant interest. He looked at Henry again and decided it was time to leave.

"I've got to go. You can stay here for the rest of the night. Marco at the door will help and ... I'll be back here before the club closes. I will make some enquiries. If you want to leave the UK, I'll come back with a contact."

"Why?" said Henry almost childish.

"If you truly want to make a choice, you need to have a choice."

Charlie stood up, so did Henry. He extended his arm and shook his driver's hand. Something he had never done before.

* * *

The redhead was back on stage. Charlie had vanished. Memories of Ireland stormed back into Henry's mind. The papers were now scattered before Liam and him. They shared the same house and had gathered in Henry's small room. Bobby had not been invited. He would be told when the plan had been fully hatched. Bobby's impatience had become far worse since they had moved out of Belfast, his restlessness a constant concern.

The papers had finally come to life, a shorthand written description of how to wire a detonator, the list of items required for the construction of a bomb. Henry had been amazed at the simplicity of its ingredients. He saw the map of the small airport with yellow highlights in a couple of places, the points at which security was at its weakest. A page with columns and ticks with their three names flashed in front of Henry's eyes, airport staff schedules, unscheduled flights. He could hear the sound of his own voice declaring sanctimoniously, "It works. We can do this anytime."

Henry raised his pint to his lips, he had nearly finished his drink. He looked at the small amount of dark liquid at the bottom of his glass. Who had decided not to go ahead and why? Had it been an intellectual exercise, a way to prove to himself and his friends how clever he was? A way to belong?

The pain of realisation savaged him. He had wanted to look after his friends as if they were family. He wanted to be part of them, just the way he was when kids had taunted him at school *"English boy, Mummy's boy, little shit we'll get your toys.*" Liam had grabbed the kid who spat at Henry by the throat and Bobby had sworn he would kill anyone who touched him. No one messed with the O'Connor clan. And Henry was one of them. But Henry Crowne would never be a killer. The well-rehearsed plan was a mock exercise. He could not bring himself to act upon it but Bobby had. To Bobby it was no mere intellectual conjecture, it was a call to arms. The seed had been sown no matter how long it would take to mature.

Henry sat back in his chair. The Vortex Club reappeared. The agony of self-doubt assaulted him. He was a nobody.

"No," said Henry aloud.

No, he would not accept this. He stood up quickly and knocked the table. A few heads turned but the music covered the noise for the rest of the room. The waitress had approached the table more concerned by an unpaid bill than a drunken man. Charlie had left a £50 note in the tray. Henry pocketed the change, uneasily. He looked at the room around him. There was nothing left for him here.

He walked out of the club and stepped onto the pavement. It was damp and cold. He zipped up the fleece that Charlie had lent him and started walking through the crowded streets of Hackney.

* * *

Nancy had taken the time to have a shower. She had checked her mobile several times. Pole had not called and she knew better than to call herself. She was confident he would let her know as soon as he had news.

The TV was on and she flicked channels. Identical pictures and comments were being repeated without giving her much to go on. She found the reporting distasteful.

Nancy pressed the TV mute button and closed her eyes. She knew there was a connection somewhere that she was missing. A way to reach Henry she had not yet thought about. She decided to go through her case notes. She opened the file that had been abandoned on her sofa and started reading through them, methodically.

* * *

Despite the plummeting temperature, Hackney Central was bristling with activity, young people moving from club to club, huddled together and speaking at the tops of their voices, cars cruising with open windows, blasting rap or techno. Henry was walking slowly, observing the sea of faces.

He had been so remote from this crowd only a few hours ago and now here he was, immersed in it with so little in his pocket that he understood once more the vulnerability of the destitute. A brightly lit shop attracted his attention. He crossed the road and stood in front of an electrical goods shop where three ultra large TV screens were relaying different news programmes. The bomb blast dominated all channels.

Henry recognised the police van that had carried him a few hours ago. He couldn't move. A passer-by bumped into him. The man was drunk, mumbling some insult. He moved on, preferring another pint to a fight. The sound of a police siren caused Henry to jerk round to see the police car rush past him. The scenes at Paddington remained so vivid, he started walking again. The noise of the street mingled with the screams surrounding the bomb site, he turned left into another street then right and found himself in a small alleyway. The activity had subsided to give way to a seediness he had not witnessed for years. Henry spotted a wine bar at the far end of the street. He walked in and sat at the bar. He fingered the £20 note he had in his pocket and ordered a large glass of red, any red would do; he had stopped being fussy. The barman stuck a menu in front of him with a choice of tapas, an indication that Henry was expected to do more than just drink. He wasn't hungry but he placed an order, anyway.

The place looked unexpectedly welcoming in contrast to its neighbourhood. On the stool next to him a man shuffled. He pulled a crumpled handkerchief from his back pocket and wiped his eyes. His friend had just come back to his seat and, extending a large hand, grabbed the other man's shoulder. Both stayed silent for a while.

"Have you heard anything?"

"I have not checked again. They said they would call as soon as they had found him."

"Yes, well. Do you trust them?"

The man next to Henry shrugged his shoulders.

"I tried to get close but there are coppers everywhere."

His friend nodded.

"I supposed they have to get to the people injured and to the …"

The friend's voice trailed. He could not bring himself to speak about death.

"The hospitals near Paddington are not responding either. Frankie always calls me after an interview. He was so proud. He thought he might get the job."

"He is a good son, your lad."

The man next to Henry took his handkerchief out of his pocket again. His mobile rang and he froze. He hesitated for a few seconds. Did he really want to know? He grabbed the phone and listened. The voice on the other side was clearly familiar as his entire body slumped.

"I don't know yet. No, Frankie hasn't come back. Look, I need to keep the line clear."

He ended the call and placed the mobile slowly on the counter torn between the respite of hope and the despair of not knowing.

Henry's food had arrived but remained untouched, his glass still full. There would be no escape. He closed his eyes in an effort to still himself. He could stand and go, but where to – another bar, another club, another country? None of these would bring him peace. He felt the agony of the man sitting next to him. No cause was good enough to inflict so much pain.

How far and why had he been involved in this madness? He wanted to know, the money, the planning? A few hours ago, Bobby's statement had read like a jumble of incoherence. Bobby, always the weakest link of the three and yet prepared to die for his cause and his friends.

The two men next to Henry had left. As they did, the barman refused their money. He just wanted to have news of Frankie when it came.

Henry looked at his food. He had toyed with it, moving a piece of omelette round his plate. He put it in his mouth and chewed it a little. But the taste of food no longer interested him.

Henry's attention returned to Bobby. His friend's confession had been madness and yet Bobby was convinced. Albert was a threat, the takeover a rigged exercise – and they had their old plan. Bobby was losing his mind. He had never discussed the impact of the peace process on his friends. Liam and he spoke less frequently than they used to. He had not mentioned Bobby in months. Henry paid his money into the fund structure he had created. He felt he was doing his bit, a convenient illusion. Bobby had lied. Did he want to know why? The imaginary calls with Henry, the revival of the old plan, the briefcase. Henry rubbed his hands over his tired face. He looked at his watch. It was 4am and the little bar was still half full. Charlie would be waiting for him until the club shut. With both his friends in jail, would he flee again, the way he had when he fled to London, the way he had a few hours ago from Paddington? He looked at his watch again in a mechanical fashion. He still had a few hours before the sun rose.

Chapter Twenty-Seven

The weather had changed so dramatically that Henry wondered whether he had walked into a brand new country. The canal path was peaceful, a few people walking their dogs or riding their bikes. The cab had dropped Henry on Upper Street Islington. Henry Crowne was now strolling along the footpath. He knew where he was going. It had come to him gradually – the answer had always been there waiting for him to acknowledge. He would soon reach his destination and in a few hours it would be over. He was glad of it.

* * *

Nancy woke with a jolt. Her phone was ringing. She answered with an unsteady hello and recognised Pole's voice.

"Have I woken you up?" Pole sounded exhausted.

"Do not worry, Inspector. At least I have had some sleep which sounds more than can be said for you," replied Nancy, grateful for his call.

"Henry has been spotted in Hackney but we seem to have lost him."

"I should try to find him before the Squad does," said Nancy. The idea had come to her yesterday as she'd been searching for clues amongst Henry's account of his past.

"Well, if you do find him before we do then please make sure he does not do anything stupid."

Despite the dire situation, Nancy could detect the smile in Pole's voice.

"Inspector, this is precisely why I intend to find him before you do," replied Nancy with determination. "I will let you know, and Inspector," Nancy changed her tone of voice for what she needed to say should be said only among friends. "I could not have had a better partner on the case than you."

She did not wait for Pole's reply. Yes, she knew where to find Henry.

* * *

The bench was in full sun. Henry had reached his final destination. He had been sitting there for a while now, resting against the back of the bench, his legs folded underneath him, hands stretched over his thighs. His mind had wandered down strange avenues since he had left Paddington. He must soon look, consider, measure the extent of the devastation but for now he was content to bask in the sun. For a few seconds more, he wanted to enjoy the simplicity of life.

He felt her presence before she laid her long-fingered hand on his back.

"Am I that predictable?" asked Henry, without looking round at her.

"No, we spoke about your first few months in London when you arrived from Ireland. You said you had escaped as far away as you could from Kilburn and decided on London Fields," replied Nancy calmly.

"Mmmmm," nodded Henry.

Nancy sat beside him, she was looking in the same direction.

"The cops will be here soon," said Henry in a low voice.

"We have a bit of time."

Henry nodded again.

"How bad?"

"You mean the—?"

"Yes," he did not want her to speak the word.

"Last count forty-seven dead, over sixty wounded."

Henry grabbed his thighs and squeezed hard, digging into his flesh but pain was no release. A question was burning him alive and yet how could he formulate it?

"Probably an Al-Qaeda splinter group, videos were posted on YouTube and sent to the press shortly before the explosion," said Nancy.

Henry inhaled deeply and forced himself to utter the words.

"Any IRA connections?"

Nancy hesitated for a fraction of a second too long before giving her answer.

"Nothing concrete."

"Which means, they supplied some of the logistics," Henry concluded without hesitation.

He looked at her for the first time since she had arrived. The intensity and pain of his look startled her.

"But we are not sure yet," she replied.

"You don't need to be sure Nancy. I know."

He shivered, the sun was still shining on his bench but the deepest cold had settled in his chest. It was time. He had been looking for words that could describe the turmoil within. And it had come to him in the dark alley in Hackney, in the little cafe he had never visited before amongst people he did not know.

He was too tired to be angry, too tired to nurture the will to destroy, a desire so intense that it negated life itself.

"I am scared, I expect you know that," said Henry.

"It is not easy to look at truth in the face, Henry."

"I am scared, I am going to pretend again I can fight this."

Nancy did not reply.

"It is time to be honest and I am not sure I know how anymore," carried on Henry.

"I could try to give you more advice or say that it takes time but that would be bullshit."

Henry managed a smile; he loved it when she swore.

"Can I ask you for something that sounds crazy? A sort of final wish before they send me to prison and throw away the key," said Henry.

Nancy nodded.

"Buy the painting, *The Raft of the Medusa*."

"Now? Why?" replied Nancy.

"Because I never want to forget. I understand what you said a few days ago about *The Raft*. It is the first piece of art that means a lot to me, no, I think it is me."

"Is it?"

"Yes, and I am tired. Tired of hating so much, tired of succumbing to the impulse that destroys."

He no longer wanted to inflict pain, a pain that could never be soothed. The word atonement had come to him with sudden and unexpected clarity.

Henry's attention switched to some movement in the far distance. The forms moving towards them had not escaped Nancy either.

"Shall we do this?"

"If you are ready, I am ready too," replied Nancy.

She had stood up.

"Remember I am not only your brief," said Nancy with kind

determination, "I am your friend. I am with you all the way."

Henry stood up too.

"Even after all this?"

"Even after all this."

They moved together towards the south side of the park. Men in uniforms were approaching them.

* * *

"Did he sign a confession?" asked Nancy.

Pole started walking the corridor with her.

"Did the Counterterrorist guys not let you see him at all after his arrest?" asked Pole, half surprised.

"Henry is not exactly thinking straight at the moment. I had to be the one informing Pritchard, his defence lawyer."

Nancy stopped to face Pole. "I don't think he cares much about what he has actually done but what he thinks he has done."

"What do you want me to do? The case is no longer in my jurisdiction," replied Pole calmly.

"Do you think it stacks up altogether? I don't, but I can't exactly tell you why," replied Nancy hoping she would catch Pole's attention.

"You're his legal counsel. It's your job to get your theory checked out," retorted Pole.

"Come on Jonathan!"

"You've got your instinct, I've got mine, Ms Wu," said Pole smiling at the elegant woman in front of him. "You don't think I am going to roll over so easily do you?"

"*Bien sûr que non.*"

Nancy smiled in return, she could indulge him. Pole blushed slightly but changed the tone.

"You never finished your story about Jacques Vergès," said Pole.

Nancy slowed the pace and took her time to gauge Pole's intentions.

"Vergès is one of the reasons I stopped practising. He contacted me when Tariq Aziz, Saddam Hussein's minister, included him in his defence team. I nearly said yes."

"What stopped you?" asked Pole amazed at the revelation.

"It was one step too far. I was so tempted by the challenge. I tried to reconcile this with my belief that all deserve legal representation but it was pure ego and nothing else I feared."

They had arrived at Pole's office. Nurani stood up to join them but Pole shut the door after Nancy. He would have this discussion on his own.

"Ms Wu, the facts are overwhelming."

"Call me Nancy," she said.

"OK, Nancy," replied Pole emphasising her name. "Let's recap on the evidence. Henry has for many years contributed to a 'charity' which we know is in reality a slush fund for the IRA. Fact. Furthermore, we know that he is the mastermind behind the legal structure, also fact."

Nancy nodded in acknowledgement.

"He has admitted concocting a plan, albeit many years ago, to bring down an executive aircraft with his pals Liam and Bobby. Fact."

"Agreed."

"We also know that his two friends are members of the new faction IRA and, contrary to expectation, they have not 'retired'. Liam and Henry have stayed in contact since they were children. OK, the contact with Bobby is less strong but he is always in the background. And we also know that Liam and Henry saw each other only a few days before Albert's plane came down."

Pole was about to continue but Nancy interrupted.

"Just so we are clear, I am not contesting this. Henry should not have contributed to this slush fund, it was stupid, in fact more than stupid. It was disgraceful altogether, but—"

"We have Bobby's confession."

"Which I find extremely tenuous," finished Nancy.

"In what way?

"As far as I can tell, they never spoke face to face about it."

"You mean always through text or phone call."

"Precisely."

"That may be a very good technique to distance oneself from Bobby. He is an unpredictable guy to say the least."

"Yes, maybe," replied Nancy unconvinced. "But it still leaves evidence behind and Henry can perfectly well justify at least one other trip to Ireland without arousing suspicions."

Pole did not reply. She could feel a shift.

"Someone else could have made those calls," she ventured.

"You would have to be able to fool Bobby very well." But Pole did not reject the idea as preposterous.

"Well, Henry has taken elocution lessons to get rid of his Irish accent. This would shape his voice in a particular way. I am a barrister. I can tell the impact these lessons have on someone's voice."

"OK, let's assume that we have one element of illogical and inconsistent behaviour. It is still unbelievably slim but what else?" replied Pole, this time more encouragingly.

"Jonathan, you are going to have to help me a bit there. Please?"

"All right," Pole replied. "The one element I find not completely conclusive, which is key to this entire story, is the delivery of the bomb."

Nancy was all ears.

"Forensic tells us that the bomb was small but powerful enough to be contained in a small space. Anthony Albert took away a briefcase from Henry's flat, more precisely from Henry's block of flats. We can't confirm that he actually entered Henry's flat."

"Bobby says in his statement that he left the briefcase in Henry's garage but never saw him take it. It is a hell of a risk to leave a live bomb unattended," said Nancy.

Pole nodded and extricated a heavy file from the piles of documents laying on his desk. He enjoyed working methodically with Nancy through the evidence.

"Henry could have, again, calculated that he did not want to be seen with Bobby but I agree it is a huge risk to take. Even for a short period of time, who would want to leave an unattended bomb in the basement? Henry now remembers meeting with Albert to give him the case but can't tell us exactly what happened. Yet Henry has an excellent memory."

Nancy stood up and walked to the window. She was looking at the Thames, letting herself gather her thoughts. She turned around to face Pole.

"And yet he has confessed."

"And yet he has confessed," repeated Pole, "and the Counterterrorist Squad need to score quickly. The latest carnage in Paddington, right on their doorstep, does not give them much of an option."

They remained silent.

"No other credible leads by the way," confirmed Pole, anticipating Nancy's next question.

Pole suddenly stopped in his tracks. Nancy read the change on his face.

"Is this worth mentioning?" she hesitated, not wanting to interrupt what could be a vital train of thought. Pole did not answer but grabbed the phone.

"Dolores, what did Adeila exactly say about the will? Yes, sorry. Hi."

Pole grimaced, indicating a major lapse in common courtesy.

"OK."

216

Pole took some notes on a pad that was perched on a pile of documents.

"Could I please have Adeila's number?" finished Pole, after listening to what Dolores had to say.

Pole put the phone down and immediately dialled another number.

"Good afternoon, may I speak to Mrs Albert please?" Pole switched on the loudspeaker.

"It is she," replied Adeila's polished voice.

"Inspector Pole here, I am sorry to disturb you but would you have a moment?"

Pole half expected Adeila to put the phone down but she volunteered a short go ahead. Pole decided there was little merit in spinning out his question and went straight to the point.

"You mentioned to my colleague Dolores Patten that you expected your husband to leave you very little in his will when he died. It might be a little too literal in which case I apologise profusely, but was there any reason why you thought he might die soon?"

"No need to apologise, Inspector," replied Adeila. "I used the term because I knew Anthony was dying. He had a terminal illness which he tried to conceal from everyone." Adeila continued unprompted. "You may ask how I knew. Well, I am sure you have done your job thoroughly, Inspector, and you must know that Anthony had an affair a little while ago. I decided to check regularly his conversation after this and had a private agency firm install a recording device in his office at home. A very boring conversation in the main, Anthony really lacked imagination. However, I learned about his illness that way together with the content of his will."

Pole and Nancy were taking in the information, already envisaging all the possibilities it contained.

"Are you still there, Inspector?" asked Adeila, somewhat amused.

"So sorry, yes of course."

"I am glad to hear I have silenced you for once. Anthony was treated in Switzerland."

"It would be incredibly helpful if you could–"

"… give you the address of the clinic?" interrupted Adeila. "Give me a few moments."

Pole could hear movements at the end of the phone. Adeila gave him the details he needed and hung up with little more than a surprising good luck.

"How can this help?" asked Nancy.

"I don't know yet, it may be nothing, but I need to understand what happened in Switzerland."

He stopped, and Nancy realised that her time with him was over. She stood up.

"You will let me know?"

"Of course, I'll keep you posted," replied Pole with a reassuring smile.

She put her hand on the door handle and turned back before opening.

"Why do we believe in Henry's innocence? *Oui, pourquoi?*"

"*Ma chere Nancy, je crois que nous avons la même réponse,*" said Pole, in his impeccable French.

Pole dialled the number of the clinic in Switzerland that had been treating Anthony Albert for the past few months.

* * *

Henry walked through the doors and the warden removed his handcuffs. Nancy felt a shock when she saw him wearing the standard prison track suit. His hair had turned silver overnight but his face looked calm, maybe resigned, she was not yet sure.

She stood up to greet him. He waved a quick hello and sat across the table but said nothing more.

"I saw Pole this morning. We learned something new," she hesitated.

Nothing of what she could say was going to change the path he had decided to embark on. As Henry remained silent Nancy decided to continue.

"Anthony Albert was terminally ill."

"So, are you trying to tell me that terminating his life a tad early was a form of mercy killing?" said Henry springing back to life. "How about the pilot of the plane, was he also terminally ill?"

This is more like it, thought Nancy, ignoring Henry's aggressive tone.

"No, I am simply giving you the facts."

"Nothing you can say, Nancy, will change the fact that I have killed these guys."

Nancy was about to reply but Henry cut her short.

"I don't care whether this is directly, indirectly, whether Bobby was a sicko who heard voices. I have known that all my life, I kept meeting them, I kept giving money. I also knew the reason, so what does that make me? A guy who thinks he still has principles because he sticks to his old school friends, a guy who believes in a cause? That's a lot of bullshit, a feel good

218

factor as long as things don't go wrong or I don't know the bloody details. I did what I did."

"No one is contesting that, Henry, but pay for what you did, not for what you think you did," replied Nancy, her tone matching Henry's.

"You have never seen a man die in–" started Henry, through gritted teeth and could not complete his sentence, the lump in his throat too large for him to continue.

"Yes, I have, bodies torn apart, the smell of blood. Do not assume you are the only one who knows about savage killings," Nancy retorted with more vehemence than he had ever heard before.

The anger and anxiety in her voice shocked Henry. They both remained silent, facing each other and not able to say any more.

"Then you know," concluded Henry.

She said nothing. He needed to find his truth. She knew the validity of the search. She would for her part keep doubting. Her intuition told her that Henry's story had not been fully unravelled yet.

* * *

Pole was standing in front of the fax machine. Documents were pouring in from Switzerland. His police contact had managed to convince the doctors in Geneva to lift the doctor-patient confidentiality. The word terrorism had done the trick again. Everything he had received so far confirmed Anthony Albert's condition. He had indeed reached the terminal phase of his illness with possibly less than six months to live. Albert had been diagnosed two years earlier and was going to Switzerland regularly for treatment. His job had brought him regularly to Geneva so no one ever suspected. Pole thought about the sheer willpower the man must have had to endure treatment and carry on his job. Rumours, of course, had circulated in the City that a lot of what he had structured was linked to the subprime market. Then again, he probably would not have cared a damn. Pole looked at the documents churning out and gave an irritated grunt. They were hardly legible. He walked back into his office, shut the door and dialled Nancy's number.

Pole had dialled from his hands-free set. He would pick up if she answered. The phone rang four times and a small click indicated that the answer phone would kick in any second:

"Oh dear! You've just missed me but fear not I will call you back as soon as I can, *et pour les Anglophiles non Anglophones,*" chimed Nancy's voice.

The message carried on in French, a story about Anglophiles not being Anglophones followed, bringing a smile on Pole's face. He needed a trip back to his roots in Aquitaine. Pole disliked having to leave concise messages on voicemails and was preparing to deliver a witty response.

"*Chère Madame Wu, mes hommages*. I am devastated I have just missed you but if you could—"

Nancy's elegant voice took over.

"*Mon cher* Jonathan, I thought we agreed you would call me Nancy."

Pole let out a short laugh.

"*Trés bien, avec plaisir*, Nancy, I am sorry to disturb you but I think I need a little help."

"I am all ears, Jonathan."

"It is proving rather difficult to obtain the documents we need from the Swiss Clinic. Using my natural charm does not seem to work, and my French has become a little rusty."

"And you would like me to add a certain *je ne sais quoi* to your natural charm," said Nancy.

"*Voila*," exclaimed Pole

"The number please, I will call you as soon as I have results."

* * *

Nancy was navigating a number of options to find the right correspondent. A young voice finally answered. She introduced herself to her *interlocutrice*, now using her perfect French. She was one of the lawyers on the Crowne-Albert Case, she explained, and was asking for a copy of all documentation that had been sent to the police. This was a matter of urgency. It was imperative that she should have access to all relevant material.

"I am very sorry," replied the voice, "but these documents are patient notes, some of them handwritten and subject to doctor-patient confidentiality."

"Of course, I can see your dilemma but you must remember that I am also subject to the same rules as you are. Lawyers always are. You could check my registration with chambers," carried on Nancy in an affable but determined voice. "It is essential for the case that we understand the extent of Mr Albert's illness."

"Well, if I could check your registration, I could courier a copy to you, this might work better," yielded the young voice.

"Very kind of you," replied Nancy as she gave Pritchard QC's number.

She would make a call and Pritchard would back her up. Nancy was calmly giving her old friend's chambers details when she felt she could press on with more questions.

"I need to complete my findings as soon as possible. It is a rather unusual case," she ventured.

"I read the story in the news. It is unbelievable that one of our patients could be involved in such a terrible thing. At least, Mr Albert was at peace with himself."

"I am so glad to hear this," replied Nancy.

Perhaps she could encourage the young woman to say more.

"It is an unusual thing to see coming from someone like Mr Albert," said Nancy tentatively.

"I did not know him so well you see," replied the voice in earnest, "but I go to the chapel very often with patients. It is a lovely place in our gardens, always full of flowers and so peaceful."

"*Et bien Mademoiselle*, you used to care for Anthony Albert?"

"Mr Albert was a very private man, but last time I looked after him he was spending a lot of time there. It was unusual because I'd never seen him there before. He looked … relieved. People come to terms differently with the end of life." She stopped abruptly, afraid she might be embarrassing the other woman with her remarks.

"I can see Mr Albert was in good hands. This is very comforting. Although he spoke little it must have been important to have a confidant."

"Well, he only spoke much about his children. When he did he was always transformed. I think he was at the end at peace with what would happen when …" again her voice trailed.

"I am taking much of your time, *encore un grand merci*," concluded Nancy.

What had Albert done next? He was not a religious man. Why such need for deep thoughts, the will? But that had been changed a few months prior.

She thanked the young woman profusely and dialled Pole's number. Pole needed to trace Albert's movements in the last few weeks before his death. Pole took the call and grabbed his mac, walking out to his unscheduled meeting in a hurry.

* * *

The tabloid press knew how to compose a headline. A pile of newspapers lay on the sofa. She was in a comfortable spot, in her favourite little coffee shop on Chancery Lane. Pole entered the place holding more papers under his arm. He had hardly had time to greet her when he saw a tantalising cup of coffee and an apricot Danish placed in front of an empty chair.

"I could have been late," he said feigning reproach.

"*Mon cher* Jonathan," replied Nancy in her best barrister voice. "You are not the type, and in any case apricot Danish turns out to be my favourite too."

Pole changed the subject, fearing he would make some corny remark.

"I presume you have read all there is to read about McCarthy's arrest?"

"Extremely precise reporting, for once the papers have done a good job of investigatory journalism. The explanations of what has happened are well researched. I suspect they had a lot of help from Whitehall."

"You mean about the large subprime business GL was running?"

"More to the point, the ridiculously large losses GL were trying to hide, at least until the merger was completed – $51 billion all told, unthinkable."

"Henry never touched that stuff, though."

"True but he knew something was up. The minute McCarthy brought the CDO team from Credit Suisse First Boston, he had doubts. McCarthy should have played his cards even closer to his chest."

"CDO?" questioned Pole.

"Collateralised Debt Obligation – product packaged with subprime loans," Nancy replied confidently.

"Extremely dodgy stuff I take it. Henry mentioned them I now remember, and before you ask, yes, we will have a chat with McCarthy about Anthony Albert and his CDOs business, although my feeling is that it won't yield anything."

"Much to my disappointment, I think you are right."

"Nancy – you mentioned Whitehall?" said Pole enjoying the use of her name.

"Ah yes, Whitehall. They know the party is coming to an end. A few economists disagreed with the government, in particular one of Tony Blair's advisers. Whitehall understand how out of touch politicians can be with real economic data. One way to monitor the real state of the economy is to let some of the City bosses court them in return for, let's say, a few favours."

"How do you know that?" said Pole in disbelief.

"The judiciary is always close to the civil service." She raised her cup of coffee with a grin.

"I am surprised that none of the papers mention Henry."

"Well, the Counterterrorist Squad is keeping a keen eye on what is being published I assume. I am also sure they do not want to advertise that they lost Henry when he was wreaking havoc at GL."

"You have a point."

"I do, very much so," said Nancy and this time Pole raised his cup of coffee.

"Enough about Whitehall. How about Switzerland?" said Nancy, ready for a much-needed update.

"Albert seemed to have behaved oddly shortly before the crash," replied Pole.

He took another sip of coffee and gave Nancy a full account.

"When will you have the results from the tapes?"

"The Swiss have a reputation for being slow but thorough, however they understand the urgency."

"Jonathan, that is not an answer," Nancy frowned.

"When is Henry's preliminary hearing?"

"Two weeks."

"That soon."

"He has confessed, remember?" said Nancy.

"I will see what I can do."

Pole took a sip of his coffee.

"Remember this is Geneva, jewellery shops everywhere so … there is a hell of a lot to go through."

Nancy nodded. The next few days would be uncomfortably quiet.

* * *

To Nancy's surprise, Pam Anderson's PA had managed to find a slot in Pam's overflowing diary, Nancy had braced herself for an exacting conversation. Pam had returned Nancy's call within a few hours simply giving her the choice of a couple of dates. Pam Anderson wanted to speak, Nancy concluded.

The lobby of Chase and Case was predictably large and possibly a little old fashioned. Nancy had decided to sit in one of the armchairs that enabled her to watch the toing and froing of Chase and Case's clientele.

She was observing with interest a small podgy man who had taken over the cluster of sofas next to her. He had arrived, ordered a coffee from the staff at reception and extricated from his briefcase two BlackBerrys, a small laptop and a number of financial newspapers. He was happily conducting his business in the middle of the lobby, his voice carrying right across the space. He did not seem to care.

Nancy saw her from afar. She instantly knew it was Pam and smiled. She saw herself as she was all those years ago as a young and ambitious lawyer. She could also see that Henry would have enjoyed being with her. There was something harmonious about her presence, the slightly less severe suit and the unexpected details of a colourful brooch pinned to her jacket.

Pam extended a slight but decisive hand. She shook Nancy's and both women walked out of the lobby.

"Let's go to the Barbican's cafe," suggested Nancy.

"Agreed, it will be quiet at this time of day."

Pam had been thinking about the meeting with Nancy and had something to say that mattered or at least mattered to her..

The cafe was empty. They chose a couple of armchairs in a secluded corner.

"Thank you for seeing me so quickly," started Nancy.

"The least I can do. How is he?", she said, finding it hard to speak Henry's name.

"Well, I would be lying to you if I said he is fine." Nancy could not pretend.

"You know about the QC," interrupted Pam.

"You mean Wooster QC's sabbatical? Yes, I do."

"I am so sorry," continued Pam in a shaky voice. "I have kept thinking about it again and again."

Nancy was taken aback by her tone of voice. She extended a hand and gently reached for Pam's arm.

"Pritchard QC is a friend and a very competent man."

"I know, but Henry was a friend too. I should have done more."

She turned her head away.

"A friend …"

It was unkind to be exploiting this sudden rush of honesty but she needed to know more.

"Any details, anything you can tell me that might help Henry."

Pam nodded. She inhaled and sat back a little.

"That is why I wanted to speak to you." Pam's voice had recovered some composure. "I will say this to you in confidence."

Pam stopped and Nancy took over.

"I understand, Henry won't know."

"Well, it was at the closing in Dublin. Has Henry ever told you about his best success?"

"He has, worth several billion dollars. You were there as his lawyer and so was Anthony Albert, if I remember correctly."

Pam blushed and glanced away.

"We had an affair." She was still looking away.

"You and Henry?"

"No." Pam was now facing Nancy with wide open eyes. "… Anthony."

Nancy was speechless. She let the information sink in and suddenly a million questions rushed into her mind, jealousy, passion, revenge.

"Did Henry find out?"

"No."

"Are you certain?"

"Nothing changed between us after the closing and Henry would never have tolerated …"

Pam could not say any more and Nancy recognised the suffering that unspoken love can cause. She could not reconcile why Pam would have an affair with Albert when it was clear that she loved Henry.

"Before you ask about me and Henry … there has never been anything."

"Because he was your biggest client."

Pam nodded.

"And because you've just been made a partner."

Pam was surprised by the forwardness of the question but she knew there was no point denying it.

"It's inconceivable but that night, in Dublin, maybe." Pam said.

Nancy bent forward a little, encouraging Pam to confide.

"Why then?"

"I thought … it was Henry. You see they have the same voice. I mean Henry and Anthony had the same voice."

"The same voice," said Nancy, trying to hide her surprise.

Nancy extended her hand and rested it onto Pam's clenched fist. She could no longer speak, the memory of her ugly affair burning in her mind. Nancy asked gently,

"Why do you think it is so material?"

"Because Anthony Albert hated Henry with such determination, I think you should know."

Nancy nodded. Pam looked at the other woman with pleading eyes but asked nothing. She slowly stood up.

"I have to go now."

Nancy stood up too and squeezed Pam's hand reassuringly.

"Thank you for your honesty."

"Just look after him."

Pam did not wait for an answer and left the Barbican café without turning back.

Chapter Twenty-Eight

"I still have not decided whether we have been unbelievably lucky or whether it would have somehow surfaced," said Nancy as Inspector Pole and she were walking rapidly along the corridors of Scotland Yard.

"I could reply that this was without doubt an excellent piece of police work," retorted Pole with a grin, "but I agree with you," he added, this time thoughtfully. "I might not have pursued it if you had not spoken to the young lady at the clinic."

They stopped in front of one of the interrogation rooms. They both knew Henry was waiting, unaware though of the content of the document he was about to read.

"What has he been told?" asked Nancy.

"Very little, apart from the fact that a letter has been recovered from Albert's lawyer in Geneva destined for him."

"And the date?"

"You mean that it was destined for him in twenty years' time rather than today."

"Yes."

"He knows."

Pole opened the door. With few formalities he placed a handwritten note in front of Henry.

It read:

I nearly started this letter with Dear Henry. How conditioned can one be, even in one's last hours? You are anything to me Henry but dear, of course, but you know that and you don't care.

By the time you open this letter a good twenty years should have lapsed, a long, long time to reflect on the human condition. It has taken a lot less than that for me to come to terms with mine.

You see, Henry, I have little time to live, six months at most says the Doc. I was told I could do so much in six months. What a joke! He does not understand men like us, he does not feel power and ambition the way we do. He does not see that a man who has lost everything he once valued, who has been stripped bare, has nothing left to him but his burning ambition. My wife thinks that I am uncouth, unsophisticated, the son of an immigrant that has never evolved to be the upper class man she wishes for, a lowlife that can barely keep her in style. My children hardly speak to me, although I suspect it is their mother's doing. You will never understand this, Henry, as your ego precludes you from loving anyone. But I would die for them, no, I am dying for them. They won't see me in my final hours, a body hooked to a machine, stripped of all dignity. In the meantime, I have become the stranger who signs the cheques and sleeps in the spare room.

So what's left? The job, but even that is no longer enough. I want what you have Henry, all of it! Why? Because I can. For all your intelligence, your immense ambition and the violence underneath, you are not a killer, Henry, but me … I am.

Did you know that I did a deal with McCarthy? Actually, by the time you read this you might have figured it out. He was so easy to convince, so wrapped up in his desire to have more, to be more, to hide all the shitty deals we did together and still be the hero of the day. I would never have lived long enough to enjoy it, the merged teams under MY NAME, so I did what I had to do.

You probably are starting to have a hint, aren't you? Can you feel on the back of your neck your hairs bristle, the slight churn in your stomach? Yes … I know you can.

So, let me tell you how it all started.

You must remember the famous closing dinner in Dublin. Everyone wondered why I was there, celebrating with you. I know, I had little to do with this god damned incredibly 'oh so clever' deal of yours and boy you did not let me forget that for one minute.

I don't think you spoke to me once but you sure spoke enough about me. By the time we all rolled to the pub you were so fucking drunk (champagne and glory are a very lethal mix) that you had finally forgotten I was there. And then it happened, your two pals, Bobby and Liam. You might have been more cautious another day but on that day of splendour you did not care.

So you poured Guinness down their throats, introduced them around. I listened, I observed, I saw an opportunity. Which one I did not know yet. I can still play the foreigner role when it suits me, I forget this altogether in the City, as you have done yourself, but there in Dublin I felt Italian again.

Liam was cautious, but somehow the gate opened up. I played the oppressed Catholic and he got friendly with me, me – your worst enemy. Bobby was getting stoned in the corner of the bar and he blabbed about the IRA. He must have scored on some good stuff and he was on a high at seeing his friend (you, Henry). He, Bobby, knew the real Henry, the City was only a cover up. What a treat this all was.

Then came the icing on the cake, if I may say. Did you know as an aside that you and I have the same voice? Partially the result of taking elocution lessons I presume, the other quirky twist of fate, at least according to the lovely Pam. I know you fancied her and I can tell you she sure did you, oh boy! But I am afraid … I got there first.

She tans in the nude by the way.

So now we have the ingredients. What am I going to do with them?

But you don't decide to do what I did suddenly, the idea slowly creeps into your mind. It does not emerge in one go, it tentatively surfaces, alternatives shock you, they come and go and you become daring. You are amazed that you can think the unthinkable and then The Plan hits you with its logical, implacable certainty. Its insanity leaves you speechless but it fascinates you. Will you dare? Will you pull it off? Will you see it through to the bitter end? If you are reading this letter then I guess I succeeded. I simply hope that in Hell where I belong I will be able to see your face when you read. But enough indulgence, back to The Plan.

I bought a top-up mobile phone, simple, untraceable and I dialled Bobby's number. For some ridiculous reason Bobby insisted on giving it to me before we left the pub, he was too smashed to care, I loved the deceit. Bobby told me he was depressed at the thought of the IRA decommissioning, a sell-out, a surrender. I stirred him up a bit, it was not difficult, so we nearly became pals. He told me a lot about you and your childhood in Belfast. I nearly felt sorry for you, not for long mind. I have no mercy, remember, neither have you.

So I called Bobby. When he replied I nearly hung up but lovely Pam had me convinced that our voices were the same and it worked. Your best pal, your childhood friend, could not tell the difference, what a coup! I had a good old rant at the fucking bastard who wanted my business and Bobby got onto it straight away. The Plan, Your Plan to bomb a small executive aircraft back in the day. I had agonised for hours, how was I going to convince him and it was there all ready to fly (excuse the pun, I am a dying man)?

So he reminded me of The Plan, in all its details committed to memory by Bobby, everything was there, impeccably thought through. I nearly got jealous, but then again, I should be graceful in victory.

The rest was easy, the money, the timing, the secrecy from Liam. For someone who looks so wasted, Bobby is pretty focused when it comes to killing. He followed my instructions to the letter, no question. I even got him to agree to leave the briefcase in your garage without us meeting – if only all my staff were as well trained.

It was easy to leave you the odd email and cryptic message that would confuse the coppers. The most difficult part will be transporting the briefcase. I have to bring a live bomb home. Adeila is wondering why I want the kids to board that week. She is a nosy bitch that one. I had a warm feeling at the idea of blowing up half of Belgravia but that would leave you off the hook – I could not do that, I'm afraid.

The airport will then be easy, I know the guys so well. The car will drop me just at the bottom of the aircraft stairs. I fly too often with them to be considered a security risk – how touching.

I will die a brutal and remarked death and you will be my unwilling murderer. In time you might even believe you did it Henry ... until you open this letter that is and then, well ...

Here we are, Henry, you alive but barely, and me dead, thankfully.

Don't be fooled by my earlier comment, I don't believe in Hell. I walked through its gates when I was born and will check out in a few days' time, oblivion awaits. Anthony A.

Henry closed his eyes, the letter dropped from his shaking hands.

A very small but painful tear rolled from his eye, traced the side of his nose in a slow but certain journey. It finished its course upon his lips, a sad, salty kiss.

Words swam: pain, freedom, hatred, peace, revenge ... and when he opened his eyes only one sentiment remained. Forgiveness

BOOK TWO:
BREAKING PO!NT

Chapter One

The room stood up and erupted into applause. Nancy joined them, crossed the platform and clasped Edwina's hand warmly. She grinned at her friend. Yes, Edwina had delivered a trailblazing speech that had provoked a robust Q&A session. She could soon be joining the most powerful women in the world, tipped to become the next Governor of the Bank of England. Edwina had discussed the offer with Nancy, in confidence.

The Women in Enterprise Conference had become the highlight in the calendar of professional women striving to make their mark not only in international investment banking but also now in the whole of the UK industry. The conference theme was the reworking of an old chestnut 'How women break the glass ceiling'. But the developing financial crisis had given it a new twist … Would all this have happened had women been at the helm? To give the debate more bite, high-profile men had been invited. The panel was well constructed, a mix of captains of industry and bankers. Nancy, the newly appointed Chair of Women in Enterprise, had agreed to act as moderator. The atmosphere had been electric as senior ladies in the audience had taken a gloves-off approach and the gentlemen were having none of it.

"One final question … one."

A sea of hands shot up, waving, snapping, eager to attract Nancy's attention.

"The *FT* will have a last say tonight … Pauline, go ahead please."

"A question for Edwina. Christine Lagarde is the Managing Director of the International Monetary Fund, Janet Yellen is almost certainly going to be appointed by Obama as Head of the Federal Reserve. Is the Bank of England ready for a woman at the helm?"

Edwina stood up again, moving back to the lectern at a slow deliberate pace.

"Any institution, private or public must consider the best outcome for what it needs to deliver. Talent will be found in a pool of diverse people and the most forward-looking organisations will not shy away from it." A roar of approvals interrupted. "I know what you are asking me Pauline – indirectly. I have only this answer – *may the best of us win.*"

How clever, Nancy thought. *An answer that will inspire the women, appease the men and say nothing about her, quite simply brilliant.*

Nancy had been a high-profile barrister practising criminal law, then became the youngest ever appointed QC at the age of thirty-five. For a very long time she had thought talent should prevail. But the latest report on lack of progress in female status had pushed her to advocate for set quotas for women at all levels of the corporate structure.

Edwina had concluded the debate with a final flash of genius. The voice of a woman who could inspire by her exemplary career.

"Thank you," Nancy said. "Thank you for the extraordinary show of support." She was broadly smiling at them and turned to Edwina with a nod. "It has been an exceptional event. I must again thank the participants for the quality of their intervention and for the quality of the audience input."

The room erupted once more.

"I know, I know," said Nancy whilst trying to appease the crowd gesturing with both hands. "Please, you know it is not completely over. We still have drinks – much-needed – waiting for us next door. You can strike up a conversation with our guests. Do be gentle with some of them!"

The room broke into laughter and the men in the audience took it in good humour. The protagonists were returning their clip-microphones to the staff. Edwina approached Nancy.

"I think it's in the bag."

"It certainly is. Did Gabriel work with you on this? I detect a forceful yet compromising approach in your speech."

"Yes, Gabs helped me … No, I meant THE appointment. Osborne spoke to me."

Nancy grinned. "Oh, I see. We must catch up. I am excited for you."

"We must, but agreed, not the place. Let's do lunch."

"Do let's – utterly delighted for you, Eddie."

Nancy moved away and started circulating amongst a crowd of women gathered on the roof terrace of 1 Poultry. She was mobbed by a group of enthusiastic young lawyers eager to speak about her experience as a QC. She finally moved on and was about to join one of the panellists, CEO of a notorious airline, when someone grabbed her arm.

"Do you really believe in that bullshit of yours?" a voice slurred. The large man was standing too close for comfort. He swayed slightly, moved backward. His small beady eyes narrowed in a vengeful squint.

"And who do I have the pleasure of speaking to?" replied Nancy whilst slowly removing his hand from her arm.

"Gary Cook, former head of trading at GL – courtesy of one of your females."

"I doubt any of these females are mine as you put it," replied Nancy.

"Yeah right, but you – you and your little friends are not whiter than white; you lot are trying to say you are better than blokes on the trading floor. That's bollocks and I can prove it." Gary's heavy jaws had clenched so hard a muscle in his neck leaped out. He had not finished yet.

"I say, how clever of you. Not whiter than white – with my Chinese ancestry that is going to be rather certain."

"Gary Cook," exclaimed a voice from behind Nancy. "Great to see you again."

Gary stopped in his tracks. The unexpected welcome confused him; then again the person who had greeted him was another man. The well-groomed young man interposed himself effortlessly between Gary and Nancy who slowly retreated. There was no point in making a scene. Gary was a loser who should not be humoured. Nancy could hear the smooth Gabriel holding the man's anger, absorbing it until it had subsided completely. Edwina had chosen well: Gabriel Steel was an impressive right-hand man. He manoeuvred Gary towards a more secluded part of the roof terrace, called for more drinks. Nancy was not sure Gary needed more champagne but no doubt Gabriel would move him gradually towards the exit and Gary would eventually take the hint. A small tremor of revulsion ran through Nancy's body. She had not recognised Gary's old and bitter face. She rubbed her hand against her dress but she needed more than that to wash away the stickiness of Gary's feel.

She entered the ladies' room briskly, lathered her hands with sandalwood-scented soap and ran cold water over them watching the foam disappear down the plug hole. An apt image of where Gary ought to end up one day. She retraced her steps but before turning into the corridor someone grabbed her shoulder. Edwina was standing close to her.

"Just had an email from George Osborne's PA. Final meeting in a couple of days' time," Edwina whispered. "Perhaps a little coaching may be warranted?"

"I somehow feel the student has surpassed the master," Nancy murmured, smiling. "But of course, I am there for you if you feel the need."

"Very much so." Edwina squeezed Nancy's shoulder gently and let go at the sound of voices coming their way.

Both women emerged from the corridor separately and as she reappeared Nancy found herself mobbed once more by a group of enthusiastic women ... the banking industry had to change its ways. One of the young women mentioned the name Henry Crowne. She must have done her homework as to who Nancy was. Nancy returned the question with a frosty look. She would not be discussing Henry at this conference or anywhere else for that matter. Then a whirlpool of questions swept her away, away from Gary and Henry.

* * *

There was only a small group of people left by now and Nancy was about to say her goodbyes when two uniformed officers walked through the elevator doors alighting directly onto the terrace.

One of the officers bent his head towards his shoulder radio set.

"Yes, I am on the roof now. There are a few people still up here."

A disembodied voice replied. Nancy thought she heard the instructions *keep them there*.

"Sorry ladies, I am PC Barrett and this is PC Leonard. We have a jumper ..."

The women looked at each other incredulous.

"I mean someone has jumped from the roof terrace. Dead I am afraid..." PC Barrett asked to see the guest list and the young security guard who had checked guests' names at the door produced it in an instant. PC Barrett turned away from the crowd and towards his shoulder radio, sheltering his voice.

"Yep, got it there. Yep ... Gary Cook."

Nancy had turned away, still all ears. She shuddered, Gary – *impossible*.

* * *

"One hundred and ninety-seven, ninety-eight, ninety-nine, two hundred. Shit!" puffed Henry as he rolled back onto the mat. He was nearly at the end of his routine in HMP Belmarsh gym. He needed to start stretching but he lay there for another minute. A small luxury in a place devoid of the comfort he once knew. He closed his eyes and a face appeared out of nowhere. He sat up slowly, eyes still closed. Was Liam also exercising in the prison in which he was? Northern Ireland Maghaberry was a tough place, a tough place for a tough boy. Liam would survive it but what of Bobby?

Anger gripped Henry again. He stood up abruptly and started stretching.

"Let go – just let go," he said softly, applying pressure to release the pain. His muscles screamed. He eased off the stretch a little.

The question had haunted Henry for months. Could Liam have done anything differently? Could he have chosen Henry rather than his brother Bobby? The police in Belfast would never have spared the life of Bobby, a faction IRA operative, a man for whom decommissioning had no meaning. There had to be a deal and Henry was that deal. And what a deal he was, a financial superstar, a city banker organising and contributing to the IRA's finances. Henry's stellar financial career masking his terrorist activities, how clever and daring – but how wrong.

"No – no choice," Henry murmured, wiping his face with a towel. He ran it over his hair. The standard prison cut had left very little of what had been a dense mane.

Yet, Henry had wanted to be chosen, always wanted to be the one. And this yearning had cost him everything. Beyond the sacrifice of his own career and hopes, he had also sacrificed lives, many lives, and for that he would pay.

Henry threw the towel over his shoulder, went into the changing rooms, stripped down and started showering. He had been apprehensive to start with. Would he find a fate in prison only reserved for the bastard of a banker he was? Would he be molested, beaten up and humiliated? But the fear had not materialised and it had faded away. He had learned to become unnoticeable amongst the Category A prisoners of Belmarsh. Even in prison Henry had managed to land in the highest ranks amongst cons, deemed to pose most threat to the police and national security. How competitive? Henry was high-risk too and on Nancy's advice he had played that card fully. He had been moved to a block in which cons shared the same Cat. A profile except – no bankers. Or at least not yet.

"Hey, good set of press-ups, man."

"Thanks, Big K. I plan to get really fit in the next twenty-five years."

"Man, you get good muscle tone here, you get respect."

Henry nodded, grabbed his towel and got dressed quickly. He still did not like to linger in the changing rooms. Another inmate had moved out of the showers too. Henry felt observed but when he looked up the man was facing the other way, going about his business. Henry noticed two entwined faces tattooed on his back – strange, the faces looked similar. Big K had already left but he would know who this was. Big K had been allocated the cell next to his and he had shown interest in Henry straightaway. Drugs were his domain and the term money laundering had his undivided attention. Big K was someone who knew what it meant to do time and worth cultivating with a few snippets of info.

Henry rang the buzzer, the security guard opened the door and informed the next guard that Henry was on his way to his cell, running the gauntlet of the next four doors to cross. At Belmarsh High Security Unit no two doors could be opened at the same time and Henry had learned to be patient with the procedure. Even the prison officers went through security checks when they entered for HMP Belmarsh High Security Unit was the most secure prison in the UK.

"Thanks John," Henry said. The guard nodded and let Henry into Cell 14 on Wing Three. The door shut with the usual heavy clunk and Henry sat on his bed. He looked at his watch, 9:47 AM – only thirteen minutes to mail time. He hoped for a letter from Nancy. It was too early for her to give news about her big night at Women in Enterprise but she might feed him titbits on its preparation. Once the post had been delivered, he would take down a heavy art book sitting sideways on his small bookshelf, from its thick spine he would retrieve his pride and joy – a small netsuke in the shape of a dog with pups. It had become a comforting ritual to be reading a letter from the outside world whilst fingering this small object, a piece of art that did not belong to prison life. Henry had allowed himself this luxury – he was ever such a good boy otherwise.

* * *

"The investment banker who jumped from the terrace of the fashionable city restaurant 1 Poultry has been identified as Gary Cook. He had recently lost his job in the HXBK takeover of GL," announced the Sky News presenter. "Mr Cook had spent most of his career at the bank. Our presenter Ken Rowe reports." Nancy was watching the news from a distance whilst opening her mail when the name Gary Cook stopped her in her tracks. She had offered to go down with PC Leonard to identify the body lying on the pavement.

She was after all a consultant with the Met. The vision of Gary's skull smashed and shattered on the ground had made her stomach heave. She had answered the police's questions as best she could, disturbed by the image that kept flashing in front of her eyes. Escaping to the safety and calm of her apartment had done little to soothe her. She had not recognised him to start with. A twenty-five-year career in the City had destroyed the image of the man she had once met. Gary Cook was a name she knew well and had hoped never to hear again. Ken Rowe had started his interview.

"We are now in front of GL headquarters on King Edward Street. GL was the subject of a takeover by HXBK four years ago, after disastrous revelations linked to GL subprime deals sunk the share price to less than one tenth of its original offer price," Ken Rowe reported. "Most of our viewers will remember the dramatic story surrounding the discovery of the subprime exposure GL was running. Henry Crowne, one of GL's own, managed to communicate GL's position to the management of HXBK, before he was arrested for his terrorist activities."

Ken moved off-centre to make way for a man who was patiently waiting in the background. The camera zoomed in and Professor James Knight moved closer to Ken.

"Professor Knight, many thanks for agreeing to answer my questions. What can you tell us about the tragic accident?"

"Well Ken, a takeover as complex as the HXBK–GL one is inevitably going to generate a high level of stress for the GL team."

"GL no longer represents the jewel in the crown it once was?" Ken was out to get the dirt on Henry's former employer and for once Nancy could not blame him.

"Absolutely, combined with the financial crisis and the revelations linked to subprime, the pressure on some of the head traders is almost unbearable."

"For the benefit of our viewers, Professor Knight, what does a head trader do? Why would Gary Cook have been in a difficult position?"

"To simplify greatly, a head trader oversees a specific type of trade. In this case Mr Cook was in charge of the interest rate book, in particular LIBOR. Again, to help viewers LIBOR is the interbank rate that underpins all lending transactions in Sterling and also other currencies. GL was the first American bank to deal with Sterling in size. Mr Cook's financial positions would have been essential when valuing the shares of GL."

"Does it have anything to do with the subprime debacle?" Ken asked with glee.

"A very important question," Professor Knight replied. "Indeed, a very good question. However, LIBOR is much broader than subprime. It underpins many instruments and all Sterling mortgages for example."

"But could Mr Cook have been linked to the contentious disclosure of the subprime book that GL was hiding?" Ken carried on.

"Gary was a very senior managing director at the bank. I can only speculate as to what he must have known," said Professor Knight letting a few seconds elapse for effect. "But I cannot see an obvious connection to the ridiculous exposure that GL had to subprime."

"Thank you for your input."

Professor Knight gave the camera a Hollywood smile and the camera moved across, zooming once more onto Ken Rowe.

"As you heard from Professor Knight no immediate link to the subprime market. Still, Gary Cook's position in the bank was central to the valuation of the shares in the takeover deal. The police have not yet confirmed whether they will treat the death as suspicious. We will know more after the coroner's Post-Mortem."

Nancy shivered. She could see Gary's face – the expression of surprise.

"No, this is ridiculous," she said and switched the TV off.

She recognised the old feeling of unease with surprise; it had settled quietly in the pit of her stomach and tightened the base of her neck. The stress of high-profile trials had left her when she had decided to hang up her QC's gown and keep her wig well tucked in its box. When Henry had placed his fateful call four years ago, the world of crime had entered her life again. His complex case had been the challenge she had forgotten she enjoyed. Pritchard QC had represented Henry; she was part of the legal team, a suitable distance from the front line of criminal law. Henry and she had grown close, an unlikely friendship on the surface, an obvious one for those who knew them both. She glanced at her watch, 10am. Henry should have received her latest letter by now. "Excellent, Henry needs to keep working on his temper. If he is going to let go of all that anger he must —"

The phone rang, interrupting Nancy's train of thought. She crossed the room, picked up the old 1930s ivory phone and gave a simple hello.

"Nancy, good to hear that you are around. It's Jonathan, I mean Jonathan Pole."

"Jonathan, *mon chère ami*. How good to hear from you. Or should I say Inspector Pole?" exclaimed Nancy delighted to hear from the other man who had entered her life at the time of Henry's case.

"How did you know I was calling you in my formal capacity, *étonnant*?" Pole slipped into French. She enjoyed the way he liked to remind her of his own French ancestry.

"I did not. In fact, I was going to call you in your formal capacity – *les grands esprits se rencontrent*."

"*Absolument*: great minds think alike," replied Pole amused.

"Now, are we talking about yesterday's incident?"

"You mean Mr Cook's unfortunate experiment with gravity?"

"The very one. I can't think of anything else. I have not gone through a red light or exceeded the speed limit I promise."

"I don't do traffic. Well, not yet anyway although I am sure Superintendent Marsh would gladly have me reassigned."

"Surely, he could not do this to one of the best DCIs in London, the one who holds the highest rate of crime resolution in the Met."

Pole was blushing at the other end of the phone; Nancy heard and enjoyed the effect.

"Jonathan – do accept a compliment from a friend, will you?"

"Gratefully accepted, *ma chère*. How about coffee to discuss the jumper?"

"Splendid idea. The usual place, say eleven?"

"Inns of Court, at eleven."

Chapter Two

The mail was late, something Henry had become accustomed to. Yet today it frustrated him. Anger, his lifelong companion, was stirring up again. Henry had learned to deny it the power it once had but today the waiting was intolerable. He could not risk unearthing his small treasure until Johnny had knocked at his door in his raspy sort of way and Henry had responded with his usual "I'm busy". A silly answer but one that gave him the sense that he still owned his life.

He stood up, breathed deeply, exhaled – letting the burn in his throat slowly extinguish. He reached his small desk in one step. He was still amazed at how much he had piled into the diminutive space of his cell: a table, a tiny bookshelf for the books he was currently reading, a chair that could accommodate his tall and now muscular body. The pile of correspondence, his most treasured possession even above the netsuke, was neatly arranged on the desk. He lifted the letters slowly to reach for Nancy's first. He sat on the chair, drawing the letter from its envelope with careful fingers.

Henry, mon ami,

This letter took me a while. I realised I had not put pen to paper for such a long time. I do not mean emails or texts. I mean actual writing, the act of my hand on paper, the slight hesitation that precedes putting down what cannot be erased. Mais enfin la voici.

A sketch of it came on the day I left you behind. The heavy doors closing on you brought a chill to my heart. So it felt right, maybe even necessary. And I have come to realise that a good letter must divulge something intimate about its writer, so I will start with my own news. I have decided to reconnect with my previous life, the one I thought I had left forever behind. Don't be alarmed and think I am recanting after talking so much about giving up the rat race. I have found an unexpected use for my old talent, my new-found bohemian style joined up with the impeccable training of this legal mind – well, you have seen the result!

Of course, you may already have gathered that I received a little nudge. It came in the shape of our mutual friend Mr. P. I want, no … I need to plunge into the City once more, but this time on my own terms. A final test, maybe? Time will tell. To be completely honest, the gentleman in question attracts my interest terribly. There you are. How about this for a confession – ha!

I think I should finish swiftly, and now that my letter lies in front of me I hope it will be the first of many. Please reply, for I know that coming to terms with the act of terror you lived through and the deceit you endured will bring you resolve. But for today I simply say – I understand. The rest is up to you.
A très vite
Nancy

The colour of the paper had started to fade. It was slightly crumpled at the top and a splash of water had blurred a couple of words. Nancy's letter had been a lifeline when it first arrived three and a half years ago. It had provided a small glimmer of light in that most desperate moment. He had so wanted to do the right thing, to show he could be a better man.

"Henry Crowne, notorious banker and IRA sympathiser, seeks to atone for his mistakes," murmured Henry. Alone in his cell, he had first thought he would go mad. But he had found that words uttered aloud had given the sentences so much more weight and instead of sending him over the edge had managed to ground him. He could not deny that the shock of conviction had been immense but he would survive. Just the way he had in Belfast. Just the way he had on the trading floor of GL. He would survive and set himself free.

Henry folded the letter lovingly and replaced it at the bottom of the pile of correspondence. His restless mind moved to the hot topic amongst the other cons on his wing, the latest arrival – Ronnie Kray. Henry had thought it a joke. Could someone seriously be called Ronnie Kray after the notorious 1960s criminal? But it was true and Big K had advised against making fun of it when Henry managed to catch up with him before bang-up time started.

"Man, this guy has the reputation for being a crackpot, a real nutjob – thinks the Krays were the best thing since sliced bread, actually before sliced bread," Big K had said with an air of conspiracy followed by a chuckle.

"Is he the guy with two faces tattooed on his back?"

Big K's chuckling face grew serious. "Not sure, why?"

"Saw a guy in the showers with that tattoo but the weird thing – the faces were similar and the Krays were identical twins."

"Did he see you or did you see him?"

"That's a bit of a technical question, mate – in the vastness of HMP Belmarsh showers I'm not sure who saw who." Henry had found it hard to suppress a smile.

"I mean it Man, you don't want this guy to notice you." Big K had run his massive hand over his shaven head. This mass of muscle was uneasy at the thought of Kray. Henry had taken note.

The much-awaited knock came at his door and Henry had to exercise superhuman control not to rush to answer.

"I'm busy."

"Letter for Mr Crowne."

Henry reached his door in one step.

* * *

Inspector Pole's solid back was bent over a low table at the most comfortable end of the cafe. Nancy moved slowly, observing Pole arranging the cups of tea and coffee together with their favourite pastries. He was moving the crockery around, neatly laying down napkin and cutlery. Nancy smiled at this display of thoughtful attention. She made some intentional noise with the heel of her shoes. Pole straightened up more quickly than he would have wanted. He too was all smiles.

"Nancy, *très heureux de vous revoir.*"

"*Moi de même* Jonathan," said Nancy undoing the belt of her orange trench coat. She was wearing one of her colourful dresses that Pole had learned to love, its pattern inspired by a Sonia Delauney design he had seen at a Tate exhibition they had visited together.

"I know, I know. How did I manage to wear the black attire of a barrister for most of my career?" said Nancy with a wry smile.

"And did you find a way?" asked Pole amused.

"Very much so. You should have seen the colour of my bags."

Pole raised a quizzical eyebrow. "Bags. I see. Could a young woman raised in France not do better than that?"

Nancy blushed slightly and laughed in turn. "OK. You got me there."

They both sank into the deep leather chairs, enjoying a leisurely conversation. Pole had nearly finished his coffee when Nancy put down her own cup.

246

"What is the story so far with Gary Cook?"

"Yes, you're right. Some more unpleasant business coming out of the City."

"It was a shock. I have seen some pretty bad things in my time as QC but it has been a while – strange or perhaps good that I have left all this behind."

"Have you? I thought you were still in touch with Henry and – are you not looking at some other cases?"

"How do you know? I thought the Arts were not in your jurisdiction."

"*Peut-être pas mais* – it is that of my good friend Eugene Grandel."

"Eugene, such a gossip. How does he manage to keep the case on track, I just don't know?"

"He manages all right. He just can't help revealing all he knows to his good friend Pole."

"Working with Eugene is fun, I must admit. Fake pieces of art that even the best dealers think are worth millions; Russian oligarchs fighting over the valuation of horrendously ugly contemporary pieces …"

"I get it," said Pole. "Blood on the street no longer appeals – I am miffed."

"For you, I will make an exception."

"And because Gary Cook's death troubles you."

"There is indeed more to it I fear," said Nancy putting her hands together in a reflective way. She was gathering her thoughts in a way Pole had learned to respect. "Everybody assumes it is suicide. But did you see the way the body fell?"

"He landed on his back."

"I think it is odd. I can't quite put my finger on it, but it is odd."

"It may be that the fall was partly intentional, partly accidental in which case the body might have fallen backward. He was trying to save himself and couldn't."

"Perhaps," said Nancy stirring slowly what was left of her tea.

"The SOCO team checked. There was no sign of struggle."

Nancy sat back and remained silent.

"The pathologist has requested an extensive toxicology report," Pole carried on, hoping it would spur Nancy to speak further.

"But the report won't be ready for a while, will it?"

"Very true; he stank of alcohol, pupils a little too dilated."

"Alcohol and possibly drugs. A bad combination. And a strange combination when going to a conference."

"Or a way to get into the right frame of mind," said Pole.

Nancy finished her tea and replaced the cup slowly in its saucer.

"Still not convinced," said Pole.

"Did you see the expression on his face, more surprise than horror or resignation?"

"Not enough to give me a new lead. You know something I should?"

"Well, Gary Cook might have been sacked from GL after the merger was announced but he was a tough boy ..." Nancy let the sentence hang.

"I am all ears and this will stay between us for the time being," said Pole reassuringly.

"That's fine Jonathan. I will tell you and frankly it no longer bothers me as much as it once did."

Pole leaned forward in an encouraging fashion.

"What did this bad boy do to have such a lasting impact on you?"

* * *

The lunch had gone well. How much could Chinese people eat? Staggering. The waiter had produced cognac and cigars of quality, Brett Allner-Smith had insisted. He would never concede that such upper-class refinements could be enjoyed in equal measure by foreigners but he had learned to be more circumspect in expressing his opinion after the Crowne affair. His open resentment of Henry as a collector not worthy of the name had brought the police too close to his business. Something he could ill afford.

The pictures of several artefacts were circulating around the table again. The quality of what was on offer was outstanding. Only a war-torn country could produce such exceptional looting opportunities. Too bad for the idiots who could not preserve their national treasures. The Americans could do little about it; most US troops had no idea of the unimaginable significance of these sites. The pillage of Iraqi treasures had started well before the 2003 conflict and it had now become a full-blown business. The black market was inundated with pieces from all the main antique sites: Babylon, Nimrud, Ummu and Ur. Brett had developed a network of knowledgeable looters who would never fail to produce large and rare pieces. And today he knew that what was on offer was simply unique.

"Allow me, please, to take you once more through the amazing array of pieces available to you."

The translator bent down and whispered into Mr Chong's ear.

"Mr Chong would be delighted to hear about the pieces once more. He would of course want to ensure provenance."

Mr Chong's leathery face had become animated over food. He had commented enthusiastically about the quality of the meal; stories of other banquets celebrating business deals had followed, interrupted by loud laughter and resounding burps and slurps. Brett had become accustomed to the etiquette surrounding such meals but the show of power still irked him.

Imbecile, thought Brett. *These have been looted.*

"Absolutely," said Brett with the most honest face he could muster. "I can most certainly provide an ample description of the site of provenance."

Again, the translator bent towards Mr Chong and whispered in his ear. Chong gave a short nod, his face closed to scrutiny. It was time to do business.

"The most exclusive piece is this 3500 BC gold jar of Sumerian origin. Baghdad's museum is searching for it but I am able to procure the object for you instead."

The translator did his duty. Chong's face remained unmoved. Brett's long experience as an art dealer had taught him to read the signs. Chong had folded his hands together in a tight clasp. His focus had moved another notch, the line on his forehead arching up with each new picture. Brett was onto a winner. This magnate of the gambling trade in Macau would buy and pay the price no matter how much negotiating he did first.

* * *

The death of Gary Cook didn't make the news. Nothing in the *FT*, a small article in the *Evening Standard* on page 20. Banker-bashing was at its height but more important matters had taken precedence. Sky News and the BBC were too busy speculating on the appointment of the next Bank of England Governor. Edwina James-Jones put the paper down and finished her espresso, two shots, no sugar – strong and bitter, just the way the battle to reach the top tasted.

She looked at her watch, 8:27 AM. In exactly three minutes her phone would ring and Mervyn-The-Oracle-King would summon her. She knew full well that the nickname The Oracle had been coined for Alan Greenspan. But was it not what all central banks' governors aspired to be? 8:29 AM. Edwina finished her espresso, crushed the cup and threw it into the wastepaper basket in one perfect arch. In one minute, she would be told that The Oracle was expecting her with the latest status report on the crisis. Today's topic would be red-hot – at what level would LIBOR become dangerous for the banking system? So much depended on the interest rate: mortgages, financial instruments, the bond market … LIBOR was traditionally fixed by a number of banks that submitted the level at which they each were respectively expecting to lend to one another. But lending had been distorted by the financial crisis and banks had stopped trusting each other. If interbank lending did not resume, the entire banking system would collapse.

Edwina had started her career on the trading desk of one of the largest UK banks. She had become the first woman head trader and subsequently head of capital markets. Too ambitious for her own good, a political animal, a cock-sucking bitch – terms of endearment often used by her male colleagues. She smiled; there would be no glass ceiling for Edwina Maude Mary James-Jones.

The phone rang.

"I'm on my way," said Edwina without waiting for an invitation. She took a look at the pile of documents she and Gabriel had prepared.

"A bloody good job if I can say so myself," Edwina smiled, tapping her number two on the shoulder. "Where would I be without you, Gabs?"

"In the same position, with an equally able lieutenant to watch your back," Gabriel responded with an amused smile.

"You're just too modest for your own good."

"Yeah, yeah, just go and get them."

Edwina opened her handbag and pulled out a small mirror. She applied some discreet rouge to her lips, brushed her blonde hair and checked the reflection of her face in the window. She was ready to do battle with the Monetary Policy Committee. Grabbing the pile of documents she needed, she turned once more towards Gabriel.

"Anything new I need to be aware of?"

"Nope, all in good shape. And nothing on Gary Cook either."

"Surprising but a welcome omission from the papers."

"Not completely surprising. I made a few calls to some of my contacts in the press."

"And what will they want in return?" asked Edwina.

"Nothing you're not going to like. Now, to your meeting please or else you will be late," said Gabriel waving her away.

Edwina headed off with a small pang of excitement in her chest. She was walking a straight line to becoming the new Governor of the Bank of England.

***

The desk, in the corner of the small cell, had been meticulously organised. A brown file was squeezed between a pencil holder and a discreet box of biscuits. Henry had finally been allowed small privileges. He had tried to be content with them: one chocolate chip biscuit after lunch and one shortbread in the evening. His universe had shrunk from the entire world to a cell barely big enough to swing the proverbial cat. Outside HSU inmates resorted regularly to self-harm or sometimes worse. And he had contemplated both. He did not miss the company of women that much although now he wished he had had more sex when he still could. The drive and desire for success had been much stronger even than the best of shags. He had had women but no commitment, chosen for company or simply for pleasure as it was expected of a successful investment banker. Even deliciously distant Pam had never broken his will. And yet the thought of Pam still made his heart miss a beat. He should have given in, taken the risk. Henry was certain she wanted him to.

His mind had drifted. The new letter he was holding felt heavy in his hands. He laid it on the desk. He had started composing a reply and was nearing the end. It would almost certainly be read before it reached its recipient. He could not indulge in deep honesty but Nancy knew him well enough to understand his moods and thoughts.

Nancy, mon amie
Your letters are always a breath of fresh air that keep me sane in this place. But two letters less than twenty-four hours apart … this is pure joy! Your latest one has also intrigued me. Something to get my brain going is most welcome as you know. I am still reading profusely but it is never enough. The course on philosophy would be interesting were it not for the level of the attendees. Of course I am a pain in the arse when it comes to intellectual pride but even the Cat. A prisoners can't spell their names – I am being a little flippant but hardly. Even the crème de la crème of the worst baddies chosen to have the privilege of spending their life in HSU are hardly challenging. The lecturer is patient and of surprisingly good quality, still I AM BORED. I know, I know, I have said this so many times and we have spoken about it equally often. Contrary to popular belief, nothing, I mean nothing, happens in prison. Unless some poor sod decides to call it a day and meet his maker (which is not unusual) or some psycho decides to go on a rampage against nonces – I hear scraps of it. Since I earned the privilege to do time within HSU as a could-escape-so-better-keep-him-doubly-locked-up con, I have been kept away from real prison life. I was indifferent to start with, not so sure now.

But enough of my rambling, I am really surprised that the suicide of Gary Cook did not attract press attention. I knew him, well enough I suppose. He was in Rates (meaning interest rates to the profane) and I used to speak to him regularly about those. I'd be lying if I did not admit this brought back fond memories. I spent all day pretending I could still be a banker: the complex products, the clients, writing deals – shit, that was FUN. Then I realised four years out of action, an eternity in the world of finance, even more so with the financial crisis. It's all over for me. But mustn't digress, Gary was a typical Rates guy: aggressive, pig-headed, an East-End lad made good. He was bright and had the memory of an elephant. You did not want to be on the wrong side of Gary. I remembered rumours circulating about his involvement in a financial scandal. I can't remember the details: it was another firm and way before my time. I am sure he got out of that one scot-free otherwise GL would never have hired him. He did piss off a lot of people eventually, so no surprise he got the black bin bag treatment after the HXBK takeover of GL. I hope you are surprised. I have finally stopped calling it a merger. Back to Gary, I am amazed he committed suicide. He was not the type. I would have rather thought he had an ace up his sleeve. He must have known his time was up at GL. The likes of Gary always feel the wind turning and prepare accordingly.

Henry was struck by the memory of his own last day at GL, a mixture of pride and bitterness. A day so memorable he could still see it unfold before his eyes with absolute clarity.

He had become prime suspect in the Anthony Albert murder investigation. He had been banned from entering GL. A decision Douglas McCarthy, GL's CEO, had taken himself.

Henry's body tenses. He is back there as he manages to enter the bank and reach McCarthy's office. The old man is not expecting him.

"Doug, you motherfucker, you were surprised," Henry says aloud. "Although, granted, you sure held your own."

Henry has kicked the door of the office open and challenges his CEO. His heart is racing now the way it was back then.

"Good afternoon Douglas," Henry points a gun at his boss. He has grabbed it from a secret compartment in McCarthy's desk. Henry can still feel the ridges of the grip panel in his hand. McCarthy is stunned at Henry's knowledge of the weapon and he wants it back.

"Don't try anything stupid Douglas, I didn't come here to kill you." Henry feels a strange blend of excitement and anticipation. McCarthy changes tack. Confrontation is not an option, neither is reasoning.

"How?" McCarthy asks, no longer hiding his amazement.

"You hired me because of the accuracy of my observations, Doug, and so I observed. The undisclosed documents, the hidden cache. I know all your dirty secrets."

McCarthy is about to move but Henry cuts him short. "I know what you are trying to do, Doug, and time is of the essence."

"That's the name of the game, I guess." McCarthy shrugs.

A pinch of admiration for the old man runs through Henry. Under threat and still in control.

"Open the top drawer nearest to you."

McCarthy does not flinch. "No."

"Suit yourself."

The gun discharge deafens them both, resounding against the windows, shattering the wood in a burst of violence Henry has not experienced for decades. Fear and shock shows for the second time in McCarthy's eyes, both men facing each other, on their guard. McCarthy moves first, desperation and rage overtaking him. Henry avoids the charge and McCarthy comes crashing down on the side of his desk. As he is about to turn back and resume his attack, Henry gives a single kick, hitting McCarthy in the face. The blow throws the old man flying across the room.

Henry grabs the file that McCarthy had concealed only a few hours ago.

"What are you going to do with it?" mumbles McCarthy, incapable of getting up.

"What you should have done, Douglas, had you had a shred of honesty in you," replies Henry.

Through a mouth full of blood, McCarthy starts laughing, stopping and starting through pain.

"You are not going to give me a lesson in ethics, are you Henry? Not you —"

Henry does not reply. He has got hold of David Cooper-James, HXBK's CEO.

McCarthy takes only a few seconds to realise what is about to happen. He summons his last ounce of strength and lunges forward one final time – straight into Henry's foot. Henry has pressed the mute button just in time. McCarthy's body curls up in the middle of the room, in a heap, motionless.

David Cooper-James is on the phone and Henry delivers the fatal documents.

McCarthy had been arrested the following day and GL taken over by HXBK only after the Treasury and the Bank of England had intervened. GL would not go the way Lehman Brothers had gone. The deal that was then negotiated had been a bloody affair. The senior management of GL took the brunt of its consequences. Gone were their dreams of a reverse takeover. They would never be back in the driving seat.

Henry found he had clenched his fists and gritted his teeth, his shoulders rounded, a man ready for a fight. He stood up, rolled his head around slowly, stretched back his broad shoulders and simply stood tall for a moment. Those days were gone and would never come back. He was in jail not because of the failed takeover or some fraudulent financial deals but because of his involvement with the IRA. Henry slowly bent forward to pick up the pen that had rolled onto the floor without him noticing. He had one final essential point to make to Nancy.

Chapter Three

The files were full of dust and unpleasant to handle but Nancy needed to take a look at the case again. One of the most crushing defeats she had ever known and Gary Cook had been at the centre of it. It had only taken twenty-four hours for the boxes to arrive from the secure warehouse in which they were stored. An express request had done the trick. Nancy had slipped into frayed jeans and an old King's College T-shirt, a very casual dress code even for this keen gardener. She had called for the main boxes that contained the summary court papers as well as some of her personal notes. Half a dozen boxes were cluttering her hallway. She had gone through most of them looking for something but she did not know quite what yet. A faded memory, a detail of the case kept pushing and prodding but still remained at bay – a piece of information relevant to Gary's death was nagging Nancy.

She opened a heavy file, the smell of stale paper made her sneeze repeatedly. She rubbed her nose vigorously and found what she was looking for, Gary's lengthy statement. Twenty years had gone by but she could still remember how cocky he had been. Nancy dialled Pole's number on her BlackBerry and turned the loudspeaker on.

"Pole."

"Jonathan, good morning, it's me. Do you have a minute?"

"*Bonjour* 'me' – and for you always," Pole said amused.

"*Bien sur, je n'en ésperais pas moins.* In particular as I have recovered some old files in which Gary Cook shows his true colours. I told you I had some details for you last time we met and here they are."

"Is that so? Now you really have my complete attention."

Pole had learned not to underestimate Nancy's instinct. It had proven invaluable in the convoluted Henry Crowne affair.

"Yes, I have gone through a lot of documents this morning and finally found what I was looking for." Nancy held back.

"OK, don't keep me guessing; you know I can't take the pressure," said Pole.

"*Eh bien, mon cher* Jonathan. Just because it is you, of course."

"*Ma chère*, I am all ears."

"Let's start with a recap of the case." Nancy said, launching into her story.

The case had arisen a couple of years after the Big Bang. Nothing to do with the creation of the universe – but rather with a fundamental change in the way the stock market operated in London. A simplification that transformed London into the greatest financial centre in the world. The change had altered the way market-makers (the people who bought and sold stocks) operated with exclusivity. Before 1986 they had a monopoly for holding stocks and shares for sale, whilst brokers were allowed to match orders for clients. After 1986 the difference was abolished together with the commission jobbers and market-makers were earning. As a result, a lot of the firms that lived off market-making were absorbed by UK or international banks. As part of that process, the accounts of those firms were scrutinised in depth.

"Gary's broking firm was part of the trail of acquisitions?" asked Pole.

"Precisely, he was then a jobber, young enough, around twenty-six, but he had been in the job for nearly eight years. Never took an exam, not even O levels, but he was as sharp as sharp can be."

"That is mighty impressive, what background?"

"His father was a typical East-End boy, made a lot of money selling antiques."

Pole whistled and could not contain a laugh.

"I find myself in the middle of *Minder* suddenly. Was his father called Arthur Daley?"

"Not quite. But not far off, although Cook was a darn sight cleverer than Terry," replied Nancy.

"I can't believe you watched that stuff," exclaimed Pole.

"And why the hell not? I tell you for a new girl like me, keen to know the ways of the world, it was the perfect intro into the world of petty crime."

"I suppose you started at the bottom like everyone else."

"You bet I did. I was a woman and I was half-Asian. You can imagine the result."

"Actually, I probably can't imagine. A story for another time, *peut-être?*"

"*Absolument*, but going back to Gary. The case should have been much easier than it eventually turned out to be. Gary's firm had been involved in taking large equity positions in a particular takeover. A classic case of insider trading."

"OK, so Gary had knowledge of the takeover before it became public and bought stocks in the company on his prop book."

"Spoken like a pro," teased Nancy. "This is what the prosecution contended. Nowadays most insiders end up in jail; the technology is there to catch them."

"You mean that in those days it was more relying on the culprit eventually bragging about it."

"Partially yes, but not Gary."

"So not the typical cocky cor-blimey type of bloke?"

"Well, he sure had the accent but he was in control. He had thought about it in the minutest details."

"What do you mean exactly?"

"I mean, he had envisaged being caught. He had not relied on the fact he would simply get away with it, like all the others, and that made all the difference."

"And you lost the case?"

"I did – no matter how hard I tried to break his arguments he remained credible, never arrogant, with just the right amount of anger an innocent man may show. The image of the typical low-class guy made good."

"And he established reasonable doubt —"

"The little git did." Nancy grabbed the pen on the table and started doodling furiously on her newspaper.

"OK, so what does that tell us in the here and now? Maybe he was a reformed character. He was young, gave himself a fright. He got away with it once, that was enough —"

"Maybe, or rather I agree that for the next twenty years he seems to have stayed out of trouble. But leopards don't change their spots. Then comes the financial crisis."

"You think that the old demons came back to haunt him and that he might have organised something dodgy because he was pushed by circumstances?"

"It is a possibility. And Gary was a bit of a lad, as most of them were in those days: a lot of booze, lap dancing clubs, and so on."

"So, Gary liked to party with the boys, very nineties of course. You must have checked whether he had confided in the lovely ladies of the various clubs he frequented."

Nancy laughed an uncomfortable laugh. "As a matter of fact I did, or rather the prosecution did – not pleasant but Gary never revealed anything material that I could use."

Pole stayed silent. He was pondering. Nancy did not like the guy for good reasons it seemed. But there was no evidence of foul play. Nancy sensed that Pole was wavering.

"I know what you're thinking, Jonathan. But by the time Gary arrived at the conference he was already completely drunk. There is no reason why I would want to make this case more complicated than it is."

"Apart from the fact that you would want to spend more time in the company of your favourite inspector."

"Jonathan Pole, you are flattering yourself."

"I am? What a shame I had managed to get two tickets for a Kodo concert at Sadler's Wells. I thought you might be —"

"Now you are talking," Nancy said with perhaps more enthusiasm than she would have wanted.

* * *

The meeting of the Monetary Policy Committee had been excruciatingly painful. Edwina was enraged by the dithering of some of its members and its lack of vision. She was advocating for another round of quantitative easing when another member was already asking for a rise in interest rates – seriously!

She entered Gabriel's office. He did not bother to lift his head. "That bad, was it?"

"Argggh! I swear I am going to strangle one of them. Where on earth did they get their degrees in economics?"

"Wrong question," said Gabriel. "The real issue is – what are they doing with that degree? Are they hiding behind the theory or are they capable of taking a pragmatic approach and embracing new ideas?"

"Well said," replied Edwina. She sometimes wondered why Gabriel had never wanted to be in the front line himself. She had pondered at length about this and was still perplexed. Surely the scar on his face was not enough to dissuade him? He spoke seldom of the accident. She knew it had taken years of patience and surgery to achieve an appearance he had learned to live with. But perhaps he was also a man who enjoyed the elaborate process of strategising, happy then to leave someone else in charge of the advocacy. If so he had chosen a woman as his advocate and Edwina had plenty of respect for a man of intellect who could make that decision.

"Do you think The Oracle will want to speak to you again about QE today?" asked Gabriel.

"After the meeting, definitely. Mervyn does not like intervention but he knows it has to be done. A second round of QE will irk him though. I need to speak to the Yanks. Can you organise a call with Ben Bernanke's chief of staff, the delightful Rose?"

"Absolutely, I will get something set up on a secure line as soon as they have arrived. I will do it myself. The fewer people know the better."

"Right you are, now. Now, what's on the agenda for lunch, nothing I hope?"

"Free as a bird," replied Gabriel with a twinkle in his eyes.

Edwina waved a finger at him and disappeared through the connecting door into her own office. She left the door open and started going through her emails.

She had begun the process of selecting what was urgent when a niggling thought kept interfering with her concentration. She opened Google and searched Gary Cook's name. Nothing. Gabriel had spoken to his contacts in the press. It would be the end of the matter he assured her. She was so close to her goal and she was damned if Gary Cook would come between her and the title of Governor.

Edwina had not seen Nancy since that dreadful night. She had looked shaken by Gary's death too. Perhaps she should check with Nancy what her take was on the matter, casually of course. Nancy had been a good friend, a woman for whom female diversity was not self-promotion but a desire to see other females succeed, even exceed her own achievements. A rare quality.

"Nancy – Edwina here. How are you?"

Edwina nodded. "Yes, me too, what a tragedy … Would you have time for an impromptu lunch? Perfect, meet you there in half an hour … Looking forward."

"I am nipping out for a short while," Edwina told Gabriel, putting on her jacket and awkwardly handling her handbag with one hand.

"Sure. What's Nancy's take on the event, if you don't mind me asking?"

"Not quite sure. I'll find out."

"She's such a great supporter of yours," Gabriel said with admiration.

"One of the few women who doesn't only talk the talk but also walks the walk. Did you know she was, and I believe still is, the youngest QC ever appointed?"

"Impressive."

"And she never mentioned it to me in all these years. I read it recently in the press. You remember the Henry Crowne affair?"

"Yes, I do. And you will be late if you don't leave now."

"Good point, till later. If The Oracle calls, let me know and I'll come back straightaway."

* * *

Moro in Exmouth Market was packed. Nancy had called and they had managed to squeeze in a table for two. She came too often for the staff not to find a place and, as always, they had managed a table "En Terrace". The sun was giving the pedestrian streets of Islington a Parisian air. Nancy's Sorbonne days were long gone but the happy memories lingered. Paris had been a revelation. The intellectual buzz surrounding the law faculty, the rebels that debated everything from politics to fashion at the Pantheon café had flung her mind open to all the possibilities that life presented. On a sunny day Exmouth Market gave her the same feeling of freedom. It had changed so much in the past five years, nearly unrecognisable, changing at the pace Islington had. Despite the financial crisis the restaurants were always full here. She wondered whether people were having fun to forget the trouble they were in or simply whilst they still could.

Moro was trendy; it was not the typical City restaurant despite its proximity to the Square Mile. Nancy quickly surveyed the inside of the restaurant before staff came to greet her. She recognised a couple of regulars: one a TV producer, the other a screenwriter. They had spoken in the past when they had all found themselves at the same art gallery preview. The small contemporary art gallery she was supporting had made the news with one of their up-and-coming artists. She sat down, content with the cosy position of her table, and opened her *FT*. She had barely started the companies section when a firm hand squeezed her shoulder.

"Hello Eddie. How are you?" said Nancy looking up and folding her *FT* neatly.

"Still fuming after a frustrating meeting at the shop. Hello Nancy. A spot of lunch with you is exactly what I need to calm down," Edwina replied with a perfect smile.

Nancy called Juan and placed the order, letting him recommend some of the dishes. Edwina pulled her BlackBerry out of her bag. She fidgeted with it until Nancy asked her what she would like to drink. Disappointingly Nancy followed Edwina with a bottle of sparking water. Edwina unbuttoned the jacket of an impeccable light-blue suit. She rearranged the pearl jewellery she was wearing and untied the Hermes scarf that sat loosely around her neck. Edwina looked around, briefly inspecting her surroundings.

"How is John?" Nancy asked.

"He is well, busy. The LSE is introducing a new curriculum and John is teaching it. The crisis has created a lot of interest in the Great Depression of 1930."

"And he is an expert on this if I remember rightly."

"He is. John in the UK and Ben Bernanke in the US.   Sometimes I wonder whether he should be in my role," Edwina said unconvincingly.

"Eddie, you know you are in the right job and John is perfectly happy in his – otherwise you two would never have worked out," Nancy said, surprised.

"I suppose that's true – still, the buggers at work are not making it easy for me."

"What do you expect? Yellen is likely to get the top job because of Obama; you've got a Conservative government to contend with."

"Osborne is more progressive than people think but unfortunately he is not the only one deciding."

"Which is why you need to keep at it, stick to your plan the way we discussed —" Nancy stopped abruptly as the tapas were being served. Juan produced plates and cutlery, arranged the food tastefully on the table and disappeared swiftly.

"And avoid any adverse publicity," Nancy finished.

"I know, the Gary Cook jump is unfortunate – and very sad of course."

"Why do you mention it? I have read very little in the press about it."

"I suppose there is little compassion for a banker taking a dive from the terrace of a posh City restaurant."

"Perhaps but I would have expected the press to like the fact that the said banker had taken a dive as you say. Still, I presume Gabriel has been on the case."

"He has. Cook had lost his job anyway. So maybe it is less interesting to crap on a banker who is no longer a banker."

Nancy was about to ask how she knew of Cook's redundancy but then thought better of it.

"Are you worried about the impact it could have on the conference's success and indirectly yourself?"

"Well, he was at the conference and he was being a nuisance."

"Yes, I am aware, he was arguing with me. I think he was extremely drunk or possibly worse."

Edwina stopped in mid-air as she was about to stab her fork in the last prawn on the dish.

"Really, how do you know that?"

"Well, I have many sources."

"I just don't want to be associated with yet another bad banker's tragedy."

"Why would you be?" Nancy asked. "Are you not overreacting a little? Even if the press made a meal of it, the conference was an enormous success, attended by women from all sectors of industry and by quite a few high-profile men too. Gary's suicide can't undo that."

"You're right, I am probably overreacting. Another bad banker bites the dust – So what?"

Nancy smiled a reassuring smile.

"You are doing incredibly well. You know that don't you?"

"Yes, yes I do. I simply need to keep going and ignore the noise. Thanks for being a friend."

"Any time, it's always a pleasure. Now let's discuss your plan in detail."

* * *

Edwina had left their lunch with a spring in her step. Nancy smiled at the invigorating effect she had had on her friend. The weather was too good to return home. She fancied a brisk walk to the Barbican: a new show had just opened at The Curve Gallery she did not want to miss. She would enjoy a cup of coffee at the pond afterwards. Her light cotton dress felt comfortable despite its elegance. Nancy caught sight of herself in a shop window and approved. She rarely spent time in front of a mirror: a shop window would always do. She enjoyed fashion. Perhaps her time in Paris, even as an impoverished student, had left its mark. She had an eye for the beautifully made, the textures, the patterns. She enjoyed craftsmanship, a taste she carried into art.

Nancy walked at a pace, still full of her time with Edwina. As ever she had enjoyed the company. But something had engaged the large cogs of her mind, a feeling, the start of an idea that would not leave her alone.

"Why was Eddie so worried?" Nancy whispered to herself.

There was no denying Edwina was concerned. Just an overreaction? No, in truth, not her style. She was under a tremendous amount of pressure, the financial crisis, the QE schedule, the ghost of the Great Depression. She was a technical person but she was also inventive, prepared to think out of the box. In fact, the crisis had brought her qualities forward. It had been the differentiator between her and her male colleagues. Edwina had come up with new ideas and Mervyn had listened.

"But why check on Gary Cook? She is busy enough."

Nancy reached the Barbican and decided to get her cup of coffee first. She sat down at the far end of the pond and took out a small writing pad from her bag. She would do what she always excelled at doing – ask herself the tough questions. To be effective they had to be in black and white. She smoothed the page on which she was about to write and started on her list.

1-why has E checked the background of Gary, in particular his latest position at work?
2-why is E concerned about an event that does not directly implicate her?
3-why has Gabriel acted upon it?
4-what is the impact of me pursuing with Pole?
5-is it suicide?

Her last question struck her with more force now it was written down.

She had started to slowly stir her cappuccino, the chocolate flower design gradually disappearing as the sugar melted in the middle of it. She stopped. Her gesture reminded her of the last time she had visited Henry. His obsession with good coffee sad and yet all par for the course.

Henry had spoken at length of his latest interest. A book, *Gang of One* by Gary Mulgrew, a real-life account of the NatWest banker extradited to the US who had found himself in one of the most violent high-security prisons there.

"I have it so easy, Nancy. He was lucky to survive and to have his sentence commuted so that he could come back to the UK, otherwise he would have died there."

"But why are you concerning yourself with what cannot happen to you?" Nancy had asked.

"Why not? Is it sad that it helps me to think it could have been worse?"

"But you know that if you carry on, try to rebuild your life the way you have done so far, you will not serve the full sentence."

"You mean twenty-five years rather than thirty?" Henry said spreading his long fingers on the table.

"I know it is not tomorrow. I won't deny it."

"The worst thing is … Nothing really good happens here. Nothing. I keep myself to myself. I am not amongst friends or even comrades. I have nothing to say to these guys. High-profile cons are less of a challenge than I thought. There is a lot of rambling going on."

"Isolation is also the sad part of the deal."

"I believed it was that for a long time. But it is more than that."

Nancy had nodded encouragingly. There was little Henry would not speak to her about.

"Even thirty years won't give me redemption. How can I show I have changed?"

"Henry, the first important thing is for you to believe that you are redeemable. Do you believe that?"

"Maybe, yes – it's about what I have done and what I want to do to fix it. And from here I am powerless."

"You mean your link to the IRA?"

"You know the score, Nancy. For years I contributed to building up their finances. The funds that Liam was running for them, I constructed them. I put the mechanism in place to ensure no one could trace them."

Henry had stopped. He had never been as brutally honest. He had admitted it of course, but it had been a mere acknowledgement of the facts presented to him.

"You always wanted to belong to the family Liam and Bobby offered to you. Northern Ireland during The Troubles was not the place for a lonely lad of mixed background to grow up in."

"I am not interested in excuses. I understand why I did it. I could have walked away. I had a brilliant job, a brilliant team and the past could have been left behind but I could not let go." Henry closed his eyes, the deep lines around his mouth arched in pain. "Whichever way I look at it, I helped kill people – a lot of people."

Nancy had remained silent. She needed the right words.

"It is in the past."

"Perhaps, but it is not good enough. For the victim's families it is the present still and will always be."

"There is something else —"

Despite the intensity of the conversation Henry had managed a smile.

"That is what I love about you Nancy. You always get to the nub of the matter."

Nancy had clasped his hand and squeezed gently. Henry had put his other hand over hers and squeezed back. She was his best friend.

"Yes, something else is troubling me —"

Nancy waited. She looked at the clock on the wall. Henry turned back to look at it too.

"It will take a bit more time than the five minutes we have left – next time."

"Are you sure?"

"I am sure." A prison officer looked in their direction and Henry withdrew his hands.

As Henry was pulling his hands away she noticed that one of the inmates was observing them, a strange fellow sporting an unmistakably fifties' haircut. His visitor, a man of similar build, was still talking to him but he was not listening. He only moved his gaze away when his visitor turned around to check what was distracting his attention. Nancy noticed the violence in his glance; even from a distance she could feel the sharpness of its blade.

"And now for something a lot more mundane," Henry said. "How can I manage to make one of those lovely cappuccinos with a flower on top?"

"That is mighty technical. But I think you'll find that the special mix I got you should do the trick. You need to find a small piece of cardboard, cut the outline of the flower, place it on the cup and spread the chocolate over it. *Et voila.*"

"Prison is good at broadening my skills." Henry sighed.

Chapter Four

The little newspaper shop was crowded with sweets of all colours and flavours. It smelt of curry and other spices Brett could not identify. He grabbed a burner phone and paid cash trying to hold his breath as he did so. The small podgy Indian man took his money hardly looking at him.

Good choice of shop, thought Brett. He had gone all the way to Mile End to purchase a couple of phones, dressed in what was the most inconspicuous clothing. His kind did not do jeans but some navy slacks together with the appropriate dress-down jacket would do the trick. He had managed to dig out an old jacket shapeless with age and kept for these occasions. Again, a clever choice.

Brett walked to the bus stop and waited for the number 205. The route would lead him back to Belgravia after a suitable number of changes. He might make the call on the way if he found a suitable spot.

Brett tried to remember where the next few stops would lead him, the City for sure. He boarded, sat down and started activating one of his phones. The screen lit up. He keyed in three numbers he had memorised: his Iraqi contact, his Chinese client, his Italian smuggler. The bus was approaching the City. Brett stood up and alighted at Liverpool Street station. He walked past the Andaz hotel towards Moorgate. The cafes, small restaurants and pubs were still full. The sun was shining and the terraces heaving with people.

"Is there a crisis, I wonder?" Brett mumbled. His complaint was disingenuous he knew. His business in art dealing had never been better. Although he had to admit that contemporary art was taking the prize. Maybe he could change his tack.

Ridiculous – his heart would always be with the classics: the exceptional craft, the complexity and skill of the old Masters. But his pocket was always empty and the sums that contemporary art yielded astronomical. The latest Basel fair had earned its participants just short of one billion dollars. One billion dollars – unthinkable.

The flow of cars had stopped and Brett crossed the street. He turned left and entered the Barbican Centre. The place was large enough for him to find a secluded spot to make the call. The brutal architecture offended his senses but somehow it suited the call he was about to place. It was already 2.30 PM; people would be leaving the pond area to go back to work. Excellent.

* * *

Her cup was empty. Nancy wondered whether she should indulge in another one?

Why not? There was no urgency today. She had woken up early as she always did and had finished the most important work for the day. She was working on the next Women in Enterprise event she was sponsoring but she was well advanced with the paper she would deliver. Her conversation with the founder of the newly created 30% Club promoting greater gender balance on FTSE100 boards had galvanised her thinking. They were still debating mandatory quotas but the day was young and the event a few months away. The young art gallery she was supporting had turned the corner. The crisis had put pressure on their finances but they had managed to survive with new commissions for their emerging artists. Charles Saatchi was rumoured to be taking an interest in the stunning photographs that were on display there, a politically loaded subject that the photographer had managed to render compelling, almost aesthetic: the *Spomeniks* of Eastern Europe. A purchase by such a discerning collector would set the gallery on a new course. And they were expecting results from the Hong Kong Art Basel Fair during which they had started to connect with Chinese galleries and collectors. Nancy had been slow to respond to their enthusiasm for China. She looked around the courtyard where the use of concrete had been softened by the lush greenery, the water of the pond that reflected a perfect blue sky. Her eyes crept up the building side to reach the large concrete blocks that formed the Barbican, a perfect example of the brutalist architecture that she could never quite understand. The sign of an era that would soon test the limits of the communist ideology both in China and what was then the USSR. Her eyes unexpectedly clouded. She cleared her throat. Why revisit a painful past that she felt she had come to terms with? She pushed it away as she always did with a resolute nudge.

Nancy had bought a number of papers before joining Edwina for lunch. She intended to look once more for news of Gary's death. Pole had promised to call her with the preliminary toxicology results as soon as they came through. There would be quite a few of these before the pathologist delivered her final verdict but it was a helpful start. Then she would put matters to rest. She certainly wanted to see Pole again but there was no need to invent some hideous crime to spend an evening with her favourite inspector. They were going to see a show together – God, it was another date. Nancy almost blushed. She had not felt this flustered for a very long time. Hesitation, her worst adversary when it came to love.

She opened the *FT* and started reading her newspaper, more about the financial crisis of course, but nothing on Gary. She leisurely moved to the next page.

* * *

A couple stood up, took their tray and moved away. Brett frowned; the table was perfectly positioned but dirty. He signalled to one of the waitresses and demanded the mess be cleared. The young Asian woman smiled and apologised. Brett hardly acknowledged her. He was about to sit down when he noticed a few crumbs left on the table. He called the Asian woman back impatiently. The girl came back flustered, apologising profusely.

"Anything else, sir?" she asked nervously.

"It will do. Actually, a pot of tea would be good to make up for the inconvenience," Brett said with a dismissive gesture.

He sat down, pulled a notebook from his inner pocket, a well-used fountain pen from another and got out one of the burner phones purchased earlier on. He composed himself for a few moments before placing the call. The people he was dealing with exasperated him but he could not show his contempt or get angry. His open disdain for Henry Crowne had brought him very close to being investigated. MI6-Steve had not been amused. A public place was the perfect environment to ring his Italian contact. He would have to show restraint.

"*Ciao Antonio, come va?*" said Brett in perfect Italian, the privilege of an upper-class upbringing. He opened his paper and looked for the crosswords. Brett would wait a little before interrupting Antonio's rant:

the state of the trafficking business was deteriorating by the minute – much easier and more lucrative to traffic people than works of art: just put them on the boat and off they go. Brett exercised patience and allowed Antonio his fifteen minutes. There was no way he was volunteering an increase in the already extortionate price he was paying to smuggle the artefacts out of Iraq and move them to their final destination.

"Back to our business if you don't mind old chap," Brett interrupted finally. "I am about to speak to the purchaser who I believe is ready to buy … Yes, the gold jar … And possibly the bust of Ishtar from Babylon."

Brett scribbled on his paper.

"I see … Can't we do it sooner? … What do you mean the Libyan route has become tricky? I would have thought the mess in which Libya is at the moment makes it easier … Gaddafi is gone and Libya is an almighty mess. I would have thought it a good thing for smugglers."

Brett looked around. He had raised his voice a little too much for his liking but the place was by now nearly empty.

"Look, I need the consignment delivered in the next two weeks. The deal is worth £50,000 to you. It's a year's salary for some people in the UK and as ever I have been overgenerous."

Brett sat back in his chair and let Antonio rant again. He knew his contact would eventually come down and agree to his price. Brett could not help smiling. Antonio did justice to the popular conception of Italians: talking, complaining and eventually agreeing to something illegal. Brett lifted his non-existent chin and winced; the Barbican architecture irked him today more than usual, such an excruciatingly ugly lump of concrete. Why on earth had this piece of brutalism become a listed building – another lefty preserving the work of one of their anarchist architect friends?

"Antonio, I have a meeting in five minutes," Brett said. "Good man. I know you will deliver as you always do in the most difficult of circumstances." Brett carried on showering compliments on his contact; a proud Italian man would always succumb to flattery. The consignment would arrive on time. Brett had given himself a large margin for error. Italy had never been the most obvious route but it was the safest for art trafficking. He had tried a few already – Greece and Turkey – but his Italian counterparts delivered not only on time, much to Brett's amazement, but also understood how to handle high value artifacts and the pieces arrived in pristine condition. Soon he would however have to increase Antonio's take. He was right the trafficking route was becoming inundated with desperate people trying to leave a region devastated by war. Traffickers simply had to put people on a boat, often without a map, and charged $5,000 per head – the maths was easy.

Then again, Brett had already made a couple of million pounds. And it was only his share of the spoil. He was asking his client to pay almost a million for the gold jar. The Iraqi rebels took half a million, Brett took his share, a neat £300,000, and the rest would go to the various intermediaries. And so what if he was helping a bunch of terrorists; it was all a matter of perspective.

The word terrorist made Brett smile. It reminded him of one of his most high-profile clients – Henry Crowne himself. The Irish peasant had ended up in prison, a delightful thought. But who could have predicted the link between Henry and the IRA? When Henry had been accused of the murder of one of his banking rivals, Anthony Albert, Brett had not believed his luck. He had been grooming Albert's wife for a while and here was Adeila, available and ready to be plucked. But it had all come to nothing and Brett had felt bitter disappointment when it turned out that Adeila had been made destitute by her husband. Still, seeing Crowne sent down for thirty years had been music to his ears. Brett had a score to settle with Henry. He had hooked him on the sale of (legitimate!) art from Asia and had wondered whether Crowne would buy some of the Middle-Eastern pieces he was smuggling in early 2004. Henry had been mesmerised by the quality of the artefacts Brett was showing him, going firm on a series of superb cuneiform tablets. The price was agreed, a hefty £450,000. And then – Henry recanted. Brett inhaled and refused to let the memory blur his focus. Crowne was in prison. He had lost most of his wealth in fines and lawyers' fees. The Irish peasant was of no use to him any longer – shame.

His newspaper was still open in front of him. He checked he had recorded the relevant information. He would soon destroy the paper and leave no trace of the details recorded on it. Brett stretched his gangly body, looked around and started walking towards Barbican station.

Nancy had finished reading her newspapers; her second cup of cappuccino was empty. The pond was deserted apart from a man sitting at the far end. She pulled the papers together and was about to stand when the man she had noticed got up, stretched and leisurely made his way towards the steps that rose to her left. She knew him. Nancy dropped the wad of papers on the table and scrambled in her bag for her glasses. She found them just in time to look at the man who was nearly out of sight – Brett Allner-Smith? Could it really be him? Should she catch up with him? She stood and started climbing the stairs too. She was now only a few yards

270

away but she slowed down, surprised by the outfit: old slacks and a tired blue jacket. Gone was the immaculate three-piece suit and the subtle tie. Brett's pompous personality did not fit the current attire. She slowed down further ... Yet the walk, the fair hair with a nascent balding patch on top, looked just like him. Nancy decided to keep following the man. She was after all going in the same direction, towards Barbican station where she could catch a bus. The man turned left, he was almost certainly going to go down the flight of stairs that led to the courtyard from which he would reach the street. Nancy decided to go straight on. She could turn a little later to follow the same route. A mobile rang. Nancy slowed. The man answered.

"Antonio, what now? I told you before, I am the one making contact."

Nancy was all ears. It *was* Brett. She recognised his voice, the contrived way of pronouncing certain common words. Irritating.

"The consignment must arrive on time. My client will not wait and more importantly my Iraqi contact will find another buyer."

Nancy froze. She was about to emerge into the open if she kept walking. She came as close as possible to the corner of the wall and waited. Brett had slowed down and was hovering at the top of the stairs.

"How much more?" Brett said, irritated by the hard bargain Antonio was driving. "No chance ... I will think about it ... I said I will think about it ... *Ciao*." Brett switched off the phone. "Bloody Italian Mafioso." Brett was on the move again. Nancy could hear his footsteps disappear down the stairs. If she followed he may recognise her, no – he would recognise her. How could he forget?

All was silent now. Nancy reached the top of the stairs. She could see Brett disappearing into the street. She followed quickly, feigning to search for some lost item in her large bag. She stood at the crossroads. Brett had disappeared into the tube station. She briskly crossed the road as the light was turning red. An impatient driver used his horn and gestured. Nancy did not bother to apologise. She entered the station and reached the platform on time to see Brett boarding a train towards King's Cross. She jumped into the nearest carriage just as the doors closed.

What was she doing? It was none of her business. If Allner-Smith was involved in some dodgy deals did she really want to know? But her heart was racing and her curiosity aroused.

"Curiosity killed the cat," she whispered. Then again, cats had nine lives and she had a few of those left in store. She stood near the doors and watched people coming in and out of the carriages. They reached King's Cross and when the doors were about to close she squeezed out quickly.

She saw Brett disappear in the distance. He was not moving towards the Piccadilly line but towards one of the exits. She followed. Outside he turned towards St Pancras and took the escalators. The Belle Epoque brasserie was packed, Eurostar travellers enjoying a quick meal before departure: a couple celebrating something important with champagne and caviar, a family of five struggling to keep the children in check. Brett hesitated. He stopped at a quiet terrace table, looked around, and sat down nonchalantly. Nancy dived into the restaurant, flashing a broad smile at a young waiter. He accompanied her towards the ideal table, providing the perfect shield. The doors were open: Nancy inside, Brett on the outside, a 50–50 chance she would hear his conversation.

"I presume you don't serve Earl Grey?"

Nancy could hear Brett clearly. She smiled; the same arrogant arse.

"You do? How amazing – a pot of Earl Grey, lemon, no sugar, and can I expect proper china?"

Nancy sat back. She was in pole position. The waiter went out with Brett's order. She could not bend forward to see what was going on and was starting to wonder whether anything would actually happen when she heard Brett's voice again, a voice discreet but audible.

"Bonjour Mohammed, votre contact anglais á l'appareil."

Nancy was surprised. Brett's French was excellent, a soft English accent but perfect grammar. He must be speaking to someone with North African origins. Brett asked to speak to *Le Capitaine* and *Le Capitaine* came online.

"Good afternoon Captain. Are you ready to ship the consignment?"

Nancy was intrigued by the switch to English. Maybe the captain was Middle-Eastern? Brett had mentioned Iraq.

"Yes, my contact can do the transfer within the deadline we have fixed … The price stays at $1.2 million … My client is ready to proceed."

Nancy stopped in mid-air, her cup not quite reaching her lips. $1.2 million was a pretty hefty sum in the world of art. Or was Brett dealing in some other products – illegal substances perhaps?

"We are using the normal route for payment … I agree we need to stay alert … The Swiss are far more cautious than they once were … I see, I will find a way."

There was a long pause. Nancy was tempted to move but what if Brett saw her? The smuggling business was a dangerous one and he would not take any risks. She knew what these people could do to an unwelcome witness.

"Very good, I believe we are done." Brett's voice had dropped. "I will get rid of this phone so any call from this number is not from me."

Brett hung up, called the waiter and paid cash immediately. His chair made of faint screeching noise as he rose. Nancy froze. If Brett looked back he would inevitably see her. He stopped for an instant, checked his pockets and carried on walking. She waved at the waiter to settle her own bill and noticed her hand was shaking.

"Serves me right. I am not Miss Marple."

When she stepped onto the terrace of the Belle Epoque Brett was nowhere in sight. She moved slowly towards the top of the escalator looking at the sea of people below. A Eurostar train had arrived. She gladly joined the crowd, safe in its midst.

* * *

Belmarsh prison had only been a name linked to one of his favourite films *V for Vendetta* until he set foot in it. A Category A closed prison, it had a reputation for housing lifers as well as those convicted for crimes carrying long sentences and within Belmarsh itself, the High Security Unit. HSU Belmarsh was a prison within a prison, a concrete block, grey and windowless. Little known to the public or even to the other eight hundred and forty-three prisoners, it had been the "home" of Abu Hamza until his extradition to the US. Getting into Belmarsh itself involved crossing fifteen gates and having fingerprints scanned but when you reached HSU the scans would start all over again. Charlie had warned him it would be no picnic. Although he had done time himself Charlie had never been a Cat. A con. He had nevertheless been an inexhaustible source of information and comfort. Charlie would not have wanted to be thanked for it. An armed robbery that had turned bloody had cost him ten years of his life; he was only eighteen at the time. He had decided on the day he had been sent down that he would walk out a free man and never return – classes, education, psychological support, he had done the lot and finally been given his chance to turn the page when he was freed on parole. Now on licence, Charlie had become a reliable limo driver, a jazz fan who had managed to land a position at his favourite club. Henry had used Charlie as his regular driver. He had guessed his heavy past, yet always treated him with respect.

"Funny how things can turn out," Henry had said when Charlie came to visit him the first time. "Here I am banged up and here you are free as a bird."

"I know. I would never have imagined —" Charlie looked shy and tense. "I hope you don't mind if I don't stay for the full duration. It got to me to walk back in here, even after all these years."

"Charlie, mate, I am simply glad you came to see me." Henry had managed to smile.

"Listen, I have brought you something, only a few pages. A sort of guide to prison life." Charlie unfolded a few crumpled sheets of paper. "It's good you know, although the bloke who wrote it was not a Cat. A con."

Henry nodded and looked at the pages. Charlie had put one hand in front of his mouth as he spoke and lifted an eyebrow towards one of the guards.

"Yeah, be careful. They sometimes employ screws that can lip-read, so watch it."

Henry had looked at him in disbelief but Charlie had done time and he, Henry Crowne, was about to find out what Her Majesty's Pleasure had in store for him.

Henry had stuck to his routine, gone to the gym in the morning and yet again worked doubly hard. He had joined the few courses allowed within the HSU, an essential lifeline to the outside world, a sanity check to ensure he was still part of the human race. He had been assiduous, even though they sometimes depressed him.

He had, naïvely, seen prison as a way of redeeming himself, a way to atone but he had started to doubt that the release he was so craving would ever be granted to him between the four walls of a cell.

He had faced reality. The murder accusation that had turned to nothing and yet had unveiled part of an unsuspected iceberg, his contribution to the IRA. The entrapment he had been the victim of had nearly destroyed his sanity, a revenge never seen even by City standards. He had in a moment of insanity and utter despair believed he was guilty. He would still believe it and would have been condemned for it had Nancy and Pole not persisted. Henry still had Albert's letter in his file. It was there in his prison cell, a few steps away from him, a few steps away from the bed on which he was sitting. He had read it only once on the dreadful and yet liberating day it had been delivered to him. A letter that was meant to reach him in twenty years' time.

Henry stretched. He laced his long fingers together and reached over his head. The crack of his long bones gave him some small relief. But the terrible question was still haunting him. How much involvement had he truly had? He had not executed the plan but he had hatched that plan. Still a teenager in search of belonging, he had elaborated the means by which a bomb could be delivered onto a plane to Liam and Bobby O'Connor. He had so wanted to be part of that tightly-knit family and yet he had escaped to London.

The City, the money and the power had made no difference. He could not let go of the violence that a Belfast upbringing had driven into him. He had done all he could to support his friends, his only friends, people who were known IRA operatives.

Albert had been a devious bastard but also a true genius. Aware of his impending death he had trapped Henry in the most methodically planned revenge. He had seen an opportunity at a Dublin high-profile closing dinner at which he had met Liam and Bobby. He had dared to think the unthinkable, using Bobby to commit the deed, his own assassination. It had worked perfectly, with implacable precision. His only mistake had been the letter. His need to triumph absolutely over Henry, to make certain he would topple him over the edge, had saved Henry. The letter that explained every single detail, the letter that exonerated Henry, had been found on time.

And today Henry was paying for what he had done: the support of a terrorist organisation. But the more he thought about his need for redemption, the more he felt he needed to use his ability, his powerful intellect, to earn that absolution. What could he do in prison? He was educated, a maths degree, a solicitor's qualification. He had built one of the most innovative teams in the world of structured products. He still read several books a week and had managed to become one of the librarians of HSU Belmarsh's small library.

The anger that had always fuelled him had perhaps abated a little. He felt much more in control. He knew he could not let it rise in a Cat. A prison, let alone within the confines of HSU Belmarsh. Henry did not fancy spending time in the segregation unit where prisoners had to spend twenty three hours a day in their cells. Henry was surrounded by terrorists, murderers; not fancy bankers who talked tough but had no idea what it would mean to deliver. IRA members had done time there before him, now replaced by al-Qaeda terrorists; so had the hardcore criminal Ronnie Biggs together with the unexpected Lord and liar – Baron Archer of Weston-super-Mare, simply known as Jeffrey Archer to HMP.

Henry had deliberately avoided the former and certainly had no desire to be further embroiled with the latter. There was no way he was giving free investment advice to a bunch of maniacs. He would probably end up with a knife sticking between his shoulder blades despite the somewhat reassuring track record of HSU – no one had ever been murdered there but there was always a first. The usual crappy disclaimer "stocks may go up as well as down" would not do the trick this time. Shame Archer had been released before his time; it might have been fun to speak to a well-educated man although Henry doubted Archer would have had to be held in HSU itself.

The greatest punishment he had to endure was a lack of freedom to do something, to contribute in some way, any way. Although the concept of reparation was bandied about a lot around the prison system, Henry felt it merely meant shut up and don't make a fuss.

But Henry no longer wanted to shut up. After the shock of incarceration, the months it had taken to absorb Liam's betrayal, Bobby's madness in executing his plan and the annihilation of his career he needed to exercise this brilliant mind of his. He needed a plan and the forbidden word had started creeping into his brain more and more often – escape.

Chapter Five

The preliminary toxicology report on the jumper, Version 1-01, was on Pole's desk. Gary Cook was a user, nothing hardcore – more recreational: a little skunk for good measure, amphetamines – a lot of amphetamines – and then something new, something Pole was unfamiliar with, nootropics. The coroner's opinion was clear. Cook used the amphetamines for sporting competition; boxing was his thing: broken nose and displaced jaw, broken fingers on both hands. Cook had been a keen boxer in his youth and still belonged to a boxing ring in the City. He must have enjoyed giving the bankers-would-be-boxers a punch for their money. An East-End upbringing was bound to have trained him in bare knuckle fighting.

Pole had visited Cook's home in South Kensington. The range of bodybuilding equipment was impressive and even more so was the private boxing ring built in the basement so he agreed about the amphetamines. He had left his Detective Sergeant Nurani Shah there to complete the search. If there was anything to find, she would. Maybe that would shed some light on the rest of the tox report.

He headed towards the coffee machine.

"Talk of the Devil," Pole said as he spotted the Detective Sergeant in front of him.

Nurani smiled. She was rattling a bag full of plastic jars of various pills. Gary Cook was indeed a naughty boy.

"What have we got here?"

"I have to say, it's pretty impressive. A great collection. And I can tell you that a lot of them are not legal. All purchased through the Internet with a particularly strong connection to an American website."

"Let's go into my office."

Pole gentlemanly gave way to Nurani and closed the door.

"How much of that stuff is used for bodybuilding and how much sends you on a high?"

"A lot of that stuff, as you put it, has to do with energy and resilience. These little red ones are amphetamines and these little yellow ones are steroids. I have not yet found the one that really sends you on a high. I am forwarding all these to the lab but I'm pretty sure that the Yankee ones will be strong."

"OK Nu, deal with the tox guys. I want to know whether any of these combined with booze would have sent Gary as high as a kite."

"You mean a kind of acid trip? Pushing him to jump?"

Pole looked at the bag. He recognised some of the names but nothing sprung to mind.

"What I can see here tells me more about pushing the body to its limits, aggression in sport, but not enough to kill the bloke. Although it might explain the arguments with people at the conference."

"Agreed, the competitive edge is more his style – the winner's drug."

"I don't see any of this making you suicidal though."

"And no cocaine either?"

"Zip, not a trace. And we have gone through the entire house, top to bottom with a fine-toothed comb, floorboards up, emptied bookshelves – you name it. "

Pole smiled at Nurani. She too was pumped up. Nothing better to draw out her skills than an investigation into the banking world. She had excelled and earned her stripes on the Crowne case. Pole did not even want to imagine the state of the house she had just searched, showing little sympathy for the grieving widow and children.

"What did Mrs Cook have to say for herself?"

"She admitted to smoking a bit of weed but she had no idea how much Gary was consuming. I gather that he was not the sort of guy who was going to share his innermost thoughts with his wife."

"Was he depressed after GL had sacked him?"

"More pissed off apparently than depressed. He was talking to his lawyers and simply volunteered that he was onto a good deal – and he was networking a lot."

"Networking – more specifically?"

"She did not volunteer much. Again, not a great deal of confidences when it came to work but she said that he was going to a lot of conferences and networking evenings at his City club."

"Old school, earn the crust whilst the Missus stays at home to look after the kids and cooks for the hunter who brings back his leg of mammoth."

"I thought I was the one who did not like the bankers."

"It's not the bankers I don't like. It's the sort of guy who still thinks women are second-class citizens."

"Hear, hear, my honourable friend" said Nurani knocking on his desk repeatedly.

Pole waved a reproaching finger at her.

"Now, now, missus. I mean it and you know it."

"I know Jon, I could not have had a better mentor," Nurani replied in earnest. And she meant it too.

"I don't really want to say this," Pole changed the subject to avoid more unwanted compliments. "But I am going to say it anyway. This suicide does not feel quite right."

Nurani moved a pile of documents that lay on Pole's single spare armchair and sat down. She was also gathering her thoughts.

"Despite what his wife says he might have felt bad about losing his job. It is not uncommon for macho guys to lose their rag. In particular if his job was given to some young buck or, worse, a woman."

"I might agree with you if he was left with nothing. But he was about to settle for a lot of money, possibly enough to start his own consultancy or hedge fund."

Nurani looked unconvinced.

"We are not in the north of England, Nu. He is not a miner or a factory worker with no hope. That sort of guy will always find something new to do. Actually, do we know how much he was getting?"

"Not yet, I have spoken to HR at GL–HXBK. I should have the final number tomorrow. The HR woman volunteered it was a generous offer."

"OK, we're talking millions. Do we know why they wanted to keep him quiet?"

"A long-serving employee?" ventured Nurani. "Remember, GL were up to their eyeballs in subprime debt. I bet you they don't want another scandal."

"What do you mean another scandal?" asked Pole, sitting up in his chair.

"I don't pretend I have new evidence but depending on the size of the deal – maybe they want to avoid another HR scandal."

"That's a very good point, Ms Shah. Maybe there is something else too that will come out. My sources tell me the disclosure of the crappy deals the City has been involved in is far from over."

"I see," said Nurani pursing her lips. Pole knew the expression well. She was frustrated she had not followed through on a potential lead.

"I'll go back and ask."

"Do. And you may want to emphasise we are not the FSA. I don't care what they have been cooking – I'm looking for a motive."

Nurani shook her head and was about to leave, eager to repair her mistake.

"Not so fast young lady. We did not speak about the new drug that was found in Cook's bloodstream. "

"Nootropics – There was nothing at his home, and we still don't have the full picture on these," replied Nurani a little too sharply.

"Really. Are you ruling them out completely? Surely it is not enough that you have not found any nootropics at Cook's house in Belgravia? Do you have a theory?"

"Well according to wife and kids, they don't use that stuff – at all. And again, we have looked —"

"I know, absolutely everywhere. Don't you think it is strange?"

"Well, I spoke to them straight after they return from Uni. I don't think they had time to rehearse the story."

Pole stroked his goatee. *A little empathy, Nu. A little empathy.* "In these days of mobile phones, I doubt they would not have spoken already."

Nurani shrugged. "Maybe. But what he was taking was not illegal, so I guess he was free to stash it at the office."

Pole sat back and remembered what Nancy had said. Gary was a party animal in the naughty nineties.

"Do we know whether these networking events involve a bit of partying afterwards? I am not necessarily talking strip joints but some private club, preferably gentlemen only unless the company involves a bunch of escort girls."

"And he would not have bragged about it to his wife either."

Nurani stood up. "Good point, I am on it."

She left Pole's office unhappy. Ms Shah was brooding a lot lately, Pole had noticed. And he knew why. A trip to the office coffee machine a few days ago had illuminated Pole perhaps more than he had wished.

"She seemed to be a good adviser on the Crowne case … and very pleasant," their colleague Andy Todd had said whilst stirring more sugar into his coffee. Nurani was leaning against the coffee machine, back towards the small corridor that led to it. Pole had slowed down as soon as he'd heard the word adviser.

"True enough, but she is not a trained officer. And she defended some pretty slimy people in her time as a QC." Nurani spoke as someone who had done a deep dive into the past of the adviser and Pole knew they were talking about Nancy.

"Perhaps, but why do you care anyway? You're up for promotion, aren't you?"

"But if there is a procedural cock-up because we have used the said consultant I can kiss goodbye to that and it's not strictly by the book anyway."

Andy had not replied and Pole had not believed his ears either. Was this the same Nurani, now all concerned about doing it *by the book*, who had proven a mercenary when it came to negotiating with the IRA for Henry's head?

Pole had retreated to his desk without a coffee to ponder on what he had heard.

Nancy was an excellent consultant and Ms Shah would have to get used to working with her if she wanted to continue working with Pole.

Pole pressed 1 on his phone's speed dial. And the phone chimed away. He grabbed the receiver and waited for Nancy to answer.

* * *

Nancy cursed as she entered the ground floor hallway of her luxurious apartment block. She had just missed Pole's call. She would call back as soon as she reached her apartment. She pushed the door open and picked up the mail that the concierge had slid through the letterbox. A large envelope attracted her attention. The paper had a different texture, unmistakably foreign, Asian she thought. She hesitated. It had been posted in Hong Kong. No, she would open it later, one thing at a time.

"Jonathan, I am so sorry I missed you. The wretched phone's ring is too low against the noise of traffic on Angel's Corner."

She listened to Pole's description of his findings without interrupting.

"So, in a nutshell, you are now also in doubt about Cook's suicide but have no concrete evidence. I'm sorry to be a spoilsport but I can't imagine GL volunteering information about any financial problems they may have."

Pole agreed.

"Well, there is one person who might be able to help," Nancy said, waiting to see whether Pole would take the bait. He did.

"You mean … Ah, sorry, a call for you on the other line. Not to worry. We have our Sadler's Wells' evening tonight so we can discuss without interruption. Looking forward."

Nancy smiled. Pole had been a solid friend for the past four years, a man whose company she enjoyed but, as ever, she could not quite make up her mind to go a little further, let alone commit. She pushed the idea aside and turned her attention to the large envelope. She moved from her lounge to her office, climbing the wood-and-steel spiral staircase slowly. She found the letter opener and cautiously slit the top of the envelope open. Inside was a letter accompanied by a newspaper article and photos – many photos. She checked the signature on the letter and recognised it, Philippe Garry. She had met him a few years ago. He had sold Henry his first important piece of contemporary art, *The Raft of the Medusa*. She had followed the evolution of Philippe's gallery with interest. He too had gone to Hong Kong, for the now much sought after HKG Art Fair. Whereas his London gallery had a clear contemporary art focus, Philippe's new venture in Hong Kong had a more open brief: contemporary, modern and some high-quality artefacts that provided unique selling opportunities.

His letter was written on an attractive sheet of rice paper.

Dear Nancy,
Join the "River Crab Feast!" On November 7, 2010 one of China's most prominent artists, Ai Weiwei, was placed under house arrest in Beijing. Since then over 1,000 people have attended the River Crab Feast at his Shanghai Studios. On January 11, 2011 the Shanghai city government, having declared the studios an illegal construction, proceeded with their demolition without appeal or prior notice.

The letter went on to talk about abuse of power *and human rights violations* and gave a link to a video of the demolition – The Crab House_YouTube – inviting Nancy to watch it, share it on social media and comment on it *"In solidarity with a friend and colleague whose freedom is under threat. They silence him, yet his voice grows louder and louder."*

Nancy froze, a shiver rippled through her body. She could not bring herself to take a look at the photos or read the article. A sense of fear she had thought no longer existed within her shook her. She sat down and dropped the letter on her office desk. She stood up again, grabbed the letter and staggered towards her kitchen. Her slender hand squeezed the banister of her stairwell for fear of falling. She wanted to tear the letter to shreds and yet the more reasonable part of her was protesting. She boiled the kettle and was about to make her much loved Sichuan tea when the name on the packet gave her a jolt – Sichuan. She thumped the work surface of her kitchen with her fist. What was wrong with her? She put the tea packet back in its jar and looked for Darjeeling. She went through her tea ritual to calm herself, warming the teapot, measuring the amount with precision. She chose her favourite mug and went back to the lounge. The letter she had thrown onto the coffee table had fallen face down. She poured some tea and sat, her hands resting on her knees. She had lectured Henry so much about coming to terms with his own past and the past had decided to catch up with her too. She moved to the sound system in the lounge. Nancy selected some easy listening music, *The Best of Julie London* and sunk into a soulful tune.

The smoky voice of Julie London transported Nancy to another time and place. She had not been born in the fifties but Nancy sometimes wished she had known America then. So much was going to happen in the world in the next forty years. Her mind was slowly drifting back to China and she was about to push it away again when her favourite song came on. The languid vocals of 'Cry Me a River' moved Nancy in a very different direction – a jazz club, the cosy atmosphere made for intimacy and the man she was meeting that night. Pole had stood up and offered a dance with such effortless charm that she had found herself on the dance floor before she had said yes. The 606 Jazz Club was full, as you would expect a good jazz club to be, yet not so packed that there was no room to move. Pole turned out to be a surprisingly good dancer.

Nancy stretched on her sofa, eyes closed. She could still feel Pole's touch; his hand on her back, fingers slightly stretched. She had tensed and then relaxed. Pole moved slowly, giving her time to adjust to a feeling she had not had for a long time and she suspected neither had Pole.

She opened her eyes; the memory was both delicious and annoying. She was not ready to fall in love.

* * *

The clock had moved very little since he had last checked it – 5:35 PM. Pole stretched and ran his long hands through his salt-and-pepper hair; he fingered the tickets in his jacket pocket and smiled. Meeting Nancy for something other than discussing the latest crime he was investigating made his pulse quicken. He enjoyed the keen feeling of expectation but he was also a patient man. There was no rush. Nancy was an emotional enigma that he wanted to solve slowly. He would soon get ready, change his shirt and tie for the inevitable black turtleneck sweater. The Kodo performance started at 7.30 PM; they had planned to meet an hour before for a pre-concert drink – 5:40 PM, Pole sighed.

Nurani knocked at the door and stepped in. Pole cast an eye at the clock again, 5:41 PM.

"What can I do for you?"

"Just had a real interesting call with HR," Nurani said, excited.

Pole raised a quizzical eyebrow. "Thinking of moving to Traffic are you?"

Nurani shrugged her shoulders. That was not funny. "Nah. They won't have me. I'm too tall – I mean GL HR."

"That's more interesting."

"Sure is. First, the woman said the package for Cook was standard. Then she said she could not comment in detail, so I asked to speak to her boss. Anyway, to cut a long story short, the Head of HR came on the line. I have a feeling that Cook was helping 'the FSA with their enquiries'," Nurani said, using both hands to shape in the air quotation marks. "GL does not want to be seen to have an axe to grind against Cook."

Pole sat up. Nurani had his full attention.

"Is he a whistleblower?"

"I don't think so, not exactly. At least not according to HR."

"They would have said so if it had been the case. Interesting, mmm. Did they volunteer any details or do they want to speak to Compliance first?"

Nurani nodded with an approving smile. Pole was always one beat ahead when things mattered.

"They are checking."

"They know. They just don't want to make a big boo-boo. And I presume they also will have to speak to their gators."

"What, alligators? I know it's banking but still!"

"You are not far wrong. I mean their litigators and other fancy lawyers. If it is what I think it is – We could have our motive here."

"Goody, a bit of banker bashing. Just the way I like it. And more information has come in, take two of the prelim tox report."

"You mean Version 1-02?" Pole asked.

"Yup, and now we not only know he was taking nootropics but he was loaded with them."

"You mean he might have ODed anyway? And how many prelim tox reports are we going to get before we get THE FINAL report? Who's the pathologist on this?"

"Someone new. Don't recognise the name but I think she is delivering in stages to help us."

"Ask our Head Pathologist to cast an eye, will you?" Pole closed the file that Nurani had placed in front of him.

"Sure, will do. But back to that nootropic stuff. Apparently it expands your brain capacity. I am checking what else it can do. And don't be impatient … the guys are giving us the info as soon as they have it so that we don't lose time."

"OK, fine but get hold of the Drug Squad team; find out if there are any reported incidents in the past month or so involving the same type of nootropics around London. And I also want to know who sells the stuff, where and how to get hold of it."

Nurani crossed her arms over her chest in mock anger.

"Already on it, sir."

"You're the best. And I am just an old fart trying to make sure he's keeping up with the younger generation," Pole said amused. "Anything else?" Pole eyed the clock again – 5:55 PM. Time to get changed. Pole closed the file he was reading with a thud and moved it onto the to-be-continued pile.

Nurani did not take the hint and sat herself down in the armchair facing Pole's desk.

"Actually Jon, I was wondering whether I could have a chat with you about something else?"

Pole looked at his watch. He had another five minutes and nodded. He had intended to leave early but if his DS needed him he would be there for her. Nurani's eyes fell on the tickets that Pole had mechanically taken out of his pocket. Pole noticed her stubborn look.

"I know you've put me forward for promotion, Jon, and I am really grateful. But do you think they'll take it seriously? I am a bit anxious."

Pole sat back and looked at Nurani closely. She was not the anxious type so why pretend? She had been equally vocal about her ambitions, so why hide it behind fake humility?

"I can't guarantee anything but you know I gathered very good reports from senior members of the force. I got Pat Murphy in Ireland to support you after your excellent performance in the Crowne case. Liam gave us the evidence against Henry, his friend, after Pat and you cut a deal with him. It all looks pretty solid, believe you me."

"That's reassuring, still I'm not exactly the typical DI, am I?" Nurani's voice trailed. She was now comfortably sitting in the chair with apparently little intention of moving. Pole looked at his watch – 5:59.

"You mean your Asian background. With the report you have it won't be a problem and it shouldn't be anyway. You know I would not tolerate any setback in that respect. If it does not go through I will be asking questions."

"I know you will, Jon."

The clock struck 6pm. Pole stood up. He was leaving right now whether she liked it or not. He pocketed his tickets, grabbed a small bag from underneath his desk and placed it on his chair, zipping it shut with a swift gesture. Nurani looked frustrated. Pole's constant open-door policy irritated some of his superiors but enthused his colleagues and juniors. Today however he was leaving on time and would resume his conversation with Nurani tomorrow. There was nothing more that needed discussing urgently about her promotion. Nurani simply wanted to hear how good she had been, was and would be, perhaps to be reassured somewhat. Had she guessed he was meeting Nancy tonight? DS Shah soon to become DI Shah might well have done. She was after all a very good cop.

"It's time. I am off," Pole said clapping his hands together.

He grabbed the bag again and gave Nurani a broad but uncompromising smile. She returned a dark look and stood up without a word.

Pole followed Nurani through the door of his office, locked it and moved swiftly towards the corridor. He was off on a date.

* * *

"Glass of champagne or beer?" Nancy had texted. Pole felt a little annoyed. She had just beaten him to the theatre. He deliberated over which was the most appropriate. Beer was a bit too copper-like. Champagne, he did not like the thought of Nancy having to buy her own glass. Champagne should be bought by the gentleman. Oh God, what to do?

"Shit, I'll go for what I like," he muttered and went for Champagne. Pole entered the building and spotted Nancy perched on a high stool at one of the tables set up in the small theatre wine bar. There was always a relaxed elegance about her no matter what she wore. Her black-and-white trouser outfit, vintage haute couture perhaps, was a perfect smart-casual choice that enhanced her tanned skin and jet-black hair. Nancy waved and gave Pole a broad smile.

"Don't worry. Perfect timing. It would have been pitiful if I had not beaten you to it since I live three minutes' walk from here," she said anticipating Pole's objection.

"You're too kind. I'll order for the interval. You look well," Pole said bending forward to kiss her cheek.

"Of course, Jonathan," Nancy replied whilst returning his kiss. "I just came back last week from a few days in France."

They briefly caught up on the latest developments in the Cook affair but there was little Nancy did not know already. Their conversation drifted into a more enjoyable chat until it was time to take their seats.

* * *

The Kodo drums were in full swing, the rhythm and intensity rising and ebbing to reach unimaginable crescendos. Pole was on the edge of his seat and Nancy was transfixed. He had cast an eye towards his companion at the beginning of the performance. Nancy had been hooked from the first beat the players had struck. The next number was about to start when Pole heard the low vibration of his phone. Someone wanted to talk but he was damned if he would even consider taking a discreet look. *They'll leave a message if it is that urgent.* Sure enough the phone interrupted again. Pole discreetly looked at his watch – only ten minutes to go till the end of the first half.

"This is extraordinary," Nancy said with complete enthusiasm as they made their way out of the auditorium. "I never would have gone on my own. Thank you."

Pole grinned. He was glad he could introduce the much-cultured Ms Wu to some new music. Next step was jazz fusion but all in good time. They reached the small table they had left an hour ago. Two glasses were waiting for them. Pole dragged his phone out of his pocket with an apologetic smile.

"Jonathan – remember, I used to be a QC. I am impressed you have waited till the end of the last piece. I would have been out of the performance like a shot."

Pole had put the phone to his ear in a distracted fashion. He was about to reply to Nancy when his focus became absolute. Nancy read his face and forgot about her drink altogether. Pole inhaled deeply and was about to apologise once more.

"Do tell Jonathan – someone else jumped?"

"No, but was found in his garage – dead in his car."

"You're going?" Nancy asked more as an observation than a question.

Pole nodded. "Want to join me?"

Nancy grabbed her bag and coat. "Who is he, if I may ask?"

"Tom Hardy, Chief Executive of the British Bankers' Association."

Nancy frowned but did not look surprised. Something was bothering her and with this new death Pole wanted to know why.

Chapter Six

The recognisable white-and-blue barricade tape had already been placed around the scene. Pole had parked his car in the middle of Holland Park. Forensics was following him. They waved as they recognised him. Nancy got out and simply observed: Pole absorbing the information, the details of what the first PC on the scene had gathered, the opinion of the paramedics. Nancy admired his effortless mastery of the situation, focused, controlled and yet inclusive. He waved her into the restricted perimeter.

"She is with me, consulting for the Met," Pole said to the other PC manning the surveillance of the enclosure. He handed a pair of gloves to Nancy and they entered the garage in which the body of Tom Hardy lay.

The odour of petrol fumes was still overwhelming. Nancy gagged but she stilled herself. She would not let Pole down. The driver's door was open and Tom had slumped in his seat. Nancy could not see his face but she noticed his hand stretched towards the passenger seat. He was still wearing a seat belt. Nancy noticed that the passenger door had been taped.

"Who found him?" Pole asked.

"His wife. DS Shah is with her at the moment," replied PC Thomas who had briefed Pole.

"You need to go in on your own," Nancy said. "I will take a look and see what I can make of it. I'll see you back at the car."

"I might be a while." Pole looked concerned.

"Don't worry. I'll make my own way if it takes you too long. I don't have another date to go to," Nancy replied with a teasing smile.

Pole nodded, smiling back, and disappeared. Nancy had learned to be guarded in Nurani's presence. She did not trust her and Nurani had made it clear she did not trust Nancy either. Too bad though; she would keep consulting with the Met whether the young DS liked it or not.

The SOCO team was setting up a tent outside the garage and a small pudgy woman arrived on the scene. She extended her hand to Nancy after removing her gloves.

"Are you *the* consultant?" she said with a twinkle in her voice.

"I did not think my reputation was that good. Or perhaps that bad," Nancy replied with equal amusement.

"Well, we all like a good gossip. And the boys are the worst." She gently moved Nancy along. "So, what have we got?"

"Do you mind if I join you?"

"Not at all. And I'm pretty sure you know the drill." She was already palpating the man's body, looking for initial clues. "My name is Yvonne Butler by the way. The Yard's head Senior Pathologist."

"Mine is Nancy Wu. I would say very nice to meet you but it may be inappropriate."

Yvonne shrugged.

"OK, no sign of struggle, position of body and face consistent with asphyxiation."

Yvonne took a small torch out of one of the pockets of her protective white overalls. "Mmmm, might have taken drugs – not uncommon in this sort of suicide," she said whilst checking one of the pupils of the dead man.

"You mean he was asleep before asphyxiation?"

"Very likely, I need to carry out a full autopsy to be sure, of course." She stood up to face Nancy. "Who is he anyway?"

"Tom Hardy, chief exec of the BBA."

"BBA?" Yvonne said moving away from the car to get her camera.

"British Bankers' Association," Nancy replied.

"Another banker! Gee, I have not even finished processing the last one."

"You mean Gary Cook?"

"The very same. Are you also 'consulting' on that one?" Yvonne asked mischievously.

"I'm afraid I am. And since we are talking about it, I presume you were there to photograph the body?"

Yvonne looked at Nancy with a hint of surprise.

"Why do you ask?"

"Did you think it was consistent with suicide to have the body land on its back?"

"A very good observation," Yvonne said, clearly convinced of the sharpness of Nancy's mind.

"And —"

"Unusual but not impossible. He was drunk and drugged. He may have lost his footing before he actually jumped," Yvonne replied as she started taking pictures. Nancy moved away slowly, turned around and said, "And Tom is still wearing his seat belt."

"Odd indeed," Yvonne acknowledged.

* * *

Nancy would have stayed were it not for Nurani. Pole had a long night in front of him and did not need a jealous spat between two strong-minded women. She smiled at the warm feeling Pole elicited but the proximity of the SOCO team sobered her up rapidly.

She texted Pole and called a cab.

The taxi drove past Sadler's Wells on the way back. The theatre was emptying slowly. An excited bunch of people were talking about the show with evident appreciation. Pole and she should have been part of the crowd and yet she enjoyed being part of his other life too. She could never be cross with a man who had a tough job to do.

Nancy entered the magnificent hallway of her block of apartments and took the lift to reach her landing. Until Henry was out of jail she would be the only one living on Floor 5. She was glad he had been able to keep the apartment opposite hers despite a crushing fine and lack of income. The tabloids had made a meal of it. How could a man involved in supporting terrorists still be able to afford such an expensive property? But Nancy knew the intimate side of the story: the childhood terror, the mixed-marriage nightmare in seventies' Belfast where Catholic and Protestant did not cohabit, let alone marry. She knew of the desperation to belong, the blind faithfulness to friendship that ultimately had brought Henry down. As ever, the barrister she was passionately believed that all should be allowed to find redemption and one day be absolved. Nancy found herself standing in the middle of her landing and opened the apartment door briskly. It was good to be home. She moved to the kitchen, made herself a pot of tea and a sandwich and removed her Louboutin Hot Jeanbi 100 with great relief.

"Really Nancy, walking a crime scene in five inch heels," she said almost amused.

She collapsed into her favourite armchair and picked up the yellow pad she now had a habit of leaving on the coffee table. She methodically reported all she had seen, smelt, heard, even touched and drew up a list of questions.

1. Suicide? Nancy did not know Tom Hardy very well but he did not seem a candidate for such an act of desperation. Edwina had spoken about his appointment as an excellent move for the financial institution he represented. The BBA was becoming old-fashioned, a lobby group for the various banking organisations and bodies that populated the City. More importantly, it was the institution that fixed LIBOR, the primary benchmark for interest rates, not only Sterling but also an impressive range of other currencies including Dollar LIBOR.

2. Financial crisis put pressure on him? Nancy poured a cup of tea. She inhaled its fragrance before taking a sip. How wonderful – tea, the cure for all ailments. She picked up the pad again and jotted ASK HENRY next to the question.

3. Tom Hardy's enemies? This would be a question for Edwina. Nancy was not entirely certain whether he had worked with her directly. It did not matter that much; in the rarefied sphere of the City's trading floors she would have had contact with him anyway. Henry might have a view as well.

4. Seat belt? This was the most puzzling part. That question would go to Pole. Or perhaps she could make friends with Yvonne. Nancy's excellent intuition was telling her it was a material element.

She looked at her watch, gone 1am. She was due to meet Henry the following day for her regular visit. Should she speak to Pole and get Henry involved? She shook her head – too early in the case. She sat back in her chair, put her legs underneath her and finished her sandwich – brown bread, plenty of butter and French mustard, smoked ham and a leaf of lettuce, delicious. She put her plate down and poured a second cup of tea, savouring the peace and security of her surroundings. Her eyes came to rest on the rice-paper letter she had received that morning.

"Not now," she said, annoyed at having left the Hong Kong letter on the table. "Too much death for one night." She stood up and disappeared up the flight of stairs to the shelter of her bedroom.

* * *

The early visiting slot opened at 9:15 AM. Belmarsh had strict rules for visitors requiring them to present themselves an hour in advance and be processed through the various gates and security checkpoints. However, Nancy was still using her Prerogative as counsel. The advantage was that she could hold and transfer documents that would never be checked by the guards. The contents of the folder she brought with her would never be examined.

The ride from Angel tube station had been uneventful. She was now sitting on the 244 bus and would arrive at Woolwich Arsenal in a few minutes. She had folded her Tate magazine and was looking at the landscape she had long since ceased to notice. Rows of low-rise buildings, squeezed between the Thames Docks and the highway, a desolate landscape for a desolate area.

She went through the gates with a crowd of people, mainly women some of whom she recognised and greeted. The early morning visits always drew the same kind of people. She acknowledged a short black woman and nodded. There was no fraternity but a certain amount of unexpected amiability. The processing started and the usual checks were performed. Legal counsels and solicitors were given their fair share of questions but nothing like the circus of what other visitors had to endure.

Nancy knew the drill too well to accept any nonsense from the prison officers and they knew it too.

"Anything else you need, officer?"

The man took his time. "Nope, all in order."

"As ever," Nancy said with the most courteous of smiles.

She was accompanied out of the main prison block to start the checks needed to enter the HSU. The small reception was carpeted, yet the comfort stopped there. The rest of the unit was bare. Nancy removed her shoes and her belongings were scanned. She walked though the metal detector unperturbed and let the guards check the lining of her suit and even the inside of her mouth. HSU guards themselves were subjected to the same strenuous checks. Nancy thanked the prison officer and moved to the meeting room.

Henry and she would have an hour and a half which sounded too little but sometimes was oddly too much. It was important to feel comfortable she had learned. She certainly had news to share but was equally keen to carry on the conversation they had started on her previous visit. Something was bothering Henry over and above his incarceration and she needed to know what.

The door clanged open and Henry entered. The prison officer removed the handcuffs. Henry rubbed his wrists, a mechanical gesture to check that his hands were indeed free rather than do away with the pain. Nancy stood up and took his hand with the usual kindness. He smiled, squeezing Nancy's hand in turn.

"Morning Nancy."

"Morning my dear."

Getting the conversation going was always a slow process. Nancy had come up with a routine that Henry liked. They would speak about his flat, the latest art exhibition, Nancy would feed him bits of gossip from the art world that made him feel he still belonged to the community of Collectors. The serious stuff would trickle through gradually.

Nancy put the copy of *Tate Etc.* on the table between them.

"Actually Nancy, I caught the news this morning. What is the story around Tom Hardy?"

"Officially, suicide – unofficially, I am not sure."

"So incredibly odd. First Gary, now Tom."

Nancy smiled. Henry was always on the ball. She told him all she knew.

"Still working with Pole as a consultant I s'pose?" Henry teased.

"I told you I wanted to reconnect somehow with my old profession. But no funny business, I promise."

"Good girl. Although I remember a particular letter that indicated otherwise."

"Argh. I should know better than to commit compromising information to paper." Nancy laughed. "Swiftly diverging our conversation, back to Tom and Gary. Do you see a connection?"

Henry pushed his chair back and lifted his face towards the ceiling. His short hair made the features of his face stand out even more. No doubt an attractive one, a resolute jaw, deep furrows slicing his cheeks and a slightly hooked nose gave it an intensity that could attract or disturb.

"A connection? That's an interesting thought."

Nancy looked at him incredulously. "You do have an idea."

"Well – I see one connection but I'm not sure whether it would matter."

"Pray tell."

"LIBOR, the interbank interest rate."

"Why? Gary was on the trading floor at GL and Tom was chief executive at the BBA. I can't see it and, yes, I know how LIBOR is being used."

Henry smiled. "I am not talking about LIBOR trading. Although it might also be a link come to think of it. I am talking about LIBOR fixing. To be more precise the process through which the banks decide where LIBOR sits daily, weekly, etc. "

"I am sorry. I feel particularly thick this morning but what's the connection between Gary and Tom?"

"You're not being thick Nancy; you just don't know these people as well as I do. Gary Cook was the guy who gave his estimate of where the bank, I mean GL, estimated LIBOR to be at. In other words, he estimated at what level GL could borrow in the interbank market and he was the official submitter of GL as far as LIBOR was concerned."

"And Tom?"

"Tom would preside over the fixing process. Not directly of course – but, still, remember BBA publishes LIBOR on Reuters."

Nancy remained silent, taking the information in.

"And how big is or rather was GL's Sterling rates book?"

Henry clapped his hands and gave Nancy the thumbs up.

"One of the largest on the market, a game changer in times of market turbulence."

Nancy's face grew serious.

"You must speak to Pole." Her dark eyebrows had come together so close they nearly formed a line. She meant business and Henry liked it.

"Well, do I want to speak to the guy who put me in this place for starters?" Henry replied dryly.

"You are being unfair. He brokered a deal to get you out of the mess in which you had put yourself."

Henry stood up, turning his back to Nancy. The prison officer reappeared.

"Please sit down, Henry."

Henry's fists were clenched but he obeyed.

"Does that mean I get to come out?"

Nancy blew through her cheeks.

"Is there any reason why you should?"

"Pole may want me to look at evidence on-screen, consult records and carry out a data search on Bloomberg."

"What are you expecting to find?"

"Nancy, if there is something to find that is market related, I will need to track it by myself and I don't want that to be done on Belmarsh's computer."

"You are not serious? You mean another banking scandal," Nancy said incredulous.

"I won't know for sure until I see the data." Henry was sticking to his guns. If Pole and Nancy wanted his help it would be done away from Belmarsh.

"OK, I'll speak to him."

"If this is LIBOR manipulation in size, it goes right to the top of the tree. You understand that?"

"You mean CEO level?"

"I mean government, Whitehall and the Bank of England."

Nancy looked Henry in the eyes. He was not joking or pretending. She thought of Edwina. Henry was perhaps overdoing it. He had been an equity boy all his working life. Was the manipulation of LIBOR a real prospect?

"I'll bear that in mind," Nancy replied. She was now keen to change the subject but did not need to find an excuse. Henry had noticed something or someone and his attention had shifted away from her entirely. She waited. Maybe this shift had something to do with what had been bothering Henry of late.

"Sorry, Nancy." A deep line was digging into his forehead; his blue eyes had grown a shade darker.

"Something's wrong?" Nancy asked resisting the urge to turn round.

"Not something – someone," Henry said slowly. "I usually don't worry about the many nutters that live round the corner from me but this one is bloody odd."

"In what way?"

"He has just arrived, thankfully not on the same landing though. His name is Ronnie Kray." Henry's attention was still on the space behind Nancy. He did not see her face drop in disbelief.

"You mean like the Kray brothers – but Ronnie died in the mid nineties."

"I know." Henry's focus came back to Nancy. "This guy has changed his name by deed poll apparently. The Kray twins are his favourite gangsters. He has carried out the inspiration a tad far for my liking – he is in here for murder and trafficking."

"Has he spoken to you?" The tone of her voice had taken on the professional edge he knew meant business.

"Not yet but he is looking, picking the moment of his choice. Charlie warned me about his type. They have a grudge and if you are on the wrong side of that grudge, beware."

"Do you need me to do anything? I can ask for a transfer at least out of the spur and —"

"I should not have worried you with this Nancy, it's the HSU after all," Henry said now more relaxed. Speaking up had had a comforting effect and Henry moved the conversation back to the topic of art. Nancy knew better than to prod for more information but she needed to stay alert. It was her turn to feel a little defocused on what Henry was saying. But Henry uttered the word netsuke and Nancy's face broke into a smile.

"I re-reread *The Hare with Amber Eyes*. I so wish I had started collecting these much earlier on." Henry had positioned his hand strategically around his face. No one would be lip-reading his words as he spoke about his new-found passion.

Nancy frowned half seriously. "And you're going to get me disbarred if you keep wanting to build this collection of yours. Without mentioning the fact that netsuke are Japanese and I have Chinese ancestry – very bad form."

Henry winked and as he did so he caught the eye of the man he wanted to avoid.

The violence of Kray's gaze hit Henry in the chest as powerfully as a well-aimed punch. Charlie and Nancy's advice evaporated in an instant. He did not lower his eyes and kept the contact going for a few more seconds, enough to tilt the balance in what was a challenge, a test of Henry's mettle. Ronnie Kray disappeared into the corridor leading back to the cells. But Henry knew he had just made his first life-threatening mistake.

Chapter Seven

TOP BANKER TOPS HIMSELF read the headline. Edwina had bought the tabloid on her way into work. She had read the article twice. She felt nauseous. Tom Hardy had been a close ally of hers for years. They had worked together, planned part of their career together. They had pushed the envelope as far as it could go … Possibly even further. And there was something that Edwina was absolutely convinced of – Tom would never commit suicide.

She emerged from Bank tube station and turned left into one of the little alleyways that so characterised the City. She had come to know the Square Mile by heart and the little passage was exactly what she needed. A secluded place to make a call.

"Gabs, it's me. Are you in already?" Edwina kept going. "Good man, I am at Bernie's. We need to talk."

She dropped her phone nervously into her bag. Gary first, now Tom – it could not be a coincidence.

Bernie waved at her and Edwina ordered two lattes, with an extra shot for Gabriel, and two croissants. She sat in the window and took a sip of coffee. As she raised her cup, she noticed her hand was shaking. Why was Gabriel taking so long? She was about to call again when he appeared through the door, his presence already reassuring her. She was almost certainly overreacting.

"Hello Eddie. What terrible problem will I have to sort out today then?" Gabriel said smiling.

"Hello Gabs." Edwina smiled tentatively. She waited until her number two had sat down. "Have you read the news?"

"Always. Are we talking Tom Hardy?"

Edwina nodded.

"Very sad," Gabriel said. "I can imagine it is a shock. You guys were close."

"Yes, we were and I am very sad but —" Edwina hesitated.

Gabriel lifted his hand to silence her. "Are you going to refer to the conversation you and Tom had in 2009?"

Edwina nodded.

"No one could have known. Right?"

"I'm not so sure."

"Why? Tom was the most discreet man I have ever met."

"Yes, but he had to act and get someone on the market to move the benchmark," Edwina said lowering her voice.

"And?"

"He would have contacted someone like Gary."

"Did he tell you that?"

"He said he had a contact at GL."

"Mmmm, I see," Gabriel replied. He took a sip of coffee. Edwina could see he was measuring the importance of the information.

"I thought I'd told you."

"Nope." Gabriel gave a negative nod. "You only mentioned Tom."

"Sorry, I thought I had. In any case, it was GL and if it was GL —"

"It was Gary Cook, I get it." Gabriel took another mouthful of coffee. He bit into his croissant and started chewing thoughtfully.

Edwina could no longer speak. Her eyes tingled. She pictured Tom's serious face breaking into a smile as he spoke about his daughters.

"Eddie, what are you exactly worried about?"

"I don't know. It is – odd. Two suicides, one after the other," her voice trailed. She avoided Gabriel's eyes and toyed with her croissant. "And these two guys were not the suicidal types."

"Do we really know that? I'm not sure."

"Come on Gabs, Gary Cook would have slaughtered half of the City before he incurred so much as a paper cut. He was a fucking bastard and fucking bastards like him don't commit suicide."

"Well, maybe he no longer could slaughter half of the City as you put it since his early retirement," Gabriel said stressing the word early. "And that got to him."

"I don't buy that, but if, and that is a big if, it explains Gary, no way does it apply to Tom. No way."

Gabriel shrugged. "I heard his marriage had some issues."

"What? Rubbish. Jane and he were a tight couple."

"That has not always been the case," Gabriel replied aggressively.

"That is very old history. They had forgiven each other."

"OK, let's assume you are right. Who would want to bump off these two guys? And why?"

"How about the very 'call' we talked about earlier?"

Gabriel looked at Edwina in a way he never had before. The scar on his face had changed colour, from a flaccid white to an angry red. He brought his hand to it and traced its outline mechanically. Edwina stopped in her tracks. There was something ferocious and determined in the movement that shocked her. But just as quickly as it had come, his amiable face returned. He moved towards her reassuringly. "The LIBOR fixing will never come out. Trust me."

Edwina nodded. Gabriel's look had sobered her down. The LIBOR matter should never be discussed; she got it now. And yet she could have sworn that she remembered Gabriel in conversation with Tom and, come to think of it, Gary at the Whitehall summer party a few months ago.

* * *

The art consignment was on its way to Macau. Brett did not want to know through which route. The less he knew about the traffickers' business the better. Half of the cash had been deposited into his Swiss account. The other half would be paid when the artefacts had been received and checked for damage. Brett hated this moment of uncertainty. His Chinese client was a reliable collector. But he would also be ruthless if the quality of the pieces did not live up to expectation. In a couple of weeks Brett would be on his way to Hong Kong. He would then make the trip to Macau on his client's private jet.

A phone was ringing. He did not recognise the ringtone at first but realised, with annoyance that it was his burner mobile.

Unexpected.

"Hello," Brett answered, cursing himself. Why had he not got rid of his phone more promptly?

Brett waited for the man at the other end of the phone to finish his long description before interrupting. "So the consignment has arrived in good order ... I will see the client in a couple of weeks and as agreed payment will be made then ... Another deal?"

Brett hung up and sat down. He should be pleased. £300,000 would be a welcome addition to his meagre income. But his trafficking contact had mentioned another deal. This assumption that Brett would be interested rubbed against the grain.

"Who the hell do they think they are?" Brett muttered.

Brett took his pack of cigarettes out but decided against having one. This was not the way it was supposed to be. He was the one giving directions. He walked to the elegant desk he had managed to salvage from yet another disastrous divorce. He took an antique decanter that had belonged to one of his most illustrious ancestors, sat down and poured a large helping of whisky. Never on the rocks. Just as his father had taught him, and his father before him. Brett closed his eyes and let the amber liquid do the trick. By the third glass he felt bolder. What if he said no? This Middle-Eastern riff-raff knew little about him: no name, no address. His only contact in London he had known for years and Brett had accumulated enough on him to condemn him for several lifetimes. But then there was the other business with MI6, that which gave him ultimate protection over and above his shabby dealings. He was not due to report on his findings for another couple of days to Steve. Brett finished his glass and stood up with a slight stagger.

"Steady old boy, or you won't enjoy your hard-earned money," Brett sighed. He stilled himself and started slowly rolling up the silk Hereke rug that spread underneath his coffee table. His index finger pressed one of the wooden slats of his immaculate French parquet, a small part of it pivoted to reveal a hole large enough to contain a laptop and some documents. Brett placed the laptop on the table, logged in – time for an update on the latest developments in Iraq. Brett received first-hand information that would never reach the public. He retrieved a small token from the safe and started stage two of his high-security log in. The remote access process lasted for a few minutes, testing his patience. When the website came live, he chose the sequence of options he knew by heart and started reading.

No new post since he last accessed the site, no military and financial developments – frustrating. The rise of a new terrorist faction had been reported. It was now a matter of weeks before the time bomb that had started ticking in Iraq after the US-led invasion failed, exploded. More turbulence and the need for more money coming from art smuggling was all good news for Brett's business. This steady source of income was unlikely to disappear soon and yet the information coming from the Middle East was alarming even for the rogue dealer that Brett was. The new type of fanaticism that secret intelligence was talking about seemed worse than

Al-Qaeda: even more ruthless, better organised both militarily and financially. Art, oil and people's donations straight from the heart of Wahhabism in Saudi Arabia. Although Bin Laden had come from Saudi too, the family was well known and it was possible for governments that were so inclined to control its business. But tracing this new group's dealings was proving more complicated. The new group also had the advantage of starting to control a region that spread over a number of countries struggling with religious conflicts – a perfect recipe. The movement had been founded in 1999 but it had failed to attract the attention of the intelligence community until recently. The word ISIS or DAESH had started circulating; no one had yet leaked the information to the press. Brett viewed this as another example of the appalling inability that America had to finish what it had started. The situation had not been aided by a Labour government run by a Prime Minister whose association with the Bush Family was questionable. Oil was a crucial link between the Bushes and the Saudis. And until recently no one at the most senior level had questioned the support that the Saudis were giving to Wahhabism.

"Very unwise," Brett muttered.

He closed the laptop with disappointment. In two days' time he would get answers from his minder.

* * *

The mortuary still made Pole queasy. It was not the sight of the flesh but the despicable smell. Pole would have felt less human if the stench of death had become habitual and he had become immune to it. He was listening to Yvonne's initial findings with an uncomfortable sense of déjà vu.

"Alcohol and drugs is my best guess at present. We need to wait for the toxicology report to confirm. Then asphyxiation by inhalation of CO_2 – took less than half an hour."

"I gathered as much," Pole said. "But a couple of things disturb me."

"Such as – not finding any booze laced with drugs in the car?"

"Right, there was nothing in the house indicating he had drunk anything or taken any pills of any kind. Odd don't you think?"

"Until we know what he took exactly, I would not draw any conclusions. He might have organised it so that he did all his preparatory business somewhere else."

"Why? And it means a lot of planning – taking booze and drugs then giving yourself enough time to get home, arrange the car …"

"He might not have wanted to leave evidence at his home address."

"Perhaps, but his suicide is going to distress his family no matter what," Pole said raising a hand. "And you are going to say that he had passed the point of no return where death seems the only option. Still, his wife was adamant all was well. He was worried about the financial crisis, obviously – but as she put it so is the whole bloody City."

"I presume you have not spoken to his BBA colleagues yet?"

"Not yet, Nurani is on the case. It's only 9am."

"I'm not criticising, just asking."

"Sorry, something escapes me and I don't like it."

"By the way, I met your *consultant*, Nancy. Very clued-up and as sharp as my granddad's razor."

Pole's face coloured slightly and he smiled at Yvonne.

"Your granddad's razor must have been a lethal weapon."

"Yep, the old-fashioned throat slitting type."

"That's my girl. She would be mighty annoyed if she heard me call her girl by the way."

"Don't be fooled Jon; all women still have a part of them that is young and cute."

"Is that so?"

"Uh-huh. And it's a bloody good tip by the way," Yvonne said, whilst removing her gloves with a precise gesture, inside out, one into the other, and immediately throwing them into the hazardous material bin.

Pole's mobile was ringing. He reached below the protective apron he had donned.

"Talk of the Devil. Nancy, how are you?"

Pole's face turned unexpectedly serious.

"I won't be long. I am with Yvonne at present, will call you as soon as I am out."

"There is nothing more for the time being. Take your call," Yvonne said waving Pole out. He mouthed "thank you" and stepped out of the mortuary into the corridor.

"Nancy, I'm still here. What about Henry?" Pole listened and broke into a slow jog towards the exit. "OK, let's meet outside the office at our regular place. I will be there in fifteen."

* * *

Nancy had broken with their usual ritual. She had arrived first and was waiting for Pole outside their favourite cafe. She waved and started coming towards him.

"I am sorry, Jonathan. It looks a little full. Let's try to find somewhere more discreet."

"Let's go round the corner. There is a small square and we can sit on a bench," Pole said, gently taking Nancy's arm to guide her to their destination. Nancy fought the immediate desire to break free and relaxed into Pole's warm guidance. He let go of her only when they arrived at the wrought-iron gate into the square and made way for her to enter first.

"So, what's Henry's opinion?" Pole said as they sat down.

"First of all, Jonathan, do you know how LIBOR works?"

"Not in detail. I know what it does broadly but do tell."

"Let me cut a long story short. The part that is relevant for us is the fixing of LIBOR. And before you even comment on the word *fixing,* it is the correct terminology. But let's call it *setting,* for our purpose."

Pole nodded. "Go for *setting.*"

"LIBOR is set every day by a number of selected banks that submit the rate at which they can borrow on the market from one another for various maturities, intraday, weekly, monthly etc —"

"Are those banks all British?"

"Good question, no. The current panel comprises a number of foreign institutions too."

"Would I be right in guessing that both GL and HXBK are members of that panel?"

Nancy gave him an appreciative look. "Spot on my dear fellow."

"And who fixes, sorry, sets, the rate for each bank?"

"Not so fast. I know you need a name but you must first know that LIBOR is set by the BBA, which receives from each bank the information it needs. The BBA discards the highest four and lowest four responses. It then averages the remaining numbers. The average is reported at 11.30 AM daily for all maturities."

"The BBA is involved? You mean the same BBA Tom Hardy was the CEO of?"

"The very same and, to answer your previous question, banks will select traders that trade Sterling – I mean Pound Sterling – and one of them will establish the house view."

"Don't tell me. That person at GL was Gary Cook."

"*Voila. Vous avez tout compris, mon cher.*"

"*Incroyable.*"

"I think you may have to dig around a lot more but, if and I still say if, there is some fixing then —"

Nancy let Pole finish her sentence. "We have the beginning of a motive."

"We have indeed."

"So, Henry put two and two together to give us our *motive*?" Pole said hovering between amusement and irritation.

"He has but I don't think he is going to volunteer anything else unless —"

"What? First of all, I am not sure I need more information from him yet. The banks might speak up if I wave the spectre of a full-blown investigation in their faces."

"That may not be very effective, Jonathan. And I can tell you straight away that the banks would rather have a murder investigation on their hands than admit to LIBOR manipulation."

"I don't owe Henry anything," Pole grumbled. "And why do you think the banks won't talk?"

"Because the size of the market that will be affected if there is manipulation is unimaginably large. I don't even know how to quantify it."

Pole jerked his head sideways in astonishment.

"I know. But consider this. LIBOR does not only cover mortgages in the UK, it also covers mortgages pegged to Dollar LIBOR. That is a hell of a lot, Jonathan. Whether you like it or not, you need Henry."

Pole stood up and perched on the backrest of the bench. His forehead had added a few lines in a characteristic frown.

"Why do I think I am not going to like his terms?"

"Because you know him so well by now. He wants to work on this outside Belmarsh." Nancy had just laid it out straight. There was no point in working on Pole to get the desired result. Raw truth was sometimes what it took. Pole moved away from the bench as if it had become electrified and a flash of anger showed in his eyes.

"Does Henry remember why he is a Cat. A con?"

"He does. More than you can imagine, Jonathan. I understand your anger at the request but frankly do you want him to work on a subject as sensitive as that from the confines of the HSU Belmarsh library?"

"I'll think about it."

"*Bien sur.* He is not going anywhere."

"I bloody well hope he is not," Pole replied vehemently.

Nancy stood up. The conversation on this topic was over. She placed her hand on Pole's elbow the way he had placed his when they had met and moved him towards the gate.

"How about we have a much-needed cup of coffee?"

An irresistible proposition ...

Chapter Eight

The laptop was booting up in the library where Henry had booked some IT time. The device was painfully slow but Henry had by now acknowledged that his days of impatience at his Tech Team were over. The screen finally came live with two icons appearing, a dog and a cat. The inmates were allowed access to computers to prepare formal documents but the functionality amounted to little more than that of a word processor. Predictably, inmates would have clicked on the cat. The prison officers had access to the system too and would have, equally predictably, clicked on the dog. The dog had, of course, much increased capability, in particular, access to the Internet. The password changed very regularly for increased security, but Henry had been able to keep track because he helped out in the library. He knew how to wipe his Internet history or access the net in incognito mode. Any sign the computer was abused and the privilege would be withdrawn.

Henry smiled and confidently clicked on the dog, entering the latest password he had managed to crack. He was in. He briefly praised his capacity for observation and deduction but time was of the essence. He could indulge in self-congratulation later. Henry moved swiftly to Google and searched under LIBOR. He remembered reading an article published by *The Wall Street Journal* in 2008 which had attracted his attention. In April of that year the *Journal* had published a controversial article on how LIBOR had been deliberately low-bowled by banks for years. Henry urgently needed to refresh his memory of what the journalist had claimed if he was going to start whetting Pole's appetite. Could he risk printing the document? Not worth it: he would commit what he was reading to memory and jot down the information back in his cell. The small library was quiet, not always an advantage. He may attract attention. Henry started a new draft of a document he was writing for Nancy. She was part of his legal team, an excellent cover if asked. He switched back to the article. *The Wall Street Journal* had as ever written a well-informed piece based on credible interviews. He might have paid more attention to it at the time had the takeover between his bank GL and HXBK not been at the forefront of his mind. The threat to his position, culminating in the titanic battle with his arch-rival Anthony Albert, had pushed this significant piece of information to the back of his mind. But his well-organised brain had stored pieces of crucial information as efficiently as ever, ready to recall these as soon as they might be of use. And here they were. The assertion that LIBOR had been understated was credible, even obvious. It was in the interest of banks at the time the credit crunch was biting to understate the level at which they estimated they could borrow from one another. The first reason was to lower the level of interest they were currently paying on their own borrowings; the second to detract from their current financial difficulties. High-borrowing costs indicated lack of confidence from other market participants. A state of play that no bank was willing to accept.

Henry's pulse quickened. He had not been this excited by a piece of news for months. His mind was racing to calculate the impact on the market. He knew the size of the GL derivatives book was around $49 trillion. He quickly extrapolated. Other banks he knew had lower exposure than GL but still their exposures were in the trillions. He sat back in his chair; the number he was coming up with made him, Henry Crowne, gasp.

"Wow, over US$300 trillion," Henry murmured. He was about to return to *The Wall Street Journal* article when a movement at the periphery of his eye stopped him. He called his cover-up document to the screen and tried to look focused. A chair moved softly close by.

"You allowed a laptop?"

"Yeah, got some legal work I'm working on," Henry said without looking up. He had recognised the North London accent of a new inmate.

"You're the IRA banker, aren't you?"

Henry lifted an eye. This guy wanted his attention badly. Even his short time in prison had taught Henry he needed swiftly to ascertain why.

The intensity of the dark eyes startled him. This young chap was a believer and no prison sentence would extinguish his fervour. He had seen the same look many years ago on Bobby's face.

"Not my favourite nickname but, yes, I was a banker who was close to the IRA. Why do you ask?"

308

The eager face broke into an attractive smile that made the inmate's dark beard look less severe.

"My brother worked at GL."

Henry closed his documents as casually as he could. His computer session was over, much to his annoyance.

"GL is a pretty big place."

"You mean was a pretty big place. The takeover has been a bloody affair."

"So I hear but frankly not my problem anymore."

"Not my brother's either; he is back in Saudi."

"Good for him, now if you don't mind. I have a class to go to."

"Certainly, good speaking to you. My name is Kamal."

Henry nodded and moved away, taking his time. The dark eyes followed him right through the doors of the library.

The chain of gates and prison officers he had to cross before he reached his cell still daunted Henry. He knew most of the guards by now: their habits, what may set them off or appease them. Charlie had warned him, never trust but be trusted. And golden rule number one: never think you are going to make friends. There is always an agenda. Henry had quickly realised that the concentration of psychopaths to the square inch rivalled that of the City. He had been naturally guarded in his City life and he remained even more so as an inmate, with a few exceptions. It was impossible to serve thirty years without any decent human contact. Big K had become a mate and could be relied on for info on the latest gossip. He would know who Kamal was. But what mattered now more than anything else to Henry was to get involved in Pole's new investigation. It was nearly lunchtime and he could bring his food tray to his cell to save time.

A short queue had just started forming, the soft shuffle of feet rhythmically following the stop-and-go along the self-service line. Henry looked around. He recognised some faces but no one he knew well, a relief. Henry put the most appetising looking lunch option on his tray. The queue stopped, one of the inmates had dropped his spoon: the only cutlery cons were allowed in prison. Henry had been shocked at first. He was not a five-year-old – but was now grateful. He had seen what damage could be done with the handle of a spoon – eyes nearly gouged out in the latest fight he had witnessed. What would some of these nutters do with a fork? And a knife, even plastic and blunt was out of the question.

The queue was moving again. Henry was about to push his tray when a clunk startled him. Someone further down the line had just joined and he wanted everyone to notice. Ronnie Kray was two inmates away. Henry moved back into line. He was nearly done, just needed to grab a chunk of bread. Kray had started whistling a tune low and the two inmates between them responded to it – they moved out of the way fast. Despite Henry's best efforts Kray had seen him and kept his eyes focused on Henry's neck, a sharp sensation at the bottom of his skull convinced Henry of it. As he was retracing his steps to move out of the canteen, the whistle intensified to a high pitch. Henry forced himself to slow down, his eyes brushing over Kray, distant. The shuffle of feet had nearly stopped. But Henry kept moving, deliberately – and he was saying:

You don't scare me.

Henry was back in his cell. The hour's bang-up time would start soon, allowing the prison officers to have their lunch. He had left Kray behind and refused to think about what the encounter meant. Henry focused instead on the all-important matter of improving his lunch. The pasta looked predictably overcooked but Henry took an assortment of dried herbs from a corner of his bookshelf and sprinkled it over his food. A luxury he had negotiated hard to obtain with the help of his former driver Charlie. There was no time for self-pity though.

Henry had work to do.

He sat down at his desk and started writing all he could remember of the article he had just read. He then proceeded to write all he knew about Gary Cook, Tom Hardy and all the people he knew whose work involved or who had an interest in LIBOR. Within half an hour he had an impressive list of names and institutions that would be involved if manipulation had taken place. Henry had spent enough time in the City, nearly twenty years, to see the signs and believe that *The Wall Street Journal* was onto something substantial. He had to make Pole listen and he would make this happen through Nancy. His intuition, a quality that had served him so well as a star banker, was again making him restless: the slight tightening of the chest, the hair rising on the back of his neck. Or was it simply the need to be doing something meaningful? Henry moved to his bed and sat down. In this diminutive space, he had found a way of distancing himself from prison life. The papers spread on his desk were alive with what had been his past. Was reconnecting a way of finding a solution to the conundrum that had been haunting him since his conviction? Was it the path to redemption he so craved?

Henry interlaced his fingers and rested his elbows on his knees, bending his tall body forward. The bed groaned slightly. The dark bubble of anger swelled again in his chest. He knew it would pass. He was learning the power of letting go. Of letting the past rise again without answering to its call. But Henry was also under no illusion. His redemption, if it ever came, would be brought about by an action perilous enough that his life might be in the balance. He was certain this liberating deed would not happen within the confines of Belmash.

The bell rang again, indicating that bang-up time was over. It was time for him to resume his work at the library. No funny business until he had spoken to Nancy though.

* * *

His meeting with Nancy had left Pole uneasy. She was close to Henry as a friend would be. Pole had never questioned how close that relationship was. But for the first time since he'd known her, the seed of doubt had been sown. Would Nancy see through Henry if he ever tried to manipulate her? Yesterday, Pole would have unequivocally answered yes but today was another day. He would have been comfortable having these doubts about anyone else but having to step away from Nancy was much harder.

He needed Nurani to deliver so that she could unequivocally secure her promotion. Her task was to force GL to talk about Cook's settlement. He had tried her mobile without success. He dialled Forensics, a little nudge on the prelim tox report's next version (V1-03, to be precise; Nurani would be pleased with his impeccable use of the reference) might yield something.

"Pole here, you read my mind … On its way. Excellent … Will check my inbox straightaway."

The beauty of not being a constant pain in the butt was that a request for high priority was always well received.

The V1-03 tox report was extensive but simply confirmed the pathologist's initial findings. Gary Cook's blood contained a cocktail of drugs including the latest kid on the block – nootropics. And, no, the nootropics Cook had taken had not been tampered with. Pole frowned. It seemed this new drug had become a real craze. Cook had not been a long-time user. Yet, Cook did not seem the type to mess with his health. The new question was why purchase nootropic drugs at all? Pole had a vague memory that they were used by Silicon Valley developers once upon a time – might still be? The V1-03 tox report was clear on another key point: the drug would have caused enhanced perception, greater brain activity. Cook was after a bit of brain enhancement. Nothing very wrong with that or indeed very lethal. Nurani would come back with what the Drug Squad may have on the tablets. Some illegal import through the Internet, not exactly a Class A drug scandal. Yet the extensive search that Nurani had carried out had yielded nothing. Why hide these? And there were some steroids as well. Another illegal drug if not prescribed by a physician. Another Internet purchase? Or perhaps a UK dealer that could deliver quality?

Pole paused for a moment. There was another place they had not searched yet. He dialled Nurani's mobile.

"You on your way back? GL is not budging ... OK, we'll speak about that when you're in the office. In the meantime, are you going to search Cook's office? ... Good girl. I'll see you after you've ransacked his office, right? What? You mean you had a proper warrant."

Pole grinned at Nurani's frosty reply.

"You need to loosen up your sense of humour, dear lady," he said, hanging up.

The combination of drugs and alcohol might have pushed Gary Cook over the edge – literally, thought Pole whilst flicking through the report. But Pole found himself drifting again towards Nancy's theory. It was out of character. Cook was taking drugs to enhance his performance, not to get on a high. So, an accident? Again, Gary Cook was not the absent-minded type. Nevertheless, without further evidence there was little Pole could do. And the idea that yet another banking catastrophe was looming sounded far-fetched. He picked up the phone and dialled Yvonne's number. Tom Hardy was still on the slab but Yvonne would not mind.

"Afternoon, anything for your old pal Pole? ... What do you mean it has only been three hours? You are my best forensic," Pole exclaimed. Yvonne was giving him lip but he got a little more information.

"No sign of struggle, just confirming – had taken a cocktail of drugs before he turned the ignition key and said goodbye to the world." Pole had started jotting down notes. "What sort of drugs are we talking about?" Pole nodded. "Need more time ... are you planning to spring a surprise on me? What? ... Still strapped in his seat. I had noticed."

Pole thanked Yvonne. He roughened up his goatee. Another unlikely suicide. He stood up, moved a couple of piles of documents around, irritated. He would wait for the new tox report on Tom awaiting a plausible explanation. In the meantime, Henry Crowne may have to wait a little longer before he was allowed to play his get-out-of-jail card if it was what he was looking for.

The voice reached Pole's ear before the man walked through the door of his office. Superintendent Marsh was visiting Pole's neck of the woods and he liked to advertise his presence way in advance. An advantage for the wary.

The smell of a profile case always attracted the politically savvy. Pole was simply surprised it had taken the superintendent this long to turn up on his doorstep.

"Inspector Pole, I hear you are on a large City case again." Marsh walked to Pole's desk and looked around hoping to find space to sit for a chat. He prided himself on walking to meet his officers, never overdoing the prerogative of summoning his people to his office.

"Perhaps, sir. But we are very much at the beginning of this double suicide and —" Pole looked at the state of his office and wished he had had time for a little tidying up. He would be reminded in a memo, yet again, of the clean-desk policy the Yard was keen to promote.

"I hear you. Although you seem to believe there is more to it than simple suicide, don't you?" Marsh was still looking around, for a seat. He awkwardly picked up the file that was laid on the only chair in front of Pole's desk. Pole grabbed it and put it on top of a dangerously high pile.

"Is that safe?" Marsh asked.

"I do lock my door when I leave for the evening," Pole replied.

"Right, right. It's a little high, that's all."

"Good point." Pole removed the file from the pile and moved it to another marginally more secure stack.

Marsh sat down, smoothing the panels of his uniform as he did so. He said nothing, the slight tap of his fingers on the armchair a cue for Pole to give a full account of the situation. Pole was considering a reply, letting the silence drag a little too long for Marsh's liking.

"Why don't you speak to me about this consultant of yours?"

Pole had not expected that question. He looked at Marsh blankly and felt his face turn a shade of pink.

"You mean —"

"Well, yes, the consultant you are using on some of your profile cases. Nancy Who."

"Wu – You mean Nancy Wu," Pole said irritated.

"That's right, as I said Nancy Wu."

Pole was about to launch into a description of Nancy's many attributes but Marsh did not seem interested. A question had been planted in his mind and it came out well-rehearsed.

"Why would she think it is not suicide?"

Pole's face froze. *Nurani, you little …*

He had sat back in his chair, about to defend a theory he had not endorsed yet. Marsh listened now to every detail. Pole had decided to underplay Henry's role in expanding on the LIBOR theory.

"In a nutshell we could be on the brink of yet another financial scandal?" Marsh summarised.

Pole nodded; much to his annoyance Marsh seemed to relish the idea.

"You realise this will need to be well substantiated. We have not even started recovering from the financial crisis," Marsh said, his lips pursed. And yet Pole knew he would revel in the thought – his team uncovering, yet again and before the regulatory authorities, another financial scandal, another feather in his cap.

"Which is why I have been particularly cautious and not wanted to inform you before I have good evidence —"

"But now that I know, I would like a daily update."

As Pole was about to protest Marsh raised an appeasing hand.

"I know you are busy, Jonathan, but I am sure that your young DS, Ms Shah, will be a good liaison – if you don't have the time of course. She is on the promotion roster if I recall."

Pole knew exactly what Marsh meant: say no and you will imply that she can't do the job of reporting to me and if she can't why are you seeking to promote her? Marsh had stood up and was moving towards the door. He half-turned back to ask his final question.

"And why don't you organise a meeting between Ms Wu and me?"

* * *

The meeting with Pole had not left her with the sweet taste of friendship she was used to. Nancy suspected that the same was the case for Pole.

"I should have thought it through a little more." Nancy sighed. She had never felt torn between Pole and Henry until now. Pole had given Henry plenty of rope to change his destiny when he first arrested him after Henry had managed to breach security at GL and assault its CEO, Douglas McCarthy. Nancy had admired Pole's sense of fairness, his ability to see through the pretence. True, Henry was a Cat. A convict and Pole would have to have an unassailable reason to involve him in his high-profile case. But Nancy's intuition was pushing her, as it had always done, to tread in uncharted territory. There was possibly one person who may have a view Pole could not ignore, her senior contact and friend at Whitehall. His insight had been invaluable when she first took Henry's case on. She had thankfully seen William a few times after they had reconnected. That meant Nancy felt less embarrassed to call upon him for yet another tip on the investigation's ramifications.

"William, what a surprise. I was expecting your PA," Nancy teased as he answered his phone. "This is very last minute but —"

Nancy did not have time to finish her sentence. "Then great minds think alike, let's do coffee at the usual place."

William would meet her that afternoon at Tate Britain – the William Blake Room. But for the first time since she'd known William, and she had known him a very long time, Nancy had the feeling he was the one who wanted to talk. He was agitated.

Chapter Nine

Tate Britain was buzzing with the anticipated effervescence the Turner Prize created. Nancy paused. She had called on William three years ago when she had decided to help Henry with his case. Her friend had been his old self with her despite his seniority; he'd assured her it was refreshing to know he would not be taken advantage of. Nancy had been open with him. She had not considered deceiving William for one moment no matter how desperate the situation was – and Henry had been in dire straits. The accusation of murder that hung over him was rooted in a mounting level of evidence that had been hard to dismiss. And yet Nancy had had doubts. William had been happy to rely on her judgement. She knew he had always been intrigued by her personality. Her ascent to the Bar, her taking Silk at such an impossibly young age, her fascinating mixed cultural background – everything felt like a challenge and an interrogation for William. He, by contrast, felt the product of an antiquated aristocracy: Eton, Oxford, the Civil Service and yet his open-mindedness often contrasted with the stale idea people had of him. William did not make friends easily; he fussed, picked and chose. Nancy felt privileged to be one of them. Not because he was fastidious but because friendship was precious, always to be honoured.

Since Nancy had become a consultant to the Met, he had been generous with his time to discuss any matter that troubled her. He had a dispassionate way of tackling a problem that helped her see more clearly. Today however William had sounded different: a slight change in the rhythm of his speech, a slight hesitation where there should be none told her he needed to talk.

Nancy walked around the rooms she knew so well to finally reach the room that displayed their favourite pieces, the William Blake prints. She glanced at her watch; she was dead on time. She turned around but William was nowhere to be seen. He was late. So uncharacteristic, she felt alarmed. She sat down again and would give it another five minutes before she rang his mobile. She stilled herself, helped by the exquisite lines of Blake's drawings. A slender but firm hand pressed her shoulder and she found herself face to face with her friend.

"Thank God William. I was getting worried," Nancy said before noticing his ashen-white face, his eyes still wide open with shock.

"Not here, let's go to the Members' Room."

They chose a quiet corner.

"So sorry Nancy. Good afternoon," William said regaining some of his composure.

"Do settle down. I will get the tea. No apologies required among friends."

William nodded and settled down into a comfortable armchair, wincing as he did so. He seemed in pain but he waved her off.

Nancy returned promptly with their favourite drink, an excellent choice of Darjeeling, and a couple of small pastries. William needed a pick-me-up.

"Shall we dive straight in?" Nancy said as she was pouring.

"I would rather you start with your news, Nancy. I am still deciding how to present what I have to say to you."

"Always happy to go first," teased Nancy. William managed the beginning of a smile.

"I am sure you have heard about the death of both Gary Cook and Tom Hardy. I am working on the case with Inspector Pole and the working assumption is that it is suicide," Nancy said after taking a sip of tea.

"You don't buy it?" concluded William. It was not a question but rather a statement of fact made forcefully. William sat back, closed his eyes bringing his hands together, fingertips touching at the level of his mouth. Nancy did not interrupt his train of thought. The process that was going through William's mind was about to deliver a verdict, a statement based on facts and experience, an immensely powerful combination.

"I think you are right," added William finally. He was leaning towards his cup wincing again in pain. He took a sip without looking at Nancy. He had not looked at her once and when he returned his cup to its saucer his hand was shaking.

Nancy was sitting opposite William, the position she liked when talking about a subject that felt like business rather than an intimate conversation. She stood up without thinking and moved next to William. She sat close to him and took his hand.

"I have never, in the twenty-five years I have known you, seen you so distraught. Please talk to me."

William inhaled deeply and faced her.

"I will. I just need to gather my thoughts. Something has happened and I don't think it is a coincidence."

"Do you know about LIBOR?" Nancy said. She was not fishing and William knew it.

"Your greatest strength as ever, my dear. To the point and no shying away from it."

"I gather the answer is yes. What happened this morning that has so thrown you?"

William took another sip of tea. He was enjoying a moment of slight reprieve.

"For a few days now, I have had the impression that I was being followed. I dismissed it to start with. There is always a temptation in my job to think we carry secrets about the workings of government; that we are at risk."

"And do you carry that sort of secret, William?" Nancy asked. "We had a conversation during the Henry Crowne investigation which I remember vividly."

"Ah yes, I said I was trying to salvage the UK financial system." William replied with amusement in his eyes. "Rather pompous I know."

Nancy's formidable memory was at work again.

"And now I ask, have you? It seems to me we are not yet out of the woods."

William hesitated.

"Why don't you finish first telling me what happened this morning?" Nancy suggested, trying to keep the momentum going.

"You're right, I felt his presence, saw someone hurrying up behind me as I crossed the road, turned a corner. And I could have sworn it was to keep track of me."

"I see. Is it the same person?"

"No. Which is why I thought I might be overdoing it. But then —" William stopped and swallowed hard. He finished his tea. Nancy picked up the teapot and poured a fresh cup, an indication to carry on and seek comfort in his favourite drink.

"I was about to cross the road. You know me, I am a creature of habit. I leave my flat in Pimlico at the same time. I always walk to work whatever the weather. The crossing is on a timer. I am an obedient citizen, I wait. It turns green. I start crossing. A white van comes out of nowhere and accelerates. He cannot *not* have seen me. I drop everything and I run. I squeeze between the SUVs parked at the end of the crossing. I can hear the scrape of metal against metal. Those two cars saved me Nancy, otherwise …" William's voice trails. He can't bring himself to say the word and for the second time today Nancy squeezes her friend's hand. William's face is ashen white again, and again his hands tremble as he reaches for his cup.

"You are certain the van was going straight for you?"

William shakes his head. "He swerved across the road to get to me. I am sure."

"Did anybody else see this?"

"The street was pretty empty – 6am."

"And you did not get the registration number?"

William shakes his head again.

"Of course, you must have been so shocked."

"I fell to the ground on the pavement, by the time I got up …"

"Have you been to the police?" Nancy asked, her stomach lurching once more. But her friend needed her to be composed. She had kept her hand on William's. He squeezed back in return. "Thank you, Nancy. You are here and I wanted to speak to you before doing anything else."

"Because I asked to speak to you about Gary and Tom?"

"Exactly right," William replied, colour coming back into his face.

"But you can't fully comment because it is one of the 'secrets', involving the government."

William simply smiled.

"Why don't I tell you about the information I have gathered and you can confirm?" Nancy suggested. William retreated into his armchair. "Perhaps, you can redirect me if I go wrong in my assumptions?"

"Much better idea," William said relaxing considerably.

"Gary Cook, Head Trader at GL, runs the Rates book. Every day he submits the LIBOR rates to the BBA. He is the voice of GL as far as LIBOR is concerned."

William drank some tea and Nancy carried on.

"Gary is leaving GL, but he seems fired up about something. Knowledge that can get him back in the race after his sacking from GL."

It was Nancy's turn to drink some tea. She was on a roll and engaged with what she did best – relentless deductions.

"Tom Hardy, Chief Executive of the BBA. The British Bankers' Association has had the huge responsibility of delivering LIBOR to the market, in all its maturities and currencies, since its creation in 1984.

It has a process and it follows it but it relies on the banks delivering an honest figure about what they estimate their own borrowing costs are. The BBA could ask questions of the banks I presume but I have never heard it reported that it had."

William finished his cup of tea. He had not said a word as his entire attention was focused on Nancy.

"LIBOR, an essential benchmark in the financial system, from mortgages for Mr Nobody to derivatives for large multinationals. And not only in the UK. I have looked it up on Bloomberg; the size of the LIBOR market is around $350 billion – I mean trillion!"

"A sensitive matter as you said, Nancy."

"Now that I have the facts, let me tell you what my assumptions are. I should have probably mentioned that I have had some crucial help from a friend," Nancy said frankly.

"You mean Henry is bored in Her Majesty's Prison?" William said.

"He is still a banker who knows how the City works," Nancy replied, a little too much on the defensive.

"He is a clever man, and I can only imagine that given enough information he will understand pretty fast what is really going on."

"His take on Gary and Tom is that LIBOR has been manipulated, probably a low-bowling by the banks to cover their true financial position in 2008–2009, possibly before, and that it may have an impact on their deaths."

William's composure evaporated again.

"If we remain hypothetical and there has been a manipulation of LIBOR then people at the highest level must have known. Bank of England. Government."

William moved his hand absent-mindedly towards his empty cup. Whilst Nancy had been speaking he had averted his gaze; now he was looking into her eyes.

"Low-bowling LIBOR as you call it may be an unorthodox way of controlling the crisis, within reason." William's voice no longer hesitated. Nancy sensed his confidence returning.

"You mean that the government may have initiated this idea?" Nancy asked incredulous.

William nodded. "I told you Nancy. We need – no, I need to salvage the financial system in this country. I did think long and hard. I have discussed the impact of the crisis with numerous people. I had to act, even if it meant using methods which …," his voice trailed off, looking for the right word, "are questionable."

Nancy was speechless. She looked at William as if she had met a totally new person. He sensed it and blushed slightly.

"Desperate times, desperate measures. Although it is really not a satisfactory excuse, I accept."

"Sorry William. I can't pretend I am not – amazed but I suppose …" Nancy couldn't really yet believe that her friend, a man she had seen as most honest and dedicated, had just admitted the unthinkable. The next question she uttered in a low voice, because it could topple yet again one of her greatest hopes.

"Who did you speak to – the Bank of England, the BBA, any particular bank?"

"No Nancy, that business has to be done so carefully, as you can imagine. I can suggest, in hypothetical fashion. I don't need to directly instruct."

"Who William? Please."

"I can't, not yet," William exhaled. His hands had become moist with perspiration. He rubbed them mechanically on his paper napkin.

"Please, don't ask me to disclose a name yet. The only thing you need to know is that the impact of LIBOR was discussed and a preference for a lower number was expressed with the relevant people."

"In other words, Whitehall, you, asked for LIBOR to be low-bowled so that the impact of the 2008 crisis be smoothed. And it actually happened."

"Correct."

Nancy exchanged a quick look with her friend and shook her head.

"I am sorry I ended up disappointing you Nancy," William said gently.

"No please don't apologise. I don't envy your position. I can understand it. I can't condone it though." Nancy frowned. "But William, coming back to you and what happened this morning – your near-miss accident. Are you telling me these two are linked?"

"Possibly, I don't know. I have felt exposed recently in a way I have never done before and I have seen a lot in my twenty-five years as a civil servant."

"I know how senior you are now. Or should I say Sir William?" Nancy managed to tease.

"A little humour at this dire point is welcome, my dear. Going back to your question. I fear I will be next; Gary, Tom then …," William said, failing to complete the sentence.

"If you are concerned you must speak to the police," Nancy said in a pressing voice. "Speak to Pole; you know he can be trusted with delicate matters." Nancy touched her forehead with the palm of her hand. A piece of jet-black hair had escaped from her hair pin. She brushed it back slowly.

"Oh God, I have been so stupid. You want me to speak to Inspector Pole for you. Is that it?"

"I understand it is a big ask but I don't want to go to the police, not just yet. I might be overreacting anyway, although I don't think so. If I come forward the police will have to investigate not only Whitehall but also the Bank of England. We, I mean the country, does not need that at the moment. The longer I delay the better."

"William, you are willing to …," Nancy looked for the word but could only be blunt, "risk your life? What happens if you are right and you are a target?"

"So be it," William said closing his eyes.

"But you are my friend. I am not sure I can let you take that sort of risk," Nancy said anxiously.

"Then I will have to find someone else," William replied determined. No one would make him change his mind. He would see it through whatever the cost, Nancy gathered.

"You know this is the right thing to do. You know," William said looking at Nancy with intensity.

"You are expecting me to speak to Pole and hope he can find the person targeting you before he strikes again?"

William nodded.

"Fine," Nancy said finally. She took her yellow pad out of her bag and started taking notes. William raised an eyebrow. "Don't worry, I write in cryptic words. Let's recap on some information. The race is on."

* * *

The phone call was short but amicable. Chancellor George Osborne had not trusted his aides and wanted to hear the news directly from the Bank of England. Edwina had assured him that Mervyn King would agree to the next round of quantitative easing.

"What does George want from his blue-eyed girl?" Gabriel asked amused.

"He wants to make sure that I will slap back the old dinosaurs who think QE is only for the rich," Edwina replied without a smile. She would have normally engaged with Gabriel in a banter about Osborne-chancellor-of-the-exchequer-blue-eyed-girl but today she didn't. What she had seen in Gabriel's eyes this morning had startled her.

"You know what that means, right?" Gabriel asked, crossing his hands behind his head and stretching.

"I am sure you will soon enlighten me."

"You're in pole position to succeed Mervyn-The-Oracle-King."

"The Oracle refers to Greenspan not King," replied Edwina tersely.

"Don't be a bore. You know I am right," Gabriel said unfazed by Edwina's tone. "Don't you want it?"

"I don't want to speculate."

"You mean so close to your goal. You're not superstitious, not you Eddie."

Edwina ignored him and kept typing the email she had been writing when Chancellor Osborne called her.

"Are you still worried about Tom and Gary?"

"No, it was just a silly idea. Forget I ever mentioned it."

"Good, I am glad you've given up on that," Gabriel said with a forcefulness that surprised Edwina again. He did not simply seem happy she had given up on the idea. He was positively pleased – as if the idea could be dangerous in itself.

Edwina stopped typing the email and looked at him. For a few seconds she saw again the cold harshness in his eyes, replaced promptly by a smile that no longer convinced her. The scar on his intelligent face looked angrier than ever. She must reach out to someone else. She must speak to Nancy as soon as she could.

The phone rang again and Edwina gave it an irritated look. *What now?* The prefix told her it was the US. She hardly looked at Gabriel.

"I need to take this call on my own."

Gabriel stood up without a word and closed the door behind him.

"Tim, good morning. How good of you to call back."

"Don't mention it," replied Tim Geithner, the Secretary of State of the US Treasury. "We are on a secure line by the way."

"Excellent, I just wanted to conclude our conversation on US LIBOR."

The governor of the Bank of England, Mervyn King, had received a memo from Geithner in 2008 alerting him to the issue that LIBOR was facing. King had delegated the sensitive project of investigating the allegations to Edwina, a mark of trust she had been proud of. Today, however she called this thorny project a typical hospital by-path if there was one. Geithner and his team were fully aware of the potential and even probable manipulation of LIBOR but the financial crisis had tied their hands. Now was not the time to challenge the way this well-used benchmark was calculated. Geithner had been more forceful of late, calling her regularly himself. But Edwina knew better than to be impressed by this show of strength. US LIBOR represented around forty-five per cent of all adjustable mortgages and eighty per cent of subprime mortgages. She had held firm since 2009 when the memo had landed on her desk. No, now was not the time for yet another full-blown crisis. If she could hold back until King retired and she was in place as governor of the Bank of England, she would have free rein to carry out the much-needed reforms. In her view, an up-tick adjustment to the benchmark would have an immediate repercussion on the mortgages it underpinned and therefore calculated by reference to it – meaning more foreclosures, more crisis. Geithner and Edwina were having a repeat conversation. As she listened to Geithner's proposition about how the LIBOR calculation could be improved, she remembered another conversation she had had with Tom Hardy when he took over as CEO of the BBA.

She had called Tom one late evening as the crisis was taking hold and had asked him for a much-needed *little* chat. She had recognised right from the beginning that this crisis would not be like any other. It was deeper because it did not affect only a segment of the economy; it affected a vast number of people whose mortgages were about to foreclose – in the US, in the UK – and take with them all the institutions that had speculated around those mortgages. Tom had been a credit specialist himself before taking on his new role. He would understand and, more importantly, trust her judgement.

It was so late when she reached his office that only a security guard was manning reception at the BBA offices on Old Broad Street. Tom came down to collect her. His equine face, normally so detached, showed strain. They hardly greeted one another and did not speak until they reached his office.

"More bad news," Edwina had said, a statement of fact.

"The worst," Tom had replied. "I am not going to dance around the issue Eddie. It's about LIBOR. I fear it's about to implode; there's no trust left in the market and the levels are being scrutinised more closely."

"Shit!" Edwina blurted.

"You are aware?" Tom asked taken aback. "Can't tell you who my source is but I have just had a memo sent to me to discuss this."

"Who knows about it?"

"You mean who suspects?"

Tom waved his hand in the air, a detail but was the implosion of LIBOR in the open?

"OK, just because it is you and I trust you." Edwina hesitated for a second. "The Yanks, but don't ask for more."

"No need."

They both fell silent, hardly looking at one another and waiting to see who would first voice a view that both shared.

"How many banks at the moment?"

"One I know of, for sure."

Again they fell silent. As they were both moving closer to what seemed an inevitable conclusion, Edwina stood up and moved towards the window. The City had fallen quiet. Even as disaster was striking, the City trading floors had closed. The trail of disaster had passed to New York, then Asia, to come back fiercer than ever at the opening of the next trading session in London. She kept her back to Tom as she spoke.

"But it means the market is panicking less …"

Tom did not respond immediately and Edwina waited for him to say the word.

"True," Tom replied eventually. She turned towards him but remained silent. They knew what had to be done next.

"Do we need more in the UK?"

Tom nodded.

"Who will ask?" Edwina said without anxiety. It was now a matter of planning, no longer debating.

Tom sat down, heavy in his chair.

"I will."

Geithner's irritated voice brought her back to the present. Did she have a plan? Of course she did but not just yet. Geithner was a decent guy and a very smart one too. She knew he would not want just to rock the boat. They both needed more time to handle the worst of the crisis. And Edwina needed to wait for her elevation. The call ended as all the previous calls had – "let's keep in touch."

But this call had also sobered her up. If she spoke to anyone, even Nancy, she was putting her career at risk. Years of hard work, planning, enduring. She was convinced that once she got the top job she would make the changes that needed to be made. She couldn't go back, not now, not when she was so close.

Her phone rang and she saw Mervyn's personal assistant was calling. Another round of emergency talks would start in five minutes and more than ever she was ready for them.

Chapter Ten

The pudgy little doorman had seen him turn the corner. Brett would soon enter the Club. The cul-de-sac in St James was suitably discreet. The Club's door, a small unassuming affair, opened onto one of the most powerful gentlemen's clubs still standing. Brett's father and his father before him had belonged. Men in his family had joined from the day when the Club had become an establishment for the nobility to meet in the eighteenth century. Brett had sent an emergency message to his handler. He could not wait for the planned meeting date. Brett hardly acknowledged the doorman who kept his distance. Brett handed over his trilby and Mac to the white-gloved butler.

"My Lord, your guest has arrived."

"Very well, do we have a quiet corner?"

"Indeed, the library as requested."

Brett nodded, satisfied with the unctuous tone the butler was using, and headed for the library.

His guest however did not bother to stand up. He looked annoyed. "I hope it's worth it."

"I wouldn't have called you if it wasn't. Give me some credit." Brett said as he sat down. "My Iraqi contact is trying to introduce me to someone new. I think this is big. I don't have all the details yet but they want me to meet him and that is unusual – in fact unheard of."

"OK, I'm listening."

"I have had two calls from them already. It's all about a one-off deal and a large, very large, sum of money. But no details yet."

"And you think it has nothing to do with art trafficking?"

"Nothing. They are talking about a consignment but I can tell they are testing whether I am interested. It's armaments or possibly people."

Brett's guest studied him for a moment. He was about to speak when drinks came through.

"Highland Park?"

"Of course," Brett replied. "What else?"

Brett noticed a faint smile on the other man's lips.

"So you think they have taken the bait?"

"Almost certainly," Brett replied as he started savouring his whisky.

"Why are you so sure?"

"Because for the past five years I have solidly delivered on my promises. Steady flow of clients, at the high end of the art market, cash payments without delays. They have also done quite a bit of digging."

"You mean about your previous trafficking?"

The remark unsettled Brett. Such harsh words should not be spoken in such an august establishment. He preferred the word facilitation.

"Well, let's say that my facilitation in the Far East has come under scrutiny."

"Who told you?"

"I still have good, in fact very good, contacts in China. They do not like people asking questions and they wanted to know who was asking."

"Is it going to become an issue?"

"No, I told them it was a particular client I knew well doing some research because of the size of the deal involved. It seems to have pacified them."

"Seems?"

"Well, I have done a lot of business with that particular Chinese client but would I trust him with my life? No."

Brett's handler did not respond. Brett had no secrets from this man, much to his annoyance and regret. The handler knew all about his art trafficking, his divorces, his financial machinations. The agency had stripped him bare. They knew details of his life he had wanted to forget about but they had handed him a deal he could never refuse once they knew they had him.

"You will soon need backup but you need to ride this alone for a little longer I'm afraid."

"I thought you might say that."

"And you were right," the man replied whilst putting his empty glass on the small table next to his armchair. Brett looked at the glass. What an exceptional drink to waste on such a thug.

"But I will make sure we are ready. I'll also see what we have picked up that might give us a better picture. We are monitoring a lot more dark-web info traffic these days."

"I will probably have to travel there – wherever 'there' is. They will want to see me before they finalise. They won't trust me otherwise."

"As soon as you know, you apply for a visa for 'there.' We will pick it up. I will then be in contact with you."

Brett nodded. Working for MI6 was not a ball.

* * *

Henry's regular routine was nearly at an end. Big K had finished his round of press-ups too and was nonchalantly moving towards the showers with the easy swagger of a Jamaican rapper. Henry had told Big K he needed information on Kamal. It may come at a cost but Henry had asked very few favours so far. It was time for him to spend some of the brownie points he had accumulated against his name. He followed Big K into the showers. At six foot three Henry was not used to having many man look him in the eyes but Big K was one of them. He relaxed, posturing would have irritated Henry in a previous life but he liked to have this slumbering giant in the next door cell, a man whose intelligence was not in question.

"What do you have for me?" Henry asked as soon as they had turned on the showers.

"Your guy Kamal is the latest bloke charged with terrorism. Comes from a rich Saudi family," Big K said as he lathered his armpits furiously. "Got caught 'cause someone grassed him up. Well-connected guy in high places."

Henry stretched his arms in front of him to lean against the wall and let the water run over his body. He needed its warmth to stop the shaking that had started as soon as Big K uttered the word terrorism. He closed his eyes and clenched his fists. Big K's voice had become distant and vague. Henry inhaled deeply and forced himself to move.

"Such as?" Henry asked, slowly running his long hands over his greying hair to lather in shampoo.

"Government, oil industry, high finance. No drugs though," Big K replied regretfully.

"Not a user then?"

"No man, prays five times a day; no booze either."

"Did he actually do something or was he the brain?"

"You mean did he plant the bomb in Paddington?"

Henry froze. In an instant, the shower room vanished. He is back in the police van that is taking him to the Counterterrorist Squad's HQ for questioning. The deafening noise, the short silence after he has been thrown around the van, the empty eyes of the dead policeman. Henry wills himself back from the abyss with an unbearable effort of strength. Big K is clicking his fingers in front of his face. Henry has turned white and his body is ice cold despite the scorching water. He moves away swiftly, embarrassed by the show of weakness.

"You were there?" Big K asked.

Henry nodded. "That's where they were taking me for interrogation."

"Shit, man."

"So, this fucker was involved," Henry managed to ask through gritted teeth. "That's why he is in here."

Henry grabbed his towel and wrapped it around his loins. He could feel Big K's eyes following him. He had just broken one of the golden rules that Charlie had given him. Do not get exposed; do not get involved.

"What do you wanna do, Bro?"

"I need to think about that. What do you want for the info?" Henry had turned back to face the other man. He had shown fear but he would not show anger. His blue eyes had turned a shade of steel.

Big K nodded. "I'll let you know."

Henry got dressed slowly, a man in control. He could not run away this time. He was composed, enough he hoped to deceive Big K as well as the guards he was about to meet along the corridors.

Back into his cell, Henry slammed his hand against the far side of the wall, the one facing the outside. The shock reverberated through his entire body, setting his shoulder on fire.

"What have these mother-fucking idiots done?" Henry said barely controlling his voice. A thousand questions assailed him. Did the prison governor not realise? Was it a way to get to him? Yet another devious plot as insane as that elaborated by Anthony Albert? Henry did not believe in coincidences. An entire career on the trading floor had taught him to trust his intuition.

"Did the little fucker not know who he was?"

Anger had crept into his belly again the way it had done so many times since his Belfast days but today he had no one to savage but himself. Henry was trembling. Out of nowhere the images that had punched him in the face in the showers resurfaced, more vivid than ever. He could smell petrol, the spilt guts. He could feel two hands grabbing him, dragging him out of the burning vehicle. He remembered the plea of one of the guards to help him with the trapped driver, his lethargy, his fear. He had been a coward on that day. Henry was shaking so badly that he had to sit on the floor and lean against his bed. He had not felt so lost since his final arrest in the quietness of London Fields. On that day Nancy had been at his side. He so wished she was here today. But prison meant solitude.

Henry finally managed to stand up and go to his small desk. Henry reached for the pile of correspondence that sat on it permanently. He would read Nancy's last letter, his greatest source of comfort. His little radio was babbling away. In a few minutes time, he would make his way to the library to start his job.

The noise of hurried footsteps hardly registered. But the thick clang of his prison cell being shut automatically punched him in the stomach. Henry rushed to the door and shook it hard without creating so much as a ripple in the heavy steal. He stuck his ear to the latch and listened hard. It had not been closed properly and Henry could just about make out a few words: him down … medics … breathing. Henry pressed his body against the door so hard he could feel the cold metal seeping into him. More hurried footsteps and now shouting voices: … not breathing … medics. Henry dropped slowly to the floor. He no longer wanted to hear. Just a few cells away, an inmate he hardly knew had decided to set himself free in the only way he could.

Henry had been asked as soon as he entered the prison system whether he felt suicidal. He had made a flippant response – me, never. But today he understood why people would regularly take their own lives. The world he had started to construct around him, the routine put in place to survive the next thirty years – God, he would be seventy by then – was crumbling around him.

He must find a way out of this hell.

* * *

Tom Hardy's preliminary tox report was in. Nurani had laid a copy on Pole's desk and she was already ensconced in the only spare chair he had in his office when he arrived. Pole still could not shake the irritation that had overcome him at his meeting with Nancy and he certainly could hardly contain his anger at Nurani's conversation with Marsh. Her intrusion into his space was only a cause for further aggravation. He was proud of his open-door policy but today he wished he had followed the more guarded approach of his other colleagues.

Pole managed a suitably friendly "What's up?" The time to speak about her conversation with Marsh had not come yet.

"Hardy's tox report just arrived," Nurani said. "Hot off the press. I have not even read it myself. Or rather finished it."

"You mean prelim to report Version 1-01 – And?" What fun to be a tease.

"Well, a cocktail of painkillers. Strong. Prescription drugs only. Something to check of course and then —" Nurani frowned, having turned the page to read the last paragraph of her copy. Her face turned dark. Pole knew the look. There was something she had not anticipated or worse she did not want to read.

Pole removed his jacket, rolled up his sleeves, stroked his well-groomed goatee and sat down. He did not bother to read the whole of the report and jumped straight to the ultimate page.

"Nootropics!" Pole exclaimed. "This cannot be a coincidence."

He pushed a pile of documents that was dangerously high, managed to extract the file he was looking for without dropping so much as a paper clip and went straight to the page on which he knew he would find the information he was looking for.

"Same nootropics," Pole pondered.

Nurani was about to speak but Pole interrupted her, unusually. "OK, so they almost certainly have the same provider. Nurani, where else can these guys stock their meds without them being uncovered by a nosy wife, housekeeper, kid or colleague?"

Nurani was not expecting Pole to take this tack. She had expected him to follow the lead she advocated. Pole tapped his fingers in succession on his desk. He was irritated at himself. He could not let his feelings for Nancy cloud his judgment but Nurani had overstepped the mark with Marsh. Nurani looked confused for a few seconds, then her face brightened suddenly.

"The gym," she said clicking her fingers.

"Well done, *mademoiselle*. The gym it is. Did you fancy a little tour of one of those posh City gyms where bankers sweat out their boozy lunches wearing Lycra?"

"Gross. I don't even want to picture it."

"Very well, I will —" Pole did not have time to finish his offer to 'do' the gym.

"But I am a devoted team player. I'll go," Nurani said all eager after all to check on the Lycra brigade.

"I knew I could count on you. Be gentle, will you? No savaging of those bankers yet. The time will come."

Nurani gave Pole a blazing smile. He nodded.

"Which will give me time to *brief* Superintendent Marsh," Pole added. "He was in fact so well *briefed* about this new *High-Profile Case* that he wants to meet my consultant."

Nurani's smile evaporated, but she kept her cool.

"Whoever spoke to him about Nancy must have created an impression. He is very keen for the meeting to be ASAP," Pole carried on, his fingers still drumming on the desk.

"Well, I suppose it is important that Superintendent Marsh meet with Nancy," Nurani said, voice in control.

"Is that so?" Pole shot her a look. "Let's hope he does not question any of my other choices." A mean reference to his support for Nurani's elevation but warranted he thought.

"I am sure he won't," Nurani mumbled as she left Pole's office.

Pole waited for a few seconds, troubled by what might lie ahead and started dialling a number on his phone.

"Some actions have unforeseen consequences," Pole said too late for her to hear. He closed the door after her. As the loudspeaker on his phone was telling him Nancy was out, he hung up.

No one would dare enter his office until he had reopened a door that so seldom remained shut. Pole moved the precarious pile of documents to the chair on which Nurani had just sat. He selected four files in addition to the one already on his desk, logged onto his computer and searched for the word that had started intriguing him more: LIBOR. A flurry of webpages appeared: definitions, fixing rather than setting, the involvement of the BBA. He sat back in his chair: nothing there that would validate Henry and Nancy's concern. Then again, it was unlikely he would easily find the information he was looking for. Pole reluctantly admitted that the use of the same batch of drugs by both Tom Hardy and Gary Cook was not taking the case in the direction he had hoped.

The idea that both men used the same provider merited attention. Nurani was now on the case of determining who that person was. This line of inquiry also focused her away from a confrontation Pole knew was coming. He no longer cared about sparing Nurani's latest desire to adhere perhaps a little too strictly to the *Rules*. If the case had to move in the direction painted by Henry and Nancy, so it would. Nurani had proven a ruthless operator in the Henry Crowne case, extracting information from

Henry's best friend Liam in the most unforgiving manner. She was right of course. Henry's secret involvement with the fundraising operations of the IRA was an unexpected bargaining chip against Liam's brother's life. But the way in which she had relished getting the deal done had surprised Pole. No, what he feared was not Nurani's wrath but rather his own antipathy for Henry. As ever he had been fair. He had kept going with the case when everyone had thought it was sealed. Even after Henry's dubious confession he had persisted in getting to the truth. And Pole recognised that Henry was smart, in fact extremely smart. If he had seen something in this LIBOR story, Pole would reluctantly have to take note.

The phone rang and Nancy's name appeared on the screen. Pole hesitated. His hand hovered, moving involuntarily towards the handset. He had to stop himself in mid-air. Pole would come to a better formulated view before he took the call and he was in no hurry to arrange the meeting with Marsh.

He came back to Henry. How could he have known? Or taken an interest?

"Option One, he is trying to get out." Pole considered the idea. Very possible: a man like Henry would suffer in prison, more than most. But Pole also believed that Henry wanted to atone. Lack of positive action would put an enormous strain on Henry.

"Option Two, he had prior knowledge." The idea sounded interesting. Henry had the most phenomenal memory Pole had ever encountered. He had witnessed it first-hand during interrogation. Henry would use the same words, recount the same facts, no deviation or omission. This had made Pole suspicious to start with, only for him to realise that this unusual behaviour for a man telling the truth emanated from a highly trained and controlled mind. Only Nancy had proven a match for Henry. The thought made Pole uncomfortable. But he was not a jealous man and his excellent ability to read characters had told him there was deep friendship between the two but nothing else. A warm feeling and small leap of his heart made Pole grin. Nancy was his, no matter how long it would take.

The light on his phone was flashing, no doubt a message from Nancy that was urging him on.

If Henry knew anything it would have to be from his GL days but Henry was not an interest-rate specialist. Nevertheless, Henry had been top management. He had used his knowledge of GL's undisclosed dealings in subprime to topple his former boss and compromise the crucial merger between GL and HXBK. Henry had revealed in a damning fax the eye-watering large loss position that GL held in subprime to the CEO of HXBK. Why would he not disclose more of what he knew now? Henry had no reason to hold back.

Pole considered the idea. Would something else have triggered Henry's interest? He was an avid reader of news, as every trading floor MD would be. Pole extended his original Google search. He combined LIBOR and news articles. The *FT*, *The Guardian*, *The Times*: a flurry of new webpages appeared. But all seemed to concentrate on LIBOR as a benchmark. He was about to give up when he spotted an article from *The Wall Street Journal*: BANKERS CAST DOUBT ON KEY RATES AMID CRISIS, (16 April 2008). Pole could not help but smile. Henry Crowne was indeed a smart-arse.

Pole's phone rang once more. He picked up still thinking about Henry and cursed his decision.

"Hello Jonathan, this is Denise, Superintendent Marsh's PA."

"Hello Denise. Is he about to pay me a visit again?"

"Nope but he wants to meet Ms Wu – URGENTLY," Denise imitated Marsh superbly. Pole sighed. "And you want her phone number, mobile number, fax number, email address so that you can invite her URGENTLY."

"Spot on."

Pole waited a few seconds, a man looking for the details he, of course, knew by heart.

Chapter Eleven

The bus lumbered slowly away from its stop outside Tate Britain. Nancy broke into a sprint to try and catch it but the driver ignored her waving arm. She cursed. Perhaps she needed a brisk walk. She left Victoria station and turned towards Grosvenor Place. Thoughts buzzed around her head like threatening insects, preventing her from creating a coherent picture of the situation.

William had asked her, no, begged her, not to reveal his identity. It was so unlike him to lose his cool, to be rattled by what could have simply been a clumsy driver talking on his mobile phone whilst driving. And yet, William was convinced he had been targeted. Could she truly leave his name out of a conversation with Pole? And, more importantly, let her friend take risks that could cost him his life? The last question made her stomach churn. She stopped to recover her breath. Nancy had defended some unholy characters in her time. She had come to consider the implications of what some of them had done in retrospect. She had managed to look at her role for the defence as an essential service justice must provide in a democracy worthy of the name. The job of the police and prosecution was to build the case following due process and according to what the law of the land permitted. Her job was to make sure that it stacked together. The promise of success, her much wanted elevation, had gradually made her lose track of what she thought of her clients. She had become supremely adept at extracting the information she needed, not to assess the value of the case she was accepting, but in order to win the battle. She recalled the moment when, at the height of her career, she had received a call from one of France's most notorious and controversial barristers, Maitre Jacques Verges. Passers-by were eyeing her with concern. She felt their attention and started moving again. She knew full well why Verges' story had surfaced.

It was reminding her of the success that warranted his contact. She had defended Vladislas Karsik successfully against war crimes. This obscure figure had never been directly involved in the Kosovo genocide but he had been instrumental in supplying armaments and logistics to the armies of Slobodan Milosevic. The prosecution had been mounted expertly by barristers she knew well and the evidence gathered was credible. Karsik had managed to keep a low profile, covering his tracks, always ensuring that evidence would be destroyed along with the people who knew too much with it. The most frustrating moment for the Prosecution had not only been to lose but also to know that Karsik was still supporting other wars from his prison cell – and yet the evidence they had gathered was far from watertight.

Nancy had reached Piccadilly. She was walking alongside Green Park and in a couple of minutes would be in front of the Royal Academy. She entered the courtyard and briskly walked into the members' room. She looked at her watch, only 3pm. Was it too late or early for a small pick-me-up? She shrugged, so what? She ordered a large glass of Merlot, chose a bowl of sad-looking olives and sat herself at the window. The meeting with William had moved her in ways she had not felt for a long time. She no longer wished to be associated with the dark shadows that power and politics cast over people. Most of all, she did not want to be responsible for someone's death. She took a large gulp of wine, passably good but it did not do the trick. The thought of William coming to any harm because she had not divulged his identity became unbearable. Nancy closed her eyes and breathed deeply. William may never forgive her. He was doing what he believed was right for his country. But he had put her in an impossible situation. She should be angry with him for presenting her with this awful choice. She picked up an olive mechanically from the bowl and chewed on it. She would call Pole, speak to him and go with the flow – when she spoke to the man she trusted more than anyone else perhaps a decision would emerge. Yes, Jonathan Pole was indeed her most trusted friend.

Her mobile rang. She fumbled in her bag, cursing, and answered with a curt "hello". A charming voice was asking her for her availability to meet with Superintendent Marsh. The worry on her face vanished. Pole must have made the right decision – he was involving Henry. If she went to the Yard now she could meet with him and speak about William too.

"Of course, I would be delighted to meet Superintendent Marsh … Today, 5pm. Perfect … It will be my pleasure." Nancy took another sip of wine. She pushed the glass away. Being tipsy now would not do.

336

Marsh was Pole's superior after all. Meeting William meant she could indulge in dressing couture. Was she too overdressed? She considered her immaculate Louis Féraud suit, black-and-grey herringbone pattern, yellow shirt that suited her tan so well, black pearl jewellery.

"No," she whispered. "A good bit of power dressing always impresses the likes of Marsh."

* * *

The call had startled Brett. He was not expecting his contact to demand another meeting so quickly. Brett was still feeling the effects of his favourite whisky. He needed to sober up significantly before making his way to Finsbury in North London. The instructions from his minder were clear: go with the flow and get as much intel as possible. Each piece of intelligence was worth harvesting for an information thirsty MI6 that needed to infiltrate the Salafi network which was fast expanding in Europe. Their Jihadi strategy was to introduce people into a country early, let them become part of the community – years, perhaps decades – before they would be asked to act. Brett's minder had been surprised that they should trust him. But the Salafi network needed access to places and people they could not yet reach. Brett had told him that this was a very specific piece of work, a narrow target, not in his view a bomb or mass shooting. But MI6 was not prepared to take the risk. Unlike the cocky little bloke that was his minder, Brett had experience of the terrain. Decades in Art's black market, navigating the trafficking world and doing business with the most dangerous of collectors, had brought him knowledge and instinct. He was on the ground. He had been there for much longer than the young MI6 Turk had been wearing trousers. And he, Brett, was still alive. He made himself a cup of strong coffee, Middle-Eastern style letting the grounds sink to the bottom of the small glass. The powerful aroma filled the room. Brett poured the liquid into a small ornate glass, took a lump of brown sugar and plunged it into the coffee only releasing it when it was about to disintegrate. The bittersweet taste sent a shiver through his body, a reminder of how his life had unfolded since his last divorce, the cruellest of them all. Brett checked his watch and released the strap. He was not taking his beloved Patek Philippe to a meeting in North London. He finished his coffee and moved to his bedroom to get ready. The shabby blue jacket and faded slacks were waiting for him still carelessly thrown onto the back of a chair. Brett changed, casting a quick eye outside his flat.

The weather was turning cold and it would soon be dark. He sat on the side of his bed, checked his new burner mobile. A text had come through confirming his meeting – Finsbury Park station, N4. Mohammed would be waiting for him there. Nothing else. Should he alert his minder?

"Not yet," Brett murmured. "If they are going to kill me it won't be today. Today they want to talk."

As he walked out of the Finsbury Park station, Brett was hit by an unexpectedly harsh wind, a sharp contrast with the snugness of the Tube. His hands were moist with sweat. He adjusted the cotton scarf around his neck and scanned the faces in the crowd: men in long white robes, white crocheted hats and well-trimmed beards; women in scarves, many of them wearing the full-face mask. Brett felt out of place despite his low key, well-worn jacket. A hand grabbed his arm and before he could say anything Mohammed was pushing him towards the exit, down the street. A car was waiting, the door opened and he was pushed inside. Brett had expected it would not be a cosy ride. He protested. They could not think he was eager or even prepared. Mohammed tried to sound reassuring but Brett could tell that he was more scared than he was. The man sitting next to him in the back of the car was wearing the requisite dark glasses, his leather jacket contrasted with the outfits more common on the streets of Finsbury. He handed Brett an eye mask.

"Put it on," he said. His voice had a slight Middle-Eastern accent that Brett could not place. Brett looked at Mohammed with an offended look.

"Come on – just to be on the safe side."

Brett protested again and hoped his mixture of disquiet and offence was doing the trick. He donned the mask and sat back. Now the real work had begun. The car was moving along Blackstock Road towards the north. He was counting the minutes, memorising the turns. They stayed in the car for just under half an hour but Brett was almost certain they had gone in a circle at least once. He felt strangely relaxed. It was not the first time he had been hoodwinked and led to some unknown destination. At least he was in the UK; he was in London – not in a foreign country run by war lords who may decide to sever any part of his anatomy including his head.

The car stopped and a large hand grabbed his arm, making him disembark clumsily. He was led through a door and the blindfold removed. He winced at the bright light coming from a single bulb dangling from the ceiling. Mohammed was with him and Brett realised that he too had been blindfolded.

"You're going on your own." Mohammed exhaled anxiously. "I don't need to be with you."

Brett nodded, avoiding eye contact. He could only have contempt for this coward, but he was of good use. No need to do damage to their relationship.

Brett progressed down a shabby corridor, paint peeling from the wall. The place was unusually warm, almost suffocating. The smell of spices and coffee told him it was lived in. The door on his left opened abruptly. The thick-necked man who was walking behind him gestured for Brett to walk in. The room was softly lit, in contrast with the corridor, a number of rugs and a couple of thick mattresses spread over the floor. A small bony man was sitting on one of them. Despite the lack of furniture, the room felt cosy. Brett quickly assessed the quality of the rugs and the throws, once a dealer always a dealer – these were not a poor man's possessions. The man did not stand up but gestured for Brett to sit down. He crouched and sat easily on the mattress to the right of his interlocutor. A faint smile brushed over the man's face. Brett had done business with the likes of him before. Brett registered. He was doing good – so far.

"We have a business deal to put to you," said the man with no further introduction. His English was fluent, educated in the US.

"I am listening," Brett replied with the coldness of a man prepared to do anything as long as it made money.

The man eyed Brett for a few seconds. Tea carried by a woman in full niqab appeared. She left the platter in front of the man and the scent of mint filled the air. He took his glass, again gestured to Brett to help himself, and started sipping at the burning liquid.

"We need to bring someone into the UK along a new route."

Brett also took a sip of tea and slowly placed the glass down on the floor in front of him.

"I don't do people," he said calmly.

"Yet," replied the man, "the price will be right."

Brett finished his tea.

"Why me?"

"You have a good track record. You smuggle unique pieces almost everywhere in the world but in particular into the UK and – you do not do people," said the man with a hint of irony. Brett paid more attention to him for the first time. His face was young enough, with the expected untrimmed black beard. His hat came down low on his forehead unexpectedly emphasising his eyes. There was a level of determination, cold and unyielding, that Brett had seen only a few times before. A pang of anxiety surprised him.

"It will be a one-off," he said

The man nodded and finished his tea. "How much?"

"Only one man, no – equipment?"

The man nodded again and clapped his hands. The woman reappeared, poured some fresh tea and disappeared without a sound.

"How quickly do you want this done?"

"Next week, possibly sooner."

Brett's hand stopped in mid-air as he was reaching for his tea.

"I need a little more time if it is to be successful."

"You don't have it."

Brett drained his glass. "£1 million," he said without flinching.

The man's eyes bore into Brett. "We will contact you."

Brett stood up. The door opened and the same thick-necked man moved him towards the door. The meeting was over and Brett knew he had won the deal.

* * *

The cell door had opened an hour ago. Most inmates had gone to the canteen to collect their dinner. Henry always made his trip downstairs at 7pm. He did not like to mix with the lot that needed to seek comfort in food. This was not food in any case. This was fuel that kept the body going. Even canteen at college had been better than that. Still, it was part of the deal. It was part of the atonement process. Today, however, Kamal's presence had made his environment taste even more bitter. He was still reeling from the discovery. Henry stood up. He had to make a move or he would miss a meal. He slowly walked along the corridor, down a couple of stairwells. Big K was not in his cell. He too liked to get his food late – "Caribbean style, man." He always smiled as he mentioned Jamaica, uncovering a set of perfect white teeth. Henry walked past an empty cell. He shivered. The sounds of the failed attempt to save the life of the inmate who had lived only two doors away came back with a disquieting clarity. Someone would be moved in as early as tomorrow Big K had told him. Henry straightened up and focused on the way ahead, slowing down his pace… He was looking down the staircase when he saw Kamal at the bottom of it. He slowed down further almost to a stop. He had not yet decided what he should do. He could turn around but the urge to face up to the little shit grabbed him. No more excuses. Henry knew his anger, the deep marks left by a Belfast upbringing. But the rage that had seized him in the gym was still fresh and potent.

"I've got to find out," he said through gritted teeth. "No matter." Henry started moving again. He forced his pace to remain measured. Every move on a Cat. A wing had to be thought through. He could not afford to be misread by the other cons, so Henry willed himself to maintain the calm appearance he liked to adopt. The queue was short. Kamal seemed to have slowed his pace too. He was only a couple of people away. He cast an eye towards Henry and for an imperceptible moment made eye contact with him. He turned back to pick up a tray and started slopping food on his plate. A politically correct prison service was offering a halal option and he took it. Henry moving along the queue hardly noticed what he was putting on his tray. Today he would eat at one of the tables. Big K had just finished and was putting his tray away when he nodded. He moved towards Henry with the nonchalant swagger of a man strolling along the white beaches of his native island.

"See who's here?" he murmured as he passed Henry.

"Yep, can't miss the beard," Henry replied. He could feel Big K's smile but did not lose his focus. Kamal had chosen a solitary table. Henry chose the corner of the room from which he could observe him discreetly. He started assessing the small built man. Kamal looked boyish, a quiet young man who no one might notice. Henry had remarked how delicate his hands were, almost feminine. His voice was soft and yet the unmistakable echoes of fierce single-mindedness could be heard by a trained ear. It was not the type of fanaticism he had been used to with Bobby or the fiery determination of Liam. It was deeper, methodical. He would not, would never be turned. Again, Henry wondered why Kamal had been moved to Belmarsh. He would check the information he had gathered from Big K with Charlie. Too much was riding on this for him to rely on only one source. He could speak to Nancy too but he discarded the thought immediately. He needed her for some more pressing issue – getting involved with Pole's new investigation. Kamal wanted to establish contact, so be it. "One terrorist to another," thought Henry bitterly. He would play the game for a while. The explosion at Paddington came back in a quick flash of disjointed images. The look of his half-eaten plate of beans disgusted him. He pushed it away and sat back in his chair. Henry would never be a killer. He had understood that on that day. But he still needed the proof, irrefutable, that he could, one day, rejoin the human race. Maybe that proof, that opportunity had presented itself and he was ready to grab it, run with it even if it laid him in the depths of hell.

Another inmate joined Kamal's table. They did not speak but when Kamal stood up the other man quickly placed a small piece of paper in Kamal's hand as he walked past. Henry slowly averted his gaze. Kamal walked past Henry's table to reach the tray conveyor belt. "Let's talk," he said.

Henry did not respond. Kamal walked past him again not expecting an answer. The game was on and Henry had an inkling as to where it was leading.

* * *

Marsh was standing at the window, in full uniform, when Nancy entered. He was poised to impress. Nancy gave him her best smile. She too was on a charm offensive. It was a formal "How do you do" all around, followed by the softer "A pleasure to meet you – likewise." Marsh locked his eyes into Nancy's as they were shaking hands and she knew she had made a greater impact than she had anticipated.

"I have read your CV, Ms Wu. Very impressive. I can see why Pole needs someone like you for the more complex City cases."

"Inspector Pole is a very capable man. I input solely on the more technical issues," Nancy replied.

"Pole is perhaps a little unconventional," Marsh added with a hint of sarcasm. He called for tea, enquired whether Darjeeling would do – yes it would, and would she prefer lemon to milk – yes very much so. Marsh offered her a seat in the more comfortable corner of his office harbouring armchairs and a sofa.

Marsh sounded genuinely curious about her background. Nancy gave him a well-rehearsed story. He kept interrupting, not in a way that was irritating but with the questions that a good listener might ask. Nancy had learned in her career at the Bar never to underestimate an adversary. Marsh was sitting comfortably, relaxed, one arm over the back of the sofa – such an open attitude, encouraging her to feel the same, comfortable and ready for a revelatory chat. If Marsh was testing her to validate her credentials, she would play the game. Even more important was to validate Pole's decision to involve Henry. Nancy volunteered a few titbits of information. She had indeed worked as a trainee barrister for the infamous Jacques Verges. She also had defended a man accused of war crimes. Nancy gave her well-rehearsed "every man has the right to proper defence in a democracy worthy of this name" speech. Marsh courteously poured more tea. His right arm was once more spread over the back of the sofa, his hand moving mechanically in slow motion patting and prodding the leather affectionately. His eyes had not for one instant left Nancy; to someone less accustomed to scrutiny it would have been intimidating.

"And your experience of the City tells you it is not suicide?" Marsh asked out of the blue. Nancy smiled, drank a little more tea. She would not be drawn out that easily. Even if Pole had agreed on Henry's cooperation. The game of influencing and toying around with arguments was on.

"I am sure Inspector Pole has told you but I was unfortunately, or perhaps fortunately, present when Gary Cook died. I saw the body."

"Your conclusion?" Marsh asked, also taking a sip of his tea, all nonchalance and yet observant.

"He certainly was drunk when he spoke to me but not that drunk. The body fell at some awkward angle."

"And Tom Hardy?"

"No sign of alcohol or pills in the car, still strapped in his seat – unexpected."

"Still a little slim." Marsh smiled. His eyes widened a little and his eyebrows moved up. He wanted to be convinced otherwise.

"But so far no personal crisis that warrants such a dramatic move has been uncovered for both – no motive. And these two men were certainly not the type."

"Cook had lost his job." Marsh had done his homework, read the file or spoken to someone who knew it well.

"Cook had been in the City for a very long time. He almost certainly would have seen this as a means to getting a large sum from his former employer."

Marsh bent forward suddenly, his knees made contact with the small coffee table that separated them. His elbows rested on his thighs.

"How do you propose we move the inquiry forward? Pole is expecting the final toxicology report on Cook imminently. Hardy's final report will follow shortly thereafter. I have made it clear it is priority." Marsh was flexing his seniority muscle to impress. Nancy gave him a "you're-so-clever" sort of smile.

"And Inspector Pole can certainly speak to Henry Crowne as soon as he has received the OK."

Marsh's head moved sideways, his eyes questioning. "Crowne?"

Nancy stilled herself. "If he is so minded of course." Had she just gone over Pole's head? Bad, very bad idea.

"Henry Crowne; you mean the IRA banker?" Marsh said slowly. "Because of his understanding of the City?"

"It's a possibility," Nancy replied. Her mind was screaming danger. She could try to force the issue with Marsh now that she had presented the idea but Pole might never forgive her. It would certainly dent the trust they had for one another. And yet, Henry needed to be heard.

"What does Pole say?"

"I have hardly broached the subject with him."

"Why not. You should." Marsh settled again into the sofa. His eyes had finally left Nancy. He could see it all: another high-profile banking case triggering much media attention. He loved it. "In fact, why don't I give Pole a ring. I am due an update in any case."

"I am due to see Henry Crowne tomorrow. Why don't I gather more information and let you know whether this is worth it? You would not want to make a premature assumption that he has much to offer." It was the best Nancy could think of to soften her blunder and delay until she could speak to Pole.

Marsh pursed his lips. She had a point. He could not sound too enthusiastic at the thought of involving a terrorist in one of his men's cases.

"Very well, I shall await your call. What time are you meeting him?"

Nancy gave Marsh the details and extricated herself from the meeting. Marsh insisted in accompanying her to the lifts where she was finally allowed to go. Nancy took her mobile out of her bag and dialled Pole's line. No connection.

"Bloody lift, come on," she blurted. The door opened and a couple of people walked in. She terminated the call, pressed the close-door button. The lift stopped again. She grumbled and pushed her way through. She would call from whatever floor she was on. Pole's landline went to answer phone, so did his mobile. Nancy left a text message marked GENUINELY URGENT …

Chapter Twelve

Pole had been elusive since they had last spoken. Nancy had tried to find him after her meeting with Marsh.

Nothing doing.

She restlessly pushed away the book she was attempting to read. But even an Iris Murdoch novel, her favourite writer, could not do the trick. She stood up and went to her large window. The light was fading away fast and it would soon be dark. She had pushed herself into the tightest of spots; a classic mistake of assuming the case was going in her direction - an assumption she should not have made. She had to reach Pole before Marsh did. Marsh had become impatient at the thought of this new high-profile case and he might give Pole a nudge before tomorrow. She would go back to the Yard today if necessary or even cross the river and see Pole at home. She took a deep breath to release the tension in her shoulders and rolled her head slowly. She wrapped her hands around her neck. The disquiet she had felt in Marsh's office at the thought of losing Pole's trust had risen a notch. The word Love floated across her mind and she pushed it away. She could never get close to anyone – lovers perhaps, but love. A small ripple of desire moved across her body and she turned her head back towards the centre of the room. The letter from Hong Kong was still on the coffee table. She focused on it with intensity, eager to remind herself why she did not want to, could not, let any man into her life. She had taken many risks in her life but that of abandonment she could not face, even after all these years.

"Why did you have to go back?" Nancy murmured, torn between anger and sadness. The pain savaged her once again.

She is running alongside the train that is taking him away, her father. The man who has enthralled her with his immense knowledge of art and philosophy. He dares everything when it comes to art, new ideas, new media; there is no limit to his skills and his inventiveness. She's barely seven when they leave China but already seventeen when he decides to go back. Deng Xiaoping has been put in charge of the National Committee of the Chinese People's Political Consultative Conference – he is not in charge yet. Her father considers him a bringer of progress. The Cultural Revolution is soon at an end. Mao is now dead. He must return to China to fight.

"With what? Your paint and brushes," Nancy said through gritted teeth. She knew she was wrong. Art has always been a powerful tool and it can make a difference.

Her mobile was ringing. She snatched it from the coffee table and was about to answer. The number was marked withheld. She threw the phone onto the large sofa. It bounced once and nearly fell off. Nancy caught it just in time.

"Bloody hell. What's the matter with me?" she said impatiently.

The ringtone was telling her the caller had left a voicemail.

"Ms Wu, I hope you won't mind me calling you at this late hour but have you given any more thought to Henry Crowne's involvement?" Marsh said as eloquently as he could. Nancy listened to the convoluted message. She sat back on her sofa and managed a half smile. Marsh was asking for another meeting or rather for the pleasure of her expert opinion as he put it.

"Well, Jonathan Pole you've just found yourself some serious competition," she mused.

* * *

Pole was in a meeting with his team, recapping on the various interviews they had carried out. He had noticed Nancy's calls. With a hint of hesitation, he turned the phone face down. Andy was recapping on their findings so far, nothing: family, friends, colleagues – not one single noticeable connection. And yet within the rarefied world of high management in the City this was inconceivable. Seniority exacerbated visibility and tightened the circle in which bankers operated. Pole was particularly keen to explore both men's work contacts, clubs and outside interests. Both Gary and Tom had worked at the same bank when juniors. They understood how to navigate the world of finance. They were experts on about bonds and interest rates. Pole's research on LIBOR had been fruitful but irritating only proving to him that Henry had a very valid point. The article published by the *WSJ* had been well researched and it had sown a doubt in his mind that kept growing the more he read around the subject matter. But Pole was not ready to yield. Nancy was probably pressing for what she believed, something she had done so effectively when she had taken Henry's case on. Pole needed more than a personal hunch; the evidence needed to stack up and so far it did not, or so he told himself. There was also the meeting with Marsh. His mind drifted a little. Nancy would know what to do, surely. Pole's slight discomfort in the pit of his stomach was not mere professional anxiety. Nancy was a strong judge of character and her help invaluable – nothing was more attractive than a strong intellect combined with a compassionate nature.

Andy was wrapping up and the team dispersed.

Pole hung around.

"Good job, even if a bit frustrating."

"I know Guv." Andy hesitated.

"But. You have an idea?"

"Not so much an idea but an – observation."

Pole raised an inquisitive eyebrow.

"It feels like something is missing. People are not talking. I am not so much saying they are doing it voluntarily, more not wanting to remember."

"That's an interesting view," Pole said slowly. "Walk with me to my office."

Andy adjusted his thick glasses on his baby face and started walking awkwardly alongside Pole.

"What makes you say that, apart from the lack of information?"

"I re-reread the transcripts," Andy said craning his neck toward his boss.

"All of them?" Pole said suppressing a smile.

"I am not losing time." Andy turned a deep shade of red.

"I'm not saying you are. And?"

"It's all about work, the office. There is nothing private. I mean, like what it was like to know these guys on a personal level. And if the guys asked – same thing really vague."

"Even with friends' interviews?"

"Specially with friends' interviews – they all talk about these guys and their work but …"

Pole and Andy crossed into Pole's office. Andy moved a pile of documents from the chair in front of Pole's desk. He took out of his pockets a roll of wine gums and offered Pole one. Much to his surprise Pole took one and started sucking on it. Pole smiled at Andy's shocked face.

"I, too, was once young."

Andy nodded, unconvinced.

"How do you want to take your hunch forward?"

"I thought I could go back into their diaries and look for lunches, dinners, parties."

"And you have already started it – so what do you have?" Pole asked. He was indeed an old guy with a lot of experience and knew a keen face when he saw one.

Andy wriggled a little on his seat. "Parties are really interesting. I mean, there is a bit more information like photos, snippets in newspapers or websites."

Pole nodded encouragingly.

"There are a couple of parties that did not quite turn out the way they should. One of them there was a brawl and the police was called – bit of a punch-up between some trading-floor guys, too much booze apparently."

Pole shook his head, pulling his mouth into a sceptical grimace. "Not uncommon I would say – most of the time the reason we don't know about it is because they don't call the cops. I mean our colleagues."

"But there is this other one where some young guy jumped from the top floor of the hotel in which they were having a party."

Pole stood up. "Keep going." He had taken his phone out of his pocket and was moving it around his hand in a rhythmic gesture.

"A young grad, apparently he had been having a bad time and couldn't cope with the pressure."

"Who was at that party? Gary Cook and Tom Hardy?"

"Yes, Guv, and a lot more top people."

"You know what you've got to do? Full list of people there, and autopsy report on this poor bugger."

Pole dumped his mobile on his desk, showed Andy out and sat back down. It would not take long for Andy to find the information on the old case file. Another excuse to delay calling Nancy perhaps? Would Marsh have called already though? 8pm. Marsh's PA would have gone home. He toyed with his phone for half a minute longer.

"Shit. I give in." Pole closed his door and was about to dial when the door opened again without a knock and Nurani entered. She was all smiles.

"You have the face of a cat that got the cream," Pole said with an amused smile. Nancy would have to wait a little longer.

"Oh yeah, the cream – or rather the little blue pills, the ones we were looking for."

"Pray tell." Pole pushed up his tall body upright in his chair.

"The gym was a good idea. We opened the lockers and found a whole bag full of various naughties and I have taken the lot to the lab."

"Did you get a list of the gym members?"

Nurani crossed her arms over her chest with a smug look.

"OK, OK," Pole said putting his hands up. "I am just a pain of a DCI doing his job."

Nurani eyed the chair that was free and sat down.

"One of the guys is going through it as we speak. I bet you we will find Tom Hardy there."

"Couldn't agree more but I am looking for another connection," Pole mused. Nurani raised her eyebrows. "Weren't we keen to find the guy or gal that sold these chaps some dodgy drug?"

"Very true, and yet – and yet."

"You're not going to buy that conspiracy crap, are you?"

"Well, I have been doing a lot of reading of late," Pole said waving at a pile of printed articles. "And I am afraid the conspiracy theory is now sounding particularly attractive."

"This is bullshit, Jon. Really, all that because *Nancy* is spinning it in order to help her mate Henry."

Nurani's voice was trembling, her eyes filled with so much outrage that Pole was taken aback.

"Temper, temper Ms Shah," Pole said, only half amused. His eyes met Nurani's and he would not yield until she did.

Nurani stood up abruptly. She leaned forward towards Pole, her knuckles planted on his desk.

"This is not on, Jon. She is not a trained investigator. She has no terrain experience and OK, perhaps she is good when it comes to fake paintings, but this is an entirely different ball game."

"And I think your way of belittling her input is, in turn, not on, Nurani. She has a huge amount of experience in the field of criminality and I am not asking Nancy to do your job or mine," Pole replied, more angered than he expected. "In any case, I do not have to justify my actions to you."

"Why not? It is also impacting the way I work on the case. And you certainly should have spoken to me about this LIBOR idea."

"What's the matter with you? You are senior enough and will almost certainly be promoted by year end. You are leading one of the main lines of enquiry in this case —"

"But," Nurani interrupted. "You are not involving me at the sharp end of the enquiry."

"Please shut the door," Pole's voice had taken on an uncharacteristically incisive edge. Nurani hesitated, yielding only to Pole's order as he was about to stand up to close the door himself. "I will not have you questioning how I run a case, not when it comes to my choice of experts. You know how I work. I don't only give orders. I do the work too including when it's hard graft. Some of my colleagues like to delegate or even over-delegate, not me. And I get results because of this – which, by the way has served you well so far." Pole paused. "I don't want to hear more of this garbage. Are we clear?"

Pole had remained seated, his tall body relaxed in his chair. Only his voice conveyed his anger and it worked. Nurani's face had turned red, her righteousness turned to concern. Pole had never spoken to her that way before. She uttered an inaudible "Fine" and disappeared, closing the door stiffly behind her. Pole sighed. "Ah, to be young and ambitious."

He snatched the mobile from where it was hiding, under a pile of articles he had dumped on his desk, evidence of his hard graft as he had put it to Nurani. The word LIBOR figured prominently on most pages. He collected the papers together, let them fall on his desk with a sharp tap. He placed the bundle in front of him. Time to return Nancy's call.

Pole's fingers moved briskly over the keypad of his mobile phone, accessing the missed call list. He tapped his long fingers on his desk, inventing a rhythm that translated nerves, or perhaps embarrassment. He should not have dismissed Nancy's views so readily. Still, he had now consolidated his view on the matter of interest-rate manipulation, had gathered more evidence on the deaths of Gary Cook and Tom Hardy. The puzzle was falling into place just the way he liked it to. Pole reached Nancy's name in the list of missed calls – seven altogether. He ran his fingers through his hair. "Something's up. Shit."

* * *

Edwina looked at her watch, 9pm. She stretched, yawned and tried to focus on the email she was drafting. Yet another email to the Governor of the Bank of England justifying the need for a further round of Quantitative Easing. Her door had remained closed and she had not checked on Gabriel. He was no doubt still around. He would have otherwise stuck his head through the door to tell her he was leaving – made some silly joke, checked she did not need him. Gabriel was the most devoted deputy she had ever had. He could have easily been in her shoes had it not been for the horrendous accident that had cost him so dear.

She rubbed her hand over her face – focus. She read aloud the last sentence of her email. "The current level of QE in the UK has reached GBP 70bn." It did not have the punch and technical quality she was looking for. She stretched again and stood up. Her mind had not been on the job for a few hours. She went to her window overlooking Threadneedle Street. The flow of traffic had died down and only the odd cab rushed past, carrying another banker eager to get home. *The activity may pick up a bit,* she thought. Most City firms no longer allowed their staff to use cabs before 9pm. The days of expense abuse were slowly disappearing. And yet so much work still needed doing to change mentalities. She rested her head against the cool glass. What was happening? She could not ignore the heavy feeling she had carried all day. Something about Gabriel had unsettled her and she could not shake it away. She moved to her closed door and eased it open slowly. Gabriel was still at his desk, working. She closed the door again. Her chest tightened, a moment of panic, then she was calm again.

The final round of meetings that would promote her to being the first female Governor of the Bank of England was playing on her mind, she decided.

I do not need this bloody stupid story: Gary, then Tom. How inconsiderate. Humour may not be appropriate but who cared? She would work another hour and then call it quits. Her stomach grumbled; she needed food.

"Gabs," Edwina said sticking her head through the door again. "I am famished. Can we order something?"

Gabriel lifted his head, rubbing his eyes underneath his glasses.

"Yep, great idea – pizza?"

"Deep, crisp and even." Edwina smiled.

"Gosh. It's not that time of the year yet."

"I know. A poor attempt at levity."

"Well, I know what Father Xmas is going to place in your stocking."

"You are convinced. Aren't you?"

"Absolutely Eddie. No one and nothing is getting in your way. Mark my words. You will be the next Governor." Gabriel winked whilst putting on his jacket. His smile was broad, perhaps too broad.

"Are you not ordering?"

"Will do that as I walk there. I need some fresh air." He turned away and disappeared.

Edwina cursed herself. She should have gone home. The work she would do after eating a pizza with Gabriel would be rubbish and she would get home late, again. But old habits died hard and it was difficult not to succumb to the investment banking macho pressure of working late. Whether quality work was produced, well that was another matter altogether.

Gabriel had disappeared for a couple of minutes. She walked to the window to see him cross the road. He had locked his PC – something he should do of course but that he rarely did when they were working late together. She quickly went round his desk, lifted carefully the chipped Oxford mug that he used to hold his pens. She found a small post-it underneath, Metatron32.

How stupid.

She entered his password. The screen on which he was working materialised. Edwina's heart was pumping in her ears.

Gabriel was checking flights to Turkey. She did not recall him mentioning a holiday nor indeed any interest in a trip to the Middle East and certainly not, she had assumed, after the terrifying accident that had cost him a deformed face and his brother his life. The dates sounded equally odd. End of the month, in exactly seven days' time. She heard the doors of the lift chime, rapidly locked down the screen and disappeared into her office. She busied herself around her meeting table, making room for the warm pizzas she could smell already. Gabriel opened the boxes, tore out the tops, took out of his jacket pockets a couple of cans of lager and plunked himself in a chair. A well-rehearsed sequence meant to make them both feel at home, the way an old couple would, Edwina thought. She was still standing when Gabriel opened the cans and gave her a surprised look – was she not hungry?

"La Reine pizza," he announced. "Thought it might be topical."

"What about yours? Sicilian pizza, extra pepperoni – that smells of La Mafia," Edwina managed to jest.

Gabriel's smile dropped for an imperceptible moment and was back again. "Anything to get the *Job* done, of course."

He grabbed a piece and took a bite. He gave an approving grunt, washed the first mouthful down with a drink from his can. "Won't you share my Sicilian Eddie? Just what you need at this moment in time …"

"As long as you share La Reine," Edwina replied short of finding something wittier to say.

"You bet I will," Gabriel smiled and helped himself. He started on his new piece and took another slug from his can. Edwina had stopped eating. The same feeling that had made her check his PC made her put her slice down. "What's keeping you so late today?" she asked forcing herself to eat her fast cooling pizza.

"There is always something to do. I need to finish the new report on the latest inflation figures. How about you? Still working on QE for Mervyn-The-Oracle-King?"

Why lie?

Edwina took her can of lager and drank from it in silence. Why lie about a holiday?

"I'm not finding the right words – frustrating," she heard herself say.

"Are you worried about anything in particular?" Gabriel asked whilst selecting carefully another piece of pizza.

She gave him a surprised look, but Gabriel was talking quantitative easing or at least she hoped he was. "Of course, I'm worried. Worried that Merv is going to say no to the next instalment of QE."

"I meant beyond that?" Gabriel's effort at being casual filled her with anger. If he wanted to ask her whether she was still thinking about Gary and Tom's deaths he should, plain and simple.

His BlackBerry rang. He was about to ignore it when the caller's ID made him change his mind. His face showed concern for a moment and closed again to scrutiny as he put the phone down.

"I'd better try to finish this wretched email," she said.

"Yep. I might disappear soon since you don't seem to need me." Gabriel stood up. As he walked out of her office door he looked at his BlackBerry again. She heard him put his coat on. A few seconds later the doors of the lift chimed open. Edwina moved to the window again. Gabriel was on the pavement in front of the Bank. He was on his phone, holding what seemed to be an angry conversation. His right hand kept thumping the air. He stopped walking, looked around and finished his conversation abruptly. Whatever Gabriel was saying was not for anybody else's ears.

* * *

Nancy's mobile had barely connected when Marsh walked through Pole's office door. Pole killed the call. Marsh walked up to his desk and this time did not bother to find a space as more files were once again sitting on the office's spare chair.

"Pole, I'll be brief. I met with Ms Wu. Remarkable woman." Marsh marked a pause. Nancy had made an impression – oh, yes. He cleared his throat. "I think we should bring in Henry Crowne," Marsh paused again.

Pole had not moved a muscle. "And let me know when he is here." Marsh was halfway towards the door when he turned back. "Well done on your new high-profile case." His voice bounced off the room outside Pole's office as he walked past desks and made conversation with the few people still around.

Pole threw his mobile on his desk and stood up abruptly. He bent forward his arms outstretched, resting on the back of his chair.

"What the fuck is Nancy playing at?" Pole clenched the back of the chair and pushed it away. He closed the door of his office. A nasty word was creeping into his mind. Was it manipulation or betrayal – perhaps both? Pole snatched his mobile from where it had landed and dialled.

Nancy's mobile was ringing.

"Jonathan, where on earth have you been? I —"

Pole interrupted. "With Superintendent Marsh." Ominous silence on the other end of the phone. "Who has instructed me to involve Henry, which I will do in my own time whether you and Marsh like it or not," Pole's tone was ice cold.

"It's a stupid misunderstanding, an overreaction, but I have something more urgent —"

"The reason I work with you, Nancy, is because you do not overreact; not a woman of your experience and even if it involves Henry," Pole's tone had the bite of a wounded dog.

"This is ridiculous, Jonathan. If you had replied to my calls you would have known about Marsh," Nancy's tone took a sharp edge Pole had seldom heard before.

"I am not at your beck and —" A knock at the door interrupted Pole. He would not have an argument with someone waiting outside his office. "I've got to go. I will call you later." Pole hung up. "Come in."

Andy opened the door gingerly.

"I have got the info you wanted, Guv, but I can come back."

"Nope. Come in," Pole said waving him in. He cleared his throat and sat down still clenching his mobile.

"I found the info about this grad, Felipe Martinez. Really bad stuff. He could not cope with the pressure apparently. That's the official version but the parents thought he was being bullied and he worked all hours – just like me really." Andy was waiting for Pole to indulge in a little banter but he just grunted. "How bad was it?"

"He was picked on by the traders – too slow at delivering the

354

documents they were expecting, not quick enough at learning how to use the systems. There is a whole report by the guy who oversaw the team," Andy replied adjusting his thick glasses in an embarrassed gesture.

"Which bank was it?" Pole started leafing through the file in front of him.

"GL, a year before they went down."

Pole stopped in mid flick. "And are you next going to tell me that this young guy was on Gary Cook's desk?"

"Spot on Guv."

Pole grabbed his phone, balanced the handpiece on some files and started dialling DS Banks, the case officer. Andy came closer and Pole indicated he should sit down. It may take some time. DS Banks was still at work and went through the most interesting elements of the case. Although GL had opened an internal investigation into the behaviour of its staff, it gave very little … a bit of a whitewash but no one was willing to talk. The other grads seem to dislike Felipe, not an Oxbridge student and certainly not an MBA from Ivy league America or the LSE.

"Why was he recruited then?" Pole asked

"Part of a Diversity programme. GL used to offer a couple of spaces to underprivileged students every year," Bank said. "What was disturbing was that his parents and even his girlfriend had not realised how bad it was until towards the end – and no one knew he was on drugs either. You've got Martinez's tox report in the file I sent, right?"

Andy picked up the file and opened it at a page he had marked with a red tag.

"Not sure whether you heard about them, but he was on —"

"Nootropics," interrupted Pole without referring to the file.

Banks whistled. "Don't tell me your two vics were on that too?"

"Yep and some amphetamines too."

"You know nootropics are not illegal, right?"

"So I gather but how these were purchased might be."

"Hmmm, maybe, but the bit that tipped the balance for the Martinez case and might be more interesting for you mate is LSD. Martinez had taken a large dose. In fact he had finished the bottle of little pills he had on him and you know what that does to anyone?"

Pole circled the word LSD in red in Martinez's tox report, thanked Banks and hung up. He was right; no one had been using LSD since the early seventies. Coke, Speed etc – these were the drugs of today's users.

And why would Cook and Hardy's tox reports not show traces of the stuff? Pole looked at his watch, almost 10pm.

"I would like to speak to Martinez's parents and girlfriend asap. And tomorrow, we go through the list of guests once more."

"What are we looking for, Guv?"

"Not sure yet, possibly someone who is the supplier of all this stuff. Anyway, well done. Go home now and get some rest; tomorrow is going to be another long day."

Andy left Pole's office with a spring in his step. Pole looked at his watch again. "Too late and not in the mood," he murmured. He wanted to go home, play a little jazz on his old-fashioned LP player and drink a decent glass of wine. Then perhaps he would have mellowed enough to forgive the unforgivable.

* * *

The short man who had followed him stood up and leaned against the glass partitioning of the tube carriage that Brett had entered. He was moving his head in short rhythmic movements, listening to music through brand-new headphones. He looked too young to be any good. Was it a warning or did they assume he would not notice? The Jihadists were trying to find where he lived. He could try to lose this chappie. But those were not the instructions of MI6-Steve. *Not his neck on the bloody line though.* Brett composed himself, he would look cautious but could not let on he was trained. The skill was to spot the shadow, assess whether it was key to give it the slip or appear unaware. Brett disembarked at Piccadilly. The crowd was dense. He struggled towards the Regent Street exit. His watch indicated 9.20 PM. He disappeared into the buzz of Soho. One of the little bars he frequented there on occasion would not take any notice of his shabby attire. More importantly, that wine bar had a well-hidden side exit he may decide to use later on. Brett sat at the counter, ordered a whisky and took his phone out. The shadow had walked in. The headphones were still on. He was relaxed. So not a complete amateur. A table had become free. The young man sat down and ordered a Coke from the waitress.

Brett was taking his time. Scrolling down his email list, replying, deleting, ordering a second whisky. The bar had become crowded. A group of gay men were at Brett's elbow: loud voices, laughter, tight bums and rippling muscles in immaculate T-shirts. Brett glanced quickly towards the shadow. He was no longer looking in his direction. Choosing a bar with a gay clientele had been a stroke of genius, Brett thought. If he wanted to leave, now was the time. The shadow would have to cross the room as soon as he had spotted Brett was no longer in his seat and wade through the group of gay men to reach the downstairs lavatory. It would take him a few minutes to spot the side door – by which time Brett would be in a cab. This time though there was no other flat, no decoy address or hotel room that stood between him and those trying to track him down. Brett looked at his empty glass. The people who wanted to employ him wanted to study him. Let them, Steve had said. MI6 was expecting him to play the game. Brett put his faded blue jacket back on and left simply the way he had come.

* * *

In the cab home Edwina finalised her email. She rested her head against the headrest and slowly closed her eyes. They felt sore and she gently rubbed them. She looked out of the window. They were crawling through the West End. She had not bothered to instruct the driver about the route she wanted him to take. She still needed to think. The BlackBerry was resting loosely in her hand. She started composing a text to Nancy. It was well past 11pm but a text would not intrude.

Must catch up. Need to discuss a peculiar point urgently.

She erased the last sentence. Nancy was busy but not so these days that she would not make time for her. Better not show concern. *Let's do breakfast.*

Edwina dropped her BlackBerry into her bag, not yet ready to commit. A nugget of relief fluttered in her stomach. She had bottled up all her concerns after Tom Hardy's death. Nancy was her best ally. The need to speak to her was growing stronger and yet, once she had voiced her concerns, how could she stop there? Nancy would put two and two together. She had been after all a most respected QC. Edwina's cab drove past the US embassy on her right. The compound's security had been reinforced. It looked more like a bunker than a Ferrero-Rocher dwelling, a sign of the times. Life felt harsher and more unforgiving. Where had the crazy eighties gone or even the rich nineties? She picked up her phone again and looked at the unfinished text. She added a few words and pressed the send button. Nancy would think it was about the appointment of the new Governor of the Bank of England. In some ways it was true.

Edwina was ready. She was ready and had more than the required intellectual capacities, the technical capacity without a doubt, but more importantly she was willing to take the harsh decisions – for the greater good.

The greater good? Edwina wondered what would have happened if she had not made the call. A futile exercise in late examination of a momentous decision, she knew. The past could not be undone, only concealed. Then again, how could she not have agreed with Whitehall? Tom Hardy had also been persuasive. He had first spoken to William Noble and eventually to her.

The taxi was driving along Holland Park Avenue. She would be home in less than ten minutes. Her husband John would still be awake, reading. She had not spoken to him either. She sagged into the seat and closed her eyes. She felt heavy, each muscle aching to release the strain and yet on constant alert. She rolled her head slowly to one side, then the other. The tension in her neck shifted a little. Her phone buzzed in her hand. Nancy had replied. She confirmed she was free. There was still time until their meeting. Edwina need not rush into a confession, at least not for now.

Chapter Thirteen

It was still dark when Nancy woke up to brew her first cup of tea. The leaves of the trees across the park below her looked shiny; a soft summer rain had cooled the temperature. A welcome relief after a stretch of hot weather that made London hardly bearable. She mechanically opened the cupboard, picked up the tin of Sichuan tea and boiled the kettle. Her eyes, still heavy with lack of sleep, could not quite focus. She consulted her BlackBerry – 4.45 AM. Pole had lost his cool and not called back. She had toyed for a moment with the idea of contacting Marsh but it was stupidly vindictive. Still, William's life might be at stake.

She made tea, walked back into her lounge and stretched on her sofa. She could doze off perhaps. But her restless mind got the better of her. She moved to her sound system, selecting her favourite Philip Glass opera. The music was low but the first bar propelled her into another world of minimalist melodies yet rich with subtle romantic undertones. She stretched again on the sofa. This time her body relaxed. She let herself be carried away by the sound she enjoyed so much and for the first time in a very long time she wished she had comforting arms around her to sooth her.

Her mobile rang. Nancy woke up in a jolt. It was not yet 7am.

"Nancy?" asked a distraught voice.

"Speaking," Nancy mumbled with a pang of anxiety. She did not want to hear what that voice had to say.

"It's Paula, William's PA," the voice continued, barely holding back tears.

"My God. He has had an accident." Nancy collapsed back on the sofa.

"Yes, he was hit by a car. He is in a bad way, in intensive care at St Thomas's."

"I'm on my way." Nancy did not wait for an answer before hanging up. A cry swelled in her throat and her eyes watered. She had not felt this helpless since she had arrived in Paris in the late sixties – a long, very long, time. The furtive images and sounds of a bygone China materialised and dissolved almost instantly. The voice of her father telling her to hide, the arrival at Orly airport after weeks of travelling … She cast aside the blanket she had wrapped herself in away and stood up almost in a panic. She looked around, disorientated for an instant. Nancy walked into the bathroom and splashed her face with cold water. Her hand searched for the towel. She brought it to her face. The soft smell of clean linen soothed her. She breathed in the comforting sent of jasmine. She took a few minutes to collect her thoughts and get ready. Now was not the time to collapse. William needed her.

Stepping into St Thomas's Accident and Emergency Department was like stepping into another world. The flow of people coming through was constant. The smell of disinfectant and human stench combined to give the waiting room its unmistakable odour. Nancy rushed to the information desk to be told that William was being operated on. Nancy held onto the edge of the receptionist's high desk and closed her eyes. Why had Pole not called back? A small hand pressed her arm. She turned back to face a pale Paula. She had been crying, her large blue eyes rimmed with red.

"They can't tell me anything until the operation is over."

Nancy inhaled deeply. She too felt like crying but she had no time now. As long as William was alive, she would fight for him, fight to find out what had happened. She swiftly brushed the corner of her eyes with delicate fingers.

"You'd better tell me all you know so far," Nancy said putting her arm around Paula's shoulders. They both walked towards the far end of the waiting room to what seemed a quieter corner.

Nancy fetched a couple of teas from the vending machine. They sat down and hugged their cups in silence for a moment. Paula breathed deeply and started.

"He came back from his meeting with you looking a little happier. William has not been his calm self of late. Not impatient but distracted."

Nancy nodded encouragingly. Paula hesitated. She had been William's faithful PA for over twenty years and speaking ill of him distressed her. Nancy gently took her hand and squeezed. "I need to know." Paula brought her crumpled handkerchief to her eyes and continued.

"He started working again on a file he had been putting together for a few years now. It must be ultra-confidential as even I have not been allowed access."

Nancy shot up an eyebrow. Paula agreed. "I know, virtually unheard of. And then he took a call on his mobile. His office door was open. He went to shut it and less than five minutes later he left with these specific instructions —" Paula drank some of her tea and cleared her throat. "I had to get in touch with you if anything happened." Nancy let out a small gulp of anguish. Why had he not called her then?

Paula continued. "I did not know what to make of it. But he looked dreadful again. I was about to ask him if he was unwell and he must have read my mind. He said it would be fine in the end."

Nancy closed her eyes. She would not succumb to anger – would not. It would serve no purpose and yet. She forced her mind into composure to do what it did best: extract the right information, uncover the evidence.

"What happened next?" she asked, knowing the answer would involve a white van. "Was he hit by a car?"

"Actually, not a car – a van. That's what an eye witness said."

"Have they found his mobile phone?" Nancy asked.

Paula opened her eyes wide. Nancy could read the shock in her eyes. How could she suddenly ask questions only someone from the police would when William was fighting for his life?

"I know how it sounds but William asked you to call me for a reason."

"The police did not recover it."

Nancy fell silent. She was deliberating. She wanted to stay at St Thomas's, huddled with Paula, waiting for the outcome of William's operation, until she knew he had been saved. But she must leave now if she was to save him from the next attempt on his life. She also must speak to Pole before Marsh did. She looked at the large clock on the wall, almost 8am. Pole would be at work and if he was not she knew how to find him. "Yes," she muttered, "I know where you live." Nancy was startled by her anger. Why had Pole not returned her calls? She was not a time-waster – he knew it. But Marsh had already spoken to him and he was now justifiably angry. Nancy stood up slowly. Panic showed in Paula's eyes.

"Are you leaving?"

"There is nothing better I'd like to do than stay with you. But I must meet someone. Someone William wanted me to talk to. It pains me to leave you on your own. Just let me know as soon as you have any news."

Paula tried to look brave. She understood the urgency.

Last night Nancy had resisted the urge to go to Scotland Yard and savage Pole. He had a point, after all. She had made a mistake with Marsh. But as the cab whizzed past the Houses of Parliament towards the Yard, she pressed the send button on a text she had just finished. She hoped that Pole would see her when she arrived or else she would speak to Marsh.

My friend William Noble is in intensive care because you wouldn't listen. If he dies I will never forgive you.

* * *

The yellow sticker that had been left on his chair told Pole that Martinez's girlfriend was on her way. Pole sat down slowly, considering the small piece of paper. He rubbed his eyes with his thumb and index finger. This new piece of evidence would matter.

"A drug deal gone wrong?" he said, transferring the post-it to the receiver of his phone.

"Morning, Guv, you saw my note?"

"Yep, and thank God I look before I sit otherwise I would be walking around with a post-it stuck to my backside," Pole replied straight-faced.

Andy swallowed a giggle, grew red and mumbled.

"Sorry, today is a grumpy day," Pole said. "What else have you got for me?"

Andy moved swiftly towards the desk.

"Went through the guest list of the evening Martinez jumped and the day Gary Cook … well, also jumped." Andy produced a single piece of paper that he put in front of Pole. "I've got a few names …"

"And the name of *particular* interest is?" Pole said.

"Not fair – you're stealing my thunder."

Pole nodded with a half-smile.

"Edwina James-Jones." Andy stabbed the paper where a name had been highlighted.

"The Bank of England woman? What sort of party was that then?"

"I don't think it was that sort of party," Andy said slowly, putting space after each word.

"I said party," Pole replied. "Not orgy."

"Well it's the City and —"

"In the eighties I would have said almost certainly; in the nineties quite possibly but 2011 – not in London, far too risky."

"It was a sort of networking event – sort of meet our senior management and senior alumni."

"So, Tom Hardy and Edwina James-Jones are both ex GL?"

Pole's phone rang. Felipe Martinez's girlfriend had arrived.

"She responded fast. Any idea why?" Pole asked.

"I got the feeling she's hoping we might reopen the case. She said she never believed in his suicide."

* * *

The small radio had been on since he had woken up at 6am. Henry had brought his breakfast back to his cell. He had hardly noticed what he had put in his bowl, porridge of some description or another. His mind had more important problems to chew on.

For the last couple of years, the prison routine that Henry had created in order to survive jail had slowed him down. There was so much he needed to reappraise. He had followed Charlie's advice, kept a low profile. Nancy had been another precious source of comfort. Even Big K had been surprisingly generous with pieces of information that proved judicious. The length of his sentence had stunned him, thirty years: the maximum term applied for an act of terrorism. The message was clear: zero tolerance for the likes of him – a rich banker and an IRA operative. There would be no mitigating circumstances for Henry Crowne. True he had been deceived by his friends but above all he had deceived himself. Denial had slowly given way to acknowledgement. He deserved every bit of what had happened to him: his best friend's betrayal, the collapse of his social standing. Yet when the verdict came, he had still been hoping for some leniency. He had survived in the City, excelled at being who he was not. He had, like so many bankers, lost track of what mattered. But in the diminutive space that was his prison cell, he had gradually learned to live again. Like a man whose body had been crushed, Henry had taken the small steps to rebuild his identity. Since his downfall he had gathered more true friends around him than he had ever had in the City – Nancy, Charlie, perhaps even Big K. And as he gradually stumbled out of the daze of his conviction, the weight that had burdened him since his arrest on the bench in London Fields had lifted. The desire to make his life count had inexorably grown.

Henry switched channels – still nothing on the deaths of Tom Hardy and Gary Cook. Henry read the pages he had written since he'd started thinking about their deaths. He knew he was right. He also knew that government and politics had to be connected to the manipulation of LIBOR.

Tweaking LIBOR, as some of the traders would put it, had been common practice for some of the large banks; infinitely small adjustments of the basis point – perhaps 0.5bps or even 0.25bps – that made a large difference because of the size of the market, from mortgages to complex financial products. But this latest manipulation of the benchmark looked like it might go well beyond what had gone on in the past. Henry was not yet sure by how much. The LIBOR market was probably one of the deepest in the world. Henry had created lists of instruments with best estimates, decision trees of who he knew would do what and for which institutions, network links to assess the ramifications of any scandal. And amongst all these names lay a killer. The containment of the 2008 crisis was at the forefront of every single government on the planet. This scandal would run deep and the argument would be convincingly the same – needs must.

Henry's isolation hit him unexpectedly. He had felt alone in the City, never expecting to build ties of trust with any of his contacts. It was all show, networking, surface friendships to get results. He had thought his true friends to be in Ireland. He would never have spoken of his hopes or fears to anybody else. But even that small sanctuary had been destroyed by Liam's betrayal. Nancy's unexpected kindness had saved him from the abyss, even Pole's remarkable fairness had helped. But this morning, as he was sitting on his small bed in his standard HMP Belmarsh brown tracksuit, he felt the stab of pain punch his stomach. He could not reach out. He had refused Big K's offer of a mobile. How he had managed to smuggle one into the HSU was nothing short of miraculous – no, it was miraculous. Henry had broken enough rules to last him a lifetime. He would abide by the rules imposed on him by HSU Belmarsh, the harshest of them all. Yet, who was he kidding? He had bypassed the prison's computer system and accessed the Internet a number of times. He had an excuse – keeping tab on the markets, a ridiculous justification of course. And there was the netsuke: no excuse for that one. Henry stood up but there was nowhere to escape to. This was arrogant, stupid … unforgivable. The familiar feeling sent a shiver down his spine. His stomach tightened again and a ball of fire burnt his throat.

Anger, no, fury.

He needed to lash out. His gym time was still hours away. His turn in the prison library was not until the afternoon. Henry removed his shirt and started rapid press-ups: fifty … a hundred. He collapsed on the floor in a pool of sweat. His arms and lungs were on fire, trembling. Henry rolled on his back. The coolness of the concrete floor calmed him a little. Images of Northern Ireland materialised. Restlessness crept back into him.

He turned over for more press-ups. This time he collapsed face down. He groaned. He had once said it to Nancy and still believed it. He had left Belfast, but Belfast would never leave him.

The memory of that first supper at Nancy's brought a sad smile to his face. He was still free then. If Nancy had been a little younger he might have fallen for her, a mistake of course. With time the friendship that had grown between them had become deep and true, its quality greater than he could have ever imagined.

Henry stood up slowly, ran cold water into the small washbasin nestled in the corner of his cell and splashed his face. He let the water trickle over his body, eyes closed. The burn of anger had subsided – for now.

"Thirty years," Henry whispered. He had taken advantage of all the facilities prison could offer to a Cat. A HSU inmate. His psychologist was a decent person. He had expected to find do-gooders at his compulsory psychological assessment; instead he had found patience and understanding, realistic, objective, yet considerate. He had to reassess if he wanted to survive the ordeal. If he wanted to keep his sanity. He had come close to losing his mind once. Anthony Albert, his most prominent City rival, had made sure of that with the implacability of the dying man that he was. Henry's certainties had been shaken to the core. The tough lad from Belfast had a much softer centre than he'd like to admit.

Henry lay on his bed, the beads of water still rolling over his skin. Memories rushed into his mind once more, disorderly until the picture of a ten-year-old boy took hold. His mother had collected him from the police station once again. It would not be the last. Why did he have to stick around the O'Connor boys? On that day though his mother had had little energy left to scold wee Henry. His father had not been seen for a few days and if he did not appear soon he would lose his job again. Henry had never quite understood what his father's job was. He simply knew he was on the road a lot. Later on, he recalled the word salesman, selling pretty much anything and everything. He never kept a job long enough to be known as anything else but The Salesman. But Henry could remember the joy he felt whenever his father crossed the threshold of their home. His little heart flipping in his chest at the sound of the heavy footsteps making the floorboards of the staircase creak. There was always something fun for him: a bright red toy car, some chocolate wrapped in the shape of a snowman. And of course, there would be the dancing. Henry on his father's shoulders, moving to a Rock 'n' Roll beat, his mother following the rhythm with delight. Then his father would once more disappear. The day his father failed to return for good Henry could have asked his mother the question – was he IRA? He heard car crash. He heard drinking too much and it was enough for him to curse forever the man he had so loved.

The sound of his tiny radio recaptured his attention. The beat of a Rock tune bounced off the wall of the small space. What a coincidence. Henry sunk back into the past. By his late teens Henry had convinced himself his father had been a partisan. Was it not much better than calling him a drunk? And what else could explain his long absences? Like father, like son. When the O'Connors asked him if he wanted in, he did not hesitate.

The bell rang in a distant present. Henry opened his eyes. Bang-up time was over and he was ready to seek his latest target, the Jihadi Kamal.

* * *

"She was very keen," Pole said leaning against the coffee machine.

"She works at the National Portrait Gallery so it's close but, still, she really wants to tell you what happened to her boyfriend two years ago – I mean according to her."

Pole entered the room and the young woman stood up nervously. Her face looked swollen. The tea in front of her had not been touched. Pole smiled kindly and put down a fresh cup.

"I am DCI Jonathan Pole. You have spoken to DC Todd. Thank you for coming at such short notice and I am sorry we have to speak to you about Mr Martinez again."

Anna-Maria Sanchez shook her head, a few curls had escaped her tight bun, but she did not bother to replace them. "It's fine Inspector. I would do anything for the Met to reopen the file." Her voice was firm and had an edge, someone used to speaking in public perhaps, Pole thought.

"I am afraid I can't promise anything."

"But if something new comes up?"

"You have my word. I will look into this again."

Anna-Maria breathed deeply and held the air in for a few seconds. She took a sip of tea and started. "This position at GL had been a dream come true for Felipe. No one in his family had ever gone to uni before him, let alone land a job in the City at one of the largest banks.

"And before you ask, yes he was stressed, but he had been under no illusions when he got the job. These guys were never going to make it easy for a poor kid to join their ranks." She had moved her body forward and her fist clenched the Kleenex she was holding even tighter.

"You mean he was …" Pole thought about the right word.

"–mentally prepared."

Pole nodded. "How about the nootropics?"

"He said they would help his brain. We argued and after that he never mentioned them again."

"But? " Pole asked kindly.

Anna-Maria sighed. "He slept less and less. He said he had to keep up."

"You know I have to ask my next question, don't you?"

"Any other drugs?" Her eyes narrowed and she clenched her fist again. "I am not going to lie to you," Anna-Maria said avoiding Pole's eyes. "We smoked a bit of weed but I swear to you, Inspector, I swear to you, we never did anything else." The despair in her eyes rattled Pole. She believed it, whether she was right or not.

"But a toxicology report does not lie," Pole spoke without pushing.

"And I can't explain why or how. But Felipe would never have taken LSD, never."

Pole's mobile buzzed in his pocket.

"Would you like to take a moment?"

Anna-Maria opened her bag to fish out another tissue.

Pole took his mobile out of his pocket and read his message, keeping the phone underneath the table – one line from Nancy.

The room disappeared around him. An eerie silence surrounded him. He must not yield. He must finish the interview. He must take the risk of losing her.

* * *

The prison-standard shirt was still hanging on the back of his chair. Henry slipped it on and was already opening the door of his cell when a familiar silhouette walked past. Three guards were following the new con who was replacing the Cell 10 suicide. The slow walk, the bulk of the body, made Henry freeze. Ronnie Kray was moving to 10. He steeled himself and stopped inside his own door. Henry rolled his shoulders, moved his head around. The palms of his hands had become moist. He rubbed them on his trousers. He walked out of his cell a full six foot three tall. Big K was out as well, his body leaning against the corridor's balustrade. Everybody on the wing had slowed their pace and everyone was watching the well-rehearsed ritual. Kray had put his box down. He was waiting, arms crossed over his chest, legs apart, a man who would not be dislodged that easily. One of the guards was doing a final check of the cell whilst the other two waited.

Kray was moving his head around, taking his time to survey his surroundings.

"Come on Ronnie, in you go," said one of the guards.

Ronnie ignored him for long enough to create what he wanted amongst the three guards.

Restlessness – no, fear.

Kray slowly bent down and picked his box up. His head turned as he did so to meet Henry's eyes. He kept looking into them until he had reached the door and as he was about to disappear he winked. And there was nothing friendly about it.

* * *

The tall frame of Pole's body appeared as a reflection in the bay window of Scotland Yard's foyer. Nancy was facing Victoria Embankment. In the reflection of her own face she could see anger and pain. A sight she did not want anyone to see except perhaps Pole. His hand landed cautiously on her shoulder and when she turned Pole's expression changed, his face dropped slightly, his intelligent eyes started searching her features.

"I know I am mighty pissed off with you, Jonathan Pole, but I am also too sad to take it out on you."

"What you need is a very large cup of good honest tea and a proper talk," was all Pole could say.

"No, what I need is you answering your bloody phone when I leave umpteen messages or even a reply to my texts."

"I know – point taken and I do apologise," Pole's shoulders had dropped forward slightly. Not a sign of contrition but that of a tall man eager to listen and share the burden of pain.

They reached his office in silence and he opened the door, making way for her to enter first. Pole moved the pile of documents sitting on the only chair facing his desk but Nancy chose the window.

"You do remember William, don't you?"

Pole nodded.

"I have known William Noble since my King's College London days."

"Not Sorbonne then?"

"Not Sorbonne. I did a Law Masters at KCL." Nancy shivered, still facing the window. "As you might recall, William is a very senior civil servant, works at the Treasury," Nancy's voice trailed. Paula's face materialised out of nowhere. Nancy turned back to face Pole. "He has been hit by a van."

Pole remained silent. The connection to his case would be made shortly but the word Treasury had already created a link for Pole to ponder on. Pole took a seat and invited Nancy to do so. She hesitated as small bubbles of anger still shook her slender frame. Pole took it in. He understood pain. A lifetime at the Met showed you an endless supply of it. Nancy moved slowly to the empty chair, drawn to the comfort Pole's presence was offering.

"Let me get us some tea. I think this is going to take some time."

* * *

Her cup of tea was empty. Nancy had finished telling Pole about her conversation with William. Pole had not interrupted and had been taking copious notes. Pole clenched his fist a few times. Something was troubling him.

"Without wanting to state the obvious, William's story validates Henry's hunch regarding LIBOR."

"I have not been idle and have done a bit of digging myself," said Pole lifting a file overspilling with press articles and other research documents. He carefully extracted a piece. "There was an article published in *The Wall Street Journal* in 2008. It was largely ignored by pretty much everybody that should have taken notice. A very good piece of investigatory journalism."

Pole handed it over to Nancy. She read without stopping and at the end released a small sigh. Pole was finally considering the impact of a large-scale manipulation of the LIBOR benchmark on Gary Cook and Tom Hardy's strange suicides. She straightened up a little and fired away.

"Anything new on your side then? The tox reports? The background checks?"

Pole smiled perhaps a little too broadly. She had turned on the charm, a sharp mind in an attractive woman – irresistible.

"On the ball as ever. Gary Cook was certainly taking a lot of little pills: mostly good old-fashioned amphetamines though, for performance enhancement. The guy was obsessed with boxing and no longer a spring chicken. But more interestingly he was also into something called nootropics. I gather it was the latest addition to his performance enhancement programme."

"Nootropics. You mean the drugs used by some of the Silicon Valley app developers to enhance their brain function? It's not so new by the way."

Pole raised an impressed eyebrow.

"No, Jonathan, I do not need any form of drug to enhance an already more than highly performing brain."

"Yep, I can vouch for that," Pole said with a wry smile. "I am in conversation with the Drug Squad; we need to find the supplier. Both Cook and Hardy used nootropics, from the same batch. Can't be a coincidence."

"Hang on, what are you saying?" Nancy frowned. "Are you saying the pills killed Gary? Or that they pushed him to jump and Tom to commit suicide too?"

"Not really but I need to be sure we are not missing anything. For a start, poisoning takes time to prove unless it's a very high dose and a very well-known substance. More importantly, the background checks have thrown us some curveballs."

Nancy clenched her jaws. "It had better be good, otherwise ..."

Pole interrupted by extending his hand and taking Nancy's. His touch was warm and firm, yet soothing. "Let me finish. Then you can get mad at me – again."

Pole told Nancy all he knew about the unlikely suicide of Felipe Martinez and the interview of his girlfriend. "She is adamant," Pole finished. "Felipe would never have used hard drugs – certainly not LSD."

Nancy frowned. "LSD? The Martinez tox report showed a high dose?"

"Enough to be detected and deemed the key factor, why?"

"Before nootropics were invented, the start-ups tech gurus used LSD as a mind-enhancing substance. I am talking over twenty years ago and am also talking very small doses. But in a small quantity LSD is supposed to have the same effect as nootropics, according to these techies – enhanced creativity, focus."

"How small is small?" Pole asked dubious.

"Maybe one tenth of a recreational dose, and not every day – and how do I know about it? One of my clients was a user – got him to become an excellent hacker."

They both paused. Pole slowly released Nancy's hand and she slumped back into the chair.

"Fine, I follow, but Gary's tox report, even in prelim form, would have spotted LSD, I presume, and anyway why would Gary go for an illicit drug when he can have access to legal nootropics?" Pole said breaking the silence.

"And you said Edwina was at this party?"

"She was, although I am not yet sure how relevant that is."

Nancy inhaled deeply. "And what is then your view, Jonathan? Does it introduce another lead?"

Pole smiled. "Thank you for keeping an open mind. We may be looking at a drug deal gone wrong although ..."

Nancy closed her eyes, her eyebrows strained and almost touching. "You mean someone flogging LSD rather than nootropics?"

"That would fit the Martinez case and perhaps that of Cook. No, I have just made one assumption which I need to check."

"In any case all this does not fit so well with Tom Hardy," Nancy interrupted.

"And it does not explain William," finished Pole. He too could keep an open mind.

Nancy opened her eyes and stood up, moving towards the window once more.

"We are missing something."

"We are missing the supplier."

Nancy moved back to Pole's desk.

"But if we abandon the suicide theory, replacing nootropics with LSD might work well. Taking too many nootropics might not agree with you but it's not going to have the same effect as forcing the dose on LSD."

"That's an interesting idea but we still don't know whether the increased dose is accidental or criminal," Pole said. "Assuming I go along with criminal intent, Gary gets supplied with a new performance little pill that is a low dosage LSD and ..." Pole waited.

"And it provides an opportunity for control either by creating addiction or ..." Nancy stalled. "Perhaps worse?"

"But —" Pole leant forward against his desk. "Gary must have trusted the person who fed him this new drug, and if it is his regular supplier he would have had a whole batch to sell – the drug squad might have had wind of this. I'll check."

Nancy remained silent.

"You don't agree?"

"Oh, I do. Gary is not going to buy his drugs from a kid out of a North London estate. He buys quality consistently if he is going down that route."

Pole pursed his lips. Good point.

"I think he knows the supplier of the LSD really well and I think this supplier has not told him about the content of this new drug."

"Something he has not tried before but that he is willing to try because it's supposed to give much better performance?" Pole asked.

"Gary is not the sort of man that is going to risk damaging his mind. He is after maximum effect to increase his potential, if he has just lost his job. He wants to remain top dog. So, he seeks something that supposedly will work better for him."

"Or he spirals downwards and takes one little pill too many," Pole said.

"If he does not know it is LSD light, maybe. And yet that would make him very reckless with his health. Not in character and, as you may recall, I know what he is capable of at my own expense."

"People change," Pole tried, fidgeting with a small elastic band that was lying on his desk.

"Not Gary."

"Are you trying to lead me where I am not yet prepared to go?"

Nancy nodded.

"What is still a leap of faith – from suicide to homicide, with intent."

"You mean murder – a completely plausible line of enquiry that you should not discard."

"Because now we have a motive," Pole added drumming his fingers on his desk. "The manipulation of LIBOR."

"Correct." Nancy's voice had an irritated edge she could not control.

Pole was pulling a piece of paper from underneath another precariously balanced pile of documents when his phone rang. His face darkened – Marsh was calling, not via his PA but directly. He hesitated but let the voicemail kick in. Nancy read his face.

"Is it?"

"Marsh? Yes, he will want an update," Pole said, dismissive. "I'll go when I am ready." Pole drummed his fingers on the side of his desk. "What is your take on Tom Hardy then?"

"Collusion. I think Tom was the intermediary or one of the intermediaries between William and Gary."

"William speaks to Tom Hardy, Head of the BBA, because the BBA fixes, I mean establishes, LIBOR daily. It's his role. Tom Hardy finds a trusted trader who can follow through because …"

"He has already done it on a much smaller scale and he is one of the submitters of LIBOR quotes at his bank GL."

"Speculation on the first assumption but correct on the second," Pole said with an approving nod. "And, more importantly, because Gary and Tom have both worked at GL. Tom would want to speak to someone he trusts."

"That's right and someone who has the ear of senior management at the bank too."

"OK," Pole said. "But from what I can. LIBOR calculation involves quite a few banks."

"True, but if Gary has already moved the benchmark in the past, he will know who to speak to and how it can be done."

Pole remained silent. If he was willing to follow Nancy along her train of thought, Henry would be his surest expert. Nancy felt Pole wavering. His face was in semi-profile turned towards the window, considering. She liked the high forehead, the straight chiselled nose – an insightful decision maker.

"Jonathan."

"OK, but where is the evidence?"

"You know who can help you with this don't you?"

Pole gave a short grunt. "But who truly benefits?"

"You mean in whose interest is it to see these two dead?"

"Two bankers dead. I am sure I can line up a number of willing participants."

"Very funny. Besides, you don't really mean that," Nancy replied casting a dark eye towards Pole.

"I don't mean it but I still have a point. My reading leads me to believe that billions of dollars or even sterling, are at stake. People will lose their businesses, their homes – the usual abomination."

Nancy paused. "I am not so sure. Because we speak of a low-bowling of LIBOR, so it means it becomes cheaper." Nancy let the question hang in the air – only one person could answer with confidence and it was Henry. "But whatever the outcome, I don't think it will be coming from one of the people ultimately affected."

"Why the hell not?"

"Because it's too soon, because it's targeting a small number of people at the highest of levels. The people who usually get away with it. My intuition tells me it is all about keeping that story quiet rather than a punishment for the damage it might create."

"I do trust that intuition of yours, Nancy, but I can't bring it as evidence," Pole said kindly.

"Targeting Gary for manipulating the benchmark, OK. Possibly Tom because he heads the BBA that accepted underestimated numbers without exercising due care, maybe. But William? No one could have suspected Whitehall."

"That's more like it. And why do I need Henry when I have you?" Pole asked, attempting to tease.

"Jonathan, I am not in the mood."

Pole's reply was silenced by the sound of Nancy's ringing phone. It was Paula. William was out of surgery and in intensive care. The prognosis was bleak but he was alive. Pole stood up and reached Nancy. He put a comforting hand on her shoulder. Nancy laid her hand on his and squeezed hard. Her elegant almond eyes had lost a little of their spark.

"I am going to – powder my nose. I won't be a moment."

Nancy soon reappeared. A drop of water had landed on her jet-black hair. She felt it run down the side of her face. She walked to the window once more and leaned against it. Pole's office was high enough to make out the line of trees in St James's Park.

Pole joined her at the window, their reflections distinct in the reflection of the glass. Nancy had collected two cups of tea. She handed him his. They drank in silence, appreciating this simple moment of peace. No need to speak to feel at ease. Nancy looked at her watch. It was nearly midday.

"How about Henry?" Nancy asked finally turning an exhausted face to Pole.

"Let me do a little more digging and I will also keep William in mind," Pole added.

Nancy's face relaxed a little. "Good, because William certainly believed LIBOR was the reason why something may happen to him."

Pole reached out for Nancy's arm. "I know William is not paranoid. I take him seriously." Pole squeezed gently and let go. "And to prove that I do I will send a couple of armed guards to look after him."

Nancy managed a smile and moved to leave. She stopped before reaching the door that Pole was about to open.

"What did you mean a moment ago when you said you had to check on one of your assumptions?"

"Let me come back to you when I have thought about it a little more. It's all about what goes into a routine tox report and what does not. You have enough on your plate though."

Nancy did not protest. She too had a little more digging to do.

Chapter Fourteen

Nancy was on her way to meet Eddie. She was at the centre of a hurricane and the eye of the storm was only a brief reprieve before it lashed out again. Everything was still in a state of flux. She took her BlackBerry out of her bag, made sure she had not missed a call.

Nothing. She pushed her head against the headrest of the cab – unbearable. She lifted her BlackBerry from her lap and scrolled mechanically through the messages. She spotted what she was looking for.

Edwina had sent her another text.

Breakfast, 8.00 AM?

She pondered on the intention behind the meeting.

"I don't need to be suspicious about everyone." But Nancy knew better. Her strength, the quality that had propelled her to the pinnacle of her legal career so fast was just that, the ability to ask the harsh question that even she did not want an answer to.

Sorry for late reply. Couldn't do breakfast but could do lunch at Nelly ... make it 12.00?

Perfect, make it Barbican. The reply was instant.

Nancy raised an eyebrow. Nelly had been a favourite for years and so much closer to work for Eddie. She would have to find out why the favourite place had lost its appeal.

Nancy wished she was sat back on the sofa of her lounge. She had created warm and peaceful surroundings with the understated aesthetic that so characterised her. Henry had succumbed to the atmosphere too, him usually so guarded. The large abstract paintings that hung on the walls still retained their fascination. They could still uplift her even after all these years. She had bought her first Rothko twenty years ago. A present to herself to celebrate her elevation – Silk at the age of thirty-five.

The youngest barrister ever to have been made QC. She was not living in her penthouse then. In fact, the painting she had bought was so large that it would hardly fit on the wall of her very small flat.

"What a ride," Nancy murmured.

Her mind drifted around the image of the room. It was her sanctuary. She absent-mindedly moved her focus towards a piece of paper that looked out of place on her coffee table. The letter she had received from Hong Kong was still open, carelessly marked by the stain from one of Nancy's mugs. It was unanswered as yet, begging to be dealt with. Was it too much to be delving into the past today? The letter had curled up slightly, an attempt to fold itself back, to mask the message that had woken her distant past up. The nagging memories had resurfaced not because of the letter but because of a taste, that of pepper. Of course, the letter had been a trigger. She couldn't deny it. She had ordered the peppercorns and they had been delivered on the same day as the letter, peppers from the province of Sichuan in China. Her father used to tell stories about their provenance and she loved the way he spoke about the most beautiful city on earth, Chengdu, and how the Chinese Emperor prized this extraordinary spice way before black pepper overtook the world.

She is sitting in his artist's studio – large pots of paints, traditional brushes and ink challenged by the more contemporary look of hardened brushes, sticks or simple rags to apply colour. She can't be more than seven or perhaps eight, crossed-legged on the floor, elbows on knees and hands supporting her head. She is looking up at him, her father, this tall and elegant man in his Mao collared shirt, unbuttoned and covered in paint.

"Not now," Nancy moaned. She opened her eyes and turned her face ever so slightly to see where she was. The cab was stuck at Smithfield Market. She stopped it and got out. A short walk to reach the Barbican would do her good.

* * *

He had not been followed to his Club, Brett was sure of it. Last night's tail must have been sufficient. He had led the young man straight to his Belgravia apartment. The Sheik knew where he lived. This was the way they would do business, once in – never out.

Breakfast was being served late for the members requesting it and his MI6 contact was keen to meet.

Unusual.

Brett did not feel *well over his head* as MI6-Steve liked to put it but he feared the moment was arriving faster than he had anticipated. It was fine to inform and be used as a data mule. He knew the drill. He knew the pitfalls. But people trafficking for the Jihadis was another ball game altogether.

Brett looked at his watch. He had arrived early and his contact was now late. Unusual too. He was tired of waiting and raised his hand to order. The waiter had just taken his order when Steve arrived. He looked tired, bloodshot eyes, hair not quite managing to look tidy. Brett could have sworn he had not changed his shirt.

"Any news?" Brett asked, not hiding his displeasure.

"Yes. You've hit the jackpot. Well done," Steve answered.

"Is that supposed to be funny?"

"Nope, just fact. By the way, you did the right thing last night. Got the tail to follow you to your flat. Good man." Steve grabbed a piece of toast as the waiter arranged breakfast on their table and wolfed it down. By the look of it he had not had dinner either.

"Uncomfortable, but I assume that is what you meant when you said I had to let them come close to me."

"Correct. Now your next move. You'll be asked to facilitate the transfer into the UK of one of their high-ranking operatives. We want him to come in."

"Do you know why?"

"Not your problem at this stage. You get him in. We do the rest."

"And what if there is more?"

"Such as?"

"Armaments, logistics. I don't know."

"We talk – at this stage nothing is off limits."

Brett's spoon stopped in mid-air. His boiled egg remained intact.

"Are you serious? Nuclear? Sarin gas?"

"Absolutely." Steve was tucking into his sausages with gusto. He had not eaten for a day it seemed.

"As long as I inform you."

"As long as you inform me."

"Can we stop playing silly arses for now?" Brett asked, opening his egg with lethal precision.

"I've never been more serious,"Steve answered. Brett eyed him closely. He was indeed serious.

"You know and I know how this is going to end up," Brett said, without waiting for Steve to protest. "This guy is going to place a bomb somewhere high profile or people are going to get shot. It would be good if you were to indulge me for once. I'm the one risking my skin here."

"Brett, you know the rules. The less you know the better it is. Precisely because you are putting your neck on the line. If these guys decide to ruffle you up a little, trust me, you don't want to have anything to say to them."

Brett finished buttering his toast and took a bite. The toast felt a little hard to swallow. He wiped his mouth ostentatiously with his napkin, took a sip of tea.

"That's a lot of bull – if I may say so."

Steve attacked a second piece of bacon. He chewed thoughtfully.

"Very nice bacon."

Steve took a mouthful of tea, sat back and crossed his legs. "Do you know Henry Crowne?"

Brett's fair complexion turned a little paler. "What has he got to do with this? You know I once was his art dealer. And for the record, I dislike this individual, this —"

"Irish peasant," Steve completed, holding his cup of tea on the arm of the chair in which he sat. "But there is a connection."

"Oooh, I see. The IRA connection."

"For a toff, you have got some brains, you know." Steve moved forward to finish his breakfast. And Brett took no offence. He did not care. He needed more information. Question was how to get it?

"Why the IRA connection?"

"Now Brett, you're gonna have to let those little grey cells of yours work doubly hard."

"Have they selected me because I know Crowne?"

"That *is* a much better question – possibly."

Brett finished his cup of tea. Poured a second cup, a splash of milk.

"But surely they must know that Crowne and I —"

"Never hit it off. Don't think they care. You know him and for their purposes that's all they want. You know how to approach him. You know what makes him tick."

This time Brett's face remained blank.

"You sold him the best part of his antiques collection – despite the fact you hated each other's guts. That takes some doing."

Brett noticed the pool of tea in his saucer. One of the waiters had also noticed and his cup was replaced immediately.

"What do you anticipate they want to do with Crowne?" Brett's voice wobbled imperceptively; being part of Henry Crowne's future demise had a delicious appeal.

"Not sure yet. I spent last night going through some fresh transcripts. His name popped up a few times."

Brett straightened up. His mind was racing. He sat back again and felt a patch of sweat between his shoulders.

"You wondering whether you can deliver?"

"I presume I can if you're asking me," Brett replied sharply.

"Wrong answer. *They* think you can deliver. We are simply happy to tag along. Don't disappoint *them*," Steve said with a grin.

"I don't intend to."

Brett turned around, attracting the attention of a waiter. He would sign the bill to his Club account. Breakfast was over whether Steve liked it or not.

* * *

On my way. Pole pressed the send button to warn Marsh's PA as he headed for Marsh's office. He did not need his boss barging onto his floor again, disrupting his investigation.

Marsh's stocky frame overshadowed Denise, his index finger following a line written on the screen and not to his liking by the sound of it. Pole stalled a little and coughed discreetly.

"Pole – finally." Marsh narrowed his eyes and moved into his office without another word.

"Sorry Sir, new evidence in the double-suicide case," Pole replied as he closed the door behind him.

"It'd better be good." Marsh sat heavily in his large leather chair and waved for Pole to sit at the desk. No comfy armchair in the corner of the office this time. Marsh was playing it very formal and Pole did not care.

Pole launched into the Martinez case, the LSD angle, the search for a possible link between the two cases using the Met's latest CCTV face-recognition software.

"You think of a drug deal gone wrong then?" Marsh interrupted.

"A possible lead that can't be ignored, Sir." Pole enjoyed the moment. He had got Marsh where he wanted him to be.

"What does Ms Wu think?" Marsh had moved his chair forward, his forearms resting now on his desk.

"She is also keeping an open mind."

Marsh nodded. "Anything else I should be aware of?"

"Nothing that is demonstrably relevant." Pole winced inside. If Whitehall was involved the pressure on the enquiry would reach a completely new level. And if he needed Henry out of HSU Belmarsh that needed to take precedent over the political elite seeking to cover their arses.

Pole rose slowly from his chair. Marsh wanted him to stay but why? His fingers fidgeted with the different Montblanc pens on his desk.

"I am expecting a prompter response next time." Marsh replaced the pens in their holders. "If you need me to support you I need to anticipate."

It was all understood Pole assured him.

* * *

The Barbican cafeteria was buzzing. The smell of coffee and fresh food made Nancy's mouth water. She had not eaten a decent meal since she last saw her friend. Their leisurely lunch felt so far away and yet the very same Eddie was waving at her from a corner table well situated near the bay window.

Nancy waved back, avoiding the suited men and women who were negotiating their way to their own tables laden with their lunch trays.

"I hope I am not imposing. You look tired." Edwina said, bending forward to kiss Nancy's cheek. "There was quite a queue so I bought something for both of us."

"Nonsense. I have had a rather unpleasant couple of days. A spot of lunch with a friend is exactly what I need, *n'est ce pas?*"

Nancy sat in front of Edwina, poured some tea and took a bite. The hot baguette was warm and tasty, the sweetness of its ingredients gave her a little taste of hope. But Edwina also looked unusually pale. Her make-up was no longer doing the trick, not managing to conceal the dark blue rings under her eyes. Nancy made idle chit-chat, reluctant to engage her friend on the thorny issue of the Governor's succession. Edwina listened to Nancy, opened her sandwich, spread some mustard on the first piece. Distracted, she let it reach her fingertips. She swore silently, getting up abruptly to find spare napkins. The scene was out of kilter: the Barbican cafeteria, Edwina's awkwardness, Nancy's own uneasiness. The sudden shift was palpable. Nancy took note.

Edwina apologised as she sat back down.

"How is your plan going, *ma chère amie?*" Nancy volunteered.

"On track, of course."

So not about succession – intriguing.

"Good. How about the markets?"

"Working on the next round of QE. Mervin is such a pussy footer," Edwina embarked on a passionate description of the process, her eyes shifting though, never quite making contact with Nancy's. She had picked up her BlackBerry several times, putting it down without looking at it. Nancy slowly extended her hand to make her stop. She smiled a reassuring smile – tell me what is wrong it said in her most persuasive manner.

"What does Gabs think about this?" A question that always provided Edwina with a way of reminding herself that she was not alone. But not today. Gabriel's name smacked Edwina in the face. She clenched her fist, tried to grab her BlackBerry again, stopped.

"I don't know," she said. "He is acting strange."

"What do you mean?" Nancy frowned. "Do you think he no longer supports you?"

Edwina shook her head. She took a sip of tea, preparing to formulate her answer with caution.

"He sounds *too* keen?"

Nancy did not have time to query this most unexpected statement. Her phone was ringing.

"Paula." Nancy's eyes shifted away from the room and Edwina.

"They are moving him. He is conscious."

She took a deep breath. "I am on my way." She let the phone drop on the table with a light thud.

"I am so sorry Eddie but a very good friend of mine is in hospital. He was hit by a van yesterday. Anyway, I am not sure he is out of danger, yet. You will understand. I must go. He's asked to speak to me."

"Anybody I know?" Edwina asked without thinking.

"William Noble," Nancy said whilst rising to leave.

Edwina's face drained of colour. She dashed out of the door, just in time to be sick on the terrace.

Chapter Fifteen

A half-eaten piece of sandwich had leaked a butter stain on the paper that contained it. It would soon reach one of the documents it lay on. Pole finished the unappetising bread. He would soon have to speak to Marsh about William or, if he delayed, Nancy would. He had seen the determination in her eyes. And yet he could not ignore the Martinez lead.

Pole left his office and reached Andy's desk. He had been running the new identification software. A way of comparing and identifying faces from a large quantity of images.

"I got the software to run the images I was sent of the party where Martinez went to and that of the party at which Cook jumped ... and I have a number of hits: a few women and one man."

"Who are they?"

"Not sure yet, Guv. I have just got the answer."

"Come on, you're the tech genius around here," Pole said with an encouraging nudge.

"Will be on your desk within the hour." Andy adjusted his thick glasses and smiled.

"And have you finished the report you were writing with Nurani on the use of nootropics? She said you had discovered evidence some could cause psychopathic episodes."

Andy fumbled with his glasses once more and spilt some of his tea as he was surfing through his own computer files.

"That's OK. I don't need it in full just yet. Just want your verdict."

"Well, I extended the search to include LSD as we discussed and it is possible to achieve an enhanced cognitive state with a small amount of LSD. You've got to be careful of course but the effects would be similar, except that with the nootropics you sort of can exceed the dose without too much damage. With LSD – well you know."

"Yep, I am old enough to know a lot about LSD," Pole said, prompting a wide-eyed Andy to fumble even more with his glasses.

"Not as a user, if that's what's worrying you," Pole replied tersely.

Andy opened his mouth but thought better of it.

"Come on – spit it out."

"Guv, it's hypothetical and all."

"And?" Pole gestured, unusually impatient.

"Unless the user did not know it was LSD."

Pole was listening.

"If someone wanted to get someone else to switch to LSD that would work in small doses. Then it would be much easier to convince that person to increase the dosage. LSD is addictive. It's a typical addiction progression. And on a particular day, if that someone needed to be given a push. They just need to be encouraged to take a little extra or —"

"Hang on, hold your horses Mister," Pole said putting his hands up to stop the flow.

Andy stopped dead, a rush of red that had started forming at the base of his scalp reaching his entire face.

"So, it is true. LSD does work like a nootropic – at least in small quantities. Because it does 'feel' like a nootropic."

Andy nodded.

"If I want to control someone or even get rid of someone and I know they are taking this LSD-substitute I do what?" Pole was moving his hand in a circle, kickstarting his brain. "I increase the dose by putting that someone in a position where he might need a boost. Like an important event, with tough competitors or people you want to impress – and if that event is on a rooftop …"

Andy had just made the point Nancy was trying to make. Pole returned to his desk. He yanked Cook's preliminary Toxicology Report Version 1-03 from a pile of documents, found the page he wanted and ran his finger alongside the long list of drugs included in routine post-mortem toxicology. He came to the part he urgently wanted to consult – Cannabis, Cocaine, Narcotic analgesics (including morphine); no LSD testing.

He came back to Andy's desk, still holding Cook's report open.

"Show me Hardy's tox report again." Pole scanned the report. "No LSD testing either but surely it would have been identified, as a foreign substance sloshing around their bloodstream?"

"Not necessarily," Andy said slowly. "LSD is one of the most difficult drugs to detect in blood. It stays there two, three hours at most."

"You mean you can't trace it after that at all?"

"Not quite; it stays longer in urine samples."

"How much longer?" Pole said as he was already preparing to dial a number from his mobile.

"Three days tops."

"Shit," Pole blurted. "Get to the lab now and speak to Yvonne. Ask her for a retest. Both Gary Cook and Tom Hardy. I'm calling her too."

Andy stood up like a jack-in-the-box, grabbed his mobile and started running. Yvonne's mobile was going to voicemail. Pole left an urgent message.

"Shit," Pole said again. He'd started writing a text to Yvonne when his mobile rang. Nancy's name came up on screen. This time he would take the call.

* * *

"Has he regained consciousness?" Pole was walking back to his office in long strides. "I see. Only briefly. But he has been transferred out of intensive care into a single room?"

Nancy's voice was muffled. He could hear she was trying to shelter it.

"You should have a couple of armed officers on the premises very shortly. They are on their way. I know, Nancy. I won't let you down." Pole scanned the open-plan office he was crossing for a sign of the person he now so wanted to speak to. Unsurprisingly, that person was not around.

"I am also sending you one of my team, young Andy ... The very same. Glad you remember him."

Pole walked into his office and started moving files around, his shoulder keeping his mobile stuck to his ear.

"I'm not overdoing it ... I want him there when William wakes up. I need the name of the caller. And Nancy, don't go and do something daring."

Pole smiled at the sound of indignation coming from the other end of the line.

"Tut, tut, tut. I know you too well. You might decide to tackle anyone who tries to get to William and that would not be a good idea."

More protestations that widened Pole's smile. She was responding to his tease, a good sign.

"In any case should you not be focusing on more important things? Such as breaking the good news to Henry. I am ready to speak to him."

Pole enjoyed Nancy's stunned silence, bade her goodbye and retrieved the file he was looking for from the pile of documents stashed on his desk. His LIBOR file was now impressive: news articles, extracts from financial publications, expert advice, searches on a number of relevant individuals involved in the calibration of the benchmark in London. He had a solid case to present to the Home Secretary requesting Henry's temporary exeat from Belmarsh. How far he would get him involved in the case was still largely undecided. Pole would not pre-judge. But having worked Henry's case a few years back he was in no doubt that if Henry put his formidable mind to work, he would bring the pieces of this financial puzzle together before anybody else could.

Pole started the request process. Marsh would back him up. At least one positive. Pole could have delegated but knew the pitfalls from having successfully extracted a convicted killer out to assist with another case. He had received a lot of flak for it at the time. Another high-profile case in human trafficking that had left people dead. A case he reopened after establishing a connection between the trafficking of young Eastern European women and a string of suspicious property deals. Both cases had started with the discovery of a body, same MO and yet a man had confessed to the first murder. Pole had had a hunch, the same hunch he was having with Henry – atonement. It happened, more often than imagined. Superintendent Marsh had been sceptical at the time, but the man Pole had trusted to do the right thing had come through.

"Denise, a good morning to you … Marsh not in a good mood. Well, do bring my email to his attention. It might cheer him up."

Pole read his submission one last time. He was about to press the send button when a shadow caught his eye. Nurani had just dropped by her desk. She still had her light mac on, and was looking for Andy. She spoke to another colleague avoiding, looking in Pole's direction.

Pole stopped and simply stared at her. She would notice his gaze in a minute. Time to have the conversation he had been waiting to have since yesterday.

Chapter Sixteen

Big K sat his massive body on the puny chair. His arms looked like a map of his personal history, tattoo after tattoo relating a story. Henry was searching for his name amongst the cards stacked up in the box at his side.

"What are you gonna do about this Kamal bloke? You can't do nothing – right?"

"I have a plan. I'm going to find out what he wants," Henry replied as he took the return book from Big K's hands. Big K shook his head.

"Man, this is not wise."

"Why is that?" Henry wrote 'returned' in the ledger of the library card delivered to Kevin Kenneth Kendal. Henry was impressed by Big K's appetite for reading, from classics to sci-fi. "Anything else for you this time?"

"I mean it, man – if you get involved with these guys, there won't be any turning back."

Henry smiled and pushed a pen into Big K's hand. He signed the register and walked away still shaking his head.

Henry mechanically consulted the clock on the wall, added five hours to calculate the time in New York, an old habit he found hard to lose. The trading floor had shaped who he was, had been part of him for far too long. It was ironic that what had put him in jail was a good old-fashioned money laundering scam. Granted, money laundering for the IRA. Still, none of the subprime rubbish that all large investment banks were peddling. He almost felt pride at the assured stance he had taken on the subject. How could he have been so right and yet so wrong in what mattered most to him?

Henry remembered with absolute clarity the first time Liam had asked him to help. Setting up a new vehicle, offshore, making the structure untraceable, a platform the IRA would use to route the funds they received from outside Ireland but also the US and the UK. The soft cap that used to circulate in the pubs of Kilburn, gathering donations, was not meant for the Red Cross. Henry had not even questioned the request; of course he would help. It had been what he had been waiting for. A way to belong, finally; a way to repay his best pals for years of friendship – he was part of that family.

A narrow figure was already settling in front of Henry, in the chair that Big K had just left and for a short moment Henry did not know where he was.

Kamal was sitting still. His intense dark eyes blinked softly and he moved forward slowly to ask his question.

"Which book do you recommend?"

"What makes you tick?" Henry replied, his blue eyes locking with Kamal's for an instant.

"The delivery of a perfectly elaborated idea."

Henry waited.

"The beauty of solving a complex equation and admiring the geometrical mosaics of the Grand Mosque of Mecca."

Henry's body tensed slightly, a muscle in his neck twitched, reminding him of the pain he had felt when the Paddington bomb exploded. The images Kamal was summoning had nothing to do with beauty; they spoke of hatred. The urge to grab Kamal's head and smash it onto the desk almost overwhelmed him. But Kamal had become part of a bigger plan. Henry had known the temptation would arise and he had prepared for it.

"Not a believer, mate," Henry replied sinking his nails into his left thigh with ferocity.

"I don't think it is true my friend. You are." Kamal's quiet determination sobered up Henry. Kamal was right. Henry had believed and despite all that had happened – the deceit, the sacrifice of all that had mattered to him – Henry still had hope.

"So, you are looking for a book about the philosophy of faith?" Henry said, sarcastic. Kamal smiled. The airy calm he displayed propelled Henry back to the Belfast of his youth when he had met the same sort of radical believer. Nothing would detract them from their missions. He had Liam and Bobby at his side then: Liam the pragmatist; Bobby the believer, the zealot.

"I have all I need for faith. Allah provides for those who seek. The Jihad is a way of life that needs to express —"

"You mean you need a way out of here," Henry interrupted. No speaking in riddles; they would come straight to the point or else Henry had no use for him.

"You like plain speaking, Henry?"

"Goes with my territory; your brother would understand."

"Plain speaking requires trust. Can you be trusted, Henry?"

Henry gave a short laugh. The prison officer looked in their direction. For the first time Kamal's composure floundered, a flash of anger showed in his eyes, receding abruptly to be replaced by the same inscrutable gaze.

"Look. You don't know me. I don't know you. I don't trust easily and I presume neither do you. But I think we both want the same thing. And you now need to choose a book or the prison officer will start asking questions."

"I will take a book on the philosophy of faith then," Kamal replied with confident humour, "a little Nietzsche perhaps?"

"This is Belmarsh library, not Oxford," Henry replied. Kamal had scored unexpectedly a point.

"Well, Henry. What else do you have to offer?"

Henry plucked a small card from inside the index box and handed it over to Kamal.

"Please sign before you leave," Henry said a little louder than usual. The prison officer had materialised dangerously close to their table. Kamal looked at the title and a faint smile brushed his lips. He disappeared amongst the bookshelves.

Henry rearranged the cards again. A surge of energy ripped through his body, a sudden burst familiar and yet forgotten. He had felt it on the trading floor in times of turbulent markets, on the eve of closing the ridiculously large deals that had become his trademark. The excitement of the chase, the taking of risk, the ruthless and clever assessment of who the opposition was. The certainty that he would, no matter what, win.

Henry's heart had started racing again yet his head remained cool. When Kamal reappeared, to sign the ledger, Henry hardly acknowledged him.

* * *

Edwina looked at her face in the mirror; she was still ashen white. She had splashed some water on her cheeks. Part of her make-up had rubbed off on the cuffs of her shirt. She looked a mess. What was happening to her? Like Alice in Wonderland, she was falling down a rabbit hole but this time there appeared to be no bottom.

Nancy had left after Edwina had convinced her it was nothing, a stomach bug probably. Nancy had accepted the explanation as she was on her way to St Thomas's Hospital. Her mind was racing thankfully in another direction. Edwina was still holding onto the sink. She thought of William and her stomach lurched again. She just managed to stop herself. It could no longer be a coincidence: Gary, Tom and now William. She would be next. But why? And who could have known? Tom and William would never blab, of that she was certain. Gary had always been the weak link, sacked from his job in the most unceremonious of fashions. The most stupid of mistakes – GL management must have known what Gary was up to. Then again, the takeover had diluted their influence. HXBK, the buyer of GL, had not discovered yet that Gary's desk was manipulating LIBOR. The questions why and who remained intact.

Edwina shook her head. It did not make sense. She straightened her skirt, rearranged her shirt and reapplied her make-up. It would have to do.

She had nearly reached her office when a hand on her shoulder startled her. Gabriel had materialised at her side without her noticing.

"My God, Eddie. I hope you don't mind me saying, but you look dreadful," Gabriel said, his face showing genuine concern. Edwina rushed into her office, Gabriel in tow, and closed the door quickly.

"Something dreadful happened. William, William Noble, has been run over." She was tearing at her jacket, shoving her bag underneath her desk. She ran a shaking hand through her short blonde hair. "This cannot be a coincidence. It's too much, too close, too …" Edwina was pacing down the length of her office. Her hands down the side of her face, a close resemblance to Munch's *The Scream*.

"Hang on, hang on," Gabriel replied. He walked over to her and grabbed her shoulders, forcing her to stop and face him. "Sit down, tell me what it's all about."

Edwina gave a disjointed account of the hit and run, the emergency operation, Nancy at St Thomas's.

"What do you mean, Nancy is involved?"

"She knows William very well – friends, old friends."

"Has he said anything then?"

"What do you mean?" Edwina sensed Gabriel's anxiety.

"Do you think he has said anything about …?" Gabriel's voice trailed.

"I don't know. If he has she's said nothing. She simply said he had been hit by a van."

"So, it could be an accident?"

"How can you say that?" Edwina shouted, shaking off Gabriel's grip and resuming her pacing. "It's impossible; don't you get it yet? Gary, Tom and now William. It's gonna be me next."

Gabriel stood still in amazement, a strange smile ran over his lips and then disappeared.

"It won't happen."

"Why?" Edwina felt her stomach churn again.

"OK. Sit down," Gabriel moved her to her desk. "Let's look at this rationally." He held his hand up before she could protest. "I know, not easy for you but easier for me. Still, by all accounts, I could also be in the frame, right?"

Edwina slumped in her chair.

"Who is … was the weakest link of all? Gary?"

Edwina nodded, exhausted.

"Tom had contacted Gary?" Gabriel carried on without waiting for an answer. "Tom spoke to you, but why would he have disclosed your name to Gary? No reason and William spoke to you and Tom – but not to Gary."

"Wait. You're losing me," Edwina said, her face on fire. "Are you implying that Gary, who is the most obvious leak, would not have known I was involved?"

"Correct," Gabriel replied, clicking his fingers.

"But so what? Explain."

"Well, if someone – and it is frankly a very big *if* – is after you because of …," Gabriel was looking for the words. "The market arrangement we facilitated, it would have had to be leaked to that someone and Gary is the most obvious person so," Gabriel said slowly, allowing Edwina to gather her thoughts.

"I still don't buy it. There are quite a few people who need to be involved to alter LIBOR in the way we discussed. Gary would have had to speak to his regular brokers and other traders. You don't decrease your LIBOR quote by 50bps without a backup story. And we are the backup story."

Gabriel's face reddened a little. He mechanically touched the scar on his face that looked angrier than usual. Edwina sagged back in her chair. Why did he look so pig-headed today? They both were a target, as simple as that.

"But Gary is not an idiot. He would have selected the right people, maybe not even mentioned us."

"How can you say that? Gary would have mentioned he was low-bowling LIBOR because the Bank of England had asked him to.

And he would have also let his CEO know. This is too big to carry on your own, even for a tough guy like Gary."

Gabriel's silence was ominous. He knew she was right.

"Anyway, I really must consider whether I need to go to the police."

"No don't." Gabriel jumped towards her desk.

"I know Gabs. You're worried about your reputation but no one needs to know you were involved. If I go down, I go down on my own."

"Eddie, Eddie – slow down, will you? You are so goddamn close to getting the big job. I just can't bear the thought of you throwing it away."

Edwina remained silent. Gabriel had as ever pressed the right button. Ambition swelled in her chest, a warm glow that could dissolve even the best resolution. Edwina James-Jones, Governor of the Bank of England. It had a certain ring to it.

She dropped her head in her hands. Raised it after a couple of minutes, looking at Gabriel with sudden suspicion.

"Why are you so sure it won't be me next?"

"Because it does not make sense. You're two steps removed."

"I don't know. I don't know," Edwina said mechanically.

Gabriel shrugged. "Just don't make any rash decision without telling me, OK?" Gabriel insisted. "OK?"

"Fine, I will."

She heard the door of her office close. Edwina noticed a bead of sweat rolling down her face. She grabbed a tissue and dabbed her forehead. For the first time since she'd started working with Gabriel she felt out of sync with him. She was on her own.

* * *

"He only regained consciousness briefly," Nancy said softly. Pole and she were in the corridor outside William's room. Her voice trembled and she grabbed Pole's arm to steady herself. The shock of seeing William's body hooked up to so many monitors that beeped and hummed, tubes sticking in and out of his body, feeding, extracting, keeping him alive – it had almost been too much.

"Understood, but Andy is staying with Paula. When he wakes up again he may be able to tell us who called him."

Nancy nodded. The deep lines etched on her forehead seemed permanently frozen there. She walked a few paces to find a seat. Pole wondered whether he should send her home but recalled the Nancy who had so vigorously defended Henry a few years ago. She would see this through.

"Don't you have someone to visit, *ma chère amie?*" Pole said with a smile.

"I know. I have missed the morning visits. But I will manage one in the afternoon. The good part of being his legal adviser."

"Is he expecting you?"

"He knows I am coming but not why."

"He knows. My request was sent an hour ago. Belmarsh will organise a bit of a surprise visit. You don't get out of Belmarsh for a jolly that easily." Pole was allowing Henry a little rope for his trip outside prison, but it would be very little rope. Pole understood why Henry had argued that carrying out controversial research on LIBOR manipulation inside Belmarsh was not a good idea but he also suspected there was an agenda. "One condition to Henry's trip into the free world."

"Which I am not going to like, *n'est-ce pas?*" Nancy replied with a fatigued yet attractive smile.

"*Peut-être pas.* I need to be absolutely certain Henry is not going to do something stupid." Pole put his hands up before Nancy could reply. "Do not tell me this has not crossed your mind. Charlie, his former driver, visits him regularly; Charlie has contacts. Promise me you will let me know if you suspect anything."

"You'll be the first one to know. The one thing Henry is not going to do is escape, for as long as I am his legal adviser it won't happen." Nancy's verve surprised Pole. Good to know she was on his side. "You're surprised, I can see it, but really you shouldn't be. Henry being on the loose with an IRA past is not what anybody needs, including Henry himself, although he probably doesn't see it that way."

They had walked away and found a few free seats in a waiting area. The faces around them spoke of anxiety and pain. Nancy felt herself drift into that mood. She locked her arm into Pole's and moved him along a little more.

"And what made you change your mind if I may ask?"

Pole looked surprised but understood almost instantly it was not a trick question.

"Andy came up with some interesting details about the use of LSD and —"

"It confirmed what I was saying," Nancy added without joy. This was not a point-scoring exercise. Pole tightened his arm around hers.

"The problem with LSD is that it does not stay in the blood for very long but we might get there in some other ways."

Nancy nodded. "What about Felipe Martinez?"

"There is perhaps a connection but not yet sure what."

Nancy stopped and sat down.

Pole's phone was on silent, but the buzz indicated that someone was trying to reach him. He cast an eye at the screen. Superintendent Marsh's PA was calling him. The big man wanted a word, again. Was Marsh getting cold feet about Henry?

Chapter Seventeen

The morning visit started at 9.15 AM. Charlie was always punctual as long as the prison officers did not exercise extra zeal. Charlie had done time and once relied on visits to keep him sane too. He had not been in Henry's league of course, never a Cat. A prisoner, but still an armed robbery that had gone wrong and turned bloody. He had not killed the woman but his brother had. He was driving the car. How stupid. He had barely turned eighteen.

Henry heard the third prison officer call his name. Yet another set of doors to go through, yet another check. Seven in all.

Charlie was already sitting at the table when Henry arrived. He rose. Henry smiled his crooked carefree smile, all for show of course. Charlie had guessed it and that made it somehow acceptable. Both men chatted for a while: the jazz club, Charlie's favourite topic; the fallout from GL's botched takeover, Henry's favourite topic. Charlie knew so many of the senior management team from having chauffeured them around from one meeting to another, most of them to be told they would not be joining the combined bank.

Henry's tall body slowly relaxed in the chair as Charlie fed him some tasty morsels. Ted Barnes, the useless little prick who had dared succeed him at the head of his team, had finally met an inevitable fate – the dreaded black bin bag treatment. Five minutes to clear his desk, escorted by HR and some security guards: just enough time to dump his gym kit into it and the Hermes scent his wife had bought him for his promotion. Henry's pulse was on a rollercoaster, slowing down then building up speed, according to who was hammered next. His breathing finally eased off. Reconnecting with the outside world proved complicated unless it was through Nancy. Charlie had warned him. Prison was a slow alienator. And Henry was no longer at the centre of City news.

Charlie returned to the subject of the Vortex Jazz Club and Henry seized the opportunity.

"Do you remember what you said to me the evening we both spent at the club before my arrest?"

Charlie's face went blank for a moment. His hand moved naturally in front of his mouth to shield a cough.

"You mean – leave the country?" Charlie's hand stayed in place. His voice had changed to a low, steady tone that punched guts.

"You said you had contacts." Henry rubbed his chin, using a similar masking technique.

Charlie's eyes searched Henry's, an uncomfortable gaze that evaluated the weight of a man. He kept drilling slowly. "I know it's tough in here for a man like you, but you really have to think this through. It will pass."

"I know you did your time and have done brilliantly well at putting it all behind you, Charlie." Henry meant it. Charlie nodded. He was proud of that.

"But something has happened inside and I need to be ready for what comes next," Henry continued with confidence.

"You've lost me there," Charlie replied, focused on the prison officer who was looking their way.

"I need to understand what it takes to leave Belmarsh."

"Look," Charlie said trying not to lose his cool. "For starters we are talking Belmarsh. And second, Belmarsh is bad enough but the HSU … No one has ever escaped, let alone tried as far as I recall." Charlie hesitated.

"I am not going to ask you to organise it, Charlie. I could never put you in that situation – never," Henry looked him in the eyes with what he hoped was the utmost sincerity. Charlie nodded.

"But I need to understand whether it could be done." Henry's voice was pressing. His jaws had clenched and released. He had to have this information.

Charlie's cold scrutiny resumed. His smooth, close-shaven face had lost some of its energy. Only his eyes had reached an intensity Henry had rarely witnessed. Henry was mad, but it also made sense.

"Just the background info, Charlie – you don't need to know the rest."

"OK. I'll see what I can do," Charlie said pushing himself away from the table slowly. "But as a friend, I can only say this – reconsider."

Henry nodded, lowering his eyes to regain composure. "Thank you."

The visit had another half hour to run but both men had fallen into a strained silence. Henry rose slowly. No point in pretending or making

Charlie feel awkward. If he had offended him or, worse, lost a friend, he would have to bear the weight of that mistake for the next twenty-five years. Henry had made his choice. He would run with it.

* * *

Nurani had finally arrived. Pole had left a voicemail that showed little of what he wanted to talk about. It was all about the case, the witness statements, the gym. Pole felt certain the gym would prove fruitful beyond the discovery of the drugs: gossip, bits of info that taken together may give them what they needed – the supplier.

Pole waved to her as soon as she looked his way. His phone rang, Superintendent Marsh's PA had not given up on him. He grabbed the phone with a swift irritated movement.

"Pole."

"He is on his way. I thought I'd give you the heads up."

"Much appreciated, Denise."

There could only be one reason The Super wanted to speak again. He put the phone down and moved to the door. Nurani had acknowledged him briefly and started making phone calls again. Marsh would try to get more from Nurani, an excellent way for Pole to provoke a much-needed conversation. He walked to her desk and asked her to join him in his office for a much-needed update.

"So, missus, what's new in the big bad world of investment banking?"

Nurani smiled and sat herself comfortably in the only free chair in Pole's office. The very chair Nancy had sat in only a few hours ago. Pole's pulse quickened a little.

"The gym was a great idea, Jon," Nurani said, praise or flattery? The latter it seemed. Praise had not been forthcoming of late, not that Pole cared for either. Or simply nerves about the approaching decision about her promotion?

"Do tell," Pole replied, his lean body well ensconced in his chair. He was, for once, enjoying the game of cat and mouse he had started.

"I've been going through a list of the members. A lot of high-profile bods there. Bankers of course but also Bank of England senior staff and people from the BBA."

"BBA!" Pole said. "You mean Gary Cook and Tom Hardy shared the same gym?"

"Correct, Sir," Nurani said emboldened. "Turns out Tom too was a gym fanatic – more a cyclist than a boxer, but still. I'm checking the CCTV cameras at the gym in case something comes up: a familiar face."

Pole remained silent. Andy would not be going through that for her. This time she would be on the front line, nose to her screen, doing the checking too.

"Bank of England could be interesting," Nurani continued.

"Have you checked the list of guests at the Women in Enterprise event and compared it to that of the gym members?"

Silence from Nurani.

"You should. It might be a good way to establish a list of connections," Pole said. And Andy would certainly not do that for her either.

"Possibly," Nurani made a face. "Andy can do that."

Pole pushed his body up into his chair. The chair slightly rotated, placing him at an angle to the desk facing the door.

"Keep going – how about the various tox reports?"

"Not yet received the final report on Hardy, a little too early. With Cook, we're done and dusted: lots of nootropics and amphetamines. But nothing that may have pushed him over the edge."

"Nothing in the batch found in Cook's locker?"

"According to the lab that batch was of poor quality; would have underperformed if anything." There was no doubt in Nurani's voice. This *was* suicide.

Pole registered – an underperforming drug needed a replacement. The ideal ambush to provide Gary with a lethal substitute.

"So far so very good," Pole smiled. Nurani looked confused for an instant then matched his smile. He was coming around to her theory. "Still looking for the replacement drug – if there is any of course," she added.

Marsh would appear any minute; he stretched.

"I fancy a coffee – want one?"

"I'll get it," Nurani volunteered eagerly.

"Nope, my turn to get it. You know me. I don't like abusing my extreme seniority." Pole smiled again and stood up. "Black, two sugars – strong and yet sweet, as ever."

"Yep, Jon. That's me."

Pole took his mobile out of his pocket. No call. He looked disappointed. He opened his desk drawer and took out some coins. He moved swiftly through the door.

"Back in two ticks," Pole said, not turning back.

Marsh was walking with his imperious stride in the direction of Pole's office. From the recess in which the coffee machine stood, he could see the back of Marsh's body. Always in full uniform but this time no idle chit-chat with the troops. Pole turned to face the grinding noise of the coffee machine, taking his time to complete the second selection. He turned his head a fraction. Nurani had stood up and she was chatting to Marsh, confident.

Pole headed back to his office with the two coffees, exchanged a few words with a colleague on his way and entered the room.

"Sir, I did not expect another visit."

"What's this story about a bad batch of pills? I thought we had agreed —" Marsh's nostrils had flared but Pole interrupted.

"We have indeed, Sir – everything of relevance," Pole said. "Here you are." Pole handed Nurani her cup. "And we have found the substitute drug, in the revised tox reports I ordered. LSD. Unquestionable in the case of Hardy, traces for Cook, but explainable due to the time lapse."

Marsh turned towards Nurani with a quizzical eye. His disappointed glance did not last, replaced by the greedy look of an animal on the prowl.

"Do tell," Marsh said settling into the chair Nurani had just vacated.

Pole started to recap for Marsh who was nodding repeatedly. Nurani retreated from Pole's office, moving backwards slowly in disbelief. She stopped at the door no longer certain what she wanted to do. Pole noticed more concern than resentment on her face this time. She could have followed the tox reports from close up but hadn't.

Pole told Marsh all he needed to know.

"And you think it is worth bringing Crowne in?" Marsh asked.

"We need to dig around the LIBOR idea seriously."

"And Ms Wu will be facilitating?" Marsh asked nonchalantly, the back of his right hand slowly gliding along his trouser leg to remove an imaginary piece of fluff.

"She will." Pole would not say more. If Marsh wanted to hit on Nancy, he would have to do better than that.

* * *

The letter was still on her coffee table. It had been festering there ever since she had read it. Nancy checked her watch yet again, pushed the cushion that she had propped behind her back. She had returned to her flat for a few moments' rest and to change for her Belmarsh meeting. She grunted and threw the cushion on the sofa, grabbed another one and tried again – a little better. This new case had pulled at her in a way she was not expecting. It had given Henry what she feared might be false hopes of freedom, possibly even, much worse, desires. William had regained consciousness for a few minutes during which he had called for her but fallen unconscious again before she got to the hospital. She moved the cushion a little again. The case had become personal on so many levels, a minefield she could barely avoid. She had never won or even lost a case in which she had suffered such an emotional rollercoaster. Being detached but never remote and aware of her client's manipulations were her core work principles.

But principles always suffer exceptions and her last case at the Bar had been such an extraordinary departure from what had been a strict code of conduct. The call that had followed from French barrister Jacques Verges was a bolt out of the blue and yet so predictable. She had considered his offer, she had seen the possibility the case offered – defending Saddam Hussein. Nancy stood up and walked to her designer kitchen: steel, stone and wood, a balance of simplicity, elegance and warmth. She put a piece of cherry clafoutis on a plate, one minute in the microwave – perfect: the slight acidity of the fruit softened by the vanilla sweetness of the flan.

She stayed with the moment, looking out of her window and refusing to consider the task that still lay ahead: to gather her thoughts and make a decision.

She returned to her lounge. She lifted the letter she'd received a couple of days ago from the Hong Kong gallery. The invitation was designed to be attractive to collectors like her. Hong Kong was still safe enough, no need to travel to mainland China.

"Serves you right for telling Henry he must come to terms with the past," Nancy said aloud. The sound of her own voice made her uneasy. She had not heard it for a while: cultured, assured, sometimes biting, sometimes cajoling – the voice of an exceptional QC.

And what did she have to say in her own defence?

She had ignored China for so long. The place where her parents had met, the place where she was born and the place she had fled during the Cultural Revolution. To this day she still did not understand why her father had wanted to go back. After all they had endured and all they had seen. Did art matter so much more than his wife and daughter?

Her mobile buzzed.

Received OK from HMP Belmarsh and Superintendent Marsh. Prep up Henry! Jon

Nancy gave a sigh of relief. The letter from China would have to wait a little longer. She was still holding the paper in her hand, the quality of which was rarely produced in the West, its resistance and yet lightness, its softness to the touch. She remembered the Ai Weiwei pieces she had seen at the Lisson Gallery, the attention to detail, the flawless production process. Surely this was in keeping with his own practice, a most excellent way to honour him. She assembled the documents she had received from Hong Kong in a neat pile. She would answer – perhaps.

For now, her priorities were William and Henry. William was secure, guarded by some of Pole's men and Paula – the fiercest of them all. Henry was about to get what he wanted, a way to prove he too could contribute. There was more to it, of course, and she would do what she did best, observe and ask when the time came the question that no one wanted to ask, let alone answer. She had an hour or so to spare before meeting Henry, time to put her thoughts in some order. Events had tumbled out, incoherent and yet surprisingly linked. She pulled her yellow notepad out of her satchel.

Nancy sat down, read the notes she had already jotted down and completed them by putting down on paper what she had learned from William.

There was no doubt in her mind that both Gary and Tom had been eliminated ingeniously. Pole was coming around to the idea. The SOCO team and the toxicology report must have turned up more evidence. She stopped writing and bent sideways to reach for her bag. She fumbled around and finally found what she wanted, the business card of Yvonne Butler, the pathologist she had met at Tom Hardy's crime scene.

"Maybe I will call after all," Nancy murmured. Whether it had been a little curiosity that had pushed Yvonne to hand her her card or simple courtesy, Nancy did not care. Yvonne answered her phone promptly, surprised but pleased to hear from Nancy. Was she free for coffee? Certainly.

Nancy had more time before making her way to meet Yvonne. Henry had been convinced from the very beginning that the deaths of Gary Cook and Tom Hardy could not be suicide. Something would have alerted Henry though to the connection. Something he had seen, read or heard in his previous life. She opened up the laptop she had fetched from her office and searched LIBOR. A little refresher on how the benchmark was calculated would give her more to go on when she met Henry. LIBOR was fixed by the BBA on the basis of submissions given by eighteen banks: before the average was calculated, the lowest and highest quotes were eliminated.

The remaining submissions formed the base of the averaging. In other words, a number of banks and hence people had to be involved. Nancy paused. Was it conceivable that someone had decided to systematically eliminate all those people? She estimated that four or five banks had to be involved for a wide manipulation to work. Henry would confirm of course or maybe she was wrong. Then a number of traders would have to be involved in each bank. This was ridiculous: a bankers' cleansing on a large scale did not make sense. No one would feel sorry for them, but still. Was she going in the right direction?

"This is the next question for you Henry. If LIBOR manipulation is at the centre of all this, is it the only reason?"

Nancy pulled her papers together, meticulously arranging them, slid them in their file and placed the file in her satchel. She moved to her bedroom to change into a suitable dress. Belmarsh visits warranted a business suit but she would allow herself a little eccentricity. She pulled out a pair of immaculately cut trousers, a black jacket with bold white stitching around the collar and cuffs and found her designer black pearl earrings. Black did not have to be boring. She sprayed a little Issey Miyake at the nape of her neck. She was ready to do battle.

* * *

The Perspex glass that separated the mortuary from the visitors' gallery left nothing to the imagination. Yvonne was running late and had invited Nancy to the finishing touches on Tom Hardy's post mortem.

"Not squeamish and you're not going to faint on me, are you?" Yvonne's voice sounded muffled through the intercom.

"If I faint I will be discreet." Nancy would not disappoint Yvonne and had seen her fair share of gore. She would rather have had Gary Cook on the slab. Nancy stopped before crossing the threshold into the viewing gallery. William's white face flashed in front of her eyes and her hands felt clammy. She breathed in deeply.

Yvonne was still in her blue overalls and looked on as one of her interns finished the sewing up. She waved at Nancy and indicated five minutes with her hand. She moved around the body, inspected the work and moved away towards the intercom again.

"Pole asked me for a revision of both tox reports. Did he tell you?"

Nancy concentrated on Yvonne's voice and told her what she knew. Yvonne moved back towards Tom's body and gave the young woman a nod.

She could finish without her. Yvonne walked towards the door, removed her gloves meticulously. Nancy left the visitors' gallery and grabbed the door frame for support before walking towards the lab door. Yvonne was changing into fresh clothes. Her blonde hair, spiky and rebellious, gave her the air of a reformed punk. She waved enthusiastically.

"Thank you for taking the time," Nancy said stretching out her elegant hand.

"Nonsense – us girls need to stick together."

"I could not agree more."

"Are you not the current Chair of Women in Enterprise?"

"I am indeed. We would have had an excellent event, were it not for the unfortunate suicide of Gary Cook."

Yvonne moved her towards the exit. She was still questioning Nancy about the WIE when they entered a Latino-looking coffee shop and Yvonne placed their order.

"Coffee and Pastel de Nata." Yvonne sampled her coffee and pastry. Her face broke into a large smile. "As good as ever. But, you don't believe it is suicide," she said, her spoon hovering over her triple espresso macchiato.

She lifted her eyes to meet Nancy's. Why would Nancy have called her otherwise? She was no fool. Nancy appreciated the sharpness of her mind.

"I am not denying it but it is neither here nor there. What do you say?"

"Why don't you ask and I will see how best I can reply?"

"Inspector Pole seems to have come round to my view that it is not suicide. I expect something helped him to decide apart from the attempt on William Noble's life."

"I am sorry about William by the way," Yvonne said with genuine regret. "Yes, the revised tox reports have shown some interesting results."

"More than simple nootropics?"

"You're right there. Traces of another substance – five days have passed but we still managed to find it. I am running tests again to be absolutely sure but it is there."

"Can I hazard a guess?"

Yvonne nodded. Her eyes creased slightly. She was enjoying the quiz.

"LSD?"

"Now, I am impressed. How did you know?"

"One of my former Silicon Valley clients. Became a user before nootropics became popular. A story for another time."

"LSD is clever. In small doses it acts like a nootropic, a capacity enhancer, but also it does not stay in the blood for very long. Hard to ID if you're not looking for it. And of course, it is extremely addictive."

"Gary took a larger quantity and that sent him over the edge – literally."

"Almost certainly – the question remains. How?"

"Suggestion of someone he trusted, boost your confidence – a man preferably and in a conference full of women. He might have felt he needed to."

"One of the guests?"

"One of the male guests, possibly." Nancy recalled the list. There were maybe forty men in attendance. Pole needed to look through it.

"Then of course, there is the story of the bad batch," Yvonne volunteered.

"Bad batch of nootropics? How bad is bad?"

"That is the intriguing thing – useless. I mean they would have produced sweet FA, zip."

"Really?" Nancy frowned. Her hand had reached for another Pastel; she took a bite. "It must be important, but I don't yet see why."

Yvonne nodded. She caught Nancy's eye and smiled.

"Now Yvonne, would I be wrong in thinking you have a question for me?"

"Am I that transparent?"

"This is – or rather was – my job." Nancy grinned.

The Pole–Wu double-act. It intrigued his colleagues and her friends. Yvonne probed a little and Nancy delivered her answer back to Yvonne convincingly enough she thought.

"Jonathan is such a special guy. I hope he has found '*l'âme soeur*,'" Yvonne said, her voice genuinely kind.

"Another Francophile – *bienvenue*."

"Nice of you to say so but not really. I expect you know Jon's family history?"

"I saw the art collection his grandmother left him. The pieces she bought after running an art gallery in Paris and London."

Yvonne's BlackBerry buzzed. She reached into her bag.

"Ah, something that may interest you Nancy." She opened the email. Her head moved as she read softly. "Faint traces of LSD confirmed on second reading."

"Which still begs the question – how? LSD does not come in liquid form, correct?"

"Usually tablets – but it can also come in liquid form when the LSD crystals are dissolved. Someone could have spiked his drink."

Nancy paused, dabbed her lips with her napkin and bent forward slightly.

"I have a theory."

"I'm listening," Yvonne replied, bending forward in turn.

"First, Gary's murder must have been premeditated." She carried on. "Whoever decided to eliminate him knew he was going to be at the venue – ideal for a jump. That person also knew Gary well enough, not only to know his drug habits, but also to convince him to try something new."

"Pop one and you're already pepped up, a little more and you're on the path to losing control," Yvonne said.

"And it's going to be so much easier to push Gary over the parapet at 1 Poultry if he is out of it on LSD."

"Which means…"

"That Gary Cook must have been invited to the event by his murderer."

"Or he knew he was going to be there," Yvonne rectified.

"Not so – a chauvinist like Gary would never have gone on his own. Someone got him there – and he would have wanted to be on top intellectual form."

Yvonne raised her coffee cup. "Pole could not have done better."

Nancy raised her cup in return. "To a fruitful collaboration."

Chapter Eighteen

The rhythmic shuffle of feet, men moving to take a tray, the sound of plates banging on the cheap Formica tables irritated Henry. He should have gone earlier but he had been too busy recapping on what he had learned so far. Nancy was coming today for a visit. He had more arguments to feed to Pole if he was not yet willing to budge. The queue stalled. Henry was holding his tray in front of his chest, the fingers of each hand drumming on the cheap plastic.

Lost in his thoughts, Henry did not immediately notice voices rising. The shouting started when the pushing began. The young man with a long fraying beard was already on the floor, his face covered in blood. He kicked the short stocky man in the groin who groaned in pain, his hands reaching down to protect himself from another kick. The siren sounded. The canteen was already swarming with guards. Henry fought the mass of bodies that pushed and shoved. The men were still fighting. The unmistakable sound of blows crashing into flesh, the muffled cries of two men who did not want to let go. Henry twisted his neck to see, struggling to stand his ground. More prison officers arrived with anti-riot equipment. Henry surrendered to the crowd that bore him away before he could see the outcome of the fight.

"Fucking idiots," Henry swore. He would have to make do with biscuits until dinner tonight.

"OK, OK, I am moving," he said holding his hands up. As he hurried up towards his cell, he saw Kamal. Already at the top of the stairs, he was observing the commotion. He was looking for something, or someone. He locked eyes with Henry and a faint smile brushed his face.

Not accidental, Henry thought. He accelerated, this time gaining ground on the inmates swarming around him, his tall body ducking, pushing, ducking.

This was not the time to piss off another inmate he had learned. Nerves were frayed at the prospect of going with little food for almost a day. Another fight could erupt any moment. But the benefit of the gym was paying off. For the first time since he had entered Belmarsh, a sense of purpose was moving him. His heart was beating a little faster, not from the accelerated pace but from something he had not felt for a long time – excitement. Kamal had slowed his own pace considerably. Henry caught up with him, walking alongside.

"I am in," Henry said looking ahead.

"This fills me with joy my brother," Kamal replied, his eyes shifting quickly towards Henry.

"I am not your brother."

"Not yet," Kamal replied. There was unexpected kindness in Kamal's voice that shook Henry to the core. Words he had heard before, words that had been spoken so long ago he thought he had forgotten – Ireland. He knew this voice and for an instant he felt like Odysseus, chained to the mast of his ship, yearning to yield to the song of the sirens. Henry clenched his fists and kept walking without another word until he had reached his cell. It was only a few metres away, up one more flight of stairs: three doors to go. Henry raised his eyes as he was turning into the staircase. But the distorted face of a man stopped him in his tracks. He was trying to cry but nothing was coming from his mouth, blood was already dripping onto the landing below. The other inmates had stopped walking. And as the noise of their feet subsided, Henry heard them. The ferocious blows that were ravaging the other man's face, rhythmic, yet muffled. The guards would soon notice that they were not moving. Whoever was doing the beating knew it; he finished with a vicious blow and threw the limp body down the stairs. The body landed with a crash of bones, barely missing Henry. The guards were coming. Henry hesitated but he could not risk it. He moved with the crowd. Walking past Kray's cell, Henry saw him leaning against the door frame. He was slowly removing bloodied bandages from his hands. His foot moved onto the landing almost tripping Henry up.

"You're next pretty boy and so is your girlfriend," Kray whispered.

Henry closed his cell door with a thud and pressed his back against it.

"I know what you are trying to do." Henry said, his head tipped back against the cold metal. "I know what you are trying to do." Henry slid slowly to the floor. He sat, head on knees, his hands on his head massaging his scalp. He could not afford to let a fight get the better of him, not now. And what was this shit about a girlfriend? Pam's scent invaded the small cell. He inhaled deeply. He could remember all the details that made him want her: not the obvious things that a man may focus on. It was the tilt of her head when she concentrated on a complex issue or the admiration in her eyes when Henry had yet again come up with a genius product idea. But how could Kray know about her? Henry stood up suddenly. There was nothing he could do to warn her. His jaw was clenched. No, this is what Kray wanted – a fight. He would speak to Nancy about it.

* * *

Edwina threw her file on the desk. She leaned against it, arms stretched, head bowed forward.

"Another bloody useless meeting – fuck," she said shaking her head, her neat bob rolling from side to side. "I wonder why we employ economists?"

"In the hope they might tell us something we don't already know." Gabriel was standing in the doorway, his gym bag slung over his shoulder, his light-brown eyes showing amusement.

"Does anything ever faze you?" Edwina asked.

"Not much, that's why we work well together." Gabriel winked. The scar over his eye pulled at his face a little. He mechanically brought his hand to it but stopped abruptly before his fingers could reach it. "I'll be back in an hour."

"Sorry – maybe I should go to the gym too," Edwina said. No matter how angry she might be with Gabriel she did not want to remind him of how his face had been damaged so many years ago.

"Yep – go and unleash some of that frustration; use some of the punchbags, clip a photo of The Oracle on it." Gabriel was already moving away, punching the air with his fist.

"Is that what you're gonna do?"

"Yep. I've booked an excellent boxing class today – just what the doctor ordered."

"Enjoy," Edwina forced her voice to sound cheerful. She watched Gabriel disappear along the corridor, heard the lift's doors click open, then shut. She moved to the window and saw Gabriel cross the street. Saw him disappear down Threadneedle. She hesitated. Gabriel's office was empty. She swiftly moved to his desk, tried the drawers but they were locked on both sides. Gabriel was a fan of the latest clean desk policy: no documents were to be left on desks, under any circumstances.

Edwina swore underneath her breath. There was no obvious place he would have left a spare key and yet a spare key there was. She had left hers with the team PA. He might have done the same.

"Clara," Edwina stood over her PA's desk. "You have a spare set of keys for our desks, don't you?"

"Of course, Eddie, all of them," Clara looked bemused. "Any problem?"

"No, I just wanted to make sure. We are all very twitchy at the moment. I'd rather have you keep our spares than having spares floating around and unaccounted for." Convincing, she thought.

"They're all here," Clara opened a little box she kept on her desk. "Colour coded: you're red, Gabriel blue, Adrian yellow and Ken green."

"Perfect, as ever," Edwina delivered one of her best smiles, the one that showed a perfect set of teeth and accentuated the little dimple she bore on her chin. "Very clever."

Clara nodded a thank you and stood up. "I'm getting myself a sandwich. Shall I get you anything?"

"That would be great please. Something fishy – in keeping with the current mood." Clara gave her a wry smile.

A few seconds later the doors of the lift clicked again.

Open–Close.

Edwina's nervous fingers reached immediately for the box. She fumbled through the tangle of keys, bit her lips and tried to pull free the blue one. It was caught with hers, red and blue entwined. Ominous, maybe? Edwina had no time to elaborate. She grabbed both keys and moved back to Gabriel's office.

The inside of each drawer was meticulously organised, unlike hers. She did not know what she was looking for, or even why she was taking such a risk, but she needed something, anything, to help her understand the growing unease that had settled in the pit of her stomach and would not go away.

Stationery was organised by categories and size. Ridiculous.

Files ordered by date and urgency.

The bottom drawer had more personal items: comb, deodorant, Kleenex (man size). She was about to shut it when a rattling sound attracted her attention. She knelt on the floor, bent forward and extended her arm to reach the back of the desk. Her fingers were moving around, feeling anxiously for the source of the noise. She retrieved a large bottle full of pills, no name. She hesitated, opened the container and tried to ease one into her hand. The pills were stuck together. Edwina bit her lips again and shook the bottle a little harder. An entire pool of them tumbled into her hand, some dropping to the floor.

"Bugger!"

She quickly poured back the contents of her hand into the bottle, dropping more pills on the floor. She was desperately picking them up, with shaky fingers, kneeling further underneath Gabriel's desk, ramming the blue pills as quickly as she could into the bottle. Clara would be on her way back by now. Edwina took a final look around her, shoved the bottle in the bottom drawer where it belonged. Pushed the key into the lock. It did not go in. She tried again, realised she was using her own key.

Come on. Come on.

Locked the drawer. Sprinted across to her PA's desk. She could hear the doors of the lift.

Open–Close.

Edwina dropped the keys into the box and turned around.

Clara was turning the corner and looked a little surprised.

"You did not need to wait. I would have brought the sandwich to you."

"I just heard the lift. I am famished," Edwina replied flustered. Clara smiled and handed over a smoked salmon and watercress on brown.

"Perfect," Edwina said with a little too much enthusiasm. She disappeared into her office clutching her sandwich in her right hand and a little blue pill in her left.

* * *

Sotheby's was preparing yet another exceptional contemporary art auction. How many exceptional art auctions could there be in one lifetime let alone a year? None, Brett estimated. But by his former employer's standards there was one blockbuster sale at least once a year. October would soon be upon them and with it the beginning of the Art Fairs season. It started right here in London with Frieze, then moved to Paris and New York. Antiquities were doing fine but were dwarfed by the magnitude of the sums that changed hands for modern and contemporary art. Brett sighed. No matter how much he tried, nothing attracted him in this contemporary gobbledygook. He did not understand the mania for conceptual art, had no time for abstraction. He could just about see the skill in early Picassos.

Walking back from his Club, he cut through Burlington Arcade and strolled down Cork Street. He stopped, looking into the windows of the better galleries. He could not see the fuss. His phone rang. He reached into his pocket, noticing the reflection of his face in the window, tired and – well – concerned.

"Antonio. What can I do for you?" Brett had called his Italian smuggler on the night he had met with his new client, The Sheik. He had put the deal to him, sparing him the details. Still he had volunteered the transaction was unusual, and possibly riskier too, but the price was also fair. The eye-wateringly large figure Brett had offered Antonio had struck the right cord.

"Yes, it is a one-off," Brett replied stopping walking altogether. His voice had stayed remarkably courteous. He had no time for Antonio to wobble. Brett listened to the habitual ranting, the lengthy description of what had been done to prepare the transfer. He was nodding as if Antonio could see him from the few thousand miles that separated them. Brett would not push back with his usual impatience this time. MI6 had been very clear. Facilitation. This Middle-Eastern clandestine had to arrive on UK soil.

Brett retraced his steps and found a little alcove from which he could speak securely.

"I don't want to hear the T word, Antonio. And anyway we deal with these people when we move art pieces around. None of our business," Brett added.

Antonio became even more animated on the other end of the phone. Brett changed ear and started walking again.

"That is why you are paid a six-figure sum of money." Brett pulled at his well-trimmed moustache. The conversation made him sick. How much more sucking up to this Italian riff-raff would he have to put up with? The six-figure sum that had suddenly pacified Antonio reminded Brett of the equally large sum of cash he was about to bank. He managed a smile. Yes, he could endure a lot more of this after all.

Brett arrived on Hanover Square, still in conversation with his smuggler. He was moving slowly towards a line of trees. The summer luxuriant greens distracted him for a moment. He entered the square and found a suitable place to sit. The timing of the clandestine transfer had to be impeccable. Clandestine X would arrive by sea from Libya. Antonio had a consignment due to leave on that same day for Europe. He used a number of points of departure from the Libyan coast. But it was always a night crossing. The route into the UK would then be a tried and tested one. Switzerland via Lugano on a truck that would cross the Italian border there. A change of truck again with another consignment, crossing into France at one of the busiest checkpoints, counterintuitive but very effective. A change again across France, a smaller van taking the deserted B roads. The final crossing from Le Havre to the UK. Two days in total.

There was no equipment. If this chappie needed it, it was travelling through a different channel. Or maybe it had reached the UK already. MI6-Steve was only concerned about Clandestine X. Brett had not asked. Antonio had fretted about the issue of armaments but their absence of it had made the mapping of the route so much easier. Antonio had almost been cheerful that day. Brett had insisted on understanding the details of the transfer and for once Antonio had not minded. Antonio was most anxious when it came to crossing into the UK, although Brett suspected that border control would be asked to facilitate. He had communicated the details to Steve and, for once, Steve had sounded mildly impressed.

"You might even pull it off," Steve had conceded.

"When the package arrives I don't have to deliver it anywhere in particular. You're OK with that?"

"We'll take it from there."

Clandestine X knew where he was going and MI6-Steve had a pretty good idea too. By Brett's best guess he was not a new arrival; he was a Brit returning from the war zone. Then again, as Brett had said to Antonio, not his problem.

"As soon as Clandestine X has arrived in Italy, I will transfer thirty per cent of the sum. Then another twenty per cent when he crosses into France. The rest when he has entered the UK."

Antonio had not even negotiated.

Brett terminated the call. There would be many more before the deal was done. He leaned against the backrest of the bench, his fingers drumming a nervous tune on the worn-out part of the wood. He breathed in the fresh air. It was time to resume his day job as an independent art consultant. Sotheby's liked punctuality. He reached into the inside pocket of his jacket for a packet of Benson & Hedges. One last cigarette would probably make him five minutes late. A small amount of subversion, how pleasant. He took out from another pocket an elegant lighter that had belonged to his great-grandfather, nothing ostentatious except perhaps the engraving *With Gratitude, Victoria*. He pulled on the cigarette and inhaled deeply. The nicotine did its trick and his jaw relaxed. He took another drag and closed his eyes.

When he opened his eyes he noticed him, a small figure hunched on a bench at the far side of the square. Brett shrugged.

Still tailing me? Ridiculous.

Brett took a final pull and flicked the cigarette away. They did not want to be subtle. That much was now obvious. He was safe until Clandestine X was delivered. But maybe the delivery of this man would only be the beginning. Henry Crowne's name popped back into his mind. Why choose him? He hated the Irish peasant with a passion and for good reasons he thought. Had Crowne not reneged on their *Ur antiquities* deal he would not had fallen into the claws of MI6. Brett pulled the gate of the square open.

"One thing at a time old boy," he muttered. "One thing at a time."

* * *

His face changed in an instant at the news, his blue eyes turning a shade lighter and the deep furrows that defined his face smoothed over. He had braced himself for it but the knowledge that he would be allowed to leave the Belmarsh HSU compound overjoyed Henry. Nancy had smiled kindly and yet her gaze had penetrated into his eyes that he thought she might have guessed. There was no time for questions. Only facts regarding the process. She would not be there to accompany him when he came out; there was no need. The Belmarsh Governor had been informed. Henry would be taken to New Scotland Yard the following morning. He would be leaving before the other inmates were allowed out. The moment of joy had quickly been replaced by the intense focus that so characterised Henry. He had taken all the details in. No need for notes; he would remember. Nancy was as prepared as he was. Her eyes rested on him, friendly, and yet for an infinitesimal moment he thought he had detected something he had never seen before, suspicion. It had vanished as fast as it had come. Nancy had defended enough high-profile criminals to know how to get to the truth. Henry was in no doubt that one day she would; it just couldn't be yet.

"One final thing before I go; they will be searching your cell," Nancy said somewhat anxious.

Henry's mouth pursed in return, almost arrogant. "Anticipation is one of the things I do best."

"Glad to hear and I hope you are right."

Nancy's irritation surprised Henry. He shook his head. No time to be an arrogant arse. "Do you know what Epiphany is?"

"The visit of the Magi to the child Jesus. What of it?" Nancy inhaled a little, just enough so as not to lose her cool.

"Bear with me. You know that the French eat *la Galette de Rois* – yes?"

412

Nancy rolled her eyes.

"And you know that they put a little token in the cake; the one who finds it is King or Queen – right?"

Nancy's eyes widened. "You haven't?"

"Yup. A little piece of my Japanese art collection has ended up inside my lunchtime bread roll. It makes it one of the most expensive buns in the world."

Nancy moved forward, her hand clenched against her mouth, hardly containing an incredulous laugh.

Henry raised his eyebrows in quick succession – who was a smart-arse after all: his netsuke in a bun – genius.

Back in his cell Henry slumped onto his bed. His body was shaking, a small rumble almost delicious. He had not felt this alive for years – before the death of Anthony Albert and his arrest for murder, before the GL takeover. He rubbed his face gently. It was only the beginning.

But at present, he suspected that the entire prison service was going after him. By now the Governor had been fully briefed. He was instructing the prison officers to carry out a full-blown search of Henry's cell. This was an exceptional situation that would warrant exceptional measures. Henry stood up. A last-minute check before they arrived, he thought. He looked at the papers he had squirrelled away, notes he had not yet destroyed. He had thought he could save them in his legal file. A file that should never be opened by any guard, prison officer, even the Governor himself but why take unnecessary risks? He tore them into small pieces and flushed them down the toilet. He picked up the pad he had used to take the notes, tore the last pages on which these had left an imprint. He flushed these too down the toilet. He looked around. His uneaten bread roll was convincingly squirrelled away with a piece of cheese inside a paper napkin. He unfolded the paper carefully, inspected the bun. He had removed a piece of crust, eaten some of the inside and replaced it by his precious netsuke, secured the crust back. He shook the bread a little, the crust hardly moved. He closed the bundle again. He was in the clear.

Henry sat down at his small desk and started a new letter to Nancy. The perfect way of creating a fresh set of prints on the pad and an equally good way of calming his nerves as the inspection was approaching.

He was still writing when the key turned in the lock. He turned towards the door and suppressed a smile.

There were three of them. The tallest of the lot, Nick, he knew well. Never trust the screws was Charlie's motto. Still Henry had to admit the prison officers of the Cat. A wing were more decent than he had expected.

"You're taking a little trip, I gather?"

"If you say so," Henry replied, still seated. Henry eyed the other two quickly: an Asian chap, small but muscular, and a bald guy in his fifties. He had seen him before handling an inmate who had pushed his luck too far with a mobile phone – not a pretty sight.

"We need to do a search before you're allowed out. You won't mind will you Henry?"

Henry shrugged. He stood up, mentally checking that all was in order. He was about to reach for his legal file when the bald guy stopped him dead. Henry turned abruptly towards him. Within a second the atmosphere changed, everybody froze. Henry clenched and released his fist.

Calm.

"This is my legal file, privileged as you know."

"Something in there I need to know?" The bald guy was still standing between Henry and the file.

"Well, all of it – that's the idea of a privileged file."

The prison officer turned to Nick. "Let it go," Nick said.

Henry grabbed the file and moved to the side wall. Papers were dropped on the floor. His bed turned upside down and the flimsy sheets left on the ground. The few bits of food he had stashed away were thoroughly fingered, including his bun and cheese. Henry forced himself not to budge.

"In case you're peckish later," the bald guy said. He pushed the bun around to the edge of the desk. One more move and it would drop onto the floor. Henry squeezed his file tight against his chest, his eyes riveted on the piece of bread.

The prison officer lost interest in his desk and moved to his shelf. Still not quite out of the woods yet. Henry had been subjected to these intrusions regularly since he had been incarcerated. They had become less frequent until today when he had become a high-profile con again.

"We'll pick you up during bang-up time. Be ready," Nick said as he closed the door with a thud. It had hardly closed before Henry jumped forward to catch the bread roll before it hit the floor. He squeezed it and pushed the air with his fist.

No one would beat Henry at his own game of hide and seek. The file would prove a useful decoy for what came next.

Chapter Nineteen

The room was small and smelled of sweat and cheap coffee. But the four plasma screens he had requested had been installed on the table at the centre of it.

Henry entered, still rubbing his wrists where the handcuffs had clasped his hands together. The buzz he had felt when he had stepped into the anonymised police car went up a notch. Someone had done a good job, tested the screens and some of the familiar trading market charts and colour-coded displays were already flickering. He walked to the monitors and started typing rapidly on the keyboard, his fingers dancing to a tune he knew so well. The tingle extended to his hands, his arms. It had been almost four years since he had last sat at a Bloomberg keyboard, so distinctive with its yellow, green and red keys. He pressed the enter button and memories flooded his mind, unstoppable. He closed his eyes for a moment. This was not the time. He keyed in more instructions and the screens came to life.

Henry turned to Pole with a grin he could not longer suppress.

"You did good. Who set this up – someone from your team?"

"Why? My team is perfectly capable. Not rocket science despite what you lot would like us to believe," Pole replied.

"You're right, it's quantum physics actually." Henry was still grinning.

Pole rolled his eyes to the ceiling. "Do you have all you need?"

"Give me five to run a few checks." Henry's long hands were running across the keys, elegantly. The screens changed again. The data mining had begun.

"Is Nancy joining us? She couldn't pick me up but still," Henry said, a little put out.

"She's on her way."

"From seeing William?" Henry said, configuring yet another Bloomberg screen.

"That's right." Pole had moved closer to the desk, standing now at the back of Henry, his tall body casting a shadow over Henry's desk.

"Sorry, I don't like people standing behind my back when I'm on my screens," Henry said half-turning towards Pole, his hands frozen in mid-air.

"Certainly," Pole replied amused by the request.

Henry faced the monitors again. "You probably think I am a prat for asking this but I have my reasons."

Pole's eyes rested on Henry, light but observing. "Care to elaborate?"

"The chap who ran the investment bank at GL used to walk the trading floor nearly every day when he was in London. He would stay there at the back of your desk – saying nothing, just watching."

"Good bullying technique. Did he get away with it?"

"Yep – for a very long time. I never took any notice, although I could quite happily have clocked him one."

Pole laughed. "And your guys?"

"I trained my team well. Polite but cool. Of course there is always a smart-arse who thinks he knows best and starts talking. That never ended well."

Henry pressed the enter button with a flourish. "I am ready to roll."

Pole's phone rang. Nancy was on her way.

"You've got an hour, Henry."

"Have a good time with Nancy," Henry said, waving Pole away with a renewed grin.

* * *

Pole was recapping for both Nancy and Henry. Nancy, focused as ever, was taking notes on her yellow pad. Henry was reclining slightly on the back legs of his chair, one arm resting on the desk turning a pen across the back of his thumb in a hypnotic motion.

"On what basis have you conceded that both Gary and Tom were murdered?" Henry interrupted.

"I don't see why that matters to you," Pole pushed back.

"It might be relevant. I need to get the full MO of the guy or gal you are looking for."

"Since I'm the detective here why don't you just let me do that – detect. You're the banker so why don't you unravel the mysteries of LIBOR for us. Then we talk."

"OK, your call," Henry replied putting his hands up.

A stack of printed documents still sat on the printer specially set up in the room. Henry stood up and distributed them to Pole and Nancy. She had been uncommonly silent until the wad of paper placed in her hand brought her back to life. She smiled to both and shook her head.

"Sorry gentlemen, I was still at St Thomas's. But here I am back and ready to go."

Henry smiled a kind smile and Pole extended a friendly hand that squeezed her shoulder. There was only goodwill in the room born out of love and friendship. Nancy sighed. Pole sat down and Henry started.

"First of all – three documents to consider: a superb article written in *The Wall Street Journal* relating to LIBOR manipulation, note the date, suggesting that LIBOR has been rigged by the banks for years. Then a rebuttal from the International Monetary Fund insisting that there was no such thing as LIBOR fixing (no pun intended) and finally a rather recent but potent analysis of LIBOR by two well-known economists corroborating the *WSJ* findings."

"The *WSJ* thinks it is an attempt by the banks to look stronger; the two economists (Connan Snider – UCLA and Thomas Youle – Minnesota) conclude that it was more a way to increase profits," Nancy said still flicking through the documents.

"So, whatever the reason, there was manipulation," Pole said. "But that is a US analysis, right?" Pole lifted a quizzical eyebrow. "And you got that info Henry in under one hour?"

"Inspector! I don't have the reputation of being a smart-arse for nothing. I was approached by MENSA you know," Henry kept rocking on the back of his chair, a faint smile on his face.

Pole grunted but let it go. No time to deflate Henry's ego.

At least not yet.

"How large are the stakes?" Nancy asked oblivious to the banter going on between them.

"Trillions." Henry answered without hesitation.

"You mean billions?" Pole frowned.

"Trillions. You are thinking purely about the mortgages. And they are real money of course but you also need to think about the derivatives."

"You mean interest rate swaps and the like?" Nancy said, confirming what she already knew for Pole's benefit. She sat back in her chair, slowly replacing a strand of jet-black hair that had escaped from her hairclip.

"That's my girl," Henry replied winking at Nancy. Pole cast a dark eye in his direction.

"*Je ne suis pas ta cocotte*," Nancy replied almost amused.

Pole made a small movement of the head in Henry's direction, satisfied that this would shut him up.

"I had a look at the audited accounts filed by some of the banks that submit quotes for LIBOR fixing – I mean the actual process." Henry expectantly waited for the question that never came.

"Yeah, yeah. I know the process is actually called *fixing*," Pole waved away Henry. "With eighteen banks submitting their quotes daily as part of this *fixing* process," Pole carried on, emphasising the word fixing with a quotation movement of both hands.

"Hey, Inspector Pole you're not just a pretty face." Henry grinned.

"An olive branch?"

"Do I need to extend one?"

"As far as I am concerned you need to extend the whole goddamn tree."

"*Ça suffit vous deux*," Nancy snapped. "You, Henry, think that either way, there was manipulation."

"Yes, I am positive. On Dollar LIBOR, I'd say I am ninety-nine per cent certain but on Sterling LIBOR I need to do a bit more work. The reason why I really need to do the work is that I may be able to determine what is really going on."

"You mean you can determine whether it is simply to make money or to save their credentials in the marketplace?" Pole asked, dubious.

"I understand you're sceptical Inspector, but I know a particular program that I can use to detect irregularities in trading patterns. If I use it and apply it to the quotes made by the eighteen banks that submit on LIBOR, I'll have a pattern," Henry said enthusiastically. He had turned away from his audience and was already finding information on the net.

"Then, I will look at the level of derivatives like interest rate swaps these banks have traded."

"Why not mortgages?" Pole asked.

"Because these instruments, unlike mortgages, are not based on hard cash but on notional amounts."

"The notional amount is not cash that moves from hand to hand but a number on which the results of the transaction are calculated," Nancy added.

"You mean it does not – exist?" Pole said with knitted eyebrows.

"Well, you could say that. There is no cash changing hands on the notional, only on the outcome. Say your swap has a notional of £200 million, that amount does not change hands but the net movements of rates on that amount will be the outcome payable," Henry explained further.

"But why?" Pole still looked puzzled.

"Because it is a risk management instrument. If I want to protect myself against a negative outcome on the £200 million I just spoke about, I enter into a swap and change the outcome – hence the term swap. I literally swap the negative outcome for a positive outcome."

Pole nodded. "Let's do a simple apples and oranges example to help a simple copper like me."

Nancy shook her head, but Henry grinned.

"I grow oranges and you, Henry, grow apples."

"Sounds good to me."

"I want apples because I am growing too many oranges but I don't want to plant apple trees." Pole was slowly stroking his goatee. "So, if you want oranges and are ready to swap your apples for my oranges we are in business, right?" Pole said waving a finger at Henry – a eureka moment.

"And as long as I don't want to plant orange trees either we are definitely in business," Henry replied impressed.

"But how many apples do I receive?"

"Very good question, Inspector," Henry was amused by the comparison. "Say today an orange is worth an apple; tomorrow however the price may change. We agree that we are going to look at these prices every three months and then we agree who gets what. If oranges go up, you get more apples. If apples go up I get more oranges."

"And ultimately you and I do that because I think oranges are going to go up and I will get more apples and I have an apple-pie factory." Pole grinned.

"Damn – you could have been a mean trader," Henry teased.

"Only now you're telling me."

"Never too late to learn."

"Back to the case Henry."

"Yes, Inspector – so for the banks the choice is between different types of interest rates, say fixed against floating," Henry said.

"LIBOR is the floating part because it resets regularly," Pole added energised by understanding what the financial markets represented.

"Correct and I think I can estimate what was happening as long as I can get to the right data."

"Do you need something else from me," Pole offered.

"Not yet. I'll see how much I can gather from Bloomberg and the audited financial reports of the banks I have in mind. I have to say though, I am not surprised it has happened. It was such an easy way of making a bit more money – this LIBOR fixing."

"But – what's changed?"

"If William Noble had not been involved, somehow I would have gone straight for the money-making angle, but his involvement changes everything."

"Unfortunately, I must say I agree." Nancy sighed.

"If you combine the financial crisis and William's involvement, you end up with a level of manipulation of LIBOR that is much more structural, probably geared at saving the banks and ultimately saving the financial system from collapse." Henry's face had grown serious. "I know this is not acceptable but I understand why a man like William may think it's necessary."

The three fell silent, each measuring in their own way the impact of Henry's findings.

"But William would not have spoken to the banks directly, perhaps the BBA?" Nancy broke the silence.

"Did he say anything that could help us?" Pole asked.

"Nothing, he was keen to protect his contact."

Henry hesitated. Should he break the news now?

But Nancy was following her train of thought.

"What do we know about the various protagonists and their connections?"

"Gary Cook worked at GL until very recently. He was the LIBOR submitter for them. Been in the market forever. He can call his pals at Barclays, RBS, Lloyds etc. But he also knows Tom Hardy, CEO of the BBA very well," Pole said.

"The very same BBA whose job it is to publish LIBOR," Nancy added.

"My guess is that Tom and Gary have spoken. We still don't know who initiated what," Pole said.

"I think we do," Henry said. "If this is a request from on high to ensure that the banks start lending to each other in order to save the financial system, then Tom reaches out to Gary. If Gary has ever been a naughty boy, it was on a small scale – maybe half a bp."

Before Pole could ask, Henry explained. "A basis point or bp is 0.01 per cent."

"That sounds very small."

"Yes, but on a very large notional – remember what we discussed earlier. These banks trade billions in notional."

"Understood, but you say it's different from what Gary would then have been asked to do."

"Absolutely, if Gary was seeking to alter the LIBOR benchmark altogether he needs to move his submission by a substantial amount to make a difference. He no longer seeks to go under the radar; he is the radar."

"I see what you mean. So now the changes are much more visible," Pole said slowly to convince himself – it sounded so impossible.

"Besides, if Gary had simply sought to improve his P&L he would have remained well under that radar and avoided Tom like the plague."

"That sounds right. So, Tom initiates the conversation with Gary – because he has been contacted by?" Nancy said, thinking aloud.

"William?" Pole said turning to Henry for confirmation.

"Don't think so." Henry shook his head with the beginning of a smile that gave his face a much younger look, the look of mischief from someone who has the answer.

"All right, do tell us, genius," Pole stood up and placed himself in front of Henry's screens.

"There is a little word missing, Inspector."

"What! I can't believe you. No actually I can believe you, *please*," Pole said pressing two fingers into his eyes to make the pain of the word disappear.

"The Bank of England," Nancy spoke the word slowly, in a mechanical voice. Henry turned abruptly towards her. Pole suppressed a smile. She had robbed Henry of his thunder – good girl.

Nancy nodded and repeated her sentence with conviction. A shadow passed over her face. Pole noticed. She knew more than she was willing to share.

"Spot on – wow, Nancy. I am impressed," Henry's face had lifted. His light-blue eyes flickering with admiration. No hard feelings amongst friends. "It's the only possible explanation."

"William, being a Whitehall mandarin, would have floated the idea with the Bank of England first, to see whether it would stick?" Pole said.

"Discussing options – all done behind closed doors. No trace of the conversation. After all there was an unprecedented crisis to manage." Henry moved away from his screens. His face lost its slight carefree expression, a deep line etched on his forehead had grown deeper.

"This is the sequence of events, I think. William is informed regularly by his contacts at the various large banks, CEOs, Heads of Risks as well as the Bank of England that the pressure on the financial markets is about to create the biggest crisis since 1930. One of the main issues is that all the banks are so worried they have stopped lending not only to Joe Bloggs on the street but also to each other. The reason: they are too shit scared about the exposure they all have to the subprime market. Banks not lending to banks: unsustainable.

"Agreed, that was all over the news," Pole said.

"If the banks stop lending to one another this ripples down the whole market and the financial system collapses. So the government wants, actually needs, to reintroduce some stability. William who is at the forefront of the effort has a conversation with the Bank of England. The Bank of England somehow accepts – in order to preserve the integrity of the system: needs must. Only one or two people are involved, no more."

"Agreed again. William himself wants one contact and one contact only to ensure maximum discretion," Pole said.

"The Bank of England in turn needs to test the plan with a trusted chum – Tom Hardy at the BBA."

"Did they really need the BBA involved?" Nancy asked. "The Bank of England knows exactly who submits in each bank, don't they?"

"Not necessarily all of them," Henry replied. "And you probably want the BBA to be picking the best candidates for the task."

"But surely top management is also involved somehow?" Pole was now leaning against the wall still in front of Henry's screens.

"Absolutely. The BBA can test the idea with a couple of traders and they will be able to tell the Bank of England whether Management may buy the idea. Then the Bank of England makes the call – to the CEO. And the instructions start coming from on high."

"But LIBOR can't be manipulated in that way only by one bank, right?"

"Right again. LIBOR is calculated on a basket of submissions, so other banks have to be involved."

"Let me see whether I've got this right," Pole moved towards Henry's desk and started leafing through a file. "Tom Hardy, BBA's director, calls his pal Gary Cook, head trader at GL. Gary tells him he thinks GL might be up for it but, at that level of alteration, top Management needs to give the OK. Tom relays that to the Bank of England, the Bank of England calls the CEO and makes a direct request."

"Uh-huh." Henry nodded.

"Tom and Gary have worked together before: same brokerage firm, then same bank," Pole was reading from a typed note. He puts the file down, one hand still resting on its cover. "They can go straight to the point. Gary starts calling his mates in other banks."

Pole was about to let go when he opened the file again and frowns. "And they belong to the same gym."

Nancy looked at him quizzically. Was it not time to put all his cards on the table?

"You mean the Embody Fitness Club?"

Pole's jaws clenched.

"Is there a need to show off?"

"That's unfair. If it was Nancy, you would be impressed."

"I doubt Nancy feels the need to outsmart everyone all the time."

"*Vraiment, vous deux êtes incorrigibles*," Nancy said standing up to stretch a little.

Pole looked at her miffed. How could she compare him to Henry?

"Let's talk about the gym," Nancy said.

"Fine," Pole replied reluctantly. "Some of the nootropics that Gary took were stored there. Although the owners had no idea that something dodgy was going on."

"And Tom?" Nancy asked.

"There were plenty of painkillers in his blood. Some opiate medication used to relieve extreme pain: post-op injuries or very strong chronic pain."

"You know that Olympic athletes train at Embody, don't you?"

"Make your point," Pole said.

"Athletes at that level do incur severe injuries that need pretty strong drugs."

"Was it your gym?"

"Of course, you wouldn't believe what people talk about when they are training together – a gold mine of info."

"And how does Belmarsh compare? Pole said closing the file with a snap.

"A gold mine too." Henry grinned, placing his crossed arms behind his head.

"Anybody from the Bank of England?" Nancy asked. The shadows underneath her eyes had darkened suddenly. They stopped Henry and Pole dead in their tracks.

"It's already 7pm. You need to be on your way back, Henry."

Henry face tightened. "Tomorrow?"

"I've asked for a couple of days. You're back at the same time tomorrow morning."

Henry turned towards the screens still flickering, scrolling down information. "Thank you."

Pole called for the guards. The cuffs were put on Henry without much consideration. He disappeared down the long corridors of Scotland Yard.

Nancy had hardly winced at the sight of Henry being taken away. An unexpected reaction that Pole had not missed. They both walked the same long corridors without saying much.

"Something on your mind?" Pole asked as they stood in front of the lifts.

Nancy sighed. "I can't hide very well from you, not that I would want to, Jonathan. But allow me a little time to think it through. I need to get this right."

The lift doors pinged open. They pushed their way into the crowd. Pole would have to wait until the morning.

Chapter Twenty

"He is crossing tonight," Brett said, his mobile stuck to his ear. He was finishing the last cigarette of his packet, inhaling deeply. The nicotine kicked in, a welcome light-headedness and feeling it would be all right on the day. Information was strictly on a need-to-know basis and Brett had so far felt that his need to know was reduced to three words *Not Your Problem*. But today MI6-Steve was precise, perhaps even helpful.

"I hear you, but until the Merchant of Venice calls me, I am in the dark." Another apt code name for Antonio; Brett managed a smile.

"Well, it's not reassuring to be reassured, specially by you," Brett took his last drag and crushed his cigarette under his shoe. If only it could be Steve's head.

Brett crossed Piccadilly over to the Ritz. He turned right towards Belgravia. A little walk would clear his brain. The young Middle-Eastern man who was tailing him this morning had disappeared. If they were still following him they were getting better at it. His new burner phone rang. Brett stopped dead. A woman with her dog almost bumped into him, barely apologising.

"They want to speak to you," Mohammed's voice was strained.

"When?" Brett reached for his Benson & Hedges in his inner jacket pocket. He pulled the pack out, flicked the top flap open.

Empty.

"What do you mean now?" Brett looked at the empty pack he had started to crush in anger; a cold sweat covered the back of his neck. This was definitely not part of the deal. "I need to be careful, Goddamn it. I can't just make my way every five minutes to your neck of the woods." Brett heard the intake of air at the other end of the phone. "Sorry, not your choice. I know." Brett never apologised as a rule – aristocratic upbringing. Today, however Brett felt for his contact.

"Fine, fine. I'm on my way home. I need to change. I will be there in a couple of hours – yes, same place."

No point in calling Steve. Bringing Clandestine X into the country had just been an appetiser he feared. He was about to be served the main course and was not going to like the taste of it.

* * *

The rhythm of her footsteps on the pavement felt angry. Nancy was beating the concrete slabs with her heels, releasing with each kick the searing sensation in her belly.

Betrayed.

Not only as a friend but also in the cause she so passionately believed in. Thousands of women, good honest women, fighting the harsh battle of equality and recognition would suffer. What had Edwina been thinking of? She was not even yet in the Governor's seat and she was already playing God.

Nancy had left Scotland Yard abruptly. Her departure would not fool Pole. She had not even wanted to hide her discomfort. But Edwina deserved to be heard. She was not, or at least not yet, one of the unsavoury clients Nancy had defended during her eminent career as QC. Edwina was her protégée. Only a few hours ago she would also have called her a friend.

Nancy reached The Mall. Plenty of cabs if she wanted to hit the City quickly. She stuck her hand in her pocket to avoid temptation. Getting to the Bank, demanding to see Edwina and savaging her was not a solution. She reached Trafalgar Square. The constant flow of cars, buses and bikes forced her to stop and wait. Today the National Portrait Gallery restaurant would be open late; she would probably not get a table for one but it was worth a try.

Sitting at the small comfortable bar, Nancy was sipping a soft Chilean Merlot. She stabbed an olive with conviction and crunched it with one bite. Deliciously spicy and garlicky. Her BlackBerry had remained untouched since she had taken it out of her bag. She had checked on William as she had settled down at the bar – no change.

The restaurant was filling up quickly; fewer tourists than expected but many regulars – artists, art critics, a couple of TV personalities. She could still call Pole. But no, Edwina deserved the benefit of the doubt. Was it not the way she had been trained? She was not yet sure and would not rush to conclusions. Nancy closed her almond-shaped eyes in a slow, calming movement. She inhaled deeply and released. In a moment she would reach this place of peace and quiet that she had learned to create so many years ago. The buzz of the bar had become less distracting. She breathed in again, letting the old habit kick in. Her mind had slowed a little more. She was reaching that space where her intuition could speak unencumbered and where she was free to consider all options.

Nancy opened her eyes. The barman was looking at her with a mixture of concern and surprise. She smiled comfortably and took another sip of wine. The young man blushed, attempted a smile and turned to serve the next customer.

She had an hour to decide.

* * *

The police van was rocking uncomfortably over the potholes of East London. Henry sat silently at the back, locked in his cubicle. The two guards sat near the door, engrossed in a low-voiced conversation. A few words drifted towards Henry – pay rise, bloody bad, prison officer badly injured. Henry had started taking mental notes of the process of transfer the second he had been on his way to central London. What would happen if the van broke down? In his last two years at HMP Belmarsh nothing of the routine followed by cons and guards had escaped him. He knew how the prison worked in all its minutiae, who the prison officers were, their habits, what made them tick or flare up. He knew the layout of the Cat. A wing, the number of steps between each security lock and to the other main parts of the building. He could have walked around Belmarsh blindfolded and not tripped once.

It had started as a way to reassure himself, a way of focusing the mind and conquer a new hostile environment. Now it was feeding the project that had been gnawing at him relentlessly.

Escape.

He could count on Charlie to come up with the information he needed. What had been tried before and had, so far, never succeeded. Inmates were receiving drugs and mobile phones through drones – several drops every night in the main prison. But what could be shipped into HSU Belmarsh?

The trip to Scotland Yard had provided Henry with exceptional information. Something he would trade with Kamal, if he needed to. The plan had started to evolve slowly and was gaining momentum. So long as he behaved and gave the guards no bother he might be allowed out again.

Henry looked at his hands in cuffs. He clenched and opened his fists a few times. He had so feared his mind would be dulled by the routine of prison life. His talent had sprung to life again after only a few lapses around the Bloomberg terminal. The flow between his deep analytical skills and the ability to synthetise a large amount of data had resurfaced almost intact and the joy had almost been overwhelming. A shiver moved down his back, rippling deliciously into his entire body. He muffled a groan. The guards had not noticed. The conversation they were having over pay and working conditions was still occupying their minds. Henry relaxed against the cool surface of metal. His mind had been freed and was feeding into a single purpose.

* * *

Need to see you urgently. Nancy pressed the send button and put her BlackBerry down next to her wine glass. She would give Edwina five minutes to reply and then call her. Implicating her without having a conversation was tempting but unfair. Once Pole knew, there would be no turning back. And he would know, either today or tomorrow. Edwina had the choice. Speak to Pole herself or Nancy would do so. Pole did not care about market manipulation but he had a double murder to solve. Edwina's career was on a knife edge. Nancy sighed. So much talent and hard work, swept away. Did she really need to go down that path? Her BlackBerry buzzed, reverberating on the counter with small jumps.

Fiendishly busy with next round of QE. Can it wait?
No.

Nancy went outside and hailed a cab. Edwina would meet her tonight.

* * *

Cook's revised toxicology report, Version V1-04 had been neatly placed on Pole's desk. A collection of coloured stickers indicated key findings. Pole smiled. Andy had as ever done a Sterling job. Nurani was nowhere to be seen. Out and about, checking on the leads they had gathered through Gary's gym and nursing her wounded pride. Caught short of the latest information on the case in front of Marsh; not the desired effect for someone nursing high ambition.

428

And yet Pole did not mind her desire to succeed. If she could only overcome her deeply entrenched self-doubts, she could be one day the finest of detectives.

Pole closed his door. A clear sign that no one should cross the threshold until he was ready to be interrupted. He read the file cover to cover, ignoring Andy's tabs, his tall body comfortable in his old armchair and his left hand playing with an elastic band he had found on the floor. He stopped the repetitive movement and straightened up. His hand hovered over his phone. He called Yvonne.

"Don't give me an earful. I know it's late." Pole pulled the phone away from his ear. "I owe you, I know." Pole was nodding away, waiting until Yvonne was done with all the things he owed her for calling her at 10pm.

"You're on speaker."

Yvonne grunted. "You're going to ask me about the traces of LSD, despite a five-day lapse between Cook's death and the latest tox report, right?"

"Yup – and the answer is?"

"No idea, but I can hypothesise."

"Hypothesise away," Pole said, firing the elastic band across the room.

"We put the guy on ice; this slows the process of decomposition. And before you ask why did I not find it to start with?"

"You said it, not me."

"I used an advanced testing method this time round, not the standard method as with any routine tox screen and the other drugs sloshing around his blood overwhelmed the initial test. This time I used a urine sample"

"And that will hold in court?"

"What do you take me for?"

"The best of the best, of course," Pole replied rolling his eyes.

"And Hardy? No fingerprints on the hose that connected the exhaust to the car?"

"None. Hardy had no gloves when we found him but we did find an old pair in the car."

"He stays strapped in with his seat belt on but puts his gloves back in the side pocket of the car?"

"Strange but correct."

"Final tox report on Hardy?"

"It will be on your desk tomorrow but he took some pretty strong painkillers: prescription drug only. The sort of stuff you take after an op or a very bad injury."

"Sporting injury for example?"

"If severe enough, yes – nerve pain in particular."

"Anything new on Felipe Martinez?"

"Nope, the Martinez tox report is clear. High dose of LSD, no question. But, I see that the hair sample analysis indicates a new habit. Not sure it's relevant."

"You mean he was not a habitual user?" Pole said, not waiting for the answer he knew. "That corroborates what his girlfriend said to us."

Pole and Yvonne fell silent.

"Jon, are great minds about to think alike. Jon, are you still there?"

"Sorry Yvonne, not sure. I mean I am here. That was great." He thanked Yvonne once more and put the phone down.

Pole stretched in his chair and looked around his office. The desk was a mess, nothing new in this. The piles of documents scattered around his room looked suitably unstable for his colleagues to grunt whenever entering. The latest news gave him a good reason to call Nancy. It was only 9.30 PM and she would still be up. He rolled the BlackBerry in his hand a couple of times. Not a good idea though. Nancy was following her intuition and he had learned not to interrupt the workings of her remarkable mind. She would call when ready.

His phone rang. Pole ignored it until he cast an eye on the screen that showed Superintendent Marsh's name. His boss was calling at this time of night – not good. Marsh had fretted about Henry. He only needed half an excuse to cancel Henry's second visit to the Yard. Pole picked up the call and was asked to make his way to Marsh's office – not good at all.

Marsh was on another call when Pole entered. He waved him in. His monosyllabic replies gave Pole an inkling about the identity of the caller. If he was a betting man he would have put his money on the Governor of HMP Belmarsh. Marsh terminated the call too courteously for Pole's liking. Marsh sat back in his chair and fired a volley of questions about the case. Pole batted them back with the coolness of a man in control.

"Crowne is delivering – was worth twisting Belmarsh's Governor's arm, I suppose," Marsh said rearranging his Montblanc pens on his desk with a meticulous gesture. "And Ms Wu was there to assist?"

Was The Super disappointed that the delightful Ms Wu had not visited him?

Pole had taken a seat and crossed his long legs, pushing his back comfortably into the chair. He straightened up a little and raised a quizzical eyebrow. "She was indeed. As ever, very much on the ball."

"And you are certain she is not too close to Crowne? Are you not sailing close to the wind a bit on this?"

Pole's gut tightened. He felt the blow he had not anticipated. The Super had not been indulged and he was flexing the muscles of his authority. Pole's light-grey eyes drilled into Marsh and retreated. A confrontation would be of no use. "That is precisely what I want. If Henry tries anything Ms Wu will be well placed to detect."

"But she was part of his legal team when he went to trial. Correct?"

Pole nodded.

"And she visits him regularly – still. Correct?"

"A lot of briefs do." Pole's focus changed. He was losing the argument that had not been made yet but would soon come. "Frankly, this is not a reason to stop Henry coming back tomorrow. Belmarsh's governor has organised the trip with prison officers that know how to transport high-profile prisoners. I am not worried about Henry escaping. However I need the intel now or I fear there might be another victim."

Marsh shifted in his chair. He had not anticipated Pole's challenge to be so well-targeted. Marsh rearranged his pens once more. "Who do you have in mind?"

It was Pole's turn to switch position in their cat and mouse game. "We are speaking to contacts at the Bank of England, Edwina James-Jones." Pole was rehearsing his arguments quickly: LIBOR, the BBA – no Whitehall for the moment.

"Is she credible?" Marsh asked.

"You mean as the next governor of the Bank of England?"

"Well, yes. You must know she is very close. First woman to be appointed," Marsh said with a small sigh. The next thing would be the appointment of a woman at the Commissioner – unthinkable.

Pole seized the opportunity; this was why they needed Henry. He kept going with details of LIBOR, enough to make it sound as complicated as it was. Marsh nodded. Pole pushed his body out of the chair and was halfway to standing up.

"And Ms Wu also knows Ms James-Jones. Correct?"

Pole collapsed back into the seat. He had been a fool not to see this coming.

* * *

The Barbican Members' Room was remarkably quiet. It was gone 10pm and the intervals for both concert hall and theatre were long over.

Nancy had chosen to sit in a secluded corner from where she could see the entrance. She sat in a comfortable armchair. Edwina would be here any minute. The knot in Nancy's stomach had tightened a little more. More difficult to control was the anger that made her right hand twitch ever so slightly. She had known the anger of the rebellious when she was a student in Paris. She had known the anger that came with fear when she had left China as it became clear to her parents that the Cultural Revolution had veered off course to the detriment of artists of any value. She had become an angry young barrister, schooled at the Sorbonne and King's College London. Criminal law had seemed apt for channelling her permanent sense of injustice. She had worked hard at understanding why and finally at letting go. But it had meant leaving the Bar, transforming radically the way she lived – and she loved it. Occasionally the beast would be summoned and Nancy resented anyone who asked her to call upon its power.

Nancy glanced at her watch. Edwina had no more than five minutes to appear, then she would call Pole. She was browsing through her call history when a swift hand stopped her. Edwina was standing at her side, arm outstretched, a desperate look etched on her tired face.

Her voice sounded strangely raw. "What is so urgent? Is William...?"

"Still unconscious," Nancy replied sharply. "Drink?"

"Yes, anything."

Nancy ordered and pointed at the seat next to her. "Tell me all you know about LIBOR fixing."

Edwina's blue eyes widened, the colour drained from her face. "You mean, the process of setting LIBOR?"

Nancy smiled thinly – was Edwina still hoping? "You and I know this is not what I am asking, Eddie." She could savage Edwina here and now but it would not help. "Let's not lose time. There is a murderer on the loose."

Edwina clung to her glass, undecided whether she should stay or flee. She took a gulp of wine. Her eyes had not met Nancy's yet.

"I hear you," she murmured.

"When I say fixing I mean manipulation: fraud, lies – and in general the type of crappy behaviour that caused the crisis in the first place."

Edwina dropped her head in her hands. "Oh God." She rubbed her nose with the back of her hand. "Nancy, I am scared."

Nancy gave Edwina a dispassionate look. Was it an act? She scrutinised her face, the clasped hands, the dark rings underneath her eyes.

"Speak to me," Nancy said in a softer tone.

"How much do you know?"

"Not the right question, Eddie. I know enough to have gathered you're involved. If you want my help, I want the unabbreviated version of events. Gary and Tom are dead. William is breathing through a ventilator. The choice is yours."

Edwina drew the light pashmina she wore more closely around her shoulders.

"I had a meeting with William a few months back. We had been talking QE …," her voice trailed. "I don't know how we came to it. I suppose it is the skill of a high-calibre civil servant – to ask without saying."

Nancy nodded. William had spoken to her when the crisis started biting – he was there to save the UK financial system come what may.

"After that we spoke of hypothetical ways and it seemed eventually to fall into place."

"Who else knows?" Nancy asked.

Edwina looked up and anger flashed in her eyes. "This is not a police interrogation you know."

"I am well aware of this, my dear, and believe you me I have attended more than I care to remember." Nancy paused.

The pressure of silence, always a powerful tool.

"Who else?"

"Gabriel is aware."

Nancy waited. It was not enough.

"He knows I spoke to Tom at the BBA and William but he does not know who Tom contacted within the banks." Edwina looked drained. She sat back, holding her pashmina even tighter.

"Only you and Gabriel?"

Edwina nodded. "We had to do something."

"As much as I would love to argue whether any form of manipulation is justified – pre- or post-crisis. Don't look so shocked," Nancy said. "People in the US are getting agitated and they have started talking."

Edwina opened her mouth but nothing came out. Nancy had found the angle of attack once more and hit hard. She sat back to see the result unfold.

"Geithner knows," Edwina volunteered.

"I bet he does," Nancy replied. "Who else in his team across the pond?"

"Not sure: a couple more," Edwina's hand moved blindly to her glass. It was almost empty.

Nancy looked at Eddie with a sudden deep sense of sorrow. So much talent and hard work. Nancy hid her disappointment.

"You must speak to Inspector Pole."

Edwina closed her eyes. Moisture had gathered underneath her blonde lashes. She cleared her throat.

"You're right. I must – and I will – but I'd like to prepare the final papers for the next QE round. My legacy: a better outcome." Edwina stopped. She met Nancy's eyes. "Give me until tomorrow morning. After that I'll speak to Scotland Yard."

"Why should I trust you?"

"Because you know that William and I shared the same view – we needed to save the system and so needs must."

Nancy gave Edwina a long hard look. "The greater good?"

Edwina gave a feeble smile. It sounded so arrogant now.

"I will be at Scotland Yard tomorrow at 8am. I hope Inspector Pole will have heard from you by then."

"He will," Edwina replied. She stood up slowly, gathered her belongings and left without another word. Tomorrow Edwina James-Jones would be history; today though she had a job to finish.

Nancy followed Edwina's silhouette. It disappeared through the doors of the Members' Room. She waved to the waitress; another glass of wine would help to dull the pain a little. She mechanically reached for her phone inside her bag. Pole had called then left a hurried text.

Marsh on the warpath – call me PLEASE. Jonathan

Chapter Twenty-One

The Tube was not moving. Defective train on the line the announcement had said. Brett cursed. He was late. Mohammed may not wait. No, he would. He was too scared of the small man in his white robe, The Sheik. Brett looked around the carriage. He had squeezed his lanky body in the last seat in the row. The space was packed. The old gentleman next to him was fingering prayer beads. His tatty clothes smelt of spices and his lips kept moving noiselessly to words he knew by heart.

The train jolted into action again and Brett breathed in. He looked at his burner mobile. No signal yet. The train stopped at Highbury and Islington. A group of women in full niqab walked on. Sweat had started to gather on his forehead. The temperature was suffocating. He stood up and pushed his way towards the opening doors.

The SUV was parked on the opposite side of the road. Mohammed had disappeared swiftly and the same Middle-Eastern man who had taken him the last time was driving. Brett got into the back, tied the cloth around his eyes. The drive seemed to take less time than before. Were they more relaxed about him?

Unlikely.

He left his mobile in the back of the car. Stepped out to be frisked and stepped forward into a different house. The man pushed the door open, removed his blindfold and waited for him to go in. The smell made Brett's skin crawl: chemicals – weed killer, ammonia? He felt a compact hand move him forwards towards the smell. Brett's stomach lurched. The man moved his head in the direction of a small stairwell. Brett climbed up moving away from the acrid vapours. He wiped his forehead before knocking at the door. No response. He tried again and the door opened ajar. He was alone. Brett stepped into a large room, a couple of different armchairs had been gathered in its centre, with a coffee table before it, and a low couch stuck against the wall. He moved towards the coffee table and spotted three photos, arranged at an equal distance face down. Brett moved closer, his mind racing through the various possibilities. Had they followed him to his club? Did they know of his MI6 involvement despite Steve's assurances? The soft draught of an opening door and the sound of the floor creaking told him his host had arrived. Brett tried to compose himself and turned around slowly.

The same young man as before signalled him to sit down. He moved to the couch and tea appeared poured by a slim young woman wearing the full burqa, her hands were gloved and Brett could see she was struggling to move around.

"You did well. I hear my Mujahidin is crossing the Channel tonight."

"Then you know more than I do," Brett replied taking a sip of tea.

A slim smile came to The Sheik's face. "I have another deal for you."

"Look, I only do art," Brett said without conviction. He would say no only if MI6 allowed him to.

"Is the remuneration not adequate?" The look was amused but the tone cruel.

Brett fretted for a moment. Some semblance of opposition, deliberation then acceptance.

"Take a look at the first photo."

Brett slid the picture towards him, still face down. He turned it over and looked at the face closely. A man, in his thirties, light-brown hair and distinct light-brown eyes, he might have been handsome had his face not been marked by some ugly scarring. Brett gathered by his countenance that he was well educated, even polished – government, Army?

"I don't know him."

"Good." The Sheik took a sip of tea and gestured. "Next picture."

Brett slid the second picture down the table, a building, The Royal Exchange. He slowly put down the photo on the table and waited.

"Now, you must know this building?"

Brett nodded.

"You work for some of the companies that rent offices there?" The man finished his tea.

"I advise on what art they put on their walls." Brett just managed to steady his voice as the unthinkable started unfolding in front of him. Beads of sweat had started to collect on his forehead. He kept his eyes fixed on the photo. If he moved them he would meet The Sheik's eyes and the man might see fear.

"I want access to this building," the voice was relaxed. He could have been asking for Brett's favourite Renaissance artist.

"Why?" Brett lifted his face and met the dark-brown eyes that had not left him since he had come in.

"It won't be a bomb."

Brett took in a short breath, surprised at the frankness of the answer. He was still dubious.

"The price will be right."

"When?" Brett swallowed some tea, the burning liquid dispersing the feeling of nausea.

"Monday, perhaps earlier —"

Brett put down his glass noisily. "Impossible."

"Monday."

Brett ran his bony hand through his thinning hair.

"I need to think."

The Sheik nodded, took out his mobile. Brett's minder appeared at the door.

"Mohammed will contact you." The Sheik said, not bothering to stand.

Brett cast on eye towards the third photo on the table.

"Some other time," came the answer.

* * *

His thumb was drumming some complex rhythm on the wheel. Pole glanced in his rear mirror, indicated and switched lane. The traffic was light. He would be at Scotland Yard before 7am. Nurani had done enough damage with Marsh, a good old-fashioned talking to was what she needed. Pole kept drumming the tune. Jazz FM was playing one of his favourite pieces by Didier Lockwood. His head started moving with a saxophone solo. Nancy was having an early meeting with Marsh to appease the great man and he would certainly not work with Henry from Belmarsh. He had managed to lose Marsh with the complexity of LIBOR. His superior would never admit to not understanding an issue, especially one that was at the centre of a high-profile case. Still Marsh would do his research too and it wouldn't be long before he caught up. Using Nancy to gain time was not his preferred choice but she had volunteered. A small pang of doubt hit him: Marsh–Nancy, nah: never.

He cranked up the radio, seeking to chase away the small bubble of anger that was threatening to burst. Jazz was the least recommended music to listen while driving: too intellectual and demanding. Pole shrugged, so what, much better than Techno – No Thank You. His mind concentrated on the improvisation for a short moment. But last night's conversation would not go away. Some idiot tried to squeeze in front of him. Pole looked at the blue light he used in an emergency. Taking out his wrath on some stupid driver would not do. He would square the impact of Nurani's conversation with Marsh with the lady herself. Nurani was unquestionably an excellent cop, resourceful and dedicated. She could not let the pressure of promotion send her off course though. She was better than that. Pole relaxed as the next tune started, confident he had found the right tone for speaking to his DS.

Pole's mobile started buzzing, unknown number. He pulled off the road and took the call. Edwina James-Jones was calling him. He recognised the name immediately, the first woman tipped to become Governor of the Bank of England but also the star guest of the Women in Enterprise Conference at which Gary had been murdered.

The conversation was short. She would come to the Yard and speak to him today about the LIBOR matter. She wanted to deliver a major report to Mervyn King this morning. Would 10am therefore do? Pole was on his way to episode two of the Henry Crowne Show. He had to reluctantly admit he was looking forward to Henry's incisive way of dealing with the case. And yes, 10am would do.

Pole resumed his driving, stuck the blue flashing light to his roof and accelerated across a red light. He would be at the office before Nancy arrived for her power breakfast with his boss. She might even have time for a quick tea with him beforehand.

Henry was already working at his Bloomberg terminals when Pole entered the room. The same dingy place, four plasma screens gave it a surreal look but Henry was smiling. "Morning Inspector. I have pulled up all the stocks and delivered a cracking model that will speed up the investigation."

Henry turned his face towards Pole. Deep circles had appeared underneath his eyes and his paler face told Pole he had not had much sleep.

"Morning Henry. Care to elaborate?" Pole placed a Caffè Nero double macchiato on Henry's desk, pulled up a chair and sat next to him.

"Ta. I am not trying to be a pompous arse. You may not agree, of course, but I spent the night reading a couple of books about this new financial model. It enabled me to spot any substantial variations in the LIBOR quotes of the banks who submit to the LIBOR panel."

"You mean that your model can detect the magnitude and time of any manipulation of the LIBOR benchmark by the banks that submitted?"

"In a nutshell," Henry said disappointed. No need to further elaborate on his brilliant idea – sulk.

"Good man," Pole replied, amused. "Although —"

"We still don't have a real motive. I know."

Pole grunted. Why could Henry never be a graceful loser? His mobile buzzed. Nancy was at reception.

* * *

"We still don't have a motive. LIBOR manipulation is what links these guys together but that's all," Pole said putting a fresh cup of tea in front of Nancy. She gave it a questioning look.

"Builder's tea, *ma chère*; nothing else will do in the morning for a good old-fashioned copper like me."

"I am sure it will be fine," Nancy said. She took a sip, surprisingly good. She leaned back in her chair. She looked around at the room they were in. Pole caught her inquisitive look.

"Superintendent Marsh is taking a keen interest in the investigation."

"And he thinks you are sailing a little too close to the wind by involving too many *outsiders*, unless the said *outsider* pays more attention to the very large —" Nancy took a sip, "ego of the said gentleman."

"In a nutshell," Pole said stiffly.

"Are you?"

"You mean do I need to be more cautious – probably, but I won't be. Not the way I work and no one will make me change that."

"Does he know about William?"

"No, and please don't think I don't care," Pole interrupted raising a hand and forcing a smile. "I can't have him making a number of calls to the Chancellor. It will stop this investigation dead."

Nancy nodded. "Yes, that is wise – to be frank I don't think William would want Osborne to be involved." She took another sip of tea to steady her nerves. "I'll be as brief as I can."

"I need you to help with Edwina too," Pole said, a way to keep Nancy close perhaps.

"That I can do. I think the conversation with Edwina will be a turning point."

"Why don't you give me a preview?"

"I won't put words into her mouth but you may find your motive to be a major cover-up involving very senior people."

"You think that Henry's list of banks that have manipulated LIBOR will give us nothing?" Pole raised an eyebrow.

"Not nothing. It will confirm our thinking," Nancy was enjoying her tea. "If my theory is right, it will show you that no one working in the banks that have manipulated LIBOR has died."

"Righto, I see where you are going. If it had been an exercise to eradicate the traders who have moved the benchmark we would have more dead bodies on our hands. And it has not happened." Pole pursed his lips in agreement.

"*Absolument, vous avez tout compris.* Hence we need to look into the rarefied space of top government institutions."

"You suspect Edwina?" Pole asked bluntly.

Nancy's jaw clenched and released. "It did cross my mind, but no is the short answer."

Pole stood up, still holding his cup, and moved to the window. The sun was playing hide and seek with some large ominous clouds. He turned around.

"You need more evidence. I understand, Jonathan, but hear me out. Two questions intrigue me."

"Pray tell," Pole asked with a flourish of his hand.

"We have had two murders and one attempt," Nancy said. She straightened herself up and carried on. "In quick succession – then nothing. Why no attempt on Edwina's life? But why does she look so frightened?"

"She is putting on an act? She realises what she's done and is frightened of being caught?"

"Edwina is a smart woman. I can't believe she would have let us come so close to her in the first instance. The Women in Enterprise Conference? Far too obvious."

"She could have an accomplice?"

"She could but here again why the conference?" Nancy's mind had become alert to a change, thoughts that were slowly gathering and ready to surface. Something important lay below that surface; she just had to stretch to grab it.

"Anything you'd like to share?" Pole asked, knowing the answer would be no.

"You must be impartial when you hear Edwina."

"That is not an answer. I am not some rooky detective." Pole gave her a charming smile. "Come on, just a little clue?" Pole shaped a small gap between thumb and index finger.

"We need to think laterally – if not Edwina. Then who and why?"

"You mean who could benefit from her involvement not being discovered?"

"*Exactement.*"

Pole's mobile rang. He gave it a dark look and was about to ignore it when he noticed the name on the screen. Yvonne was calling.

"Why did you not call the landline?"

"And good morning to you too Inspector. "

"And good morning to you Yvonne – sorry, you're on loudspeaker."

"Good morning Nancy; making sense of this case yet?" Yvonne said with a smile in her voice.

"Morning Yvonne – any clue from you would be most helpful."

"Well, I have something for you." They heard the muffled sound of paper. "Here we are. Working on Hardy's forensic for the final tox report. I promised Pole it would be on his desk asap. You recall that the passenger door was taped with some heavy-duty parcel tape, right?"

"All around the window to seal any gap that the hose pipe carrying the exhaust's fumes had created." Pole said. He could see it clearly. "And the same tape was used to fix the hose to the exhaust."

"Spot on. Well, I noticed that the tape was jagged and therefore had not been cut with a sharp instrument. That got me thinking," Yvonne waited. "Anyone with a view – no?"

"Someone cut it with their teeth," Pole said snapping his fingers.

"Hey, don't burst my bubble," Yvonne said playfully. "But correct – and I found saliva which gave me DNA but —"

"Not the DNA of the victim," Pole finished. "He never taped that tape to the hose."

"Nope. And before you ask there is zero match on the database, nothing on NOMAD."

"You're a star." Pole said.

"I know – only to be eclipsed by dear Nancy of course." Yvonne was enjoying the tease. "I will leave you guys *alone.*" She hung up with a tut-tut in her voice.

Pole tried to ignore the slight blush on Nancy's face.

"Let's see what Ms James-Jones has in store for us then."

"Enjoy. Let's see what Superintendent of Police Timothy Marsh has to say for himself then," Nancy said.

Her eyes met Pole's. There was only defiance and humour in them – somewhat reassuring to Pole.

* * *

Henry was sitting back in his uncomfortable chair, rocking on its back legs. Pole's coffee had been drunk long ago and he was craving more. He had completed the financial model that was about to reveal which banks had moved their LIBOR submission artificially. It had started to churn from live data at 9.17 AM. Henry looked around the room for the first time, a drab little place not so dissimilar to the cell he occupied at HMP Belmarsh apart from the larger size and the lack of a window. Pole could have at least provided him with a coffee machine; he was not asking for The Ritz.

The door opened letting in a draught of much needed fresh air. Henry did not bother to look at who had come in. He wanted to strike the right note and was still appraising his handiwork. Pole had been daring in choosing Nancy as a consultant when Henry's case had turned nasty. Granted he evidently had a soft spot for the lady but this was not the sole reason. Nancy had proved to be an asset to The Yard. If Henry could prove to be an asset too, the plan would work.

A cup of fresh coffee materialised on his desk and the refined scent of Nancy's perfume announced his friend. Her face looked even more tired than his own.

"I know what you are going to say. I should have thought twice before stepping into the world of crime again."

Henry stood up and brought a second chair close to his. Nancy deserved more attention than he had given her recently. He could never take her for granted. Her face had sagged a little and her high cheekbones that made her face so attractive had become more pronounced. He had not seen the deep lines etched on her forehead since the days of his trial.

Henry's prosecution had been more than just facing accusations that made him a monster. He had had to face the cost of betrayal. Yet, she had never shied away from her commitment to helping him.

"I would never criticise you for believing in someone, perhaps too much," Henry said as she sat next to him.

"You don't have to do it, Henry. I am quite capable of doing this to myself."

Henry took his cup of coffee and stirred in some sugar. "Friendship takes two things to be called just that, I discovered at my own expense – time and obstacles."

"You are so right and I know this too. I even take pride at being a good judge of characters but this time, well …" Nancy closed her eyes and sighed.

"You shouldn't regret fighting for the causes you believe in."

"Perhaps, but I will not advance the female cause by backing the wrong sort. It will do ten times more damage."

"Still, damn sight nobler than the IRA. Although of course, when I was part of it, it never felt that way."

The door banged open, interrupting their conversation. Pole walked in, took a chair, turned it around and straddled it to sit down.

"Your friend's in the clear," he said, crossing his legs underneath his seat.

Nancy's body straightened up a little.

"James-Jones not in the frame then?"

"Don't rub it in Henry, please," Nancy said with a mix of impatience and tiredness.

Henry's face dropped. "Sorry, I did not mean it that way."

"How did you get that name anyway?" Pole asked, pleased at the rebuff.

"Bank of England involved, Edwina main speaker at the conference where Gary's killed and," Henry hesitated. "Nancy upset, so —"

"How do you know she is not involved?" Nancy asked, invigorated by the news.

"Her alibi stacks up for Gary. Still need to check CCTV cameras but she was speaking to a lot of people so we'll get there. For Tom, she was working until late with one of the sub-committees she chairs. Again, we'll check but there are CCTV cameras everywhere around the Bank of England, so difficult to slip out without being seen."

"Accomplice?" Nancy forced herself to ask. Her hand clenched slightly. Only a few years ago this would have been a routine process. But today it felt harsh. She had yielded to a quality she had tried to ignore for too long, compassion. She had no regrets.

"Don't think so," Pole said. "She is scared not of being caught but because she thinks she is next."

"I know you are going to tell me I am a smart-arse but don't you think she would have been done by now?" Henry ventured.

"Your point?" Pole shot back.

"What if someone is trying to save Edwina's bacon?"

"Henry has a point." Nancy nodded.

Pole stood up slowly. "Right. Let's have another conversation with Ms James-Jones. Nancy, care to join?"

* * *

Pole and Nancy were retracing their steps towards the rooms on the upper floors.

"Whether we like it or not, Henry has a point."

Pole grunted. "How was your pow-wow with Marsh?"

"Predictable – a lot of ego management; I'm not sure I delivered." Nancy shuddered.

"I sincerely hope we can nail this one before he knows about William." Nancy reached for her shoulders and pressed hard on them. She needed to relieve some of the unbearable tension. She stopped and leaned against the wall for a second. "I'll be fine," she said anticipating Pole's concern.

"You should speak to Gabriel, her number two. He understands better than anybody the politics around Edwina's job at the Bank of England, perhaps even better than Eddie herself," Nancy said still massaging her neck.

"We did speak to him after Gary's jump. Remind me. What does he do exactly?"

"He has been working with her for over ten years. His father was a diplomat with, I believe, a long stint in the Middle East. He speaks quite a few foreign languages – Arabic, Farsi as well. Very bright young man."

"Why is he so faithful to her?" Pole had stopped walking.

"I can only guess but his appearance makes him a little shy of crowds."

"He is the guy with a scar on his face," Pole said, his memory jolted. "What happened?"

"No idea. You need to ask Edwina. She knows and yet never speaks about it at his behest."

They started walking in silence again.

"If she gets the job, he gets a boost to his career too?" Pole asked one hand on the door handle.

"*Absolument*," Nancy said.

"*Compris*." Pole eyes had lit up with the bright spark of realisation.

* * *

She looked bewildered. Edwina had aged ten years in one hour. She answered Pole's questions in half-disjointed sentences. The ceaseless pressure to reach the top, the financial crisis and now Pole's interrogation had broken down Edwina's resilience. She would soon have to salvage what she could of her career in the LIBOR manipulation scandal that was about to explode.

Nancy sat on the other side of the tinted glass, anger gradually replaced by sympathy.

What a fool. But she still felt raw, disappointed not so much for herself but for all the other women who had taken Eddie for the perfect role model.

Some of Edwina's answers drew Nancy back to the room in which she was sitting. Of course, her elevation benefited Gabriel. Of course, he was at the conference, he is her right-hand man and, yes, he has the same alibi as her on the day of Tom's murder.

"Could he have left for a few hours?" Pole was prodding.

Edwina seemed less shocked than Nancy would have expected by the implications of the question. She was thinking hard. Yet she was not willing to give up on Gabriel just to keep Pole at bay.

"We worked separately on certain issues." Edwina hesitated.

Pole was on the attack again. "Why is Gabriel not in the running for the Governor's job?"

Nancy winced. It was a slap in the face.

"You mean because he is a bloke?" Edwina blue eyes had turned dark, her brows were knitted so tight they almost touched one another.

"No," Pole was not letting go. "Because he is just as good as you are."

"Point taken," Nancy murmured.

"He is not comfortable with large audiences and certainly not with the prospect of fielding press conferences."

She had refused so far to talk about the scar, a pledge to him?

"But if you're sacked because of LIBOR, he goes down with you?"

Edwina's face changed once more. Reality had sunk in – hard, raw, unbearable. Her left hand travelled to her stomach. For a moment Nancy thought she was going to be sick.

"Yes, if I go, he goes." It had been softly spoken, a whisper.

Pole had stopped the savaging. He pushed the untouched glass of water towards her. Edwina took a sip and put it down with a trembling hand. She now knew.

It was over for her.

"But he can get a job anywhere."

Pole had sat back in his chair, considering. Nancy saw from the tilt of his head she knew so well that he was running with a new line of thought.

He terminated the interview and let one of his team process Edwina.

"She is not telling me everything." Pole had joined Nancy in the viewing room. "Stay with her but don't do anything —"

"Silly." Nancy managed a faint smile.

Pole was so close. He could put his arms around her and pull her to his chest. But he mustn't.

"I'll get to the truth," Nancy nodded, breaking the moment. She too never took no for an answer.

Pole had no time to reply. His mobile was buzzing urgently. His face said it all – Emergency.

"St Thomas's – Is he all right?"

Nancy sat down abruptly, her eyes wide with worry. William had been targeted again.

"He is fine but whoever has targeted him has given my guys the slip. I'm going." Pole squeezed her shoulder with all the affection he could muster.

"Careful too," she managed to articulate.

"Always – you need to go to Edwina."

"Yes, of course."

Pole disappeared but Nancy was still sitting. She shook herself out of her slumber. Edwina would be out soon.

Nancy retraced her steps and entered the room in which Henry was still working.

"Don't ask please, no time, but can you find all you can on Gabriel Steel?"

She was already on her way. She stopped, turned back and laid a burner phone on his desk.

"Call me – my number is there under my name. The phone won't lock."

Henry gave her an approving look. This woman was the business.

Chapter Twenty-Two

This morning

Brett reread the text and threw the mobile on the sofa. It had spoilt a perfectly good breakfast – full English this Saturday morning accompanied by an excellent cup of Jamaican Blue Mountain coffee.

MI6-Steve had been *crystal clear*, as he put it. Do whatever they ask you to do – sound reluctant if you think it will work better but facilitate. Brett had given up asking why. Yet today he felt he deserved a bit more of an explanation. The Sheik had proven to be an unexpected cross between Jihadist and shrewd businessman. He almost certainly despised Brett and would eventually seek to do away with him.

9am

Brett texted back. He would walk towards Harrods at nine this morning, a man would bump into him, lift his wallet and escape on a scooter with his accomplice. Brett would report it two hours later. The card he used to enter The Royal Exchange building would be in his wallet. He would also leave a message with the firm that employed him as an art consultant but, because today was a Saturday, they would not pick up the message until Monday morning. Credible enough, he thought. Brett sent a message to Steve from his other mobile. He took his cup of coffee and looked through the window of his lounge. He was high enough to see the tree tops of Eaton Square. A name entered his mind and he smiled. One thing was certain. Crowne would not be enjoying a leisurely breakfast this morning. Brett moved from the window to his kitchen and poured the reminder of the coffee into his cup. That thought made his final cuppa delicious.

* * *

They had not exchanged a word. Edwina collected her personal effects and Nancy waited with an odd sense of déjà vu. She had waited at this exact same desk for Henry after his first interrogation. But this time she hoped she would not have to assemble a defence team for Edwina.

Edwina averted her gaze. Slinging her small rucksack over her shoulder she spoke to Nancy in a murmur.

"I must go back to the Bank of England – now."

"Let me come with you."

Edwina hesitated but she did not have the strength to say no.

"I need to check – to be sure."

Nancy nodded. They walked out and she hailed a cab. As she entered the cab Nancy felt someone was staring at her but she had no time to look around. Edwina was already telling her her story. Gabriel had changed, perhaps in small increments she had not noticed until she could not ignore it any longer: a new gym craze she never thought he had, holidays booked at the last minute and not mentioned. Edwina had found an online airline ticket to Turkey – he always spoke about his holidays: trekking the Himalayas, walking the trail to Machu Picchu. *I live to travel* was his motto.

Edwina's face had become animated as she spoke about the details that had been haunting her for days. There was also Gabriel's detachment over the death of Gary and Tom, the lack of concern over her own safety, let alone his.

The keys jingled in Edwina's hand. They never left her key ring. She fished around for a little parcel in her top drawer. She handed it to Nancy. Nancy's phone was ringing before she could unfold the paper to reveal its contents. Henry was calling.

"Two things I managed to unearth, but not verified —"

"Never mind that, tell me."

"When his father was UK ambassador to Saudi Arabia, Gabriel got very interested in the Salafist movement – Don't ask me how I got that."

"And number two," Nancy said.

"He and his brother were caught in the 1998 Nairobi attack on the US embassy. His brother lost his life and he got badly injured. Nancy, where are you?"

"Bank of England – will call you later."

She had delayed contacting Pole. Edwina might not share her findings if she called him too early. Nancy unfolded the scrap of paper Edwina had handed over to her. She carefully retrieved the smooth and oblong object, held it between her thumb and index finger: a little blue pill similar in size and colour to the one Yvonne had shown her.

"Where did you get that from?" Nancy asked.

"Gabriel's desk," Edwina said. "What does that mean Nancy? I can't think anymore."

"One thing I am sure of Eddie. It's time to call Pole." Nancy reached for her BlackBerry. She could see its black corner sticking out from underneath a piece of paper Edwina had just moved. Her hand was hovering when she saw the expression of terror on Edwina's face.

"Good morning ladies." Gabriel walked through the door. He had a gun.

* * *

The young policewoman looked exhausted. She was at the end of her shift. Brett couldn't believe his luck. She took his statement. Theft of a wallet.

"Would you be able to recognise the assailant?"

"Not really, they were on a scooter." Brett did not lie. He did not need to.

"Any valuables in the wallet?"

"The usual, credit cards, some cash and – oh yes, my office ID card."

It was all finished in less than fifteen minutes. He texted Mohammed – *Done*. Now the clock was ticking.

* * *

The burner phone rings. Henry casts an eye towards it. Maybe he should let it go to voicemail? Nancy almost hung up on him the last time he phoned her to give her some goddamned good intel. Still, Henry grabs the phone with a swift movement and presses the green button. He is waiting to hear Nancy's voice and has already prepared some flippant comment but the occasion does not materialise. There is a rustling noise, paper being moved, then voices two … no three: one man, two women and one of them is Nancy's.

Henry feels a cold sweat coming over him. He has moved in the danger zone of equity trading and spent enough time in prison to know that something is badly wrong. He cradles the phone in the palm of his hand. He mustn't hang up.

"Move away from the desk – hands on heads," the man's voice says.

"Gabs, what are you doing?"

"That is a really stupid question coming from a top-notch banker like you Eddie," the voice carries on.

Henry makes sure the phone is now on mute. He must reach Pole.

* * *

As Gabriel makes his grand entrance, Nancy hits the call button. She prays Gabriel does not find the phone, otherwise …

Gabriel's face is drawn, his eyes glitter with fever – he has not slept for a while. He has moved slowly towards the desk so that Edwina and Nancy have retreated to the far end of the room. Their hands are resting on their heads. Nancy is slow and deliberate. She does not want to stumble. It is not the first time she has had a gun pointed towards her. She gives a discreet look in Edwina's direction. She is doing much better than she thought she would. She can see the struggle on her face, moving from anger to fear. A vein pulses in her neck and her jaw is clenching so hard, Nancy can almost hear the gritted teeth.

Gabriel is now at the desk. He is fumbling around the drawers. His back has turned against the large windows, his face in the shadows. Nancy's focus has moved from his face to the gun. It glimmers in the sun that has come suddenly through the window.

"Where is the key to your desk?"

Edwina stays silent. "I will shoot you Eddie, if that's what you're wondering – and Nancy. Teach you to be such a nosy bitch."

"Desk is open," Edwina's voice is a little croaky but no longer scared. Gabriel looks at the desk. He is thinking. Nancy measures what it will take to stop him. There is nothing heavy enough. She follows Edwina's glance, a small letter opener on the side of the desk, hardly visible to someone who does not know it is there.

Gabriel moves towards the door and points the gun at Edwina.

"Go to my desk, get the black gym bag underneath it – any funny business and I shoot her," his head jerks towards Nancy. Edwina moves slowly, hands still over her head. Nancy moves towards the desk very slowly too but Gabriel has noticed.

"You stay where you are. You move and you get it in the stomach – very painful I've been told."

"Why?" Nancy puts on her you're-so-bright-why-are-you-doing-this look.

450

"You're not in court any longer. Don't try that lawyer bullshit with me," Gabriel speaks with disdain. He has both women in his firing range. They need some time.

"I'm not, but if I am going to die I'd like to know why."

Edwina is back with his gym bag. She drops it in the centre of the room and moves back to her original place.

"Not so fast – go to your desk, slow and easy," Gabriel is enjoying his moment. "Good girl – open the second drawer on your right. There is an envelope stuck to the inside."

Edwina moves as slow as she possibly can. She sits, opens the drawer and drags every move she makes. She too has realised that time is on their side. The envelope is well concealed. She fumbles.

Gabriel is impatient, but she convincingly looks clumsy. The packet comes loose. She retrieves it, walks slowly to where the sports bag lies and drops the packet onto it.

"Is it about your brother?" Not Nancy's best-phrased question she knows but she has to try.

Gabriel reaches mechanically to his scar. His finger is tight on the trigger.

"How do you know?"

Nancy explains.

A few precious minutes to save their lives?

* * *

The floor on which William is recovering is swarming with police. Pole pushes his way through to find Detective Constable Todd. Andy's face is starting to swell up. He is going to end up with a decent black eye.

"I am impressed," says Pole. "Did you manage to see the guy?"

"He got me from behind and knocked my glasses off," Andy slurs with a pack of ice on his cheek. "But I've got something else for you, Guv. "

His laptop is on the chair next to him. Pole sits down and helps his DC by holding it open for him.

"You remember that program – face recognition," Andy sucks in some saliva from the corner of his mouth. "I found a match that does not tally. "

He gets to the image of a young man, medium-build, fair-brown hair and a nasty scar across his face. "He was not on the guest list." And the image shows the man speaking to Felipe Martinez.

"You've done brilliantly," Pole says standing up with a jolt.

"But," Andy struggles. "I don't have his name yet."

"And I do," Pole says already halfway down the corridor. He is calling Nancy but her phone is engaged. His phone buzzes back and Pole answers before checking the caller.

"When were you going to tell me about William Noble?" Marsh asks. His voice is calm but the undertone furious.

Pole's mind goes blank for a second – shit; he was not expecting this. He has no time to reply anyway. Marsh wants him back at The Yard, now – Pole's phone goes dead.

Pole is back in his car, siren screaming, dialling hands free. "Nurani, are you at base?" Pole goes through a pedestrian crossing that flashes green. "I know Marsh is looking for me." He can't get angry with her. He needs her to save time with Marsh. "Check with Crowne. If he has anything good I will need it. Yep, I need a very large bone to throw Marsh."

The door opens and Henry turns. He recognises Pole's deputy as she approaches his desk. Henry's face must say it all as she freezes. She sees the burner phone in Henry's hand. The phone is on loudspeaker and she can hear Nancy's voice.

"She's at the Bank of England with Edwina. Gabriel – I mean Edwina's aide, is with them and he has a gun." Henry nods.

Nurani grabs her own phone and calls her boss.

"Hostage situation?" Pole's focus is absolute. "Get to Marsh and tell him what you know."

"You need me," Henry grabs Nurani's phone from her. "Inspector Pole – I know the bank's layout. I know where they are."

"You're on."

Pole hangs up and is already on the phone to SO19, the Met Specialist Firearms Unit.

Pole is running. He is speaking to Commander Ferguson. He crashes into Scotland Yard whilst agreeing an intervention protocol with Ferguson. He meets Nurani in the corridor.

"I'll deal with Marsh," she says before he has time to ask. "I'll delay as much as I can."

Pole nods. It is good to have the old Nurani back at last.

He runs into Henry's room and signals Henry to follow him.

"He is with me," Pole says to the bemused prison officers who see Henry walk free from the room, which they have guarded all day. One of them opens his mouth to speak. Pole is already at the end of the corridor with Henry in tow. He pushes Henry into the lift, still listening to what is being said on the burner phone.

"Nobody moves until I arrive. I'll be there in fifteen minutes," Pole gives his final instruction to Ferguson. Another caller is trying to reach him, Superintendent Marsh. Pole ignores him.

* * *

The siren is screaming at the traffic. Pole is leaning forward, hoping it will make the car move faster. Henry has cranked up the volume of the phone as high as it will go. He too is bent forward but his ear is to the phone trying to follow the conversation above the noise of the siren.

"How do you know?" Gabriel says.

"I noticed you and was interested to know who Eddie was working with," Nancy lies convincingly. Gabriel thinks she is a meddler; let him think. "You looked so protective of her."

Gabriel ignores the compliment. "What do you know?"

"That your brother died during the US embassy bombing in Nairobi in 1998," Nancy speaks slowly. She is factual. Gabriel does not want pity.

"Is that it?" Gabriel is stirred up enough by the memories that won't go away. "Are you not forgetting something?" Gabriel's face is ashen and the redness of its scar almost unbearably fresh. He is on the brink. Nancy hesitates. "Your face?"

"That – and the rest of my body," he yells. "Moronic Yanks. They think they know better, can do better than anybody else. Reality is not Hollywood. These fucks think they can blast their way around the world – Vietnam, Somalia, Afghanistan, Iraq ..." He is ranting, fact and grudge intricately mixed. "They interfere with people they don't understand. Always more money, more power. And what does our pathetic government do? It follows – because we have a special relationship." Gabriel has adopted a derisory tone. He gestures and for an instant his gun is out of focus.

Nancy sees it now. It's all about revenge – not justice or fairness. She has seen it so often. "You blame the British for what happened?"

"Who else? Who else could be so incompetent?"

Nancy keeps talking, keeps asking. She has seen Edwina move ever so slightly towards the desk, towards the paper knife.

"You think you can change the course of events if you are at the top of the Bank of England? Economic policy can be a powerful tool."

"Who says I am interested in economics?" Gabriel takes a step back. His face has changed again. His eyes bore into Nancy. He has been waiting for this moment since he entered Edwina's office. Edwina grabs the knife and lunges forward.

The sound of a firearm discharge shatters the entire room.

* * *

The siren has been turned off as he charges down Poultry. Pole screeches to a stop. Gabriel is still rambling – US embassy, Nairobi …

Keep talking.

Pole enters the main hall. The security guard slowly raises his head from his newspaper. Pole flashes his ID.

"We have a hostage situation, Edwina James-Jones – SO19 on their way."

The guard's face takes an extra few seconds to react. It is not the Saturday he was expecting at the Bank.

Pole's phone rings. ETA, seven minutes.

Henry has been listening to the conversation. He nods negatively. "I think Nancy is running short of ideas."

"Shit." Pole looks at his watch: seven minutes.

Too long.

"Where is Edwina's office?"

"Fifth floor, corner left – lifts very close." Henry says, facing the security guard for confirmation. "Right," he says, snapping his fingers at the guard.

"Right."

"Is there a service elevator?" Pole is already moving towards the back of the building. The security guard finally springs into action. "Yes, and you won't be heard when you arrive. You'll need my pass." Pole runs towards the other lift, Henry alongside him. They head for the fifth floor.

"You should not be here."

"No one is going to cry if a terrorist banker gets done trying to stop another terrorist banker."

"Don't be an arse – Nancy will never speak to me again."

Henry has nothing to say to that. Blast! Pole has finally shut him up.

The door of the lift opens with a soft ping that sounds deafening to both men. They hold their breath. The guard was right – they are at the other end of the building. A couple of doors separate them from Edwina's office.

Nancy has asked another question.

Keep talking please … Pole opens the first door softly, a short walk, the second door. He can hear voices. Henry indicates with his hand a right turn, then a left. "If the door is open, the corridor will be partially visible – our best bet is to crawl alongside the windows," Henry murmurs.

Pole nods. It's time to switch off the burner phone. Henry hesitates. Pole grabs it and presses the red button. He turns away abruptly so Henry cannot see the dread on his face.

Pole is in front. He can see the door of Edwina's office and movement. Gabriel is well positioned to survey the corridor. They have to crawl their way to the windows. Henry gives Pole the thumbs up. He will do anything now to get to Nancy. So close and yet so far.

Pole is at the window. He can hear Gabriel's voice distinctly.

"Eddie, this is a stupid idea," he says, ironic.

The sound of a firearm discharge shatters the entire room.

* * *

Pole jumps through the door, ready to slam Gabriel. But the man is already down, half of his skull shattered, the unmistakable smell of blood seeping into the air. Henry is at the door too, frozen by the sight. Pole is about to rush towards Nancy when he notices a floating red dot that hovers across Gabriel's back.

"Shooter," Pole screams. He lunges towards Edwina, who is closer to him, and drags her to the ground. Henry pulls Nancy behind a filing cabinet and they both drop to the floor. Pole is on his mobile to the SO19 commander.

"What the fuck are you doing, Ferguson? Who told you you could shoot?" Pole is beside himself. He is still sheltering Edwina with his body, but the red dot has disappeared. He turns his head towards Nancy as he speaks to Commander Ferguson. She mouths *I am OK.* Pole's attention reverts to the man on the floor. He squeezes his phone between his ear and his shoulder. Pole is about to move forward when he stops.

"What do you mean your team is not yet in position at The Royal Exchange?" Pole signals everyone to pull back. "Shit, we have a rogue shooter. Understood, we are not moving until you've secured the area."

Chapter Twenty-Three

Brett picked up the morning papers at his Club but nothing could distract his mind. Why had MI6-Steve insisted they meet again so quickly? Brett had sent a secure email to him reporting the wallet trick as agreed.

Steve materialised in front of his chair forcing him to drop his paper. And his handler finally looked worried. Brett removed his glasses with a nonchalant hand.

"What's up my dear fellow?" Brett asked, his eyes catching those of one of the butlers.

"Your wallet."

"What about it? I told you I have reported it as agreed."

MI6-Steve plonked himself into an armchair. "The content, I mean your pass, has been used already. Is it too early for a glass of something"

"Never too early." Brett ordered two Glenlivets, no ice.

"The Sheik has used his new operative. The Royal Exchange – this morning."

"You mean?"

"Yes, at least one man – dead."

Brett looked towards the bar. Where was the goddamned whisky? He stuck a finger into his shirt collar and moved the tie away from his neck.

"You're not in the frame, if that is what's worrying you." Steve was also looking at the bar with impatience.

"Really? I'd like to be sure of that. Who is – was this chap anyway?"

"You don't need to know —"

Brett interrupted before Steve gave him more rubbish about the need to know basis.

"You don't get it, Steve. I am certain The Sheik showed me his photo when I went to see him."

Two whiskies had materialised. Steve finished his first. "You need to play your cards even closer to your chest."

"Closer than I do already and those cards will be tattooed to this famous chest of mine."

Steve ignored the humour. "You're about to move centre stage according to our latest intel. Don't worry about what you hear or read on the news. We manage the flow of information. Your main concern is to keep The Sheik happy – whatever it takes."

"What's in it for me apart from staying alive?"

Steve paused. He had not expected this. His little beady eyes flashed with amusement. "You pull this one off and you won't have to see me or MI6 ever again."

Brett remained poker-faced. "Righto, and you have the authority?" Brett waved at the butler again. He did not wait for Steve's answer. "One condition – what did the man in the picture do?"

Steve pushed himself back in his armchair, fingertips touching and hands in front of his chin. "He had infiltrated the Bank of England but —"

"He did not quite deliver," Brett finished.

The whiskies arrived and Brett raised his glass to Steve. Something he had thought he would never do.

* * *

The deflated atmosphere was palpable. Henry, Nancy and Pole were holding their cups of tea the way a child might hold his blankie.

A ringing noise came from the computer. Henry cast an eye towards it. There was no point now but Pole welcomed the change of subject. "What's the verdict on the banks?"

Henry raised an eyebrow but Pole looked serious. He turned towards the screen and read aloud: Barclays, RBS, Lloyds, Deutsche Bank, UBS, GL.

The last name brought Nancy back to life. "You're sure?"

"Well, this is my first stab at it but I'm pretty certain that those guys have been up to no good. Not that it is relevant now."

"Not so – LIBOR is still at the centre of this investigation. Edwina got far too involved." Pole's voice had an edge Nancy had rarely heard.

"Edwina won't survive that scandal," Nancy said. It may not appease Pole but it might go some way to releasing his anger. "I wonder whether Gabriel had pushed to get the deal with the banks done too."

"Ambition always gets out of hand," Henry spoke without resentment. "And I should know."

Nancy managed a smile. She turned towards Pole. "What was in the sports bag?"

"A couple of passports under different names, airline ticket to Turkey —"

"Gabriel was on his way to the Middle East?"

"Almost certainly. I am not sure why he was silenced yet. The team is going through the lot: computer, phone, flat. I have the feeling though that we were not the first ones there."

They returned to their tea for a short moment, each retreating into their own thoughts. Henry broke the silence.

"It would have been an incredible tool for market manipulation or money laundering if a group had unfettered access to the Bank of England Top Management." Henry's voice trails. The thought is both chilling and exciting.

"You mean a terrorist organisation?" Nancy asks.

"Far-fetched." Pole shrugs.

"No," Nancy and Henry reply in unison.

Pole's mobile rang. Belmarsh's van had arrived. Henry's fist tightened around his teacup.

They stood up. Nancy hugged Henry warmly. She didn't care. Pole stretched out his hand, "Thank you." Such a small but important phrase. The door opened. It was time.

* * *

Green Park is bustling with activity. A pink fireball, aged six, is on a collision course with Nancy. The future Olympian is not looking where she is going: her head turned back, checking whether her friends are catching up with her. Nancy moves away. The parents apologise. No harm done, not today at least. Nancy walks home. The sun shines through the thickness of the trees. It bounces off the windows of the adjacent building. She fancies an ice cream.

Pole has promised to call in the evening. She suspects it may not be to talk about LIBOR and her pulse quickens ever so slightly. The grass has not yet lost its softness. She removes her shoes and her toes dig into the lawn. An ancient memory is surfacing. Mixed emotions roll into her chest. If she had had to die on the floor of Edwina's office, she would have regretted not taking Pole's affection seriously.

Memories of China finally break free: The Cultural Revolution, her father. Not today, she is not ready.

Nancy spots a bench drenched in sunlight, unexpectedly empty. Not for long no doubt, but presently it offers her the solitude she needs. She plunges her hand in her light mac and fingers a piece of paper. The paper Henry handed her as they said goodbye. She sits down and looks at the sky. Pure blue. The weather may be kind for a while.

Nancy, dearest friend

I could not miss this occasion to write a letter that I know will only be read by you and you alone. Writing to you has been my lifeline; thank you for never giving up on me.

There is not much time and though I feel there is so much I want to say I will have to be brief. I have been restless. Not about my sentence. I deserved it. But it is about going beyond it. If it was right to make me pay for what I did, don't I somehow deserve to be given the chance to show I can change – that despite everything I am redeemable?

You will hear or see things in the next few weeks that might make you doubt me; please give me the benefit of the doubt.

You will be asked to interfere or even stop me – I beg you, don't.

You may even be told that I have killed myself or been killed. I will never let this happen.

Trust has been at the core of our friendship – believe in me one last time. I know what I must do.

Henry

BOOK THREE:
NO TURNING BACK

Prologue

The blindfold sits heavy over his eyes. Henry fights the desire to adjust it and show his apprehension. He has been led down a series of long corridors; at least they feel that way. They must be underground judging by the lingering smell of damp and mould that had puzzled him at first. The floor feels smooth underneath his feet. Someone has used strong detergent on the floor but it hasn't managed to cover the smell of decay.

By his own estimation, Henry has been sitting on this small uncomfortable chair for fifteen minutes, perhaps longer. He spreads his long fingers carefully on his thighs. He does not want to fidget or, worse, show trembling.

"Hello Henry," says a voice that sounds familiar.

He turns his head slightly. To his surprise he is not sitting directly in front of the door but side on. He does not respond.

"Do you know why you are here?"

Henry still does not answer.

"Remove the blindfold."

A pair of hands pull at the material and his eyes hurt even more. The mask comes off but Henry keeps his eyes shut.

Should he open them? If he does he will know the man's identity and there will be no turning back.

"I am here to offer you a deal … a one-off chance." The voice is smooth and convincing. It is what he has been wanting to hear since he walked through the doors of HMP Belmarsh. Henry inhales deeply and opens his eyes. The light blinds him and he jerks his head sideways, raising his right hand to protect his face. A strong spotlight has been placed above him. He need not have worried about the man's face as it's hidden in the shadows.

"Do you know why you are here?"

"Because I'm — a City banker?" He still can't bring himself to use the past tense.

"Wrong answer."

Henry's head falls imperceptibly. He will not be defeated by the shame that eats him alive every day.

"Because I'm – a terrorist?"

"That's a much better answer."

The man moves his head, indicating to the guards still standing behind Henry's chair that they can now go. His handcuffs were removed when he was pushed down on the chair. How very confident of the men who have brought him to this place.

But what could he do, deep underground in one of MI6's bunkers?

"You're growing very close to Abu Maeraka?"

Henry shrugs. "You mean Kamal?"

"Who else did you have in mind?" The man is still in the shadows. But Henry can almost distinguish his shape. He is medium height but his shoulders are impressive. He has turned away for a short moment, enough to light a cigarette and its red dot now glows at his mouth. Henry almost wishes he had taken up smoking in jail. Only cigars, of course, to celebrate the obscenely large deals he used to structure and close in his investment banking days.

Henry does not answer the man's question. He has questions of his own. "Did you get him transferred to Belmarsh?"

"Does it matter?"

Henry's throat tightens. These fuckers have been playing him all along. Anger, his old friend, grabs him again. It swells in his belly, a rumble that is familiar and exciting. Henry exploited that feeling so often when he worked in the City.

But no more.

He must stay in control. He must push away the images that haunt him: the Paddington bombing, the bodies, the smell of burning flesh and above all his cowardice.

Inhale – Exhale.

The man has moved behind him. Henry feels his proximity. Two strong hands land on his shoulders and the acrid smell of smoke assails his nostrils. The man is speaking in his ear. Henry does not understand what he is saying now … it is a foreign language, something throaty. Henry has heard it before, around him, Middle-Eastern – almost certainly Arabic.

"Have you told anyone of your plans with Abu Maeraka?" The hands have tightened and the breath in his ear becomes hotter, the fetid smell of cigarettes repulsive. Henry's fingers are digging into his thighs, his body stuck to the chair.

Powerless.

The door opens with a crash and men pour into the room: four, five – maybe more. They grab Henry's limbs; push him back into a contorted position. A damp cloth sticks to his face and water starts gushing over it. The wet cloth has become so heavy, it clings even closer to his nose, to his mouth. His breathing slows. His head is leaden. His mouth gasps desperately.

Breathe – Breathe.

His chest is about to explode and at the very last instant the man removes the cloth.

"What is your plan?" The voice is so calm.

The room has become hotter as more men come in. They jostle to tear Henry's clothes from his body and he can't move. He should run. He should resist but remains frozen.

Powerless.

The cloth comes over his face again. The water fills his nose, his lungs. This time he will drown.

He screams a noiseless scream that no one can hear.

Chapter One

Midnight, Inspector Pole stretched, moving his tall body gently so as not to disturb Nancy. He picked up his BlackBerry, scrolled down his emails. Nothing from Andy and no text either.

Promising.

He placed his hand over Nancy's and squeezed gently. She moved a little closer, rolled her face towards him slowly, "Mmmm". The music they had been listening to, a new Philip Glass piece Nancy had recently discovered, had just finished. Pole smiled. He looked at her slender body, the loose silk trousers and blouse that accentuated the curve of her waist and breasts. He turned sideways to face her more fully, resting his head on his bent arm. He squeezed her hand once more. Nancy's eyes fluttered open and she stirred with a smile.

"So sorry Jonathan." She moved one arm lazily over her head, stretched, bent her arm and facing Pole rested her hand on his shoulder.

"It's midnight after all," Pole replied. Nancy falling sleep in his company felt more like a sign of trust than boredom.

"Any news?"

"Nothing," Pole replied, placing a kiss on her hand. "In my profession no news is not always good news but tonight I —"

The unmistakable buzz of the BlackBerry interrupted him and Pole rolled his eyes. Nancy chuckled.

"Pole," he answered.

Nancy bent forward to grab the yellow notepad that now lived permanently on her coffee table and handed it to him with a ballpoint pen.

Pole started to scribble.

"Are you serious?"

The person at the other end of the phone confirmed a piece of information. Pole cast a quick eye towards Nancy. He did not like what he was hearing.

"Fine. With you in a few minutes."

Pole's interlocutor seemed in turn surprised.

"Yes, I said a few minutes. Yes, I know where this is." Pole hung up.

"Should I get ready too?"

"Body found at the entrance of the Regent's Canal – tied to a trolley."

"Is that reason enough to be calling you?" Nancy asked, dubious. "Someone's death warrants attention, of course but …"

"No, only the quirkiest cases go to your friend Pole."

"Do tell – the suspense is killing me. Metaphorically that is."

"The man has been identified as a well-known criminal, on the INTERPOL most wanted list."

"And?"

"I can't hide anything from you – he was a prolific art thief, Italian with deep mafia connections." Pole had finished tying his shoelaces. He stood up. Nancy had already sprung off the sofa and was running barefoot towards her bedroom.

"I'm grabbing a pair of shoes, be with you in two ticks. I am a consultant with the Met after all."

"But perhaps I should check first what this is all about?"

"Nonsense, Jonathan. If art is involved you know you need me."

"Do I?"

"*Absolument mon cher*," Nancy said from inside her bedroom.

Pole put on his jacket, pocketed his BlackBerry and moved towards the door. Nancy caught up with him.

"*Andiamo*." She closed the door of her apartment behind them. "Let's see what the Italian Mafia has in store for us then."

* * *

Islington High Street was teeming with people. Nightclub goers, restaurant goers, cinema buffs – an eclectic mix of age and culture that so characterised her neighbourhood.

A group of giggling girls was heading towards Camden Passage, dressed in black but each sporting angel wings on their back and headbands with flashing bobbles – a hen party going to The Ladybird Bar, no doubt.

Nancy was walking alongside Pole watching his determined pace.

He had placed himself between Nancy and the pavement kerb as any gentleman worthy of the name would do. She recalled the first time one of her older colleague in Chambers had walked in this way and offered her an explanation.

In the days when pavements were either small or simply non-existent, a gentleman would walk between the lady he accompanied and the road, shielding her from the splashes of mud, soiled water or sometimes worse. Nancy smiled but said nothing.

She slowed down to let a couple of Punk men, complete with Mowhawks and safety pins, cross before her, losing a little ground to Pole.

He was already focused on the case. He had called the officer on site to request the pathologist he trusted and her team. Yvonne Butler might not be available but someone in her team would be. He stopped abruptly as they were approaching the canal from behind the Angel.

"I am sorry – was I going too fast?" Pole's face was hardly visible in the shadows of the night but Nancy could see the lines of his forehead gathered close together.

"Don't flatter yourself, Jonathan. You'll never be too fast for me."

Pole laughed softly and brushed a strand of hair away from Nancy's cheek.

"Are you ready for it? It won't be pretty."

Nancy rolled her eyes but smiled. "Jonathan, I am not the squeamish type. I could not have done all those years at the Bar if I had been. And in any case we ate our dinner some hours ago."

Pole did not move, for a moment unconvinced by this show of bravado. But Nancy had seen her fair share of nastiness. She would somehow cope with whatever the canal was about to reveal.

The musty smell of all but stagnant water told them they were near. Nancy recognised the stairs that led from Colebrooke Row to the water's edge. Already a couple of police cars were parked near the steps. A few passers-by had gathered, together with residents concerned or curious about the latest disturbance.

Pole flashed his ID as he approached the uniformed police. "Good evening officer."

"Good evening Sir, PC Leonard, Sir," the young woman said, glancing a suspicious eye towards Nancy.

"Ms Wu is with me. She consults for the Met."

The young police constable moved sideways. She nodded towards the towpath.

"Not a pretty sight, Sir."

Pole stopped at the top of the stairs, looking down on the scene. He hesitated.

"How bad is it?" Nancy asked with an even voice.

"He has been – beheaded." The young woman shuddered.

"Is it your first time at a crime scene, PC Leonard?" Pole asked kindly.

"No, Sir, but I haven't come across one of these before," she said moving her head towards the canal. "And they left his wallet in his jacket pocket – nothing stolen."

"So not a robbery gone wrong then?"

"Doesn't look like it —" PC Leonard was interrupted by the static of her radio. "Yes, he has arrived, Sir."

Pole thanked her and turned towards Nancy.

"I'll be fine, really." Nancy's voice had lost a little of its assurance but she would not backtrack and let him down now. Pole nodded.

The body had been covered up with a blanket. Pole walked towards it and, crouching, lifted its corner carefully. He pulled back slightly but forced himself to inspect the corpse thoroughly. He let the blanket fall back and stood up, his tall body towering over the dead man. He looked at Nancy standing only a few feet away and shook his head.

"You don't need to see that," Pole said with kind determination.

Nancy hesitated; the protest she had prepared stuck in her throat.

"This is butchery – an execution."

"And the fact that whoever has done this has not bothered to hide it, is what? A warning?" Nancy offered, relieved she could direct the conversation away from the body itself.

"Almost certainly."

"Who is the victim? You said he was on the INTERPOL most wanted list. Strange to be found in the middle of Islington, *non*?"

"*Très bonne question*, as ever."

"Good evening Guv. Good evening Ms Wu." Pole was interrupted by a young man in thick glasses.

"Nice to see you again, Andy." Nancy extended her hand and DS Todd shook it awkwardly. The light was bad but she could have sworn she saw reddening cheeks.

"Massimo Visconti, Italian from Venice, established a reputation as an inventive art thief, organised a number of high-profile heists, caught as the result of a tip-off and managed to escape before serving his sentence." Andy was reading from his notebook. Pole cleared his throat. "Sorry Guv,

I thought Nancy, I mean Ms Wu, would want to know the details."

"I do indeed but I think your boss is more interested in what you might know already about the murder – weapon used, witnesses, that kind of thing."

"Right, right," Andy delved into his notebook again. "Got the name of the guy who found the body, he was walking his dogs; actually, the dogs found the body. As for the weapon, we are still looking – we have a team doing a fingertip search of the area —"

A series of calls interrupted Andy; something had been found.

The three of them moved swiftly towards a part of the towpath covered by undergrowth and empty bottles discarded thoughtlessly. An officer was flashing his torch in the direction of a piece of metal that shone in the light, his long stick pulling back branches to keep it in sight.

"It's a large knife," Andy said flashing his own light on it. "And there is a lot of blood on it."

Nancy moved closer and shone the small torch she had borrowed from Andy on the knife that had been dumped in the undergrowth.

"OK, well done: bag it, send it to the lab – you know the drill," Pole said, moving away to look in the opposite direction. "Forensics have arrived – Yvonne." Pole waved.

Nancy ran the beam up and down the part of the weapon that was visible. She gave Andy his torch back.

"Is it a knife? I'm not so sure …"

Pole joined her and for a moment the pronounced features of his face in the shadows looked grotesque. "Let's see what forensics has to say. You remember Yvonne, don't you?"

Nancy smiled "Absolutely. No one would forget Yvonne."

"Come on, what's on that great mind of yours?" Pole asked before they reached the team in white protective overalls waiting for them at the bottom of the canal steps.

"It's not a large knife, Jonathan. It's a short sword, probably antique by the look of the decorations I saw on the hilt. And I think I have seen something very similar once before."

* * *

The laptop was still open on his coffee table. Brett cast an eye towards the ornate XVII century French clock sitting on the fireplace mantelpiece – it was gone 1am. He had almost finished the report he was writing for his minder. MI6-Steve had been clear: a report every time he met The Sheik.

Brett looked at his empty whisky glass, hesitated then shrugged. He only had a few words to add. A final glass of the amber liquid would do no harm. He stood up, walked to the small bar absent-mindedly swinging the elegant tumbler from the tip of his fingers. He ran his hand over a stylish bottle. His lips arched in the type of smile he had not had for a long while.

The unexpected outcome of dealing with the requests of his latest client was the ridiculously large sums of money he was prepared to pay. Brett opened the bottle and poured a generous measure into the thick crystal glass, enough to appreciate it, but not enough to be called greedy. At £2,500 a bottle, this forty-year-old Highland Park had to be savoured.

The ping of an email interrupted him. He screwed the top of the bottle back on with an irritated gesture.

An email at this hour, on his hyper-secure MI6 laptop, did not bode well. Brett moved back to the seat he had abandoned to recharge his glass, sat down heavily and opened the message.

"Massimo Visconti is dead – let's meet tomorrow, 8am."

Brett sagged back into his leather sofa, his throat so tight he could hear the laboured sound of his own breathing. He looked at his glass and pushed it away.

"Visconti dead," he murmured several times, forcing himself to hear the words. The Master of Thieves, dead.

Brett had entered the world of art theft, dealing with terrorists from the Middle-East knowingly, yet his sense of British superiority had convinced him he would always prevail.

With Visconti's death, the solid rock on which that certainty was built had just been chipped – a small but noticeable chip.

Chapter Two

The shrill sound of a bell interrupted his sleep. He tried to push it away but its persistence told him he could no longer ignore it. The memory of a nightmare surfaced. Henry opened his eyes and for a moment did not know where he was. He gulped in some air.

Yes, he could breathe.

The Belmarsh High Security Unit bell kept ringing. Henry moved his arm across his eyes, just one more minute to let the fog of his mind clear. He counted to thirty, turned on his side; just a few more seconds before he was ready to face the routine of washing in the small basin squeezed into the corner of his cell, collecting his breakfast from the prison canteen and starting Day 1,365 of his thirty-year sentence.

The countdown had started in 2008 and it was only mid 2012 ... Henry ran his hand over his chin, the black stubble that, to his delight, had not yet started turning grey unlike his hair, had also grown rough and uncomfortable.

Henry stretched his muscly body. He craned his neck to look at the watch he kept strapped to the head of his bed. No time to dither. Kamal would have been awake for a while, rising for his first morning prayer and now he would already be on his way to breakfast.

Henry threw back the covers, jumped into his standard prison uniform, a sad-looking tracksuit, tidied his bed and left the cell. He had twenty minutes for the morning meal and would put this time to good use.

Kamal had already settled in front of his tray, at the agreed right-angle to the canteen's door. He barely moved his head when Henry arrived. Fraternising outside allocated times was not encouraged within HSU Belmarsh. It was with good reason that the High Security Unit, a prison within a prison, had a reputation for being the most secure in the UK.

Henry moved past Kamal towards a table in the opposite corner of the room. His spoon was balancing precariously over the edge of his tray. One move sideways to avoid colliding into another inmate and it fell to the ground.

Henry grumbled. Dumping his tray on the table at which Kamal was sitting, he bent down to retrieve the wayward item of cutlery.

Kamal lifted his foot slightly, enough for Henry to place a small piece of paper underneath it. Henry shot up again, dumping the spoon on his tray in a gesture of disgust.

The prison officers would be paying him attention by now. He carried his tray to the table he had chosen, cleaned the spoon on the small paper napkin he had collected with his breakfast and started eating his porridge. The guards' attention moved to Kamal. The young man stood up, his small frame almost childlike, his demeanour reassuring.

No one meeting him would have branded him as a terrorist: the strength of his beliefs betrayed only by the intensity of the large brown eyes that observed and never yielded.

The officers relaxed. Kamal moved slowly to the conveyor belt on which he placed his tray. It disappeared into a small opening in the wall, beyond which no inmate had access.

Henry looked at his watch, 8.25am. Another five minutes and he would be returning to his cell. Big K was nowhere to be seen, preferring most mornings to take his food to his cell – a small luxury he seemed to particularly enjoy.

Henry's gym time would be coming up right after bang-up time had ended at 10am. He would catch up with Big K then. Big K's activities and connections in drug dealing had earned him the privilege of spending time at HSU. He certainly was a flight hazard and Her Majesty's Prison services were not taking any chances.

"Man, I'm so dangerous they've locked me in here." A raucous laugh would always follow. But with the kudos HSU brought, also came boredom. In his more truthful moments Big K would sit on one of the benches in the gym, towel slung over his powerful neck.

"I tell you friend, I am out of here as soon as I can get parole. I am a reformed bloke." Henry never failed to nod convincingly but could a leopard, one of the mightiest big cats, ever change his spots?

His mind drifted to another tough prison in another county. Northern Ireland Maghaberry was a harsh place. Would Liam and Bobby feel as restless as he felt? Henry pushed the thought away. It would lead him nowhere to reminisce.

Perhaps.

Henry sought to change. No, he had changed. The terrible anger that had seized him for most of his adult life had started to be channelled differently. The shock of incarceration, of having to face his involvement with the IRA, had almost destroyed him.

His brilliant banking career, which had made so many of his colleagues envious, had been damaged without any possibility of repair. No one in the world of finance ever recovered from money laundering for a terrorist organisation and so it should be.

For his part Henry was done with that world of power and excess. He was looking for something different. He needed to prove to himself that he was not the monster he had been made to feel during his trial. He had come to understand his motivations but now this was no longer enough, he wanted more. Forgiveness might never be within his reach, but he could perhaps hope to atone.

Within the confines of his prison cell, within the rarefied atmosphere of the most secure prison in the UK, how could he achieve this?

Henry pushed his empty plate away and took another quick look at his watch – 8.29am. He stood up, following in Kamal's footsteps, and made his way to Cell 14. He walked past the officers with the same amount of disinterest he had shown them whilst coming in.

Would the small piece of paper that was stuck under Kamal's shoe make it all the way to his cell? A small amount of honey, used to sweeten the tasteless porridge served daily, might do the trick and keep it glued in place. A pang of anxiety ran through Henry, accompanied with the inevitable tinge of excitement.

So far, so good it seemed. The now familiar bell rang again. Inmates were returning to their cells and when their doors clanged shut the choking silence of HSU Belmarsh fell on them again.

* * *

Henry's letter rested on her desk. Nancy touched the paper with the tip of her fingers. It was not a letter really, more a rushed note, quickly penned in the tight handwriting she knew so well, the inclination of the letters always tilting to the right and the short paragraphs developing ideas with ease.

But Henry's note had brought a chill to her heart. Nancy read it again, trying once more to decipher the hidden message within it, not yet certain of its full impact.

Nancy, dearest friend

I could not miss this occasion to write a letter that I know will only be read by you and you alone. Writing to you has been my lifeline; thank you for never giving up on me.

There is not much time and though I feel there is so much I want to say I will have to be brief. I have been restless. Not about my sentence. I deserved it. But it is about going beyond it. If it was right to make me pay for what I did, don't I somehow deserve to be given the chance to show I can change – that despite everything I am redeemable?

You will hear or see things in the next few weeks that might make you doubt me; please give me the benefit of the doubt.

You will be asked to interfere or even stop me – I beg you, don't.

You may even be told that I have killed myself or been killed. I will never let this happen.

Trust has been at the core of our friendship – believe in me one last time. I know what I must do.

Henry

Nancy ran her slender hand over the letter and left it there for a moment. She could not reply to Henry's message. It had been placed abruptly in her hand as Henry was leaving Scotland Yard for Belmarsh, his time away from the HSU having come to an end. Nancy sighed and folded the letter. The flow of a constant correspondence that had passed between them had been broken. The feeling of unease that had started gnawing at her since she had first read Henry's words had grown stronger. She could not confide in Pole. Nancy had let Pole grow closer, intimate, but that intimacy had consequences. Should she choose between her allegiances?

"No," she said replacing the letter in its folder. "Not yet."

From the time she had organised, then joined Henry's defence team almost four years ago, her support for him had been unwavering. It was love of a very special kind, not one that called for crumpled sheets and intimacy. It was the love of deep friendship, that of two people who understood each other.

There were no excuses for what Henry had done. He too was adamant that he must bear the consequences of his actions. But perhaps it was the hope that some goodness still remained, untapped, ready to be given a chance, that made him a man one could not turn away from.

Nancy had been given that chance when she had decided to move away from the Bar and concentrate on the world of art. Perhaps Henry deserved that chance too? Her BlackBerry buzzed, the vibrations spreading into the wood of her desk and into the tips of her fingers.

"*Bonjour* Jonathan; don't apologise please." Nancy smiled at Pole's protectiveness.

"It is a sword – a Mashrafiya sword."

"Let me grab my pad." Nancy stretched to dislodge a yellow pad buried under a pile of opened documents and pulled it towards her. She pressed the speaker button.

"I am very impressed." Pole's voice tilted into the base register. "You did say it looked like an antique sword and it is."

"Very glad my hobby can be put to good use."

"Do not tell me you are a specialist in Arabic artefacts?"

"Alas no, I simply test my skills religiously with the weekend FT Quiz and this name crops up regularly. I am just a bit of a snob when it comes to general knowledge." Nancy chuckled.

"I had half wondered whether this was the result of one of your cases. I couldn't quite imagine that your other passion would have got you close to such a weapon and the countries where you might find one."

"You mean the contemporary art scene?"

"*Bien sûr.*"

"You would be surprised how prolific art is in the Middle-East, daring and irreverent too – Iran, Iraq, Lebanon. The Istanbul Biennial." Nancy could summon in her mind dozens of pieces by artists she had come to know well. "These artists risk their lives for their art. *Pardon* Jonathan, I am digressing."

"Not at all but perhaps a conversation over dinner?"

"And what a good idea that is." Nancy's voice was all smiles. "Still, let's talk about the Mashrafiya now. Has Yvonne come up with anything?"

"Too early for forensic results." Pole hesitated. "I am glad you did not see the result of its use though. I have seen quite a few cuts in my time, but this was one of the worst."

"In what way?"

"Deliberately brutal." Pole's voice lost some of its colour. "Not only to the victim but to the people finding him. It was meant to shock."

"Any theory about why?"

"Nancy," Pole's voice became softer. "I am not sure you need to be involved in this one."

"Jonathan, really? I have dealt with war criminals and various other unscrupulous individuals. I don't scare easily."

"Which is precisely what scares me," Pole carried on before she could protest. "I have some news that will interest you and it involves Henry."

Nancy's mouth dropped; for a moment she could not say anything. Her throat tightened as her eyes fell on the folder that contained Henry's letter.

Had Pole guessed or, even worse, seen it?

"The SFO has been in touch with me. One of their lawyers has requested help on a case involving a suspected high-profile banking fraud."

"You mean the Serious Fraud Office?" Nancy managed to say with enough composure.

"The very same."

"Pray, tell." Nancy inhaled deeply and pushed the folder away. "They have not said very much yet, but I gather the SFO hopes to use Henry's expertise in banking and financial structuring matters. They have heard about the way Henry helped with resolving the LIBOR scandal case."

"Ah. That case has done the rounds in well-connected legal circles."

"I know. It has at The Met too. Superintendent Marsh has not stopped talking about it. It's almost embarrassing."

"You're just too humble, Jonathan." Nancy teased.

"Anyway," Pole changed subject swiftly; his personal qualities were never his favourite topic. "I would of course have recommended that you be involved but —" Pole stopped for a short moment and Nancy's heart missed a beat. She could hear the rustling of paper. "— the SFO lawyer had asked for you already. Her name is Marissa Campbell."

"*Je suis très flattée, mon cher ami.*" A little French helped defuse the anxiety of not telling the whole truth. "Both you and Marissa have thought of me." Nancy cringed. Was she sounding obsequious? "Do we need to adjourn somewhere for —"

"Lunch. *Absolument,*" Pole suggested with enthusiasm. "Our favourite place, 12pm?"

"Our favourite place it is," Nancy replied without hesitation.

* * *

The drab little office smelt of over-brewed coffee and sweat. Mark Phelps stood up, moved to the small window that overlooked an outside wall stained with the dirt that pervaded Trafalgar Square.

There was little light in the room, the only thing he could see distinctly was his reflection in the window. The investigation team had left the room. He wrapped his long arms around his body and squeezed.

His body started shaking a little, a tremor that came in short bursts and ran from his neck down to his belly. Mark moved away from the window. He had to sit down. The clock on the wall indicated 9.35am.

He had spent almost fourteen hours with the SFO team that Marissa Campbell was leading. They had offered to stop at 1am but he had too much to tell.

A draught of fresh air startled him. Marissa Campbell walked in with another two cups of bitter coffee, sugar sachets and small tubes of milk. She sat opposite Mark and pushed a cup towards him.

"You should go home," she said.

"I should. I should." Mark sipped at his coffee, eyes fixed on nothing.

"Why hesitate? You can say what's on your mind, Mark. It's only the two of us."

Mark inhaled a small gulp of air. "Is it all worth it?"

Marissa smiled a tired smile and nodded. "It's a valid question."

"Only time will tell, I guess but I'm glad I said it all straight away, otherwise I might have faltered. I still can't quite believe I'm accusing my employer of fraud. That bank is one of the largest investment banks in the City."

Mark dropped his gaze on his solid wedding band; the tan of his body made it look more noticeable. He had told Marissa his wife believed he was travelling on business.

Marissa picked up on where his eyes had fallen.

"Are you worried about your family?"

"How am I going to tell my wife I am almost certainly putting in jeopardy my lucrative career at the bank. A career I have been fostering for the past ten years?"

"Perhaps by explaining you could no longer stay silent about what you have uncovered ... She must know you are an honest man."

"I'm not sure it will be much comfort when the papers start talking about me even if they don't mention my and I become Bank X's whistle-blower."

"It is not your fault if that bank has been caught the 2008 financial crisis. And if its management has decided to save its independence by not accepting the UK government bailout, over and about saving it from collapse."

Mark stretched his body, in a half-hearted movement that felt tired. "Asking too many questioned about how far the bank was willing to go to preserve its autonomy and the method used did go down well. They'll know it is me."

"Your name will be protected. You know that?" Marissa's solid body was hunched over her cup. If she was tired, she did not show it. Her dark eyes rested on him with confidence. Mark nodded.

"Did you ever see this film with Russell Crowe ... The Insider?"

"It's the UK ... not cut-throat America."

"I'm not so sure it will make much difference. I doubt a whistle-blower in the financial sector is ever going to find a job again.""Have you spoken to Helena yet?"

The name of his wife spoken within the confines of this horrible little room took the wind out of him. He ran a weary hand over his face.

"I haven't told her yet."

Marissa nodded. She knew how hard it would be and she was not going to judge him. Mark looked grateful for her patience.

"Today. I'll tell her today."

"It is a brave decision to report your employer Mark. Remember that."

Mark nodded and moved away from the subject to one that gave him some confidence.

"How soon are you going to launch the case?"

"You mean prosecute?"

Mark nodded.

"You know how this works; it will take time, a long time."

"And what should I do in the meantime?"

"Go back home. You're tired and making a decision now is not a good idea." Marissa's broad shoulders had moved across the table a little more.

Her hands stretched over the table, reaching out to him to give Mark strength. She was there for him, an able person, a decision-maker who could keep hold of the rudder in a storm and never let go.

Mark looked out of the window, trying to gauge what the weather was like outside.

"It's fine out there; you'll be fine." She had moved away from the table, calm. Mark finally stood up, gathered his small rucksack, now empty of the folder, USB keys and CDs he had brought with him the day before.

The lightness should have been a relief, yet his hands gripped it tightly, wary. Marissa moved closer, ready to grab him if he fell.

Mark managed a smile and pushed his chair against the table. "And you are telling me you can get help from someone who understands the City well? An ex-banker you said?"

Marissa nodded.

"Oh yes. And I also know the right person to make sure he co-operates."

* * *

The taxi dropped him at the top of a small alleyway in St James's. Brett paid and left a small tip. He could not be bothered to collect a few pennies. More importantly he was keen to hear what MI6-Steve had to say about Massimo Visconti.

Brett was, for once, eager to meet his minder. That thought irritated him. Still, he had played his hand rather well so far with his latest assignment, and there was more, much more to come.

He barely acknowledged the doorman, walked straight through the club to the smoking room and let himself drop without much ado into one of the armchairs. Steve was late.

Did it mean anything?

Could The Sheik have discovered he was with MI6? Could he have discovered Steve was his minder? Could he? … Ridiculous.

Brett steadied himself. He was a Brit and Brits did not succumb to absurd paranoia; now was not the time to lose one's cool. He looked at his watch for the umpteenth time – 9.11am.

One of the waiters he knew well offered him a selection of newspapers, but he waved him off impatiently: 9.15am.

Another five minutes and I am leaving, Brett muttered, fidgeting with one of his cufflinks – 9.19am.

Brett stood up, hoping that his impatience would summon Steve. He looked in the direction of the door, hopeful.

Nothing doing.

A couple of members had stopped their conversation to give him a curious look. Brett ignored them and they quickly went back to their business. Brett sat down again abruptly. He was safe in the club and certainly less so outside. What would he do if Steve did not turn up? He had been given specific instructions to follow in this eventuality. He was trying to recall what the process was. But when Steve had spoken about the possibility, Brett had dismissed it.

Arrogance today was not his best friend.

His mobile buzzed.

Delayed, wait at Club, must speak urgently.

Brett shuddered, grateful that he had stayed. He waved at one of the waiters and ordered his usual breakfast: two eggs, boiled, two pieces of white toast, marmalade and the club's special English Breakfast tea, with whole milk. (Brett did not believe in drinking milk that did not taste like milk).

"Eggs runny, marmalade thick cut, toast slim cut. I do not like doorsteps." The waiter didn't hesitate, reassuring Brett that he was indeed among like-minded people and that his breakfast instructions would be, as ever, followed to the letter.

Steve finally arrived, sinking into the armchair opposite Brett's as Brett's breakfast was served. He waved at the waiter. "The same," he said not bothering to greet Brett nor acknowledge the man taking his order.

"That bad, is it?" Brett always enjoyed needling MI6-Steve whenever he could and yet he was relieved to see him this morning.

Steve's podgy face looked a little leaner than usual. His receding hair stood in small clumps sticking out in all directions.

His expensive suit looked out of place on his body. No doubt MI6 had indulged him with a handmade, Savile Row suit. After all, he could not meet his contact Brett in one of the most exclusive London clubs dressed in a Marks & Spencer's outfit, even a three-piece.

"I have spent the best part of this morning – and it is only just after 9am – trying to find out about Visconti's murder." Steve bent forward, elbows on knees. "All this is on account of you because —" He stopped to let the waiter serve him his breakfast. "Actually, could I also add bacon to my order?" Steve said, turning towards the gloved man … no need for please or thank you he had been told. "Not the streaky stuff but crisp."

Brett started tapping impatiently on the arm of his chair. Steve ignored him. "Where was I?" Steve added another spoonful of sugar to his tea. Brett remained silent. He ran a couple of fingers slowly over his slim moustache and waited. Unbearable, but the well-bred English gentleman in him knew how to endure pain.

"Yes. I would not want to lose one of my best assets."

"And why would you lose me?" Brett asked, slowly moving his hand towards a fresh cup of tea. His fingers rested for a moment over the delicate handle of the bone-china cup.

No, they were not shaking.

Steve grinned, uncovering a neat row of white teeth. "I am so glad you knew it was you I had in mind. Still, back to Visconti, we are now certain it was an execution, mujahideen style. So, some questions for you, old chap." Steve cracked the top of his egg open; pieces of shell scattered over his plate. He ignored the mess he had just made.

Brett inhaled deeply.

How could Steve be British and not know how to open a boiled egg with civility?

"You had some questions?"

"A couple." Steve carried on whilst buttering his toast. "First …Any inkling from your latest acquaintance?" Steve hesitated … cut his toast into two triangles and started munching.

"And the other question?" Brett asked, having not yet touched his own breakfast.

"Do you feel exposed?" Steve had been concentrating on a perfectly crisp piece of bacon until then. He put down his knife and fork and looked at Brett with unusual graveness. Brett opened his mouth, closed it again. He pushed his lanky body into the back of the comfortable leather armchair.

"Are you concerned? And for that matter should I be concerned?" His desire for humour at Steve's expense had vanished.

"Why don't you answer my first question?"

"Well, I have absolutely no idea. I might be of use to The Sheik, but I don't think he sees me as one of his buddies."

"Fair enough." Steve moved on to a second piece of toast. "There was a third photograph when you met him to arrange for his sniper to enter the Royal Exchange in London."

The bluntness with which Steve had mentioned the Royal Exchange marksman, conjuring images that even Brett had found hard to stomach, unsettled him. "There was, but as I told you he never showed me who or what it was."

Steve finished the second piece of toast, chewing the last mouthful thoughtfully. "Did you know Visconti – well, I mean?"

"You mean, rather, did I ever do business with him? Before …" Brett cleared his throat. The thought of how MI6 had managed to secure his services still rankled him. The name Henry Crowne surfaced as a bad memory linked to Brett's MI6 recruitment; it was almost nauseating.

"Yes, yes, before we got you to work for us." Steve replied with a small wave of his hand.

"His business was a little different from mine. More paintings, some of a classical nature, old masters ... then a lot of modern stuff." Brett waved his hand dismissively. "But his greatest successes were in the Middle-East. When he started in Iraq, he was the first to handle antique pieces looted from the main historical sites back in the early nineties, even the Baghdad museum – very daring and lucrative, but well before my time."

"Glad to know the thieving community benefits from its specialists too. What are you going to tell me next? You had business cards indicating that as well."

Brett ignored Steve. He was just an undiscerning East-End boy. "In short, I have not seen Visconti for years. His reputation in the market has suffered since he was caught, of course. Then again, you are the guy in the intelligence service. I am surprised your various snooping operations have not been more effective."

Steve grumbled.

"Park that question then. How about question two?"

"If you had not called me in the middle of the night to tell me about Visconti, I would have said all is well."

Steve cocked his head. "Then again, we are talking terrorists."

"So you think there a but?" Brett held his cup in mid-air.

"The very question I have been asking myself since last night. I can't think of any." Steve rested his cup of tea on his lips before taking a sip. "... And zero contact since the Royal Exchange and the transfer of Clandestine X."

"None," Brett confirmed, his jaw clenching.

Steve finished his second egg. His plate was empty and he was eyeing Brett's. Steve poured a little more tea in his cup.

Brett wondered for a short moment what it was Steve wanted to ask and yet seemed reluctant. The realisation of what it was hardly surprised Brett ... he was not done with MI6 by a long shot.

"You want me to get in touch with The Sheik to offer my services again, don't you?" Brett said calmly. He should have known that MI6 would not let the trail go cold so readily.

"Yes." Steve pushed his squeaky-clean plate aside. "We have an idea about what might draw The Sheik out."

Chapter Three

Henry had left the letter half-finished. It languished on his small desk since he had abandoned it. It was the first time that words did not come easily when writing to Nancy. Had it been a mistake to be so truthful – at least as much as he could be with his feelings? He did not fear betrayal. That she would never do.

Never.

But she might guess; she might decide – despite him asking her not to – to interfere in order to save him. Henry shook his head, a slow soulful movement.

"You've saved me already," Henry murmured.

He rolled his pen across his thumb and caught it back with his index finger before it fell off, repeating the move in a rhythmic fashion.

The decision he had made had taken hold like a plant taking root and ensnaring a tree, spreading inexorably over the many months he had spent at Belmarsh. It had felt foolish, daring, stupid, the only way, impossible: a merry-go-round of emotions.

But now he had decided he would apply his immensely skilled mind to the task. Redemption would never be found within the sterile walls of a prison cell, let alone in a unit like HSU Belmarsh in which the inmates were so well guarded that absolutely nothing could happen to them. Or so it seemed.

The arrival of Ronnie Kray had changed the balance of this rarefied world though. As crazy as it may sound, a certain Reginald Murphy had decided to change his name to Ronnie Kray by deed poll. His ambition to emulate or even surpass the deeds of his idol seemed well on track from what Henry had gathered.

Henry had started to find out at his own expense that Kray was not a man to cross. A bad joke about what Henry considered a ridiculous tattoo on Kray's back had almost cost him dear.

Today Henry, the once ambitious banker, bent over backwards not to be noticed. He wanted to blend into the crowd of HSU inmates so as to further his master plan.

Escape.

No one had ever achieved this feat before, no one – from the most notorious gangster to the most wanted Russian spy. But Henry had a plan, the first building block of which he had laid securely.

Henry pushed the letter away. He was not in the mood. He reached for his legal file and extracted from it a list he had been assembling since he had last visited Scotland Yard, the compilation of possible scandals financial or political or both, that the regulatory authorities or the Serious Fraud Office might want to investigate.

Being allowed out once more was essential for the plan to work. He must find a way, through Nancy or perhaps Pole. Henry ran his hand over his short hair. Could he stomach using his friend to achieve his purpose?

No, it would have to be Pole.

What was the price he was prepared to pay to show he could rejoin the human race? And what was the point of showing there was goodness in him if it had to be done by exploiting Nancy?

Henry stood up, irritated that the thought had entered his mind. He crossed his cell in one long stride, leaned against the wall, his back pressing against the cold surface. He needed to exercise, to burn the tension in his body, control the fire that raged in his belly.

Only thirty minutes to go before gym time. Henry removed the top of his tracksuit. The heat of exasperation had spread to his entire body. He reached his desk again and looked at the list.

– Manipulation of foreign exchange rates, also known as FX
– Insider trading; Henry had spotted some interesting movements in the stock market
– Circumvention of sanctions directed at countries on a restricted list: Iran, Iraq, North Korea
– Bribery linked to sales of armaments in the Middle-East, most likely Saudi Arabia

Henry dismissed the first two, perhaps too obvious and an overkill for the use of his remarkable mind and his knowledge of the financial markets as well as its players. The last two on the other hand were promising.

Doing business in the Middle-East had always been a complex issue for Investment Banks. Most countries in the Middle-East that respected Sharia Law would never consider interest-bearing investments such as loans or bonds but instead purchased equities, without hesitation.

The idea was to introduce an element of risk sharing between investor and client and remove the risk of punitive high interest rates. Not an entirely ridiculous idea after all: at least these investors had not been involved in the subprime market that so very nearly crashed the world markets in 2008.

Henry would be manning the HSU library for a couple of hours in the afternoon. Could he risk logging onto the computer there to access the Internet? He was allowed computer access but only to operate it as a word processor. The Internet was out of the question and so of course was email.

The prison officers, however, had different log-ins that allowed them more freedom in order to fulfil some of their duties. Henry had never even asked about Internet access. He had simply observed the place the officers' hands landed on the keyboard, the slight hesitation before entering their passwords.

Henry had spent most of his career as a banker, almost twenty years, on the trading floor of large investment banks. He had not only memorised the very special keyboard that traders used, the Bloomberg keyboard, but he also operated the standard one effortlessly. A great advantage in deciphering the passwords of the guards.

Fraternising with prisoners was discouraged within HSU Belmarsh and this suited Henry fine. The most innocent of questions might have aroused the suspicions of the highly trained officers. Courteous but distant was Henry's motto. He had cracked the last two passwords, but he was under no illusions; one day he would hit the wall either by being discovered or by not being able to good guess the passwords.

He stood up, stretched one long arm over his head, then the other and moved once more to the only part of the cell wall that was free. He stood with his back against the cool surface and let his body slowly slide down to the floor into a squat. Then he sat on the floor, crossed his legs and started breathing slowly and deeply, his latest discovery for relaxation.

His well-exercised muscles released gradually, his mind rested in stillness, thoughts floated in and out, ephemeral. A new skill that eased the anger and harnessed it, this time perhaps for good. He emerged on the other side of this ocean of stillness, rested. His mind came to and started measuring the impact of what he would need to do next – the permutations, possible outcomes – discarding what would not work in the process. His focus was complete, yet his body was relaxed. He would do what he needed to do to achieve his goal and the plan that he had honed looked solid.

Henry's mind now moved in another direction. Why had Kamal been sent to Belmarsh? Unquestionably for his terrorist's activities, but why on the same spur?

Kamal, the man who had masterminded the Paddington bombing, the very event that had almost cost Henry his life. His back tensed, his knees trembled. Henry could hear the sound of the bomb again – the barely human cries of the wounded ripping the silence of the cell apart.

Breathe in. Breathe out.

There was nowhere to go in his six-by-ten-foot box. Unlike Paddington, there was no escape, no running away.

Breathe.

Henry slowly rolled his head around. His mind floated over to a new question. One part of the equation had not revealed itself yet but his progress with Kamal meant it almost certainly would soon.

* * *

A few drops fell on her head and Marissa cursed. She had started to walk towards Scotland Yard. She needed some fresh air after an exhausting night with her key witness. Whistle-blowing was no small beer. No matter how much the law sought to protect him, Mark's life would never be the same again.

She accelerated her pace. Her umbrella was safely tucked away in one of the drawers of her desk. No chance it would get wet, unlike her.

How many years since she had left Barbados? Twenty? No, twenty-one at the end of this month. A black student attempting the impossible – to become a barrister in London. She smiled at the picture forming in her mind: the tall, almost masculine frame of a young woman arriving at Heathrow Airport, uncomfortable in the heavy clothes she had purchased for a fresh life in London.

One suitcase and one designer leather bag, brand new, purchased by the family as a farewell present. The brand was nothing too ostentatious, Mulberry, and yet instantly recognisable. It was by now well-worn but still she could not bring herself to discard it. The rain asserted itself and Marissa started to run – only a few yards to go. The pun almost made her laugh.

She entered the offices of Scotland Yard, shook herself, releasing the beads of water that had formed on her cropped hair. She no longer tried to straighten her unruly mane. Her style was clean cut, close to her skull. The security guard gave her a disapproving look. She ignored it and presented her work badge.

"I have an appointment with Inspector Pole."

The guard scrutinised her badge for longer than was necessary, switching between the photo and the face in front of him but there was nothing to be done about it – she was indeed Marissa Campbell.

"Take a seat. I will call Inspector Pole's office."

Marissa moved to the reception area where seats were arranged in a semicircle. She did not sit but instead turned towards the large bay window to watch the rain lash down in large sheets of water, almost tropical. She had never worked with Pole before but knew Nancy Wu well, a woman she admired greatly.

Despite her high-profile career Nancy had always found time to mentor students from her *alma mater*, King's College, and Marissa had been lucky enough to be one of them. Nancy had offered her pupillage when no other chambers would give her a chance; more recently, Nancy had been the only person she could confide in. The only one who knew how to listen to Marissa's anxious calls about a large case she was dealing with, without asking questions that might compromise her integrity.

Exceptional, Marissa nodded.

The outline of a tall man materialised in the window, his reflection only a dark silhouette. Marissa turned to face him.

"Inspector Pole. Pleased to meet you." Pole extended a friendly hand. Marissa shook it, firm but warm. His intelligent eyes were already at work, but his smile was no fake, a man she could do business with.

* * *

"I looked at the file that HMP Belmarsh sent me. I can see why he might be a good resource," Marissa said, flicking through a large set of papers she had spread over their meeting table.

"Boredom is the worst enemy of someone doing time within the confines of Belmarsh's High Security Unit and Henry is doing thirty years," Pole said.

"That level of security risk?" Marissa asked, her large dark eyes resting on Pole with calm. The delicate features of her face had a benevolence that didn't match the strength of her voice.

"With his IRA background he is at the top of the list. Although some would say the IRA has been decommissioned."

"What about the New IRA or whatever they care to call themselves these days?"

"Well observed," Pole replied raising an approving eyebrow. "Henry's friends were certainly part of that so, yes, HMP needs to keep an eye on him."

"Then it will be good to work with Nancy." Marissa grinned. She enjoyed speaking to Pole, a perfect stranger, and recognised his skill of putting her at ease.

He must have done his research and knew she and Nancy were close. But she felt obliged to ask questions she had not yet had time to clear with her former mentor.

"She is part of his legal team ..." Marissa let her sentence hang hoping for additional information.

"And she is keen to keep her client a law-abiding con," Pole carried on with the flash of a smile.

Marissa nodded. She spread her hands over the open pages of the HMP document, still assessing its content. "I can't hide it from you. I am delighted Nancy has agreed to be part of the team."

"Then I won't hide it from you either, so am I. I have worked with her on some pretty high-profile cases, much to my benefit."

"You mean the LIBOR scandal involving the Bank of England?"

"The very same. And Crowne went straight to the heart of the matter, by the way. As much as I don't like to admit it, he is a very *smart arse* to quote the man himself."

"I gathered that. The additional advantage, of course, is that he no longer works in the City, yet remains perfectly knowledgeable about the way it operates."

Marissa moved a few pieces of paper around, replacing them neatly in the file in a different order. She extended her firm hand, brought her coffee cup to her lips, and drank in small cautious sips.

"I presume you can't yet share the details of the background of the case?"

"You know the rules as well as I do, Inspector. But perhaps I can ask a few questions about what you estimate Henry's skills are and you might get a sense of what is going on."

"Fire away."

"How much does Crowne know about the Middle-East?"

"He has done business there," Pole replied, lifting the file that he had compiled. He went straight to a couple of pages at the back of the folder and started reading.

"He worked on certain investment funds specifically designed for that region called Sukuk funds. Those investments are compliant with Sharia Law." Pole kept reading. "Crowne specialised in equities which were key assets in those funds."

"Which countries?" Marissa asked. She put down her cup. Her eyes had turned a shade darker.

"UAE, Oman, Qatar and Indonesia."

"Indonesia is irrelevant," she said. Pole stopped reading. "Apologies, I should not have interrupted."

"He took a trip to Saudi Arabia. Not sure what the outcome was on that occasion. It was just before the takeover between HXBK and GL, the bank he worked for, was announced."

"You mean he had to stop working on this deal because of the takeover announcement?"

"So I understand."

"I hope you won't mind if I borrow your file?"

"That's the reason I brought it with me."

Marissa raised the cup to her lips again, realised it was empty, crushed it in her hand and dumped it in the wastepaper basket. She moved slowly and deliberately as if continually aware of the impact she might have on her surroundings.

"Was he closely involved with the rescue plan for GL during the financial crisis?"

"No. He was excluded from the merger team."

"He was never tasked to find finance to rescue the bank or a bailout solution?" Marissa moved her body forward, leaning over the neatly arranged papers lying on the table.

"No."

"That must have been painful," she observed neutrally. If she was going to work with a hotshot from the City, she wanted to know how to manoeuvre him to her advantage.

"I will speak to the SFO director." Marissa picked up Pole's file and her own.

"And I will speak to Superintendent Marsh." Pole ran his solid hand over his goatee. "He will be keen on this new high-profile case."

"In the meantime, I will organise a meeting with Nancy if you don't mind." Marissa's eyes lit up for a moment. She would relish being involved with her former teacher, mentor and friend on a par.

What a thrilling prospect.

Chapter Four

The brightness of the light always made the contour of each instrument sharper. Pole recoiled from the smell. Invariably the mortuary had the same effect on him.

Yvonne had been working on Massimo Visconti's body since she had arrived at 8.00am. She had been swabbing, bagging meticulously and was about to start the heavy work on the cadaver's internal organs when Pole arrived.

She stopped working for a moment and Pole was grateful for it.

"Morning Jon. Want a preliminary on my findings?" Yvonne said lifting the visor of her protective headpiece. "I don't need to tell you what the cause of death is. Serrated blade to the throat."

"I can see that very well thank you, a severed head is usually a good indication," Pole grumbled.

"Yeah. But you will see that the jaggedness of the cut means that the perpetrator took his or her time."

"Could the perpetrator in fact be a woman?" Pole asked with a frown.

"Well, it might explain the structure of the cut. It is not a clean slash either because of the desire to inflict pain or because it was difficult, perhaps both."

"And the sword we found?"

"Almost certainly the instrument used. It all seems to match but I will confirm this with final tests, blood etc."

Yvonne moved to the sword that had been placed back in its evidence bag. She opened the bag carefully and drew the blade out with her gloved hands.

"It's old, very old, perhaps even an antique, well preserved though, and sharp. In fact, it has been sharpened recently probably with the intention of killing. I have swabbed the victim to check for metal residue."

Pole was leaning against the wall, his tall body braced against it, his arms crossed. He craned his neck to see what Yvonne was pointing towards. She lifted her head and smiled. Pole took his time to walk over to her, eventually coming to stand over the beheaded body.

"I see what you mean about the cut."

"If you look at his wrists and ankles, you can see he was in shackles. He was not killed immediately after his abduction. These bruises have taken time to set and the skin is badly damaged."

"You think he was locked up for a while. Any idea for how long?"

"He had lost weight, I think; the skin is slack in places. And he was severely dehydrated so I would say over a month, perhaps longer."

"Any other signs?"

"Apart from the fact that he was probably starved, and not allowed to shave or wash. I will tell you more when I have finished the examination of his internal organs."

Pole moved slowly around the body, taking in the details as Yvonne was pointing them out to him. His breathing had slowed down to a minimum, little gulps of air that prevented him from smelling the only too familiar odour of decomposition.

"For what it's worth," Yvonne carried on, slamming her visor back down, "I think it's a warning."

She selected a scalpel and started on the Y shape incision. Pole willed himself to move steadily back to his place against the wall. But Yvonne shooed him away with a wave of her hand.

"Don't need you here," she said without looking at him. "I'll let you know as soon as I have some meaningful results."

"Good," was all Pole managed to say.

"And I don't need you fainting on me."

* * *

The gallery had just opened its doors. A simple white cube with a small recess, large enough to house a select number of art pieces. Phillippe Garry emerged from the diminutive office nestling at the back of the gallery, balancing two cups of Sichuan tea on a small tray. Nancy smiled as he advanced towards her, always attentive to her needs.

"Here you are Nancy. You converted me to Sichuan. I hope you like my choice."

"So kind of you Phillippe but I don't need the VIP treatment really." Nancy chuckled. "Although I am very appreciative of it of course."

She took the delicate bone-china cup and saucer and sat down on the wide windowsill alongside the pamphlets describing the gallery's latest show.

"I have gathered as much information as I could on the Chinese name you mentioned but I haven't had much luck. I also have the feeling my contacts are not being forthcoming."

The cup wobbled in Nancy's hand and a little tea spilt into the saucer.

"How clumsy of me," she said.

Her elegant hand put the cup and saucer down on the floor to look for a tissue in her bag.

"Please don't worry," Phillippe hurried back into the tiny kitchen. He took a little while to find the required paper towel.

Nancy was grateful. The emotions rising in her chest were not yet ready to be witnessed. He might have sensed it, giving her time to compose herself before he reappeared.

Phillippe mopped up the spilt tea carefully and threw the paper into the wastepaper basket in a perfect arch.

"Once a cricketer, always a cricketer," he smiled kindly.

"Thank you for taking the time but don't worry if you can't find more. I was not expecting there would be much in any case."

Phillippe nodded. "And I very much appreciate your involvement with the Ai Weiwei crisis. Strong support from high-profile collectors and friends, especially with your legal background, can only help."

Nancy drank a little tea before she replied. The warm liquid with its delicate fragrance helped to soothe her choking throat.

"I am always glad to help." Nancy took another sip. "Thank you for being discreet and for not prying."

"For you, Nancy, any time."

She attempted a smile. "What else is happening in China that is worth noting?"

Phillippe launched into a passionate description of the younger, subversive artists he supported. The challenges they faced from the state that was by no means ready to hear dissent.

The lines on his forehead moved, arched, settled again, expressing admiration and anxiety in turn. Nancy sipped her tea in silence, occasionally nodding, but despite her desire to listen she couldn't concentrate.

She could no longer leave the task of finding the artist she was looking for to Phillippe. It was too complicated, perhaps even dangerous. She needed to speak to Pole. A warm ripple moved through her body. Was he not the man she most trusted, whose affection she was finally learning to accept?

Phillippe's voice had stopped in mid-sentence. His iPhone was ringing. He pulled a face. A client. Nancy nodded smiling and was glad to let him take the call. She was in no fit state to have a decent conversation about art. Her mind was elsewhere.

When he came back, she rose slowly, put on her coat and moved to the door.

"I hope I have not chased you away," Phillippe said in a sorry voice.

"Not at all. I need to get on with my work." She smiled a reassuring smile and bade Phillippe goodbye. She stopped as she was about to leave the gallery.

"Mo Chow was my father. Under his artist's name. I should have told you earlier. I'm sorry … It's a complicated story, perhaps for another time."

She smiled again and drew the light coat close to her chest, clasping the collar tight with her hand. Phillippe nodded, stunned by the revelation. He simply raised his hand to say goodbye.

Nancy walked out and across to Central Street, took a sharp right. Her pace accelerated. Her chest was tightening and she hated the sensation. She would not be helpless or tearful for a man who had left his family behind and never told them why. She crossed another street; a car sounded its horn. She ran to avoid it.

"Get a grip," she muttered between gritted teeth after waving the driver an apology.

She closed her eyes and remained motionless for a moment.

Yes, she would speak to Pole.

* * *

The metal steps responded to his weight. Henry's light jog reverberated through the stairwell structure. He turned right when he reached the ground floor. Time for Association.

Kamal had already settled in his favourite chair. A couple of the other inmates, all of them sporting beards of various shapes, were assembled on the few chairs next to him. Their conversation was animated but Kamal stayed silent. He listened.

As soon as Henry arrived in the room, a couple of them walked away, not rushed, a natural enough looking move to go to speak with other prisoners. Henry had been struck by the need other people had, including the worst of offenders, to congregate.

People from completely different backgrounds, who would have never spoken in the outside world, conversed regularly, exchanged tips on how to make the suffocating atmosphere of HSU Belmarsh a bearable living hell.

Henry took his time.

He spoke briefly with Big K, the striking giant who was doing time for drug dealing on such a large scale he was deemed a flight hazard. They had a little banter about the latest rugby results.

Henry moved to the water cooler, poured himself a glass and finally reached Kamal's corner. He sat down in the armchair opposite, reached for the paper that had been left on the chair and started reading, his back turned to the people in the room.

"Got your message," he said.

Kamal gave a small nod. His eyelids fluttered. Henry turned a page, the paper now resting on his crossed legs, his foot beating an irregular rhythm.

"No one has ever escaped from HSU Belmarsh," Henry said, his head bent over the newspaper. He did not look at Kamal; he did not need to. The convention to discuss this explosive matter was clear. Whoever was doing the talking had their back to the room.

"People get transferred out. Usually after having spent a long time in here." Henry turned another page.

"You and I haven't done enough time." He drank some of his water. "Or rather you and I do not want to wait for that long."

Kamal had picked up the novel he was reading. He broke the spine of his book slowly. It cracked gently, a small sigh of relief.

"Three ways of doing it. Become seriously ill. Attempt suicide or …" Henry pushed his tall body into the back of the chair. His muscles felt like iron against the worn material.

"Take the opportunity of a trip outside Belmarsh."

Kamal had started reading. He turned a page and smiled.

What did Henry want him to do? Betray his brothers, pretend that he had changed his mind, that the Jihad no longer meant anything to him?

"I know what you are thinking," Henry said, moving to another section of his newspaper, "but look at me. If you can convince them they need you and they do —"

Kamal closed his book and looked up. Someone was coming their way. Henry kept reading an article about the impact of the banks' financial rescue package. "The UK government bailed out these idiots back in 2008 and for what?" Henry said as a shadow spread over his paper. He half turned his athletic body towards it.

"Interested in the ramifications of the enduring financial crisis?" Henry asked, still holding his newspaper open.

"You're turning the pages of that newspaper awfully fast, Henry," Prison Officer MacKay said.

"I am a fast reader," Henry replied folding the paper out neatly. "You will find that the analysis of the banks' exposure to the subprime market on page four is still a great underestimation and that the one on LIBOR fixing on page six is barely scratching the surface. That's the *FT* for you. I didn't bother after page ten." He handed over the paper to MacKay with a broad smile, finished his glass of water in a couple of gulps and stood up.

"Terribly thirsty today. Must get another cup." Henry took his time to reach the water cooler. MacKay had taken the paper and skimmed through the articles. Kamal had returned to reading his book.

The familiar bubble of anger had swollen in Henry's belly as soon as MacKay had spoken. He let it rise without responding to it. In a few minutes he would be using the rowing machine that was permanently available in a secluded corner of the room.

Patience that had eluded him for most of his career in banking was becoming an essential ally. Henry crushed the paper cup in one swift gesture and dumped it with the others in the rubbish bin.

Henry turned to survey his surroundings. Big K was in a conversation with an ex-FSB agent, the intelligence service that had replaced the KGB after the USSR was broken up in 1991. They had discovered a common passion: chess.

And Big K had assured Henry he was receiving prime information about the Russian mafia and their appetite for cocaine. So much for being a reformed con.

"You are doing a market survey inside HSU Belmarsh?" Henry had laughed.

"Man. If the guy has got info."

"Yes, but nothing comes for free in this world. You told me that. What will he want in return?"

Big K had punched Henry's shoulder in slow motion.

"My man Henry is learning the ropes," Big K had chuckled.

Henry turned towards the small enclosure with the rowing machine inside. He checked the book. No one had reserved the slot starting before his but there was someone using it.

He waited against the wall for the inmate to finish. The grunts that came from inside the enclosure stopped. A few swear words for good measure. The gulps of someone drinking water, *no Lucozade at HSU Belmarsh – Lord knows what a sugar rush would do to some of the inmates,* and the man was out.

The rowing machine was free.

Henry entered the enclosure, adjusted the seat and bent forward to lock the resistance in position. He straddled the centrepiece, sat down and started pulling on the handlebar. Someone was leaning against the partition separating the room from the enclosure.

Henry recognised the overpowering scent. The sickly smell of Ronnie Kray's skin made his stomach heave. Kray's skin condition after covering his body with tattoos required special ointment, the smell of which followed Kray like a warning.

No matter, he was proud of those tats, a celebration of his idols: the famous Kray Brothers. Henry had first noticed the twins' heads inscribed on Kray's back at the gym.

"Minnie-me is pushing it a bit far," Henry had quipped. "One head perhaps but two – the guy who did his tat must have had a stutter." Big K had liked the joke and his laugh had bounced off the walls of the gym. But there are no secrets in prison and Henry's little joke had got back to Kray's ears.

Breaking Rule 101 of remaining unnoticeable in jail had been a stupid thing to do and Henry was starting to feel the brunt of it.

Kray stood silent, running his eyes over Henry as he started his session.

Henry stopped, adjusted the seat and started to pull again, a slow and rhythmic action that made the machine groan under his effort.

He looked straight ahead. Henry had had plenty of similar intimidation attempts when he worked on the trading floor and would not allow Kray to get under his skin.

Kray had started humming a low tune that could hardly be heard, a wasp buzzing around, looking for an excuse to sting. Henry accelerated the pace, the machine groaned louder.

The hum grew a little keener. Kray had dropped his hands across the low partition. He was slowly moving them inside the space, a progression measured and unstoppable. Henry's body was now covered in sweat, yet the hum had not stopped. His heart was pumping fast.

Could he push himself one notch up?

Should he push himself one notch up?

He increased the cadence, his muscles screamed, the machine protested but Henry did not care. Oxford's rowing team might have been impressed, not Kray though. The humming gained in intensity. Until suddenly it stopped.

"Have you booked a slot?" Officer MacKay asked.

Kray's hands had slid back outside the partition wall. He turned slowly towards the guard. "Thinking about it."

MacKay opened the book and pointed to a slot.

"15:30; put your name down." He handed a pen to the other man.

"Too late." Kray turned around, resuming the hum of his little tune. He took his time to walk away.

"Do you have beef with Ronnie Kray?" MacKay asked Henry as he was wiping his face dry of sweat.

"Not that I know of."

"Good. I don't want to have to separate you two and send you to the box."

Henry nodded. The box was not part of the plan.

* * *

"Are you taking the car? Helena shouted from the bottom of the stairs. She waited for a reply before climbing up a few steps and standing on her tiptoes to shout again.

"Mark? Are you taking the car?" She enunciated each word and waited again for a reply, her slender hand resting on the banister for balance.

A door opened and Mark called down.

"Not sure, why? Do you need it?" Mark's latest acquisition, his last folly before he decided to become a pariah of society, at least the society they were both involved in, was Helena's favourite car.

They had always wanted to drive a Jaguar and now they did. Mark waited with a faint smile for a reply. Helena was looking for an excuse to deprive him of his – their – favourite toy.

"It's going to rain, and I'll be on the motorway. Going to visit Mum," Helena said less convincingly than expected.

Mark moved to the top of the stairs. His wife was waiting; a full head of blonde curls brushed her shoulders. Her face lifted towards him with an irresistible smile. How could he say no?

He had another meeting at the SFO, going over his account of events one more time. His face darkened at the thought and Helena read the change in him immediately.

"Doesn't matter."

Mark darted down the stairs and caught her before she had turned away. He put his arms around her, a gentle, folding embrace.

"You can drive my car," he said brushing a kiss on her forehead. It was the least he could do.

Since he had told his wife about the whistle-blowing case the mood in their relationship had changed. Perhaps predictably it would take a little time for her to accept what was going to happen.

Helena returned his kiss, a quick peck on his lips, a smile, another peck, a little more insistent. She pushed him away gently.

"I need to hit the road before the traffic builds up."

Mark lets his hand slide away from her waist, helping her with her coat. The keys lie in a large ashtray, a souvenir from a trip to Mexico they took so many years ago he can't quite recall the date. He has always resisted her attempts at getting rid of it. Helena opens the door and waves a quick goodbye, with final instructions about food, kids, pets. Mark leans against the frame of the door, watching Helena slip into the car, a schoolgirl walking into her favourite sweet shop. A rush of cold air makes him shiver and he prepares to close the door.

The burst of heat and its force are staggering.

It propels him to the bottom of the stairs. His head hits the wall. The gale that has burst into his home stops him from breathing. It all goes black.

Chapter Five

His faded navy slacks felt tight around the waist. Brett pulled his stomach in, his chest out and took a glance at his image in the full-length mirror of his bedroom. He disliked this shabby look and even more what his trousers' waistline was telling him. He was putting on weight.

He released his breath and walked away from the mirror, unstrapping his Patek Philippe watch. He laid it carefully on a small table he used to arrange the necessary items a gentleman should own: cufflinks, lighter, leather wallet and cigarettes.

He would not be wearing or carrying any of these on his trip to North London. The Sheik had asked to see him after a couple of months' silence. Brett had not needed to find an excuse to see him after all. A good state of affairs but a worrying one too.

Brett sat down on the Louis XV bed, his hands stretched over his thighs, the material absorbing the film of moisture that was forming on his palms. Since accepting the deal The Sheik had offered him a few months ago, Brett had been operating well outside his comfort zone.

True, MI6-Steve had been surprisingly supportive. And the deal Steve had in turn offered to Brett for his continued involvement with The Sheik's terrorist organisation had been too good to ignore.

"You pull this one off and you will never have to hear from us again."

Now that Brett had had time to think about it, he was not certain that day would ever come. One did not deal with the head of a new UK terror cell with impunity. Brett had enough contact with the Middle-East to realise that.

A new organisation was growing in strength and might well surpass Al-Qaeda in the region. MI6-Steve would know that too. Still, the idea that he might *pull it off*, as Steve had put it, excited him. The assurance that he would keep the cash he had made from art trafficking and more recently the money The Sheik had paid him, persuaded him too.

How long would that money last? Brett would cross that bridge when it eventually came. He had been born into money and the aristocracy – a rare combination.

The money had evaporated but the title had remained, a useful tool for a skilled fraudster. Brett clasped his hands, cracked his knuckles and stood up.

He grabbed his old, shapeless jacket, pocketed the new burner phone he had just activated and made his way to the tube station. He sent a text to Mohammed, his London contact, as he was walking towards Hyde Park Corner. His phone pinged back. Mohammed had replied.

Brett did not bother to check the text. It was clear that the usual routine for meeting The Sheik would be repeated and he could expect the same treatment as before.

A large SUV with blackened windows waiting for him a few streets away from Finsbury Park Station. A couple of bulky men in black leather jackets shoving him into the back seat. A blindfold.

A journey that circled around the same area a few times in an attempt to make him lose track of his surroundings. The rough frisking on arrival and then The Sheik.

Every time another house, another room but the same figure clad in white robes, a crocheted white hat on his close shaven head and a jet-black wiry beard.

The phone pinged again. Brett squeezed the phone in his jacket pocket and muttered an insult. "What does this moron want?" He was on his way and would be, as ever, punctual. Or had the meeting been cancelled?

Brett found himself torn between the relief of deferment and the excitement of wanting to know what The Sheik had in store for him. He yanked the phone out of his pocket and started reading.

New meeting location: Manor House tube.

He should have known, a last-minute change of location to destabilise him, perhaps to frighten him too. Nothing would ever be predictable with this lot.

Fear was the trademark of all Jihadi groups and he could feel it even in the heart of London. Brett acknowledged the text and hurriedly climbed down the steps leading to the platforms.

* * *

502

Pole accelerated, using the siren on the roof of his car to attempt to move the traffic out of the way. He went through a red light and DS Andy Todd sitting in the passenger seat closed his eyes. Pole might have smiled were it not for what he knew he would find at the end of his journey.

His mobile, placed in its holder on the car dashboard, was relaying with difficulty his conversation with Marissa.

"When did you last speak to him?" Pole was asking, changing gear again to slow down, blocked this time by a lumbering bus.

"Last night. No, this morning. It was around 3am when he left the SFO office." Marissa's voice was barely audible over the screams of the siren.

"I need to join you." She said several times as the message began breaking up.

Pole increased his grip on the steering wheel, banged his horn and moved up a gear again. "Let me find out first what has happened exactly. Are you on your own?"

Marissa's voice became garbled again. "No. With —"

"Can't hear you."

"In a meeting with Nancy."

Pole slammed on the brakes in front of the first police cordon at the top of Kensington Park Road. Andy lowered the window, showing his badge to the PC on duty.

"I'm nearly there," Pole said, killing the siren. He moved his car more cautiously along the street into which he had turned. There was another police cordon ahead, a couple of officers with dogs and paramedics being held back until the zone had been secured.

"Where are you?" Marissa's anxiety was real and Pole could not pacify her. For all he knew Mark Phelps could be dead. A dreadful situation the SFO would never have contemplated and for which Marissa alone now shouldered the responsibility.

"First I need to speak to the Counterterrorist Commander on site." Pole was not ignoring her but trying to assess the situation.

"Your call," Marissa said. "I am not going to lie to you. I don't want to have to handle this on my own if Mark ..." her voice trailed.

"I'll let you know as soon as I can." Pole jumped out of his car and moved quickly towards the site of the blast. The unmistakable smell of explosive and burnt metal almost choked him. He covered his nose with his hands briefly. The memory of another explosion flooded his mind.

Paddington.

He could see the bodies strewed around, hear the moaning of the victims and picture the police van that was transporting Henry Crowne to the Counterterrorism Command Headquarters cracked open like a discarded nut. Henry had been lucky to survive.

"Guv," Andy materialised at Pole's side. "I think it is Commander Ferguson," Andy said adjusting his heavy glasses.

"Yes, and for once I am not going to grumble at being involved with someone I know at the Squad."

"Was it the Commander who responded at the Royal Exchange?"

Pole nodded and moved forward. A couple of heavily armed officers moved towards them and were about to stop them when Commander Ferguson's voice pulled them back. "Let them through."

"Pole, you again," Ferguson said waving him in.

"Car bomb?" Pole asked without bothering to greet the other man.

"'fraid so, with someone in the car unfortunately." Ferguson was moving towards the vehicle, the SOCO team was also moving towards it from the other side of the road, some of them still kitting themselves up for the task ahead.

"We have just cleared the area and allowed the paramedics to enter the house. Some poor bugger is trapped under the door it seems."

"Is it too early to know who the driver is?" Pole asked, the hand in the pocket of his raincoat squeezing his BlackBerry.

"We have just arrived. But the car is registered to a Mr Mark Phelps." Ferguson waited. If Pole was involved, he had details on the case that were relevant to it.

"Is he the person in the car?" Pole asked instead. Ferguson gave him a dark look but volunteered. "Not sure it's a man."

Pole nodded, relieved at the thought that Mark Phelps might still be alive and yet dreading to find out the identity of the dead person. It was likely to be a relative: wife, sister, daughter? Pole ran his hand through his greying hair. No matter who this was, the life of the Phelps family had changed forever.

"What's your involvement in all this?"

"Let's go into the house. I don't want to speak to you about it in the open." Pole was already moving towards the home.

Pole was already moving towards the home as voices came from inside it. A man was lying on the ground, dragged it seemed by one of the paramedics.

504

Someone was shouting, "He's stopped breathing." One of the paramedics was already doing CPR. A young woman rushed to the ambulance, returning with a defibrillator.

Another woman cut open his T-shirt exposing a bloodied chest. The paramedic applied the pads; the man's body arched up. The young woman took the pulse.

Nothing.

The paramedic rubbed the pads, applied them to the man's chest a second time. The body arched again, hanging suspended in mid-air for a few seconds and dropped back onto the ground with a thud. The young woman felt for the pulse once more. She nodded.

Everyone on the scene had been standing stock still, frozen, joining together in hope for the life of a man they didn't know. Mark Phelps was transferred onto a stretcher and moved into the ambulance.

Pole and Ferguson walked quickly to join the paramedics as soon as they realised Phelps was alive.

"Where are you taking him?" Pole asked.

"Are you family?" The young woman pushed back at the intrusion.

"No. Police," Pole produced his ID card.

"St Thomas's emergency."

Ferguson spoke into his radio. The victim couldn't travel unaccompanied.

Pole let Ferguson organise Mark Phelps' secure transfer to hospital. Andy had already started gathering information, speaking to the SOCO team inside the house.

Pole was happy for him to take the lead on this. He has a call to make.

* * *

The clunk of the lock shutting automatically was for once welcome. Today Henry greeted bang-up time. For an hour, he would not be expected to interact with other inmates or be disturbed. He walked to the small bookshelf he was allowed in his cell, evidence of his good behaviour, chose a large art book and moved to his bed.

He removed his trainers, placed his flimsy pillow behind his back and sat cross-legged in what had become a comfortable position. The book had been well thumbed and yet handled with care.

He opened a page at random and started reading. The prison officers were having their lunch but there was always a possibility that one of them, still on duty, might open the latch of his cell door.

The spine of the book cracked with the soft sound of a crisp waffle and Henry pushed the hard cover slowly apart. It came off to expose pages that had been glued together. Henry felt along the ridge with his finger and dislodged a small piece of cotton wool. It came loose and a small object slipped out of it.

The netsuke rolled into his hand, no bigger than a walnut. He turned the small piece representing a dog with pups around his fingers a few times. He let it rest in his palm and suddenly squeezed it hard. Its ridges pressed into his skin.

He inhaled and slowly let go of the breath. The exquisite piece of art represented everything Henry longed for and what he had lost.

He rolled the netsuke around his hand, stroked his fingertips along the back of the dog, appreciating the delicate carving of its nose and ears, the intricacy of the tiny pups suckling their mother.

A voice in the corridor made him jump and he hurriedly replaced the object in its cache, squeezing the cotton wool back into position. The book sat in his lap and he waited. A few minutes elapsed. Henry relaxed and started reading *Art & Today*, one of the best introductions to modern and contemporary art he had read so far.

Henry smiled at the picture that his random opening had selected, an installation in New York's Central Park called *The Gates* by Christo and Jeanne-Claude, in 2005.

His smile dropped. He had seen this extraordinary piece on one of his trips to New York that winter. The pictures in the book did justice to the power of the piece: red gates, thousands of them organised into two rows, meandering around a frozen Central Park, where snow lay on the ground, trees were bare of foliage but clad in ice.

He had agreed with a contemporary review then, that their installation made you see a place, a landscape, differently. That day, it had made him notice the beauty, vastness and fragility of Central Park.

Henry shut the book and closed his eyes. An unfamiliar sense of peace had settled on him since he had made up his mind about what he must do next – a sense of peace but also a sense of purpose.

It had taken him four years since he had been thrown in jail to formulate what had been haunting him, from his responsibility for Anthony Albert's death to his involvement with the IRA.

Even though the reconciliation process had started and

decommissioning had been ordered, he had continued helping the IRA with their finances, so keen was he to belong, to repay Liam and Bobby for their unwavering friendship when he needed it the most and also perhaps to find a connection to the father he had lost so young.

But he could no longer excuse his behaviour – nor did he want to. He needed to prove if only to himself that he could be better than what he appeared to have become.

Henry threw the pillow away with one hand and lay back on his small bed. The frame creaked a little underneath his weight. He held the book against his chest, heavy. Henry opened his eyes and lifted the book over his head. He felt free from a heavy burden. He knew what it would take. Something that might perhaps cost him everything.

Kamal had plans for him. He had suggested as much during their coded conversations. Henry did not need to be a genius to work out why he wanted his involvement.

Henry had been a banker, a brilliant banker. He had managed to keep the finances of the IRA hidden, inaccessible to the most extensive of investigations. Something new was happening in the world of terrorism in the Middle-East.

Kamal, or Abu Maeraka – his warrior name – had convinced him that something more powerful, more extreme was afoot. Another new organisation that needed someone to help with the money they were already amassing. Would they trust a non-believer though?

Perhaps not, or perhaps for as long as they required his services and then ... But it was all part of the yet-to-be-revealed master plan and, if Henry was right, also the reason why Abu Maeraka had been transferred to Belmarsh on the same wing as Henry.

Henry stood up in one jump. His well-trained muscles responded to the command instantly. He replaced the art book on its shelf and lifted out a much smaller one he had recently been lent. The *Holy Qur'an* in Arabic with an English translation. Kamal had not told him about the book.

Henry had simply one day found a little parcel of green silk on his chair. Kamal had not bothered to give Henry a simplified text. It was a Qur'an with a translation but no commentary.

The perfect way to lure a man of Henry's calibre, whose intelligence was his greatest asset and his biggest downfall. Henry replaced the Qur'an on the bookshelf too. There was nothing wrong in trying to understand the way of thinking of the people he wanted to join – at least for a while – but now was not the time.

His watch indicated he had another few minutes before bang-up time was over. He returned to his bed, stretched out again and reviewed the status of the financial market in his mind.

He had succeeded in cultivating his good reputation as a model inmate, keeping himself to himself in the hope that the next fallout from the 2008 financial crisis would provide him with a get-out-of-jail card of a more permanent nature.

The world of banking was still far too messed-up not to produce yet another spectacular outrage. His involvement in the LIBOR scandal had proved decisive. Even Pole had given him due credit.

He sensed that the next shocking incident was around the corner, and he, Henry Crowne, was ready for his next move.

* * *

"What did Ferguson say?" Marissa asked, a small muscle at the edge of her mouth twitching with nerves. She straightened up, her solid frame shielding the back of her chair. Nancy nodded. She too wanted to know.

"It will take some time to analyse all the components of the bomb but from what has been gathered so far it was motion activated: it detonated when the car started to move." Pole pushed his chair back.

"Can we tell the origin? I mean I've heard it's possible to trace the maker of a bomb." Marissa clasped her hands so hard that the knuckles had turned white.

"It will be given top priority, no doubt about it, but my guess is that we will find most of the components originated from within the UK – such as the timing device and the motion sensor. Our best hope of finding something that helps with more specific identification rests with the explosive itself —"

"But the bomber?" Marissa interrupted.

"If we can trace the origin of the explosive it will tell us something about who is involved and possibly who the bomber is, assuming he is known to the Counterterrorist Squad."

Marissa remained silent. Her face had frozen. She absorbed the information, trying to make sense of what it meant.

"Does Mark Phelps know?" Nancy asked.

Marissa nodded, took a deep breath. "He is in shock but, surprisingly, he remembers everything."

She broke out of her frozen stance and spread her hands over the table.

"He knows about his wife?"

"That she didn't survive the blast … Yes." Marissa held her breath for a moment.

"It's the hardest thing I have ever had to do." She dropped her hands into her lap. "I have prosecuted dozens of cases and yet …"

Pole glanced at Nancy and stood up. "I'll get us some fresh tea, shall I?" She blinked in acknowledgement.

"If you are blaming yourself, don't," Nancy said as soon as Pole had closed the door. "It won't help in any way. More importantly, how could you have predicted this?"

"But I can't help wondering whether there were signs I missed."

"Because of who is involved in the case?"

Marissa stood up, went to the window and leaned her head against it. "That is what I like the most about you Nancy, always going straight to the point. I liked it very much during my pupillage years, but it is tough to bear when you are on the receiving end of it."

"I'm sorry Marissa," Nancy said, coming alongside her and extending a friendly hand. "I didn't mean to be insensitive."

"But you are right, this is no time for self-pity. The best thing I can do now is help you find the frigging bastards who did this." Marissa spoke with feeling, the attitude of someone who understood injustice and who would not shy away from tackling the cause of it.

There was a rasp against the door and Pole entered with a tray bearing some appetising looking biscuits – no doubt snatched from the tin of one of his colleagues – and some freshly brewed tea. Pole placed a cup in front of Marissa and Nancy. Everyone drank in silence but the biscuits remained untouched. Marissa waited.

"There is no immediate rush to decide what your next move is going to be." Nancy's voice was calm, hoping it would help.

"Mark came to us, I mean the Serious Fraud Office, about six months ago." Marissa had sat down again. "He had been working for HXBK for ten years as a very senior compliance officer, so he saw a lot of privileged information. About a year ago his boss was taken ill. Something sudden, a heart attack I believe. Anyway, he had to step in."

Marissa drank some tea. "To cut a long story short, he came across documents that his boss hadn't had time to file. During the 2008 crisis the UK government offered a bailout programme to enable the banks to escape bankruptcy. I am sure you remember the likes of RBS and

Lloyds accepting the offer. Of course, no government pulls together a programme like that without wanting shares in the institution they intend to salvage and taking some level of control at board level."

"You mean government officials on the board of these institutions, complete scrutiny, reducing the risk profile of the deals done by the bank?" Nancy asked.

"That's right." Marissa nodded appreciatively. "HXBK had found an alternative solution. A private investor."

"Someone out there was willing to invest enough money to salvage them, despite their involvement in the subprime market?" Pole asked incredulous.

"That's correct." Marissa nodded again and this time her stiff shoulders relaxed Nancy remarked. She had found a team that was more on the ball than many of her colleagues and the light in her eyes said so.

"Were the terms of the share purchase commercial and who was the investor?" Nancy asked.

"A state in the Middle-East. I can't say more at the moment and no, not at all, the terms of the share purchase were reasonable bearing in mind the circumstances. It's what happened subsequently to the money HXBK received that has become an issue."

Marissa opened the file she had been guarding closely and handed them each a copy of a short document. "A sum of money representing a large portion of the original investment has been lent back to a fund registered in Panama."

Nancy speed-read the document, still listening to Marissa.

"In itself a fund registered in Panama is legal," Nancy said.

"Very true but the question is who is the Ultimate Beneficial Owner of the fund? So far we have not been able to determine who the UBO is."

"And you suspect this UBO is someone representing the Middle-Eastern State that lent the money?" Pole had finished reading the document too.

"That's right."

"Mark thought it was the case too. Otherwise he would not have contacted you?" Pole turned his BlackBerry face down as several messages kept appearing on its screen.

"Mark had a conversation with senior management, at CEO level, and the answers he received were less than convincing."

"How so?" Nancy frowned, drawing her elegant eyebrows together.

"A final document was issued confirming the verification of the identity of the UBO, but that identity was never made available to Mark and the excuse made that the identity was politically sensitive complete non-sense. The complexity of the structure of the fund's ownership was not particularly transparent either." Marissa finished her tea. "When Mark's boss returned, he told Mark in no uncertain terms to close the file and stop questioning a transaction that had already been finalised."

"In other words, don't ask the awkward questions," Pole added.

"Mark's involvement in high-profile transactions almost completely dried up at that point."

"If you don't have the identity of the UBO you don't have a case." Pole handed the document back to Marissa.

"No, not a chance."

"This is the reason why you need to speak to Henry Crowne," Nancy said also handing the document back.

Reluctantly, Pole nodded. "We do need Henry."

Chapter Six

Andy was pacing up and down in front of Pole's office. He was speaking to someone on his mobile phone and waving a sheaf of papers.

"What's all this extra activity about?" Pole asked with a faint smile.

"Got some results on the Mashrafiya, Guv." Andy looked disappointed as Pole's face remained blank. "The sword that was used to behead Massimo Visconti."

Pole slapped his forehead. "That sword, the Mash ... whatever."

"Rafiya," Andy's mind was already on the next piece of news. "I have managed to find out where it came from."

"You mean it has some special origin?"

"It was stolen from a museum in Iraq during the last Iraqi war. But this particular piece is very important. It is supposed to have belonged to the man who fought alongside the prophet Mohammed."

"Go on," Pole said opening the door of his office and waving Andy in.

"The museum in Baghdad was ransacked a number of times but very thoroughly after the fall of Saddam Hussein."

"I see what you are getting at," Pole said dumping the file Marissa had prepared for him to a dangerously high pile of papers. The pile wobbled. Andy held his breath. Pole sat down hardly noticing. "You think Massimo Visconti had something to do with the theft of this sword?"

Andy sat down in slow motion, a wary eye still on the pile of documents. "Yeah, Guv, I do."

"And? You can't hide anything from me you know." Pole leant forward, elbows on his desk, hands clasped together over another bundle of papers.

"I also think ..." Andy took his time to speak the words, "...he might have known his assailant."

"That is a pretty big assumption. From having possibly stolen the Mashrafiya to being slaughtered with it and by whom – the person who asked him to steal it in the first place?"

"I know, Guv, so I spoke to DCI Grandel." Andy waited for Pole's reaction.

"That's a good idea. With his long experience in stolen art he must have a view. What did good old Eugene have to say for himself then?"

"He confirmed that Visconti was heavily involved in art trafficking out of the war zones in the Middle-East. He was on the ground way before anybody else dared chance it according to DCI Grandel."

"Who were his contacts in the region? Do we know?"

"According to DCI Grandel, Visconti had already realised that he had to work with the fighters on the ground, get very close to the local people. In particular the rebels in Iraq who needed funds for the war against the US and the government it supported there."

"You mean Al-Qaeda?"

Andy nodded.

"So after nearly ten years of playing happy families with a number of terrorist groups, looters and so on Visconti comes to a sad end. But why? What changed?"

"That's what I'm trying to find out. He was arrested, remember."

"But he escaped." Pole had started to fiddle with a rubber band and stopped, keeping the elastic fully stretched.

"You don't seem convinced."

"It's not that, Andy. It's what comes next if your theory is right."

"You mean …" Andy's chubby face dropped.

"Yes, what does it mean if we prove Visconti was murdered in the middle of London by a terrorist cell?"

Andy's blue eyes darted from Pole to the papers he had prepared for his boss, attempting to articulate a response to the chilling question.

London. Terrorism. Last bomb from the IRA, 1993. Then 2007 the Al-Qaeda bombing happened.

"So no, I am not saying you are wrong," Pole released the elastic band. The car bomb that had just killed Mark Phelps' wife could well validate Andy's findings.

Superintendent Marsh would shortly be addressing the press. The Home Secretary would almost certainly chair a Cobra meeting to discuss the event. But Pole did not want to overreact. Andy needed to find proof.

"Shall I go back to DCI Grandel?"

"That's a good plan. Get all the information he has available on Visconti. Do we know what he stole? Do we have the names of people he dealt with? You know the drill."

"On it, Guv." Andy adjusted his thick glasses, leaped out of his seat and left Pole's office, already dialling Grandel's number on his mobile.

* * *

The blindfold had been knotted too tight. Brett could feel the pressure against his eyes but did not dare loosen it.

He gathered the car that was taking him back was not the one that had driven him to his meeting with The Sheik. It had been cleaned recently, the smell of detergent mixed with an overpowering rose-scented air freshener almost made him throw up.

Brett had known that a tough meeting would happen one day but perhaps not so quickly and not so openly brutal. There was nothing physical, at least not yet, apart from the tight blindfold and the rough way he had been frisked when he had got out of the car that had picked him up from Manor House tube station.

The change of pick-up address had already unsettled him. But again, it had been intended to. The journey had taken longer than the usual thirty minutes or so. The pattern of the journey had also changed.

Brett had relied on his training, spotting the turns that indicated the car was going around in circles. This time though there was very little circling around the same area. By his reckoning the drive had taken a little more than forty minutes in a straight line. He was taken deep into the suburbs, the heartland of a community he knew nothing about.

The blindfold had only been removed when he was in the meeting room. The place was dilapidated, the floorboards bare, the wallpaper had been torn down, taking with it pieces of plaster. The house had no heating and the cold seeped through his body as he stood wondering once more whether this was a meeting or an execution.

Should he sit down on one of the mattresses that were lying on the floor? Perhaps not. He had been brought here as a warning. He was intended to be scared and he was, but more importantly he should show that he was.

Someone walked through the open door. Brett jerked back. The Sheik waved to him to sit down. His eyes focused on Brett with a coldness he had not yet witnessed.

514

The Sheik sat down on a mattress opposite Brett's, drew a photograph from a brown envelope and threw it at Brett's feet.

"Do you know this man?"

Massimo Visconti's face, the unmistakable large brown eyes, the slightly hooked nose and strong jaw – a charm that seduced all. Brett held his breath for a few seconds. Should he deny it? But it would not make sense. Visconti was too well known in the art-trafficking world. He had nodded hesitantly.

The Sheik's face relaxed slightly. Brett saw he had passed a test.

For now.

"It's been in the news," he mumbled. Perhaps he could glean more information?

The Sheik threw several more photos onto the floor. It took almost a minute before Brett could make sense of what he was seeing and when he did he scrambled to his feet and stumbled to the back of the room, reeling in horror.

He coughed and reached for a handkerchief in his trouser pocket. He wiped his mouth and face with it.

The Sheik had not moved, terrifyingly patient.

"Why?" Brett mumbled, immediately regretting the question.

The Sheik invited him back onto the mattress Brett had left so abruptly.

"I reward well but I punish harshly."

The Sheik had pulled another photo out of the brown envelope. Brett's eyes closed.

"Please, no more."

"This one has his head still very much on his shoulders." He handed Brett the picture.

Another attractive face was looking at Brett from a photo that had been professionally shot: dark blue eyes, furrows that cut deep into his face, a decisive chin and a mane of dark hair. It was a man Brett once knew well.

Brett fidgeted in the back of the car. They were a good thirty minutes into their journey back. The car had turned in a direction he was not expecting, taking another route to deliver him back to a tube station.

Brett kept his mind occupied, replaying the second part of his meeting with The Sheik. Yet the pictures of Visconti's mutilated body kept appearing in front of his eyes. He pushed away those images to concentrate on the face of the man who was very much alive.

Henry Crowne.

* * *

The drip bag would need replacing soon. Marissa wondered whether she should call the nurse. Mark was asleep and she felt awkward at the thought of waking him up, at the thought that the woman at his bedside should have been his wife, not her. Never had she had to face a threat to the life of a key witness or the devastating consequences a case might have on a family.

She had organised protection under the witness protection programme, but it had always been a successful pre-emptive move.

Pole had been efficient without being overbearing. Mark's children had been collected from school on the basis of an emergency, taken to Mark's parents and the police were guarding the house. At least they were all safe.

Mark stirred, perhaps disturbed by Marissa's intense gaze. She stood up carefully and placed her large, heavy hand on his.

"Mark," her voice cracked a little.

He turned his face slightly and opened the eye that was not covered by bandages. His mind was adjusting, extricating itself from the fog created by medication and pain.

"Hi," he mumbled. He turned his head a little more towards the glass of water on the bedside table. "Thirsty." Marissa brought the plastic tumbler to him and helped place the straw in his mouth.

She wanted to say something meaningful, but she could not think of anything. What could she say to the man who had almost lost his life, lost his wife and would almost certainly spend the rest of his existence looking over his shoulder?

Mark took a few long pulls of water and let his head fall back again on the pillow, eyes closed.

"Shall I leave and come back later?" Marissa asked.

"No." Mark remained silent and Marissa thought he might have fallen asleep again.

"Children?" Mark asked, opening his good eye again and fixing it on Maria with a look of anxiety.

"Yes, they are fine. They are with your parents under police protection."

It was excruciating, Marissa's stomach was a lump of lead in her midriff. She could not let him down. He had trusted her when he came to the SFO. "Mark, if you want to stop?"

"No." The same determined word surprised her.

516

"No," Mark repeated. "She can't have died," he slurred, "for nothing." The bandage restricted his jaw. "Catch the bastards."

Marissa squeezed his hand. "I promise."

* * *

"Enter."

Marsh was in a foul mood today, Denise, his PA, had warned. He had asked her to rearrange an entire week of meetings to fit in an interview with *The Times* on a prickly subject.

Pole straightened his tie and gave Denise a wink. She gave him the thumbs up. He walked into Superintendent Marsh's office.

"Good afternoon, Sir."

"Pole. Good afternoon." Marsh was now on the charm offensive it seemed. Pole had barely told him about the SFO request for a contact to be found that could both speak to HMP Belmarsh's governor and the Home Office but Marsh's well-trained ear had picked up the tone.

Another high-profile case.

"What does Counterterrorism Command say about the bomb?" Marsh asked, settling deep into his chair. His eyes glinted with interest. Pole cringed. The body of Mark Phelps' wife had scarcely reached the mortuary and Marsh already wanted something he could deliver to the Press.

"A motion device triggered the explosion, Sir. CT Command is being very cautious in making assumptions." Pole sat down before being invited to. Marsh would have to wait until Ferguson, the commander in charge, gave him more information.

"Right, right. Of course, we would not want to jump to conclusions, would we?"

"We certainly would not, Sir."

Whatever the conclusions about the bomb and the Mashrafiya, they would hit Marsh's desk only after they had hit Ferguson's and Nancy's.

"The SFO has confirmed they intend to request assistance from Crowne, I presume?" The very large piece of news Marsh was savouring.

"They have indeed, Sir. I have prepared a draft request on their behalf to be sent to Belmarsh and the Home Office. Assuming your backing of course."

March gestured consent as if Pole did not need to ask.

"Understood. However —" Marsh moved his body forward in an

abrupt fashion, forearms on his desk. "I will want to know all of the details and I mean *all* the details of this operation."

Pole nodded, with pursed lips. "Absolutely Sir, as ever."

His omission in the last case involving Henry Crowne and Nancy, an attempt on the life of one of Whitehall's most senior civil servants, had irritated Marsh greatly. Pole had managed to plead urgency and he had had a point. Marsh knew it. Nevertheless, he was the man in charge and Pole had better remember it. Pole remained impassive as Marsh scrutinised him for a sign – anything indicating he was already not quite as transparent as he was intended to be.

"Good," Marsh finally said. "Take me through the SFO case and why they want Crowne."

If Marsh thought Pole would make any mistakes when explaining why they needed Henry, he would be disappointed. Marissa and Nancy had done a superb job of briefing him and, much to his surprise, he was getting the hang of all the City jargon too.

"You must have read that during the financial crisis in 2008 the UK government offered a bailout facility to UK banks." Marsh nodded; so far so good, he was following.

"However, one of the banks that could have benefited from such an offer decided to go elsewhere to find the necessary capital." Pole sat comfortably in his chair, legs crossed and moving his hands as he spoke. "Bank X – the SFO is seeking to avoid disclosing the name – was funded by a Middle-Eastern country and therefore raised enough capital not to need the UK government bailout."

Marsh wriggled on his chair. Mentioning the Middle-East always had an effect on senior Met officers.

"What the SFO has discovered through a bank employee who contacted them is that a large part of this cash has been lent back to a fund in Panama. The structure of the fund is complex. This means that the SFO has been unable to determine who the Ultimate Beneficial Owner of the fund is."

"Is this illegal?" Marsh asked, arching his mouth in a doubtful fashion.

"It is not, Sir, unless the fund is structured/designed for illicit motives or the money is used for illegal purposes." Pole was enjoying himself. Marsh, an intelligent man despite his voracious ambition, was starting to struggle.

Pole 1 – Marsh 0.

"How illegal then?" Marsh rearranged his collection of Montblanc pens on his desk, each received after a new promotion no doubt.

"The whistle-blower, Mark Phelps, has information indicating illegal activity."

"Which is what? Drugs. Weapons. Human slavery?"

"None of those, at least as far as we can tell, but rather the very fact that the money received by Bank X has been lent back to the Middle-Eastern country that invested it in the first place."

Marsh opened his mouth, closed it. No, he would not ask the question that was burning his lips. Was this illegal too? "Is this whistle-blower reliable?" Marsh asked instead.

"Very. The SFO is convinced of it and Marissa Campbell, an experienced prosecutor, as well." Pole briefly locked eyes with Marsh. "And by the look of it the bombers thought as much too."

Marsh pulled away from his desk. "Clearly." Marsh remained silent for a minute or so.

"If Mark Phelps has been targeted, I assume Bank X is his employer?"

"That's correct, Sir." Pole kept his countenance.

Blast. Marsh 1 – Pole 1.

Marsh grinned, satisfied. "So why call it Bank X still?"

"As far as Crowne is concerned, the documents he sees will be redacted. The SFO does not want the case to be contaminated. If he finds the UBO, his findings will be based on the Panama fund structure only, no other inference."

The Super pursed his lips, pondering the validity of the argument. Not that the SFO director would take any notice of his opinion but it was good feeling one could perhaps present a different opinion.

"I see the point," Marsh said slowly. He was formulating his next question in the most neutral fashion he could think of. Pole was expecting it but he would be damned if he was going to make it easy for his boss.

"Are you using your consultant, Ms Wu?" Marsh avoided Pole's eyes. He sounded almost innocent.

Pole suppressed an ironic *Certainly Sir, shall I also organise dinner?* and simply shrugged. "Unless you have any objection to it."

"No, not at all," Marsh volunteered, perhaps a little too keenly.

Pole coughed, a feeling he was not familiar with rising slowly in his chest, a shade of jealousy perhaps.

"Although I still have to receive formal confirmation from the SFO, they are likely to be comfortable with our arrangements." A little disingenuous of Pole since Marissa had specifically asked for Nancy to be involved with the case. Marissa almost certainly had more confidence in Nancy than she had in Scotland Yard.

Nancy had been a brilliant QC before she gave it all up, and an even better mentor. It was clear to Pole that Marissa would never forget the time she had spent as Nancy's pupil.

"Let me speak to the SFO director – only if that would help, of course." Marsh's keenness must have been clear even to him.

"I am sure it will be perfectly fine, Sir," Pole rested his crossed hands on the side of the chair. He was not prepared to facilitate another meeting between Nancy and Marsh. The last time had almost soured his relationship with her. Even though Pole had made much progress with the delightful Ms Wu since then, he was not taking any chances. The little bubble of jealousy burst into a sense of joy.

Marsh was talking again and Pole caught only the end of the sentence.

"Call the governor, now."

"Absolutely," Pole said, hoping he was not committing to some ridiculous requirement for The Super.

Marsh sent him a quizzical look but started dialling, switching on the loudspeaker.

The deep voice of HMP Belmarsh's governor answered.

"Phil. Superintendent Marsh here. How are you?"

Marsh was on the offensive again. Another high-profile deal that would further his career.

* * *

The seventh door had just clanged shut. Henry stretched his arms and legs to be frisked once more before being allowed out of High Security Unit Belmarsh for time with his visitor.

Nancy had left a message that she would see him during the early afternoon visiting slot. It was not her usual day and Henry was excited. Something was afoot. He had scanned the news bulletins on his small radio in search of a clue. There was nothing he could put his finger on.

Frustrating.

Had he been on the trading floor he would have browsed through Bloomberg and Reuters and almost certainly had a good idea. He could have tried the library and attempted to log in, bypassing the restrictions imposed on inmates, as he had done successfully a few times now. But he judged it was not worth taking the risk. He needed to keep his powder dry for when he knew exactly what he was looking for.

The door to one of the inner yards opened. Henry hesitated. Confinement in HSU sometimes made him shy of walking outside the compound. The urge for freedom he then felt was often unbearable.

The fresh air hit his face. The weather had turned bitterly cold. He had felt it even from within the stuffiness of his cell. He walked over the threshold slowly, closed his eyes and inhaled.

Gusts of wind brought with them smells of cooking: mutton, onion and something else he could not quite define. He called it the Belmarsh smell, a smell one recognised just the way one recognised the smell of one's own home when walking in, with perhaps something particular to a prison: fear, despair, anger mixed with an infinitely small grain of hope for those who could find it.

Henry arrived in front of the next set of doors without noticing. The clunk of yet another set of locks reminded him that he had to keep moving. He turned his head briefly towards one of the yards reserved for HSU prisoners and noticed the small silhouette of a man walking slowly on his own around the perimeter, two guards in attendance.

"Henry?"

"Yep, sorry." Henry moved quickly inside the warm building and along the corridor. He did not know who the inmate was but had heard from Big K that several prisoners were deemed such high-risk that they were never allowed to mix with the others.

Henry had smiled. He was not deemed such a high risk and neither was Kamal.

A mistake? Or a plan?

Nancy was already sitting at a table in the meeting room when Henry entered. She had brought newspapers with her that she was arranging in front of her. Her briefcase was underneath the desk, neatly aligned with the legs of the table. Henry stopped, smiling.

They were allocated an hour and a half which often was too short but surprisingly had also proved too long on several occasions. It was almost always a shock to meet someone from the outside world: the clothes, the scent of freshly washed laundry or simply soap, a new hairstyle – and with Nancy, the fragrance of Issey Miyake.

She lifted her head, aware that someone was watching her and she broke into a smile.

"Do you have some good news?" Henry asked with a wry smile whilst bending down to put a quick kiss on her cheek.

"Perhaps." Nancy pushed a few papers towards him. Henry read the headlines in a low voice.

The UK government bailout – an update was RBS too big to fail?

Barclays says choosing Qatar as investor perfect decision ... TSB rescued by Lloyds. Will it work?

"OK, these banks have all been exposed to the subprime market in London. Nothing very new here." Henry said as he speed-read the papers. Nancy nodded but said nothing. Henry ran his hand through his short hair, irritated.

Could it be that his mind was becoming rusty? It had been over four years now since he had left the trading floor and four years since the banks had been offered a bailout. He scanned the papers again to find a common denominator.

"Aha. The UK government bailout programme," Henry said, a cheerful look on his face. "That's the point, isn't it?"

Nancy smiled in acknowledgement.

"Exactly right." Her face looked kindly amused, the almond shape of her eyes a little more pronounced, her lips gently arched upward.

Henry pushed the papers away and crossed his arms over his chest, ready for more.

He was needed again.

His breathing had become faster, hope bubbling up in his gut. Yet he did not want to acknowledge what he was hoping for, a little Celtic superstition perhaps.

"I won't keep you guessing," Nancy said. "The Serious Fraud Office is proposing that you assist them with a particularly complex investigation."

"The SFO?" Henry frowned. His heart was now beating fast, the short hairs on his neck standing up.

"That's right. They are preparing a request to go to the governor of HMP Belmarsh as well as the Home Office."

"Wow, I'm speechless," Henry said. It was an honest answer. He would have never dreamt the SFO would need him, but hey, why not?

"Same conditions as previously?" He asked. It almost felt routine.

Nancy leaned forward, arms on the table, hands crossed. "

Absolutely. I am to be appointed consultant to the SFO and Inspector Pole will be the official liaison between The Met and the SFO."

Henry rolled his eyes but broke into a smile.

"Pole, I would never have guessed. Still, I shouldn't grumble, better the devil you know."

"You were almost friends the last time you two worked together."

"Of course, we were trying to save you."

They both fell silent as the scene unfolded again in front of their eyes. The gun's discharge, Pole and Henry rushing into the room to rescue Nancy and her friend, glass shattered all over the floor, a man down, blood … so much blood.

Nancy had turned pale and Henry extended his hand, squeezing hers.

"I'm sorry, I didn't mean to bring back those memories in such an uncouth fashion."

"I know." She cleared her throat, squeezed his hand in return and slowly let go. "I can tell you a little more about the case; not much though, but perhaps enough to get that impressive brain of yours ticking."

"Am all ears."

Nancy summarised what Marissa had told her: the investment in Bank X by a Middle-Eastern country; the fund and its complex structure. Henry's focus was absolute, taking in every detail until Nancy had finished.

"Where is the domicile of the fund? Can you at least tell me that?" he said after a moment.

"Panama."

Henry grinned, uncovering a set of regular teeth. He crossed his arms behind his head, nostrils flaring.

"Panama, hey. I was wondering when the issue of fiscal paradises would surface. It seems it now has."

Nancy arched her eyebrows. "Really? Let's hope the governor will agree to let you out then."

Henry's smile broadened even more. "He will. Your good friend Pole will make sure of it and, if not, I can guarantee Superintendent Marsh won't hesitate to assist."

"But before I agree to support the SFO too, I want to have a little chat with you about something." Nancy opened her briefcase and placed an untidy piece of paper she had taken out of it in front of Henry.

"Would you care to elaborate please?" Nancy asked, her eyes on Henry. "If it means what I think it means … I will not be walking through these doors again for a very long time."

"I know – a bit melodramatic – very Irish. I get some strange ideas within the confines of HSU. It always passes." His smile had become rueful. He had known the question about the note he had written to Nancy a few months ago would come up. He did not regret writing it and simply hoped he could be convincing enough now.

"So just a bit of the blues nothing more dramatic than that?"

"Absolutely." Henry's smile did not falter. His heart raced a little. He didn't like lying to Nancy, but it was the only way.

"Escape out of HSU is not an option, you know that." Nancy leaned forward and placed a hand carefully across her mouth so that no one could lip read what she was saying to Henry.

"I know – the most secure prison in the UK." Henry's shoulders sagged sightly. "I am convinced of that."

Nancy searched his face. He felt his smile drop but she pulled back. He thought she was convinced.

Now the game was on.

Chapter Seven

The frisking was done professionally. She was glad however when the heavy prison door closed shut, leaving her outside and Henry still inside.

Nancy was only half convinced by Henry's explanation. The HSU was an impressive environment, a smaller community of inmates imprisoned within the main body of Belmarsh prison itself.

The prison officers too were different, better trained at identifying problems early and under strict instructions not to fraternise with the prisoners. But even if Henry dreamt about freedom, no one had ever escaped from HSU Belmarsh.

She felt reassured. Her experience of visiting Henry regularly had convinced her that no one would ever change that.

The bus arrived. She climbed on board and found a seat at the far end. She had been followed by a couple of other women. She recognised one of them, also a regular visitor. Her son was doing time for GBH, assault on his girlfriend and mother of his unborn child.

The younger woman was talking to the older one animatedly. The meeting with the prisoner she was visiting must have gone well, leaving a small glimmer of hope that he might change his ways and that there could be happiness once he came out.

The two women would leave the bus at Hackney Central and take a tube that would deliver them into the heartland of gangs' territory: high-rise estates riddled with drugs, weapons and abuse, a place where few policemen would ever venture. It looked cliched and yet sadly too familiar.

Nancy sighed; poverty in a country like the UK was a disgrace. What was the excuse in this place of abundance? It was not India. Or China with 1.4 billion people to feed.

Her body shuddered; she pushed away the memories of China. Nancy looked at her watch, almost 4pm. She could be with Pole in half an hour if she got off now and hailed a cab. Would it be unprofessional to distract him in the middle of two murder investigations? Nancy rested her forehead against the window of the lumbering bus.

The words of Phillippe, the young gallerist who had kindly agreed to help her with her search for her father, came back to her. "The trail goes cold after 1989." She opened her bag, fumbling with the zip, grabbed her BlackBerry and sent a text to Pole. She could hold back no longer. She had to know.

Pole replied within minutes. Nancy smiled. She sat back in the taxi she had been lucky to find quickly. How much more was she prepared to tell him about her childhood and her greatest fears?

The taxi swerved wildly, the cabbie banged his horn and lowered his window to give the cyclist a piece of his mind. He had barely avoided a man on his bike with a child seat at the back complete with a small passenger.

Nancy was thrown to one side, causing a searing pain in her right shoulder. The pain grew in intensity going way beyond what the impact should have provoked. Memories of another bike flooded her mind, uninvited.

Her long hair has been braided in an equally long plait that has not been undone for days. She wants to scratch her scalp but she is too frightened to let go of her father's back. Her father is pedalling fast. She is barely holding on. The small child seat on which she is perched has been built by him, a rackety affair that has done a good job of carrying her this far but now is threatening to collapse at any moment. She hears her mother call after them. They must reach the safety of their next stopover before it is dark, before the roads are deserted and the red guards prowl the streets. Nancy sees that they are in a city, people moving like ants, relentless, unstoppable. Her father slows down and a few people stare. Her mother is a foreigner and easily recognisable despite the scarf around her hair – just a little effort and they will be safe.

They turn off into another street, away from the main road, then take another turning into a smaller lane. Her father stops and takes her into his arms. He is almost running. Nancy sees her mother move her bike alongside her husband's, as she clasps her father's neck. Her mother catches her satchel on the handlebar of the bikes; they collapse with a loud clatter. Her father drops Nancy in front of a wooden door and runs back towards his wife. Out of nowhere four young men in uniform have appeared … red guards.

A door opens and shuts. She is in; they are out. She wants to cry but one hand covers her mouth, and another grabs her shoulder in an iron vice, "Don't say anything." The use of English stuns her.

Nancy heard another voice in the distance. She had taken hold of her shoulder trying to ease an overwhelming pain. The cab had stopped, the cabbie was speaking to her from the car's open door – "All right? Hurt?"

Nancy opened her eyes. She could hardly hold back the tears. She managed a breathless, "Don't worry – it's fine; an old wound."

* * *

Pole had once again arrived before her. She slowed down and spent a few moments observing him. His tall body was bent over a small coffee table. He had managed to secure their favourite spot, a couple of comfortable small sofas alongside the bay window, secluded from the rest of the cafe and its clusters of armchairs and couches.

She sometimes wondered whether he used his police ID card to secure the spot. He had ordered pastries already. Her latest favourite, introduced to her during a trip to France, the Ile de Ré, a little island close to La Rochelle.

These chaussons aux pommes, a kind of apple turnover drizzled with coarse granulated sugar, had awoken her taste buds and she was delighted she had found them in the middle of London.

Pole had a knack for knowing when he needed to be there first to welcome her; perhaps he heard it in the tone of her voice. This simply reflected the skill of a successful DCI and yet his ability to read human feelings always impressed her. It was one of the things which made him so immensely attractive.

Nancy started walking towards him. Pole had just finished rearranging one of the small sofas when he saw her. She was now all smiles and so was he.

"Jonathan, *mon cher ami*, always full of thoughtful attention when I need it the most," Nancy said putting one hand on his shoulder and standing on tiptoe to kiss his cheek.

"*Très heureux de l'entendre*," Pole kissed her cheek in return and bent forward to help her with her coat. "Did it not go as well as you expected with Henry? I would have thought —"

Nancy pressed his arm to interrupt him. "No, he is raring to go, just as we expected." She sat down, inhaled deeply. Pole sat opposite her, patient. He was there, as always. ready to give her all the time she needed.

Nancy looked into Pole's face, his intelligent eyes that creased ever so slightly near the temples when he paid attention, the famous goatee, now more salt and pepper than when they first met, and one immense quality above all.

Truthfulness.

"I have been thinking about this for a while now," she finally said whilst pouring the tea that had just arrived. Pole nodded encouragingly. He was pouring his own tea, a slow careful movement, mindful of not disturbing the atmosphere of confidence.

"It's about —" Nancy hesitated. Did she really want to do this?

"The past?" Pole ventured.

Nancy felt her lips tremble. "Thank you, yes, it is, very much so." She took a sip of tea. "It's about someone from my past." Hesitating once more, she looked into Pole's eyes. He let her gaze deeply into them. Her right hand started shaking ever so slightly but she could only see immense kindness in front of her.

"It's about – my father."

* * *

The cab almost felt comfortable. It was an old model, the cushioned upholstery had seen better days and so had the scuffed floor. Marissa pushed her body into the left-hand corner, squeezing herself between the window and the backrest. It was oddly cosy.

She spent a few moments observing the driver. He too had seen better days: short white hair barely covering his skull, hunched over the wheel, hands knotted with arthritis and yet smoothly weaving his taxi through heavy traffic.

She closed her eyes and rested her head against the window. Mark's bandaged face and hands sprang to mind, interrupting her train of thought. She buttoned up her coat, shivering. Was it truly what he wanted to do – carry on with the case? He was still so raw and shocked. She had never hesitated in prosecuting even the most tedious of cases. But today was different. Her large dark eyes felt moist. She opened her handbag, fished out a couple of tissues and ran them over her face.

She was about to arrive at the Serious Fraud Office where the director was waiting for her. Under his leadership the SFO had regained much of its lost reputation. He was unlikely to let the human factor interfere with the decision to follow through.

"David is going to want to prosecute. No matter what," Marissa whispered. David Black had made it his mission to restore the agency's relevancy.

He had reopened the LIBOR case after his predecessor had decided not to prosecute bankers, consequently revoking the previous decision. If there was sufficient evidence, he would want to forge ahead.

She asked the cabbie to drop her at the bottom of Trafalgar Square, paid and stepped out into the cold. She raised the collar of her coat and brought it close to her face. The wind was pushing mercilessly into her.

She moved at a slow pace, each step making ground against the gusts and sudden squalls of driving rain. She was getting wet, but she would not hurry, wanting to gain a few precious minutes before having to face a decision she did not want to make.

She entered the SFO building, greeted the receptionist with her usual nod and took the lift to the third floor. She ran her hand over her thick short hair, brushing off the raindrops.

She almost smiled: the advantage of African hair … it was hard for it to get wet. Her mobile phone buzzed, reminding her why she was back in the office. David was waiting for her and his texts made it clear.

Marissa was sitting in a narrow chair in front of the director's desk. He was pacing down the length of his office, rehearsing the speech he would deliver to the Attorney General, his boss. The LIBOR scandal was at the forefront of his strategy to charge the bankers who had manipulated the benchmark. LIBOR served to fix interest rate levels not only in the UK but also around the world, a $350 trillion scandal.

Even he had gasped at the figure. How far could he go in holding the banks and the bankers to account? And now this new scandal, another bank to prosecute. This was exactly what the SFO needed after years of lacklustre performance.

Marissa shifted a little. The wretched chair made her self-conscious of her size, and yes, it was not supposed to be comfortable to be in the director's presence. David stopped and peered over his narrow, blue-rimmed glasses.

"Your view, Marissa."

"I think he has decided to carry on."

David looked puzzled. "You sound unsure."

"He has barely recovered from the shock of the blast and from losing his wife, of course." Her voice trailed.

"I am not talking about Mark Phelps; understandably, his decision isn't final yet." He moved to his desk and sat down heavily. "I am talking about you. Your views on the case. The evidence looks solid so far."

"We still need to demonstrate that the Ultimate Beneficial Owner of the fund that received money from HXBK originates from the same Middle-Eastern country that invested in them in the first place."

"A circular transaction of the worst kind." The director smirked. "You've found a banker that can help, haven't you? I read Crowne's résumé. This case should be a walk in the park for him."

"Perhaps." Marissa's large hand moved a few sheets of paper around the file she had laid open on the desk.

David leaned back in his chair, one hand swinging the glasses he had removed.

"Marissa, we can't afford another BAE Systems failure. Surely, out of all people, you know that too."

Marissa froze for a few seconds. She had been expecting a reference to the case that still haunted her but perhaps not so soon.

Not being able to properly prosecute BAE Systems for bribery in the sale of armaments to the Saudis had been the worst moment in her career. What amounted in her view to a mere slap on the wrist for BAE and a pardon granted by Tony Blair to the Saudis, who had invoked national security, had been a severe blow.

"I know, Sir; how could I forget?" Marissa straightened up.

"You were not helped by the previous director, of that I am aware. But I am here to give you all the backing you need."

"It is very much appreciated."

"Come, come. What is it?"

"What if he changes his mind?"

"I presume we are back to Phelps. It is your job to convince him otherwise."

"He has two children. He may not want to risk their lives too." Marissa rearranged the papers again, meticulously aligned them in a neat pile. She could feel the heavy scrutiny of her boss's eyes. It was almost impossible to escape his astute and prodding attention.

"Are you reluctant to prosecute because you fear more lives will be lost?"

"I think that is correct, Sir." Marissa lifted her face and looked at him calmly. She was glad he had prised the question out of her.

He stopped the rhythmic movement of his hand. The glasses stood still in mid-air. His icy gaze rolled over her like water over a duck's back. The lady was not for turning, at least not yet, but she knew he would keep trying.

"They will benefit from the witness protection programme if they need to."

"Which has had mixed results," Marissa answered.

"If we give up now and he yields to intimidation, others will follow suit. These people will use the same techniques again and win."

Marissa held her breath. Of course, he had a valid point. But what was she expecting from such a seasoned lawyer?

"He is under armed protection, the Counterterrorist Squad is in attendance, and from what I can tell, Inspector Pole is a man who gets results." The director had resumed swinging his glasses from the tip of his fingers, round and round they went.

"His wife is dead," Marissa spoke without conviction, trying to find the argument that would perhaps stop or at least delay the wheels of the SFO from moving forward inexorably.

"It's a tragedy, an abomination but not prosecuting will not bring her back. More to the point, her murderers will have achieved what they wanted."

Marissa felt her tense body give a fraction. Her shoulders had been braced since she had started the conversation and her feet were itching to leave.

"I know you have a point, Sir, but I need to be absolutely sure that Mark will not change his mind and cave in at the last minute," Marissa said. Perhaps an argument that was giving her a little more time to assess her own feelings about the impact of the case on Mark's family.

"And it is also your job to make him feel secure enough not to want to cave in, as you put it." The director put down his glasses and stretched his hands over the desk's surface. "I understand it was a shock. You may not believe it but I understand. You know though that the only way to do the wife justice is to find and prosecute the bastards who did it."

Marissa locked eyes with the director for an instant – manipulation or compassion? She didn't know.

She slowly closed the file.

"I will speak to Mark."

* * *

531

Sotheby's Cafe was buzzing with a fauna that Brett hardly noticed. Afternoon tea was being served and much champagne being consumed, Brett could tell.

He navigated the tables, managing to avoid the long legs and Louboutin high-heeled shoes of an ultra-chic brunette. His eyes lingered a little too long over the legs that had almost tripped him. She did not mind the look nor did she move away – ruffians, plenty of money but little education.

Brett recognised the stocky frame of MI6-Steve. It was the first time Steve had arranged a meeting outside Brett's club or some facility regularly used by the agency.

It felt rushed or perhaps it was just that Brett did not like the fact that his ability to anticipate the moves of his associate had been thwarted.

Afternoon tea had arrived, a mountain of cakes and finger sandwiches into which Steve was tucking hungrily. Brett sat down without a word.

"It's a good table, relax. We can speak without being disturbed."

"If you say so." Brett was in no mood for risk-taking.

"Care for tea?" Steve was already pouring Brett a cup. He was almost jovial.

"Was it part of the plan?" Brett asked as calmly as he could muster. He so wished he could turn the plate of cakes onto the little rat's head.

"Which part of what plan?" Steve had wolfed down what must have been a coronation chicken sandwich going by the look of the yellow stains on his fingers. He wiped them on his napkin, scrunching it in the process.

Brett stopped Steve when he tried to finish pouring him tea. Afternoon tea was served with lemon. He waved at one of the waiters who was too busy serving a group of Asian women to notice.

Brett stood up, made his request known and came back to the table.

"I saw the pictures of Visconti's body." Brett had decided on another tack. His stomach felt queasy. He took a sip of tea, forgetting altogether about the lemon slice he was so eagerly awaiting.

He cleared his throat discreetly. MI6-Steve's face lost some of its glee. Brett had not mentioned this when reporting on his meeting with The Sheik. Steve put down the sandwich he had just grabbed.

"You should have said." It was not a reproach; an indication rather that MI6-Steve could have been better prepared. "And no, I didn't think The Sheik would show you the photos."

"Yes, well. I don't think I wanted to speak about it then. But this is not the reason we are here. As much as I dislike Crowne, I need to speak to you about him. And I find it easier to speak to you about him face to face." Brett took another mouthful of tea. He so wished they had met at the Club; he could have ordered a much-needed glass of whisky.

Steve bent forward. He would wait for Brett to be ready to tell his story. He had seen too many of these executions not to know the effect it would have on someone who saw a beheading for the first time – even in a photograph.

The slice of lemon arrived, a little slim but it would have to do. Brett refilled his cup, dropped the lemon into it and stirred.

Almost acceptable.

"You may not believe it, but in all my years dealing with these people, selling their looted artefacts and art pieces, I had never seen a Jihadi execution." Brett closed his fingers tightly over the handle of his cup.

"The slaughter of the kafir, the infidels." Brett stopped. The pictures materialised in front of his eyes. His stomach heaved. He brought his napkin to his lips for control.

"You don't need to give me the details," Steve said. "I have seen enough myself. I understand." He moved his glance away for a moment, stirred too by the dread the photos were meant to inspire.

"The question that matters now is why?"

"A warning." Brett tried to gather his thoughts. "I don't know why though. Everything has gone smoothly so far and," Brett stopped in mid-sentence. "You don't think they know about …?"

Steve shook his head.

"You would not have made it out alive otherwise, no matter how much they need you. And if they had wanted you to deliver something for them and then execute you, they would not have warned you."

"Right. Right."

"How much do you know about Visconti's business?" Steve asked.

"In my art business —" Brett started.

"You mean your trafficking business," Steve replied, glad of the diversion.

"No need to be crude." Brett frowned. "Visconti was known to be one of the best at supplying almost any piece his clients wanted. He was connected all over Europe, in particular Eastern Europe, the Middle-East, of course, and Asia."

"OK, so you know he was a crook who stole art from anyone but in particular from museums and war zones."

"Well, some of his thieving, as you call it, has saved some exceptional pieces from destruction."

Steve rolled his eyes. "Not going to argue with that one. What else?"

"It all went very badly when he was caught with a stolen piece from one of the best-known museums in Venice."

"And after that?"

"He escaped. But you know that already." Brett put the cup he was holding back on its saucer abruptly. "Then I assumed he had retired, but perhaps not." Brett pursed his lips in a dubious pout.

"Would he have started the old business again?"

"I don't think so." Brett wiped his mouth slowly. "There would have been a buzz in our community and my contacts would have told me."

"You've heard nothing?"

"Not a word." Brett felt genuinely puzzled. "Are you testing me?" He had no time for Steve's games.

"I'm not trying to trick you. Visconti was up to something, that much we know."

"What? The great MI6 lost track of a well-known art trafficker – shocking." Brett looked suitably distressed.

"No need to rub it in." Steve grumbled. "Not our pad anyway; we're not the National Crime Agency."

They both fell silent. The leftover sandwiches and cakes looked unappetising. Brett called for a fresh pot of tea.

"Still," Brett said, playing with his cigarette pack. "I don't understand why the photos."

"There is perhaps an explanation," Steve mused, toying with a piece of uneaten bread. "If Visconti worked for them and he did not deliver they may …"

"Ask me to deliver instead." Brett shook his head. "Shit, what have you dropped me into?" Swearing was not part of Brett's education but at that very moment he no longer cared. "Some crappy weapon deal, Lord knows?"

"Very possibly," Steve replied, his bulldog face more serious than ever.

"You mean, almost certainly,"

"Whatever you need, we can provide."

"Don't be ridiculous – you mean bodyguards, a bulletproof jacket and a change of identity?"

"Well, remember what we agreed."

"A clean slate to start again and a fat bank account. As long as I live long enough to enjoy it, which at the moment is starting to look rather unlikely."

"You don't know what The Sheik has in mind and Visconti didn't have the backing of MI6."

"So. Anything I need, hey?" Steve was onto something big and Brett could feel it. Brett waited.

"Fine," Steve grunted. "Anything you need."

Brett poured a fresh cup of tea. "I meet The Sheik again in a couple of days." He took a content sip.

"Glad to hear it." Steve poured himself another cup of tea in turn. "And to accompany this excellent cuppa, how about the topic that brought us here in the first place?"

Brett shot a dark eye at Steve. Did he really have to be such a tiresome arse?

"You mean Henry Crowne?" The name almost stuck in his throat.

"The very same." Steve grinned.

Chapter Eight

The library was empty, and today's librarian was taking his time, checking the cards he had taken out of the filing box. These showed the names of everyone who had either borrowed or returned a book.

Henry was sharing the job with a strange-looking man, thin as a wire, an equine profile and an unusually high forehead. The Doc had a reputation. He had been convicted for prematurely terminating the life of several of his patients; to him, euthanasia did not only apply to cats and dogs.

Yet, the Doc was incredibly well read and at times Henry almost forgot why he had been convicted in the first place.

Almost.

"Library shutting in fifteen," The Doc said, his nose still stuck in the cards.

"Just finishing a letter to my lawyer. Won't take five." Henry sat down in front of the computer and moved to the right screen.

The Doc raised one eye and finished replacing the cards in the box. He did not care what Henry was up to as long as it did not impact him.

Henry started typing on the keyboard. He had once more cracked the password that allowed him access to the Internet, access reserved only for the prison officers. The PC provided for inmates was designed to facilitate writing to their solicitors and other officials.

Two icons to choose from: a cat and a dog. The corny humour of assigning a cat to the cons and a dog to the officers still made Henry smile. Today he had clicked on the dog and the little pet had responded to its master's voice; Henry was in.

The password was complicated enough but Henry had taught himself to touch type. A skill he deemed essential for a man who prided himself on his quick and error free email replies.

Henry had also noticed that although the screen was shielded from viewers its reflection could be seen in the shiny surface of a steel cupboard behind it. He simply had to be patient and keep an eye on the guards' fingers when they typed. The password was changed fortnightly and Henry had kept up with the change.

He was searching for articles on Serious Fraud Office lawsuits. The SFO had had mixed success in prosecuting high-profile cases. The BAE Systems debacle must still have been rankling badly.

In 2004 the SFO had started litigating against the company for making illegal payments to government officials to win deals relating to armaments. It had made payments to several governments in Africa and the Middle-East.

The allegations covered payments handed over to an unnamed Saudi official in relation to the £40 billion al-Yamamah arms deal between the UK and Saudi Arabia. However, the case had been dropped after the UK government argued the enquiry might upset the UK–Saudi relationship and threaten national security.

BAE paid a record UK fine of £30 million in 2010, "for failing to keep reasonably accurate accounting records relating to its activities." The SFO confirmed there would be no further prosecutions, including of the individuals identified in the fraud. BAE had taken measures to implement a better ethical and compliance culture.

Henry smiled a knowing smile. Could any arms deal be done without a large backhander? He doubted it, or perhaps he was too cynical. Henry continued reading.

The US Department of Justice had also pursued BAE and had received almost the entire amount of the final fine – over £400 million. Well done the prosecutors of the DOJ, Henry thought. The conclusion of the case had not ended well for the previous SFO director, Robert Wardle, who had narrowly escaped being charged with perverting the course of justice.

Henry looked at the clock on the wall. He did not have enough time left to finish his research. The Vincent and Robert Tchenguiz case looked embarrassing, but the discovery of its details would have to wait.

"The SFO needs to score," Henry murmured.

The Doc pushed his chair back noisily. It was time to leave. Henry closed the article he was reading, erased his browsing history, printed the letter he was supposedly writing.

One of the prison officers had arrived and was doing a circuit of the library. He checked what Henry had printed without reading it, a quick glance showed it was harmless. Henry left slowly. Bang-up time would start shortly, an hour back in his cell, followed by free time for dinner and then lock-up for the rest of the night.

Henry's mind was buzzing despite his nonchalant pace. He had to mine the SFO story further. He had also started browsing Panama in the hope he would find snippets of information telling him what the interest was in this particular fiscal paradise.

But nothing obvious had come up. He knew the place well from numerous trips and had looked up the name of the law firm he had worked with there in the past, Mossack Fonseca. There was nothing relevant on their website apart from the usual corporate ads detailing how easy their shell companies were to set up and maintain.

Henry left the long corridor that led from the library. Another officer was waiting for him whilst the first guard was locking up. He found himself in the common room where the inmates socialised during the day.

They were allowed twelve hours outside of their cells, not a bad ratio. Henry slowed his pace further, scanning the perimeter for troublemakers. To his relief Kray was not around. Big K had also disappeared and so had Kamal.

Perfect timing.

He did not want to have to face anyone, including Big K. No matter how much he enjoyed the banter with the Jamaican giant, Henry needed to put down on paper what he had learned. Try to find a pattern and get an angle, anticipate why the SFO sought his expertise.

It had worked superbly well in the LIBOR manipulation case. He just needed to pull another similar trick out of his hat and he would get closer to his goal.

The door clanged shut behind him and Henry felt almost free in his cell. His heart had not sunk as it usually did at the sound of the bolts closing, a regular reminder of where he was. In one step he reached the little table he called his desk. The word gave him hope that when he sat down at it he could still produce work worthy of that name. He pulled a pad from underneath some books and started writing.

A list of all the countries he had used to structure complex transactions: Europe, the US, Asia, as well as all the small jurisdictions that offered legal advantages. Nothing ever illegal when working in banking.

But a clever understanding of the differences in the laws of each place had allowed him to take advantage of discrepancies. There was however one noticeable exception – he placed a star next to the place he had used for structuring the funds and accounts the IRA once used.

Now those were illegal – good old-fashioned money laundering. His hand stiffened and he stopped. There it was, in black and white, his commitment to what he thought had been his father's cause. He put his pen down for a moment.

The pain of betrayal surged into him like a tidal wave, threatening to drown him. He pressed his hands over his trembling thighs and the spasm going through his body eased off. It had become easier not to succumb, to let the feelings course through him and then be released.

Was it the passage of time or the faith in the plan he was meticulously pulling together?

Perhaps both.

The plan was shaping up as he had hoped it would. The word that had been haunting him no longer felt fantasy but reality.

He would escape the most secure prison in the UK: HSU Belmarsh.

* * *

Low tide on the River Thames had dropped the waterline of its banks. Nancy had walked for a while along the path that led to the water's edge. It was not a route she knew well nor one that would take her back to the safety of her apartment. Pole had been full of attention. She had never felt surrounded by so much kindness and, dare she say it – love. He had patiently waited for her to tell the story of her father, questioning seldom but always with tact.

Nancy leaned towards the water, her forearms resting on the stone wall. The colour of the Thames had turned icy grey, the swells within it giving the river an occasional silvery glimmer. She pulled up the collar of her coat and fished out from its pockets the gloves she had forgotten to put on.

She had allowed Pole to jot down a few notes, mainly dates and names. Early memories of her childhood in China – the visits to her mother's family in the UK, their escape during the Cultural Revolution since her father had become one of the artists the Chinese government wanted to "re-educate" – had come flooding back.

"I never speak about it," Nancy had said to Pole.

"In your own time." Pole had extended his strong but elegant hand, wrapping it around Nancy's fingers and she had almost cried.

She was not yet ready for this ultimate show of trust.

"My father left us – after almost ten years in Paris." Nancy had taken a gulp of tea to dissolve the lump that had swollen in her throat.

"You mean he left to go back to China after the Cultural Revolution was over?" Pole had helped by putting it into words for her.

"That's right. He had great hopes for China once Deng Xiaoping took over." Nancy struggled to continue, and Pole pressed her hand gently again. Nancy squeezed back so hard she thought she might hurt him.

"I'm sorry," she said releasing Pole's hand and withdrawing in shame. Pole captured her wrist loosely.

"It will take a lot more than a tight pinch to hurt a well-weathered DCI like me." His smile was reassuring, his eyes a mixture of affection and gentle tease.

Nancy groaned. "I have to know, Jonathan." She raised her wounded eyes towards him. "Oh God, sorry. I am not very good at giving you the right background."

"This is not a Scotland Yard case. It is you and one of the most important events …" Pole's voice trailed off.

"I need to know whether he is still alive," Nancy had spoken quickly. She felt exhausted. She let her body drop back into the small sofa she had been sitting on. For a moment she closed her eyes and when she reopened them Pole had moved next to her. She rested her head against his shoulder and for a while there was nothing left to say.

Pole's BlackBerry buzzed and he sent the call to voicemail with a click. Nancy straightened up slowly.

"I need to gather some proper information for you. I have an old file." Her voice still sounded uncertain. Pole's phone rang again, another click. He would not be rushed. Nancy managed a smile and gently cupped his cheek with her hand.

"The great DCI Jonathan Pole is needed."

Pole kissed the palm of her hand and returned her smile.

"I am sure they can wait a little longer."

Nancy had sighed. "Thank you."

Nancy was now on her own. She turned her back away from the river. She leaned against the wall, facing the Globe theatre. She wondered whether she was right to dig up the past. Her father had left France for China in the early eighties. He had written a few letters but then silence. Whenever he wrote it had always been about the new government, hope for the future, the artist's role at the centre of the people's revolution. He never asked about her, never wished her mother, his wife, well.

The anger sizzled within her. She would not surrender to it though, not any more. Still, she was unsure what the result of a confrontation with reality would be. She thought about Henry. His own anger had led him to where he was, a grubby prison cell and a thirty-year sentence to go with it. Could it have been her?

Perhaps.

She had, after all, worked with the famous Jacques Vergès when he had defended Klaus Barbie for crimes against humanity. He had called her back when he was hoping to mount the defence of Saddam Hussein.

A vicious gust of wind made Nancy shiver. It was time to head home. She decided to leave the heart-aching questions for another day. Another case demanded her attention and she was glad of it.

* * *

"Slow down." Pole broke into a slow jog towards the lift doors on the ground floor of Scotland Yard, pressing his mobile against his ear "I'll be with you in less than five minutes."

Andy had received news from the Counterterrorist Squad and Commander Ferguson was agitated. He had delivered the information to Pole's DS as, "the Inspector was nowhere to be bloody seen," quoting the man verbatim.

Pole did not regret the time spent with Nancy. He had devoted enough years to The Met; his personal life, for once, would come first. Andy was pacing outside and almost rushed into the lift as Pole walked out.

"That important, hey." He could never be cross with Andy, who was sometimes puppy-like but so goddamn bright.

"Ferguson says that the material used for the bomb underneath Phelps' car matches the Paddington bomb."

"Let's go into my office." Pole pushed the BlackBerry deep into his pocket. Perhaps he should have answered the call after all.

They both walked in silence. Pole closed the door of his office and sat behind the desk. Andy moved the pile of documents occupying the only other chair in the room and sat down.

"OK, what do we know?"

"Ferguson is categorical. Same components used for the Paddington bomb. The one that almost killed Henry Crowne—" Andy stopped abruptly. Pole knew all about the bomb that had exploded near the train station four years ago. He had been called to the scene as it had just happened and witnessed the carnage it had left behind.

"Two possibilities," Pole said. "Either the same person built the bomb, or we have the same explosives supplier." Pole started playing with a large paper clip he had found on the floor. This was not the news he wanted to hear.

"Ferguson's conclusion exactly."

Pole remained silent. Loose connections were coming together forming a web of improbable links. The bomb that had targeted Mark Phelps the SFO witness, the explosion that had almost cost Henry his life and Henry being dragged out of Belmarsh to work on the SFO case. What of the Islington canal execution?

"Guv." Andy was waving tentatively.

"Sorry, just thinking…" Pole didn't yet have a theory. "Never mind, I need more time to elaborate. What does Ferguson want to do next?"

"He would like to speak to you about Mark Phelps and the witness protection programme."

"Has he spoken to Marissa Campbell?"

"No, he wants to speak to you first."

Pole was about to call Ferguson, his hand hovering over the phone.

"How about Visconti links to the Middle-East? What did old Grandel say?"

Andy looked lost for a second. "You mean —" as if answering his own question, he carried on. "DCI Grandel confirmed that Visconti was very well connected with a number of looters in the Middle-East. Well-known terrorists raising money by selling artefacts – particularly in Iraq."

"Does Grandel think that could be a motive? One of his deals going wrong?"

"Not sure, Guv. Visconti was arrested in Italy and had been serving time until he escaped."

"How long did he serve?"

"A year and a bit."

"Hardly any time then. Was he caught for trafficking Middle-Eastern pieces?"

"No, he tried to organise the theft of a well-known painting in one of the main museums in Venice. He managed to steal it but got caught with it in his possession.

"DCI Grandel thinks the buyer got cold feet because of the publicity and Visconti didn't have time to shift the piece before the police found him."

Pole sat back in his chair. Was the old link between Visconti and the Middle-East relevant or was he trying too hard?

"And does Grandel think Visconti tried to reconnect with his previous contacts?"

"That is his assumption. Visconti was sighted in Geneva shortly after he escaped and then nothing."

"Good work. Keep digging. What about INTERPOL?"

"Nothing yet."

Chapter Nine

A distant sound of locks opening, the cell flooded with light.

"Hello Mr Crowne." The voice was far away. Henry could not quite place it. He squinted into the harsh neon light overhead.

"Hello Mr Crowne; you don't mind if we check your cell, do you?"

Henry rolled over on his side, threw the sheet and blanket to the bottom of the mattress in a slow and uncertain move. He swung his muscular legs over the edge of his diminutive bed.

"Sure," he mumbled, rubbing his eyes.

It was a good sign. The governor of HMP Belmarsh had decided, once more, to allow him outside the compound; the downside – impromptu checks of his cell.

Henry had undergone a few of these searches when he had been asked to assist Pole and Nancy on the murder enquiry linked to the LIBOR scandal. He was ready for what came next.

However, one of the new prison officers on his wing was keen to show he could do the job to an exacting standard and Henry had been a little anxious – all right, very anxious. His small art piece, his netsuke, could have got him into real trouble and, worse, it would have cost Nancy a lot too. But no one had outsmarted Henry Crowne on that day. Complacency meant mistakes and he was not about to let himself down by being smug. Gone were the days of investment banking.

His legal file marked in bold letters LEGAL & PRIVILEGED was sitting on his desk. An irresistible decoy for any prison officer worthy of the name.

The three guards moved noisily. Henry stood up and donned his tracksuit bottoms. He moved to the head of his bed, waiting for instructions.

John, a short stocky man, was in charge. Not a bad chap, but all officers appointed to HSU Belmarsh were discouraged from befriending inmates. No small talk, which Henry regretted.

He had always been good at it, creating an atmosphere of trust in which people enjoyed working. He had struck the right tone, though, courteous without being obsequious, but detached. He did not seem to want anything from anybody.

The file did the trick. Officer number two, tall and wiry, a man whose name he did not know, was already moving towards the desk. He had been brought in on the task from another wing within HSU. Henry waited a few more seconds before protesting.

"Hey, that is a privileged document," he said raising his voice.

"So you say," the tall man replied. He had picked up the file from the desk, not opening it but threatening to.

"That's the law and I know my rights," Henry replied, crossing his arms over his chest.

The other guards had stopped searching. No one wanted a confrontation. John took the document away from the other officer, looking at the outside before putting it down again. "It's the same one I saw last time we searched."

"And the one I take when I see my legal representative."

The search resumed. Henry cursed himself. He should have pulled back a little. The guards were now moving around his bookshelf. Some books were opened and thumbed, then came the turn of the heavy art book that hid the netsuke.

The spine cracked. Henry held his breath. The guards would have to look into the spine to see the little bundle and even if they did the small clump looked like paper.

"You like your art don't you, Henry?" John asked. He was still perusing the book, looking through the images.

"Are you saying I could start a collection?" Henry shot back. Shit, what am I saying? he thought. A small film of perspiration formed at the back of his neck. Henry tried to look amused. He hoped the sudden tension in his body would not betray him. John kept going through the pictures. The sound of an object dropping on the floor almost made Henry jump. His legal file had been left on the side of his desk and it had now fallen to the floor, its contents lying on the ground.

Henry almost burst into laughter. It had all been about this goddamn file after all.

"Sorry," the tall officer said with a grin, already gathering the papers together. Henry moved towards them quickly. "I'll do it." He knelt and bunched the papers together in a disjointed move, pushed them into the folder and hugged it to his chest. He looked suitably annoyed and the guards took note.

An excellent decoy indeed.

Any information worth remembering he would never store on paper but rather in a place no one else could access – his brain.

The search lasted another ten minutes. The art book had been left on his chair, pushed around every time the officers moved to access another part of his cell. Henry's back was now resting against the wall, his eyes in the distance.

He forced himself not to look at the book precariously balanced on the seat. One of the guards bumped into the chair and this time the book almost fell. John caught it with one hand. "I wouldn't want your collection to get damaged." Henry felt the punch in the gut.

Had John guessed?

The officer threw the book onto his desk, gave the other two a nod.

"Very funny," Henry managed to mumble.

He collapsed on his bed as soon as they had left and did not move. What if they came back? His cell was a mess and he was now fully awake. He waited in complete stillness for a while.

Finally, he stretched and a small bubble of contentment burst in his chest. The decoy had worked. Wheels were in motion and he was once more allowed outside HSU Belmarsh. Kamal would be aware of it and yet Henry was not entirely sure what the other man's plans would be. Would he attempt to escape at the same time as Henry? What Henry was sure of was that Kamal and his group wanted him for his knowledge of banking and finance. He had built an impenetrable maze of companies and bank accounts for the IRA. The money that had been taken to finance the IRA decommissioning had never been found and its origins would remain unknown for ever. Someone with such capabilities was invaluable to a new ambitious Jihadi splinter group.

Henry started tidying his room. It did not take long and once done he sat on the floor, back against the wall, knees to his chest. He dropped his head back, resting. The last piece of the puzzle was still missing. What if it never came?

Henry groaned. He must trust his instinct. It would. It had to.

Henry did not believe in coincidences. Kamal Al Quatari known under his battle name as Abu Maeraka had been transferred to HSU Belmarsh on Henry's wing the minute he had been found guilty of terrorism.

There were three wings in HSU but the man who had almost cost Henry his life had been transferred to his wing. Henry's jaw tightened. He pushed away the images that were trying to force their way into his mind.

The smell of burning petrol filled his lungs. He stood up abruptly. He needed to walk away from the scene. He took off his T-shirt and, lying on the ground, he started a series of press-ups: thirty, fifty, one hundred.

Henry collapsed face down. His heart pumping in his chest, his throat on fire. He turned on his back and let the cool surface of the floor calm him down. It helped. The images of Paddington receded. The bomb exploding near the police van that was taking him for questioning had been the turning point he needed. The driver of the police van had died and his colleague had been trapped in the vehicle. Henry had not had the courage to help.

He sat up, grabbed his T-shirt and wiped the sweat from his face and his body. He bunched up the garment into a ball and threw it into the corner of the cell. He knew why he had joined the IRA.

He had wanted to believe his father belonged. Wasn't it better to think he had died a partisan's death rather than a drunk's? Liam and Bobby had given him a sense of belonging. And perhaps their cause had been just, but nothing justified the killing of innocents.

Nothing.

Henry walked to his washbasin and ran his hands underneath the cold water. Whose blood was he trying to cleanse? He splashed his face, moved his fingers through his greying hair. Atonement would only come one way.

A life for a life.

The thought pacified him somewhat. After the months of agony during his trial and the early days at Belmarsh a glimmer of hope had emerged. A flicker of light he had learned to kindle.

His need for redemption had astounded him. He had realised he would never be fully forgiven for what he had done but he could perhaps show he could be a better person. The plan he had slowly elaborated was bold, perhaps as bold as the one that had brought him down four years ago. But unlike the man who had wrecked Henry's future, Henry was willing to risk his life and face death. The lies and manipulation that had sent him to prison had only been devious at best.

Henry lay down on his bed again. He had a couple of hours before breakfast. And he needed a sharp mind for what was coming next.

The piece of toast popped out of the toaster with a small mechanical click. The smell of warm bread made Brett's mouth water. He started buttering his toast and checked the tea had brewed long enough. He opened a jar of his favourite marmalade. It was all looking appetising and yet something essential was missing, a butler.

Brett could not help smiling at his own delusions of grandeur – gone were the days of *Downtown Abbey*, an absolute tragedy. He moved to his lounge, placed the buttered toast on the table and activated the screen of his laptop, special edition, MI6 encrypted.

Steve had sent additional information that might help him with The Sheik's request. Brett had acquired a reputation for gathering information and in particular information of a sensitive nature on his clients. It had helped him to cut deals, to know their tastes and how far they would go for a piece they truly desired.

The Sheik wanted everything Brett had on Henry Crowne. Brett had looked a little puzzled but he was not prepared to argue after having been shown Visconti's pictures. He had assured The Sheik he would do his very best. It was a balancing act, neither too much nor too little or his own head would be next.

The file was extensive and Brett was surprised. This was not a last-minute cobbling together of information. It had taken time, perhaps years, to gather. Some parts were blanked out. Still Brett could see considerable effort had been used in finding out who Henry Crowne truly was.

Brett bit into his toast, white of course, none of that wholemeal rubbish. The idea of delving into Crowne's life rather changed his mood.

The family history was unexpected. A mixed marriage forty years ago in Belfast was unheard of. There had been speculation about Henry's father's IRA affiliation. It looked likely despite the lack of evidence. The puzzlement was Henry's father's marriage to a British woman.

Perhaps it was a cover-up. Henry's father's death attributed to a UVF assassination reinforced the idea. This part of the document was heavily redacted, and Brett's curiosity was piqued. Steve might one day indulge him.

Brett kept reading.

As for Henry, outstanding academic results, a move to London with a career in law then investment banking – a UK bank, a Swiss bank and finally GL, one of the most successful American banks before the 2008 crisis. Brett hated to admit it, but Henry was a very clever man.

Then entered Brett Allner-Smith, his good self, into Henry's life. All the pieces of art and antiquities he had sold to Henry – listed, with prices, provenance whether legal or illegal. Brett felt almost nostalgic. But not quite.

Henry was only an Irish peasant trying to look the part. He chuckled at the news that Henry had taken elocution lessons to rid himself of his Belfast accent. And yet Brett could never forgive Henry for leading him straight into the claws of MI6. Brett poured some fresh tea. The little coward had recanted on a deal involving a stolen Iraqi artefact that had almost cost Brett his life.

Brett had offered Crowne, the man whose deals earned him millions in bonuses, an exceptional piece, a piece every museum would want to own. Henry had been keen; so many of these pieces went missing. It was almost his duty to salvage one of them. Brett had been cautious to start with but eventually trusted Henry's desire to own something no one else could. At the eleventh-hour Henry got cold feet.

"One million dollars," Brett said aloud. It was the sum he owed his Al-Qaeda contacts for the artefact and these people did not accept credit.

Brett drank his tea and pondered. Now Crowne was in prison and he, Brett, was involved in a potentially lethal operation that far exceeded his appetite for risk. No time to feel sorry for himself though; if he played his cards right he would escape the clutches of MI6 and the money he had made would go a long way towards restoring his past standing.

Brett resumed his reading. The dossier was now dealing with Henry's involvement in money laundering for the IRA. The fund structure Henry had used had never been completely uncovered, essential pieces of the puzzle were missing and by the looks of it Crowne had not been willing to cooperate.

Brett read through all the documents in one sitting. He kept sipping his tea and whenever his cup ran dry he poured more without stopping his reading. It was riveting and almost – creative. He put his cup down and started putting together a sheet of information for The Sheik. The Sheik would be impressed. He pulled towards him the notepad that already lay on the table and started writing.

Out of nowhere the images of Visconti's body resurfaced. He stood up, feeling giddy. Brett leaned forward against the table. The moment passed.

Never feel complacent; that was the only way to stay alive.

The black and white photos had turned yellow around the edges. An elegant young man in a three-piece suit, yet sporting a Chairman Mao collar shirt, a young woman with long dark hair, a short dress with broad stripes and insert pockets that interrupted the lines – she could remember the dress, she thought.

Both are all smiles. He has wrapped his arm around the young woman's shoulders and she has her hands on the shoulders of a little girl called Nancy. Nancy turned over the photo and looked at the date. By then her parents had left China as the Cultural Revolution was biting hard.

They had just arrived in Europe after months of travelling through the Chinese countryside to escape the communist regime and finally reached Hong Kong, then France. Nancy shuddered. She had kept very little that could remind her of that era but somehow this faded picture of three happy people had been hard to let go of.

She had gathered together the few documents she had kept that related to her father. She adjusted her dressing gown, drawing it tighter. Her hands were freezing despite the pleasant temperature of her apartment.

She was still somewhat puzzled by her renewed desire to find her father. It had started a few years ago when she had decided to give up the law after a remarkably successful career as a QC. She paused at the thought. Any regrets?

None whatsoever.

Having more time to think about the direction of her life had perhaps allowed her to let her true emotional needs emerge or perhaps her aversion to being attached despite the keen attraction she felt for Pole had caught up with her.

She could no longer argue that her busy job was taking her away from possible relationships or that men do not like to date a woman of keen intellect in a position of power. Her intellect was certainly intact, but she had become a philanthropist, patron of the arts and collector. Nothing very scary about that.

Nancy moved to the kitchen, a modern and aesthetic space – wood, steel and stone – with plenty of room to cook and enjoy a gathering of friends or entertain a single person. She smiled at the memory of her first dinner "*en tête à tête*" with Jonathan Pole, both a little nervous and both trying to be humorous about it.

The gurgling of the kettle was interrupted by a sharp click. It snapped

Nancy out of her reverie and she started preparing a fresh pot of tea. She always took pleasure in this simple ritual but today it had become a little less enjoyable.

She saw her mother, so very English yet so very carefree, making the same gestures. But this time the attractive young man of the photo has disappeared. Her mother looks tired, sleep deprived through lack of news. Silence tearing at her soul every day. The ghost of her father floating over them both since his departure for China, ever since the letters he had promised stopped coming.

By then Nancy had decided to push memories of her father away, push them to a place they could no longer be reached and could no longer hurt. Nancy, the rebel who dissented as a matter of course at The Sorbonne, was merely dealing with her loss.

She knew that now more clearly than she had known then. But she also understood that her indecision, her reluctance to commit to a man, was rooted in this pain she had ignored for so long.

Nancy was back in her lounge. She was drinking tea. She didn't quite know how she had got there.

A few months ago she had almost lost her life and the chance to respond to Pole's affection. Her stomach tightened at the thought.

"It is time." She must move on. It was somehow ironic though. She, who had been so instrumental in helping Henry come to terms with the rage that had almost destroyed him, was now on the same journey. Harrowing, laborious but worthwhile.

She hoped.

Nancy returned to the photo, the old documents; she started on her yellow notepad to do what she had done best all her life, to ask the hard questions.

Chapter Ten

A crust had started to form on his bowl of porridge. He laid the tray carefully on his small desk, opened the salt sachet and sprinkled it over his breakfast. He always preferred eating porridge the Scottish way.

He began eating, taking his time. Henry had rarely eaten in his cell since he had made contact with Kamal. He was careful not to break the pattern of his daily routine. Anything out of the ordinary would attract the attention of the prison officers. Today was different. He was once more allowed outside HSU. The guards would understand he might not wish to show his excitement or apprehension to the other inmates.

Kamal would also know that Henry was on his way to Scotland Yard. He had assured Henry that, God willing, he would organise an escape. Henry's goal had been set. Even if his outings became a regular occurrence he would never feel he had given enough until his life was in danger.

Henry finished the porridge, moved to his bed and sat down cross-legged with his mug of tea. He had expected Kamal to have a crack at the rhetoric about "the fight", "the Jihad", but he had been remarkably silent.

He had simply demonstrated to Henry how other Muslim inmates were devoted to him. One of them was sent to the box, a room with nothing inside apart from a Perspex window, for instigating a fight. A couple of other inmates had tasted the segregation unit, a place where prisoners spent at least twenty-three hours in their cells every day, for breaking HSU rules. Kamal or Abu Maeraka, always affable, always discreet, was slowly building his army within HSU and perhaps outside.

Henry suspected that the guards were not fooled by his manners but knew could they do nothing about someone who was polite and did not seem to cause trouble. He was a true leader of the kind that inspired total devotion.

Henry had mentioned the Qur'an, after finding the small book in his cell. It had been clever to say nothing beforehand, to let Henry wonder why it had been put there. "You might want to understand how my brothers think," had been Kamal's reply when Henry had questioned him about it. It was unobtrusive and clever. Would Henry be asked to join the faith once he was outside?

Henry drained his cup. He pushed the thought aside. For now, he needed to anticipate what Kamal had in mind for their escape.

He had never entered a deal in his City banking life without having the upper hand or at least without having an ace up his sleeve. This situation was different though, more fluid. He needed to think on his feet, to be prepared for all eventualities and also to be physically ready.

He had trained his mind ruthlessly for more than twenty years in investment banking and on the trading floor. Today he would train his body, pushing himself to the limit alongside Big K. Henry might even regret leaving Big K behind.

Henry stood up, grabbed a small towel which he slung over his well-developed shoulders and walked out of his cell. His porridge would give him plenty of energy since, after all, it was a decent breakfast.

"What's happened to your taste buds?" Henry murmured with a sigh. Gone were the days when he would have returned a boiled egg to the kitchen because it was not cooked to perfection. Henry prepared himself to run the gauntlet of the gates he had to cross before arriving at the gym. He would be frisked a few times in the process. Nothing so strenuous ever happened in a standard prison compound, even on the Category A wing, which housed the most dangerous criminals. But this was HSU Belmarsh and no measures were spared to ensure maximum control over the inmates.

Henry entered the gym where Big K had already started his routine. He had his back turned against the wall facing the door. Henry had never thought about it before but realised now that none of the machines had their backs turned to the door – so no one could sneak up from behind.

Big K was in full swing. The rowing machine was moaning under the strain of his efforts. Henry set himself up a couple of machines away, arranging the weights tray. He added to the set left behind by a previous inmate. Henry stretched against the wall and when he was done started exercising. One of the officers at the far end of the room observed them for a moment, then looked elsewhere.

"Not at breakfast this morning?" Big K asked as he slowed down the pace.

"Nope, felt like a little bit of privacy in my deluxe three by nine suite." Henry replied as he pushed hard on the traction bars.

"You're out again?" Big K slowed down a little more, the machine now purring comfortably.

Henry exhaled loudly. "Can't hide anything from you."

"Lucky bastard, man; you're gonna breathe some proper fresh air." Big K shook his head.

Henry smiled. "You mean the shitty fumes of the van that's going to take me to the Yard and the crappy air of the crappy room in which they are going to squeeze me?"

"At least that's proper kinda pollution, right?"

"As opposed to what?" Henry pressed on the traction bars harder and heard the weights hit the top of the machine.

"The BO of all the guys who don't shower after exercise. Man, I don't get it; show some respect." Big K replaced the handlebar in its holder, wiped the sweat from his face and drank from the plastic cup he had brought with him.

The guard looked in their direction again. Big K had moved towards the wall at the back of Henry's machine and started stretching.

"Any news about Ronnie Kray?" Henry asked before his next move.

"Zippo. He's been unusually quiet after he tried to piss you off. Think John had a chat with him." Big K groaned as he changed legs. "That guy is a real nut job – unpredictable, know what I mean?"

Henry started quick repetitions, pumping hard and unable to reply.

"Got news on Kamal." Big K was almost hesitant.

Henry squeezed the traction bar and pulled a couple more times on the weights. "What's the word on the street?"

"You know he was transferred straightaway to HSU after being sentenced?"

The officer stood up and started walking around the room. Henry replaced the traction bar. He added to the weights tray again and re-started his routine.

His muscles screamed under the pressure. The guard walked past them and returned to his seat. Henry stood up, walking behind the back of Big K's machine to start stretching. "And?" he said, running the towel over his face.

"Kamal got busy during his trial." Big K detached every syllable, "Radicalisation."

"You mean he radicalised some of the other detainees?"

"Yup. And he got others to do it too, recruiting guys like you and me." Big K paused. "The guy is real bad news, man."

"Thanks for the tip." Henry was almost at the end of his weights routine. "How do you know that anyway?"

"'Cos he got his guys in the main prison units and so have I."

Big K had moved away from the machines for a final set of stretches. He was clocking up a lot of goodwill which he would want to cash in sometime. Nothing came for free. But if Henry was smart enough, he would be out of here before he found out what Big K's price was.

* * *

The police officers at the door checked her ID, three of them, wearing body armour, heavy weaponry and earpieces plugged in.

They looked the part and Marissa was almost reassured. She walked into Mark Phelps' parents' home. Another police officer, a middle-aged woman this time, in civilian clothes, greeted her. Mark and his children had been moved to the back of the house. The terraced property in Holland Park was not dissimilar to the one Mark had just left. After the explosion the house had been boarded up and forensic specialists were still working their way through the crime scene.

The smell of cooking surprised Marissa and it made her mouth water: a mixture of vanilla with a hint of cinnamon, her favourite spices. Someone was preparing comfort food for a family in distress. Marissa gingerly entered a spacious room, photos in different shapes of frame on every shelf. Mark was sitting on the sofa with his arms wrapped around his children, huddling together in silence. The pieces of cake that had been placed in front of them were barely touched. Marissa stopped, her imposing frame intruding on their intimacy.

"Hello Marissa," Mark said in a tired voice, his face still partially bandaged and his bruises shading from yellow to blue.

"Hello Mark," Marissa took one step forward, undecided. "If this is not a good time …"

"It won't be a good time for years to come," Mark replied. He kissed his girl and his boy of the top of the head. "Come on guys, perhaps you could check whether grandma needs your help."

The little girl wriggled away but the young boy clung to his dad even tighter.

"We'll watch a Disney movie a bit later. OK, big guy?" His son nodded and slid off the couch, fingers still stuck in his mouth.

Mark's mother appeared in the doorway. She brought Marissa a cup of tea and poured a fresh cup for her son. She gently squeezed his shoulder and as she turned away he squeezed her hand in return.

"Any news?" Mark asked as he was taking a sip of his tea.

"Nothing new yet, I'm afraid. At least nothing that's been communicated to me." Marissa sat down in the armchair closest to him.

"You said someone would help with the case." Mark shifted a cushion that no longer felt comfortable against his back.

"That's right. A woman called Nancy Wu; someone I know and respect hugely. She is a former QC. She practised criminal law for years and has a lot of experience in white-collar crime." Marissa would not mention Nancy's representation of war criminals. Why muddy the waters?

"Her name sounds familiar," Mark said. "How do you know her?"

"I was her pupil when I trained as a barrister."

Mark nodded. Marissa was expecting more questions but instead he closed his eyes and let his head rest against the back of the settee. Marissa waited. Perhaps it was too soon. She put down her cup silently. Mark opened his eyes again.

"Mark?" Marissa moved her body forward as much as she could, whispering.

"Mmm?"

"I have to ask." Marissa inhaled. "Are you certain you want to carry on with the case?"

Mark arched his unbandaged eyebrow in surprise. "I would have thought that the SFO would be very happy."

"Of course, the director is ecstatic, but I am not the director and I will support you in whatever you decide to do." Marissa's face was smooth and open. She meant what she said.

"I don't think I will change my mind, Marissa, but thank you for giving me space." Mark moved his body again trying to find a more comfortable position. "Besides, they will crucify you if they learn you haven't secured my participation."

"That's my problem." Marissa tightened her mouth, determined.

Mark ran his hand mechanically over his bandages. "Unless you're not confident of a successful prosecution."

"No, it's not that," Marissa interrupted, placing a hand on the sofa next to Mark. "I will fight for this, believe me, but I will not push you to do what you do not want to do."

Mark nodded.

"Anyway, maybe it's time for me to go back to where I come from."

"Barbados."

Marissa smiled, a beautiful broad grin that shone like the sun of her own country.

"Don't you have family in the UK though?"

"Oh yes; some of them arrived in 1948. Have you heard about the Windrush generation?"

"Should I have?"

"Don't worry, not many people have unless they're part of that community or deal with immigration issues for those who didn't think it necessary to have papers. The policy of the current Home Secretary, Theresa May, means there's a hostile environment."

"Tell me." Mark winced as he moved forward to replace his cup on the table. Marissa hesitated but then why not? It was an important part of the UK's history that was seldom talked about.

Marissa spoke about the first wave of people from the Caribbean who had arrived after the Second World War to help rebuild the country. The first boat that carried them was called HMT *Empire Windrush*. It was the beginning of waves of immigration between 1948 and 1971.

With the continuing labour shortage in the UK many of them settled. "Many of those people have been here for decades, have families. But, unfortunately, often have no official papers."

"Surely, they must be entitled to something?"

"Strictly speaking, no – unless they have applied successfully for leave to stay." Mark was about to question her again. "A story for another time." Marissa smiled.

"Will you find someone on the banking side to help with the case? You said you would since it is important." Mark asked after a moment.

Marissa froze. Until now she had not thought about it, but how could she explain to Mark that the man about to work with him on the SFO case had been condemned for financial terrorism?

"We are looking at options," was the best Marissa could think of, off the cuff. Not entirely false. Crowne had not been confirmed yet. She would work out later how to break the news to Mark.

* * *

With a croissant stuck in his mouth, a cup of coffee in one hand and a couple of files under his arm, Andy was struggling to retrieve his pass from his trouser pocket.

A hand holding an ID materialised in front of him and Pole opened the door of the large open-plan room in which his team worked. Andy shook his head and mumbled something that sounded like thank you.

Pole rolled his eyes and smiled. "Have your breakfast, then we can talk."

Pole moved to his desk, dumped his mac on a pile of documents, sat down and booted up his computer. He was expecting results from forensics yet anticipated no surprises. He picked up the phone and dialled Yvonne's number.

"Analysis confirmed," Yvonne said by way of greeting.

"Blimey, bad day already?" If Yvonne was abrupt, something was up.

"A partial set of prints is giving me trouble."

"Relevant to my case?"

"Possibly, I'll tell you tomorrow – and don't ask me whether I have run them through IDENT1."

"I wouldn't dream of it," Pole teased. No point in badgering Yvonne further.

Andy had materialised in front of the desk, his files still under his arm and a few crumbs of croissant scattered on his pullover.

"Good news, Guv," he said moving files from the chair that stood in front of Pole's desk so he could sit down. Pole extended a hand and took the files from his DS. "That would be useful as we have nothing new from forensics."

"Eugene, I mean DCI Grandel —" Andy grew a little pink and Pole laughed. "Don't worry, half of the force calls him by his first name. A couple more meetings and he will ask you to call him Uggie." Andy nodded and carried on in a rush of words.

"Well, the thing that is interesting about Visconti and his trafficking is that he uses – I mean he used to use – the Libyan route."

Pole pulled a face. "OK, backtrack a little."

"Yes, sorry Guv. I've been wondering who and where his connections were in the Middle-East and how he would go about doing his smuggling." Andy waited, his large glasses almost down to the tip of his nose.

"Don't hold back. This sounds good."

"Visconti knew his way around and he had never had trouble smuggling art before."

Pole nodded to indicate he was listening.

"Then he gets killed – worse, it's a proper barbaric slaughter. So there is a message, a message really worth sending to whoever."

Pole moved his chair to get closer to his desk. "You think it's got nothing to do with art."

"Exactly." Andy clicked his fingers. "What if he decided to change tack. He'd been burnt on the art scene with his arrest. He was done on the art market front but …" Andy's face had turned pink again and the dimples in his cheeks made him look mischievous.

"He has a trafficking route he can use."

"Maybe he tried to find another market, using that route?"

"Keep going."

"If he knows the Libyan route well because it's the one he's used for years, perhaps he wants to be part of the other trafficking that happens on that route.

"Don't you think he would have known he was going to piss off the other traffickers?"

"But maybe he was desperate or —" Andy smiled. "He had a new source from a different place?"

"You mean not coming from Africa? I assume I am right in saying that Libya is mainly used for trafficking out of that continent."

"I'll check it out."

"But you already have an idea about the alternative "market" don't you?" Pole stopped fidgeting with his BlackBerry.

"My guess – either drugs or armaments." Andy waited for the effect the last word would have on his boss.

"Armaments? You mean supplying weapons to people in the UK?"

"I think so, Guv."

"And I think the Visconti case is seriously hotting up, if you can find more to substantiate your theory. Call the NCA. I'll speak to Ferguson at Counterterrorism Command."

* * *

The trees had almost completely lost their leaves. From the vast windows of her lounge Nancy could look out on the gardens surrounding her apartment block. The sky was low and heavy. She rubbed her arms vigorously with her hands and shivered. It was barely 10.30am but she felt exhausted. The road back to China, to her past, was proving long and hurtful.

The buzz of her BlackBerry took her by surprise. She turned away from the window, hesitant.

It could be Pole.

She crossed the space to the coffee table quickly. Marissa was calling; another ring and it would go to voicemail. "Just this once," she murmured.

The voicemail kicked in. Nancy waited. Her finger hovered over the button that allowed her to access her messages. She shook her head. The bitterness of her past was encroaching on the work she enjoyed doing but she had to allow it to surface.

The art book she had left open on the table, begging to be read, was calling her back to China. Ai Weiwei's desire to reconnect with ancient techniques of production, praising handcraft associated with Imperial China, had unsettled her.

She is sitting at a table, a piece of paper, a pot of black ink in front of her and a brush in her hand. Her father is teaching her calligraphy. He is both patient and demanding. She has repeated the same movement to create the same ideogram so many times she can't count any longer.

He has told her about the pressure of the brush on the paper, the inclination of the hand, but above all, the intention – the moment of stillness that precedes the act of creation, the slight hesitation and the movement that gives life to a word.

Her father is a modern artist yet the skill of the old helps him to conceive and execute. He won't compromise – no matter how much the new Maoist thinking is trying to compel him.

Nancy muffled a cry with her hand and dropped the pen she had been holding absent-mindedly since she had sat down on the sofa. The Chinese ideogram for girl was staring up at her from the first page of her notepad – the first word her father had taught her because it is simple and because it is her.

She turned the pad over gingerly, as if it was burning her fingers, torn between the desire to rip out the page, destroying it with a crush, or let the memories of her father flood back in.

Marissa's message was now awaiting her, the buzz of her BlackBerry telling her so. Nancy brought her chin down to her knees, huddling them with her arms, it was all too much.

Marissa's call would have to wait. Her artist friend, Susan, had offered to give her lunch and today this is what she would do. To escape once more the echoes of her past.

* * *

Marissa had started on her report for the SFO director. She had penned its outline on a sheet of paper and was about to type a new document when she went back to her mobile phone again. She had left a message for Nancy half an hour ago: no reply. The numbers displayed on the screen told her it was lunchtime already. She hesitated – perhaps a little more work before she joined her colleagues in the queue for sandwiches? She checked her messages again as if it might make a text from Nancy materialise.

Marissa sighed. She pulled together the documents that had spread over her desk during the course of the morning into a well-ordered pile.

Her unfinished conversation with Mark was still hanging uncomfortably over her. He had to trust her and to foster that trust she had to be transparent. But how could she release the information about Crowne to him in one go without jeopardising the case?

"Hello Mark, you are about to work with a terrorist."

She extended her arm and reached for another file, on which the title Henry Crowne/HXBK was written in bold letters. She lifted the cover but did not start reading the documents she almost knew by heart. She needed a chat with Nancy and she also needed some air.

Marissa stood up, approached the window and spotted a faint glimmer in the sky. The sun was trying to pierce through the clouds: she could do with a few rays, even if they were weak, on her skin.

Trafalgar Square was surprisingly empty. Even the street artists in their Yoda or Pokémon outfits, hovering in mid-air, had given today a miss. She gave her scarf another twist around her neck and turned her face towards the sun, seeking its warmth.

She spent a couple of minutes with her eyes closed, trying to imagine she could feel the meagre rays on her skin. A cold gust of wind reminded her it was time to start walking again. She crossed the road and entered the St Martin-in-the-Fields Crypt Cafe. The place looked busy. It was lunchtime after all.

Marissa bought a bowl of soup and some bread. It would be enough as she was not particularly hungry today. If she hurried, she could sneak upstairs into the main body of the church to hear one of their free lunchtime concerts. The programme included Debussy's Clair de Lune, a piece for piano she could play herself.

The front pews were almost full, a mix of students who had come to support their friends and family members eager to make sure the church was not empty for the performers' first recital at St Martin's.

Marissa sat in a quieter back row, near one of the great stone pillars that supported the balcony. She lowered her eyes, leaning against the uncomfortable stiff wooden frame of the seats.

St Martin's was a good place for meditation she had found, a quiet space to turn within and seek guidance, so very different from the vibrant church she used to visit with her family on Sundays, and yet a place where she could experience the same joy.

The music almost startled her, but the meditative calm of Debussy's piece took her over instantly, her fingers moving with each note the young pianist was playing. She liked his touch, evocative of a breeze – speeding up and slowing down the tempo of the piece following his own inspiration, just the way Debussy had instructed.

More Debussy pieces followed, and Marissa was transported – the young artist's playing was so fluent. She wished she could be sitting there in front of an audience, playing the instrument that had always inspired her the most, the piano.

A vibration in her bag reminded her suddenly that it was midweek, and she had an urgent case to go back to. She discreetly slid along the pew and disappeared through one of the side doors. She scrolled down her messages to discover a text from Mark.

I need a chat and need to do this outside my home – I'm on my way.

The words punched her in the stomach. She checked the time. The message had been sent forty minutes ago. If she rushed back, she might just make it before Mark arrived. She ran down the steps that lay at the entrance to St Martin's. The crossing light had turned red.

She waved frantically towards the car that had started coming her way so she could cross. Her pace accelerated even more once she was on Trafalgar Square; she ran towards the rotating doors of the SFO offices. People were exiting the premises, slowing the doors down, and she had to match their unhurried pace.

She heard the receptionist call her name. "You have a visitor."

When Marissa finally walked into her office, she saw Mark standing over her desk, a file open in his hands and through his fingers she could read the name Henry Crowne penned in large letters.

Chapter Eleven

The studio space was beautifully peaceful and yet busy with creativity. Susan had not bothered to tidy up for her friend's visit and Nancy liked it that way. The colourful and almost tactile drawings her friend was working on had had a soothing effect.

Nancy sipped her coffee, almost ready to listen to the long list of calls that queued for her attention. Her phone buzzed again, a text message followed, and a sense of guilt sent a small shiver along her spine. She apologised to her friend, moved to the back of the studio and listened to what Marissa had to say.

Mark had discovered Henry would be the financial expert helping on his case … he knew who Henry Crowne was … Mark's reaction had been fury and disbelief.

"No," Nancy blurted. She ran her hand through her thick jet-black hair, hardly able to wait until the end of the message. She dialled Marissa's number – engaged. She left a voicemail of her own. She was going to the SFO to see her.

Her friend smiled kindly when Nancy made her excuses. It was urgent and she believed her. Nancy dashed into the first cab she could find. Less than thirty minutes later she was arriving at Trafalgar Square.

Marissa was waiting for her in the lobby of 2–4 Cockspur Street.

"Let's go for a coffee," Marissa said.

"The Crypt, St Martin's?"

"Good idea. We may need a miracle."

They both walked in silence. This time the Crypt Cafe was almost empty with plenty of tables to choose from.

"This is a disaster," Marissa sighed, collapsing on a chair.

"Is he determined not to speak to Henry?"

"He went mad – almost literally – when he realised who Henry Crowne was."

"Had you not mentioned to Mark you might involve someone like Henry beforehand?"

"I did but I didn't want to release Henry's name until we had the all-clear from the Belmarsh governor ..." Marissa's voice trailed. "And then there was the bombing and after that I was not sure it was a good idea altogether."

"Is there something else?" Nancy prodded a little.

Marissa hesitated. "No."

Nancy did not pursue the matter. She would return to it later though.

"What did Mark exactly say if I may ask?"

"First an incoherent explosion when I entered my office. I have never seen him like that. Months of tension, then the raw grief coming out all in one go. My colleagues almost called Security."

"What then?"

"He refused to work with a terrorist, a coward who kills innocent people, who targets decent folk like him and his family."

Nancy fell back in her chair. "I can't say I blame him for his reaction," she eventually said.

"I hadn't done a great job in preparing him either." Marissa's long fingers were pushing a couple of forgotten breadcrumbs towards the centre of the table.

"We have all been shocked by what happened."

Marissa kept playing with the crumbs, not meeting Nancy's eyes.

"Is he still prepared to go ahead with the case?"

Marissa raised her head, surprised. Her large brown eyes lit up and she managed a smile. She recognised the Nancy Wu QC she had known and admired in the past.

"You're always prepared to go to the point and never shy away from the hard questions."

"Always. And I am glad you remember." Nancy gave her friend a kind smile. "So, yes, does Mark Phelps still want to testify in this whistle-blowing case against the large UK bank he works for?"

Marissa swept away the crumbs with the back of her hand. "He does."

"Then, I'm afraid, we need Henry to work with him."

Marissa remained silent.

"I understand your reservations. You don't know Henry and you have never worked with him, but I assure you, if you want to unravel this complex financial structure, he is the best."

"Perhaps if you were to speak to Mark," Marissa ventured.

"That's a good idea. You need to remain the person he trusts in all of this. And I am expendable."

"It's settled then."

"It is indeed."

* * *

The radio was chattering in the background. Bang-up time had started at 12:45pm sharp, allowing the officers to have their lunch.

The news bulletin he was listening to was interrupted. Henry's attention focused a little more on what was being said. A couple of words made him hold his breath.

Explosion. Bomb.

The radio presenter on BBC4 was describing an explosion that had happened less than twenty-four hours ago in Notting Hill Gate. Henry sat on the edge of his bed, rigid. The story unfolding on the radio was punctuated by flashbacks. "The Metropolitan Police acting in conjunction with Counterterrorism Command have confirmed that the bomb was planted underneath a car."

Henry hears the deafening noise of the explosion that rocks the van in which he is sitting.

"Speculation about the target."

His body hits the ceiling of the van; everything goes black.

"The identity of the victim has not been confirmed."

The glazed eyes of the dead officer who looks at him but can no longer see.

Henry stood up in a jump, grabbed the radio and squeezed so hard he heard it crack under his grip. He threw it on the bed. The radio station was almost lost and he could now hear only a few jumbled words.

He must know what had happened though. His fingers fumbled with the wavelength button, tuning in and out – "act of terror". The presenter had moved effortlessly on to the next topic. Henry's body went limp. The question that had been haunting him for years surfaced unexpectedly.

Was he up to it? Could he join them and defeat them the way he had planned?

Behind this new bombing was Kamal's cell. When bang-up time was over, Henry could go and find him and finish him off. He could snap

Kamal's neck like a twig. He knew how to do it. The images played in front of Henry's eyes, mesmerising.

Kamal's face contorted.

Kamal's eyes emptying of life.

Kamal's body going limp.

Henry's breathing had become short, his fists squeezed so hard they hurt, but in that moment pain felt good. He slammed his fist against the wall.

It was all fantasy, though, for Henry Crowne was no killer. He had learned that on the day of the Paddington bombing but perhaps he could be taught?

Henry dropped to the floor and lay on its cold surface. He must learn to pretend if he was to fulfil his plan. He must learn to pretend to share Kamal's belief. But was it too crazy? HSU Belmarsh was stifling but also safe in a strange sort of way. Once he was out on his own, there would be no one to look after his back.

No Liam, as there had been in Belfast.

No Nancy, as there had been during his trial.

No one.

Henry heard the bolt on the cell door being released and for once wished it had not come so soon.

* * *

"I'm on my way to see Mark." Nancy was walking towards St James's. The traffic was solid and she would only catch a cab when on Piccadilly. Pole had listened to her account of the latest development without interrupting. He would never say he was enthusiastic about facilitating Henry's second trip out of HSU Belmarsh but he had seen the results previously and there was no denying it – Henry was impressive when it came to banking expertise. Nancy understood his point of view. If something went wrong during Henry's transfer, Pole and The Met would be in the firing line.

"I agree, this is going to be difficult." Nancy waved down a taxi. She accelerated her pace to reach the place where it had stopped. She was glad she had chosen a pair of comfortable Chanel pumps. She kept speaking to Pole in between giving the cabbie directions. Pole would have to speak to Superintendent Marsh.

"Give me some time before you speak to The Super. We don't know yet whether Mark will change his mind."

Pole seemed undecided and reluctant to formalise Henry's trip out of HSU Belmarsh if Mark was refusing to work with him.

"I am not going to force the issue, Jonathan. I don't want to get Henry out of Belmarsh at any cost."

Pole had hit the nail on the head though. A gentle or perhaps not so gentle reminder that her friendship with Henry could not blind her.

"I understand the risk to your reputation, too." She wished she could have had the conversation with Pole in person, though perhaps he would have seen her unease, or perhaps he could hear it in the tone of her voice?

"The point I really want to make to Mark is that if he is serious about unravelling the financial structure that underpins Bank X's money flows between it and the Middle-Eastern state in question, he needs an expert."

Pole was agreeing, albeit reluctantly.

The cab was now well on its way to Holland Park and Nancy told Pole she had to go. It was time for her to gather her thoughts for what would be a very uncomfortable conversation.

She took her yellow pad out of her satchel, started listing the points she had made to Pole and added one she had not mentioned.

What did Henry's letter mean?

Despite Henry's best attempts at reassuring her, Nancy was still grappling with the feelings that the letter had elicited. Henry was not someone who rambled on paper. For all his faults, Henry was solid, and she doubted he had written something to her that was devoid of meaning.

He had brushed the letter off as the after-effect of the life-threatening situation they had found themselves in. Nancy was not convinced. She wished she had spoken to Pole at the time but it had felt like a betrayal of Henry's confidence. And now it was even more difficult to speak to Pole about it.

The taxi slowed down, and Nancy replaced the pad in her satchel. The three armed police officers looked suitably impressive from a distance. Pole had called Commander Ferguson. She was expected. She paid the cabbie and moved at a slow pace towards Mark Phelps' parents' home. She kept telling herself that if Mark really was serious about the case he needed Henry's help.

If.

Nancy stopped for a moment. The terraced house looked peaceful, the small front garden well-kept and welcoming, a typical prosperous family home. Nancy crossed the road and presented her driving licence to the two policemen guarding the house gate.

She was allowed through the garden gates and presented the document again to the other armed officer before ringing the doorbell. The chime of the bell sounded cheerful and out of place. This was not a home that invited drama or pain, but a cosy place built for the joys of family life.

A plain clothes policewoman appeared at the door and let Nancy in. She asked Nancy to wait in the hallway, no doubt checking Mark was up to receiving a visitor. Nancy's eyes scanned her surroundings. Photographs had been hung all over the walls: African animals, foreign landscapes, Masai warriors with their beaded necklaces and spears.

"Mark will see you."

The policewoman's voice made her jump, its neutral tone felt almost like a rebuke. Had this man not had enough? Nancy fought the desire to turn back.

She entered a large lounge, warm and welcoming. Mark was facing the bay window. In the garden, despite the cold, his children were playing football with their grandfather. Nancy paused. She could see Mark's face in the glass's reflection – bruised and scared.

"Good afternoon Mr Phelps, my name is —"

"I know who you are," Mark interrupted. He moved with difficulty towards the couch. Nancy waited. She looked at the broken man taking a seat and her throat tightened. The conventional "I am sorry for your loss" felt inadequate and unseemly.

Mark indicated she should sit down.

"Thank you for seeing me." There was a genuine feeling of sympathy in her voice. Mark nodded and for a while they both sat without saying more. He was observing her, and she let him take time to speak first.

"So?" Mark's face barely moved when he spoke, his lips hardly pronouncing the words.

"You have been told, I'm sure, that I consult with the Metropolitan Police as a former QC."

Mark nodded.

"I have been asked to assist in the supervision of a person, a former banker, who can help with the case the SFO is preparing against the bank."

Mark closed his eyes. His hands tightened on his knees.

"Are you not forgetting one essential detail?" he managed to articulate. His good eye opened wider and fixed Nancy with anger or perhaps even hatred.

Nancy sat still. She understood suffering, the need to inflict pain in return. Her calmness was compassionate rather than detached.

"I'd be a fool not to mention it."

"Then why have you come here?" Mark's voice was trembling, any minute now he would unleash his fury.

"Because I understand that you have chosen to keep going with the case despite what it has already cost you."

"Find someone else," Mark replied without hesitation.

"We could try." Nancy paused. "Yes, we could, but I am not sure we will find the person we truly need."

Mark attempted to laugh. His face twisted instead in pain, his throat almost choking.

"The person we are talking about —", not mentioning Henry's name seemed less provocative – "used to be one of the best financiers in the City but also —", she took her time to formulate the last limb of her argument – "but also someone who understands how criminal organisations operate. He knows how to put together a fund structure that is opaque enough —"

"Find someone else," Mark interrupted.

"The people who are good at mounting these structures are seldom caught because they do not implement them."

"Must be someone else ... arrested?" Mark had hesitated for an almost imperceptible moment.

"And because very few financiers behind bars will share their knowledge to unravel these funding structures, unless they can cut a deal. If we are talking about those who are free – how many will have the courage to do what you have done?" Nancy's voice had lost a little of its composure. She too was passionate about exposing the truth.

Mark's face dropped onto his chest so that Nancy could no longer read his expression. "I want you to leave." Mark had raised his head just enough so he could speak.

Nancy gathered her belongings, taking her time. Perhaps he did not mean it? She had detected a shift, she thought. She finally rose and moved towards the door. Her heart sunk in her chest. It was as much Mark's defeat as hers. He would never unravel this conundrum without Henry's help.

"Goodbye," she said as she reached the door.

Mark rose slowly and made his way to the bay window to resume watching his children play. Nancy walked all the way to the main road at a slow pace. Could she have been more convincing without appearing manipulative? She pulled her scarf tighter around her neck, the cashmere felt warm and comforting against the bitter cold of the wind.

She had reached the main road. It was time to speak to Pole again.

A small patisserie looked promising with plenty of empty tables at the back of the shop. She ordered and settled in the far corner, secluded. She took out her BlackBerry and paused. Hesitation was not helpful when it came to running a case – she could be measured, considerate, open-minded but today she felt the flux of the situation, a situation she could not control.

Pole and Marissa needed to know she had failed and yet she felt she had made a connection with Mark. For an instant he had seen her point of view. She dialled Pole's landline number. The voicemail kicked in. She switched to his BlackBerry.

"Pole." His tone sounded formal. She was interrupting.

"Sorry Jonathan, I will call back later."

"No, please – tell me."

Nancy gave him the details of her meeting. He did not interrupt. Unusual.

"Have I stunned you into silence, *mon cher*?"

"It is disappointing, I must say – is there anything that could make him change his mind?"

Pole now seemed keener to facilitate Henry's involvement. Perhaps he had spoken to Marissa again.

"I'm not sure. I thought he hesitated. Something happened fleetingly but then he asked me to leave."

"He needs to think it through. We should not have hoped to convince him that fast. Let's give him more time."

"I like your optimism. His emotions are very raw. He needs to let reason speak, but it is too early."

"Will you tell Marissa?"

"I will. And will you inform Marsh?" Nancy was expecting one of Pole's humorous remarks about Marsh's keen interest in Ms Wu.

"Let's wait a little," Pole replied. Nancy said her goodbyes and returned to a tasteless cup of tea. At least it was warm.

* * *

Pole dropped his BlackBerry on the small table.

"Mark Phelps is not budging."

The young man opposite bent forward, elbows on the plastic top.

"That's a shame but I have the impression that that is not the end of it?" His light brown eyes read Pole in an uncomfortable fashion. Pole was not used to being on the receiving end of interrogations.

"We'll have to see."

"Crowne has to help on this case."

"I understood you the first time around." Pole's eyes locked briefly with the brown eyes.

"I know you understand, Inspector, but you need to do more than understand; you need to help."

"As long as 'help' does not mean breaking the law, I am good."

The young man shrugged. "A little accommodation with the truth perhaps?"

"What about Marsh?"

"Not your problem."

"Are you joking?" Pole crossed his arms over his chest.

"I am doing anything but joke, Inspector."

Pole stood up. "Unless Marsh is in the loop, I am not doing anything." The young man pulled away from the table; his chair screeched.

"You might," he said stretching his arms over his head, "reconsider. Ms Wu, a very attractive woman I have to say, is looking for her disappeared father?"

"How do you …?" Pole's shoulders dropped slightly.

"Know? Never mind that. But how about a good old-fashioned you scratch my back and I scratch yours?"

Pole did not reply. He could have clocked this arrogant little arse.

"You know your way back out The Cross, Inspector."

Pole grabbed his raincoat and disappeared through the maze of corridors.

* * *

The car had stopped abruptly. The driver swore in what Brett recognised was Arabic. His third meeting with The Sheik had yet again been arranged at the last minute. Brett had grumbled about it and Mohammed, his contact, apologised profusely, but what could he do? It was The Sheik asking. Brett had known Mohammed for years and he would not have believed him to be a Jihadist. But Mohammed had been recruited to serve The Sheik and there was nothing he could do except do as he was told.

The car gained speed once more, driving through the streets of North London. Despite the blindfold, Brett knew they were going around in circles.

The underground station at which he had been picked up by the man in the leather jacket had changed once more. More precautions, more checks, his burner phone had been switched off and the battery removed – all this could mean only one thing.

A large operation was in the offing.

The car went over what he thought might have been the threshold of a garage door, or onto a pavement, and stopped. Brett was manhandled out of the vehicle, roughly without being violent, just enough to instil fear.

Brett played the part, suitably scared, but still with it. The scared part was becoming increasingly easy to act, whereas being with it …

The blindfold was removed and the large man who had been leading him by the arm through the corridors of the house they had entered indicated a door with a movement of his head. Brett stepped in and found to his surprise The Sheikh already there.

No greetings necessary.

The Sheik indicated that Brett should sit. The mattress on the floor was thin and had seen better days.

"What have you got for me?"

"As much information as I could gather in the amount of time I had." Brett handed over his dossier: printed documents, photocopied news articles, photos. Everything he had gathered on Henry Crowne over the years Crowne had been his client and everything MI6 had allowed him to disclose without arousing suspicions.

The Sheik grabbed the file and started leafing through it, taking his time to read the parts that seemed important to him. A faint smile moved across his serious face.

"Do you have a USB key with these documents?"

Brett fished the key from his jacket pocket and placed it on the floor.

A woman in a niqab entered noiselessly. She placed a tray carrying two glasses and a large brass teapot on the ground. She poured the liquid and disappeared without a sound, invisible. The Sheik extended his hand and took a glass; he was still reading. Brett took the other glass and pulled a face, his fingers scorched by the searing liquid inside. The Sheik was still holding his – immune it seemed to pain.

"How did you get all that information?" The Sheik asked taking a sip of tea.

"It's taken time – almost ten years' worth of work. I ask a lot of questions and I work with people who can find information too."

"Who are these people?"

"People who specialise in identity theft." Brett wriggled on the mattress; it was uncomfortable more ways than one.

"I want names."

"It is unlikely the names they operate under are their real names. It might not be very helpful."

"That's for me to decide."

Brett squirmed. The Sheik raised his eyes for the first time since he had started reading the documents, the cold stare of a man who had killed many times, without giving it a second thought.

Brett took a pen out of his inner jacket pocket and started jotting down names on the envelope The Sheik had discarded on the floor. He handed it over and as he did The Sheik's body relaxed a fraction.

How interesting, Brett thought, you too are under pressure. This was more than just a terrorist cell seeking to wreak havoc in London.

"One last question." The Sheik finished his tea. Brett waited.

"Would he join the Jihad?"

Brett's mind went blank for a short moment. Surely he could not mean?

"Crowne." The Sheik's eyes drilled into Brett.

"I don't know."

And that was an honest answer.

Chapter Twelve

Marissa had spoken to Pole. Marissa had spoken to Nancy. She now needed to speak to Mark or perhaps it was too soon. Tomorrow the SFO director would want to hear about "progress".

If Mark persisted in refusing Crowne's help and yet was still determined to be the SFO's main witness, he had to measure the impact of his decision. Maybe she could convince Mark he did not need to meet the man or perhaps she could simply not tell him of Henry's involvement.

She discarded the latter idea the minute she formulated it. Mark had to trust her and she had to trust herself.

"I need a walk," she spoke aloud, an affirmation. Marissa stood up, grimaced and arched back a little, hands on her waist. She looked at the piles of documents neatly arranged on her desk: read with annotations – read, needing further comments – to be read (the largest pile).

She hesitated. She could take some papers to read at home. She could take a cab to Battersea and walk the rest of the way. She could log in from home. She could …

"I need a walk."

Marissa logged off, dropped a loose paper clip into the stationery holder on her desk, shrugged on her coat and walked towards the bank of lifts. She caught the reflection of her body in the large windows of the SFO office, a tall form stooped with tiredness.

Trafalgar Square was impossibly clogged up with cars. She did not bother to wait for the pedestrian light to turn green and moved across the road towards Parliament Square. She took a woollen cap out of her coat pocket, a cosy hat she always carried once the winter had started and adjusted it on her head. Marissa gathered pace. She thought about which route she would take today, turning towards Victoria; once there she would jump on the 344 bus.

The walk had loosened her body a little and her mind felt more alert. Marissa had given Mark her word he could choose not to go ahead with the case. The SFO director would never accept this though, not after the string of disappointments (the politically correct term) the SFO had encountered.

For her there was the BAE Systems case – yes BAE had been charged a heavy fine. $450 million was a considerable sum but most of it had gone to the US Department of Justice. And what of the employees who made illegal payments on behalf of the company – nothing.

The UK had invoked national security and Saudi Arabia was pardoned by Tony Blair whilst he was prime minister. The sale of armaments in return for bribes – a practice supposedly rampant in the industry – was a case worth fighting for and yet she felt it could have gone so much deeper.

She was already on Parliament Square and stopped at the traffic lights, close to the kerb, her feet ready to move the second the little man had turned green. She felt the pressure of the crowd behind her, as eager as she was to reach their destination. Marissa stepped back a little. The traffic that was whizzing past felt somehow too close. The pressure on her back surprised her. There was no space left to move. She pushed back more decisively, a couple of men protested. She apologised. She looked around. No one was paying attention to her.

She was now turning into Old Queen Street and the flow of people eased off. She looked behind her. A couple of women, chatting and crossing the road. Marissa slowed down and her mind drifted back to Mark. Mark in his hospital bed, Mark at his parents' home, with his children – the images kept coming but did not provide her with any answers.

She turned around again – fewer people still. In the distance, a car turned into the street, drove slowly past and disappeared around the bend of the road.

The Counterterrorism Command offer of protection popped into her mind. What would murdering her achieve? Someone else would take the case.

Marissa broke into a slow jog. She thanked her American friends for convincing her to wear running shoes on her commute. Her bag was now rhythmically banging against her back. She was only a couple of streets away from one of the main roads.

Once at Buckingham Gate she would hail a cab. A car drove past again at a steady pace. Was it the same car? Marissa accelerated her jog into a run, crossed the street as the lights turned red, the sound of car horns following her. She kept going and, as she reached the other side, put her hand up, dashing into the taxi that had stopped.

The cabbie looked at her in the mirror. "Are you OK, luv?" She nodded, too shaken to speak. She turned and looked through the back window.

The SUV she thought she had seen driving past her was a few cars away. No, this was ridiculous, the black SUV looked like any other black SUV. She took a tissue from her bag and ran it over her face. The black SUV had moved up and was now stopped alongside her cab, one lane away. She moved forward towards the intercom.

"We're going to Scotland Yard," she shouted, her eyes wide open.

The cabbie turned down the radio.

"What's that luv?"

"Turn around, turn around; we need to go to Scotland Yard."

"All right, all right – calm down," the cabbie grumbled. "I need to get out of the one-way system first."

Marissa sat back and squeezed herself into the corner of the cab furthest from the SUV. Her mind was racing. She could get out again, could try to get a cab going in the right direction but what if they were after her?

No chance of escape.

The SUV was stuck in traffic too; if they were going to attempt anything they would have to wait until they could move away safely, surely?

Marissa fumbled in her bag, found her mobile phone, hesitated, and then called Commander Ferguson's number – engaged.

The traffic was moving in her lane; the SUV was still stuck. The cabbie moved to cross into a new lane. He managed to squeeze between two undecided drivers – there were now two lanes between her and the SUV. The SUV was moving now, also trying to change lane but with less luck than the taxi. Marissa tried Ferguson again – still engaged.

"Shit, shit." Marissa could see the SUV pushing against the traffic despite the protestations of the other drivers. It would not be long before it would be level with her cab – then what?

"Can we try to go a little faster please?" Marissa asked. Her voice must have sounded desperate and the driver registered.

"You've got a problem?"

"Perhaps. I really need to reach Scotland Yard."

The cabbie opened his window again and indicated he needed priority, another cabbie let him in and they started to move faster out of the traffic jam. The SUV was stuck again, and Marissa felt hope. Her body now half turned, looking through the rear window.

"No. No," she cried raising her hand to her mouth.

A figure had jumped out of the SUV and was crossing the lanes that separated them. The gun was pointing in her direction, the gunman running towards her cab.

"What the fuck?" The driver blurted as he looked in his rear mirror. The cabbie sounded his horn; the traffic moved faster. He turned into the Embankment to the sound of gunfire being discharged. He did not stop until they reached the Yard.

* * *

"Ferguson is on his way." Pole put a cup of tea in front of Marissa. His gesture was slow, not wanting to scare her, knowing she needed time to recover. Marissa nodded, the tissues she had used to wipe her face still in her hand.

"The cabbie is fine by the way; a bit shaken but fine."

"Good," Marissa barely managed to utter. Pole sat down as well, drank some tea and waited. She stretched a quivering hand towards her cup, wrapped her other hand around it. Her mouth opened and closed. Her eyes were moist, but she recovered and cleared her throat.

"You need a statement from me?"

"Let's wait for Ferguson. There's no rush. You're safe here."

Pole's voice was reassuring. There was nothing wrong with being scared.

Pole and Marissa drank their tea in silence. Pole didn't need to fill the time with meaningless words. If Marissa needed to talk he would be ready.

When Commander Ferguson arrived Andy Todd also joined them.

"You think you were followed?" Ferguson asked as soon as he had finished greeting Pole and Marissa.

"I think so. I had not given my safety much thought, even after Mark's wife." Marissa was still struggling with each word. Her face strained with the effort of concentration, of trying to remember and to be accurate.

"The SUV drove past you twice?"

"I think so."

"The shooter?"

577

"Small man." Marissa covered her eyes to still herself. "Small person. Five foot two or thereabouts, dressed in black – balaclava or hoodie."

"Anything else that springs to mind?" Ferguson asked.

"It was so quick…" Marissa's jaw clenched. "There was something unexpected…"

"In your own time." Pole cut through Ferguson.

"The gunman raised his weapon as soon as he was out of the SUV as if he wanted everyone to know he could do this."

"These guys are not afraid of dying…" Ferguson shook his head.

Pole waited to hear more but Marissa looked spent. Perhaps this particular individual had more to prove.

Andy was taking notes in his notebook. "We need to have access to all CCTV cameras in the area and around Buckingham Gate."

Ferguson nodded. "Can you deal with it?"

Pole did not have to ask. Andy had stood up and disappeared the moment the request had been made.

"I doubt we'll find them by tracing the vehicle. It was probably stolen and will've been set on fire and completely trashed by now," Ferguson said.

"But people make mistakes."

"Not these guys." Ferguson moved to the window. He looked outside. It was dark and blustery. "In the meantime, we need to get you home safely," he said to Marissa. "I'll send a team to secure your flat. If it's too complicated, we may need to move you to somewhere safer." Ferguson commanding voice softened a little. "Does that work for you?"

"Yes, fine. I'm fine. Thank you for asking." Marissa's rigid body sagged a little.

"Perhaps a friend or family member could stay with you?" Pole's voice, warm and comforting, somehow made it worse.

"I hope you find these fuckers and you have no mercy," Marissa said, stunning both Pole and Ferguson into silence. "I need to powder my nose and I'll follow you."

"Tempting instructions," Ferguson said once Marissa had left. Pole nodded. He had joined Ferguson at the window.

"Something bothering you?" Ferguson asked. "Apart from also being tempted to follow Ms Campbell's instructions?"

"Yes, but I'm wondering," Pole ruffled his goatee with his knuckle. "Who might be next?"

* * *

The doorbell buzzed a couple of times. Nancy moved swiftly to the intercom to let Pole into her building. She left the door of her apartment on the latch and ran to the kitchen. She had decided on a good old-fashioned blanquette de veau for their supper later on. First a private view at one of the contemporary art galleries she supported in Islington for the oening of her favourite sculptor, Bernard McGuigan, followed by *dîner a deux*.

Pole knocked and entered.

"I'm in the kitchen, Jonathan," Nancy's cheerful voice called.

"You shouldn't leave the door on the latch you know," Pole said walking into the kitchen with a bottle of red wine and a bunch of white lilies.

Nancy had donned oven gloves. The smell of slow-cooked meat filled the room with a delicious aroma when she opened the Le Creuset casserole lid. She stirred the stew with a wooden spoon, lifted it to her lips – perfect.

"It's not been a good day, I think?" Her smile had disappeared. She took another spoonful and presented it to Pole.

"Sorry, I shouldn't bring it home. Good evening Nancy," Pole blew on the spoon's contents and took a bite. He smiled at what was good old comfort food. He put the wine and flowers on the table. He hugged Nancy gently, kissing the top of her head and pulling back.

"What's happened?" Nancy asked taking off her oven gloves in a sharp move and placing her hands on his shoulders. "Another —"

"No, no," Pole interrupted. "But it was a close shave."

Pole sat down at the kitchen table. Nancy opened the Nuits-Saint-Georges he had brought, poured out two glasses without tasting the wine first and listened carefully to Pole's account of Marissa's near miss.

"How is she taking it?" Nancy took a sip of wine, ignoring how good it was.

"Very shaken to start with, of course, but she's bounced back pretty quickly."

"You mean she is damned pissed off?"

"That's a good way of putting it." Pole smiled. "But she won't be put off that easily from working on the case."

"Quite the contrary. I've known Marissa a long time and I'd say missing their target is the worst these people could have done." Nancy raised her glass to her friend. "Courageous is definitely Marissa Campbell's middle name."

Pole swirled the wine around his glass, more in a meditative gesture than to let it breathe. He finally took a sip. "The question now is, what next? Or perhaps who's next?"

Nancy stretched her hand over Pole's. "What are you worried about? That these people are on a murder spree?"

"That's a possibility. If the intention is to intimidate or murder key witnesses, in a case that is not even a full case yet, they will target whoever it is they feel they need to target."

"It would be almost impossible to reach Henry in HSU Belmarsh," Nancy said.

"I'm not worried about Henry."

"You think I might be a target?" Nancy pulled a dubious face.

Pole drank a little wine. "You are the go-between connecting Henry and Marissa."

Nancy squeezed Pole's hand again. "For all we know, Mark may not want to work with Henry and Marissa may have no other choice but to agree to that."

They had moved to Nancy's lounge whilst talking, sitting close on the sofa. Pole looked absorbed in something he seemed to have recalled.

"Jonathan? Is there anything else?"

Pole shook his head. "No, you're right. Let's go to this art preview you've been raving about." Pole finished his glass, forgetting to comment on the excellent Nuits.

He was keeping something from Nancy. She couldn't figure out what.

* * *

The small gallery nestling in Islington's back streets was already packed when they arrived. Nancy pushed the large silver globe serving as a door handle, and she and Pole entered Phillipe Garry's gallery.

Philippe welcomed Nancy with a warm hug. He shook hands with Pole and insisted on bringing them a glass of wine. Pole looked around at the diverse crowd only contemporary art could produce.

He felt immediately at ease amongst this eclectic mix of bohemians and collectors. Nancy greeted a couple of artists she knew well and introduced Jonathan. "Jonathan Pole, a friend".

They smiled, inquisitive, but before they had time to launch into personal questions, Pole started to comment on the quality of the pieces displayed around the gallery.

"Bernard's craft is truly impressive." Pole had picked up a thing or two about art, to Nancy's delight, and she joined in the conversation. "My favourite piece remains Ecstasy."

The other artists argued; perhaps the latest abstract pieces Day and Night or Ode departed from the well-known McGuigan figurative work but they were inspiring. Phillippe joined the debate. If they could wait until seven-thirty, Bernard would be arriving from the countryside then. He was finishing installing a large piece in the garden of one of his main collectors, but he would arrive later.

Another younger artist she had not seen for a while came to say hello to Nancy. Pole started a conversation with a seasoned collector, Audrey.

The room buzzed with opinions, news about current work being conceived or art pieces being purchased. A young man in a hat perched on the back of his head and dressed head to toe in black was gesticulating in front of the largest sculpture on display, elaborating on the technique, the material used and the impact the piece would have on the art market.

"This is crazy, have you seen the latest figures? Frieze Art Fair was again a complete success. The galleries sold eighty per cent of their art stock by the end of the first preview day."

"I heard they had done so even before that," a young woman in a vintage Alexander McQueen dress replied.

Pole moved towards the small office and casually consulted his BlackBerry.

"Any news?" Nancy asked as she presented him with a fresh glass of wine.

"Sorry." Pole took the glass and gently tapped Nancy's.

"Don't apologise. I am very impressed you have spent almost a whole hour without looking at it."

"I am glad my efforts at being civilised have borne fruit." Pole smiled.

"In fact, I am impressed full stop." Nancy raised her glass to him. She saw a little warmth rising to Pole's cheeks.

"I'd told you I can talk the art talk too," Pole teased.

The rumble of voices changed, suddenly turning to an acclamation. The door opened and a man with a mane of thick grey hair and a friendly smile entered. The artist had arrived.

Time to go back to the party.

* * *

Henry heard the bolt of his prison cell door releasing. Another visit before he was due to leave the compound, normal procedure. He would be expected to be ready before the inmates were allowed out for breakfast and would return after night lockdown had started.

The most senior of the prison officers came in. Henry was sitting on the bed, reading a book he had borrowed from the library, something of quality but not contentious, *A Brief History of Time* by Stephen Hawking.

"Change of plan, Henry. Your trip has been postponed." The guard withdrew without further explanation.

"Wait." Henry jumped from his bed, but the door had already closed. "Wait." Henry slammed his hand against the door. The small window latch opened. "I don't have any more information. I'll let you know when I have some news." The latch closed again.

Henry lifted his fist to bang against the door once more. It took all his determination and more to stop. If the guards were toying with him it was not the time to rise to the bait. Henry spread his hands on the door. He needed to scream.

What had happened? Why had Nancy not contacted him?

His mind was fluttering, a bat caught in a confined room, bumping into the walls and never finding a way out. His cell closed in around him. He needed space but there was none.

The desire for self-harm returned. He had never succumbed to it when he was a teenager in Belfast. Always fighting the temptation to test his resistance to pain. The street fights alongside the O'Connor brothers gave him enough deep cuts and bruises, sometimes broken bones, to satisfy his thirst for torment.

Prison was a new form of slow-burning torture. Henry was the first one to recognise he deserved his sentence but going through with it was another matter.

Henry's body was now trembling with anger. The old foe had returned, summoned by the unexpected outcome of the officer's visit. He needed to speak to Nancy. But there was no mobile, no phone he could use at this time of night. He would have to wait until the morning, queue at the telephone booth and finally place a call.

Henry returned to his bed in one step, threw the sheet and blanket to the floor and yanked the mattress from its base in a vicious move. The chair hit the desk. The carefully arranged books and papers shook, some fell to the ground. Henry did not care. He rolled the mattress, sat on the impromptu punching sack and started pummelling it with blows. He kept going, hitting, swearing, hitting again. A painful memory hit him

He can only hear the shots. The short sharp burst a gun makes before it hits its target.
It is August. The weather has been pleasant since the beginning of the
month. Henry's mother is visiting a friend in Ballymurphy. She does not know
that the British army is about to launch Operation Demetrius. It is holiday season
so she has decided to spend time with her friend whose son is Henry's age. The
house overlooks the green. The day has started like a normal day, breakfast with Henry
and Patrick running around the house before they finally sit down to eat toast and fried
sausages. Henry's mother and her friend are sitting at the window, smoking cigarettes.

Men run past shouting. Everybody goes quiet. Even at the age of four, Henry
knows when he must stop talking. Men in uniforms of the Parachute Regiment run
after them. There is no shooting at this stage, just running. His mother moves away
from the window and asks the boys to go upstairs.

And then it starts – the gunfire. The shots are coming from somewhere on the left,
from high up. His mother freezes at the bottom of the stairs. She calls them to come
down now. Where is safe? They huddle in the kitchen. His mother's friend is still at the
window. One man is down on the ground. She screams.

Another man with arms over his head moves slowly towards the body. He is shot
as well. A few moments later a man in a white collar, a priest, takes his handkerchief
out of his pocket, moves it over his head. He is looking around, hoping the marksmen
will see his white flag. He walks steadily; surely, they wouldn't dare. A few minutes
later Father Hugh Mullan collapses; death is instantaneous.

Henry couldn't feel his fists. The past refused to let him go. The sweat
was pouring from his body; it soaked his T-shirt, his tracksuit bottoms. He
rolled onto his side, banging his back against the leg of the bed. He could
hardly breathe.

He no longer knew whether he remembered the actual killings or
whether he recalled the story told by adults around him. Ballymurphy had
rarely been spoken about. Henry's eyelids fluttered open.

His cell was in a mess. He did not care. He had until the morning to
make it look presentable again, to keep up appearances. But for now, he
wanted to stay with the violence that burned within him.

Henry sat up and shuffled towards the only part of the wall that was
wide enough for him to lean his back against. His mind had quietened
down somewhat. Lashing out in the privacy of his cell was the only way
to control his anger.

Nancy had not called. There must be a delay that could be overcome.
Henry had done good research on the topic of fiscal paradises and he
knew the people well.

He knew the countries that sell passports – real passports – to the Russians, the Middle-Easterners and others in search of a new identity. He knew that Cyprus and Malta are used extensively to launder money. He knew these people open bank accounts, create companies, trusts, structures with so many layers that the Ultimate Beneficial Owner of the funds will never be found. Unless you are Henry Crowne, of course, because he knew all the tricks.

Henry stood up warily. The cell had been plunged into darkness. He fumbled towards his desk and switched on the wall light. Time to clean up the mess.

I just need to speak to whoever is running the case. I can make a difference.

When he had finished, Henry ran a wet flannel over his body, washing away the rest of the anger.

He moved to his bed and lay down. He must prepare for a day of waiting and hoping.

Chapter Thirteen

Nothing had managed to lift Marissa's spirits this morning. She had made herself a cup of her favourite Jamaican coffee, a couple of pieces of crunchy toast with guava jam – nothing doing.

The images of the shooter aiming at her kept coming in front of her eyes as soon as her mind stopped thinking. She had called the SFO director late last night; she had explained the interference as she had decided to call it.

An attempt on her life sounded too grand or perhaps too scary. The long silence that had followed her account of events had said it all. It was up to her to decide whether she wanted to go ahead. "I'll support you in whatever you do," he had said.

No "your life matters more than a bloody case", not that the SFO director would have sworn in front of his staff.

Marissa was ready for work and time was moving on. She could not quite bring herself to go out and make the call.

"It must be shock," Marissa grumbled.

The intense determination she had felt last night had been replaced by a sluggishness she did not know herself capable of. Her mobile rang. Nancy's name flashed on the screen. Always there when you needed her.

Marissa held back a sob. The mobile went to voicemail. But as Nancy's name disappeared from the screen Marissa felt the urge to speak to someone. She rang back.

Marissa didn't have to say much to Nancy before her former mentor suggested coffee and a chat. As she was about to leave, a young woman stood in the hallway. Marissa had almost forgotten the presence of the young police officer who had been dispatched for her protection. She stopped Marissa, reminding her she would be calling for a car to drive her to wherever she needed to go.

The car arrived and Marissa was asked to sit in the back. She did not know what to say to her police escort. The young woman was now speaking to the driver about the best route to take, avoiding traffic or slower roads. Marissa turned her face to the window and absent-mindedly watched the scenery go by.

The Groucho Club was buzzing at breakfast time: artists, TV producers, aspiring young and not so young actors, were huddled into groups, joking and whispering in a conspiratorial manner. It certainly was colourful. Marissa felt a little out of place with her plain black suit, white shirt and severe haircut. Nancy waved at her from a table in the Brasserie.

"Thank you so much, Nancy; you're always here when I need you." Marissa said as she sat down.

"The least I can do. How are you holding up?"

"I'm not sure." Marissa hunched over the small table. "Last night I was so certain; now I'm not so confident. I'm not frightened, which is odd too."

"You're still processing what happened." Nancy laid her hand on Marissa's arm and squeezed gently. "We can simply have breakfast without talking about it."

"No. Well, I'd love a coffee, but I also need to discuss options."

"You mean yours as well as Mark Phelps'?"

Marissa wriggled on her chair, a direct question but to the point. She waited for the coffee to be served.

"These people won't stop at anything." Marissa's eyes had darkened, and her voice had acquired a new hard edge.

"I agree, but the real question is – will the fact that you stop working on the case make any difference to the outcome?"

Marissa stopped stirring her coffee and looked at Nancy in surprise. "Are you saying Mark will remain a target for the rest of his life?"

"That is part of the problem. We can't be sure, but can we take the risk?" Nancy said.

Marissa liked the collective "we". It was her and Nancy very much together on this case.

"If it were the mafia, we would know what to do, but here we are in uncharted territory."

"I'd say these people are worse than the mafia."

Marissa's hand wobbled and she put her cup down. "Mark has been outed anyway as a whistle-blower. He is protected but the harsh truth is that he will lose his job. Bank X is probably shredding documents as we speak."

"He is almost certainly past caring about his job by now. It is more a question of survival." Nancy's calm and ability to dissect a case had always impressed Marissa.

"The only hope is to find out quickly who is behind the Panama structure. Then enrol Mark and his family in the witness protection programme."

"And we are back now to the thorny question surrounding Henry Crowne's involvement."

"Mark has not made contact by the way."

"But does he know what happened to you?"

Marissa drank some coffee; her face lit up, a little bit of goodness in a cup.

"Not yet. But I will tell him," she said, unhappy at her own procrastination.

"It might —" Nancy shook her head, "No, I think it will make a big difference."

"Don't you think he will be even more reluctant?"

"Mark hesitated when I spoke to him – only once, but he did. I think the rational part of him wants to use Henry."

"But why would the incident …" Marissa drank a little more coffee, "…of last night, convince him?"

"The only way to take some pressure off his family is to find the ultimate owner of the funds and even, perhaps, the people who are also funding the terror cell."

"Nancy, that is the huge leap. Do you really think he will think about it?"

"My guess is he has been spending all this time thinking of the permutations. He will not rest until his wife is avenged. He trusts you and needs you to help. With this latest attempt the pressure has escalated. He can't afford to make the wrong call and I think he knows it."

"Even if Mark is concerned about me, I am not so concerned about myself."

"This is why he trusts you. He also knows you will respect his decision."

"The SFO director will bypass me. I realised this last time I spoke to him."

"I can imagine." Nancy topped up her cup of tea. "Does Mark really need to know you are working with Henry?"

"Of course, I could keep it from him." Marissa frowned. "It wouldn't be honest though."

"Mark only needs to see the outcome of Henry's findings. He has already given us all the information Henry needs. So what difference does it make if Henry works on it without Mark knowing?"

"I suppose it could work."

"As long as you still want to take the case on." Nancy said with a kind smile.

Marissa sat back in her chair, drinking her coffee in small gulps.

"The time for hesitation is over. I'm in. I won't let the bastards get away with it."

"Quite positive?" Nancy asked, her face now serious.

"It won't be another BAE Systems." Marissa finished her cup. Time to resume her work at the SFO.

* * *

The small queue for breakfast moved rhythmically: tray, plate or bowl, eggs or porridge, toast with a very small piece of butter wrapped in foil, marmalade or jam. Gone were the days of luxurious breakfasts at the Four Seasons Hotels or the Shangri-La, an endless choice of foods catering to international tastes.

Henry shuffled with everybody else. Kamal would want to speak, he thought. Henry had not given any dates confirming when he was meant to be let out, but a substantial delay would alter his credibility or, worse, affect Kamal's plan. Henry scooped a couple of greasy eggs onto his plate, chose two pieces of toast that seemed edible. He poured tea into a plastic mug and sat down at a table from which he could watch the crowd moving in and out of the canteen.

One of Kamal's latest recruits appeared at the end of the line. He started shuffling too: eggs, toast, tea. He walked to a table close to Henry's and sat down so that he was facing him. He ate his breakfast slowly, observing the other inmates who chose to sit away from him. This seemed to suit him. The young man glanced at Henry a few times.

A couple of officers sat in the room. There was never any privacy at HSU Belmarsh. Henry was just about finished and expected not to hang around. He saw the young man drop the flimsy paper napkin that came with the cutlery to the floor.

Henry stood up and moved towards the conveyor belt for trays. As he walked past, he told the young man about the napkin; he bent down to pick it up, thanking Henry. This is what the guards saw.

"When does he want a chat?"

"Library, this afternoon."

It was all Henry needed to know.

* * *

The library had just opened. Henry had taken a seat at the small desk, opened the box containing index cards for books borrowed and returned using a key the officers had given him. He was waiting. The library opened every day for a couple of hours with a rota of librarians picked from a list of "suitable" inmates.

Henry was alone for the first fifteen minutes. He stood up, went around the bookshelves. No new books had arrived. He went on to a small window, the pane of glass was opaque and thick but it was the closest he would get to daylight. He had not heard from Nancy although the post was late yet again and had not arrived before he had to leave his cell.

A couple of inmates entered. Only a limited number of people were allowed into the library at any one time. It was all very efficient; inmates wanting to use the library would take a number and wait until their number flashed up on a board. They were allowed fifteen minutes inside, no longer.

"Cashier number five," Henry murmured with a tired smile. The anger of the previous night had sapped his energy. He just wanted to have a quiet day, but Kamal might have other plans.

Inmates picked up books. Henry filled in the cards. They left.

Uneventful. Perfect.

The clock was moving forward; a few more inmates came and went.

Henry walked out of the library to pour himself a glass of water, looking down the corridor in a nonchalant way. Only twenty minutes left before the library closed. Irritation had been replaced by anger and, more worryingly, doubt.

Did Kamal know something Henry did not?

Henry slumped into his chair, then straightened up and checked the cards one more time. He would let off steam with a workout on the rowing machines after the shift had ended. He needed to stay calm. If the Jihadi group Kamal belonged to was serious about building a financial empire, they needed him. Didn't they?

The soft steps of someone walking in refocused his mind. Kamal had put down a couple of books on Henry's desk without a word. He was now browsing the bookshelves. Henry could hear the soft movement of books being taken out, the cover being opened, the pages turned, the slight effort of returning the book to its place. Kamal emerged from the row of shelves with one book, a biography of Richard Wagner – intriguing.

The guard had popped out for a minute, ready to close the library for the day.

"How is life treating you Henry?"

"Not bad?" Henry replied whilst filling in the card.

"Ready for a change of scenery I understand." Kamal's face was soft, his long beard left uncut, a sign of rebellion that made him look more like a poet then a murderer.

"And you?"

"Always ready for what God presents me with."

"God and I are not on speaking terms," Henry replied, miming the need for a signature on the card.

"Not yet, not yet." Kamal signed and pushed the card forward but did not let go of it when Henry tried to pick it up. "Be ready."

"For what?"

"Be ready."

Henry let go of the card. It was not good enough. But Kamal simply left the card on the desk and walked out.

Henry stood up abruptly and fought the desire to follow Kamal, slam the door of the library shut and punch him in the face. Instead he stretched.

Patience. Henry consulted the clock on the wall, ten minutes to go. He walked to the window again, turned his back to the door and pretended he could see through the frosted glass.

He heard him before he saw him walking through the door. The low whistle that preceded him everywhere he went. It was not a tune, or at least not one Henry or anybody else had ever heard before. It was animal-like, a warning the way a dangerous creature might announce itself.

Ronnie Kray walked through the door.

Henry turned back in a flash.

"We're shutting down," he said walking back to the desk and closing the box of indexed cards.

"Still five minutes mate," Kray replied with a wink. He walked straight to the far end of the library and started browsing through the shelves.

The whistle had started again, covering the noise of books being moved around.

The officer came in, banged his fist against the open door. "Five minutes. Make your choice." He was standing outside the door.

What could happen now?

Henry relaxed and took out the card with Kray's name on it. What a ridiculous idea. Change your name to emulate some fucked-up bloke, who did, after all, spend more than twenty years in prison.

"Bloody idiot," Henry muttered. He looked up to find Ronnie Kray standing in front of him.

The fist that flew in his face was barely a surprise to Henry. Henry threw his body to one side, but Kray's blow caught him on the edge of his head. The chair screeched and bounced against the wall. Neither man had made a sound.

Henry stood up before Kray could come around the table and throw his second punch. Henry had hunched forward, fists at the ready. Kray launched into him head first, trying to catch Henry in the stomach. Henry swirled to his right too late. The knock propelled him against the wall. He contained a yelp, rolled sideways on the floor to find that Kray had caught his shoulder against the bookshelves. He had fallen on one knee.

Back on his feet Henry took a defensive position again. The scream of a whistle did not stop Kray. He took the chair that was now lying on the floor and hurled it with all his might at Henry.

The back of the chair caught Henry's shoulder and threw him against the row of books. The lot collapsed with a clap of thunder.

Other guards had arrived, running through the door, sticks at the ready, and then slowly approached the two men.

"Come on. You don't want to do this." One of the officers was doing the talking. The others advanced steadily towards Kray. Kray ignored them.

Henry had retreated between the other shelves. He could see Kray's face, intent on inflicting damage, eyes crazed, a mix of hatred and glee. Kray had been waiting for this and there would be no reasoning with him. All Henry wanted to do now was to be his victim. He could not be sent to The Box.

Could not.

The guards were at each end of the bookshelves. Kray lunged forward with a scream that stunned everyone. Henry braced himself for impact once more.

The Kung Fu leg kick propelled him against another lot of bookshelves, books tumbled again. Kray dashed forward, slipping on the books and falling to the ground. The guards threw themselves on him, four of them. Their sticks came down on his back, arms and legs. One of them managed to pin him to the ground with an armlock.

It was over.

Henry had not moved. His face was throbbing. His chest burning with pain. Two officers grabbed him by the shoulders, stood him up and handcuffed him. They would sort out later who had done what. Henry wiped the blood coming out of his mouth and nose on the side of his shoulder.

Henry's mind was working fast. Damage limitation was essential to avoid The Box. "Bloody idiot" had been directed at himself. He thought he had made a mistake. The story might hold. In the distance he could still hear Ronnie Kray, yelling, swearing, spitting.

One of the guards opened the door of the corridor leading away from the main area of HSU. Henry found himself in front of a room he did not know. The cuffs were removed and he was pushed into it.

"Wait in here, Crowne." The door closed shut and Henry limped to one of the chairs. He sat down slowly.

"Fuck, fuck, fuck," Henry mumbled. He lifted the bottom part of his T-shirt and wiped the rest of the blood that had started congealing on his chin. "It can't be happening now."

* * *

"These are my conditions," Mark said, a calm voice that had not lost its determination. He had insisted he wanted to see Marissa at the SFO offices after she had told him about her own brush with death.

Marissa looked at the sheet of paper listing Mark's conditions in neat yet rather large handwriting. She nodded.

"I agree with most of them."

"But?" Mark asked somewhat surprised.

"About Crowne?"

"The IRA banker," Marrisa's voice tightened.

"I am not sure this is entirely practical?"

"I don't care, Marissa. I can see he is the right man for the job and this is my demand for working with him."

"I've thought about it too. I have no desire to work with this — monster either but I need to squeeze every bit of information from him, and I mean everything. I am not letting these —" Marissa stopped herself from swearing, "these other monsters get away with it."

"How about this Nancy woman?"

Marissa hesitated. How much was she prepared to tell Mark?

"She is a very smart woman. I have worked with her before. She is an extremely good lawyer."

Mark waited. It was not what he wanted to hear.

"She does know Crowne very well, too."

"A little too well?"

"I'm not saying that."

"What are you saying, Marissa? That perhaps she might not be objective?"

Marissa hesitated for a fraction of second. She had not asked herself that question.

"I don't think so," she replied slowly. Mark picked up on it.

"Why are you hesitating?"

"Because so far I have had no cause to doubt her." Marissa's mind had been made up. She needed to steer Mark away from the dangerous waters into which he was wading. "In any case, I will be the one dealing with her directly."

"And with Crowne as well, as agreed?"

"Agreed." Crowne was a terrorist but at least he was behind bars. To her the IRA felt dated but somewhere, very deep, in the darkest part of her soul, she understood what being the conquered people, the underdog, meant.

Marissa focused on Mark again. He had dropped his chin against his chest, a sign he was reflecting, she had learned. She gave him the space to think. She poured some water into two glasses; the gurgling of the bottle emptying sounded almost too loud.

"Are you sure you want this confrontation?" Marissa pushed a glass towards him.

"No, I'm not sure. But even if I never see him again, I need to ask him why."

Marissa nodded. "Then I will ask him whether he agrees to meet you."

* * *

HMP Belmarsh's doctor shone a light into Henry's eyes with a small torch, left right, left right. He inspected his nascent bruises.

"Quite a fight, wasn't it?"

"More an aggression than a fight." Henry grumbled.

The doctor kept prodding Henry's body for other signs of damage.

"Why did you have this fight then?"

"I told you this is not a fight…I didn't start this."

"But you must know why Ronnie had a go at you?"

"It's Ronnie we are talking about. here I've got no idea what goes through this guy's head." Henry's anger had risen into his belly. Did this idiot not know Kray was a nutjob?

"Still, you've received quite a pasting."

"It's only because I protected myself and didn't retaliate."

The doctor raised a quizzical eyebrow. When did inmates not relish a good fight?

Henry inhaled deeply. He did not need to be rattled by this little asshole, Kray had done a good enough job of that.

"In my experience there is always a trigger."

Henry managed to shrug, wincing as he did so.

The doctor moved back to his desk. "You'll live."

Henry nodded and started to slowly get dressed again.

Why Henry had not kept his mouth shut was a question that would come later in the privacy of his own cell.

The doctor looked at the two officers.

"I don't think he needs to go to the hospital. I'll come back tonight to check him over again."

"Come on, Henry." One of the officers nodded in the direction of the door. Henry dressed in the standard Belmarsh tracksuit still covered in blood and followed them. He had not asked where he was going. At the bottom of the stairs one of the guards started climbing towards Henry's cell. Henry limped in the same direction. They were taking him back. Henry stepped into Cell 14.

"Get changed," said the officer he knew. "The governor wants a word."

Chapter Fourteen

From a distance Pole could see Andy standing at his desk and gesticulating, whilst talking on his mobile. He stopped abruptly and bent down to jot some illegible note in his notebook.

Pole smiled. Working with his newly promoted DS was a treat. There was something almost childlike in the way Andy engaged with his job so enthusiastically. Pole's DS hung up but kept talking at the screen as if reprimanding it for not delivering the answer quickly enough.

"I am not sure it will take any notice," Pole said.

"Guv," Andy turned around with a small jerk, but Pole's amused face gave him confidence. "I've got some really interesting news."

"Very good, shoot." Pole leaned against the desk, arms crossed.

"I confirmed, well I think I confirmed, the route that Visconti was taking to smuggle the art pieces and artefacts out of the Middle-East war zones."

Pole nodded, "Go on."

"I am ninety-nine per cent sure he's been using the African route: Libya, Malta then Italy."

"What's the alternative?"

"From Tunisia to France or sometimes Southern Spain."

"Are there no direct routes? I mean from the Middle-East?"

"Not really. The most direct route would be to Turkey or Greece."

Andy had brought a map of the countries surrounding the Mediterranean onto the screen. He had drawn the routes in different colours, making them easier to distinguish.

"What leads you to believe Visconti was taking the African route?" Pole said. "Choose a less obvious route to avoid detection?"

"That's one of the reasons I think, but it may also be that it is where he had the best contacts for smuggling."

"Who else is using that route for trafficking?"

"The Narco unit told me that drugs are smuggled along a completely different route. People trafficking drugs established their routes before any of these were mapped and they don't like to mix."

"Armaments, as you suspected?" Pole bit his lip. This case was getting bigger by the minute.

"That's much more interesting because that's where the lines are getting blurred and Libya is in such a state of flux that weapons transit through it all the time."

"To where, do we know?"

"The whole of Africa. CT Command was pretty adamant."

"Nowhere else?"

"Nope." Andy moved his mouse and new lines appeared on his map of the Mediterranean and Africa. Pole moved to the back of Andy's chair to take a better look.

"How about migration?"

"You mean people?" Andy turned around surprised.

"Why not?"

"That's an interesting idea, Guv. I'll dig around."

"How about INTERPOL?"

"Haven't had much luck."

"Let me make some calls too. In the meantime, take me through the chart."

"As far as weapons are concerned, African trafficking goes through the Libya–Tunisia route then moves to Malta and Italy. The Middle-Eastern trafficking goes through Turkey; they have various entry points through the Arabian Peninsula."

Pole was following the various colours on the chart with his fingers. "That's a pretty good map you've put together." Pole straightened up and resumed his previous position, leaning against Andy's desk. "Visconti departed from the norm. He took the risk of taking a much longer route for the trafficking of his goods, I presume to avoid detection."

"Overland that's got to be true, but I'm not sure it holds when it comes to sea transfer."

"Which is why he would probably have stopped first in Malta?"

"A short stop to secure the goods and then carry on to Italy." Andy nodded approvingly.

"Hey, I too am a bear of some brain." Pole grinned. "What's next?"

"I need to find out whether Visconti changed any of his MOs and

I need more evidence to prove that he moved from art to armaments."

"Or people," Pole added. "Anything else?"

"Well." Andy adjusted his thick glasses. "I've got the feeling —" Andy stopped, hesitant about how to put his idea across to Pole.

"I don't care about diplomacy. Come on, say it how you see it."

"I'm not sure CT Command is telling me everything."

"I'm sure they're not."

"I asked whether they had Visconti on their radar and they were pretty vague."

"Vague is good." Pole clicked his fingers. "They can't say categorically no, or they might be misleading us."

"What if it's national security and all that?"

"Then they need to tell us Visconti is off limits."

"Would someone else be leaning on them?" Andy asked, candidly.

Pole hesitated for a second. His DS had just raised a tenuous link he had not yet considered. "What do you mean?"

"Other agencies."

"Let's first see what Ferguson has to say before we jump to any conclusions." Pole patted Andy on the shoulder. "Doing a really great job. Keep it up."

Andy beamed a smile and went back to work.

Pole's face darkened when he crossed the threshold of his office. He closed the door and pulled a brand-new phone out of his pocket. Time to call MI6.

* * *

The smell of bland meat, boiled cabbage and mashed potatoes made him retch. Henry had taken his lunch to his cell and left it on his desk. He was not hungry. The bruises on his face had started to change colour: pus yellow and dirty blue. He touched his cheek gingerly. It had almost doubled in size despite the pack of ice the doctor had given him.

Henry looked at the plate that was getting cold. He fought the urge to throw it into the toilet. He reached for a small tin of herbs stashed away on his shelves and sprinkled a pinch over the dish; perhaps it would help.

He sat down and put a forkful of mash in his mouth. At least he did not have to chew any of it, for once overcooked was a good thing. He kept going until his plate was empty. It was fuel for survival. Whilst eating, Henry was mentally going over the meeting he had just come back from.

HMP Belmarsh's governor had not been happy. He had spent half an hour being lectured about fighting, privileges to be reconsidered and, of course, was he fit to be released to help with the SFO case? Henry had remained silent, contrite, repeatedly making the point that he had been attacked. The CCTV cameras would tell. But no fight ever started unprovoked. The governor dismissed him; he would be told later what his ruling was.

The familiar clunk of the cell door's bolts told Henry it was bang-up time. He stretched his arm towards the biscuit tin. Another clunk surprised Henry. He pushed the tin back and turned around painfully. Someone had just released the bolts and would enter his cell in a few seconds.

"Hello Henry, put your shoes on and bring your coat."

Henry's mind went blank. Shoes. Coat. He was leaving the compound. Was it so cold outside that he needed a coat? He could not quite tell. The temperature in HSU was almost constant, hospital-like, a temperature that made you limp and comatose.

He remembered – the segregation unit was at the other end of the large structure that made up HMP Belmarsh.

"Hurry up, I haven't got all day." The officer moved his hand in the direction of the landing.

Henry sat on his bed, fished out his shoes from underneath it and fixed the Velcro into position. There were no shoelaces allowed in prison. From a small wardrobe Henry pulled a duffel coat Nancy had hurriedly purchased when he had been sent to HSU. It was not the place where an inmate should be wearing an Armani camel coat.

He started walking, one officer in front and one at the back. He did not want to ask where he was going. He did not want to show he cared or that he was scared.

Henry went through the fourteen checks it took to exit HSU:
- body checks
- name checks
- metal detectors

As Henry approached the small reception area within HSU his stomach somersaulted. True, he went through the same area when he was out on exercise. But today he was turning left towards the governor's office again. He would be told he had instigated the fight with Kray. No matter how much Henry had argued, he had lost the argument.

He would now be told how long he would spend in the segregation unit. He would almost certainly lose some of his privileges as well. All this for two small words: "Bloody idiot". He could scream at his stupidity. Who was the bloody idiot now?

Henry stopped beside the door leading to the outside.

"Sit please," one of the guards asked. Henry did as he was told. He could not give up so close to his goal. He had to argue his case again: self-defence, never had a scrap with anyone before, a saint – by HSU standards of course. At six foot three and with four years of solid gym training he could have inflicted damage on Kray but the only injury Kray could show would have come from the guards. But would they want to admit they had savaged him?

This was hopeless.

"It's cold outside," one of the guards warned. Henry nodded and slowly moved his arms into the sleeves of his coat. He adjusted the collar and stepped inside the yard where another two guards were already waiting for him.

A large van was parked outside. He almost ignored it until one of the guards opened the back door. "In you go."

Henry could not hide his surprise and he caught the amused look on the guard's face. He limped for a few seconds towards the open door and before he could take it all in the handcuffs were put on him and he was pushed inside.

There was already a guard sitting in the van, a man he had not met before. The second guard sat down in silence opposite his colleague. The van lumbered out of the gates. Henry let his head fall against the cold metal of the cage in which he had been locked up. He was leaving Belmarsh.

The plan was still on track.

The excitement was so intense he needed to calm down and chat.

"Any chance of some water?"

The officer he did not know grabbed a bottle from underneath his seat. He stood up, walking cautiously and hunched forward to avoid falling when the van suddenly hit a pothole. He slid the bottle through the bars without a word and went back to his seat.

Henry opened the bottle and drank the water in one go. He closed his eyes and tried to quieten his thoughts. It was an astounding outcome. Who could have cut a deal of that magnitude with Belmarsh? The SFO needed him badly. A reassuring thought.

Henry brought his mind back to the last time he had left HSU. The LIBOR scandal had been about to explode, and he certainly had been instrumental in its uncovering. He smiled at the memory. The UK government, the Bank of England and quite a few top executives in the City were about to feel the pain.

His smile broadened at the idea of working with Nancy and Pole again. He had almost enjoyed working with Nancy's *favourite inspector* as he liked to tease her every so often. Henry stretched. His mind now felt alert once more. He thought about the case that Nancy had outlined. It would take no time to help them find out who the mysterious ultimate beneficial owner of the fund was.

The van slowed down and stopped for a little longer than Henry would have expected at a set of traffic lights. It took a sharp right and went over what felt like a ridge. The angle of the van tilted forward.

They were no longer following the road but going underground. The van was moving slowly. It took another sharp turn to the right and stopped altogether. For a moment everything was silent and almost peaceful.

The door of the van opened with a metallic thump and both guards got out, leaving Henry alone in the cage. He had forgotten his watch and could not tell how much time had elapsed since they had left Belmarsh. Twenty minutes perhaps, half an hour at most.

The heating in the van had been turned off and the cold was seeping through the metal frame. Henry moved around. He leaned his back against the part of the van that connected with the driver's seat. He stretched his long legs and waited.

The door of the van opened again, a small gap to start with. Henry stayed put. His heartbeat had risen, and he started breathing slowly, ready to deal with whatever life was about to throw at him.

A squat young man entered. He was wearing a sober blue coat and a pair of black leather gloves. He sat as close as he could to the cage, crossed his legs, one foot in the air. "Hello Henry." He spoke with an imperceptible smile.

His voice did not try to disguise a faint East-End accent. "I'm glad we finally get to meet." He uncrossed his legs, moved forward, now elbows on knees. "And I feel certain that you've been expecting the call." The smile broadened, uncovering a neat row of teeth, sharp and dangerous.

"What makes you say that?" Henry asked folding his legs under the bench.

"Experience. And the help of the few people who know you well."

"There aren't that many of those around." Henry's face expressed certainty, perhaps a hint of irony.

600

Contact, at last.

The young man ignored this. "I have a deal for you."

"How about an introduction first?" A negotiation; finally, something Henry knew he excelled at.

"OK then, you can call me Steve for the time being."

"And later on?" Henry pushed.

"We're not there yet," Steve said, his small eyes drilling into Henry, searching for the weak spot and finding it already. "You're an angry man, Henry."

Henry fought the desire to tell the little chap to bugger off. He smiled instead. "It's a good asset on the trading floor."

"But it's something that gets you killed in my world."

"And what is your world?"

"Intelligence." Steve's amused eyes were roving over Henry again, gathering much more subtle information than the police had ever done.

"OK, intelligence about what?"

Steve laughed, a resounding don't-give-me-that-bullshit laugh. "You have spent four years at HSU Belmarsh with some pretty high-profile characters and you have befriended Kamal, sorry Abu Maeraka, so what do you think?"

"Cards on the table straightaway, hey." Henry was almost impressed.

"No time to lose, mate." Steve leaned against the side of the van.

"What do you want, information?" Henry was not going to make it so easy. Cards on the table but one ace up his sleeve.

"That's rather obvious." Steve looked disappointed.

"What's in it for me?"

"Need a bit more; you tell me what you can give me, and I'll tell you how much it is worth."

"No." Henry had pursed his lips. He moved to sit next to Steve on the other side of the cage. "I'll tell you what I want, and you tell me what I need to do to get it."

"Ambitious. I like it." Steve nodded with appreciation.

"Get me out of Belmarsh." Henry locked eyes with Steve.

Steve stood up, walked to the other side of the van but did not walk out. He was thinking.

"Hypothetically, if I said yes, *if*, you'd have to deliver something pretty big to me, something no one else can."

Henry had stood up too. He leaned against the bars of the cage, casually so.

"How about the financing structure of a new terrorist organisation?"

Steve moved closer. He was much shorter than Henry, but he did not feel threatened. "Now we're talking."

Steve moved away. "I'll contact you again."

"Is that it?" Henry hands now clung to the bars of the cage.

"Yup. I need to organise a few things before the next step."

"How do we make contact?"

Steve took a small picture out of his jacket pocket, on it the face of a man, looking serious, taken to fit an official badge.

"He will be your contact." Steve moved the photo so that Henry could see. Henry squinted. His eyelashes batted a few times.

"You're not serious, are you?"

"Couldn't be more serious, mate." Steve replaced the picture in his inside pocket and grinned.

Chapter Fifteen

The same dingy room, the same smell of sweat and bad coffee – Henry recognised it immediately. He loved it. It had been fun to work on the LIBOR case with Nancy and Pole here, despite the dramatic twist that could have cost them their lives.

Still, it had been a breakthrough for Henry, a way to consolidate his plan, to see how to move forward. Today the stakes were even higher. He had had no time to take stock of what Steve had said and what his proposition meant. MI6 needed him. Now he knew why.

Henry rolled his head from side to side a few times, inhaled deeply and exhaled slowly counting from ten to one. The palms of his hands had gone moist. He rubbed them on his thighs. So much was riding on this meeting. He was about to meet the SFO prosecutor, Marissa Campbell.

He dragged a chair across the floor away from the small table that would become his desk. It screeched, sending a shiver along his spine. He sat with an effort at the main table. He stretched his hands over its top, fingers spread to the limit. He was not ready the way he would have liked to be.

A soft noise startled Henry. He rotated his body with a wince to face the door. Friend or foe? He shook his head in relief at the sight of her.

Nancy had walked into the room carrying two cups of Benugo coffee, his favourite.

"Good afternoon." She smiled.

"Good afternoon Nancy." Henry stood up and bent forward to give Nancy a kiss on the cheek. She almost dropped their coffee as she spotted Henry's bruises and swollen face. She hurriedly put the cups on the table and dragged him into the light. "Who has done that to you? I need to report —"

Henry lifted his hand. "No need to panic. It's under control."

"What do you mean?"

"The nutcase who did this will be spending a lot of time in the segregation unit."

"Are you certain?"

"Positive."

Nancy looked unconvinced. "Positive." Henry repeated, bending forward and finally kissing her cheek, a gentle human touch that almost felt awkward. This was one of the other punishments he had to endure in prison. Human contact was either violent or non-existent. Nothing in between.

Henry handed her a coffee, they sat down and started drinking in silence.

"Inspector Pole is on his way," Nancy changed the subject.

Henry's jaws clenched and his look darkened.

"Surely, you can't be that annoyed at working with Pole again?" Nancy said surprised. "Henry? I thought you had made your peace."

"So sorry Nancy; getting out of HSU makes me nervous." It was the best he could do. Pole's involvement in the case had taken on a new meaning. A pang of sadness shook him. He had to lie to her.

She looked at him still in doubt. "Are you sure you are OK? Is something troubling you?"

Henry shook his head. He felt a distance opening between him and Nancy, a small gap but a break, nevertheless. He had not thought about it but now, in her presence, he understood how much he had felt included, encompassed in a field of friendship that was seamless. And the fact that he was about to lose it wrecked his heart.

"I'm fine working with Pole, really." Henry forced himself to smile.

"I'm sorry," Nancy said laying a friendly hand on his shoulder. "You had plenty of time to prepare last time you were allowed outside Belmarsh; today has been very rushed."

"Why was that?" Henry's hopes lifted; perhaps she knew about MI6?

"The attempt on Marissa. The bomb that was meant for Mark Phelps delayed the procedure to approve your helping us, but this time —"

"What do you mean? Another bomb?" Henry had turned to stone.

"Have you not been told?" Nancy said surprised. She gave Henry the details of what she knew. He listened in silence. First Mark Phelps, now Marissa Campbell's unsuccessful shooting. The implications almost overwhelmed him. After all, he had been branded, no – he had been a terrorist too. Would these people still want to work with him? The thought hit him square in the chest.

He took a gulp of coffee. Something to keep his throat from closing. His focus went for a moment. He pushed away the question that was crushing him.

Who would be next?

Their coffee was almost finished. Nancy started taking documents out of her satchel. Her yellow legal pad and unassuming biro came out as well. Henry welcomed the disruption. He picked up the pen between his thumb and index finger and inspected it.

"What on earth is that?"

"It's called a pen I believe." Nancy smiled coyly.

"Don't you have anything more decent to work with?"

"You mean a Montblanc pen, Cartier?"

"Or even a good old Parker. With proper ink, I mean."

"And it has taken you four years to realise that I cannot abide writing with any of those. Tut, tut, tut. Where has your sense of observation gone?"

"Ouch, point taken." Henry was still holding the pen the way he would a piece of junk.

"We do not receive tombstones or ridiculously large corporate presents when we close a case. Unlike you bankers."

"Ex-banker if you please. And Pritchard QC did have a very large collection of excellent pens if I recall." Henry was enjoying the light banter.

"Indeed, a point on which Pritchard and I strongly disagree – my rebellious nature and my old communist upbringing," Nancy replied, equally enjoying the tease.

"You, a commie?" Henry arched his eyebrows in genuine astonishment.

"I did tell you my father was a communist; remember I am half-Chinese from the mainland of China not Hong Kong."

"Of course, you did say. And the years at The Sorbonne."

"*Absolument, rebel de la gauche.*" Nancy nodded.

A knock on the door stopped them in their tracks. It opened and Pole entered followed by a tall black woman.

Henry stood up, uncertain whether she would want to shake hands. He thanked Nancy mentally. She had helped him once more to feel he was human after all.

Pole extended a firm hand towards Henry. Their eyes met and Henry knew he had been told not to make his life difficult. Pole introduced Marissa Campbell as the SFO prosecutor dealing with the Bank X whistle-blowing case.

She extended an equally firm hand and shook Henry's. Her broad face was amiable, the face of someone you could confide in. Perhaps wrongly. Her willingness to shake his hand after what she had gone through impressed Henry. She sat herself in front of him, impassive. She was here to do a job and a job she would do.

Marissa took over and started by recapping the facts of the case.

By 2009 Bank X had refused the UK government bailout programme. It had instead received funding from a state in the Middle-East. So far, so very good; nothing wrong with this.

However, a large proportion of the funds raised had been subsequently lent to a Panama fund, the ownership structure of which was complex. It had been impossible so far to establish who the ultimate beneficial owner was.

The suspicion was that the same Middle-Eastern state was benefiting through some of its government's officials. And this was a circular transaction UK legislation did not allow, in clear contravention of the law.

Mark Phelps, the whistle-blower, had had access to information that supported the suspicion, and he was ready to speak up. But the documents he had been able to collect were insufficient to bring about a conviction. The SFO needed the details of the Ultimate Beneficial Owner, the UBO.

Henry nodded a few times. He could already think of a number of ways in which he could disentangle the fund legal structure and find out the name of the UBO.

"How much do you know about Panama?" Marissa directed a first question at him.

"I understand how the system works." Henry moved nearer the table and spread his long fingers over a set of documents Marissa had just put in front of him. "May I?"

"That is why you are here, right?" Marissa shot back.

Henry ignored her tone and started going through the file, speed-reading the details it contained. "I'll need more time to digest the information, but I can see already that complex layering is going to make it very hard to find the UBO."

"Yes, we gathered that."

"You would like me to disentangle the ownership structure and trace the individual or individuals at the top."

"That would be helpful." Marissa blinked. It would be bloody marvellous. Henry made a metal note of her tic.

"What do you need?" Pole asked.

Henry tapped his fingers on the side of the table. "I need a couple of Bloomberg terminals. Like last time, set up to access live market data. Access to the web." Henry locked eyes with Pole again. If he wanted to facilitate he needed to provide the right tools for data mining. "And, a burner phone."

"Shall I also provide you with the keys to your cell?" Pole shot back.

"That would be really nice. However, the governor at Belmarsh may not be that forthcoming."

"Let's calm things down a little." Nancy moved her arm across the table to separate the parties. "Perhaps we should remind ourselves why we are here."

"Well put," Marissa added. "We are hoping to unveil significant criminal activity."

"Why the phone?" Nancy asked.

"Because I need to make a call to a former contact. He won't talk if he knows the call can be traced."

"And you won't give us the name, I presume." Pole looked unhappy. Henry's contact was outside his jurisdiction. Henry understood why Pole would rather focus on finding out who the relevant person was at the end of a long line of connections but this was not the way it worked in the murky world of tax evasion.

"Spot on, Inspector," Henry replied, giving him the thumbs up.

"Ms Campbell, would you agree to my suggestion?" Henry's voice almost trembled. It was her he needed to convince.

"I will support it to the extent you can demonstrate it is necessary and I can see progress in the unravelling of the structure of the Panama fund." Marissa had relaxed suddenly. Perhaps she had seen enough of Henry to sense that she could trust him to deliver the information needed. Perhaps it was something else altogether. Henry did not care. All that mattered was that she was willing to work with him.

"Which countries are you intending to call?" Pole asked.

Henry sat back and thought for a moment. "I may need information along the way from Malta, but my first port of call will be Panama."

"And in Panama?" Pole was not letting go.

"Mossack Fonseca, the largest law firm in the country."

Marissa nodded. "If you can get something out of them, I'll be very impressed."

"Then prepare to be amazed." Henry almost smiled.

* * *

"Your guest has arrived, Sir," the porter said, whilst taking Brett's trench coat and trilby hat.

"Has he?" Brett would have been annoyed at the news in other circumstances, but MI6-Steve's early arrival could mean only one thing.

Trouble.

Brett walked without stopping through his club. A few people he knew were reading their newspapers, expecting to be greeted, but Brett had no time for common courtesies.

Steve had selected a suitably secluded corner. Brett caught the young man unaware as he moved towards the chairs, a first since Steve had become his minder. He was observing a couple of men speaking loudly about their views on the current government. A lot of posturing and very little depth. Steve might have been amused by the shallow conversation. Instead he seemed to survey the people Brett frequented. His small beady eyes, roving in their direction unnoticed. Brett resumed his walk.

"It is unusual to find you here before me." No need to be civil with Steve. He might even have been disappointed if Brett had been polite.

"Thought I might pick up some intel." MI6-Steve grinned. "But I gather you also have some important info for me."

Brett sat in the armchair opposite Steve's. He did not want to face into the room whilst discussing his findings about The Sheik. A gloved butler took Brett's order – Glenfiddich, no ice – but no need to specify – the butler already knew.

"The Sheik is contemplating turning Crowne into a Jihadi." Brett barely contained a smile. How was that for a piece of news?

"Good," Steve replied, swilling his glass of whisky in slow motion to dissolve the ice that swam in it.

"Are you being flippant for the sake of it?" Brett's nostrils flared. The East-End boy was annoying him more than usual today. His glass of whisky appeared as if from nowhere and Brett almost thanked the waiter. He took a large mouthful hoping it would help.

"Nope, just very happy to hear they think they can do that."

"Enlighten me then."

"It means they are starting to trust him."

"And what if he gets —" Brett looked for the right word, "turned?"

"Don't worry about that. That's my problem, not yours."

"Not so. I need to know whether to encourage The Sheik or not."

"Do you think they will listen to your opinion on a matter like that?"

"He just did. So why would he ask if he didn't want to know the answer?"

"To test you. To see whether you have an agenda; whether you want to place Crowne."

Brett stopped for a moment to consider Steve's point. True, he had not thought about that.

"You did good by not lying about your opinion by the way. He would have guessed in any case. Which is why the less I tell you the better."

"You're looking after my interests now?" Brett sniggered.

"No, looking after my interests, but since you are part of my interests …"

"And here I was, hoping."

"You need to keep your powder dry for what comes next."

"Are you intent on talking only in riddles today?" Brett drummed his fingers a few times on the arm of his chair.

"Be patient, I am coming to it." Steve took a mouthful of whisky. "I believe you are about to be asked to arrange the transfer of another consignment out of the UK."

"You believe or you know?" Brett sat back in his armchair.

"Let's say we are ninety per cent certain."

"That sounds pretty certain to me. Anyway, I presume the next request from The Sheik will be armaments."

"Have you been told already?" It was Steve's turn to sound miffed.

"No, my dear fella," Brett savoured his small success. "I might be a toff but I do have a brain, as you yourself remarked a few months ago."

Steve whistled softly and grinned. "Go ahead, and …?"

"When The Sheik asked me to bring Clandestine X into the UK, he didn't mention armaments and I was keen to stress that suited me fine. And it does." Brett took another sip of whisky. "Then, there is the shooting – the one that caused the death of the young man at the Bank of England. And the other – execution." Brett felt strangely queasy. He did not do emotions but the latest development had been a little too much even for him. MI6-Steve nodded encouragingly.

"A couple of days ago, The Sheik saw me and produced the photos of Visconti, as you know."

This time, Brett felt sick. He braced himself and a bead of sweat rolled down the side of his face. He quickly wiped it away with a white cotton handkerchief.

"You think it's a way to 'incentivise' you to do the things you don't want to do. Like armaments?"

"That's what I think," Brett gulped down more whisky to clear the nausea.

Steve finished his glass and looked at the small lump of ice still dissolving at the bottom. "Possible."

"What if it is something – lethal?"

"Brett, all armaments are lethal. That's the point."

"I may only deal with antiquities, but I know what a gun is for," Brett replied dryly. "I mean extreme weapons: chemicals, nuclear?"

"We will be tracking the parcel. You know the route; that is all I need. Just keep The Sheik on board."

"Do I have a choice? Unless I want to finish like …" Even Brett couldn't bring himself to be sarcastic about Visconti's death.

"We are getting deeper into this project."

"You mean I am."

"No, we are. You have just become one of our top priorities. You should be flattered."

"No, I should be mightily scared."

Brett finished his glass and put it on the table. Time to leave the comfort of his club.

Chapter Sixteen

Pole and Henry were walking alongside each other, the prison officers who accompanied Henry walking a few steps in front of them. Pole slowed down a fraction, Henry matched his pace. The distance between them and the officers increased a little, then a little more until Pole felt able to speak.

"You spoke to Steve Harris?" Pole murmured.

Henry nodded. Pole glanced at him. Henry's body had tightened. He was on the alert, looking straight in front of him.

"Why you?"

"Convenience and …" Pole hesitated. There was not enough time to speak about Nancy. He was not even sure he wanted Henry to know about the quest for her father. Should he trust Henry and tell him about the deal he had cut with MI6 to gather information on China?

The officers stopped in front of the lifts, in a few seconds they would turn around and see the two men lagging behind.

"Past history." Pole added swiftly before quickening his pace.

It was too late for Henry to ask another question. Pole noticed the clenched fists in the tight clasp of his handcuffs. They had entered the lift and Pole still could not quite read Henry's mood.

Anger – as ever. He was not surprised or even concerned about it but could the essential ingredient their relationship needed to work together be found? He did not know. Pole would have to work a little harder than he had anticipated.

Trust would not come easily.

They reached the end of the long corridor at the back of the Scotland Yard building. A high security reinforced door opened onto a small inner courtyard. The back door of the prison van was already thrown open. Henry got into the vehicle without looking at Pole. The van door slammed shut and Henry was on his way back to HSU Belmarsh.

Pole almost felt sorry for him. He ruffled his goatee and stayed in the yard to watch the van pass through the heavy gate that led to the street. An icy gust of wind made him shiver. He walked back through the corridor and towards the room where Nancy and Marissa were debriefing about what Henry had said.

Pole had noticed a nascent shadow on Henry's face. Henry did not seem the sort to grow a beard. A silly idea, of course; why should he not?

No, Henry was close shaven, clean-cut, the blade doing its job close to his jaw and close to his throat. It seemed important and yet Pole could not make it out yet.

* * *

The door had shut behind them. Nancy had barely said goodbye to Henry. It felt inappropriate to demonstrate their closeness in front of Marissa.

Marissa had been outstandingly controlled. Not a hint of nerves or anger, after what she had just gone through. Remarkable. Her eyes had followed the two men leaving the room, her heavy frame tilted forward, ready to follow them. Nancy cleared her throat. Marissa's body twitched, awoken from her concentration.

"What do you think?" Nancy asked, moving to the chair Pole had occupied next to Marissa.

"Very bright. Not what I expected – intelligent of course; I thought he would be – but not as brash or arrogant as I had anticipated."

"You think you can work with Henry, despite …" Nancy hesitated. Should she bring terrorism into the conversation? She, who never shied away from the hard questions, was uncertain.

"Despite his IRA connections?" Marissa asked. "You look surprised Nancy. Wasn't it you who taught me to ask the tough questions?"

"It seems the pupil has exceeded the master." Nancy laughed, joining fist and outstretched hand in the sign of a Kung Fu master.

Marissa hesitated and joined Nancy in a giggle; it was nice to be a little less serious.

"I'm not so sure about that but I'm glad you feel that way nevertheless." Marissa carried on smiling. "And to answer your question, I can't deny it, it is unnerving to be working with a former IRA operative. But now that I've met him …"

"I'm glad of it. He will deliver what he has promised."

"I have no doubt about it. He is – on a mission." Marissa's face became thoughtful.

Nancy nodded. Henry was dedicated, almost obsessed with the idea of redemption. A subject he spoke regularly about. But Marissa had put her finger on something new. Something had moved in Henry's attitude. Nancy could not quite fathom what, unless she took his letter at face value.

Marissa's voice came back into focus. "… burner phone might be difficult."

"But we won't leave the phone with him all the time and we may even be able to limit his access."

"You mean narrow it to a specific country?"

"For example."

"A good idea. Still …"

Pole knocked and walked in. Nancy smiled as she turned in his direction. He had stopped inside the door frame, making sure he was not interrupting an important conversation.

"Come in; it is your interrogation room after all." Marissa said.

"Just making sure I'm not intruding on something essential." Pole smiled. "You may have been talking fashion or hairstyles."

"That is so not PC." Marissa chuckled. Her smile broadened to uncover a small gap in the middle of a set of otherwise perfect teeth.

"Then what? Henry's long list of must-haves?"

"That's more like it." Marissa kept smiling.

"Superintendent Marsh is going to have a fit," Pole mused. "I like it."

"Perhaps I should be the one asking?" Nancy's eyes sparkled, teasing him.

"Not a chance." Pole crossed his arms. "I am keeping my powder dry for a better occasion."

"You mean there will be a better occasion than asking Marsh to let Henry have a phone?"

"Absolutely. No doubt. Obvious." Pole replied almost serious.

"Am I missing something glaring?" Marissa questioned, amused.

"Hardly." Pole gestured dismissively and came to sit at the table. "Going back to the case, how much are you prepared to disclose to him?"

"I'm not sure yet. Let's see how he gets on with what he's been given so far."

Pole dropped his head forward a fraction. Considering.

"What if he needs to meet with Mark Phelps?"

The room stood still for a moment. Nancy felt her stomach drop at the memory of her meeting with Mark.

"I've spoken to Mark myself. He's had time to think." Marissa aligned a paperclip on the wad of documents in front of her.

"Has he changed his mind?" Pole sounded dubious.

"Somewhat. He can see that Henry is the right person to help deliver the evidence for the case."

Nancy felt almost relieved but there was a chill in Marissa's tone. "If he simply does not want to deal with him directly it should be workable, but is there something else?"

"There is. Mark wants to meet Henry, just once, to talk about his involvement with the IRA."

A deep intake of air came from Pole. Nancy was mildly surprised. How strange? Perhaps this is what she had felt when she had spoken to him. The need to make sense of it all. The need for a confrontation with his tormentor. It brought victims some release, made it easier for them to move forward.

Nancy felt two pairs of eyes on her waiting for her reply. She was Henry's principle contact. What would he say?

Accept? Refuse?

"Maybe this is a good way for Henry to atone?" Pole said, serious. No banter about Henry's famous need for redemption. Something he liked to tease Nancy about every time she brought the subject up.

"Maybe." Nancy could genuinely not decide.

Henry's desire to make amends was to be on his own terms, he would choose how and when to do so. Would the Henry-in-control-of-his-destiny agree to see a victim – not his victim, but nevertheless a victim of terrorism? A terrible reminder of the depth of his failure.

"I need to think about how I approach him about this." She spoke slowly, beginning to gauge what it would take.

"Otherwise …" Marissa let the sentence hang. It was not a threat, simply fact. It was Mark Phelps' price for assisting with the investigation.

"We understand," Pole said.

Marissa stood up, wincing as she did so. She rubbed her back and opened her satchel, methodically pushing her papers into it.

"Henry is due to come back tomorrow morning first thing. Belmarsh likes to get him through their gates before the other inmates are allowed out."

Marissa nodded. "I'll be here."

He stood arms stretched, legs apart – a vulnerable position he had learned to cope with. The prison officer frisked him, ran a metal detector up and down his body. Henry turned around to complete the check.

He was only through gate three. Another five to go before he reached the inside of HSU Belmarsh where he could move a little more freely. The journey back from Scotland Yard was always a deflating experience – as he had learned the last time he had been allowed out. Today had been particularly testing. The guards that had been around when MI6 first made contact were the same and yet they had behaved as if nothing had happened. Henry's mind was racing. He had to find a way to deliver the Ultimate Beneficial Owner of the Panama fund structure. He had been restless through the entire return trip at the thought of the plan coming together, at Kamal – Abu Maeraka's – words. He was also concerned. Henry would be allowed only minimum contact with inmates from now on.

Still, he could not be denied a shower or gym time. And he needed to have the conversation, not about Abu Maeraka's ploy for escaping, but about Nancy – no one must target her or the deal was off.

The usual metallic sound almost startled him. It was another door being opened. The routine checks started all over again. How many times did you need to frisk someone to be sure he was not carrying anything on his body?

The thought of smuggling something inside his backside had felt repulsive to start with but what would he now accept should his freedom depend on it? Suddenly the idea did not sound so distressing after all. Henry almost smiled. Give him another ten years and he might consider it a perfectly good option.

Henry stopped before the final door. It was almost 7pm and dinner was now available. He was asked to move into a small room; he would be brought some food, almost certainly cold and barely edible. But, hell, he had been allowed out, yes ... out. He would gladly eat a piece of cardboard if it meant he could keep visiting the outside world.

The officers had left him on his own. He started shaking again, a tremor born from excitement and danger. Henry stood up and stretched his tall body. It felt heavy and muscular.

"Be ready," Abu Maeraka had said. He was. He wanted to shout the words in his throat building up to a roar.

Henry stretched again. Could he ask to go to the gym? The concern for Nancy stole most of his enthusiasm.

The small spy window carved into the door opened and closed almost instantly. Another inmate stepped in carrying a tray. Not someone Henry knew, even by sight. There was no eye contact; the guard was surveying the young man's every move. As he placed the small tray on the table, the young man brushed aside the small paper napkin that had been hurriedly placed on top of a plastic spoon. The paper towel dropped to the floor.

Henry froze. The young man mumbled an apology, picked up the napkin and disappeared as quickly as he had come. The door banged shut after him.

Such a clumsy gesture and yet such an important one. Was Abu Maeraka speaking? Be ready.

Or could it have been a genuine mistake? Henry replayed the scene in his mind. The very slow movements to place the tray on the table, the young man's hand trembling as he brushed the napkin away, his back hiding his movements from the guard – too deliberate. Big K had warned Henry. Abu Maeraka was building an army, his influence growing stronger every day. But wherever the young man came from, HSU or main compound, the message was clear … Be ready.

Henry looked at the unappetising-looking pizza on his plate – a piece of cardboard, hey. He wolfed it down. It was fuel for a purpose.

* * *

Nancy and Marissa had left. Andy wanted a word. Marsh, The Super, wanted him – now. But he would have to wait his turn. Pole locked the door of his office and actioned the security pad that required a code to open it. The latest in security measures.

His second mobile phone was ringing. He hesitated, but what was the point in delaying. He needed to speak to Harris anyway.

"Harris," Pole kept his voice bland, no sign of anger, none of anticipation.

"Inspector Pole." Harris was waiting. He held all the cards, at least for the time being. Pole clenched his jaw.

"He has made a number of demands. In particular, one for a mobile phone." Pole elaborated further and gave Harris the details.

"A phone, good. Just make sure you limit the range and we will do the rest."

616

"Right," Pole replied. Harris seemed to have anticipated Henry's request, or had he suggested it?

"How has Marsh reacted?"

"I am about to have that conversation." Pole's voice took on a stubborn edge. He would not be pushed to discuss every step of the enquiry whether Harris liked it or not.

"Don't worry, Marsh is far too keen on his new high-profile case and he will be delighted to know Ms Wu is involved." The tease was hardly bearable.

Pole did not reply, torn between giving Harris a piece of his mind and terminating the call. "My secret weapon. Marsh will never say no to her."

Pole could hear the smile in Harris' voice, good shot it said. "I gather."

"How far are you with Crowne?" Pole asked.

"As much as I would like to show you the big picture, Inspector Pole, I am afraid I can't discuss with you the —"

Pole interrupted bluntly. "Harris, don't give me that bull. This is not the first time I've worked with MI6 so don't piss me off unnecessarily."

"I genuinely can't tell you." Harris sounded serious. "But I can tell you that I will keep Ms Wu and Ms Campbell safe."

"Now somehow that does not give me the warm glow it is supposed to," Pole replied. "Since you have mentioned Ms Wu perhaps you can tell me where your investigation into her father's disappearance is at?"

"It is China, and it was thirty years ago – very little has surfaced so far, a few cuttings on him as an artist and that is about it, and yes, before you ask, I am trying."

"You are trying, Agent Harris, I am glad even you admit that." Pole had moved to his desk, pleased with his pun. "Any timeline?"

Harris sounded interested enough in finding out more about Nancy's father. Pole asked a few more questions. Harris replied patiently and Pole wondered …

"Do you have any particular interest in Mr Wu?" Pole was unexpectedly direct. He was listening. There was a short intake of breath, a slight hold and release. Harris' voice remained even.

"None that I can think of, but I will let you know if that changes," Harris carried on. "Before you go, Inspector Pole, it would be good if you could arrange for Crowne to be on his own tomorrow between eleven and noon."

"I'll see what I can do." Pole hung up and threw the mobile on his desk. He slumped into his chair. Dealing with MI6 meant that he would never be one step ahead. There were too many moving parts he could not see, was not told about. As for being kept safe – Pole's experience told him otherwise. He was certain Harris would choose the security of his asset over and above that of Nancy or Marissa.

Pole's mobile rang. He grunted.

"I'm on my way Denise."

"The great man is waiting for you. Impatiently."

"I am walking as we speak."

"No, you are still at your desk wondering how to get what you want from him." Denise's voice had a cheerful tone that Pole trusted. She had been Marsh's PA for as long as Pole could remember. How she had delt with The Super for so long was a mystery.

"Can't fool you, can I?"

"No. You have two minutes to materialise in front of his door."

"Now, I am walking."

* * *

Marsh was outside his office speaking to Denise, when Pole arrived. Pole slowed down in the hope The Super would walk into his office without noticing him but was out of luck.

Marsh straightened up and looked towards Pole over his half-moon glasses. He waited for his DCI to approach and walked into his office without a word. Denise rolled her eyes. Pole moved an eyebrow up but there was no time for pleasantries. The great man had been waiting.

"The latest please?" Marsh asked as he sat down behind his desk. Pole resisted the urge to ask him which case he wanted to discuss; he needed to convince Marsh about the phone.

"The first meeting with Crowne was a success. I think the SFO prosecutor is impressed and convinced he can help."

"You think or she is?"

"She is."

Marsh shot Pole a look. "Timetable?"

"A series of daily meetings for the next three days. There is a lot to go through and the SFO needs to speed up the information gathering phase. They are willing to support Crowne in facilitating his requests."

Marsh suddenly moved forward in his leather chair. "What does Crowne want that is contentious then?" His voice showed that he was weighing up the impact of a dangerous situation. No matter how much

Pole disliked Marsh for his brusqueness and political ambition, his mind was sharp.

"Top of the list – a burner phone." Pole gave it to Marsh straight, there was no need to be subtle with him.

Marsh's eyebrows rose and stayed like that until he had sat back in his chair.

"I see. And the SFO is willing to support this?"

"As long as we limit the range of the phone."

Marsh nodded. "Which destination?"

"Panama."

"I don't like it but you and the SFO are going to tell me that there is no other way, right?"

"Right."

"What does Ms Wu think?" Marsh's eyes moved away from Pole for a short moment. Pole straightened up a little. "She also believes it is not ideal —"

"Of course," Marsh interrupted. "Perhaps we can discuss options."

"I am not certain you will —"

"I'll ask Denise to arrange a meeting," Marsh interrupted again. "Please let Ms Wu know."

"Shall I tell the SFO we have a delay?" Pole made a final attempt.

"No. But let them know I need a second opinion."

Pole left a few minutes later. Perhaps Nancy could pretend she had a headache. A permanent one at the thought of meeting The Super.

Chapter Seventeen

"I suppose it would be too much to ask to be allowed gym time or even fifteen minutes on the rowing machine?" Henry asked as he was walking alongside one of the officers.

The small podgy man smiled. "Don't push it. You've been allowed out, right?"

"That doesn't mean I was able to run a marathon along the banks of the Thames, John."

"A good set of press-ups in your cell should do the trick." John was still amused. He had been working in HSU Belmarsh for almost two years. His time was due to end soon, much to Henry's regret. John had managed to be pleasant without compromising the *Sacro Saint Dicta* of HSU – "Thou Shall Not Fraternise With The Cons."

"Perhaps a shower after the set of press-ups, then?" Henry twisted his nose. "I don't want to offend my Scotland Yard colleagues with a good dose of BO and give Belmarsh a bad reputation."

John laughed outright. "It'll take more than a pongy con to give HSU Belmarsh a bad reputation. It's got one already."

"Still, I am meeting with two ladies tomorrow." Henry pleaded jokingly.

"I'll see what I can do."

Henry nodded and prepared to enter Cell 14. He slowed down a little, crossed the threshold and stood there until the door was shut. He could feel the metal against his back. Henry's body swayed gently, an oscillation that gradually pushed him inside the room. He forced himself to move slowly to his bed, two steps. He sat down, using his breathing as control.

Inhale – exhale.

Adrenaline was still coursing in his veins – everything was now possible.

620

"Everything," Henry murmured.

He let his mind drift, coming back to one word in focus. He had lived a boring but sheltered life since he had started his sentence. He hoped the four years spent in an environment in which hardly anything happened had not blunted his mind and his ability to anticipate danger. He would very soon find out.

Kamal was ready. Henry was still puzzled at the thought. Be one step ahead of the competition had been his motto and he had never failed. Today he was prepared to let someone else make a life-changing, even life-threatening, decision on his behalf but it was the price he had to pay.

Henry relaxed into the thought. Kamal and the new Jihadi group he was helping to build needed Henry Crowne. He certainly could construct a financial empire, unassailable and capable of churning out hundreds of millions. But a new idea was forming in his mind. Kamal had another motive perhaps.

Henry scratched his nascent stubble. He had always hated the idea of growing a beard but needs must. He would have to fit in and look dedicated. He picked up the small book wrapped in a delicate silk scarf. It was only 9pm. Time to read a few verses of the Qur'an before sleep.

* * *

Yvonne's phone rang for a while before someone picked up. The mortuary was not a place where matters were rushed. A young voice asked for a name. Pole replied he was returning Yvonne's call and the next minute the pathologist was on the line.

"I have something to cheer you up. Perhaps."

"How did you know I needed good news?" Pole's voice sounded almost offended.

"'Cos you're having to deal with The Super."

"How did you know? Never mind. What is it that is so cheerful in the middle of explosive devices, cadavers and other forensic paraphernalia?"

"I sent the bullet that was recovered from the taxi carrying Marissa to ballistics and there is a bit of forensic evidence on it."

"The suspense is hardly bearable."

"I have a partial print."

"OK. That could cheer me up. I can hear there is something more."

"Yup. That partial fingerprint is pretty close to the one I found in a previous case."

"Go on."

"The Royal Exchange sniper."

Pole's entire body tensed. Images and sounds jumble in his mind. The noise of a bullet shattering a window and the thud it made when it hit its target, Nancy and Edwina barely sheltering from the shooter, the man dead on the floor.

"Jon, Jonathan, are you still there? Hello ...?"

"Yes, sorry. I'm back. I mean I'm listening." Pole's voice sounded faint. He leant against the desk.

"Flashback," Yvonne's voice was professional but considerate. "Happens a lot."

"Right. Thank you." Pole cleared his voice. "Would someone have been that careless?"

"More often than you think. In particular with bullets. And this is only a partial print, don't forget. I don't have enough to identify the person, but I have enough to establish a connection between the print on the bullet that almost killed Marissa Campbell and the one which exploded Gabriel Steel's head."

"And I presume the same gun."

"Correct."

"And how about ...?"

"Visconti? Lots of prints on the sword and zero matches on IDENT1 so far, but I haven't finished."

Pole remained silent.

"I agree entirely," Yvonne said.

"What now? Can you also mind read?"

"You were thinking so loud I couldn't fail to hear. All this could be connected. I'll focus on the fingerprints."

"Thanks Yvonne, good to know we are on the same wavelength. My intuition —"

"Intuition! I'm a scientist. If I ever even whispered the word intuition I'd be branded a hysterical woman."

Pole managed a laugh. "I promise I won't mention it to The Super."

Pole hung up and looked at the long list of calls he had to return. Nancy had suggested a late dinner. He sat down and started his round of calls. He would be damned though if he missed an evening with the woman in his life.

* * *

"Will we see you at the wedding, old chap?"

Brett lifted an eye from his newspaper. He replied without asking the other gentleman to join him.

"Almost certainly, the young Earl of Coventry is finally tying the knot. I wouldn't miss it for the world." Brett barely smiled. He had no time to waste on such pleasantries. A few more words were exchanged, and the intruder retreated.

Brett resumed reading his paper, barely managed a few lines and checked his watch again. MI6-Steve was late, very late. Brett tried to pay more attention to *The Telegraph* article speculating about the death of Massimo Visconti: mafia – Sicilian or Russian? It was all about art smuggling – perhaps Italian old masters or even antiquities from further afield.

The paper had taken Visconti's death as an excuse to lament the theft of art in war-torn countries. "Better that than letting it be blown to pieces," Brett murmured with contempt. He dropped the paper and ordered a second whisky. He was meeting The Sheik again the next day, another request at short notice for a conversation in which he would be asked to deliver an impossible deal. Armaments of some horrendous nature. Antonio, his reliable Italian smuggler, wouldn't like it. Then again, if the price was right …

MI6 had promised back-up and he needed it, preferably now.

Steve was over an hour late. Even by his casual standards when it came to timetables, this was alarmingly late. Had something happened to him? Brett pushed the idea away but as time passed it kept creeping back into his mind. His handler was not a man he would have chosen to mix with – still, he was his protection, as his link to the agency.

The whisky arrived. Brett inspected the amber liquid through the thick crystal of the tumbler, an elegant Victorian Royal Scot Diamonds piece. He took a mouthful and closed his eyes.

Surely, if something had happened to Steve, he would have been contacted by now – although there were no mobiles allowed in the club.

Surely, they, whoever they were, would have sent a note.

Brett straightened up; this was ridiculous. The whisky was not helping, and he resented it. He would finish his glass and make a plan – back at home he could activate his emergency code.

The sound of a body dropping heavily into a chair startled Brett.

"Did you miss me?" Steve asked with a grin and a wink.

The tumbler shook in Brett's fingers and a few drops landed on his immaculate trousers. Brett brushed them off with the back of his hand and suppressed a curse.

"That much, hey." Steve turned towards the gloved waiter who had appeared noiselessly at his elbow. "The same thanks."

Brett would have liked to summon outrage at the way Steve was being so matey – name your drink, don't thank the waiter for crying out loud –but he was too relieved to indulge in his favourite pastime: correcting MI6-Steve in the ways of the upper classes.

"The reason why you are late had better be a good one."

"It is but …"

Brett pursed his lips. "You can't tell me."

"At least not yet." Steve nodded. "We're picking up a lot of activity outside the UK. Too early to give us a lead."

"So that's it – no intel I can use, nothing." This was not the support Brett had been waiting for.

"Not quite. It is almost certainly about movement between countries."

"Really, I would never have guessed." The sharpness of Brett's voice amused Steve.

"You may want to prep Antonio up."

"Let me handle Antonio as I see fit."

"I reckon it will be armaments this time around," Steve interrupted Brett. His face had turned serious.

"I thought you had no idea."

"Not enough details though."

"Is that supposed to be reassuring?"

"It's not. Don't care whether you're reassured, Brett. I care whether you're still alive at the end of this deal."

"I don't believe one word."

"And to make matters even better, I think you've just been promoted by your Jihadi pal."

"To state the obvious, he is not my Jihadi pal. And what do you mean promoted?"

"You're about to replace Visconti – again unofficial." Steve emptied half of his whisky in one gulp.

"Was Visconti one of your – assets?" Brett's eyes had locked with Steve's.

"Nope. I don't even know whether anyone tried to recruit him."

"Let me rephrase the question. Is the fact that someone tried to recruit him what got Visconti killed? He was one of the best operators —"

"Hold your horses," Steve interrupted. "When it came to stolen artefacts, paintings and the like, perhaps, but armaments is a different matter altogether."

"And why would I fare better?"

"You got me." Steve raised his glass and drained his whisky.

Brett tapped his fingers on the arm of the leather chair. "Do I facilitate anything?"

"We've had this conversation before, yes. Anything goes."

"But before, it was hypothetical; today …" Brett let the sentence hang. He could not quite believe what he was letting himself in for.

"What matters is that we track the payload."

"But Antonio does not tell me the route he takes. That is the deal. I only see the merchandise when it arrives."

"And that is what we want."

"So, you don't care that some ridiculously dangerous item – nuclear, chemical, whatever – transits through Europe."

"I didn't say that but if it's the price to pay for dismantling this terror cell …"

Brett had bent forward towards Steve as the conversation progressed. He now sat back in his seat. "Anything else?"

"Try to find out more about Crowne."

"You're not serious?"

"Extremely."

"And what am I supposed to find out? Whether they are going to get him out of jail?" Brett sniggered. His fair complexion had turned a shade of pink, making the roots of his hair almost look white.

"That would be ideal." Steve replied. He was not jesting.

Brett put the glass to his lips, realised it was empty. Another one? What the hell, it might be his last. He looked in the direction of one of the waiters.

Brett remained silent for a moment. Was MI6 genuinely expecting Crowne to escape? The answer seemed straightforward after all. Yes, they were.

"You want to recruit him, don't you?" Brett asked suddenly.

"You don't expect me to answer that question?"

"The idea of sending the peasant to the hell that is the Middle-East war zone has some appeal."

"Whether it has some appeal or not, it's off limits."

Brett sat back again. He had scored an unexpected point against MI6-Steve and he savoured it.

"If you know what is good for you, Brett, just let it rest." Steve's biting voice slapped Brett out of his mood.

"Fine, I'll see what information I can gather tomorrow."

* * *

The warm smell of food made Pole's mouth water. The small restaurant's top-floor room was packed, yet Nancy had secured a corner table that commanded the entire space and felt cosy. She was reading a book, her head slightly tilted forward, a pair of Chanel glasses shielding her eyes. Pole reached the table in a few long steps. Nancy lifted her face with a broad smile, small lines creasing the corners of her almond eyes.

She removed her glasses and lifted her face to Pole. He bent forward and kissed her cheek. Nancy closed her eyes. The brush of his lips on her skin felt delicious.

"Sorry I'm late." Pole sat down on the banquette next to Nancy.

"Don't apologise, Jonathan. The book I am reading is keeping me excellent company."

"Which book am I competing with?"

Nancy laughed. "Nothing can compete with you, *mon cher*, but, if you must know, Murakami."

"*Kafka on the Shore*," Pole added smartly. "Even a copper like me has read the man who is tipped to be the next Nobel Prize winner."

"*Mais je n'en doutais pas moins.*" Nancy pressed her fingers into his hand. "Let's order, I'm famished and so must you be."

The menu looked appetising and they chose a mix of peppery lamb, seabass cooked in lemon and herbs, okra fritters and roast aubergines. The waiter brought a tasty plate of beetroot hummus with freshly baked lagana bread for starters. Nancy and Pole enjoyed the first dish, sharing their impressions of the food they were eating. It was good to take pleasure in having dinner together.

The conversation drifted onto the latest art show they had visited together. Pole had been enthusiastic about the artist he had not known before, Bernard McGuigan. He spoke about his grandmother, her art galleries in London and Paris, opened in the fifties. "She would have loved his sculptures," he said animatedly.

"She must have met some of the biggest names in modern art. And so must you."

"She did, although she had a preference for the quieter, more obscure artists. Or artists that once were famous but have somewhat faded from memory; although she was a great fan of Kupka or Dubuffet."

"You own a Kupka, *n'est-ce pas?*"

"*Absolument*, although I have a few more on loan to museums."

"She had a very avant-garde taste, right until she sold the galleries, you mentioned before."

"She was fond of videos and installations way before they became popular; Joan Jonas in particular was a favourite. And we are talking early seventies."

"I am impressed. I can't quite get to grips with some video installations, I must say, but Jonas, she is a giant of that medium."

Pole spoke about the artists he had met. Nancy was listening but at the same time her mind was wandering towards another time. Pole gently took her hand. "What is on your mind? I'm talking about art which you always find uplifting but somehow I feel it is dragging you down today."

Nancy sighed. "I'm sorry. It's just bringing back some memories; Paris, artists in the seventies …" She squeezed Pole's hand back and left hers in his, safe.

"Your father?" Pole's voice was cautious, only murmuring the words. Nancy nodded and her face changed. Her radiance had disappeared; it was sad and overcast. The memories of China rolled back like thundering clouds.

"I can't hide anything from you. Well, I'm not trying to anyway."

"I know it's not easy. I'm afraid I've not made much progress since we last spoke about it." Pole had moved closer, his shoulder almost touching hers. She ran her elegant hand over her hair and tugged a strand that had escaped from the clasp behind her ear.

"I'm not expecting you to find anything significant this early on. It was over thirty years ago, and I haven't heard from him for almost as long."

"Still, it's important to you. I don't want to let you down."

"Jonathan, *mon cher ami*, I can't ever imagine you letting me down." Nancy had tilted her head towards him. "And I also hope you won't do anything you shouldn't to get the information."

"*Moi. Jamais,*" Pole said mockingly offended.

"*Vraiment*, Inspector Pole. I know what you are capable of." Nancy squeezed his hand once more. Pole remained impassive. Being involved with MI6 to solve her father's disappearance fell squarely into that category.

"May I ask a question?" Pole became more serious.

"Of course." Nancy drank a little wine.

"Why now? After so long."

Nancy pulled back slightly and considered her answer.

"Maybe because I feel ready. It would have been impossible – too difficult – when I was working." Nancy's eyes focused in the distance, conjuring images that did not speak of happiness.

"You needed to hold it together when you were a QC, emotionally." Pole ventured.

"That is a good way to put it."

"I can understand," Pole said.

"Time to move on. I can't spend the rest of my life hesitating." Nancy's voice wobbled a little. Pole moved his shoulder even closer and she rested her head on it lightly. They stayed silent for a moment before Pole murmured quietly.

"Shall I take you home?"

"Please."

Chapter Eighteen

The coffee grinder made its crunching noise, its small vibrations rippling through her fingers. Marissa opened the lid and closed her eyes. She inhaled deeply the rich aroma of freshly ground coffee beans. She poured the coarse powder into the cafetière, an old-fashioned two-part affair. The water had boiled and reached the right temperature. She poured it over the coffee in small doses, making sure it was wetted through.

Marissa touched her face gingerly. The bump on her forehead she had got diving to the floor to avoid being shot, had come down and the bruise near her eye had darkened. At least a black eye on a woman of colour might be less noticeable. Marissa chuckled at the thought. Finally, a small advantage.

She was wearing her usual black suit, white shirt uniform. She was allowing herself a quick cup of coffee before the police car came to pick her up. Crowne would already have arrived. She had left it to Pole and Nancy to speak to Henry about his proposed meeting with Mark Phelps.

Against all odds, Marissa had decided to trust Henry. His rebellious nature chimed with her own, although she was grateful, she had never been dominated by it and plumbed its depth. She dropped a lump of sugar in her mug and drank in small sips. She never stirred her coffee, enjoying its bitterness being gradually replaced by the sweetness of the taste once she reached the bottom of the cup.

Marissa understood only too well the temptation to seek revenge. Black and female in the legal profession, let alone the judiciary, had not been easy. King's College London had been a bedrock of support, helping her assuage her frustrations. With Nancy as a master and mentor during her pupillage, she had learned to gain in confidence. She could not have hoped for a better role model: similar experience, equally ambitious and above all the same determination to preserve their integrity.

It was still early, and she had absent-mindedly moved to the lounge whilst drinking her coffee. The space was dwarfed by the grand piano she had positioned beside one of the bay windows, not too close though to avoid exposing it to the sun.

She lifted the keyboard lid and ran her fingers over the white and black keys. She placed her cup on the floor, leaned over a little. Her hands moved quickly, playing the first bars of Debussy's 'Clair de Lune'. The melody brought back the unhappy memory of her meeting with Mark. Music was her sanctuary. It should never have been violated in that way.

The doorbell rang. At the same time her BlackBerry buzzed with a new text. The police car was waiting for her. She gently closed the keyboard and finished her coffee, enjoying the sweetness of the last gulp. She moved back to the kitchen, looked around: everything was in its place, tidy and organised. The doorbell rang again. She hesitated; a wave of anxiety surprised her.

"I'm outside." Marissa recognised Pole's voice.

Her knees wobbled and she grabbed the door handle for balance. "Is everything all right?"

"Yes. Don't be alarmed. I was just on my way to work and thought I'd give you a lift and use the official car as an escort."

Marissa opened the door, struggling with the bolts.

"Sorry, I didn't mean to worry you." Pole's tall frame loomed in the hallway.

"I'm going to be a bit jumpy for a while." Marissa closed the door behind her, secured all the bolts. She tested the door handle. Pole called the lift but when it arrived, she could not quite remember whether she had switched on the alarm. She cursed between gritted teeth, went back to check whilst Pole held the lift doors open. She hurried through the same ritual. When they reached the ground floor, Marissa slowed down. "Did you want to speak to me about anything in particular?"

Pole smiled. "Direct in your questions, just like Nancy taught you."

"No point in beating around the bush with you, Inspector."

Pole led her to his car and opened the passenger door to let Marissa in. She nodded an appreciative thank you. The escort car's engine was running. It moved alongside Pole's. The officer in the passenger seat lowered the window.

"I've checked traffic around the bridges across the Thames. Battersea is our best option."

Pole had also lowered his window. "OK, you're in the lead. I'll tune into your radio frequency in the car to follow your route."

"Fine by us." The officer closed the window and the car moved forward at a measured pace. Pole checked his rear mirror. No one behind him. He pulled out.

"Going back to *your* question about *my own* question Marissa," Pole said with a smile that did not reach his concentrated eyes. "I wanted to know what you thought about Henry."

"Off the record?"

"Off the record."

"As financial criminals go – and I have seen my fair share of them – I like Henry Crowne. Before you choke, I know this isn't what you were expecting me to say."

Pole shook his head in disbelief. "What is it with you lawyers indulging a criminal like Henry —"

Marissa interrupted. "I said financial criminal. I did not say terrorist. As far as that is concerned …" Marissa stopped. She was about to condemn Henry for his IRA affiliation but before she could continue the police radio interrupted.

"Inspector Pole, change of plan. There's an accident on Wandsworth Bridge, all traffic re-routed to Battersea. We are re-routing to Lambeth Bridge."

"OK, your call," Pole answered. He looked again in the rear mirror. The traffic behind was still light. Nothing out of the ordinary. Marissa had stopped talking, observing him as he drove.

"You were saying," Pole asked. "Terrorism is a no-no."

"Surely, you don't think I'm condoning it?" Marissa feared her voice sounded somewhat forced. Could Pole have read her hesitation? Or was he simply trying to put her at ease during the ride?

"There are quite a few barristers who try, genuinely, to understand why people resort to violence. Any form of violence, including terrorism." Pole indicated, turning right into a maze of smaller roads. The police car was still comfortably close.

"That's true but it's also part of their job. I don't deal with those people."

"Even money laundering?"

"Point taken."

"What about the BAE Systems case? Bribery paid to Saudi Arabian officials." Pole kept an eye on the lead car and one on Marissa. "I too read the papers."

"And I presume you did a bit of digging around before you agreed to work with me."

Pole chuckled. "Once a copper, always a copper. Got to know the background." A small moped had come alongside the lead car. Its basket bore a Deliveroo sign and the driver was checking his watch. Pole's attention switched to the bike , Marissa noticed. It seemed well used. The driver's jacket was bulky, enough to hide a weapon. The traffic light went amber, then green; the driver swerved in front of the lead car and disappeared into the distance.

Marissa fell silent as well. Pole relaxed, the lead car moved on. It picked up speed again. Pole accelerated, ensuring no car moved in between. They were on the approach to a large roundabout. A few cars were already waiting in an adjacent lane. The lead car indicated right, accelerated then veered to the left, almost turning back on itself. Marissa heard an unfamiliar noise that did not bode well.

* * *

Pole hears it again, the noise of tyres exploding on impact.

"Marissa, brace position," Pole shouts.

He looks into the rear view mirror, reversing – a bullet hits his windscreen, the glass cracks but holds. Pole picks up speed. Marissa muffles a scream, head on knees, hands over ears.

The police officers in the other car jump out, taking up position. Pole hears retaliatory shots. A van moves to block Pole's retreat. Pole changes gear, moving forward towards the crowd of police officers advancing towards them under the cover of cars parked along the street.

Another shot hits the car from behind. Men in balaclavas get out of the van. Pole counts at least two. He increases his speed and brakes furiously sending the car sideways, his flank exposed to the shots. The men fire rounds in his direction.

"Stay down," Pole shouts. "The car can stand this."

The glass of his window takes a bullet; another one and it will explode. An officer is running in the direction of Pole's car. Pole manages to manoeuvre his tall body onto the back of the car. He opens the door as the officer arrives. The officer starts firing, giving Pole and Marissa cover to leave Pole's stranded vehicle.

Marissa has opened her door but she has to be coaxed out of her seat. Pole helps her to crawl towards other officers who have just arrived.

Pole crouches behind another vehicle. Marissa has been extracted from the danger zone.

Pole glances in the direction of the shooters from behind the bonnet of the car protecting him. He sees a small rucksack moving rhythmically with the blast of gunshots. Pole hears a cry of pain. He retreats to check none of the officers have been hit.

One of the gunmen is limping between two cars, takes another bullet and rotates with a jerk. Pole loses sight of him.

The rucksack he had spotted keeps moving away from the scene. He waves at the officer closest to him.

"Another shooter, five cars down."

The officer nods, starts inching slowly towards the spot. The rucksack has stopped.

The officer yells. "Drop your weapon." The gunshots start again. The rucksack has moved behind a large tree. The officer has moved into position. The rucksack suddenly moves backwards, in a flurry of gunshots.

The attacker has reached a small alleyway and disappears into it. Pole stands up and starts running after him. The gunman picks up speed. Pole accelerates. He can't see a gun. Pole can only hear the pounding of his feet on the pavement. They reach a main road. The shooter doesn't stop, effortlessly avoiding the cars.

Pole follows but is less nimble. He slows down, almost hit by a car. He does not stop to apologise when the driver angrily sounds his horn. The gunman increases the distance between them. He now turns left, running along the central reservation of the road. Pole swears. He needs to cross the road before he can follow.

Which is the closest tube? Lambeth North.

Pole races across the road again. Cars barely avoid him. The shooter is now on Kennington Road. He jumps over the protective railing and runs between the cars almost in a straight line, fearless.

Pole climbs over the rail further down the road. He pushes himself as hard as he can. A mass of people is coming out of the tube station. The attacker jostles his way through. Pole makes a final effort and bursts down the stairs of Lambeth North.

The crowd is too dense. He slows down and when he reaches the corridors, looks around and tries to spot the man he has been chasing. Pole does not want to create panic or, worse, a hostage situation.

For all he knows the shooter still has a gun and bullets in it. He scans the tide of people: a young woman fiddling with her mobile, two men in baseball caps. Pole vaults over an entrance gate and considers the direction of the tube line. He can hear the rumble of the next train approaching. He reaches the bridge that straddles the two platforms.

People have started to gather towards the edge of one of them. He must make a choice. He climbs down the stairs two by two as the train appears. He thrusts his tall body forward. And he sees it, the small rucksack at the end of the platform. The doors have opened, people pushing through to get out, people jostling to get in.

The warning beep sounds, the doors about to shut. In a final effort Pole reaches for the rucksack with one hand and the hoodie with the other. The rucksack comes loose and slides along thin arms; a plait of thick black hair escapes from the hoodie – a scarf – a woman. Pole freezes. The doors close and the train lumbers away. She never looks back.

Pole gathered himself together. Had he been chasing the wrong person? But surely the owner of the rucksack would have resisted it being pulled away? He unzipped the bag impatiently. It was empty.

"Shit," Pole blurted. "Shit."

He ran back up to the concourse and knocked at the window of one of the ticket booths. The man looked up, taking his time and putting down a newspaper. Pole shoved his ID onto the glass and indicated he needed to come in. The man adjusted his glasses, suddenly jumping to attention and moving quickly to open the door.

"What can I do for you, Officer?"

"Do you have access to CCTV cameras and can you call Waterloo?"

The elderly man looked blank.

"I'm in pursuit of a suspect."

"Right. Right." He grabbed the phone and dialled promptly. "What does he look like?" Pole clenched his fist. The description was ridiculously bland: small build, black trousers, black hoodie and scarf – and a plait of dark hair.

"Where is your CCTV camera access log?"

The phone was ringing.

"Do you still want me to call them?"

"Yes, tell them I am looking at CCTV footage to get a better description."

The old man waved Pole towards the back of the ticket booth. Pole walked into a small room, smelling of food and coffee. A weary young man stood up. Pole showed his warrant card again.

"I'm in pursuit of a suspect, direction Waterloo. The train left three minutes ago."

The controller keyed instructions into a portal he had called up on his monitor. A number of screens appeared, replaying the event. Pole could see himself holding the rucksack, stupidly stunned.

"Go back a couple of minutes." Pole was searching. "There. There," he shouted, pointing at the screen. He looked at the small figure, weaving her way through the crowd towards the far end of the platform.

The other man came into the room. "They're waiting for you on the phone." Pole nodded. "Can you send these images to Waterloo Station and the British Transport Police?"

The young man nodded matter-of-factly.

"Hello, this is Inspector Pole. I am following a suspected attacker in a firearms incident. Your colleague here is sending you a picture of the suspect. "He ..." Pole hesitated. "I'm not sure whether it's a man or a woman, but this person is armed and certainly dangerous."

The woman who had taken his call responded immediately. The trace was in motion. Pole went back to the weary young man.

"Can you roll forward and switch to the train itself?"

"Sorry mate. Can't do." The man shook his head. "You have to ask the LUCC to see the footage of what's happening on a train."

Pole shook his head, exasperated. He should have remembered; only the London Underground Control Centre had access to the camera footage from trains.

"Not my fault mate." The young man had become almost animated.

Pole ran his long hand through his salt-and-pepper hair. There was nothing he could do at his end for the moment. He gave his contact details and walked out of the station towards the site of the shooting. He called Andy. The images gathered at Lambeth North were on their way to him and he would call the LUCC. Pole broke into a jog. Marissa was unhurt when he left. He hoped it would still be the case when he returned.

* * *

Pure luxury. Henry had been allowed a proper coffee from the Caffè Nero close to the Yard. Andy had obliged and he would be eternally grateful. The same arrangement of screens had been set up as the last time he helped Pole, together with a Bloomberg terminal and a printer. No mobile phone yet but it would come. Henry just needed to be patient and start impressing them as he had before.

A very large wad of papers had been left for him to go through. It looked disproportionately big on the small desk where it lay.

Henry smiled, cracked his fingers in a ready-to-tackle-anything gesture and started keying in instructions on his BBG keyboard. He liked the colour coding of its display, specific to traders or research analysts.

He called up the names of several law firms he knew that could put together complex legal structures of the type Marissa had mentioned. Mossack Fonseca was still at the top of the list.

Their website deceptively plain but effective, the four-branch logo that represented them a well-known trademark distinguishing them from the other Panamanian firms. Henry checked whether the website listed the contact names and telephone numbers of people working there.

But no, only one enquiry number, just as it had always been. The reputation built on forty years of servicing the world with legal, yet obscure corporate structures had to be preserved. Henry pondered. His contact would probably still be working there, but if not, he knew how to trace him. Mac would be aware of Henry's fall from grace, but that eventuality had been thought through and worked out a while ago. Henry also suspected Mac would not want to be the subject of an international search warrant.

Henry seized upon the pile of documents and went through them methodically, underlining the details he needed to commit to memory.

For Bank X, the rescue package extended to UK banks by the government had been unpalatable. Treasury representatives sitting on the board meant an unwelcome intrusion of civil servants lacking the understanding of risk taking in the international banking sector.

The offer from the Middle-East on the other hand had been much more appealing. Henry grinned a wicked grin. The name of the Bank and the Middle-Eastern state had been blanked. Who did they think he was? Some newbie who did not know his way around banking?

He had heard the news at the time of the offer and could still remember it clearly. HXBK was the bank which had bought his previous employer GL for almost nothing. The press had been all over it for days.

What the press had not been told about was the arrangement between HXBK and an obscure Panamanian structure that was soon to receive a substantial amount of the money diverted from the cash injection HXBK had received.

Speculation had been high that Saudi Arabia would once more increase its exposure to the financial sector in the Western world. But the

Saudi Sovereign Fund had made their fair share of investments and Henry had discounted them immediately.

The two remaining candidates were the UAE and Qatar. Qatar was the most interesting. It had started to show interest in building up its Sovereign Fund investments and HXBK was an ideal candidate.

The stock was depressed. Henry went to his Bloomberg screen and dropped HXBK's share reference into the BBG search engine. The stock had dropped by seventy per cent at the beginning of the 2008 crisis.

"Shit a brick," Henry blurted. "Time to buy."

And this is what Qatar had done four years ago.

How far would a bank go when its management had been grabbed by the throat or possibly somewhere even more painful?

Henry nodded. "Far – very, very far."

Chapter Nineteen

Brett had hoped The Sheik would want to see him at a reasonable time when he had been told the day before they were having a meeting. But a text he had received on his burner phone had simply said instructions would arrive at 6am. The promised instructions duly arrived at 6am on the dot, giving Brett scarcely two hours to get to the meeting place at Tottenham Hale.

The old navy-blue slacks and the faded jacket would be the first clothes he wore today. Brett checked his MI6 laptop as he ate a quick breakfast. No further news from Steve. Where was his minder when he needed him?

Typical.

Brett made his way to Knightsbridge tube station. It was far too early for the shops to be open, but a few staff were already starting to arrive. At 7am it seemed Belgravia was only just waking up. Brett's burner phone buzzed. What now? The sound raised his hopes – perhaps a cancellation.

Further instructions had come through. Mohammed would be meeting him at the station. The game was on.

Sitting in one of the deserted carriages, Brett tried to occupy his mind. His nervousness had increased in recent days and the last meeting with The Sheik had been, well, frightening. Brett did not like to admit that he had been scared. It was fine to be fearful in the Middle-East, constantly on one's guard. He had taken many trips to countries close to war zones to meet his trafficking contacts. Even in countries like Egypt, the UAE or Qatar he had remained careful.

But Brett objected to being frightened on his very doorstep in London. Granted, Tottenham Hale was not exactly his neighbourhood. Still London was his stomping ground and he wanted to roam around it freely. He checked the cheap watch he had bought the day before.

He might arrive early. No matter, Mohammed would be there early too. Brett liked Mohammed, a cultured, mild-mannered man who had become embroiled in the trafficking business to clear debts he could not repay otherwise.

The Tottenham Hale sign appeared through the window. Brett disembarked and walked towards the tall escalators. On the concourse he looked around him. The once white tiles on the walls looked filthy. Brett moved around the large open space that lay in front of the station.

Trees bare of leaves seemed strangely petrified. The few concrete benches were mostly empty. Mohammed was there, hunched over a cardboard cup bearing the name of the local caf. Brett walked towards him and sat down abruptly, making him jump.

"You're early." Mohammed looked startled.

"So are you," Brett replied. Mohammed took his own burner phone out of his pocket to send a quick text. "They're just around the corner. Waiting."

"Well, it seems everyone's early then." Brett's stomach rumbled quietly. He did not want to think why. *Focus, focus on what's coming. That's all.*

The heavy SUV pulled up alongside the pavement. The door opened and the same ritual started: eyes blindfolded, burner phone confiscated, bundled up in the back of the car between two large bodies.

It took them more than half an hour Brett estimated. A thick-necked man pushed Brett into the corridor. The place was different again. How many people were willing to let The Sheik use their properties?

Brett snapped back to the moment. Focus.

The frisking was rougher than usual. Brett let his body go. He hated being touched but he had learned not to resist. Somehow the feel of a relaxed body that seemed non-responsive to the intrusion discouraged the intruder.

Brett had entered a large room that looked more lived in than the places where he had been taken before. Rugs, thick mattresses covered with colourful throws and large cushions to sit on. The smell of spices and a sweet aroma Brett could not define. He was left alone and stood in the middle of the room waiting – five minutes, ten minutes.

Brett finally moved to the mattress that faced the door and sat down. The door opened and a black figure entered, full niqab, hands gloved, bringing tea in a glass silver pot and two glasses. She did not look at Brett, simply laying the tray on the low table in front of him. She poured the tea and left.

The silence with which she moved was remarkable, almost gliding, her feet barely touching the ground. Her long dress rustled with a faint noise, yet her manner felt familiar.

The smell of sweet tea made Brett's mouth water; steam rose from the glasses in long lazy coils. A couple of minutes passed. It was excruciating and intended as the perfect way of preparing Brett to succumb to the demands that would be made of him.

Brett stretched his hand towards the glass; he was not ready to admit defeat yet. The door opened and Brett hurriedly withdrew his hand. The Sheik entered and sat down without a word.

"You do not drink?" he asked with a faint smile.

"I would have, but you arrived." Brett's face remained smooth.

The Sheik nodded, took his tea and sipped the burning liquid. Brett followed in silence.

"Visconti was a great disappointment." The Sheik refilled his glass. Brett's gut tightened, the horror of the pictures he had seen only too fresh in his mind.

"I have a deal that needs to be delivered quickly."

"Armaments?" Brett's voice sounded wooden.

The Sheik lifted an eyebrow and broke into a broad smile.

"I thought you did not do armaments?"

Brett's mind snapped back into action. "You mentioned Visconti."

"Only that he had disappointed me." The Sheik's eyes scrutinised Brett, his posture, his face.

Brett shrugged. He could feel the sweat gathering at the back of his neck.

"Visconti had given up on art; arms seemed the next thing to try, I assumed." Brett moved towards the teapot and refilled his glass. Was this credible?

"Why would you assume it, and why would that be of interest?"

"He was a competitor; it's always good to know what a man like him would do." The pitch of his voice had risen. He sounded on edge.

"You have not been a disappointment so far."

"I'm not certain I feel reassured." Brett sounded scared; at least he did not need to fake the way he felt.

"What do you know about armaments?"

"Very little." Another honest statement.

"Unfortunate."

The panic rising in Brett's gut made it gurgle again.

"But I am not in need of arms. I will need to move two of my people out of the UK, very soon."

"Two people?"

"Very soon," The Sheik added.

"How soon?" Brett was almost happy, people not armaments and out of the UK – good riddance.

"I will let you know. Be ready."

Brett straightened up. It was time to speak about his favourite topic – money.

"Two million." The Sheik had read his mind.

"That sounds reasonable," Brett managed.

The Sheik stood up. He moved towards the door and repeated before he left, "Be ready."

The door remained open. Brett rose unsteadily to his feet and stood for a moment. Who would be worth that amount? He did not have time to think about the answer. Much to his annoyance he had to use the lavatory.

* * *

"Too severe, too funky, too short." Nancy was standing in her walk-in wardrobe, flicking through the clothes rack. She was meeting Marsh in a under two hours. "This is ridiculous." She chuckled. "Pole can't think I am dolling up for The Super and I'm not. Still a good bit of power dressing can't hurt."

She kept going through her outfits, shifting the clothes hangers rhythmically.

"*Ha, voila.*" Nancy smiled. "*Parfait.*"

Grey pencil skirt, just above the knee with a discreet black and white line woven into the material. She took it off the rail and held it against her. To go with it, she chose a black jacket, with black leather lapel and cuffs, over a simple pearl grey silk top – Vivienne Westwood at her best.

She dressed quickly, the way a busy professional woman learns to. She walked to the bathroom, applied some light make-up, fastened her hair with a simple clasp. The final touch was a pair of Chaumet white gold earrings. She was ready to do battle. Marissa was counting on her.

She heard the ring of her BlackBerry from within her bag and moved swiftly to her bedroom.

"*Bonjour* Jonathan," Nancy's voice had a smile in it until Pole interrupted.

"Where are you?"

"I'm about to leave."

"I'm sending a car, a police car, to pick you up."

Nancy closed her eyes and dropped onto the bed. "What's happened?"

"Another attempt on Marissa's life." Pole's voice was rasping. "I'm on my way back from the scene."

"Is she ...?" Nancy felt her eyes prickle.

"No, sorry. I should have said. She is all right but very shaken though. It was close."

"You think I'm in danger?" Nancy inhaled slowly. She cared less about her safety than that of Marissa.

"You're working on the case. I'm not taking any risks." Pole's voice shook a little.

"Fine, I'll wait for the car and I'll let Marsh know I might be delayed." Nancy's voice changed tone. "Were you in the car too?"

"Well ..." Pole hesitated.

"Bastards – find them."

"I intend to." Not in the mood to tease Nancy for using strong language, Pole continued, "Let me know when you are done with The Super."

"*Dés que j'ai fini.*" French always made Nancy feel closer to Pole, a language that was not the first they had learned as children yet which bound them together.

* * *

Marsh was on the phone when she arrived at Scotland Yard. The ride in the police car had been uneventful. Nancy had rehearsed what she would say to The Super to convince him to accept Henry's demands. She doubted though that he needed much convincing in the first place. She let her head roll back against the headrest. Memories of William Noble's hit-and-run surprised her. Another friend who had almost lost his life in one of the cases she was involved in – a chilling thought.

She pressed the release button of the window and let some fresh air into the car. The sharpness of the cold struck her face and made her shiver. The female police officer in the front passenger seat turned around. "Are you all right, Ma'am?"

"Absolutely. But it's kind of you to ask."

Nancy returned to the question that was preoccupying her. Did Henry have a plan? She was increasingly sure he had. The letter had said it all along no matter what he now pretended.

There was no doubt in her mind that he needed to be able to telephone his contact to deliver the UBO in the Panamanian structure. It was vital to the success of the case and if the range of the mobile could be restricted then ... She sighed. The female police officer looked at her in the rear mirror. Nancy attempted a smile. So be it – if Henry needed a phone, she would help him get it and perhaps be more circumspect. Something she had hoped she would never have to do with Henry.

It was Pole she wanted to see now. If he was concerned for her, she was concerned for him. How close had it been for both him and Marissa?

Marsh's voice had tailed off. He was finishing his call to another member of his reporting line it seemed. Marsh's voice had risen too many times to remain polite and Nancy was sure she had heard the F word being used almost as often as it would be by the gangs of Hackney.

Denise, Marsh's PA, had kept her company until the great man appeared on the threshold of his office. The Super, in full uniform, as was to be expected, greeted Nancy with profuse apologies, but no, it was she who was late she replied. The exchange of playful courtesies irritated Nancy. It was hard to smile. She felt her face freeze when she first tried. She tried harder and the result must have worked. Marsh was almost blushing.

"I hear the latest development could affect you?" Marsh said putting a hand behind her back, almost touching her. The gesture was intended to be considerate without being invasive, protective perhaps.

"I have asked Inspector Pole to make sure you have the required protection."

"How very kind." Nancy thought she would lose it. Pole did not need to be told when people who worked with him needed protection. She quickly sat down, keen to come to an agreement with Marsh about the subject of her visit.

Denise entered with a fresh pot of tea, one of Marsh's quality brews that he prided himself on offering his visitors.

"I'll pour. Thank you Denise." Marsh sat himself in front of Nancy in the chair he had the habit of choosing when they met. Marsh remembered how she took her tea – how very charming. Nancy took the cup, proper china, that he was extending to her. Her patience was in short supply but needs must.

"So you have come to suggest I allow Crowne some additional liberties." Marsh's tone was as sweet as his tea, two sugars – in Nancy's view it spoilt the taste of a perfectly good cup.

"Not exactly." Nancy drank a little tea and extended an elegant hand to put her cup down. Marsh raised a quizzical eyebrow.

"I am here to make sure we measure the impact of his request and perhaps only then acquiesce."

"You're not convinced we should allow him to have a mobile phone?"

"That's correct. I don't have the technical skills to determine how securely we could monitor his phone or limit its range."

"I'm pretty certain that can be done. But, of course, I'll seek confirmation from my technical people in trace and make the suggestion."

Nancy nodded. "The other question is, why does he need a phone?"

"To make contact with someone who can deliver the required details relevant to this Panamanian structure, I presume."

"I agree, but is there any other way it could be done?"

"You mean, for instance, use a local contact to take a statement?"

"For example."

Marsh shook his head. "It wouldn't work because the informer would have to disclose his identity and even with guarantees I doubt they would take the risk."

"How about other social media? Opening an account solely for that purpose?"

"Possible, but then again, for it to work it has to be untraceable. I mean the contact would have to be established using an anonymised PC not on the grid."

"So it's tricky." She drank some more tea, pausing for Marsh to consider the impact of his own analysis of the situation.

"And it is much more difficult to circumvent the security protocols surrounding an account than to simply use a burner phone."

"I'm sure you are right." Nancy managed another gracious smile.

Marsh leaned back in his armchair. His gaze appraised her for a second. "What does he intend to achieve by contacting this person?"

"The answer to the SFO question lies with the UBO, the Ultimate Beneficial Owner, of the complex Panamanian structure and without that —"

"They cannot prove the circularity of the transaction between Bank X and a certain Middle-Eastern state."

"Exactly right." Nancy had finished her tea.

It was already decided, and Marsh must have known it but appeared to indulge by detaining Nancy a little longer. "What else could he do with the phone?"

"Get in touch with his former IRA contacts. But if the range of the phone is limited it will make it difficult. He could try to persuade his contact to get in touch with the former IRA on his behalf. But with the decommissioning going ahead I doubt they would respond. In any case HSU Belmarsh is the most secure prison in the UK."

Marsh's face dropped, struck by the directness of her answer – no frills, no trying to argue Crowne's case, a no-nonsense statement unusual in the realm where he operated.

His nascent smile said it all … he liked it.

Nancy adjusted a lock of hair that had come loose. Marsh found the gesture surprisingly seductive.

"Right, yes, well." He straightened up in his chair. "You're right. HSU Belmarsh's security record is impeccable."

"Precisely."

Marsh allowed himself one more minute of what seemed intense cogitation. "Provided my tech team can limit the range of the phone, I shall authorise it."

The exercise of power motivated by ambition. Nancy sighed, the downfall of most driven men.

* * *

The lift doors had just closed on a so very courteous Marsh. Nancy had given him a slightly rigid goodbye, thanking the great man for his enlightened decision. As soon as the lift started moving, she plunged into her bag, fishing out her BlackBerry. Reception was patchy and she kept trying to dial Pole's number. When she reached the ground floor, the call went through. Pole's line was engaged. She sped towards the next bank of lifts, leaving a message that she was on her way.

A mass of people walked out of the lift she was hoping to board. She gave way then squeezed in before the doors closed. On reaching her destination she dashed out but a tall figure stood in her way.

Pole was waiting for her. She barely resisted the urge to throw her arms around him. Pole grabbed her hand and held it tight.

"I could have slaughtered Marsh," Nancy's voice trembled. "You are fine though."

"All in one piece." Pole's voice was also shaken. "And Marissa is fine too, although she could do with a friend at the moment."

"I'll go to see her in a minute but …" Nancy hesitated. People had just walked out of the lifts. Pole reluctantly let go of her hand. "Let's have two minutes to ourselves."

Pole smiled. They stopped at the coffee machine in silence, walked into Pole's office and, with the door closed, stood alongside each other at the window. It was good to simply be together.

A quote by Saint-Exupéry came to Nancy's mind: "Love is not to stare at one another but to stand side by side."

Chapter Twenty

When Nancy entered the room, Marissa was still in her coat, her right hand clutching her collar up to her chin. Nancy slowed before moving towards her friend, startled by the dread she could see in her eyes. Marissa tried to articulate a few words but her chattering teeth made the sentence incomprehensible.

"I'm so sorry." Nancy moved quickly to her friend, arms outstretched. She hugged Marissa for a moment, her slender arms surprisingly comforting. Marissa nodded and sat down, still wrapped in her coat.

"It was awful," she eventually managed, eyes in the distance.

"Pole has spoken to Commander Ferguson. They've increased the security around Mark Phelps' residence," Nancy said as if reading her mind.

"Good," Marissa managed to articulate. A knock at the door startled them both. It opened gingerly and Andy popped in his head with an apologetic smile.

"Can I bring you anything?"

Both women shook their heads with a thanks. The door closed with a small creak.

"Do you know what I really need?" Marissa said in a recovered voice.

"A bar of Belgian chocolate? A nice French patisserie?" Nancy teased gently.

"No. I need Pole and Ferguson to catch those bastards and make them suffer."

Nancy stretched out her hand and squeezed Marissa's shoulder.

"I'm not quite sure about the suffering bit but Pole will catch them – he won't rest until he does."

Marissa stood up, still uncertain on her feet. She grabbed the edge of the table. "I'm fine," she said responding to Nancy's concerned look. She closed her eyes, inhaled and released the air slowly.

"Let's go and meet Crowne. We have business to do."

* * *

Henry had considerably advanced his review of the new batch of documents that had been left for him. The first instalment of files had given him a broad understanding of the construction of the fund that was receiving cash from HXBK. The second was giving him more details about the transaction itself.

He had started sketching out diagrams of the corporate ownership, reconstructing the multi-layered levels of companies, partnerships and funds that made the structure challengingly opaque.

A draught of fresh air. Henry recognised Nancy's scent and lifted a smiling face. His smile dropped almost instantly. Nancy looked grave and Marissa at her side, awful.

Henry's stomach tightened. He did not want to ask the dreaded question. "Have the Jihadists managed to —"

"Everyone is fine," Marissa simply said.

Henry stood up, hesitating. He arranged chairs around the table so they could all sit down. Nancy picked up the diagrams he had left on the table.

"These are looking encouraging." She nodded appreciatively.

Marissa picked up the pages. "Let's go through them together." Henry gathered it was all about being business-like.

"Good idea." Henry clapped his hands and moved documents around, fishing out a piece of paper stuck at the bottom of the pile.

"First of all, Bank X is one of the banks that did not join the UK government rescue programme. It found other means to survive its capital crisis and to buy another competitor that was defaulting, namely GL, my previous employer.

Marissa lifted an eyebrow. "You know who Bank X is?"

"I know which banks needed rescuing back in 2008. I know, or rather know what was, their management style. I can narrow down the number of banks that would have looked elsewhere to two – Barclays and HXBK."

Marissa gave a small laugh. Her eyes searched Henry's face in open amazement. Henry had received the files barely twenty-four hours ago. He had been locked up for the past four years in Belmarsh. "Did you already know about this?"

"Nope ... but I still read the news and I spent twenty years in that business."

"You think Bank X is ...?"

"HXBK of course. Their management team would never have stomached what RBS and Lloyds had to accept in order to receive the rescue package. The thought of having to agree to change the board composition to include government officials – never."

Both women remained silent, but Nancy gave a small, content nod. "HXBK had to raise cash, first to survive and then to hoover up competitors that went under, as I said previously. They raised cash from their existing shareholders – about nineteen per cent. I checked this morning on Bloomberg. The rest was raised by selling shares to a number of financial institutions and sovereign wealth funds."

"You were still at GL when it happened?" Nancy asked.

"Just about." Henry shrugged. He had not known at the time his downfall was imminent. A pang of regret came and went. "I do recall the terms of the UK government's rescue package."

"You think the terms were not generous enough?" Marissa asked

"It's not that, but HXBK wanted to buy the competition on its own terms, not to be dictated to by the government who to buy or not buy. They needed that deal."

"Though the price for GL was not astronomical. All is relative, but in investment banking terms I remember the price was around £700 million?"

"Wow, Nancy, spot on." Henry clicked his fingers. "On the ball as ever." Marissa smiled. "Nancy is always on the ball."

"I'm flattered," Nancy returned the smile, "but I still don't see what difference it made. That is not such a large sum after all."

"Correct but remember HXBK acquired GL because of the large losses GL had suffered buying subprime assets." Henry waited expectantly.

"It needed to raise further capital to absorb the GL losses and satisfy the regulator." Marissa was nodding her head.

"Absolutely and remember, it did raise an additional £7 billion from its Middle-Eastern friends – namely the UAE and Qatar."

"That is your working assumption – UAE and Qatar as UBO?" Nancy asked.

"Yup. I think we are going to find someone in one of those countries at the top of the complex corporate structure we are trying to unravel."

"Have you made any headway with that?" Marissa's expression had livened up. Talking about the case she so wanted to bring to court energised her.

"I have." Henry closed the file that was open in front of him. He placed it on the floor, next to several other files he'd organised in his own way. He picked up another folder.

"The loan by HXBK is not in itself a problem," Marissa's voice was trailing.

"But it's who the ultimate recipient of that money is – I get it," Henry replied. He picked up a few pieces of paper, checked the data briefly and presented them to the two women.

"The company that received the loan was incorporated in Panama. Nothing wrong with that as such but the disclosure rules when it comes to ownership are far less stringent than in the UK."

"That's right." Marissa moved towards the table.

"The company's shareholding is split between other companies and foundations by using nominee companies." Henry was pointing towards numerous boxes he had drawn on his diagram. "The foundation that holds shares in the nominee companies is formed in Lichtenstein."

"And we are not going to know who the actual person is who holds the shares in the foundation because Lichtenstein does not disclose either," Nancy added.

"Correct." Henry nodded. "If we find that person, I'm certain it will be yet another company."

"How could HXBK have run this through their compliance department successfully?" Marissa asked.

"I think the Ultimate Beneficial Owner must have been disclosed but only to a very small number of senior people. The identity of that person is sensitive. Hence the limited disclosure, justified by the need to protect that individual," Henry replied.

"That is precisely what Mark said." Marissa ran her hand over her face. "When he asked the question about the UBO, he was told to mind his own business. Senior management had given their approval."

Henry leaned back and crossed his hands behind his head, thinking.

"I wonder." He changed his mind and moved back towards the table. "I wonder whether Marsh will let me have a mobile phone?"

"He'd better." Marissa looked up. "Otherwise I'll get the SFO director on his back and Marsh won't know what's hit him."

Henry's reserved manners had registered with Nancy and she kept her eyes firmly on him. He met her gaze reluctantly. She wanted an honest conversation. Something Henry was not prepared to have – at least not yet.

* * *

"From Lambeth North to Waterloo then he disembarks and leaves the underground system." Andy and Pole were following the slim silhouette in a dark hoodie which exited the tube carriage, walked up the stairs in no great hurry and left Waterloo Station, merging into the mass of passengers. Pole had kept his suspicions about the gender of the attacker to himself.

"And then …" Andy switched to another CCTV camera installed on Waterloo Bridge roundabout. "He reappears along the embankment towards the National Theatre." Andy switched to a CCTV camera near the IBM building. "I think I can pick him up again going towards Bernie Spain Gardens. Same hoodie but slightly different colour I think: he could have changed if the hoodie's reversible. Then I completely lose him in the Gardens."

"How many cameras around the Gardens?" Pole was hunched over the back of Andy's chair.

"Not many, two." Andy pushed his chair back and Pole moved out of his way. He grabbed a chair, sat down and rolled it towards Andy's desk.

"What did you see after he entered the Gardens. I mean around the area?" Pole had taken out his BlackBerry, spinning it around his hand.

"Well." Andy pushed his glasses back up the bridge of his nose and speeded up the images: an old man with his dog appeared, a couple of youngsters fooling around, a woman with a pushchair.

"On the other camera – a couple talking, finishing a shared cigarette —"

"And having a snog." Pole added with a smile. Andy's cheeks had become a little pinker. He kept moving the images forward; more pictures danced their crazy bop. Pole had almost given up.

"Then twenty minutes later a group of women, in niqab, leave together."

Pole straightens up. "Did you see them arrive?"

Andy scrolled back to the time he had lost the gunman, then back a couple of hours before. "No, I can't see them come in. At least not up to a couple of hours before the incident and not from the cameras we have."

Pole scratched the back of his head. "Are there other entrances to the Gardens not covered by CCTV?"

Andy moves to another screen, a map of the area. "Yes, Guv – the lane from OXO Tower."

Pole nodded. "And where is the group of women going to?"

Andy moves the images forward. "Towards Blackfriars – shall I ...?"

Pole's phone buzzed. "Yvonne, what have you got for me?" He pulled his notebook from his jacket pocket and scribbled a few words, at an uncomfortable angle.

"Great news, thanks. I'm with Andy; can I call you back in a couple of minutes?" He ended the call and turned back to Andy.

"This is what I would like you to do please – track the women back, find out where they came from and how many of them there were when they arrived in the Gardens. How many of them left?"

Andy was already working the cameras.

Pole disappeared into his office, already on the phone to Yvonne again.

"Well done Jonathan Pole." Yvonne sounded genuinely impressed. "How did you know?"

"I didn't think Jihadists wore long hair, even plaited."

"You mean you nearly got her?"

"Nearly is unfortunately the word."

"You must tell me more next time we meet." Yvonne voice was ringing with excitement. "And you're right, there is a difference in fingerprints between male and female, ridge density is indicative of gender difference. It's not one hundred per cent but pretty close and is irrespective of origin or race."

"So, the partial prints you found on the bullets at the Bank of England and in the cab that was driving Marissa are both female?"

"Spot on. It didn't cross my mind to check to be honest, since they were only partials, but hey."

Pole sat down at his desk, still processing the news. Despite what he had seen at Lambeth North Tube, he was amazed.

"The shooter is a woman."

"Don't be so shocked. Women can be pretty lethal too. I open up cadavers all day."

"But at least they are dead, right."

Yvonne laughed. "Think about the Peshmerga too."

"You mean the Kurdish fighters?"

"Yes, they are some of the most feared fighters in the region and they are all women. They fought alongside the US marines in Iraq in 2003."

"How do you know that?"

"A story for another time."

"Aren't the Jihadists different? I didn't think Al-Qaeda used women, not as fighters."

Yvonne pondered. "That's a point. Perhaps they are changing their tactics?"

"Anyway, thanks for that. It gives me something to go on."

Pole ended the call. He was about to go back to Andy with a new set of instructions when he stopped. He stood at the door of his office and reached into his inner jacket pocket for Agent Harris' burner phone. He took it out and looked at it, considering.

Ferguson at CT Command would need to know. Harris could not ask him to hold back that information. But Harris had been clear – anything new about the terror cell was to come to him first. Pole swore and closed his door.

He moved to the window and placed a call to the only number entered in the phone's speed dial. The reply was almost instantaneous.

"Pole here. You told me you were working on an Al-Qaeda cell presence in London?"

Harris simply confirmed.

"How likely are they, would you say, to use a woman sniper?"

The silence at the end of the line pleased Pole.

"What do you mean? A woman?"

"Chromosomes XX. I'm sure you have heard of them."

Pole did not wait for a reply. He gave Harris the details of his discovery. The chase down to Lambeth North, the tracking to Waterloo Station, the long plait of dark hair, the fingerprints. As he spoke Pole could sense a deepening feeling of unease in Harris' silent attention.

"Keep me posted, even the smallest details, but particularly if you manage to track her location."

"What do you think it means?" Pole asked, doubting he would get an answer.

"Give me a few hours – if there's anything important, I'll let you know."

Harris hung up. Pole sat down on the only free chair in his office. He was starting to see where this case was heading, and it took the wind out of him. He thought of Nancy with a chill. He could not discuss this latest development with her, a great pity. How was he going to keep her safe without telling her everything?

Andy knocked at the door, gesturing urgently.

Pole waved him in.

"Guv, I know where the women went."

Pole would not give Harris a few hours after all.

* * *

"Another burner phone," Henry teased.

"What do you mean another?" Nancy was still holding the much-coveted device.

"I seem to recall you lending me something very similar a few months ago."

"Certainly not – not the same make or model, and hardly any roaming facility."

Henry laughed. It was a happy moment. In this dingy meeting room, situated underground, with prison officers waiting for him outside, all that mattered was that he was allowed time alone with Nancy.

"They've limited the range to Panama?"

"That was the deal. I tried to call the UK – engaged tone."

"No worries. All I need is Panama." He was still in a good mood. He did not want to think ahead. Just live in the moment: a good cup of coffee, a close friend, possibly even his best friend, and doing what he excelled at.

"I presume you will want to be on your own when you call your contact?" Nancy's voice was kind.

"Afraid so, yes. I need to make my contact feel comfortable and I don't expect he will want to speak to me immediately."

"You have an agreed process for this type of …" Nancy was looking for the right words, "emergency contact."

"That's the sum of it." Henry nodded. He had always appreciated Nancy's way of asking questions. Soon he would no longer have the benefit of her wisdom. He felt a cold trickle of ice run along his spine and shivered.

"It's almost 12pm in London and 7am in Panama. A little too early but not by much though. Another half hour and I'll make the call."

"What makes you think he will talk?"

"Because he will not want me to give his name and details to the UK police. He wants to stay anon – the John Doe of the Panamanian Legal System."

"So, what's next?" Nancy wanted to be clear about Henry's strategy.

"I get enough information to enable me to go back through the chain of ownership until I find the UBO." Henry was rocking slowly on the back legs of his chair, a rhythmic motion that seemed to help him think. "I guess it will be a convoluted business that will eventually lead me to the Middle-East."

"Is that the reason why they have pursued Mark and Marissa?" Nancy sat on the chair next to Henry, her legs crossed at the knee. It was an inexplicably seductive pose and Henry could not help but smile. Pole was a lucky bugger.

"No one knows what that money is used for and I guess someone wants it to stay that way."

"Strangely, I don't feel threatened." Nancy pouted; it sounded odd, she should.

"Pole will be looking after you." A shadow crossed Henry's face that he hoped Nancy had not noticed. Pole would certainly do his bit, but Henry had given an unequivocal message to Kamal. *Whether Marissa or Nancy are kafir or in your way, do not touch them – otherwise the deal is off.* Henry meant every word. If anything was to happen to Marrissa, let alone Nancy he would never work for Kamal's organisation even though it would cost him his way to freedom.

"Do you think the case will go through?" Henry changed the conversation away from the danger zone that emotions always were for him.

"You're thinking about the BAE Systems debacle?"

"Yup, not the SFO's finest hour, despite the large fine."

"Marissa is doggedly determined. She will see this through – even more so now."

Henry looked up at the clock on the wall. He smiled an apologetic smile at Nancy.

Time to make the call. It was all down to him now.

Chapter Twenty-One

"The Sheik wants you to extract people?" MI6-Steve could not disguise his surprise.

Brett had settled in the cab that had just picked him up outside Green Park tube station. A new initiative from Steve to avoid meeting yet again at the club.

"That's what my email said, I believe." Brett remained stony faced.

"Names?" Steve ignored Brett's patronising tone. His ability to ignore Brett's comments made Brett furious. Steve was well in control of Brett's life.

"What do you expect? It's far too early." Brett took a sip from a bottle he had bought before boarding the cab – though water was not what he needed to soothe his battered ego.

"Did he give a number?" Steve unwrapped a piece of gum and popped it into his mouth.

Steve's jaws masticated the gum nervously. Brett cringed.

"Yes. I did also mention that in my email. Why do you insist on making me repeat myself?"

"Al-Qaeda does not extract people."

Brett frowned. For the first time since he had started working for Steve, MI6 was giving him important information. He did not have to grovel, beg or get annoyed as he usually did.

Unexpected and worrying.

"What are you saying?"

"I'm not sure yet – we're picking up some activity on social media; recruitment attempts on a large scale that have a different slant to the usual guff."

"How different?"

"More radical, more organised."

"Than Al-Qaeda?" Brett pursed his lips, incredulous. "Is that possible?"

"Why not? Splinter groups happen all the time. The question is whether they can turn into something new that will be successful."

"They feel organised and established in North London. The Sheik never meets in the same place, but I always have the same driver and contact meeting me."

"Exactly my point?"

Brett nodded. "True, they could be limiting the number of people I meet for security reasons, so as not to expose the network."

"Possible or else it means they're a small unit that's growing but doesn't yet want to go public."

"The chap who got a bullet in his head a few months ago at the Royal Exchange might disagree with you if he could," Brett replied with feeling.

"He was another Visconti. That's all."

"What do you mean by public?" Brett asked.

"Exactly that – challenge the old Al-Qaeda group that's perceived as weak, particularly since Osama Bin Laden's death."

"If that's the case, The Sheik feels pretty secure and in control."

"Do you think he's a Brit who has returned after fighting the Jihad?"

"You're the expert." Brett took a mouthful of water and looked at the cab driver. It felt uncomfortable to talk in the back of a taxi. "I'd say almost certainly. His manners, his spoken English – he's well educated I'm afraid."

Both men remained silent, pondering on what they knew might validate Steve's view.

Brett kept casting an eye at the streets the taxi was taking them through. Steve noticed. "It's safe. Better than another meeting at your club."

Brett locked eyes with Steve. "If Henry Crowne was one of the people who needed 'transportation' would it confirm that a new terrorist group is about to be formed?"

Brett enjoyed the result of his question. Steve's eyes darkened, his lips tightened into a straight line. He stopped his furious chewing.

"Being a smart arse isn't always a good idea in the world we inhabit."

Brett ignored him. "Perhaps, but looking for a financier with experience of organising money laundering for terrorist organisations like the IRA would validate your view. This splinter group as you call it needs and wants to get the money side of things right so it can fight its war."

"Brett, I've told you before. You're rather smart for a toff; however this time, take my advice, don't get involved."

Brett raised an eyebrow. "Thanks for the tip but, unfortunately, I am involved."

Steve grumbled a pain-in-the-arse answer and gave Brett a new set of instructions. The world of art trafficking was morphing into the trafficking of things Brett did not care about, people.

* * *

The big hand of the wall clock was moving towards the top of the hour. In one minute, it would pass that important point and Henry would make the call. The room was empty. Nancy had left. Pole was nowhere to be seen which told Henry something was up.

The clock struck 1pm. Henry stopped playing with his pen, running it over the back of his thumb and catching it as it came around, a clever little move very few managed. A smart arse, always a smart arse, Henry sighed.

He tested the phone he had been given by placing a call to Mossack Fonseca, the law firm in Panama. The notepad he had arranged in front of him was more for show than note taking. It had reassured Nancy who now walked everywhere with her yellow legal pad. He smiled at the thought.

Henry dialled the number he had memorised so many years ago. Many phone numbers had changed but he was certain that this one, his emergency number, would still connect. The phone rang and the answer phone at the other end spewed its message.

"This is Henry; call me back."

He resumed playing with his pen, round and round it went. The saying "a watched kettle never boils" amused Henry. This particular burner phone was about to become too hot to handle.

It took his contact less than fifteen minutes to ring back, a record, Henry reckoned. He let the phone ring once, twice. Holding his nerve.

"Crowne." The person at the other end of the phone stayed silent. Henry's voice had sounded steady. He needed to close the deal. "Mac, this is Henry Crowne. Are you OK to talk? My phone can't be traced."

"OK."

"I need a name."

"Who for?"

"That is not relevant; you know that."

A small intake of breath at the other end of the phone and Henry carried on.

"You knew this call would come one day, right?"

"The IRA has decommissioned."

"But you are still in Panama to handle the winding down of some of its funds and because you have branched out – right again?"

"As cocky as ever, Henry."

"Yup."

"What's for me in the deal?"

"I keep your name out of it."

"For how long though?"

"If I haven't grassed you so far, why would I do it now? I'm serving my sentence, as I'm sure you know."

"I've heard."

"And if I had wanted a reduction, you would have been done by now."

The line stayed silent for a moment.

"You know that it's easy to trace this call."

"To where, Panama? Big deal. You are calling me from a location that has no relationship with your office or house there and Panama is not renowned for its CCTV camera network."

"Glad to hear you thought it through."

"I always do Mac; so what's it gonna be?"

"What do you want?"

"The name of the UBO that sits at the end of a long corporate structure that starts in Panama."

"Any idea who is at the top of the ownership chain? Are you looking for someone in particular?"

"You tell me. I've prepared a document; it's on its way to you."

Henry selected the image he had photographed earlier and attached it to a message. "You have all you need on that."

"Got it. This is your new emergency number." Mac repeated a string of digits twice.

"I'll call you tomorrow."

"Not enough time."

"Tomorrow Mac, end of your day. You know the ropes better than anybody else."

"Can't promise." Mac hung up. Henry slumped back in his chair, his entire body jolted, and he closed his eyes. Small beads of perspiration gathered on his upper lip. Had it worked?

He had a long twenty-four-hour wait to find out.

"I'm certain." Pole's voice had hardened as Agent Harris repeated his question. He worked for the Met, but he was not a goddamn idiot. "I don't do counterterrorism – it's Ferguson's pad – but my team can definitely trace a suspect."

"How far have you gone?" Harris had shifted his phone. Pole could hear him typing on his keyboard.

"You mean do we have an address? Not yet, but we're rather close."

"Have you spoken to Ferguson?"

"No, we agreed – you first."

"Thank you." Pole was surprised but did not let it show. Was it a way of gaining his trust?

"I can't hold back forever though. How long do you need?"

"'til the end of today."

"That might work. I'll ask my man on the case to dig around more before we release the information." Pole grunted.

"Let me know when you do."

"You have an asset on the ground?"

Pole heard the smile in Harris' voice. "No comment in the interests of national security."

"Before you go …" Time for Agent Harris to deliver. "How about your enquiry in China?"

"Ah, Mr Wu's possible demise? I have something for you, Inspector Pole; not much but the beginning of a trail."

"Good," Pole replied. "It would be even better if I could take a look at this trail's beginning before the end of the day."

Harris laughed. "I'll have an envelope dropped to your office – before you call Ferguson."

"Much appreciated."

"I like a hard bargain, Inspector."

"Glad to hear it."

"And Inspector Pole, call me Steve."

"Things are going to move fast." Pole had perched on Henry's desk. His tall body leaned forward, hands on knees.

"You've spoken to Harris?" Henry almost felt comfortable with Pole.

"I have but that's not where I got this from."

Henry considered Pole for a moment. He was playing with his burner phone.

"Why do you do it?"

Pole crossed his arms over his chest – a no-go area.

"OK. OK," Henry said raising his hands. "You're just keen for me to get the bullet I deserve."

Pole rolled his eyes. "You don't really believe that crap."

"I just don't like it." Henry pouted like a sulking child.

"I don't like it much either but I'm your MI6 go-between and that's that."

Henry stood up, taking a few steps in the boxy room he had learned to like. He leaned against the wall.

"Why the warning?"

"You are a pain in the butt, Henry. Let's say you are about to find yourself a little over your head if you're not careful."

"You're kidding. The IRA wasn't exactly a friendly bunch."

"Granted but you were a key operative and your roots were in Belfast. Here you're just a tool."

"So what's the plan?"

"Harris has not graced me with the details. You're his asset and if I were him, I know where I would want you."

"Which is?"

"Out." Pole locked eyes with Henry. For the first time since they had met, Henry felt concerned. He hesitated. "You mean?"

"Out, escaped, gone and I presume at his service to infiltrate whatever he thinks he needs to infiltrate."

Henry's face froze and grew a little paler.

"Don't worry. I have been told in the interests of national security etc, etc."

"And you are fine with that?"

"As long as it doesn't end up being a bloodbath, I guess I am."

Henry moved back to his chair, uneasy. Pole changed the subject.

"When are you expecting a reply from Panama?"

"Tomorrow, his evening, so late here – 10pm."

"I need to let Marsh know. We'll send a special dispensation request off to the Home Office and Belmarsh."

"Understood." Henry thought for a while and Pole let him be. The atmosphere was almost relaxed.

"You think I should accept," Henry's voice trailed. He was asking Pole for advice.

"What can I say Henry? But knowing you, you need a purpose."

Henry shook his head in disbelief. He had been waiting for this moment for years. It was perhaps just around the corner. He thought of Nancy. He pushed the swelling pain away; not now, not in front of Pole.

"Have you finished your day?" Pole asked, standing up to leave.

"Not yet, I just want to go through a few things on the Internet; read through the docs Marissa left me again."

"I'll speak to Marsh now. Any problem, I'll let you know."

"How?"

"You've got a mobile, haven't you?"

"But I thought with a range limited to Panama."

Pole tapped his nose with his index finger — who was the clever boy after all?

* * *

Marissa sat back in her office chair. It was not the request she had expected from Mark Phelps. Her hand hovered over her phone. She withdrew it in a slow gesture that gave her time to think.

Why did Mark really want to meet Henry?

To confront the monsters that had taken his wife? The idea felt strangely out of character. She certainly needed Mark to testify when the case came to court. As a protected witness she might be able to spare him an appearance in court.

She returned to Mark's request. She could not imagine him coming to blows with Henry. And how would Henry react? She needed them both on the case. Could she perhaps delay the request until it was too late, until Henry was no longer allowed to leave HSU Belmarsh?

She could then organise a meeting in the confines of the prison environment. But Mark was an intelligent man; he would see through this. She could not lose his trust. They were so close: this case would not go the way the BAE Systems case went.

She picked up the phone swiftly and dialled Nancy's number.

Nancy replied after a few rings, a little breathless.

"Marissa — is everything all right?"

"Yes, sorry, I should have told you myself."

"I mean over and above you being targeted, dealing with the case and —"

Marissa interrupted. "You need to convince Henry to meet with Mark."

The phone remained silent.

"I'm sure you are reading my thoughts," she said at last.

"I know how it may sound."

"Now that you're close to getting some answers, what would you say if Mark asked you to stop? If he wanted to pull out. You did say earlier you wouldn't want to push him – but what about now?"

Marissa took a deep breath, ran her tired hand over her eyes. Then she smiled; she had just been subjected to what had made Nancy such a formidable QC – the ability to ask the tough questions.

"You're right. I would find it almost impossible now," Marissa said. "You know why, don't you?"

"Because you do not want to have another disappointment."

"I can't hide anything from you." Marissa smiled faintly.

"You can't because you don't want to; you want to get to the truth. You don't want Henry to stop cooperating either." Nancy paused. "What is the chance of Mark pulling out if he doesn't meet Henry?"

"Very high."

"For what it's worth, I think Mark needs to make sense of what happened."

"A question for you, Nancy – how will Henry react?"

Nancy inhaled deeply. "I would lie if I said I was certain." She paused again. "Speak to Pole. He will have a view on the question." To her amazement she felt Pole was better qualified to answer than she was.

Chapter Twenty-Two

The brown envelope was sitting on his desk. Pole hesitated. He had been closing the door of his office quite a lot recently, rather uncharacteristic of him.

He looked around for the letter opener, an instrument he used to use regularly, now made redundant by email. Where was the damn thing when you needed it?

Pole considered the state of his office. He would never find the implement quickly. A pair of scissors would have to do. He looked around, twisting his tall body this way and that.

In the end he simply lifted the flap of the envelope which came unstuck without much damage. Pole peered inside – photocopied documents, official-looking papers and some photos too.

He carefully turned the envelope upside down until its contents lay on the desk. He took one of the photos out and gazed at it.

An elegant young man in his early thirties was looking back at him, slim and of medium build. Pole concentrated on the face: delicate cheekbones, high forehead, intelligent almond eyes and the smile – perhaps not a smile, more an expression of the lips, that was both uncertain and humorous.

Pole was shocked by the likeness; there was no doubt in his mind that the young man in the photo was Nancy's father, Li Jie Wu. Pole turned the picture over. A date had been stamped on it, April 1980.

A bunch of papers had been bound together with a clip. They were old travel documents. China was just coming out of the terrifying period that the Cultural Revolution had been. Chairman Mao was dead, and his wife and the Gang of Four had been arrested. Travelling to and through China still had to be authorised though.

Pole wondered how Agent Harris had managed to find these but why should he care? The address on one of the documents was in Chinese with a translation: Shanghai to start with, then Beijing, then Chengdu, the main city of the Sichuan province. Chengdu, the place where Li Jie Wu was born and raised; his place of ancestry too.

A timid knock at the door startled Pole. Andy was hovering in the doorway with a look on his face that Pole knew well. He had found something that might have escaped a less discerning mind.

"I did a lot more digging, Guv, and I managed to follow the women after they left the tube station."

"After they left Seven Sisters?" Pole cautiously replaced the documents he was reading in their envelope and sat down, waving for Andy to do the same.

"That's right, Sir. They were all chatting happily, but I had a feeling they were protective of one woman amongst them."

Pole had called up a Google map of the area on his computer screen. Andy dragged his chair towards Pole's desk to help him track their movements. He picked up a pen and moved it across the map.

"They crossed the street, went into Page Green Common, walked through and crossed the road on the other side, but when I looked more carefully, I could see that one of them was missing."

"Well done. Does she reappear later?" Pole's voice had a new ring to it, the edge it took when the chase was on.

"No, but a car, a black SUV, arrives on the Green ten minutes afterwards."

Pole nodded expectantly.

"It parks underneath the trees then it leaves very quickly, driving back towards Finsbury Park. Got the reg number and ran it through ANPR. The number plate does not exist."

Pole smiled. "But you managed to track it because …?"

Andy chewed his lip. "Traced it by creating a new number reg that can be tracked by the system. Then the system recognises it because —"

He stopped abruptly, judging that the minutiae of his handiwork might not interest Pole. "To cut a longer story short, Guv. It went to a garage, rent a car place in Finsbury."

"That's a brilliant job."

"And." Andy grinned. "I managed to pick up a similar-looking woman walking towards Wilberforce Road. She then entered a small hotel. After that nothing … can't trace a woman in full niqab."

"But a few women came out just wearing a simple scarf."

"Correct. I'm following through."

"We're closing the net." Pole's voice had an edge again.

"Are you speaking to Commander Ferguson?"

"Why do you ask?" Pole felt put on the spot. Did Andy suspect he was holding something back?

"If you give me a couple more hours, I might be able to track down where she actually went."

Ambition is sometimes a good thing. Pole nodded. "Granted, then we can discuss what you find."

Andy walked out a little bit taller, his plump body shaking with trepidation – puppy turned bloodhound. Pole liked it.

He sat back in his chair, an eye on the MI6 envelope. He could indulge himself for a few more minutes. Pole let more documents slide out into his hand: reports of political and artistic activity it seemed. Names of art pieces that the authorities had classified as subversive, mainly paintings, but also some sculptures that embraced Western modern art trends.

Despite the poor quality of the images and the paucity of the vocabulary describing the pieces, it was evident that the art was executed with confidence and spoke, at least Pole felt, about social anguish, individuality and reform.

The documents were dated up to 1989, the year of the fateful Tiananmen Square protest that saw the tanks of the Red Army kill ten thousand people.

Pole replaced the contents in the package. The search for Nancy's father went cold after that date it seemed.

* * *

Nancy had unpacked the small sculpture and it lay surrounded by protective bubble wrap on her settee. She ran her fingers over the stone and smiled. It felt both smooth and coarse at the same time. The profile of the young woman had the angularity of a Modigliani, yet the affirmation of a contemporary piece.

Pole's instinct had been spot on. It would look striking in her newly redecorated lounge. She had done away with the mural on the far wall and allowed the area to be painted plain white, space for more art. The first purchase had been made with Jonathan, a new painting by one of her friends, the artist Susan Rosenberg. The hanging of the piece had been a celebration, accompanied by a glass of excellent champagne.

She moved closer to Susan's piece, a colourful abstract piece unique and uplifting. Pole had moved into her life effortlessly. Yet it had taken the trauma of the previous case they had worked on together to make it happen. She needed his company; no, more, his affection. Nancy stepped back from the piece. Why could she not speak the word that kept wanting to be heard but not acknowledged?

Love.

She shook with irritation at her own inability to face her feelings. She, so very able to ask the harsh questions when working on a case, could not bring herself to ask the simplest one when it came to emotions.

Was it why she had formed a friendship with Henry, understood him, two people wrestling with their feelings? Pole had never been jealous of Henry and he was right. Their affection was of a different kind. She admired Pole for being able to recognise this and never trying to oppose it, despite his reservations.

Nancy drifted away from her lounge, into her office at the far end of her apartment. She looked in, uncertain why she had moved to that room.

Pole. Henry. The Letter.

She moved a strand of dark hair away from her face, still on the threshold of her office. She had to speak to Pole about The Letter. The equivocal note Henry had slipped into her hand a few months ago, both ominous and hopeful.

Her BlackBerry's ringtone interrupted her deliberations.

"Jonathan?"

"*J'ai besoin de vous,*" Pole said. "In a professional capacity." A small wobble of embarrassment in his voice. "Marsh is being difficult."

"Well, I do not mind you needing me in whatever capacity," Nancy teased. "I'll do my best to convince The Super, *mon cher ami.*"

"And you will succeed, *je le sais.*" Tease happily received.

The thought of China floated into Nancy's mind. But why ask? Pole would let her know as soon as he had received news that was worth relaying.

It was good to have utter confidence in someone. It was reassuring, a feeling Nancy rarely sought but that she discovered she enjoyed. The burden shared felt so much lighter.

Pole was showering her with instructions regarding Marsh. She didn't mind for once, carried by his silvery voice, a warm rich authoritative baritone that cared.

"Jonathan, Jonathan," she finally interrupted. "I'll be fine."

"Of course." Pole stopped abruptly.

"Is Henry still at the Yard?"

"Not for long. I thought it would mollify Marsh and the Belmarsh governor if we sent him back early today."

"Good thought." Nancy hesitated. Whilst talking to Pole her hand had started fumbling with Henry's letter, burning her fingers. But what could she say now? And would it mean Henry not being allowed out of Belmarsh again, so he would be unable to obtain for Marissa the information she so badly needed?

"Nancy, are you still here?" Pole's voice interrupted her thinking.

She pushed the letter away. "Yes, I'm just wondering when the best time is to see Marsh."

"I'd speak to Marsh's PA and grab a slot as soon as possible if I were you," Pole said. "Do you fancy a drink afterwards?"

"*Une proposition irrésistible.*"

"I might be a little late."

"I'm in no rush. I'll wait for you with a good book."

The Super was behaving like a petulant child. She hung up and dialled Denise's number immediately. Marsh needed to be acknowledged as the important man he was. She did not mind putting on the charm as long as it bore fruit and it would.

* * *

Brett had taken the call. It was the first time Mohammed had spoken to him on his burner phone.

"The Sheik wants to know whether you are ready?"

The sharp answer that was on Brett's lips stayed there. "I'm working on it. I told him I don't —"

Mohammed interrupted. "I don't know the details." And it was obvious he did not want to know either. His job was not to argue with Brett but to deliver the messages.

Sly, Brett thought. The Sheik would no longer communicate with him directly but put pressure on him through Mohammed. Brett had to say yay or nay and nay was out of the question.

"I'll be ready by the end of today. Say at what time?"

"It's imminent." Mohammed's voice had lost its rich Middle-Eastern tone. It had become the flat voice of a scared man, hardly uttering his words for fear of saying the wrong thing.

There was no point in giving Mohammed a piece of his mind.

"What's the process?"

"I'll meet you tomorrow with a new burner phone. The instructions will be sent on that," Mohammed finished with a cough of relief.

"That's a little slim," Brett protested, again why bother but it was good to vent.

He drew a blank from Mohammed, predictably.

"Fine, and I presume as usual a text one hour before the meeting will tell me where to go?"

"Sorry, yes."

Brett killed the call. His hands shook a little. He no longer was in control of the trajectory in which his business and possibly his life were going.

"Fuck." Brett threw the phone onto a chair. It rebounded and almost crashed on the floor. "Fuck. Get a grip."

He pulled back the exquisite Hereke rug from the floor, pressed hard on a couple of boards and a small opening appeared. He took out his MI6 laptop and logged in. The five minutes it took to go through the security protocols lasted an eternity. He sent an email to Steve – *will be told details of transfer tomorrow.*

The response was almost instantaneous. Steve was tracking Brett's emails, unexpectedly. Brett almost wished he could go back to the time when Steve took a couple of days to reply.

Shall we meet at the club?

Not now. I will find another way of communicating with you. Back in touch tonight.

Brett walked to his Louis XV antique desk, took out the Highland Park bottle of whisky and poured a large glass. Hell, the bottle was still half full, and he might never get to finish it. He took a mouthful and let the amber liquid do its trick. He topped up the glass and walked back to his armchair.

Brett took a more reasonable sip, grabbed another mobile phone he had prepared. Time to call his Italian contact and prep him up: flattery, more money no doubt, more flattery, perhaps a few veiled threats he might have to take the business elsewhere.

Yes, it would work.

* * *

Ferguson was on his way. He was bringing two of his team to review Andy's findings. There was nothing Pole could do to prevent it and he was almost glad Ferguson was coming. Agent Harris could not stop that.

Nancy was with Marsh, no doubt getting The Super to where he needed to be. Henry had left for Belmarsh and arrived without incident. It all sounded perhaps a little too smooth.

Marissa's name flashed on the screen of his BlackBerry.

"What can I do for you, Marissa?"

"Mark Phelps would like to meet Henry."

Pole's eyebrows shot up. "A confrontation?"

"I don't think so," Marissa replied slowly. "He needs to understand. Make sense of what has happened."

"Victim meets perpetrator. Do you think it will help?"

"I spent a long time with him this afternoon. I think it is important and —"

"You're worried he will pull away otherwise."

"Mark could meet him at the Yard."

"I can clear this with Marsh but, Marissa, who will tell Henry?"

"Nancy could."

Pole was about to reject the idea. But it seemed Nancy was brokering every delicate situation and making a splendid job of it already. Pole grinned. It was good to be vindicated about involving her.

"Do you think he will accept?"

Pole moved around his office whilst thinking. "To be frank I'm not sure he is ready."

Pole turned towards the clock on the wall. Ferguson was late.

Unusual.

Marissa stopped, alerted by Pole's lack of focus.

"Sorry Marissa. Nancy is probably the best person to speak to Henry but don't expect him to rejoice."

Pole terminated the call by wishing her good luck and moved to Andy's desk. He had not heard either. Pole returned to his office. He would give Commander Ferguson another fifteen minutes and call.

He did not have to wait too long. The door of his office closed abruptly. Ferguson stood in front of his desk, alone.

"We need to talk."

Pole pointed to the chair in front of his desk. Ferguson dropped the files covering it on the floor unceremoniously, his face like thunder.

"I received a call from MI6."

Pole nodded, a few sharp pins prickling his spine.

"It seems that your case involves one of MI6's assets." Ferguson moved his fingers giving the word assets an air quotation.

"I see." Pole did his best to look surprised. Ferguson was too incensed to consider his reaction closely.

"Which means that I have to delay any intervention with this bloody lot your chap has traced."

"Why delay?" Pole knew the answer and he did not like it.

"I don't know. It's not uncommon to launch an assault and isolate the MI6 insider but there is always a risk."

"What do you want me to do?" Pole asked, hoping the answer would be nothing.

"Stay put until I get MI6 onside. I have not said my last word. National security is as much my concern as theirs."

Pole agreed, giving a few words of support as Ferguson was leaving. "And make sure your chap does not speak to anyone about what he has found. I don't like leaving this hanging but I've no choice, so keep it safe for me."

Pole nodded again and watched Ferguson disappear into the corridor. Pole's usual sound judgement was about to be tested to the full, he feared.

* * *

Superintendent Marsh was walking out of his office when she arrived. His face was a little red and unwelcoming. He made an effort to greet her and apologised immediately.

"Emergency meeting I'm afraid. I'm so very sorry I have to cancel just as you are walking in."

"Don't worry, Superintendent. I understand the pressure you are under."

Marsh straightened up a little; a compliment would always go a long way.

"It is very kind of you. Unfortunately, I cannot delay, but walk with me and we can talk."

They both made their way towards the bank of lifts. Nancy spoke about the request from Mark Phelps. To her surprise Marsh was not in the mood to argue. He agreed with the request, would speak to the Belmarsh governor and did not foresee a problem as long as the meeting was organised at the Yard.

"Something on your mind, Superintendent?" A bold question from Nancy perhaps, but why not?

"National security is on everybody's mind," Marsh volunteered.

His BlackBerry was ringing. "Pole, I'm coming your way."

Marsh bade Nancy goodbye, with a rapid bow. She had never seen him so anxious. He was taking Pole with him to his meeting and that could not be a good sign.

Chapter Twenty-Three

Pole could hear him before he saw him. Marsh was coming his way and evidently also on the warpath. MI6 was throwing its weight around and intruding into the Met's operations. He did not like it.

Pole stood up in anticipation.

"Ah, Pole – glad you are still at your desk."

Obviously. Pole bit his lip. "How can I help you, Sir?"

"You've spoken to Ferguson I gather."

"Yes, he came in to talk about our latest findings." Pole waited for Marsh to say his piece. Marsh's face had the livid colour of anger, his dark eyebrows gathered in one straight line.

"You mean your team has been able to track the shooter?"

Blast, Ferguson had spoken to his superiors already. "Although I wanted to discuss with Ferguson in detail to make sure."

Marsh did not even bother to rebuke Pole. He was keeping his frustration stored up for someone else to feel.

"Right, I've asked the Home Office to call an emergency coordination meeting. The constant interference of MI6 has to stop." Marsh was playing politics but Pole had indeed noticed MI6 interference; he was at the centre of it.

"I wouldn't know, Sir."

"Of course, you wouldn't."

Perfect answer and Marsh was still not asking the right question – who had given MI6 the heads-up?

"When is the meeting taking place?"

"Now. We are expected in fifteen minutes. You can brief me in the car about the evidence you have gathered."

Pole shrugged his jacket on. Picked up a file Andy had been compiling. Marsh was rehearsing his arguments with him: interference – trust – cooperation.

Pole fell back a little when they reached the ground floor on their way to Marsh's car, enough to send Nancy a quick text.

With Marsh – will be late, *vraiment désolée*. Jx

He had pressed the send button before wondering whether the x was too much.

When they reached the Home Office, Commander Ferguson and the Head of CT Command in London had already arrived. The Home Secretary and his aide were in the meeting room, having a final conversation behind closed doors.

A couple of people, a tall wiry man and a Middle-Eastern-looking younger man, sat in a different corner. MI6 didn't mix. The aide to the Home Secretary opened the door and everybody walked in. Pole followed Marsh. They all shook hands and introduced themselves.

Agent Harris was not there. Pole breathed a sigh of relief until one of Harris' colleagues mentioned he could not attend as urgent matters required his attention.

The Home Secretary set the scene and the squabbling started immediately. Pole observed the people around the table. Ferguson and his boss were facing MI6. Marsh had positioned himself a little off-centre but on Ferguson's side. Pole found himself relegated far out, a place he felt comfortable with.

"What do you mean, your asset is irreplaceable?"

"Commander Ferguson," the lean-looking man interrupted. "Infiltrating these cells is not easy. You know that as well as I do, so yes, our asset is irreplaceable."

"This cell is posing an imminent threat to the public," Ferguson's boss cut in. "We need to take them down now."

"I would agree if my undercover officer was warning me of an imminent strike, but his very reliable intelligence does not say that there is one planned."

"Nothing planned. How about the attempted murder of a key witness and a prosecutor in a high-profile case?"

"You've done a pretty good job so far of stopping them." There was a hint of humour in the thin man's voice.

"This is preposterous. We need to see your intel now." Ferguson had raised his voice.

"I can't comment in the interest —"

"Don't give me that crap," Ferguson growled. "You're not the only one defending national security."

"Gentlemen, gentlemen," the Home Secretary had raised her hands to calm the situation down. "This is not helpful."

"We are monitoring them closely. We will know if they try something else. In the meantime, this operation has given us the opportunity to discover more about what we believe is a new terrorist organisation."

"You mean a new cell in London? We know that already." Ferguson's face only showed contempt.

"I don't think you heard me right, Commander. I said organisation not operation."

The room fell silent. Marsh looked at Pole, then at the Home Secretary. Ferguson and his boss exchanged a surprised look.

The Middle-Eastern looking MI6 agent took over.

"We still don't know whether this is a splinter cell and new offshoot of Al-Qaeda, but we are seeing fresh movement on social media, a new way of talking about the Jihad, more aggressive, more ambitious."

"And you think they are in the UK? Why?" Ferguson's boss's voice showed genuine interest and doubt too. This was far too big to ignore or rebuff.

"The tactics for recruitment are different. They are prepared to recruit outside the traditional Muslim community."

"Can you substantiate that?"

Both agents remained silent.

"What do you need CT Command to do? Sit on our hands?"

The Home Secretary intervened before anybody started arguing again.

"You need to hold back until we position our asset. After that they are all yours," the thin man said.

"And dispose of them, which is what CT Command will do." The Home Secretary left no room for argument. Ferguson and his boss exchanged angry looks.

The MI6 agents savoured their victory.

Marsh had not opened his mouth until this point, a wise move Pole had to admit.

"How can the Met help?"

"Let us have what you've got so far, and we can all be on the same page." The lean man had turned towards Marsh and Pole.

Marsh turned to Pole. "And what do you think?"

Seven pairs of eyes started scrutinising Pole. For a split second he felt like a rabbit caught in the headlights.

"Perhaps you can liaise with Inspector Pole and keep me in the loop?" Marsh said irritated at Pole's lack of an immediate reply.

Pole simply nodded an "Of course". *They know already and they know I know.* Pole caught the eye of the Middle-Eastern agent. The message had been received. A few moments to agree contact points and updates then people disappeared. The Home Secretary left first. She did not want to be cornered by anyone.

Before they separated Ferguson's boss turned towards Marsh. "I'd like to know how MI6 got wind of our operation so quickly."

Marsh shrugged it off. "That's their job."

"Going home?" Marsh asked Pole as they were walking out of the Home Office.

"Not yet, Sir. Going back to the Yard – a few things to tidy up."

"Right." Marsh stood for a moment on the pavement. "You were very quiet in there."

"It's really not my scene," was the best Pole could think of.

Marsh eyed Pole. "Ferguson's right, of course. How did MI6 get hold of the information?"

Pole raised his shoulders, hailed a cab and disappeared.

* * *

The smell of bacon made Henry's mouth water. He did not take his eyes off the monitors. It was almost too good to believe. He had already started work on his Bloomberg screens. Pole was at his side in three long strides.

"Morning Inspector. Peace offering?" Henry nodded towards the bacon sandwich wrapped up in greasy paper. Henry had almost forgiven Pole for being his MI6 go-between. He had pondered long and hard over the choice and had to admit Pole was the ideal candidate.

Outsmarted. How annoying.

"Morning Henry." Pole handed Henry his breakfast. He took his usual position, half sitting, half leaning against the makeshift desk. He looked tired and perhaps nervous.

Henry waited for an update.

"What's new on the market?"

Henry cocked his head. "Really, Inspector. You're not going to ask for my advice, are you?

"Hey, I too have a pension."

"Equities. And more equities, in the US in particular. They are heading up for a new bull run and don't be scared about the odd market retreat." Henry grinned.

Pole nodded. "Sounds good." He put down his own coffee and took a longer look at Henry. "Any news at your end?"

"What do you mean?" Henry was genuinely puzzled until the penny dropped.

"You mean?"

"That's right."

Henry's face grew serious. It was true; he had not had direct contact with Kamal and the current regime imposed by Belmarsh made it difficult for him to see any inmate.

"Nothing. I am not allowed to join the others, even for dinner, and I leave before breakfast."

"But I am sure there are ways of communicating."

Henry remained silent. He recalled the message he had received two days ago.

"Something springs to mind?" Pole kept prodding.

"Not really. The food is as bland as ever although they have not thought of poisoning me yet."

"That's the Bolsheviks, Henry, not Jihadists. They prefer the knife."

"I know but, hey, the Irish like the knife too."

Pole withstood the punch. Henry regretted throwing it as soon as it was said.

"Where is Nancy?" Henry asked. He could do with someone to smooth the conversation between him and Pole.

"She'll be in soon."

Surely Pole could be more forthcoming.

"When are you calling your contact again?"

"I'll try at 8pm this evening. It's more likely the answer will come later though, but I'll try."

"You're sure of yourself, aren't you?"

"I know you think I'm an arrogant prick but yes, I am sure. I know too much about him so he has no choice."

A rhythmic knock at the door made them both turn their heads at the same time. Nancy's elegant silhouette appeared in the doorway. They were all smiles.

"*Messieurs*, I'm glad not to be walking into a match of fisticuffs."

"Never," Pole and Henry chimed together.

"Good news. The Super has decided that in the interests of the enquiry, ha ha, the SFO case being so high-profile etc etc, he will ask the Belmarsh governor and the Home Office to let you, Henry, stay at The Yard until midnight today."

"You're the best." Henry stood up but stayed back a little. Pole was in the way. He graciously moved back. Henry landed a small kiss on Nancy's cheek, almost shy.

"Marsh sounded a little frazzled, Jonathan. He gave me all I wanted with hardly any need to convince him."

Pole's face managed to convey astonishment. Both Henry and Nancy were waiting for specifics. But he moved his hand vaguely – a no-idea gesture that failed to convince.

"Shall we see where we've got to?" Nancy changed the subject.

"Sure." Henry called up a few documents he had saved in a protected folder specially created for him. "Aren't we waiting for Marissa?"

Nancy avoided looking at Pole. "She's coming later."

Henry called up on screen a complex diagram showing all the layers of companies, trusts, foundations and partnerships that had accumulated, one on top of another.

Panama to start with, then a trip around the world of tax havens and finally a box with a large question mark, the Ultimate Beneficial Owner. No matter how complex a structure was, and this one could have won a prize, there had to be an individual or individuals involved at the end of the chain.

Nancy looked at the different boxes stacked together, and colour coded to indicate the type of legal relationships they had. She was suitably impressed, certainly with the structure itself, but also with Henry's grasp of the legalities surrounding the chain of ownership in this maze of international arrangements.

"I too was a lawyer once, remember." Henry smiled his naughty-yet-clever-boy smile.

"Of course, Chase and Case. Was law not interesting enough for you?"

"I was an Irish boy working in a very closed shop environment. They may eventually have made me partner, but it would have been long after all my peers and I was too good at structured products to wait that long."

Pole moved to Henry's side to look at the diagram as well. Henry nodded his approval. Pole had remembered that he did not like anyone standing at the back of his chair, a remnant from his days on the trading floor during which the head of investment banking would prowl the floor in search of a victim.

"I'm still puzzled. How could compliance at HXBK let this go through?" Pole asked.

"Because there was a disconnect. Some senior people, close to the Ultimate Beneficial Owner, did the review of the structure."

"If the UBO is linked to the state that bought shares in HXBK to support their capital during the 2008 crisis, then that is a problem. Circular transactions of that type are illegal." Henry tapped the screen where the empty box lay.

"My other question is what is this money being used for?" Nancy said.

"Exactly. That should have worried the senior management."

"They are too keen to do business with the big oil producers," Henry replied to Pole.

"Your guy will tell us who the UBO is?" Pole still sounded dubious.

"Yup. And he will tell me how we can track him down, too." Henry crossed his arms behind his head and stretched his long legs underneath the table. He loved this. It was almost as thrilling as concluding some of the ridiculously large transactions he had the reputation of closing in his previous career.

Almost.

Unfortunately, in a few hours' time, instead of celebrating his success in an expensive restaurant, guzzling vintage champagne, Henry would be heading back to Belmarsh.

But just now, sitting between Nancy and Pole, Henry was enjoying the moment.

Pole's BlackBerry rang. He frowned, gestured an apology and walked out of the room. Henry relaxed a notch. It was good to be alone with Nancy.

"What's going through that great mind of yours?" Nancy turned on her chair to look at Henry.

"I'm simply enjoying the chase." Henry sounded playful.

Nancy moved her hand to the side of her neck and rested her elbow on the back of the chair.

"You haven't answered my question."

Henry sat at his screens looking away from her. *Please let it not be the letter.*

"Nancy, you may not believe it, but I have learned to live for the moment and I am enjoying this particular one."

Nancy let it go. She was preparing a difficult question. Henry prayed again, please let it not be the letter.

"I know you are expecting me to ask a difficult question."

"If it's about that stupid letter?"

"It's not. It's an unusual request."

Henry turned to face her. What could be so unexpected that he had not thought about it already?

"Mark Phelps would like to meet you."

The bolt of fire that punched him in the gut drew a small intake of breath from Henry. Lost for words, Henry stared at Nancy. The sudden numbness in his limbs became unbearable.

Henry opened his mouth, unsuccessfully. Was it a joke? Was Mark Phelps insane?

Nancy let him be. She gave Henry space to understand the request was real. She got up, poured two glasses of water, and handed one to Henry. He finished the glass in a couple of gulps.

"Is this why – I'm not?" Henry closed his eyes, fighting back tears he thought he no longer had.

"He needs to understand, to find some peace – and in order to carry on with the case, this is his request."

Henry dropped his head in his hands. He stayed silent for a while.

"What can I say that will make a difference? That I'm a bastard of a terrorist, that I regret what I did?" Henry's voice oscillated between pain and anger.

He stood up, walked to the wall. He spread his hands over it, his forehead resting against its cold surface; he was fighting emotions, despair and …

Shame.

"And if I say no?" Henry spoke, still facing the wall.

"He will almost certainly no longer be a witness in the case."

Henry turned his head slowly.

"Does he want to …?" Henry was searching for the word.

"I don't think he wants to make you feel …" Nancy tried to find the word Henry was looking for. "Inhumane. He is not that sort of person." Nancy had stood up as well. He felt her move in his direction. But he did not want to be approached. He moved to another corner of the room.

"Let him, then. Let him tell me what a monster I have been. Yes, let him."

Nancy froze. Her kind eyes were on him, trying to soothe his torment.

"You know this isn't true. You are not a monster."

"To you Nancy perhaps, but others – and who could blame them?"

Nancy was about to continue but Henry lifted a hand.

"We don't need to speak about this any longer. I will see him. Please go and tell him."

He needed to be on his own to prepare for what would be the most difficult conversation of his life.

Chapter Twenty-Four

The underpass smelt of urine and rotting food. Pole looked at his watch again. He had arrived a little early. He kicked a beer can that lay on the ground, the sound of it rolling on the rough asphalt reverberated along the walls. Almost too loud to bear.

Hurried footsteps were coming his way, a man's shoes. Pole was on his guard. Agent Harris turned the corner and broke into a slow jog.

"Ferguson's boss is wreaking havoc at the Home Office," he chuckled.

"You're not concerned?"

"Nope. What we've got is too big."

"I suppose it is."

"You spoke to Crowne?"

Pole's jaw clenched. He nodded.

"Anything I should be aware of?"

"Such as?"

"Change of mind, change of mood – trying to contact other people in the old IRA world."

"I am his go-between, not his confidante."

"But you're talking to him to find out, right?"

"As much as I can; it's not my job to snoop."

Harris gave Pole a broad smile. He unwrapped a piece of chewing gum and popped it into his mouth. "Trying to stop smoking." He kept grinning.

"Is that it?" Pole looked at his watch again. He could not be away for long in the middle of this political minefield.

"Got a message for Crowne." Harris grew serious. His beady brown eyes darkened. It was time to do proper MI6 business.

"My source tells me that it will happen in the next twenty-four hours."

"What if we don't get the information we need to keep bringing him back to the Yard?"

Harris shrugged. "Find a way."

Pole took a step closer to Harris. That was not the deal as he understood it. Harris carried on chewing his gum. Even in the shadow of a towering Pole he was relaxed.

"I know it's going to piss you and a lot of other people off, but things are in motion and I don't decide on the timing. I can only give you the heads-up."

Harris was right but Pole stayed close for a moment longer, restraining the urge to stick his fist into the other man's face.

"Would do you little good, Inspector. It's not me you need to slam, is it?"

Pole pulled back.

"You and Ferguson will get the cell but first we need to let them do what they are planning to do with Crowne."

"People are going to get hurt," Pole snapped.

"We'll try to minimise that."

"How?"

"My problem, not yours."

"That's not good enough."

"But it will have to do. You and I know what we've got is too big for it not to go through."

"What if Ferguson finds out?"

"Why would he?" Harris had stopped chewing his gum and his eyes drilled into Pole – *don't even think about it.*

Pole turned around in one swoop, running one hand through his thick hair.

"If this thing goes wrong, I'll find a way to get to you," Pole spoke over his shoulder.

"Fair enough but you're underestimating what my team can do."

Pole kept walking away.

"Speak to Crowne and have a little faith in Her Majesty's Secret Service." Harris sounded surprisingly honest.

* * *

The day was going to be long and slow. Henry found himself looking at the wall clock yet again – a watched kettle. He needed to be doing something more than re-reading the file Marissa had left with him. Still, it was a welcome distraction from what had been haunting him since he had been told he would be meeting Mark Phelps.

He pushed away the thought of the meeting. He needed to concentrate on the task at hand, re-read the file, possibly spot something new and make the call to Mac in Panama.

But he had agreed to the meeting. It was the right thing to do. It was what the reformed Henry must do. Nothing had prepared him for the feelings that assailed him once Nancy had left him alone. He had gone to the wastepaper basket and nearly thrown up. His body was still feverish at the thought.

In the end, the idea of a meeting had given him greater resolve. He would see his plan through.

The sound of a text message delivered on his burner phone brought him back to the here and now. Mac had given him a time to call. The man had been busy all night. Henry breathed deeply. He could still make good on his commitment and the code he had used with Mac in their conversation still worked. The answer was ready for delivery and he would not have to wait until 8pm.

Henry deleted the text, stood up and poured himself a cup of water from the water cooler. It was all working towards the point of no return from which there would be no turning back. Henry was pouring a second cup when the door opened. Pole came in, eyebrows knitted, an expression that had seldom left his face in the last few days.

"Next twenty-four hours; get ready."

Henry's cup wobbled, spilling a little water at his feet. "Shit," he blurted.

"Leave it," Pole said.

Henry walked to his chair and slumped into it, cup in hand. He squeezed it so hard he heard the crunch of the plastic ready to split. His throat had closed. He could not swallow anything.

Pole moved a chair, turned it around and straddled it. "Harris is certain."

"But how?" Henry lifted his eyes and scrutinised Pole.

"He did not care to elaborate."

Henry put the cup down, slowly, not trusting his movements. He rubbed his hand over his face, pulling it down to form a strange grimace.

"The Belmarsh lot won't be able to communicate. I can't meet anyone until I'm back for good."

"Think about what happened in the last two days; there might have been a sign." Pole had crossed his arms, resting them on the back of his chair. He too wanted to validate Harris' information.

"It has always been very vague." Henry picked up the plastic cup. He hesitated, froze and finally lifted the cup to his lips, drinking in small gulps, hoping Pole had not noticed.

Pole stood up. "Let me know if something comes to mind."

Henry nodded – and both men knew MI6 was right.

* * *

Her back was turned to him when Pole entered the open-plan space. Nancy was talking to Andy. Pole slowed down his pace. Nancy had pulled her jet-black hair into what looked like a complicated bun. Her slim figure was twisted into an elegant pose, hand on Andy's desk partitioning, hips at an attractive angle. Pole forced himself out of his state of languorous admiration.

Andy must have told Nancy he was approaching since she now swirled around. Her smile was courteous, but her eyes relished their contact with Pole's.

"I spoke to Marissa. She will let Mark Phelps know Henry has accepted."

Pole's office phone rang. Andy picked up.

"It's Commander Ferguson."

Pole pulled a sorry face.

"Don't worry, but Jonathan, *j'ai besoin de vous parler.*" Nancy's eyes conveyed an urgency that surprised Pole.

"*Bien entendu.*" He disappeared into his office, door closed. Nancy was still speaking to Andy. Pole hoped Andy would not talk about the shooter. He had been clear with Andy; no one must know, no one – but Nancy had her ways with young men and come to think of it with a number of not-so-young men too.

Ferguson was raging on the phone. MI6 was not budging and would Pole at least give him something; he almost said please.

Pole clenched a fist. He did not enjoy keeping essential information from CT Command and yet Harris had been clear. He sat down and kept talking to Ferguson: options, who to call next. Pole gave some snippets of information as he spoke.

What if he was wrong? Pole stood up again. He had not felt so unsure of his instincts or his analysis of a situation for a very long time. Even the protracted case against Henry had not challenged his judgement as much.

Marsh's number appeared on another line.

"Ferguson, got to go; Marsh is calling me."

He ended one call and took the other. The bark of Marsh's voice irritated Pole. "I spoke to the Home Office again. They are reconsidering their position." Pole grunted. Marsh could certainly pull the strings of power, silent when needed, reaching out to the right people when necessary.

"You don't think it's a good idea?" Marsh snapped.

"We just don't have the full picture, Sir."

"Perhaps not, but we have a bunch of Jihadi on our streets that might attempt a terrorist act. I'm not happy to delay. In particular with the quality intel your team has dug up."

Marsh had a point. He failed to mention the enormous kudos he would derive were the Met at the centre of the arrest. Despite this Pole could see where Marsh was coming from.

"Shall I come your way to discuss strategy, Sir?" Always a good argument – the S word had a hypnotic effect on The Met's management and Marsh could never resist it. The meeting would give Harris a little more time to get organised.

Pole hung up, shook his head and walked off in the direction of Marsh's office. Nancy would have to wait a little longer before he could devote his attention to her.

* * *

Andy's voice sounded distracted as Nancy's eyes followed Pole's tall body moving swiftly towards the lifts. Something was up. She had felt it when Henry, Pole and she had been talking in the morning. The atmosphere was friendly, perhaps deceptively so, with no more sparring between Pole and Henry, she having to play the schoolmistress separating two rowdy boys.

Andy kept talking in the background, his voice suddenly more pressing. Nancy snapped out of her thoughts and forced her attention back to the young man. He was pointing at his screen. News alert. "I need to call Inspector Pole."

Nancy read the news alert on Andy's screen.

Prisoners have barricaded themselves in one of the wings of HMP Belmarsh. The prison is now in lockdown. Five anti-riot units and a negotiator have been dispatched.

Text kept coming.

Two prison officers have been seriously injured, one is in a critical condition. Hostage situation not confirmed.

"What's your mobile number Andy?"

Andy kept an eye on the screen whilst giving her the number.

"I'll give you a missed call so you know how to contact me."

She could not reach Henry on his burner phone.

The lifts were full. It was almost midday and employees were already going for their lunch trying to avoid the inevitable queues. She squeezed near the door, fighting the influx of people. Level 3, Level 2, Level 1, Ground Floor; almost everyone got out. She pressed Level -1 a few times; someone dashed in and the doors reopened. She tried to remain civil. As soon as they reached Level -1 she burst out of the lift and ran all the way to the room in which Henry was working. One of the prison officers outside was on his mobile. The news about Belmarsh was spreading like wildfire.

Henry was typing furiously on his keyboard when she entered. The noise of the door made him jump.

"You've seen the news?" he said returning his attention to the monitors.

"Who are they?" Nancy had moved to his side, reading the information that was scrolling through Bloomberg news.

"Nothing on that yet." Henry responded, calling up another screen from the Reuters information platform.

"It only came up on the Met internal info line a few minutes ago."

"No time at all."

More data had started to appear.

Some of the prisoners have been heard shouting Allahu Akbar. Fear that a number of hardcore radicalised inmates have taken over Wing 2 at Belmarsh is growing.

Henry's body froze in a strange position, halfway towards the screen, his fingers in mid-air, immobile.

"What does it mean? Henry?"

No response came. She shook Henry by the shoulders.

"I don't know."

"Oh, come on," she almost shouted. "This can't be a coincidence."

Henry's eyes met hers and she could see hurt. "Sorry. I'm sorry. I shouldn't infer —" Nancy's phone rang. "I'm with him now." She mouthed Pole's name to Henry.

"Why?" she said. "This is ridiculous." Nancy felt the lump in her throat growing. "I will."

"What's happening?" Henry had turned his entire body sideways so that he could face her.

"The Belmarsh governor wants you back at HSU right away."

"This is ridiculous," Henry blurted. "I haven't finished."

"This is what Pole thinks too, and for once Marsh agrees."

"And that is what you have to convey to the prison officers outside."

"Correct." Nancy looked serious.

"Wow. I never saw you as a bodyguard but hey!"

"I may not look it but I sure can hold my ground."

"I don't doubt it and it seems you're going to be tested right away." The door had just opened.

* * *

Mohammed was running his prayer beads through his fingers, thumb and index finger, rolling them one after the other. Brett could see him in the distance, eyes focused on the door. He half stood up and sat down again as Brett made his way over to him.

"Is The Sheik too busy to speak to me?" Brett's sharp tone sent a shiver of angst down Mohammed's round body.

"Shhh, not so loud."

Brett rolled his eyes and sat down. Mohammed half extended his arm in the direction of one of the waiters and tea materialised.

"Didn't know you were religious," Brett remarked after he had tasted his tea, a rather good and fragrant beverage, he had to admit.

"Who told you that I wasn't?" Mohammed's eyes darted around the room in fear.

"Relax. I've simply never seen you with prayer beads before."

"Helps the nerves."

Brett raised his glass in acknowledgement.

"You'll receive a text in the next twenty-four hours."

"And you got me here to tell me that?"

Mohammed did not reply. He waited for a couple of men to walk past their table and settle in another corner of the room.

"He has this for you." Mohammed handed over a large envelope. "To be opened when you are home."

"Obviously." Brett took the envelope. It was light and had no markings.

Brett finished his tea in a few gulps and left the tea shop without another word.

He walked down the large street, came to Seven Sisters tube and started walking down the stairs. He stopped to consult the tube map. Two people were following him, he was sure. He had seen their shadows when Mohammed had stopped talking.

Brett moved to the platform and sat down waiting for the next train. He leaned against the bench backrest, an eye on the people tailing him. He was pretty sure they were not supposed to be discreet. The Sheik had one message to communicate.

Remember Massimo Visconti.

* * *

"Crowne, Belmarsh governor wants you back to HSU now."

"On what grounds?" Nancy stood between the two prison officers and Henry.

The men looked at each other, incredulous. "Look lady," one of the officers started.

Wrong title.

"To begin with, young man," Nancy interrupted with eloquence. "You address yourself to me in the appropriate manner. Secondly, there is an understanding between the Home Office, the SFO, the Metropolitan Police and the governor that Mr Crowne needs to provide us with his assistance to gather vital information and that he will not be returned to Belmarsh until he has done so until late today."

"Perhaps but Belmarsh governor's just called us to tell us he wants him back at HSU."

"You mean Mr Crowne? May I remind you that since the 2004 Home Office reform inmates are called either by their first name or addressed as mister."

The second officer had said nothing so far. His calm contrasted with the irritability of his colleague, a puffed-up sparrow – all feathers and no weight.

"That does not change anything." The sparrow's face was turning crimson.

"I heard you the first time." Nancy was not budging.

"My colleague is right, Ms Wu. Perhaps you could check with Superintendent Marsh?" The polite yet determined tone of the other guard surprised Nancy.

"I will do so or, even better, speak to Inspector Pole."

"I think Superintendent Marsh might be the one deciding."

Hurried steps came down the corridor. Pole opened the door briskly.

"Shall we speak to Inspector Pole first?" Nancy's voice had taken on a relentless sharp edge. "These gentlemen are intending to take Mr Crowne back to HSU Belmarsh right away."

"Yes, I've been told and haven't had time yet to speak to Superintendent Marsh about it. For the time being, Henry stays put."

"But the Belmarsh gov —"

"I am aware." Pole snapped.

"Perhaps you should try him again?" The other officer said.

"Is this because of the riots?"

"We have not been told why; simply to bring Mr Crowne back to HSU immediately."

"It may not be safe."

"HSU Belmarsh is the safest prison in the UK, Inspector Pole."

Nancy liked the game Pole was playing. He too was playing the clock. If the riots escalated, Belmarsh might not be accessible and in complete lockdown.

"Not if the riots escalate into a complete lockdown."

"Mr Crowne is an HSU inmate. He must be returned to HSU. That is the procedure." The guard's calm was putting pressure on Pole. He shrugged.

"Still, I'm not comfortable with the risk that this entails."

"Let's see what Superintendent Marsh has to say."

Pole gritted his teeth and pulled out his BlackBerry. A text had arrived and he read it quickly. Pole pressed the recall button.

"Pole here. I am returning your —" Pole was interrupted by a flow of words. They sounded angry as they drifted out of his phone.

"Yes, Sir - if this has been agreed – understood, Sir."

Pole killed the call.

"You can have Henry."

Chapter Twenty-Five

It was happening.

The hairs rose on the back of Henry's neck when the two prison officers bundled him into the high security vehicle parked at the back of Scotland Yard. Nancy muffled a cry of anger with a quivering hand and Pole looked defeated.

It was not the sort of goodbye he had hoped for. Henry rested his head against the metal frame of the van and closed his eyes. He could feel the cuffs tight around his wrists. Not long now until they were off.

At Belmarsh, the breakfast they had brought him before he left for The Yard had angered him to start with: a bread roll roughly cut and already buttered, a glass of juice red in colour, a small lump of jam – must have been strawberry. He had drunk the juice and hardly touched the bread.

Henry had not thought about it until Pole had asked the question. But now he was in the van taking him back to HSU he was wondering. Was it a message? The events of the day kept intruding: the discussion with Nancy and Pole, the call with Mac and Pole's warning, the conversation he had agreed to have with Mark Phelps. He shook his head, opened his eyes. It had been there all day waiting for him to decipher, a subtle but perfect reference to his Catholic upbringing – a Last Supper allusion, bread and wine. Henry recognised Kamal's hand, subtle but to the point. The van had stopped. Henry braced himself, a few minutes elapsed, then the vehicle resumed its journey. Henry moved his head a fraction to survey the two prison officers that sat close to the door. An odd pair he thought. The young chap was nervous, perhaps a newbie in his role as escort. The other officer seemed inscrutable, his calm almost eerie.

The van stopped again, this time at the side of the road. Henry could feel the movements of the van being reversed and driven into a parking bay. The walkie-talkie crackled and the young guard responded. The conversation was mostly happening at the other end with monosyllabic responses from the guard until finally he formed a complete sentence.

"That route won't delay us too much." He bent towards his colleague, informed him of the decision. The other nodded. "OK, let's do that."

Henry made his entire body let go. But what had he been expecting?

The van restarted with a jolt. Henry tried to ease off the tension that was building up steadily in his body. He rolled his shoulders, moved his neck, breathing deeply in the process.

He settled back against the cool metal. His mind drifted back to the case, to Mark Phelps. The fear he felt at having to face a victim who was not even his victim had startled him.

He had spent the time between working on the case thinking about it: what he would say, what the responses might be. Sorry was never going to be good enough even to start with. But maybe he could explain why he had followed the path he had taken, with honesty. That perhaps was all he had to offer.

He was not sure it would be sufficient, that it would fulfil the hope he nourished. The hope that something in his life was salvageable, that he was redeemable … The thought of perhaps escaping the meeting with Mark did not bring him joy or release. To Henry's greatest surprise he wanted to have this honest conversation with a victim.

The collision with the front of the van reverberates through its entire structure. The two prison officers brace themselves against the handlebars of their seats. Henry is thrown against the iron bars that separate his seating area from the guards'. The pain in his shoulder is searing, his mind takes him straight back to another van, to the explosion that marked his descent into hell. The walkie-talkie has fallen to the floor; it buzzes like a wounded insect – someone is calling urgently.

One of the guards grabs it.

"Is he hurt? I'll go and check."

"We shouldn't open the door until we're inside Belmarsh," the younger guard says, agitated.

"I need to check whether we killed this guy. Right, right."

Henry collects himself. His mind throws up images he does not want to see. He smells gasoline. He smells fire. He looks around in anguish but there are no flames to see.

The door of the van opens and shuts. People have congregated outside it seems: Henry can hear voices. The young guard is verging on panic. He stands up and peers through the protected windows. He cranes his neck but cannot see what he is looking for.

Banging on the door, the walkie-talkie crackles again.

"OK." He hesitates. More banging at the door again, not insistent; just a come-on-open-up-it's-only-me type of knock.

He complies and the cross of the M4 carbine strikes him square in the face. He has no time to pick himself up from the floor; the second blow crashes over his skull.

The older officer who went to check the incident has come back, his weapon in his right hand. He takes his keys and starts unbolting the door keeping Henry locked up. Henry looks at him, numb. He has been thinking about this moment for months and now he cannot move. The sound of a police siren yells in the distance. Henry steps away from the door.

The officer moves forward. "Cuffs," he says.

Henry moves in slow motion. He had not expected it to happen this way. He no longer knows what he was expecting. The cuffs are off. The guard turns around and throws a bundle of clothes at him. "Put these on." A dark hoodie, a pair of black waterproof trousers and jacket, a black helmet.

Henry's head is held in a vice. He could say no. He looks at the young man on the floor, blood already coagulating on his head wound. Who is he kidding – there is no turning back. A few final images and he knows – Liam, Nancy, his father.

He is putting the clothes on quickly now, hoodie, waterproofs. The guard is impatient, even suspicious. The look of fanatical hatred smacks Henry in the face. Hesitation has been swept away from him. He puts on the helmet and gets down from the van.

Outside, the motorbike that had slid under the front of the vehicle is still there. Two other men are pointing M249 sub-machine guns at the driver. Even locked in his armoured vehicle, the metal is no match for the penetration power of the ammunition.

The driver is holding his hands up over his head. Two motorbikes are parked either side of the van. There is no traffic in this side road they diverted into. One car has driven past, accelerating.

It seems that in the middle of Deptford no one wants to know about a police van under attack. The guard fires up one of the bikes. A loud moan comes out of the van.

Impossible.

Henry snaps his fingers in the direction of the gun that sticks out of the belt of one of the bikers. The guard hesitates. Henry snaps up the visor, his face has grown cold. What is he waiting for? Henry grabs the gun the guard has handed to him, walks back to the van.

Two loud firearm discharges and Henry straddles the bike that is waiting for him.

* * *

Nancy was still on her call to Marissa. Pole was on his way to his office. He knew what was coming next. Assailed by doubts, he could not bring himself to speak to Andy who had received yet another call from Ferguson's team. Henry had been gone barely an hour when a text pinged on Pole's burner phone. Pole closed the door of his office and leaned against it.

Call me now.

He felt the urge to throw the phone against the wall.

He pressed the call button instead.

"Crowne is out."

Pole remained silent, his throat dry, incapable of speech.

"Are you there?"

Pole grunted. "Casualties?"

"Not sure but you need to be on your way to the scene."

"Marsh?"

"I'll deal with him."

"Ferguson?"

"Ditto."

"I'll call you when I'm there."

"Good."

Pole's siren let him blaze through the traffic, the longest twenty-minute drive of his career. He had just let an ambulance overtake him.

He parked his car in the middle of the road and walked quickly towards the officers already on the scene. He showed his badge. "Any casualties?"

One of the officers moved his head towards the van without a word. Pole's gut tightened as he looked inside.

"Hello Sir. What's your name? Can you hear me, Sir?"

Pole recognised the young man who had been so keen to take Henry back to Belmarsh. His face had started turning blue and the force of the impact had no doubt crushed some bones.

"I need to speak to him please." Pole flashed his ID again.

"And I need to assess him first." The paramedic held her ground. The tall woman had turned back to the patient.

"We may have some extremely dangerous people on the run and an abduction."

She hesitated. Her colleague had kept asking questions and the young man was coming around. He recognised Pole.

"Where is Crowne?"

"Gone."

"The other guard?"

"Gone."

The young man closed his eyes and for a moment Pole thought he had passed out. The paramedics moved Pole out of the way but the young man fluttered his eyelashes in an effort to focus.

"But – did not." His mouth was dry and the paramedics helped him with a damp tissue. His eyes moved towards the side of the van.

"Did not – kill —"

"They did not kill you?" Pole asked.

The young guard batted his eyelids, yes. "Crow —"

"They did not kill Crowne?"

Frustration flashed in his eyes. "Me, me."

"That's enough Inspector. I need to take him to hospital."

Pole let the paramedics do their job. He moved to the side of the road. The driver of the van was wrapped in a blanket, sitting sideways in the police car that had arrived first on the scene.

"Are you OK?" Pole asked. He meant it.

"Fine. I didn't see it coming."

"Can you tell me what happened?"

The driver took a sip from a water bottle and started his story. He did his best to give a fair account and Pole did his best to take coherent notes.

"I thought he was dead – the boy," he finished.

"You mean because of the beating?"

"No because of the gunshots – two of them. I thought that's it."

"He was shot at?"

"As I said two shots."

Pole finished taking notes and headed back to the van.

He bent forward in the direction the young guard had indicated. Two bullets had penetrated the metal. Pole stood up, hands on hips, thinking the unthinkable.

Someone had fired two shots at the young guard at point-blank range and missed.

The paramedics were loading the stretcher onto the ambulance. Pole ran to them. He lunged forward for one last question.

"Who shot at you?"

"Crowne."

The woman was about to be rude to him but Pole managed to add, "Crowne missed you?"

A look of relief went through the young man's eyes. He had delivered his message. He moved his head slightly and the stretcher disappeared into the van. The female paramedic closed the door forcefully in Pole's face.

Pole walked away from the scene and found the recessed entrance of a small building. Harris had to know.

"You're certain?" Harris asked after Pole had told him what he knew.

"Certain, I checked the van – two bullet holes. He could not have missed him, not unless he did it on purpose."

Harris grunted. "Why the fuck did he have to get involved?"

"To save a life," Pole shot back.

Harris did not reply immediately but Pole sensed he was holding his tongue.

"Leave it with me. Send me the names of all the people on the scene: police, paramedics —"

"Got that already," Pole replied irritated. Who the hell did he think he was?

"Good man – shoot me a text. We need to make sure the story that comes out on the news is the right one."

"What else do you need from me?"

"I'll let you know."

Pole sent the text and replaced the burner phone in his inside pocket.

His sole consolation for the events of the day was that Harris would soon be dealing with Henry directly.

Henry Crowne had not gained the reputation of being the smartest of arses for nothing as Harris was about to find out.

* * *

The bike was using the back streets of Deptford. The other bike had disappeared. No doubt to avoid identification.

The bike stopped. Another man, also dressed in black, visor down, was waiting for them in a small alleyway.

"Ahmed is going to take you to where you need to go."

Henry nodded. Ahmed pointed to a bag on the floor. "You need to change clothes."

Henry slammed the visor up. "On the side of the road? Why?"

"It's good enough here."

"That's ridiculous." Henry glanced at the two men. There was no way he could make a run for it. And to go where? He removed his helmet, moved to the back of the alley and stripped out of his Belmarsh jogging pants. He grabbed what was in the sports bag. Another set of dark clothes.

"Underwear."

"No fucking way," Henry said. He had already put on the trousers and was not going to expose his manhood to these two in the middle of the street. He put on the jumper with ferocious determination.

The officer and Ahmed exchanged a few words in what Henry knew was Arabic. Ahmed relented, unhappy. Henry had already made a friend.

The ride continued through an area Henry knew nothing about. They hit a main road that seemed to be going towards the river.

The weather was overcast and a few droplets of rain started hitting Henry's helmet. The downpour came in a wave of unexpected strength. It was pelting down on Henry's shoulders, seeping through to his back like a glacial drip. People were hurrying out of the way.

The bike stopped at a set of traffic lights. Henry cursed. He wanted to be somewhere dry. In the distance he thought he recognised the skyline. When the bike turned left he knew where he was – the Cutty Sark.

They were near the Thames but Henry could not recall a bridge over the water in that direction. The bike turned again into an open space. Henry was about to tap the driver on the shoulder when they stopped in front of a strange construction. It looked last century, round and squat – similar to the Greenwich Observatory.

Ahmed and Henry alighted. Ahmed made his way towards a set of lifts, pushing the bike. Henry read the name Greenwich Foot Tunnel. The lift was empty. Ahmed pushed the bike into it and they rode to the bottom of the tunnel. Ahmed fired up the engine again and they started their journey underground and underwater. The noise of the bike was deafening, bouncing off the walls of the tunnel. Henry looked back. But there was no one coming out of the lifts.

Minutes later the bike had reached the other side. Ahmed loaded the bike yet again into the lift and when they emerged on the other side Henry recognised the unmistakable shape of Canary Wharf. A cold piece of ice dropped into his stomach – his old life was gone forever. He straddled the bike again. They made their way north.

* * *

Nancy and Andy were reading the news that had started rolling onto Andy's screen when Pole arrived. Her body no longer showed a relaxed nonchalance but complete tension.

Nancy was fidgeting with one of the buttons of her jacket. Pole could not hear what she was saying but Andy had turned his face towards her and looked concerned.

Nancy's face was pale and her eyes shone with the fever of anxiety.

Had Henry been taken?

"Guv – did you get my call?"

"I did."

Andy looked puzzled. A question was forming on his lips but Pole cut it short.

"Speak to Ferguson; matters might have changed."

"Let's go into my office." He tried to sound reassuring. Nancy had not uttered a word. "How come —"

"I was called as soon as the van hold-up was reported." That was not entirely wrong. Nancy sat heavily in the chair in front of Pole's desk.

"Wasn't there anyone closer?"

"We are talking Henry Crowne."

"But still?" She lifted her head towards him. "Can't you tell me?"

Pole breathed in. "A couple of police cars had arrived before me but I am The Met contact."

No, he could not tell her.

Nancy grew even paler.

"The van was held up. They took Henry. Whoever they are."

Nancy's focus on him was a mixture of fear and scrutiny. Her almond eyes had changed shape, a little narrower perhaps. It could not be the whole story and she knew it. Pole ached.

He wanted to tell her all he had seen, to use her skills openly and comfort him he had made the right decision ... but he wanted to protect her too.

Nancy bent forward unexpectedly, placing her head in her hands.

"I need to speak to you about a letter," Nancy said slowly. She hesitated and lifted her head. She was looking straight ahead, to the place where Pole should be sitting. A sense of unease had settled in the room. She was working out how best to explain. Her face told him so. He had seen the same line of her eyebrows and the frown on her forehead before. But today he was not certain he liked her need to gather herself before speaking to him.

"Is it about Henry?"

"Who else but Henry Crowne," Nancy's tone had an edge Pole did not recognise. "Henry gave me a letter. She was still looking at Pole's empty chair. "Not a letter really, more like a note, handwritten – when he was last allowed out of Belmarsh."

"You mean after the Bank of England hostage situation?" Pole's voice was incredulous.

"That's right. I don't know when he wrote it but he gave it to me just before he left for Belmarsh."

Pole stayed where he was, leaning against the wall and its large window. He could not bring himself to sit on his chair, behind his desk – too official.

"It was a strange sort of note. I mean the tone was strange." Nancy shook her head. "I'm not describing this right." Her hand tightened, frustrated. "It felt out of character; someone who had had a revelation. I took it seriously but perhaps not seriously enough." The words were excruciating.

"Did he mention escaping?" Pole cursed his bluntness.

"No, of course not," Nancy had finally turned to face him. Her protestation felt unconvincing.

"But it was implied?" Pole was surprised by his own calm. Perhaps aided by the fact that he too already knew.

"It was – a possibility." Nancy agreed. She had turned paler again. Her hand had risen to her throat in a protective gesture. "I'm sorry, Jonathan." Nancy's eyes had lost a little of their spark.

Pole left the window and came to lean against his desk close to Nancy's chair. He pushed his hand through his hair and left it there for a moment.

"Why did you not say?" Pole's gaze rested on her hands.

"Because it looked impossible – HSU Belmarsh – and he needed some hope. I thought it would all dissipate eventually."

"Is that all?"

Nancy pulled a quizzical face. "You mean I'm his legal brief – that too of course."

Pole did not reply, and Nancy looked stunned. "You don't think …?" Her voice wobbled. "He is a friend, maybe a bad choice …"

698

"And what am I? A friend too?"

"Jonathan you are much more, so much more than that —"

The buzzing noise of a mobile phone interrupted. Pole's BlackBerry was still on his desk where he had left it. Pole pressed his hand to his jacket pocket.

"I must take this."

He walked out of the office and through the open-plan space in long strides, finding a small corner where people went to have coffee.

"Spoken to Ferguson – they have the go-ahead to mount an assault." Harris was uncommonly serious.

"Where is Henry?"

"Just been delivered there."

"What do you mean – the address Andy mapped?"

"I know what you are thinking," Harris carried on. "But it will work and also get Ferguson off my back."

"Does he know?"

"That Crowne is there? No – and it will stay that way."

"How?"

"That's my business." Harris shot back. "Ferguson will ask you to be there; act surprised."

Pole stood in the corner, burner phone still in hand. A few people had tried to join Pole, but his glare had told them to find another spot.

What was the idiot doing? Catching Henry again after his escape. For what – sending him back to Belmarsh with a more credible story.

Perhaps it was time to speak to Nancy about all of this. She had levelled with him. Her last words had rung true and he had not been able to tell her he believed her, that he had pushed too hard with his last question.

He had never doubted her. It was friendship with Henry on her part although he had often wondered what Henry's true feelings were.

Pole walked back to his office to find it empty.

"Shit." He dialled her mobile – engaged.

Call me. This is URGENT. PLEASE. Pole sent the text.

Where had she gone?

* * *

Nancy had been saved by her own BlackBerry ringing, showing Marissa was calling. She too had been told of Henry's disappearance. She had no details either. Was it an abduction? What was Henry thinking of if he had masterminded this? But it was HSU Belmarsh. Had she facilitated?

"What an absolute idiot I've been," the words stuck in Nancy's throat. Had she been played all along?

She was walking fast, on her way to meeting Marissa. Nancy accelerated her pace further. She was fleeing Scotland Yard and the scene of her mistakes. She could still see Pole's face, his controlled anger and perhaps even his disappointment. The last words she had spoken she would have wanted to deliver differently. She was not even certain she was ready to utter them in the first place.

Curse Henry. She shook her head – idiot, you bloody idiot.

Nancy tried to focus on what there was to salvage. She slowed down. *Where was Henry's burner phone?*

She found herself in front of the SFO building near Trafalgar Square. She fumbled with her BlackBerry to let Marissa know she had arrived. A text flashed on the screen. "Call me". It was from Pole. She hesitated. She might not want to know what the rest of the text said.

Marissa was pacing up and down the SFO lobby when she saw Nancy outside looking at her mobile. She dashed out.

"Do you have fresh news?"

"Very little." Nancy shook her head.

"Pole?"

"Not much on his side either." Nancy's voice wobbled a little. She cleared her throat.

They walked back into the lobby in silence and found a couple of large chairs. Marissa flopped down into one of them.

"I can't even start to think about what this means for the case."

Nancy sat down. *Was there hope?*

"We need to find out what happened to Henry's burner phone."

Marissa leaned her head against the back of the chair. "It will only give us a number."

"Perhaps, but his contact is still expecting a call; we could try to speak to him." She refused to be beaten.

Marissa looked at her surprised. "I doubt …" She did not need to elaborate further. "And then there is Mark Phelps."

Nancy stood up. This was unbearable. She needed to find a way, a solution to this mess. She needed to make the feelings that were slowly creeping into her heart go away.

Anger and shame.

Despite her brilliant legal mind, she could not see a way out of the impasse.

Chapter Twenty-Six

They entered through the back yard. Henry could hardly make his way amongst the piles of objects covered in plastic that had been left lying there. He suspected he might not want to know what was being stored underneath them.

Ahmed opened the door. Another man was waiting for them inside, solid build and thick neck, black leather jacket. Not the Jihadi look Henry was expecting. But Henry recognised in his eyes the same determination he had seen in some of the IRA men he had known well, and in Bobby's.

The door shut behind him. Ahmed removed his helmet and the three of them stayed silent for a long moment.

Was he up for it?

Too late.

The black leather jacket man gestured with his head. Henry followed him into a large room with flaking paint and rising damp on the walls. A young man was already sitting on a low bed covered with a thick blanket.

A few rugs had been thrown on the floor, some cushions. "As-salaam Alaykum," the man said with a smile, exposing a row of perfect white teeth that matched the whiteness of his robe and crocheted hat.

"Wa Alaykum As-salaam." Henry did not hesitate, laying the palm of his right hand against his heart.

"Sit Henry." The Sheik gestured towards another low bed that looked old and tattered. "We have much to discuss."

Henry removed his shoes and sat down, fighting the urge to identify a way out of the room.

"Abu Maeraka has told me you should join us," The Sheik carried on. He stopped as the door opened and a woman in full niqab entered. The tray she carried was laden with food and the delicious smell made Henry's mouth water. She poured some tea into two glasses and left without a sound.

"But you must tell me about yourself."

The educated accent of The Sheik amazed Henry. This was not an ignorant thug. He had been schooled in the UK and his fluency indicated higher education.

Henry nodded and drank some tea. He thought about apologising for perhaps looking aloof. After all he had just escaped from prison, but he changed his mind.

This was a job interview; no mistake about it. This one would not end with a simple handshake and a "will call you later" if it had not been successful. The parting words would be a bullet in his head or a knife through his throat.

A challenge – at last.

Henry was factual. Ireland, the IRA funds, investment banking and most importantly the fact that he had been caught not because of his carelessness but the vengefulness of his enemy, Anthony Albert.

The Sheik was silent. Henry saw from his relaxed face that he was doing well. Henry bent down to take the glass that had been refilled with tea.

The lights went down.

* * *

Pole is standing at the door of a large vehicle parked one street away from the target. Harris is speaking to SO19, Ferguson is all rifled up, balaclava rolled up on his forehead, raring to go. Harris is passing two photos around the assault team.

"These are my agents – do *not* shoot them." Harris keeps repeating. Each officer looks at the photos and nods.

Pole knows that one of the photos is Henry's. He hasn't been shown the other one. Harris is too preoccupied with his assets getting out of the op alive.

Pole knocks at the van door and enters the mobile control room. Two people are manning the screens: a man and a young woman who seems to be in charge.

She is checking whether properties within the perimeter have been evacuated. Ferguson is now standing behind Pole, pressing Control for quicker results. Time is of the essence and so is the element of surprise.

The young woman pulls her headphones down abruptly. "We're all clear."

"Roger that." Ferguson adjusts his earpiece, one final comms check and the balaclava comes down together with the night vision goggles.

"All right lads, let's go." He is already walking outside amongst his men. Harris has joined Pole in the van. "I hope they don't bollocks this up." Harris is chewing on his piece of gum furiously. Pole nods.

Pole hears the woman's voice give instructions. "Controlled evacuation complete on the North side; we are clear to breech."

The lights go down.

Both Harris and Pole are looking at the screens tracking SO19's progress in infrared light. The colour is a strange monochromatic sepia.

For the untrained eye it is not always easy to make out who is who. Harris is bending forward over the officer manning the screen, but the other man does not notice. All his attention focuses on the action unfolding in front of him.

The first phosphorus bomb goes off.

Pole can hear the shouts. "Armed Police – get down, get down." And the shooting starts, short bursts, screams, retaliation.

Harris pops another gum in his mouth.

"Fuck, they are shooting left, right and centre."

Pole feels his stomach tightening. He is powerless and he hates that sensation.

On the ground floor, a couple of targets are hiding in a room that controls the bottom of the stairs. The burst of sub-machine guns is incessant.

Ferguson has spread his men; three of them are looking for the back door. Another of Ferguson's team crawls on the ground and delivers another phosphorus bomb into the room. The cries become shrieks.

The three men dispatched to the back of the house find a way in. Ferguson and his team climb the stairs, cautious, guns at the ready. More gunshots and a body hits the wall at the top of the stairs.

"Where are you guys?" Harris is anxious. His people are in the middle of this shooting match and a stray bullet is all it takes.

Ferguson's team is doing a room by room sweep. Two women are screaming, hands in the air.

"Get down, get down."

They fall on their knees. It takes only a second for the smaller of them to pull a gun from underneath her dress and discharge it at one of Ferguson's men. The retaliation is ferocious. She will never pull the trigger again.

"Officer down. I repeat officer down."

"Shit." Harris swears as each room is cleared.

Pole has not uttered a word. He is used to violence but not of this intensity.

Ferguson's team is now on its way to the second floor. They ascend the stairwell without encountering resistance. The first door they check is locked.

The burst of a machine gun and the door explodes into splinters. The windows are open, a man in a white robe is about to jump, gun in hand. A burst of bullets stops him before he can escape through the window. His body hesitates and slumps back into the room.

Harris leaves the van before the officers can protest. He runs towards the backyard, pushing on his earpiece to keep it in place.

"They are in the backyard," he shouts. "Don't shoot them – my guys are in the backyard."

Pole turns towards the screens again. He can see the muzzle of several machine guns pointing at two men on their knees at the bottom of the fire escape.

Ferguson's men have pulled back. One of the silhouettes collapses on the ground. The other man stands up slowly and turns towards him helping him to stand up as well.

Henry is rising to his feet.

The blanket on his back is barely keeping him warm. He is chilled to the marrow. One of his hands is clinging to the rug. He can't quite recall how it happened, but he is also clutching a cup of tea. Harris is speaking to his other agent, Wasim, the officer who helped Henry escape. They are surveying the carnage again, accounting for who in the world of terrorism has been eliminated.

Pole has been barely listening. Henry knows what is on his mind. He wants to attract Pole's attention, to indicate he needs a word, but his body is not responding. He wants to rest and simply feel he is still alive.

Henry focuses on Pole's face in the distance. Now that he is looking at Pole, Henry notices he is strangely attractive. His personality speaks through his body. The way he holds himself. The way he talks or listens. He moves, assured and yet restrained. Henry envies him for a second, but the thought passes almost as quickly as it came.

Whatever Henry is, he is not a jealous man.

Pole finally moves away, extracting himself step by step from the conversation. The others don't notice.

"How are you feeling?" Pole has found a space next to Henry at the back of the van.

Henry gives a small nod. He tries to clear his throat, "Alive."

Before Pole can respond he summons all his strength.

"I have something for you – and Nancy." His voice sounds cloggy. His teeth start chattering. He inhales. He can do this.

Henry puts his tea down very slowly, each move costs him an enormous effort. His fingers fidget underneath the blanket. He is getting something out. He can feel it underneath his fingers.

Pole looks at Henry's hand. It cradles in its centre a small mobile phone SIM card.

"Take it."

Pole registers and he cannot help but smile.

"Everything is on it. I wrote notes as messages. Nancy should have all she needs."

"Including?"

"The UBO – yes."

Pole has taken the SIM card. Henry cradles his tea for comfort.

"But I thought …?" Pole doesn't need to formulate his question. He has the answer. "You didn't give us the correct time for the call to your contact in Panama."

"I was worried you would somehow track the calls." Henry is drinking in small gulps.

Pole shakes his head.

Harris and his agent have almost finished.

Pole has slipped the SIM card into the inner pocket of his jacket. Henry has almost finished his tea, his gaze remains on the empty cup.

"There is a lot I would like to say to Nancy but …" He stops and drinks the dregs. He cannot be shy. There will not be another occasion. "Tell her I wished I could have said goodbye and that …" He hesitates because he wants to get it right. "She has been the best friend I could ever have hoped for."

Pole nods. He understands and there is nothing equivocal about it. Henry has fallen silent. He feels the lump in his throat swelling.

"Are you sure you want to do this?" Pole's eyes are searching Henry's face.

Henry inhales and manages a smile.

"It's my path – chosen – the only way I can make sense of all the mistakes."

"Redemption?" Pole asks.

"Perhaps, one day."

They feel Harris' eyes on them. He approaches slowly. He is happy to let them have a few more minutes it seems. Soon Henry will disappear with the other agent, into the underworld of Jihadism – yes, he can have a few more minutes. Pole hesitates to leave but when he does it is with a *Thank you* that means much to Henry.

Harris has taken Pole's place at his side. "Ready?"

Henry let's his body slump, in a slow move against the metal frame of the van they are in. There is one more thing Harris needs to help him do, one final meeting he needs to have before he surrenders himself to MI6. It crushes him it won't be with Nancy. But the man he has in mind needs it more than she does.

* * *

It was way past midnight but she would not be asleep. Pole had called Nancy to tell her he was on his way. When the door of the lift opened on her floor, Nancy was waiting for him. She looked pale and almost fragile in a long woollen dress that hugged her body close. Her eyes searched his for an indication of what had happened but also to see how he felt. She waited for him to get close and slid her arms around his body, her head dropping against his chest. Pole felt the firmness of her embrace and he closed his arms over her, breathing in the scent of her hair.

"He is alive." He repeated. "Henry is alive."

Nancy nodded and lifted her face to his. "Tell me."

The SIM card was lying on the coffee table wrapped in a piece of tissue. She was looking at it without sadness or joy. She turned to Pole.

"It's all on there?"

"Yes. You and Marissa have all you need to pursue the case." Pole was sitting next to her on the sofa, one arm around her waist.

"It may sound ridiculous but I always assumed I would be the last person to see him if something happened," Nancy's voice trailed. "I don't even know what I really mean by that. I would never have allowed him to ..."

"This is what he wants; perhaps, rather, what he needs."

"Henry fighting for Queen and Country?" Nancy said.

"No, he is fighting for himself – no one will ever own Henry Crowne and if they think they do they will be bitterly disappointed."

706

"*C'est vrai.*" Nancy pushed her body back into the comfort of Pole's embrace.

She rested her head on his shoulder.

"I am sad, Jonathan; he had become a friend. There was something good striving to come out but somehow I don't think the confrontation with Mark would have given either of them closure." She shut her eyes.

Pole took her hand and placed his lips on her fingers.

"And he valued your friendship above all." Pole kissed her fingers once more.

Nancy opened her eyes and gave Pole a gentle smile.

"And you, *mon cher* Jonathan, know that you are much more than a friend."

* * *

The head grip is brutal. An arm is locked around his neck in a nutcracker choke that is strangling him – in a few seconds he will lose consciousness. His hands try to grab the attacker's limb with little success. He summons all his strength and shoots his elbow into the man's stomach, his fingers into the man's eyes, the grip loosens. Henry rolls around and twists with vicious strength the arm that has choked him. Wasim falls and slaps the floor. Henry releases him and collapses next to his instructor. It is intense training.

"That was the best you've done so far." Wasim throws a bottle of water to him.

Henry nods. He opens the bottle slowly and drinks, surveying his surroundings yet again. The place he has been moved to with Wasim is almost derelict. They left London after the shooting a few weeks ago and arrived in Manchester late at night. He has only come back to London once since then. Harris almost gave him up, when he set his conditions to join MI6.

"You're not in a position to ask yet, mate."

"But I'm your best bet to infiltrate these people in Syria."

"Shit, I knew you were going to be a pain in the arse to handle ..." Harris has grumbled. But he has delivered.

Henry is standing in the garden of Mark Phleps' parents. He is wearing the red uniform of a postman and has been given a bundle of post. He has one hour to talk to the man who has so wanted to speak to him. MI6 has spotted a reoccurring window in Mark's routine. It's Henry's only chance.

His breath is shallow, and his mind fuzzy ... does he always have to push himself to the limits?

Henry knocks on the glass bay window and holds up the letters in his hand. Mark looks up from his book. He is a little startled, but he stands up with a wince and moves towards the door. Henry drops the items to the ground and steps back in a reassuring gesture.

Mark opens and asks a question, bending down to grab the post. Henry doesn't catch what he says ... it doesn't matter. He takes a deep breath and with a slow but clear voice begins.

"My father was an IRA man."

Mark is frozen on the spot. His eyes have widened and there is more disbelief than fear in them.

Henry removes his red cap, revealing his face so that Mark is in no doubt about his identity.

"Now ... Why?" is all Mark manages to say. Henry's escape from HSU Belmarsh has been all over the news.

"Because you wanted that conversation ... and I need to explain ..."

"Don't expect forgiveness ..." Mark spits out.

"I have made many mistakes, but I am not that much of a fool."

Mark steps back and returns to the seat he occupied earlier. His face has sagged. In the deem light of the lounge he looks much older than the picture Henry has been shown ... Henry walks in. He hasn't been invited but he knows this is what Mark wants ... what he needs.

Henry sits down in front of a man whose life has been devastated and simply tells him about what made him who he had become.

As he remembers the London meeting, Henry can feel Wasim's eyes on him. Wasim has learnt to let Henry return to that moment without interruption. A moment of intense truth Henry is still wrestling with. And Henry is grateful for his patience. Henry nods his appreciation.

Wasim Khan is the other man infiltrating the new terror group for MI6 but unlike Henry he is a Muslim. Henry suspects Wasim Kahn is not his real name and that he is working under legend. What were the chances he'd have a name exactly matching that of a famous cricketer?

Henry stands up. He snatches the towel that has been thrown on an old set of pipes. It has seen better days and has started to smell. Still, he wipes the sweat from his face. Wasim is waiting for Henry to sit down next to him.

"I have made contact again." He moves a cloth over his thick neck. His manners are strangely considerate for such a powerfully built man.

"Are they ready?"

"They are."

Henry never speaks about Agent Harris or MI6 with Wasim. He has been told very clearly on his way to Manchester. He does not initiate conversation. He does not take risk. Wasim knows when they can talk safely.

Wasim has checked the cameras he has set up around the perimeter. They are alone. The sympathisers who come to bring supplies won't come during the day, but it pays to be careful.

Henry is burning to ask the question *Am I ready?* but it would sound weak. He also knows that the only person who can convincingly answer is himself.

"How?" Henry asks instead.

"Boat across the Channel to France. After that, I have not been told."

"Why haven't they told you if you are coming too?"

"They have alternative routes and will decide at the last minute; more secure that way."

"Have you made the trip to Iraq before?"

"No, but I've been to other places …"

"Such as?"

Wasim does not reply immediately Henry must learn that he can't ask all the questions he wants. "Pakistan," he volunteers.

Henry nods. He is learning fast from his trainer about the way of the jihad. The training camps, the brutality towards those who cannot make the grade.

"They want you safely delivered," Wasim carries on.

"Are you coming back to the UK after that?"

Wasim grins. "*Inshallah.*"

"Sorry, a no-go area," Henry replies with raised hands.

Henry stands up, walks to the broken windows that have been patched up with mismatched wooden planks. Nancy's image springs into his mind and she feels far away, not only a few hundred miles, but as if she now belongs to another world. He turns back, away from the window, and as he does, Wasim nods.

"You're ready."

SPY SHADOWS

The most wanted INTERPOL fugitive,

The most destructive Terror Group in the world,

The most impossible British Intelligence Services' mission...

Henry Crowne, disgraced financier and former IRA operative has escaped London's top high-security prison with the unexpected help of MI6.

His mission...infiltrate an emerging terror group that has already claimed many lives in the West and threatens to destabilise the Middle East further. Henry's perilous journey leads him to the group's centre of power in Syria and Iraq. His aim, to meet the elusive man who runs a merciless war against those who oppose him.

But Henry decides to help Mattie Colmore, a war reporter hostage. Can he still hide in plain sight, bring back the information the West desperately need to defeat Islamic State and save Mattie at the same time?

* * *

SPY SHADOWS is a political and espionage thriller, the fourth in the "Henry Crowne, Paying The Price" series. If you liked Rob Sinclair's SLEEPER 13, L.T Ryan's NOBLE BEGINNINGS or the TV series MacMafia or Spooks, you will enjoy the twists and turns of Freddie P Peters' latest fierce-paced thriller.

Discover it now...

Dear Reader,

I hope you have enjoyed reading HENRY CROWNE PAYING THE PRICE BOOKS 1-3 as much as I have enjoyed writing them … Perhaps I can now ask for a small favour? Please take a few minutes to write a review on Amazon, Goodreads or Bookbub. Thank you so very much!

Don't forget FREE access to the genesis of the trilogy as well as FREE chapters, or receive information about the next book in the series.

Join Freddie's book club at <u>www.freddieppeters.com</u>

Looking forward to connecting with you …

Freddie

List of French Expressions
with English Translations

French Dialogue	English Translation
Absolument	Absolutely
Absolument mon cher	Absolutely my dear
Absolument, rebel de la gauche	Absolutely, left wing rebel
Andiamo	Let's go
Bien entendu	Certainly
Bien sur, je n'en ésperais pas moins	Of course, I could not have hoped for more
Bienvenue	Welcome
Bonjour mohammed, votre contact anglais á l'appareil	Hello Mohammed, your English contact speaking
Ça suffit vous deux	Enough you two
C'est vrai	It's true
Compris	Understood
Dés que j'ai fini	As soon as I have finished
Eh bien	And so
En tête à tête	Face to face (romantic and intimate)
Étonnant	Astonishing
Exactement	Exactly
Ha, voilà. Parfait	Ha, here we are. Perfect
Incroyable	Unbelievable
Je le sais	I know
J'ai besoin de vous	I need you
J'ai besoin de vous parler	I need to talk to you
Je suis très flattée, mon cher ami	I am very flattered, my dear
L'âme soeur	The perfect match
Le capitaine	The captain
Les grands esprits se rencontrent	Great minds think alike

Ma chère	My dear (female)
Ma chère amie	My dear friend (female)
Mais enfin la voici	But finally, here it is
Mais je n'en doutais pas moins	I had no doubt about it
Messieurs	Gentlemen
Mon ami	My friend (male)
Mon cher	My dear (male)
Mon cher ami	My dear friend (male)
N'est-ce pas	Isn't it
Peut-être pas	Maybe not
Peut-être pas mais	Perhaps, but
Très heureux de l'entendre	Very glad to hear it
Une proposition irrésistible	An irresistible offer
Voila. vous avez tout compris	Here you are, all clear
Vraiment	Really
Vraiment désolée	Really sorry
Vraiment, vous deux êtes incorrigibles	Really, you two are incorrigible

Glossary of Technical Terms

Term	Meaning
ANPR	Automatic Number Plate Recognition
IDENT1	UK central database for biometric identification, fingerprints etc.
NCA	National Crime Agency
SOCO	Scene of Crime Officer
SO19	Special Firearms Command of the Met
SFO	Serious Fraud Office
UVF	Ulster Volunteer Force
INTERPOL	International Criminal Police Organisation

Acknowledgements

It takes many people to write and publish a book … for their generosity and support I want to say thank you.

Cressida Downing, my editor, for her no-nonsense approach and relentless enthusiasm for books…mine in particular. Lucy Llewellyn for her expertise in design and for producing a super book cover, yet again and her team Catriona, Aimee and Melanie. Helena Halme, an author in her own rights, for giving me confidence in marketing my books.

To the friends who have patiently read, re-read and advised: Kate Burton, Alison Thorne, Elisabeth Gaunt, Anthea Tinker, Helen Janececk, Mandy Little, Prashila Narsing-Chauhan, Adrian Lurie, Geraldine Kelly, Malcolm Fortune, Tim Watts, Gaye Murdock, Kathy Vanderhook, Kat Clarke.

Finally, a special thanks to ARCADE Gallery for providing plenty of fantastic contemporary art, and to my artist friends for providing plenty of inspiration … Susan Rosenberg, Bernard McGuigan and Tom de Freston.